BE CAREFUL OF DEALS MADE WITH GODS
IN THE DARK

NEVERMORE

MIRANDA LYN

Dustjacket Cover Design—Tairelei

Copy Editor—Megan Visger

Maps—Virginia Allyn—www.virginiaallyn.com

Hands Art—https://thewonderwitchemporium.com/

Print Chapter Heading Art—https://lilaraymond.com/lettersbylila-links

CONTENT WARNING: Threats of Violence, Language, Explicit Sexual Content, Gore, Mention of Child Endangerment

TRIGGER WARNING: Violence, Death, Murder, Imprisonment, Mentions of Drug and Alcohol Use, Kidnapping, Torture, Grief

Also by Miranda Lyn

FAE RISING:

BLOOD AND PROMISE

CHAOS AND DESTINY

FATE AND FLAME

TIDES AND RUIN

UNMARKED:

THE UNMARKED WITCH

THE UNBOUND WITCH

THE UNBLESSED WITCH

THE NEVER SKY SERIES:

TILL DEATH

NEVERMORE

EVERMORE

www.authormirandalyn.com

DEDICATION

To everyone who lost their way but found themselves in the dark—
this is for you. And to coffee, without whom none of this would exist.

A NOTE FROM THE AUTHOR

Dear reader,

I felt it necessary to drop a quick little note to let you know what you're getting into. Nevermore is the first of a duology within the Never Sky series of standalone stories. These stories can be read on their own, however, this story needed two books. You can read Nevermore without reading Till Death, but you'll need to read Evermore to complete this story.

I tried to make it happen in one book, but as you'll soon see, Paesha needed some room to dance. She's always loved the stage and she was adamant she keep the spotlight a little longer. And I've learned from experience to let the characters take the reins on their stories.

Happy reading, friend. I'm so grateful for you.

Miranda Lyn

PROLOGUE

6 years ago

SOME WOUNDS I CHOSE, knowing they'd never heal. Listening to those tiny sobs for the hundredth time, I now understood that to be the first lesson Quill would ever teach me.

I pressed my forehead against the cool, wood door, feeling the vibrations of those heartbreaking whimpers travel through my skin. My fingers hovered over the doorknob, trembling. The knob taunted me. Just a quick turn, and I could end this torment. End the suffering that sliced straight to my fucking soul. The whimpers of an orphaned child were a song that should have never been written. But it was a song I knew by heart long before this little girl stumbled into my arms. It was a song I thought maybe I wrote myself when I was ten years old.

I couldn't open that damn door. I knew better. I knew if I did, I'd be opening a wound that would never, ever heal. The

1

moment I laid eyes on that tiny, tear-stained face, I'd be lost. My resolve would crumble.

I'd sworn to myself, to the universe, that I wouldn't let myself love her. If I did, he'd find out. And he'd use her like a weapon against me. She didn't deserve that. Distance was safer for both of us. Ezra and I had both known that when we'd stood in that room the day the Maestro had tried to use her to trap me into a bargain. The day he'd traced his disgusting fingers over my scar and smiled.

Yet here I was, my heart fracturing with each muffled cry that seeped through the cracks of the door. I could almost see her in my mind. Tiny, huddled in the corner of her new room in our house, her little arms wrapped around her knees, face buried in the folds of the oversized t-shirt she wore. Her dark curls would be wild, sticking to her tear-streaked cheeks. Those big blue eyes would end me.

My hand tightened on the doorknob. One twist, one push, and everything would change. I'd be responsible for this tiny, fragile life. I'd have to mend scraped knees, chase away nightmares, teach her how to tie her shoes and read bedtime stories. I'd have to love her fiercely and unconditionally. There would be no going back for me.

But she deserved that, didn't she? One person that would end the world for her.

The sobs grew louder, and suddenly I remembered the crushing weight of being utterly, completely alone. No one to dry my tears, to hold me close and whisper that everything would be okay. No one to chase away the monsters that lurked in the shadows, both real and imagined. No one to care if I lived or died, if I disappeared into the cracks of the city never to be seen again.

If I was smart, and I'd survived this long by being ruthlessly practical, I'd remember she had others. Thea, with her quick smile. Elowen's steady presence. Even Orin's fierce loyalty. But they couldn't teach her what I knew: how to recognize the Maestro's traps, how to read the shadows before they swallowed you whole. They couldn't understand the particular shade of loneliness that colored both our abandoned souls.

They weren't enough. It had to be me. She needed me.

So, I opened the fucking door.

She didn't flinch when I sat on the edge of her bed, didn't retreat into herself like most broken things do. Instead, those blue eyes found mine and held on, patient beyond her three years. She knew, somehow, that I needed time. Maybe she did too.

We sat in that loaded silence, two fragments of the same shattered mirror, reflecting each other's wounds. I wasn't supposed to have children. She wasn't supposed to be anything more than leverage, a pretty piece on the Maestro's chessboard. But sitting there, watching her tiny fists grip the blanket as she waited, I knew we were about to rewrite all those "supposed tos."

"You're lonely, aren't you?" I whispered, the words falling like tears between us. And in that moment, I felt it, not just her loneliness, but the way it tangled with my own, forming something new. Something unbreakable.

I

I'd paid the grave digger three extra coins to bury him at night.

    I'd fallen to my knees and begged every god to keep the sky clear. Wearing white for the first time in my life, I hoped the light from the stars and moon would shine so brightly, he could look down upon this rotting world from Death's court and see my sorrow. See my aching soul and know my heart only beat for him. Yearned for him. Needed him. But there was no light at all. And, in answer to my prayers, it'd poured that night.

The rain had lashed against my body, soaking through the delicate fabric of my gown. It clung to me like a second skin, a cloak of despair. The grave digger worked diligently. His shovel sliced through the mud with a sickening squelch and each heave of dirt upon the coffin was a twist of the knife in my chest.

I'd stood sentinel as the hole swallowed him up. My love, my heart, my reason for drawing breath. Gone. Consigned to the depths of the cold, uncaring earth. The gods had forsaken me. But then, they'd made no promises in the first place.

Tears mingled with the rain on my cheeks as the final shovelful of soil had thudded into place. The grave digger, his task complete, slunk away into the shadows, leaving me alone with my grief. I sank to my knees, unbothered by the ruin of my dress.

"My love," I'd whispered, my voice raw and broken. "Wait for me in Death's court."

Years passed, each one a heavy burden upon my soul. The pain of losing Ezra had dulled to a constant ache, soothed only by the presence of a child we'd taken in. But my heart never forgot the way it felt to watch from the shadows as Death's Maiden slid that blade across his throat. When the opportunity arose to see him again, to find him in Death's Court, I took it, leaving those I'd loved the most behind, but I hadn't died and, as it turned out, I didn't belong in the realm of the dead.

In the chaos that had followed my journey here, I hadn't taken the time to remember the true depth of my relationship with Ezra. I thought the moment we were reunited, I might've burst from joy and everything would come crashing back to me, but instead, I'd treaded lightly, my mind taking precedence over my heart. Protecting me. Reminding me I never wanted the pain of losing someone I loved so much again. Even if it was with him. I'd learned to build walls after he died. I'd just never expected he'd stay on the outside of them too.

Though something between us remained. All of our shared dreams. A treasure chest of memories. The first time we'd kissed. The first time he'd confessed his love to me, eyes nearly glowing with anticipation as I uttered those words back in the middle of a rainstorm.

"Walk with me," Ezra said, pulling me away from the thoughts running rampant in my mind, away from the guilt.

He held out his hand, knowing I would take it. And I did, still comforted by his touch. The ever-present chill of Death's Court felt a little less biting with his hand in mine. We walked beneath the starless sky, our path lit by the glow of two moons haloing the ominous castle in the distance. But each step was like ripping a piece of paper a little further in half. I was confident my soul was actually ripping. That somehow being here was breaking me. It was wrong. All of it. I couldn't tell a soul though. I wouldn't let myself be vulnerable. Still, I needed to leave. Desperately.

I looked up into Ezra's eyes, just as vivid as they were in life, stormy with an undercurrent of softness only those closest to him had been privy to. I forced myself to concentrate on the feeling of his fingers wrapped around mine, the aura of familiarity they radiated. That connection was still there. Still beating. Maybe the dissonance gripping me by the throat, pushing in on my nerves, slowly strangling me, wasn't him at all, but this place.

He cleared his throat, pausing to swipe a lock of dark chestnut hair from my face. "I've decided we won't stay in the castle. I'll ask Orin for our own space."

"Ezra," I began, placing my hand on his chest. "We should've made that decision together. I know you mean well, but I can't stay here. You know I'm not... I haven't died. I can't explain it, but my soul knows I don't belong here. Every day, it's getting darker. I have to find a way home."

He gripped my hands. "We don't know the rules. Give me time."

"I promised her I'd come back."

"You promised me things too, Paesha."

I knew that tone. The one that was meant to be protective. The period at the end of a statement. But I couldn't let it go just because he wanted me to. "She's only a child."

"She is not you!" he barked. "I know you look at her and see yourself. The innocent girl sleeping in an alley, the depravity of your childhood. You remember your fear and your pain. You look at her and you remember your father and that's what kills you the most, isn't it? But you have to stop. She isn't your responsibility, and you know that. She'll be cared for. Ro promised."

"Ezra." Tampered fury flared in my chest as I dropped my chin. "Don't make this harder than it already is. You won't like the outcome."

"Don't you love me?"

That pit in my stomach grew. "Of course I do."

He looked at me long and hard with those eyes that always saw all of me—the girl who loved him, the woman who wanted to live... and leave. His voice was soft. "But it's not enough."

"I can't explain it. It's like something inside of me is broken. Or sluggish. It's not right. I'm not meant to be away from her. Quill isn't my daughter, but there's a bond there, and leaving Thea and Elowen to care for her isn't enough."

Running a hand down my arm, he sighed. "I think you're just scared for her. She'll be okay, and you know it."

I'd forgotten how much talking to Ezra about something I didn't agree with was like talking to the broad side of a building. He heard me all right, but he didn't give a shit about what I was saying. And usually, after I rolled over in an argument, it would all come around that he'd been right in whatever the conflict was anyway. Or that's how it seemed when I was blinded by his love. But now? Now I kind of wanted to punch him in the dick.

The rose-colored glasses I'd worn had come off, and the small bits of him I'd made excuses for, the pieces of him that commanded control, were suddenly suffocating.

I'd needed that when I was younger. Someone to guide me. Someone to make the hard decisions in life. But after his death, though it'd taken time, I learned to live for myself, rediscovering the independent little girl that'd been abandoned on the streets of Requiem when I was far too young to survive.

And then I had Quill. A doe-eyed, little magic wielder with far too much innocence in a world so dark. A beauty abandoned by her parents just like I had been. She helped me learn to smile again, to find joy in the simple things. In her happiness, mostly. She'd been a light. She'd been healing. And like an asshole, I'd left her behind, chasing what I thought I wanted instead of realizing what I needed was right in front of me. I needed Quill just as much as she needed me, and each hour that passed was filled with silent regret. I wasn't her mother, yet I'd abandoned her all the same.

But what could I do? How was I supposed to tell him I didn't want to be here? How the fuck was I supposed to get home anyway? It's not like there were more enchanted mirrors just thrown about.

Silence fell over us like a thick blanket, muffling everything. He had no idea the woman I'd become without him. And honestly, neither did I, until now. The tension was shattered as a brilliant light exploded across the court. It filled every crevice and corner, lit the dead fingers of every branch surrounding us. The chill that had constantly nipped at my skin was replaced by a breathtaking warmth.

Ezra looked around wildly, shielding his eyes from the light. "Run." His command echoed through the trees, but I found myself rooted to the spot. He snatched my arm, his fingers biting into my skin. "Paesha!"

I jerked free just as the glowing form struck, snatching him by the neck and hanging him in the air. Ezra went limp. A scream sliced through the realm, and it took several seconds for me to realize it was mine.

I whipped around, heart racing as I searched for help. For Orin to come running, but everything was still and silent. I turned back, blocking the light, squinting to try to see the details of the massive figure holding Ezra above the ground.

"Stop. Please," I begged. But the glowing figure didn't answer.

Instead, Ro stepped out from behind him. The one person I was counting on most to keep Quill safe until I could get back. Fucking perfect.

"You can't be here. You have to be with Quill. You promised."

With her chin high, she gripped the edges of her golden gown, looked behind me, then bowed in a graceful dip. "Kneel before your highest god, Reverius the Supreme Sovereign, the Unerring Arbiter of Beginnings and Endings, and the Keeper of All Realms."

Shadows billowed along the ground as Orin, a man that'd been like a brother to me, a man that'd held me through my grief and lifted me on the hardest days, filled my periphery, falling to his knees. Deyanira, always close behind him, followed suit, though I knew that stubborn, protective nature of hers was likely fighting it.

I saw no more, heard no more words beyond the stillness in those dangling legs. How could I have come so far and not loved him as he'd deserved? How could I have longed for his arms, yet forgotten how to find comfort in them?

When Ezra dropped with a thud, he scrambled backward, loosening the dread circling my heart. Of course he couldn't have died a second death. He slowly took a knee beside me, his eyes squeezed tight, hands trembling with obvious fury.

The searing light radiating off the figure burned so bright, my eyes quickly tired. The voice of the sovereign rattled me to the core, shaking my bones and causing every nerve to tighten. Whatever words he said in those moments were lost to me. I didn't care about who he was or why he'd come. Until Ro's eyes locked onto mine and she spoke within my mind.

Focus.

Fuck off, I retorted, though I wasn't sure if the weird mind chatter worked both ways. Judging by the defiant curl to her lip, I'd have bet it did.

Still, her command worked as the big, bad god's words to Orin became clear, shooting through the fog of misery that'd been there so long, I hadn't even noticed it. "The final gift is a portal..."

A portal.

My eyes snapped to Ro. *Get the hell out of my head.*

So demanding. She smirked and suddenly I wanted nothing more than to punch her in her perky little nose.

The god of things, or whatever his name was, swiped a glowing arm through the air and a large door appeared in the forest. The void between the frame rippled, revealing a glimpse into Requiem. "This is the world from which you come."

My heart stopped. Actually stopped beating.

Now you see.

I glared at Ro but said nothing back, fully consumed by the decaying streets of home only paces away. But the vision rippled and changed into a vast ocean. The change was like a laceration. Like dangling food before a starving man and then ripping it away.

"This is another of your charges," the god of god things was telling Orin. "The Astral Seal is a world with great order and balance far vaster than your Requiem." Again, the picture changed. Mountains and forests and winding rivers stared back at me.

Go back, I begged.

The Keeper of Memories doesn't care for the fleeting thoughts of mortals, girl. He cannot hear you.

What part of 'fuck off' didn't you understand? Was it the fuck part? Should I spell that bit out for you?

Ro's trill of laughter echoed through my mind.

I cleared my throat to rid myself of the sound. His name.

What was his name? "Reverius, Keeper of Realms and Sovereign of Sovereignty things, can we please see Requiem again?"

"Unerring Arbiter of Beginnings and Endings, Supreme Sovereign," Ro said, eliciting a glare.

"That's what I said."

"These other worlds are not for you, Huntress," the glowing god answered. "But this one is, and I can see your heart's desire."

The Syndicate house appeared before us, my home for so many of my healing years. But it wasn't the house that nearly swept me to my knees. It was the backs of Elowen and Althea, the women that lived with us, as they held hands and stared into Quill's tidy bedroom. My whole heart, my precious girl, lay in her bed with her dog snuggled in a tiny circle beside her as she shook with tears.

"Oh, gods," I breathed, stepping forward to reach a hand toward Quill.

And it ripped me to shreds to see her sorrow and know I was the cause. I'd left her. Just as her parents had. Just as Ezra had when he'd died. Just as Orin and Deyanira had. A never-ending cycle of abandonment plagued her, but I knew my absence would be the worst for her to endure. Because not being with her was the worst for me too. Gods, I hated myself.

"Your realm has fallen," Reverius said quietly, yanking me back to Death's Court. "With no present ruler and your Fera in distress, there can be no peace."

"Fera?" Deyanira moved like a wraith, coming to stand at my side. She knew that little girl was my weakness. She knew I'd stared into those big, blue eyes and promised her I'd come back.

"Quill is rare," Ro answered. "Special. She is known as a Fera, which means the bearer. At a baser level, her unique power allows her to bear the emotions of others, sometimes carry them when they grow too heavy, and ultimately manipulate them, should she choose it. Her power has been lost for a millennium. And with eternal mourning, she will bring down that world, and the rest will follow. Because sadness is only a root from which anger grows."

Oh gods. I couldn't blink. Couldn't breathe. How many nights had Quill curled up beside me as I drank too much and mourned the loss of Ezra? How much of my pain had she had to bear at such a young age?

"No." Deyanira balled her fists at her side, ever the fighter, as she snapped at Ro. "You said you were going to help her. That was our bargain."

"I've been called back to Etherium." Ro tucked her dark hair behind her ear. "I'll still help as I can, but my role is vast and demanding."

Deyanira shifted forward. Her fingers twitched as she reached for her dagger. But it was immediately swept away with dark shadows. Orin's protection. Still, she fought. "You're such a liar. I did all of this for you, and you're just... leaving?"

"Such is the way of gods," the glowy one said.

Deyanira cleared her throat, shooting him a glare. He'd done something to steal her words.

Heart aching, I shuffled forward, determined to take the heat off her, but also desperate to get home. "Tell me how to go back. Can't I just walk through this?"

I knew those words would be hard for Ezra. I likely loved him. But even as we were trying to adjust to this new normal, my heart and obligation was curled in a ball crying. And if it couldn't be stopped, if she was left to sadness as no child should be, she would bring the worlds down. She would change into something else. Something born of my abandonment. I forced myself to look into Ezra's storming eyes. I expected a torrent of emotions. The betrayal and hatred. But of course it wasn't there. Because Ezra wasn't a monster. I had loved him for a reason. I'd mourned him for a reason. He was good. And kind. And everything I ever wanted back then. Staring into those eyes, I hesitated. It was only a second, but it was there, the depth of my love for him stirring within me. I should have cherished these moments more. Realized it was Death's court poisoning my mind and not reality. But the life in me felt so anchored to a realm of the living, it was too hard to accept the realm of the dead. "I'm sorry, but I will come back to you. Wait for me here and I will come back. She needs me."

"Seventy years is nothing compared to an eternity together," Ezra answered, pulling me into his arms. "I would wait a thousand lifetimes."

The promise of eternity with him wrapped around me left me feeling uncertain. As was my prerogative, I had no idea if I truly wanted that. Maybe I did. Maybe it was only my desperation to leave that made him so undesirable. Maybe I was actually terrible for thinking that. I kept my eyes down as I turned back to Reverius ready to walk into that portal.

"I've allowed the gods to return to Requiem. There is no immortality among humans anymore. No need for Maidens. Humans will live and die by fate alone, as it should be. There is no path back for you, Huntress."

I straightened, nearly choking on a breath. "What?"

"You stand in a realm of the dead, living. The Aurelian Gate is only for those touched by Death. Deyanira was marked by him at birth, but you cannot return to Requiem. Should you try to pass through, you will simply die and return here."

"That..." I shook my head. "You're supposed to be the supreme god of the fucking realms. You're telling me that little girl is going to burn it all down, and there's nothing you can do because... why, exactly? You're the master of beginnings or whatever. You can create worlds, but you can't just send me back to save everyone? What the fuck?"

"Tongue," Ro snapped.

I responded with a solid middle finger.

"There is a way," Reverius said, his authoritative nature consuming the air around him. "But all magic comes at a cost."

"Then pay it," I snapped.

"Why should I? Perhaps the Ether calls to me, Huntress."

"Bargain with me, then," I said, stepping toward him, desperate to change his mind the only way I knew how. "Let me try to save the worlds you damn so easily."

"Speak your terms, Huntress," the god said, the edges of his form darkening, if only slightly.

I was about to do something reckless. Something that went against the very nature of my resolve. Something I'd vowed to never do again after being trapped in a bargain with my old boss for years. "Send me back and I will pay the cost. Whatever it is, I will pay it."

"Paesha," Ezra and Orin said in unison.

Ezra continued, "Absolutely not."

Deyanira shifted at my side, whispering, "You can't mean that, Paesha. It's too dangerous."

I spun with a glare. "Everyone dies, Maiden. Everyone. Not just die. They cease to exist. You, me, Orin, Ezra, our family. The Syndicate, every soul across the realms if what he says is true. Tell me you wouldn't make the same deal, pay whatever the cost to save them."

I hardly saw her slight nod before the world around me stilled. The god's presence wrapped around me like a silken cocoon, separating me from my friends, though I could still feel them beside me. I tried to move, to search the blinding light for an explanation, but I couldn't.

Couldn't move.

Couldn't breathe.

Couldn't blink.

What is this? The words were meant to be internal thoughts, but the shiny asshole answered as clearly as Ro had, rattling my mind.

Blissful privacy, Huntress.

Could you maybe blow out the giant light so I can see the form I bargain with?

Are those the terms?

You're lucky I can't roll my eyes right now. Those are not terms. That was simply a request.

Denied.

Prick.

His stoic voice lost all sense of formality. *So, we're insulting gods now?*

Look, you're in my mind. I can't be held responsible for my thoughts. If I spoke them aloud, then fine, damn me to purgatory or whatever. But here, there's no tiptoeing for comfort.

Fair enough, though sadly, we don't have a lot of time for this... riveting conversation. There was a falter in his voice, followed by a flicker of light.

I knew what he was doing. I'd seen the Maestro feign weakness to quicken the pace of a lopsided deal. The less time you had to cover the terms, the more likely you were to miss the giant net falling over your freedom. But I'd already agreed to the cost. However entrapping the net was, I'd already been caught.

Then speak the terms and let's get this over with.

You can leave this realm of Death behind, Huntress, but you can't go to Requiem. You will have to start in Wisteria, in a city called Stirling and find a way back to the Fera. But it won't be easy. The paths between worlds are twisted and tangled and meant only for gods and realm walkers to travel. And since the fall of the realm walkers, only the gods are able.

16

Then how did I get to Death's Court?

The amount of power the goddess used to bring you to this realm was vast. She will feel the loss of that for centuries if you're successful. Otherwise, she will fall with the rest of us, and it will not matter.

Maybe you should care more.

Seek the path, Huntress. Start at the place they call the Hollow.

Who are they? Be more specific.

A deep, exasperated sigh followed. *The people of Stirling. Now focus if you want any chance of survival.*

Oh, so now we care about survival. Got it.

If you find the path, don't let yourself forget the reason for walking it. You must save the realms for the Fera.

The weight of his words fell onto my soul like the burden they were. But then I realized what he'd said.

For or from?

Perhaps both. As for the bargain's terms: if you have not returned to the Fera in seventy-five days, you will lose all your memories and be stuck in Wisteria forever. The worlds will fall to peril and it will be because of your failure. There will be famine and death and warfare beyond anything you can imagine. You will know you are at fault, but you'll never know why. When you return to the present, you will only speak your agreement to these terms and nothing else, so others may bear witness. None can know of this bargain or where you come from. Only me. You'll walk obediently forward and through the Aurelian Gate.

And if I don't agree? I needed a minute. Just a minute to think this through, to comb through the terms and make sure I completely understood what I was agreeing to. But I was not afforded that luxury.

I could hear the god's evil tsk in my mind. I could even feel the hint of a smile on lips I'd never seen as he answered. *Oh, my dear. Don't you remember? You've already agreed.*

Shock slammed into me as the veil fell and I was once again

standing within the decay of Death's court. I turned, staring only at Ezra. My heart hammered in my throat. My vision faded to only him as I spoke the only words I was allowed. "I agree to your terms, Keeper."

"What terms?" Orin demanded, surging forward. "What did you do?"

But before he could get to me, before I could be stopped and the deal broken, I spun and took a single step backward. Silently I mouthed, "I'm sorry," just as Quill's sweet face flashed into my mind and the portal swallowed me whole.

2

I wasn't a saint. Not a god or a conqueror. I was likely closer to the villain than I was the hero. But I was never reckless. Calculating at times? Yes. But foolish? *Never.* Except now, apparently. When everything that would happen from this point forward was a matter of life and death, not just for me, but for all existence. And it all boiled down to one precious little girl that needed me to find a way home.

Still, as I stood cast into a world that wasn't my own, stuck in the aftermath of a foolish bargain with a god, I was lost for the first time in my life. I added a new title to my growing list of things I'd found myself becoming.

Desperate.

Bits of wind and ice lashed my face as I studied a boy peddling his wares. Deep brown eyes keen and his fingers nimble, he wore a wool coat that was far too small and a hat that smothered his ears. But he reached expertly into his patron's pockets without their knowledge. I'd watched him for hours, chatting with passersby as he tried and failed to sell them things. But his fingers were quick and nimble. No one suspected a child. A fact I'd also learned at his age.

Mostly, children were innocent, untarnished by the complexities and poisons of reality. But watching the adept little thief from my spot in the shadowed alley, I realized some things were universal. Hatred. Love. Desperation. Even hunger.

I was no different than the boy. In a matter of three hours, I'd stolen a cloak, a letter opener, and half a bottle of liquor so potent it'd probably keep me warm for a solid week, even in these frigid temperatures. It wasn't shelter. Or food. But those would come.

"Four silver! Get your mask. Fifteen silver! Get your invite. Might be real, might not." The boy brushed messy, brown hair from his face, the frozen locks of ice leaving a trace of dirt behind. "Salts invited too. Four silver! Get your mask!"

"Travers McKinney, you get your ass inside and stop trying to scam these good folk outta their wages. Tithe's coming."

"They could be real tickets, Ma! The Silk man said—"

Puffy cheeks reddened as she leaned so far out the window, I thought she might fall. Perhaps they were immortal here, too. "You'll catch your death on the word of the rich, you fool."

Guess not.

The boy's face turned sour as he held frozen fingers up to his mother to show her his coin. "Least I'll have a coin for safe passage to Death's Court."

I'd chosen him specifically. Kids were smart, and they knew things without knowing they knew them. They watched. They listened to obscure things. But if I waited to approach him any longer, the woman hanging outside of her window would likely coax him in.

The bitter fingers of a frozen breeze wrapped around my neck, blowing strands of chestnut hair across my face. I lifted my shoulders for warmth and stepped out of the alley, moving toward the boy. The moment my feet hit the bricks lining the street, a tug on my cloak pulled me back. I spun, eyes falling on another child.

"Don't do it," he said, his sunken cheeks and lack of color to his skin haunting. "The tickets aren't real. I heard the Silk man say it."

"I'm not interested in tickets." My eyes flashed to the hand still gripping my cloak as I wondered what a Silk man was.

The gaunt boy, who couldn't have been older than ten, followed my glance, but didn't pull away, instead digging his fingers into the fabric tighter. "What you want from him, anyway?"

He glared across the street until I saw it. The jealousy in his stare. The hint of envy souring his face. The eyes of a child were the unyielding sentinels of truth, and in my most desperate days, they rarely steered me wrong. But to pit the boys against one another, to lean on a suspicion was risky in a foreign world. One where I didn't know the laws or what made people tick. Still, I had to try.

"He promised me he knows where the Hollow is. I'm just visiting, you see, and I don't know exactly how to get there."

"Oh." He adjusted his round cap with a small brim in front, no doubt made of wool and the only thing keeping him warm. "Well, I could help you. I been there once."

"I wouldn't want to be a bother and I'm sure your friend over there can manage."

"No, it's not a bother. I wouldn't even make you pay." Something foreign crossed the boy's face, something that should have been a warning had I been less trusting of children. "Give me a story instead."

"All right, that sounds like a fair deal. What kind of story would you like to hear?"

His dark green eyes narrowed, a victorious smile crossing sunken features. "Tell me about a time you fell in love."

A handsome face flashed into my mind, followed by immediate heartache, mourning, and then a feeling of regret. I opened my mouth to speak, to tell him of the man I'd loved and lost and recently reunited with. But as those words came to me, as I grappled to hang onto them, the feelings, the memories, anything tangible... vanished, fading like a dream hours after waking. I stumbled backward, searching and searching my mind until I realized I must have been mistaken. There was no man. No mourning. No regret. Nothing.

I'd never been in love.

But...

No.

I pressed my hand to my chest, pulling away from the boy. "I'm so sorry. I think I've only been in love in my dreams."

His smile widened until it edged on the side of unnatural, causing the hair on my arms to stand and my heart to plummet in discomfort. "Thank you for your story, Huntress."

Ice cold shock slammed into me at a title that I owned but hadn't shared in this world. "But I didn't...?"

He stood a little straighter, like a dancer before the curtain raised, the gray color in his cheeks turning pink and vibrant. "There's an inn at the end of this street. You'll go past it, turn left toward the Parlor. Walk until your feet hurt and you see a big stone bridge. Follow Grimwater River east a little. There's an old green cart that sits outside the Hollow. But don't tell no one you're going there. It's a secret. I'm supposed to tell you to find the Lord of the Salt if you want to find your path." He spun on a heel, and tore off down the street, so quick it wasn't worth the effort to chase him down.

That arrogant god had promised a path home, and apparently riddled it with creepy children to mock and guide me. At least I'd given nothing away with his bargain. Hadn't even had a story to tell him. But he'd called me Huntress and I couldn't help but circle the burning question as I started toward the Hollow.

What other secrets about me had this meddling god revealed to his pawns? And why?

3

Huntress. Glorified thief. That was my only value to everyone that never mattered. My father, in the end, who'd traded my skill for his own pleasures. My former boss, the Maestro, who'd taught me to steal before I knew how to read. Even the others who danced on stage with me. I was only a pickpocket. A crook. But I was really fucking good at it.

I had grown up on the streets, learning from the wicked and cunning. Every lesson was a brutal necessity for survival. Each trick, each scam, each theft, a necessary step out of the filthy and desperate world I'd danced in. I clawed my way up, not out of some romantic notion of a better life, but because the alternative was a slow, painful existence.

I'd come a long way since that poisoned childhood. Which wasn't saying much, but some people never grew up that way. They never knew the fear of starvation. The desperation found on a bone-chilling winter night. They knew nothing of self-deprecation or giving away every bit of yourself and your dignity for basic human needs.

I'd become a ballet dancer as a child, with aspirations of fawning crowds and tossed bouquets, maybe even heart-swelling love. But as I grew into a woman, those foolish dreams were swallowed whole by a man that coaxed me onto a different kind of stage. Before an audience that craved lust and a glimpse into the waning pride of a naked dancer.

With every step and spin, every inch of my skin I showed, I'd learned to lock away tiny bits of me, bits of my soul that I could protect from reality. Those pieces were only ever shown to a handful of people. I knew how to love ferociously and protect like a wild animal. Because the few that earned it, deserved it, and those that fell short were simply stepping stones to a better life.

Working for a crime lord, I'd danced among higher society, draped in stolen silks and adorned with ill-gotten jewels. I crafted a persona of elegance, but beneath it all, I was still that poor child, fighting tooth and nail to stay one step ahead so I'd never have to sleep curled up behind a pile of garbage in an alley again.

Bitter wind gnawed at my skin as I walked along unfamiliar streets. The city of Stirling differed vastly from the rotting edifice of Requiem. Every building here was made of stacked stone like looming castle walls topped with intricate carvings. I felt so small. Lost even. But nothing was as disorientating as the narrow, winding cobblestone streets and alleys. A fact the boy had failed to mention in his hurried explanation. Still, I marveled at the buildings, their stone facades weathered and worn, as if they had stood sentinel for centuries.

Horse-drawn carriages clattered along the uneven streets. The drivers hunched against the cold, their breath puffing out in misty clouds. The horses' hooves struck the stones with a rhythmic clip-clop, but something felt wrong, opposite of Requiem. There was life among the homeless there. Dreams among the people. Here? The long faces of strangers rushing by lacked color. Vibrancy. Smothered by the dense fog creeping along the frozen streets.

The heavy air seeped into my bones, the gray, dull world stealing any sense of beauty in the vacant sky above. I pulled the stolen cloak tightly around me, its heavy fabric offering a feeble barrier against the biting cold. Each step was a battle.

As I walked, the crunch of my boots on the frosted bricks added a solitary rhythm to the cadence of the muted city. I could have danced to it, lost beneath the never sky of a foreign world.

But as of now, I was a vagabond. An intruder. With no home, no resources except what I'd stolen, and not a single plan beyond finding the Hollow. And now, apparently the Lord of the Salt. Everything was foreign and unsettling. My magic was thoroughly unanchored here in Wisteria. I'd spent a lifetime familiarizing the swell of power within me to the streets, alleys, people, and even the stones of Requiem. And though I didn't plan to stick around this city for long, I still dragged my fingers down the walls, brushed unsuspecting strangers, and let magic unfurl enough to give me a small sense of familiarity. I could hunt almost anything. People, paths, things, but because all magic requires balance, and a price paid, I could only find the things I'd already found once. Things I'd touched and seen. Random buildings in a foreign world included. I kept my head hidden within the dark walls of the stolen cloak and continued following the directions from the eerie boy.

I knew it was foolish, but what choice did I have? Without a doubt, he'd been sent by the god of god things. And now, I was bound to my bargain with that meddling fucker.

"Don't get too close to them," a woman sneered, gripping her child and yanking him away from a vagrant stooped over an open fire. "Pure trash, the Salt."

The boy, with a rigid spine and finely pressed suit, tucked in closer to his mother. "Yes ma'am."

If I had a coin, I would have passed it on to the dirty, bearded man, if only to soothe the wound of such cruel words. Instead, I walked by, letting the warmth of his fire creep over my skin as I passed him the flask I'd stolen.

"It's not much. But that's all I have."

His kind, sunken eyes met mine, the crow's feet growing at the corners as he shared a smile, unaware of the way I brushed my fingers across his in the exchange, nor the hint of power. "I thank you, Miss. Beware the Silk."

Salt vs Silk. Got it.

I dipped my chin and continued on my way. On and on I walked, eradicating the feeling of floating through a mysterious world with every bit of magic I planted in it. It was impossible for me to refrain from using power. Anchoring myself to people and things came as naturally as breathing. When I hunted, seeking the location of those things, that was always a choice, but I had no control over marking, beyond touching as many things as I could. Still, the use of it wore on me. Exhaustion crept in, unfamiliar and worrisome. I'd never had an issue using magic in Requiem, but I knew power was rarely an endless supply. Everything came with a cost, and for me that cost was typically light fatigue. This was heavier. As if it were taking from me.

A giant man approached, his steps sure as he held a book before his nose, eyes scanning the page rather than where he was going. I turned, looking into a warmly lit shop as I planted myself in front of him. Right on cue, he slammed into me. I'd been prepared, of course, gripping his wrist to keep us both from falling over as I... collected him, in a sense, marking him with power.

"I uh... sorry, Miss. Didn't see you there."

"Good book?" I asked, eyes down, so as not to be memorable.

"The Seventh War of the Division: A Lesson of Gods."

"No." I feigned shock. "I've just finished a book on the second war. Do you mind if I take a peek?"

The tall man handed the book to me with a nod just as a creepy, masked figure stepped out from around a corner up the road, the inky black robes they wore heavily contrasting everything gray around us. With a small release of power, I quickly handed the novel back to the man. "I can't wait to get to it."

I didn't stick around for his reply. I'd simply wanted to mark the book. As I continued on, getting closer to the mysterious figure, the rapid pulse of curiosity within me quickly changed to an odd feeling of dread. I struggled to pull a breath into my lungs by the time I was within five paces of the ominous being standing at the mouth of the alley. But it was only a cloak. Perhaps the black mask with delicate golden filigree was odd for me, but the man hadn't seemed concerned with the figure at all.

Maybe I should have turned and ran, but as I allowed myself the tiniest glimpse of the dark robe, the silver crest on their chest told me two very important facts. One: they were linked to a leader in some capacity, be it enforcement of law or huntsman, and two: running would paint a target on my back. The paranoia I felt was unwarranted. I'd done nothing wrong.

Two paces now, heart racing, I shoved trembling fingers into the folds of my cloak, grazing the handle of the letter opener I'd stolen from an unsuspecting merchant. The temperature dropped as I neared. Warning bells of peril pealed across my mind. My nerves, vibrating with unmatched fear, came alive the second I stepped past.

Run. Run.

But those thoughts had come too late. Strong arms reached

forward and captured me, dragging me into the darkened alley as I screamed.

A massive hand slammed over my mouth. He spoke in a monotonous tone. "You stole from that man and will be punished. As stated in the Code of Arms, Section Seven-Twenty, Subsection C: Thievery shall not be tolerated within the realm. Those suspected of such crimes will submit to questioning."

I lashed out, trying to scramble away. "Get your fucking hands off me. I stole nothing."

I was strong and limber and had stamina for days. Pushing off the adjacent wall with my feet, I sent us both careening down the narrow space, my adrenaline surging to life as he held his grip on me. He whipped me around, slamming me into the wall. The back of my head ground into the building. With long fingers wrapped tightly around my throat, I forgot about the cold. I forgot about the Hollow. I thought only of the fear. Of my own vulnerability. Of how foolish I'd been to let my guard down. Staring into the mostly hidden eyes of whatever this monstrosity was, my limbs trembled. He squeezed tighter. So tight I was sure he'd sever my head from my body with pure brute strength.

"You will submit to testing." His voice was so eerie, muffled behind the dark mask, I couldn't tell if it'd been in my head or spoken aloud, but it coated my fear all the same. "Stop fighting."

"Go ask him if he is missing something," I grunted, swinging an elbow until it bounced off his hard head.

"Enough of this." With only that as a warning, a fist of steel cracked my skull, connecting with my eye. Stars exploded across my vision. Searing pain followed. I could only see out of one eye now, the other rapidly swelled shut as terror threatened to overwhelm me and my body stilled.

Fight back, I pleaded with myself. *Be strong.*

My lungs burned, desperate for air around his firm grip. I

thought of Death's Maiden, an assassin in a world of immortals who took no shit and succumbed to no one. A woman who'd become a friend to me when I hadn't deserved her. If I died here and now, would our reunion be a celebration or an admittance of my defeat? And then how long until the realms fell because of it?

Fingers still tightly locked around my throat, the cloaked man pulled me from the wall, lifting until my feet dangled. I tried to pry him away to no avail. I kicked him between the legs, but the bastard didn't flinch. As my vision continued to worsen, I did the only other thing I could think of. I sank my thumbs into the holes of his mask, burying them into his eye sockets. His scream was more of a guttural howl, an inhuman bellow that originated from the depths of his tortured soul. It echoed through the narrow alleyway, bouncing off the grimy walls and gaining momentum with every ricochet. A wet, squelching sensation encompassed me as my thumbs buried further into the soft jelly of his eyes, and my stomach rolled with revulsion. But I fought back the bile burning my throat. I could not be weak. Fragility was only for people that'd never been broken. Those that were forged in the fire of their own ruin became harder, sharper, unable to shatter again. Or so I tried to convince myself.

The man's grip around my neck loosened, and he staggered backwards, releasing a string of garbled curses. His hands flew up to cover his ruined eyes, and he stumbled, falling to the ground with a heavy thud.

I gasped for breath. Desperate to keep from panicking further. I couldn't be caught. I couldn't be bound to this world in any capacity. Each gulp of air was like inhaling shards of glass; sharp and cold, they stabbed my lungs until tears filled in my eyes. My throat burned from the trauma, every beat of my pulse throbbed painfully against the tender flesh.

Pushing myself onto shaky legs, I looked down at the writhing form of my attacker. Blood seeped from beneath his hands where they were pressed against his face. He moaned and rolled. His body convulsed in pain. But I felt no mercy. No remorse. Fucker.

Through my one good eye, I watched the man turning to the side with a groan. His hand slipped in the puddle of blood, but still he tried to rise.

What the fuck?

He was relentless, a monster that refused to stay down. My mind raced, desperately searching for a way out of this nightmare when I remembered the letter opener in my pocket. I lunged forward, a scream tearing from my raw throat as the blade plunged into his chest, piercing through layers of dark fabric and sinking into yielding flesh. I watched, holding my breath as he took his last.

His last.

I'd killed a man.

In Requiem, murder was a rarity, a fate delivered by one person only. I turned, retching violently onto the grimy alley floor. The acrid stench of vomit mingled with the coppery tang of blood, creating a nauseating smell that clung to my throat, gagging me. I wiped my mouth with the back of my hand, smearing a streak of red across my skin.

My back collided with the frozen wall, sending a chill so penetrating through me, I stood frozen, replaying the last moments. I'd fought men before, sword in hand, cutting them down. But there was comfort in knowing they wouldn't die. That if their deaths came, that marking would never be on my soul. Only the Maiden's.

But if I'd killed a man—I gasped. Orin would come.

Tears blurred my vision as I sank to my knees, the icy cobblestones biting into my skin. I wanted to go back to Death's

Court, to find another way to Requiem. To the familiar streets and the comforting embrace of those I loved. Fuck this awful, dingy, colorless place. I needed the warmth and simplicity of stage lights, the rush of adrenaline as I danced, and the sense of belonging I'd fought so hard to achieve. The simplicity of winning over a crowd and walking away at the end of a show. Because I was not a hero. And this task was too great.

I knelt there, waiting for him as a figure emerged from around the corner. Hope flared in my chest, a desperate prayer that it was Orin. But it was not Death, come to reap a soul. It was another of the masked guards. His dark robes billowed in the frigid wind.

He looked down at his fallen comrade, then back at me. I gave him no time to react. I bolted to my feet and dashed the opposite way down the alley, but half blinded, I didn't see the other two. Nor did I see the fist before it slammed into my face. The second blow struck like a thunderbolt, a searing flash of pain exploding behind my eyes. My head snapped back, skull cracking again against the unyielding stone wall. Stars burst across my vision in dazzling pinpricks of light before everything went dark. Why the hell hadn't Orin come?

4

She was stunning, as she always had been. Though dressed like a doll in layers of pretty lace, she stood on a pile of bodies, bathed in the blood of the innocent. The curls in her hair were soaked through with blood, the red enveloping her signature golden brown.

Eight years old. She was eight years old.

Stepping toward the child, toward my Quilly, heart in my throat, I did not look down. Did not consider who I stood upon as I climbed the hill of the fallen to get to her.

"Quill." I tried to keep my voice calm, still, void of judgment. But only anguish and despair seeped from my lips. Only a cry of pain. Not for those below me. Not for the slaughtered. But for the soul of the child that had shattered the world. The Fera.

She turned to me. Nothing but hatred rolling from her glare as she bared her teeth, letting her power race forward, overtaking the way my heart ached for her. Her control over emotions, hers and those around her, had grown. It suffocated everything I felt; transformed it into something wild and furious.

"I love you, Quilly. Please don't take that away from me. Let me love you. I don't want this anger. Take it back."

"You left me," she roared. "You were supposed to return."

"I'm trying. I'm trying so hard."

The child soared forward, so close I could see the blood spattered across her skin like freckles, so close I could hear the tremble in her cry. She sank into herself, into the child I'd known her to be and not the monster that waged war in a broken realm. Tears of blood streaked down her round face. She turned, surveying the slaughtered before falling to her knees. "I think I hurt these people."

"It's not real."

She looked up to me, as she did the day I'd met her and swept her away from the monster that'd been my boss. She and I were the same. Kindred spirits.

I knelt, reaching my hand forward to tuck a wild curl behind her ear. But my fingers passed through.

"Are you mad?" she whispered, staring down at the ground. "Can you forgive me?"

"Of course I can. You and me against the world, remember?"

But, as if she hadn't heard me at all, she reached for someone below her, a body discarded within the masses. The child tried to clear red hair from a familiar face, streaking it with blood instead.

"Paesha will be home soon and she can fix this, Thea. She can fix me. You'll come back too."

My stomach rolled as I stared into the vacant green eyes of a woman that'd been a sister to me.

Sorrow coated me, stealing my ability to think and breathe. Growing like a thorn in my throat, refusing to let me swallow as tears burned my eyes. Thea. Nevermore to laugh. Nevermore to love. Nevermore to dream.

"It's not real," I whispered again, to myself more than the child that could not hear me.

But then the world flickered and faded, the bodies vanishing to nothing as a familiar being soared forward. She shined so bright her dark skin practically glowed, matching her perfect smile. Ro, the meddling goddess that had promised she would help protect Quill.

"You failed," I said through clenched teeth.

But she didn't react to my hateful words. Instead, she only repeated words she'd already said to me, as if reminding me why I'd chosen this.

"She will bring down that world, and the rest will follow. Because sadness is only a root from which anger grows."

"No shit. But how am I supposed to get back to her?"

Though her mouth moved, whatever words she uttered were silent. Less than a whisper. Nothing at all as a piercing pain ripped through my body and wrenched me out of the horrible nightmare.

5

A silent scream lodged in my throat as I writhed in agony, disoriented by the sudden transition from dream to reality. Everything hurt. But the pain sat behind a torrent of fear.

I hung suspended by my arms in a place so dark, if not for the moonlight trickling in through one small window, I'd have never guessed it was a prison. My shoulders protested in agony. My wrists were tender and raw from the chains hanging from the ceiling. The pain was a wildfire, consuming my limbs with a searing, unrelenting heat that left me gasping for air and struggling to hold on to consciousness.

One thing held me anchored. One thing sank its talons into my mind and held me in the present. Beyond the pain. Beyond the unknown. Something strange. A song. A melody that felt as familiar as it did foreign, tossing me through the oddest sense of déjà vu in a world I'd never been. But something about the song coated even the sharpest pain, soothing it, if only for a moment while my thoughts raced to remember where I'd heard it.

"H-hello?" I whispered, unsure if I'd conjure help or another of those demons.

Behind the bars of the prison cell across from mine, a hunched figure shifted. I had to squint through my one good eye to bring them into focus. A slight groan and several movements later, he crept across the floor of his cell, not bound by thick chains as I was.

"Please. Please help me."

The face of a man shifted into the moonlight as he pressed his sunken cheeks to the prison bars. His long beard, silver and matted, grazed the floor. Wild eyes looked up at me. "Say nothing to the Cimmerians, girl. Not a word. Be strong but silent, lest they take everything."

His words were powerful. The only offering he had in such conditions.

"I need to get down," I said. "My hands are numb and my shoulders are on fire."

The old man laughed. "Be grateful for the numbness." He moved his fingers forward, pushing them through the bars until they stroked the stream of moonlight.

I nearly vomited. Gnarled and broken, void of nails and stained black with rot, the old man's fingers were a haunting testament to the horrors of this place. His laughter echoed through the hollow prison, wrapping around me. "Numbness," he croaked between breaths, "is a blessing."

The melody hung thicker now, winding through the cells, past the crumbling walls, and into my throbbing skull. My pulse hummed along with the rhythm as if recognizing an old friend. I hated it and needed it in equal measure. I didn't want comfort.

"Can you hear it?" I whispered, wincing as the chains dug deeper into my raw wrists.

The old man's laughter waned, replaced by a solemn silence. "Aye. It began when you were chained."

"Are we alone?" I asked, my voice shaky from the cold and fear, but desperate to hold a conversation, if only to keep myself conscious.

"We're never alone. The Cimmerians watch and the song observes. Newly observing."

"We're being watched by a song?" I asked. The ridiculousness of the idea helped distract from the throbbing pain that continued to engulf me.

"Aye, girl. Sounds have eyes, walls have ears, and shadows play with the minds of men."

The old man's cryptic words hung in the frigid air between us. The chains rattled slightly, vibrating with the rhythm of the song that was somehow watching us as I felt it wrap around me like ribbons.

"Is there a way out of here?"

His laughter returned, harsh and brittle. "Escape? If I knew a way out, don't you think I would have taken it?"

"How... How long have you been here?"

"Time? Time is an honor we do not have. It slips through our fingers like sand in a sieve."

He must have been losing it. His words grew more twisted and their meanings practically useless. I needed him to focus while he still could. "Can you see anything from your angle? How many cells are there? Is there another prisoner here? Please."

"I grow weary, child."

"Please," I managed, beyond the thick lump in my throat. "I can't stay here."

The old man sighed heavily, his thin chest rising and falling like a ghost ship on a stormy sea. He turned his gaze to the window barred with rusting metal. "There is another. One more, far at the end. The song. Then there is only desolation and tortured souls that have long since departed."

"The humming is a person? One other?"

He fell into a long pause, his eyes glazing over as though lost in the past. "Yes. The other. The one who hums. The rest are gone. Taken by the Cimmerians or simply dead. Their bodies left to feed the starving rodents."

The old man's eyes flashed with intensity. The humming stopped. He leaned into the bars. The dampness of his ragged clothes and the sour rot from his lack of hygiene struck me hard. "Remember my warning, girl. Say nothing. Give nothing." With that, he retreated to his corner, his silhouette blending into the darkness of his cell.

I swallowed, trying to drown the fear welling up inside me. The sound of chains echoed through the prison once more as I shifted my weight from the tip of one foot to the other. Somewhere, beyond the confines of my cell, heavy footfalls echoed. Each thud felt as if it landed directly on my chest, threatening to steal whatever breath I managed to draw into my burning lungs.

I forced my uninjured eye open despite the spots dancing in my vision. Perhaps the wound to my face was a mercy. With one green eye and one blue, if I ever escaped, they'd know me instantly. I wrapped my mind around that single blessing as the stomps drew nearer. I wanted nothing more than to let my head hang and pretend I'd died, but I doubted they'd be so easily tricked and truly, I needed information from them as much as they needed it from me.

Two guards entered, their bulky shadows blotting out the faint moonlight that leaked in from the small, barred window. Their eyes remained hidden behind those dark masks with intricate designs etched into them. The Cimmerians were the guards from the alley. And I'd killed one of their brethren.

"She wakes," one said, voice muffled behind the metal.

"Murderer," another hissed, shoving a key into the door of my cell and twisting.

I held my breath. Half in fear and half from pain, as trembling caused my limbs to burn. I tried, gods I tried to keep from crying out as the man moved forward, pulled a whip from beneath his robes and sliced it through my cell, shredding the cloak I still wore. Warm blood leaked from the fresh wound, blooming across my stomach.

"Confess to your crimes."

White light lanced across my vision as another strike came, hard and fast. Hot tears streamed down my face. The only thing I could hold on to were the words of the crippled old man. *Say nothing. Give nothing.*

There was a profound silence. The only sound was the rhythmic thump-thump of my heart and the ragged breathing of the Cimmerian. He snarled, pulling his whip back for another strike. It came faster, more furious than before, the pain hot and cold simultaneously.

I couldn't hold on to my silence. In misery and agony, I let out a wail that surely rattled the rusted iron bars as much as the chains holding me. I hated it. I'd broken so easily. How could an old, decrepit man last for so long, when I'd gone mere minutes before making a sound?

The low, ominous chuckle of the Cimmerian guard turned my veins to fire and rage. Fuck him. Fuck the god that'd sent me to this hellhole to die. Fuck the realms. They could burn. I was not a hero.

I was not a hero.

I squeezed my eye shut, preparing for the next strike. Only Quill's beautiful blue eyes kept me company as lash after lash shredded my skin to ribbons. Across my stomach, my thighs, even my neck.

Unable to see a thing, I listened as the guard stomped across the cell. The sound of shifting chains echoed through the small space, accompanied by the hiss of metal on metal. Only then did I realize I'd been spun around. He circled me again, though raising my head to follow him was a chore.

"Speak and I will release you from your chains."

I bit my tongue and couldn't feel it. The slice of my teeth was nothing compared to the ruination of my body. Of the skin hanging from bones. My clothes were nothing more than shreds of fabric soaked in blood.

I took three more lashings across my back before the world faded away.

"Pity." The old man's voice dragged me from unconsciousness.

I lay on my side in a puddle of dried blood. The humming returned, coating me, wrapping around me as if it were only mine, speaking to the dancer I used to be. Never again.

"Come," he said. "Come closer to your bars, child. Let me see your face."

I couldn't move at all. Not an inch. I'd been dropped to the floor, and the chains were gone, but I was sure my cheekbone had been broken in the fall.

"You must fight through the pain, or you will die here. Move."

"Water," I rasped.

"You broke. Though it was clear your mind had already protected you. You begged for mercy." He shifted forward, those gnarled fingers gripping the bars in front of him. "That is why they released you. But they will be back for more. Do better."

"Water," I repeated.

But he only responded by humming along with the tune seeping through the old prison until it lulled me back to sleep.

WHEN I WOKE, stars spun in a dizzying dance over my head. Or maybe that was just the blood trickling into my eyes. I didn't know. I didn't care. Dawn was breaking, streaks of merciless light pouring through the tiny window near the ceiling, illuminating the dried blood and dust floating in the stale air.

A day had passed. But had it only been a day? Might I have been here longer? How long had I been unconscious? Did they bring me here first after knocking me out in the alley? Had I been drugged? The sluggish weight on my mind made me think so. I'd already lost track of the pressing countdown delivered by a god that didn't care about the realms. Maybe that was always his plan.

I peeked into the old man's cell with pity. I knew he'd been here longer, was far older, and had likely been through far worse than me. Maybe I was weak. Maybe I was nothing more than a vain dancer from Requiem, shoved into a bargain I had no right making. Maybe I wasn't a hero, but I was more than this. If he could be strong, so could I.

"There," he whispered, pointing to the corner of my cell. "Get yourself over there and drink, lass, before the rain freezes."

I turned my head toward the window, letting my one good eye follow the trickling rain. There was no question of pride here. I'd drink rain water off a prison floor if it meant I'd live. But I wasn't sure if I could make it all the way over there.

"Start with your fingers, one at a time. Good. Good."

I wanted to cry. I wanted to scream. I wanted to give up. But that soft voice of a tortured soul would not let me. So, I moved. I crept across the floor, letting my tears fall. Everything hurt. Still,

I pushed. Until little by little, I crept across the floor and sank my fingers into the water.

"See that? It tastes of victory."

I hadn't been able to lift my head, only turn until my lips pressed into the puddle and then I drank. The tang of water shocked me. Whatever this flavor, it certainly wasn't victory. But it was something. If only a morsel of comfort. I closed my eyes and listened to the stranger's haunted humming. The lament was sad, languid and beautiful. And though sometimes the singer's voice broke, and I could only imagine silent tears filled that space, they always continued. Perhaps in their own way, it was a rebellion against Wisteria's evil guardians.

But when the song abruptly stopped and the guard's stomping began, I felt a small piece of my heart break. I wasn't ready. I'd never rise again after another beating. I could feel it in my bones.

The old man cleared his throat, dragging my attention to him. He pressed one gnarled finger against his lips, and then he began humming the haunting tune. The cloaked figures returned, but this time, rather than facing me, they gathered around the cell across from mine. I couldn't breathe beyond my panic. He would never survive a lashing like the one I had yesterday.

A Cimmerian knelt before the other cell, dragging his baton across each bar as he taunted. "So you know how to make noise, old man. Confess to your crimes."

"No," he answered, his voice far weaker than it had been. Likely coated in fear. Had he truly never made a sound until now? He'd done that for me? Stealing their attention and saving me. And there was nothing I could do as they wrenched open his door and grabbed him. I held my breath as they dragged the old man from his cell and down the hall. His eyes locked with mine as he pressed his lips into a fine line and dipped his chin.

And though I couldn't hear him, nor could I be sure, I thought maybe he mouthed, *be strong*, before they faded out of the light.

The echo of their departure reverberated in the grim silence of the cell block. The old man's vacant space stared at me, a terrible reminder of my own inevitable fate. I lay there for ages, watching the light appear and disappear through the window as time passed. Days passed. I could guess seventy-two days remained at this point, but it would only be a lie I told myself for comfort, counting down my own demise.

The person down the row who hummed the tune did so on a cycle. I knew when they slept. When they wept and when their heart hurt the most. Their song changed, melting into another based on their mood it seemed, reminding me of Quill. Of how everyone around her knew how she felt, simply by proximity. Because that was her power. And likely her damnation. Everyone's.

I slept, woke, searched for the old man, and slept again, my body trying desperately to heal. The water had long since dried before I woke to the old man staring at me from across the way. He said nothing, didn't move at all as those forlorn eyes spoke of the horror he'd been through. His cheeks were more sunken in than they had been, and dirt and blood stained his long beard.

"I'm sorry," I whispered.

But he simply blinked and turned away, his broken body moving more slowly than mine. I stared at the rise and fall of his shoulders, listening to the harsh rasp of his haggard breathing. Only then did I realize the muted singing had stopped. The Cimmerians were coming again already.

Though still laying on the cold ground, I balled my fists and prepared myself. They would come for me this time, and I would shout from the rooftops, demanding it if I needed to. I could be strong. Just as he'd been. I would be his shield, just as he'd been mine.

The stomping boots matched the cadence of my heartbeat as they approached, their masks as ominous today as they'd always been.

I stared into their eyes, lifting myself into a sitting position.

Come and get me, you fuckers. I'm ready.

The second the door swung open and the guard gripped me beneath my arms, I quickly learned I was not, in fact, ready.

6

The guard's touch was harsh and brutal, like the bite of frozen steel against raw skin. His fingers tightened around my arms with a crushing grip. I resisted, but my little act of defiance seemed to amuse him as he yanked me up with an effortless tug.

The low, mocking chortles of the Cimmerian's laughter slipped into my ears, crawled deeper down, and squeezed my core. I sucked in a shallow breath and squared my shoulders. I would not give them the satisfaction of seeing me wilt. Though it pained me, I reached forward, brushing my fingers over the keys on his belt as I fought. He gasped and pinned me with a glare before he kicked me in the stomach. I fought no more.

They dragged me down the dimly lit corridor, shoving past the other empty cells. Try as I might, I couldn't see a figure beyond the bleak darkness, no proof of anyone with a voice of pure honey. But I wasn't able to dwell on that, entering a room bathed in horror. The scent of old copper invaded my nostrils, a potent stench of rust and blood. The room was dominated by a table in the center and its wooden surface was stained with the things I didn't want to know about. Wisps of chilled air licked at my face as the masked guards threw me onto it. And I was too damn afraid to fight back.

Leather creaked and metal clanged as they bound my wrists and feet. One of them towered over me. "Confess to your crime, murderer."

And though he peered over the side of my face with an eye still swollen shut, I could see the hatred beyond the mask. The fury in his eyes at what we both knew I'd done. "Do you think you're better off waiting for the prince? He will come. And he will take."

I bit the inside of my cheek to keep from answering. Not that I knew shit about the prince, but the urge to spit at the guard was overwhelming, if only my mouth weren't so dry. I stared at him and said nothing, a hateful sneer my only response. The prince could come and take what he wished, but he would never own my spirit. With that thought alone, I allowed a small grin to curl at the corners of my mouth, my gaze never wavering.

The Cimmerian's breath hitched, and his hold tightened. Then, with a growl of pure loathing, he spun around, gripping a knob attached to a wheel. The anticipation alone made me nauseous, but I squashed it down. If I vomited, I'd choke on it and that was the least of my worries.

The guard slowly turned the wheel. The ropes around my wrists and ankles tightened. The first cracks echoed throughout the room in a horrifying promise of torment. Pain spread through me like wildfire, consuming everything in its path with a vengeance that could rival an inferno. Each crack was a symphony of agony, a cacophony that threatened to pull me under its cruel rhythm. It didn't take long for the tears to start, torrid trails sweeping down my face.

"Confess," he snarled again, the word dripping from his lips like venom. The satisfaction in his eyes made my stomach roll.

Yet, amid the blinding pain and guilt, I found an ember of resolve. It was tiny. As frail as the old man's voice, but it was there, my only hope. If he could endure this torture, then so could I. For him and for all the others who may have lost their lives on this godsdamn table.

The Cimmerian let out a low growl. Creepy fucker. His focus shifted from inflicting pain to decoding my insolence when I made no sound. His hands stilled on the wheel as he leaned over me, his mask only inches from my face. "This is nothing compared to what awaits you."

I could hear the smirk in his voice, taste the satisfaction he took from every second he held me on the brink of death. But he had no idea that Death was my friend, and I would be greeted with joy when I left this wretched world behind.

"I can stop," he whispered, spittle hitting my ear. "I can stop as soon as you speak the words. Did you hunt my brother down before you killed him? Did he leave that pretty mark on your face?"

I closed my eyes and pictured Quill's lovely smile as the groan of the wheel began again and the ropes pulled tighter around my wrists and ankles. Fire blazed beneath my skin, searing and lancing up along the bones of my arms and legs as my body was stretched on the rack. I bit down hard on my tongue. Blood filled my mouth, but I refused to give them the satisfaction of a scream. It happened in my mind though. Ripping me apart on the inside long before the contraption did on the outside.

With every pull of the wheel, I felt a part of me losing hold, slipping away into a deep abyss where the pain was but a dull echo. Yet, there was a fierce stubbornness in me that refused to let go completely. I clung onto the image of Quill's smile; each strand of laughter tinkling in my ears, each sparkle in her eyes forming an anchor to reality. It was pathetic and I knew it, but it was all I had.

The closest Cimmerian growled in frustration, slamming a hand against the table. "I will break you."

The one that'd been silently watching by the door lunged to grab the wheel as the other did the unthinkable. He threw his entire body weight into the spin. The only thing that saved me as the lights went out was one merciful Cimmerian's opposing grip on the wheel that was bound to rip me in half.

I WOKE BACK in my cell, the song once more coating me, though I no longer found comfort in the tune of a stranger. My waning awareness was a pendulum, swinging precariously between consciousness and oblivion. In the half-light, shadows danced on the cold stone, taunting me with their freedom.

"Are you awake?" I whispered, staring at the hunched figure across the way. He'd groaned occasionally. Moved a little, though every time I woke to check on him, it seemed to be less and less. I'd dragged my broken body across the floor one inch at a time to be near the old man. I couldn't help him. I couldn't even help myself. But at least I wasn't alone. And for that, for the whispered song and the ragged breathing, I was grateful.

"I am sorry, child," he finally said. "In the end, I wasn't as strong as I hoped."

I swallowed the lump in my throat. "Don't say that. You were strong. So strong." I could feel the tickle in my nose as I clamped my teeth together to hold back the tears. "Please don't leave me. I don't want to be alone."

His response was no more than a shallow breath.

"I don't even know your name."

Again, nothing.

"I'll tell you a secret. Stay with me and I'll tell you. When I was young, I read to escape the reality of poverty. I read every story about heroes I could. They slayed their enemies with weapons on battlefields. They were warriors that ran to war, determined and screaming. And I've only just realized that's not what a hero is, is it?" I swiped away a tear, talking, if only to drown out the ache in my heart as the song from down the hall began to fade. "There's no such thing as heroes, not really. Only fools. Fools and kind old men."

I stared for hours and hours with no response, waiting in that awkward pause before the end of a performance and the first clap. Waiting until my ears rang in the silence. Waiting until I was sure his was the last voice I'd ever hear. When the doors down the hall opened, I closed my eyes, ready to accept my defeat and end this misery. But harsh voices echoed through the space. Not the guards, but someone else.

Two figures emerged from the gloom, their whispering voices feverishly bouncing off the stone walls. They bickered as they approached, becoming louder and clearer as they neared my cell.

"Are you sure it's this one?" a feminine voice said in a voice like honey that echoed through the stone chamber.

The other answered, his tone low and quick. "Thorne is never wrong."

I peered at them through one eye, unable to make out many features beyond their matching blonde hair as they quickly slipped by.

"I can't see anything in the dark," the woman said, "But what in the world is that awful smell?"

"Trust me, you don't want to know. Just breathe through your mouth and keep looking. He's got to be around here."

"Oh, gods. I can taste it."

The man chuckled before walking back toward me.

My mind was at war with my broken spirit. Should I call out to them, hoping they were here to rescue someone? Or was this a trap? Did I care, really? I was ready. Done with my time in this wretched world.

"Here," I managed. "Please."

The man stopped, kneeling before my cell. "Hey there," he said, as if speaking to a wild animal before calling over his shoulder. "Harlow? We've got a problem. Toss me the keys."

I blinked up at the handsome man. "You have to be quiet. They'll hear you."

He snatched the keys from the air and shoved them into the lock with a snort. "Trust me, they won't be hearing anything for a long time. It's the next round we have to watch out for. Can you move?"

I tried to pull myself up, praying to any god that would listen to give me strength and let these people be saviors. I thought maybe the machine used to stretch me had broken my back, but I'd been able to move my legs and arms, even if only a little.

With a groan, defeat poured over me. If I admitted how bad off I was, they would probably leave me here. There was no rescuing a burden. But try as I might, I could not pull myself to my feet.

"I can do it," I promised. "Don't leave me here."

"Don't worry. We're not leaving you behind."

The woman grumbled, rummaging through her leather satchel. "We didn't plan for this. She needs some extra help, Archer."

He whipped his head to look up at the woman. "Don't."

"You have to. Look at her."

The pity filling his eyes as he studied my broken form sent a flush of embarrassment through me. I'd never let myself be vulnerable. Not once. And here I was, at the mercy of strangers.

Archer, the man, nodded grimly. "Fine." He leaned in, whispering to me. "I have to use magic. Don't be frightened."

"And be quick about it," another man's voice barked from down the stone path between cells. "They find us here, we're not walking away."

Archer nodded, laying his hands on me.

I shook my head. "Wait. There's another. A man. He needs you more than I do."

Harlow rushed closer, voice raising in pitch. "Where? Where is he?"

I flicked my eyes to the old man's cell. "In there."

"Oh, gods. Oh, gods," she said moments later, gripping the iron bars and rattling. "The keys. Give me the keys."

Archer tossed them, and with an easy catch, she spun, shoving them one by one into the lock. "They aren't working. Why aren't they working?"

A hulking figure stepped into the faint light, his build unlike anything I'd seen before. Broad and tall, he filled the space entirely. He looked at me first, but looked away just as quickly. "Get it done, Archer," the man commanded. "Do it now."

Archer pressed his hand to mine gently. "I'm only able to speed the healing process. But brace yourself. It's going to hurt like hell."

"Can't be worse than when it happened," I whispered, closing the only eye that would open as I pressed my lips together.

"Hold on to me then," Archer said.

A deep breath reverberated from within him. A sensation like molten honey began to seep into my hand, warm and soothing until it festered, heating beyond anything I'd ever known. As if ignited by an unseen flame, the heat consumed me.

Invaded every inch of my body with a punishing fervor unmatched by any torture I endured. My breath hitched in my throat, and I clung to Archer's arm, the cool feel of his touch offering a cruel contrast to the agony racing through my veins.

The stone floor pulsed in rhythm with the cataclysmic pain. Each shockwave rattled my bones and shook my sense of reality. Sweat beaded on my forehead, trickling down into the corners of my eyes, blending with the tears that were now flowing freely.

When the pain faded, though my tears were still fresh, I opened my eyes—both of them—to see Archer smiling down at me. "Would you look at that," he said, brushing away a blood-stained lock of hair. "Your eyes. They're two different colors."

"I know," I groaned, rolling over to get to my feet, realizing I was covered with a cloak that wasn't mine. "I've seen my face before."

"Oh, pretty and funny." He moved to his feet as he held a hand out. "A rarity. Now we've got to get going, prisoner. The next round of Cimmerians are coming."

My head snapped to the old man's cell. "Where are the others?"

"The keys weren't working. They saw what they needed to see. We have to go."

"No. We can't. He needs help." I grabbed the bars, rattling them, ignoring the pain that echoed through my body. "You can save him."

"I can't—"

"Yes you can. I know where the keys are. I saw them. Wait here."

"No. We have to go. The other guards—"

"I can't leave him," I shouted, already halfway down the hallway, dragging my sluggish magic forward. I didn't bother searching the other cells. I knew what I would find there. Absolutely no one. Because there hadn't been another prisoner. There hadn't been a person humming. The magic that'd comforted me, the song that'd felt familiar belonged to the old man. And if I could save him, if we could get to him soon, perhaps he would sing again.

I flung the door to the torture room open, slamming to a halt at the scene before me. The guards... they'd been brutalized. Beaten beyond recognition. Killed. Blood coated the floor, turning my stomach. I wasted no time, though. I couldn't give any thought to what that giant man had done in here. Instead, I swiped the second set of keys I knew to be hidden in a jar, and darted out of the room before Archer could catch up. I'd process that nightmare one day. I'd sit with the vision of my torturers and find peace with their end. But not today.

Today I had to save a life.

Racing down the hallway, the keys cold and slick in my sweaty palms, I ignored Archer's shouts as I shoved them home and twisted, the lock giving way.

"We have minutes. We have to go. It's too late for him."

"Please," I begged. "Come help. It's not too late, I promise. It's not. I'll carry him."

I couldn't abandon the old man. Not when his voice was the only music that could drown out the cacophony of terror that resonated through this prison. I fell to my knees before the old man's frail body, now close enough to see him. His face, etched with years of hardship and wisdom, was as still as the grave. Eyes that must have once sparkled with grand tales were now dim and unresponsive. The wrinkles that framed his eyes had hardened into permanent grooves, carved by the tears he shed this final day.

I was too late.

I couldn't save him.

My heart broke into a million pieces as I remembered why. He'd taken my place. He hadn't even known me.

I threw myself over his still body. "You are a hero. I lied. There are heroes."

A warm hand fell heavily on my shoulder.

"I didn't even know his name," I whispered.

"His name was Atticus, and the world is far worse off without him."

7

Sad and aching, I followed Archer out of the prison. I hadn't been locked in the bowels of a castle, but rather, trapped in a tunnel system below the city. We climbed jagged rocks up and up until he pushed a half-hanging door to the side, and we stepped onto a path so narrow we had to walk sideways, shoulder to shoulder, until it widened and eventually we were deposited back into the city. He'd said very little, seeming to understand my grief, and I'm sure he had his own version to work through. He'd clearly known Atticus, and I was fairly certain that was who they'd come to save. Not some broken woman, tortured within an inch of her life, trapped in a foreign world.

The towering buildings grew out of the ground. The stone walls reaching to the sky did little to light the streets at night, but at least they staved off the icy wind. I had no idea how long I'd been down there, and had no one to ask. The last time I counted, I had sixty-eight days left, but even that was a guess, because I'd been unconscious for some of the time.

Archer reached back into the hidden alcove, feeling around

in the dark. He produced a large bag and tossed it to my feet. "We'd meant this to be for Atticus," he said quietly. "It's not much, but it's better than what you've got. It'll be dangerous to wander the city like that, as I'm sure you know. Obviously, beyond this point, we can't be seen together."

He unclasped his cloak. Beneath it he wore a very fine, five-piece suit: impeccably tailored, a midnight blue so dark it was nearly black, with silver buttons that glimmered in the weak sunrise. It was not the attire of an adventuring rogue breaking prisoners out of dungeons. It was that of someone respected, someone formidable, someone important. A Silk, if I'd gotten the hierarchy here right.

"Do you have somewhere to go? Someplace safe?"

It was only then that I realized the cloak I wore didn't belong to him, but rather the other man that'd said little and escaped as quickly as he could. I contemplated my answer. I couldn't lead him down a path of questions for me. "Of course. I'll go home."

"You sure? It's Tithe today."

"Yes. I'm sure." I reached up to remove the borrowed cloak, having no damn clue what he was talking about, and no ability to ask without raising suspicion. "Return this to your friend and please tell them both thank you."

"Keep it. It's yours now." He pulled a pair of leather gloves from his pocket and slid them in place before pulling out a wool hat and slipping it over his golden locks. "Good luck out there."

With that, Archer set off into the early, early morning, leaving me alone in the vast expanse of the city. I watched his retreating figure until he was nothing but a black dot against the labyrinth of stone buildings.

I was alone now, completely and utterly alone. The reality of it bore down on me like an anvil, threatening to crush me under its suffocating weight. I was in a foreign land with no allies or friends, just the memory of an old man and a vague idea about where to go, should I be so brave to fucking try again.

I opened the bag and found a change of clothes and a pair of sturdy boots. The clothes were simple. Rough-spun tunic and trousers of deep gray blended with the city's dull backdrop. Surprise, surprise. I was pretty sure yellow wasn't a color that existed in this horrible place. Not that I loved yellow, but damn. Thankfully, the boots were sturdy. They were slightly too big, but they'd do.

Ducking back into the narrow alley, I changed quickly, peeling off the tattered remnants of my prison garb. A plethora of voices sounded from the depths of the underground tunnels. I froze. Unable to think. Unable to move. Suddenly, as if the ground was swept out from under me, I was consumed by fear. If the other Cimmerian guards had found those two bodies, and I was missing, they'd make their own assumptions about what happened, and the city would turn into a manhunt.

That was inevitable. But if I could shake off the inability to move, I could get a head start. There was nothing at first. I was weak, and honestly scared. Suddenly I was nothing more than an abandoned child again, locked into my own body, unable to function. I pushed and pushed against the feeling of dread, willing my feet to run, heaving the bag of soiled clothes over my shoulder as I moved. I had no idea what kind of power lurked through this world, but I sure as hell wasn't going to leave any more of my blood lying around to find out.

The second I approached a group of vagrants gathered around a fire, I tossed the whole bag in the bin and watched it burn, gripping the edges of my borrowed cloak silently. It was made of a heavy woolen fabric that fell around my shoulders like a mantle, too big, but I'd never complain.

I didn't linger, noting how the people around began to shift, whispering more frequently to each other. Clearly they dreaded the rise of a new day, and in such a miserable place, I couldn't say I blamed them. I moved quickly, purposely keeping my head down as I headed back toward the place I'd met the boy. I'd have to start my trek to the Hollow over.

The city was slowly waking up. People were leaving the buildings in packs, filling the streets as they seemed to move as one, in a dance they must have performed every morning. The grind, the monotony. If any of them had a clue what was happening below their streets, none showed it.

I made a sharp turn into an empty alley, pressed my back to a frozen wall and slid down, allowing myself a single moment of vulnerability only when I was alone. I hadn't been a stranger to the streets in my life, but it'd been so long, I'd forgotten how deep the chill could sink into your bones.

Still, I knew if the sun fully rose and anyone saw me caked in dried blood and dirt, the guards would follow. Water dripped steadily from a gutter, building a puddle in the alley that was mostly ice. But with no more shame, and desperate to keep myself concealed, I plunged my face into the freezing, shallow water.

The cold stung, a raw, icy pain that ignited every nerve in my face. I gasped, the icy shock seizing my lungs. My hands, now numbed by the chill, worked mechanically to scrub away the evidence of where I'd been. Archer had healed the marks. Atticus's clothing had covered me. The giant's cloak had warmed me, and with the blood gone, it would be like it never happened. Except my mind would never forget the sound of my own breaking point.

With a determined and trembling hand, I washed away the layers of filth that clung stubbornly to my skin. Each swipe seemed to peel away more than just grime; it removed parts of my old identity that no longer served me in this hard new world. The dancer. The woman bound to a dark burlesque show. The woman who'd been so sad, though I'd never had a reason.

I scrubbed until my skin was raw, shivering as the icy wind bit into my wet face and hands. I dipped the ends of my hair into the puddle, knowing I'd have to braid it. Without soap, or at the very least, deeper water, I didn't have a prayer of true cleanliness.

When I was done, and frozen to the bone, I rested my head against the stone wall once more. Tired. More tired than I'd ever been in my life, I let the stranger's gifted cloak provide me with the only warmth this city would ever offer.

As dawn slipped into morning, I spotted a carriage making its way down the street. Elegant yet inconspicuous, it was hitched to a pair of dapple-gray horses that moved with a graceful rhythm. Always gray. My eyes were drawn to a large trunk attached to the back. It was bound securely and had the sheen of a well-oiled chestnut. Beside it, a few other bags and boxes were strapped down, evidence of a long journey. Perfect.

With a cautious glance around, I got up from my hiding spot, weaving through the crowd that began to fill the streets. The city's activity masked my approach. I couldn't say I wasn't afraid. I'd been accused of stealing when innocent. But I knew better this time. Knew to trust my instincts and run, should I feel the urge.

There was no room for fear or morality now; survival required all parts of me, including the ones that needed to adapt to this shitty place. The carriage stopped to allow another cart to pass by. Taking advantage, I stepped casually behind it and gently unlatched the trunk to find clothing, jewelry, and a few scattered books. But it was the wool gown that caught my attention. A deep emerald green, far too grand for a street rat. It would provide warmth against the gnawing freeze of the city and serve me better than Atticus's worn trousers. Plus... color.

Without hesitation, as other's shoulders brushed mine and no one paid any attention, I grabbed the gown from among the scattered belongings and folded it under my cloak. The heavy wool felt comforting against my chilled skin, a promise of warmth to come. I snapped the trunk closed again, cringing at the sound that echoed louder than it should have.

I shifted away, fading back into the alley, allowing myself to feel how heavily my heart beat with fear as soon as I was alone. Out there, in the world of strangers, I couldn't feel. I couldn't *be*. Only blend. The world was not a stage. I was not a hero.

Slipping into the warm dress. Braiding my hair. Sliding the cloak over my shoulders. Each of these things felt so normal. If only I wasn't so lost. Now that I blended in a little more, I continued on my way, following the directions I'd been given to the Hollow once more, seeking the Lord of the Salt, and hopefully some kind of arched door of magic that would lead me home.

As I made my way back towards the spot where I'd met the boy, I noticed the city was alive now in a way that was both alarming and intriguing. No one smiled. No one talked. People looked over their shoulders, hustling to wherever they were meant to be.

I treaded lightly, watching as the others had done. A buzzing sound filled the air. Growing louder and louder as I moved. I turned, deciding to hide, rather than be caught on the streets during whatever was happening, but two Cimmerians slipped out from the block behind me. Spinning once more in a collected panic, I locked my fingers on the edges of my hood to keep my face hidden, and continued on my path, nervous because the sound grew louder and louder. Every turn I could take was blocked by a masked guard, baton in hand, shoving more and more people forward.

I drew back, stalling, panicking, my heart in my throat. The only thing I could see was the blood on the floor I'd lain in while imprisoned. The waning rise and fall of Atticus's chest. Could only hear the crack of the whip and the Cimmerian's calculated laugh.

The buzzing was gone, replaced by the shuffle of feet and the quiet whispers of people. They were everywhere, filling the street so that no horses could pass. No one could move beyond the barrier of the prince's masked guards as they shouted and herded people down the street like animals to slaughter. My heart stopped beating. Whatever warmth I'd gathered from the borrowed cloak left me like a scarf in the wind.

I didn't realize I'd stopped moving until someone slammed into me from behind and I could feel more than see the guard's attention turn to me. There was no escape. Nowhere to run. A Cimmerian's firm grasp dug into my arm as he yanked me toward him before shoving me forward, forcing me into the crowd of people.

"We come in the name of the king," he growled as I stumbled on a brick, colliding with a woman dressed in layers of wool, carrying a screaming child on her hip.

It was strange, though. These guards, identical to the ones I'd faced, claimed to work for the king, when before, they spoke only of the prince. So which was it?

"Tithe is announced in the name of the king," another of the Cimmerians further down the road barked as we were herded forward. "You pay your taxes or the price for withholding His Majesty's revenues. Silk or Salt, makes no difference today."

Oh fuck. Tax day.

Men, women, and children crowded the streets, some in threadbare clothing and some dressed warmly in fur-lined cloaks, the occasional shouting barely discernible over the long distance of people. Children clung to their mothers, their screams piercing through the tense morning. The sound was heart-wrenching, a high-pitched counterpoint to the low grumble of adult voices, which were either choked with fear or seething with barely contained outrage. The crowd jostled forward, shoulders pressed together, feet tripping over uneven stones and each other.

I moved as I needed to, trying not to lose it. I needed to keep it together to make a plan but what the hell could I do? Lie? Steal a fucking name? Gods. My heart pounded as I was pushed along by the mass of bodies. Each step felt like I was marching closer to the edge of a cliff I was meant to jump from. Hands trembling, not just from the cold, but from the terror that gnawed at my insides, I moved. Cinching my cloak tighter around me, I attempted to block the bitter cold and the over-whelming sense of vulnerability. I scanned the walls. The streets. Even the people seeking some form of escape or refuge. But the relentless tide of humanity offered no sanctuary. My fear was mirrored in the wide and worried eyes of everyone else. No one had a plan, it seemed. I was one of many, all doomed.

We were shoved through the narrow streets until they opened up into a vast city square. In the center, a large canvas tent had been erected, dark fabric flapping in the icy wind. The tent held more Cimmerians, the detailing on their masks gleaming coldly in the pale morning light. Those masks were designed to intimidate and it sure as hell worked. Other men stood behind tables stacked with ledgers and chests filled with coin as if this were a holiday and paying taxes, the celebration.

The tension in the air pressed against my skin like a warning and a damnation. Because what the fuck could I do? What money did I have to pay a tax man? And that wasn't even the biggest problem. Those ledgers most likely held the names of every man, woman and child living in the city. When I gave mine and there was no record, what would happen? Would they have a record of outlying cities? Of course they would. Taxes were everyone's burden, not only for those that lived close to the king. And it wasn't like I knew the name of a different city to lie.

"Move along!" one of the Cimmerians barked.

The crowd surged forward in response, a wave of desperation and submission. A mother nearby clutched her child to her chest, her eyes hollow with exhaustion and worry, but the child's sobs had quieted to weak whimpers. A man beside them muttered curses under his breath, his fists clenched in fury.

My panic rose until a lump I couldn't swallow formed in my throat, making it hard to take in a full breath. The closer I got to the front, the more my mind raced. I had to think of something, some way to survive this.

A plump, older woman, with glasses sitting on the edge of her nose and no barrier from the cold beyond the apron tied around her waist, looked over at me. I could only imagine the fear that she must have seen to make her stop and share a hesitant smile. "Don't be afraid, dear. Eyes forward, chin high. Perhaps we will find leniency."

But as the guard shoved her, and she continued on, swallowed immediately by the crowd, I knew she was wrong. There would be no leniency for me. A murderer. A stranger. My only mercy was Archer's healing of my mangled face, hiding the violence. My only hope was that none of the guards got a look at my mismatched eyes. One green and one blue were hard to hide.

The line edged forward and I could actually feel my nerves rattling. Further and further we went. One step and then another. Closer and closer to the tables. The heat of the crowd pressed against my back, but inside, I was frozen, trapped in a nightmare I couldn't wake from. I'd never get back to Quill if I was locked in a prison again. I'd die there.

I watched in horror as a Cimmerian seized an old man from the throng. His frail frame barely resisted, his eyes hollow and resigned. The Cimmerian's grip was unyielding. The old man stumbled as he was dragged toward a cart encased with heavy bars, and so full of people, limbs stuck through. Each solemn face within wore nothing but defeat. Perhaps the horrors of the Cimmerian's torture chamber were not a secret. With a brutal shove, the guard thrust the old man into the cart and slammed the door shut with a metallic clang, sealing his fate.

A familiar face lurked behind the cart, standing within the crowd of people that'd already been shuffled through. Archer. The line stopped moving for a moment, so I watched him carefully. The way his unblinking eyes stared straight ahead before he quickly swirled a finger in the air to give a signal.

I followed his line of sight to another man on the outskirts of the chaos. And then, almost like the strike of a snake, that man purposefully slammed into someone in front of him, gripping their arm to keep the stranger from falling before patting his chest as if asking if he was okay. When the stranger turned back to face the crowd, I wasn't surprised to see the other, the one Archer had signaled, slip a handful of stolen coins into a giant red pouch and vanish into the crowd.

They were thieves. And honestly, the man wasn't very good at it. What kind of monster chooses a moment like this to pickpocket a crowd of distraught people? Especially when he was a Silk. Dressed in layers of warmth and fine clothing, there was no questioning his status.

Disgusting, really. Not that it mattered. Not that a single person in this chaos did anything but battle through their fear and panic as the Cimmerians continued to shove the crowd and bark orders.

"The king?" a massive man in threadbare clothing shouted, not ten paces from me. "The king, my fucking asshole. This is done in the name of the prince. The king would never stand for this."

"Is he here to say otherwise?" one of the overseers at a table shouted above the crowd. "Where is your precious king to save you? Not here." He looked around, feigning shock. "Because these are his orders."

"Fuck you," the protestor countered, lowering his head and running forward like a battering ram, likely trying to flip the table. The crowd parted as the man screamed in fury.

But he was caught effortlessly by a nearby guard. The flaps of the tent flew open and a dark-haired man wearing a silver crown emerged, a coy smile on his face as he approached. He slid a hand down his pressed suit, glaring over the crowd as if he'd been waiting in the wings for someone to step out of line. All the herded people, the Cimmerians and those along the side-lines bowed, me included, albeit slightly delayed.

"Hold him," the royal demanded, stalking forward as the defiant man was shoved to his knees. The man, who I assumed was the prince, reached out, gripping the naysayer's chin. "Please, repeat yourself, so that all may witness the crime before the punishment."

As if a bucket of icy water had been dumped on the man's bald head, he stopped immediately, his eyes widening with fear the rest of us had already practically bathed in. The protestor's body trembled, the once invisible line between pride and sheer terror obliterated in an instant.

"Repeat yourself," the prince said again, enunciating each syllable in a cold demand.

A woman in front of me cried out. She'd been quiet, and though she'd nearly swallowed the sound, as one, the Cimmerians turned toward her. I wanted to reach out to her. To find a way to hide her from their brutal wrath. But I was not a hero and in minutes, I wasn't even going to be able to save myself.

8

The moment one of the prince's guards pulled a pair of pliers from his pocket and handed them over, I knew what was going to happen. I'd seen copious amounts of torture and severed limbs in Requiem. No one died at the hands of my old boss, but plenty broke.

I couldn't look away. From the fear thrumming through my veins, the viciousness of this world, or the biting cold that held me frozen in place, I wasn't sure. But I watched, as still and silent as the rest of the crowd. The protester trembled on his knees.

"Prince Farris," he managed, "Please." The regret in his voice was clearer than the chill in the air.

A Cimmerian grabbed the sides of his head at the temple and squeezed until the man turned a dangerous shade of purple. "You will address His Royal Highness properly."

My stomach turned when he screamed in agony.

The prince smiled down at him. "Petulant children must be taught a lesson in justice, isn't that right?"

A dark stain spread across the front of the victim's trousers.

The sight of his humiliation was both pitiable and terrifying, an indication of the merciless grip the prince had on his people. The prince laughed, arching his eyebrows while reaching into the man's mouth with the pliers, brutally stretching his tongue as he pulled it further than it should have been able to extend.

Farris's eyes, cold as the stone beneath my feet, scanned over the crowd, each person a potential participant in his next act of brutality. It was a game to him, a spectacle of power and pain that left no room for mercy. This wasn't about justice; it was about terror.

There was a difference between the prince and the Maestro. My old boss would see an act done and never dirty his hands. He wouldn't revel in it. The prince leaned over and whispered in the man's ear, then turned to the crowd with a sinister smile. He even waited, tapping a toe as the man cried out in pain. Only when he silenced, only when I was sure I could see no more, did the dreadful prince draw his blade and slice the tongue from the man's mouth, splattering the bricks with rich, dark blood. For a single moment, the world remained still, shocked. But as if that horror was no worse than everyone's plight, the people began moving forward again, and the prince walked casually back to his tent.

I was shoved closer and closer to the head of the line. I'd slowly made my way to the side, nestled behind the woman with the apron that'd spoken so kindly to me. Another commotion at the center table halted everyone as a woman cried out. Searching beyond the plump woman before me, I was still not close enough to see all the tables, but I did catch Archer again, his face tense as he held onto the shoulder of a black-haired child. They both scanned the crowd. I turned slightly, hoping to keep from drawing attention to myself as I caught his comrade across the way, reaching into the pocket of another onlooker.

"You there," a collector called, pointing directly at me. "Come forward."

I swallowed my heart back down my throat as every nerve came alive. Tucking my arms closer to my sides, I meant to step to the man's table, but he shouted again. "In the apron there holding the child, Tilly Page, don't dally."

"Gods help me," the kind woman whispered as she shuffled forward, surrounded by children.

Looking down, afraid to watch the woman's demise, I edged forward until the tips of my borrowed boots scraped a massive golden circle inlaid into the cobblestone streets. Squished between all the people, I managed a quick glance around the outskirts, noting we'd been shuffled into a giant city square, encircled by more of the towering buildings I'd come to know as the staple of Stirling. But this place, this golden mark, was special. Just a hint of knowledge that might be useful to know, should I ever get out of this.

I took a sharp elbow to the back, reminding me to move. Forcing me to be next in line. To give my name. A name they would not find. To pay coin I didn't have.

"Please," the woman in the apron said to the man with the ledger. "It must be enough. That's all I have. What good can come from depleting your own orphanage?"

"Your Grace!" the collector shouted over his shoulder, though his eyes remained glued to Tilly Page.

She called out, nearly falling to her knees as she stumbled over a child. "Please."

I didn't breathe. The children didn't stir. The world buzzed with fearful anticipation as that royal fucker stepped out of his tent again, another smile on his hideous face. He gestured for the man to move to the side and slid into his seat, running a gloved hand over his giant book. The prince slid a finger down the page of the ledger, stopping beside a name and tsking. "Seventy-two coin. Last time, you were given respite for three days, Tilly."

"Yes, Your Grace. And my dear husband Atticus trekked all the way across the city to pay on the final day."

I swallowed my gasp. *Atticus.* Did she know? Oh gods, had this poor woman just learned of her husband's death?

"As he should have. Do I look like I deal in charities, Mrs. Page?"

"N—no, Your Grace."

The tremble in her old voice was gut-wrenching. His dark eyes narrowed, causing my ears to ring with fear for her. She'd been kind, in her simple words to me. The children surrounding her, children from an orphanage, were quiet and just as strong as she was. Yet we would all witness another tragedy this day, it seemed.

I forced myself to breathe.

To think.

But as the prince rose, I knew there was nothing I could do. "Stocks or prison, Tilly, I'll be generous and let you choose since your husband isn't brave enough to stand in your place this day."

"No," she cried out again, reaching for the small girl clinging to her skirts. "You mustn't. Atticus he—"

"I'm not interested in your excuses."

Because you know he's dead, I wanted to say.

The prince lowered his chin at the two Cimmerians as a commotion broke out beside us. "Stop. Wait. Stop." The boy that'd been standing with Archer cut through the crowd, his tousled black hair a mess as he pushed through the people in his way, not at all bothered by the danger as he shoved past me, nearly knocking me over and ran up to the prince, dropping the red coin pouch on top of the giant ledger. The pouch with the stolen coin...

"I'm not so good with my numbers yet, Your Grace," the boy said with a formal bow and panting breaths. "But I think all the coin is there."

"Convenient..." The prince scowled, dumping the bag to scan the wares. "Eighty-four. I'll consider the extra a bonus for my trouble."

"But—"

Tilly's hand slammed over the boy's mouth. "Mind yourself, Ruben. Of course. Thank you, Your Grace."

She rushed the children away. Distracted by her timely rescue, I'd forgotten one very important thing. I was next in line. And the prince was staring straight into my soul.

"Hello lovely," he crooned as I was shoved forward. "What a glorious treat. May I have your name?"

Every muscle in my body tensed, my mind racing frantically, searching for a way out, but I was paralyzed, trapped in the nightmare unfolding before me.

His creepy, dark eyes shifted between mine, studying them. Did he know? Had they seen my eyes?

"I'll need your full name, of course."

My name. Paesha. Paesha Vox. But he wouldn't find that within his ledger. I stopped breathing as my final seconds of freedom swallowed me whole.

"Cat got your tongue, beautiful?"

Panic. Panic had my tongue. And fear.

I opened my mouth to speak, to squeak, to force out any word I could manage, but I was interrupted. A long, heavy arm slid across my shoulders, wrapping around me as a man two heads taller than me plopped a brown leather bag onto the books. He leaned in toward me, speaking so quietly, only the prince and I could likely hear. "You wouldn't believe how long it took me to find you. Sorry, darling."

Every nerve in my entire body shot to life, trembling

beneath the stranger's touch. I'd never felt so trapped, and I'd been magically bound to a crime lord. I slowly turned, careful to school my face as I realized who'd planted himself beside me. The large man that'd come with Archer and Harlow.

"You... you two know each other?" the prince asked, staring only at the massive stranger that'd taken my side.

"I hope so, considering we're married, Farris."

Ice shot through my veins.

"Your Grace," the prince corrected, though I'd hardly heard it above the sharp ringing in my ears.

Did he just say married? No.

Hell no.

I bit the inside of my cheek until my mouth filled with the metallic tang of blood. This was a game of pick your poison. Death by a prince or murderous stranger.

The man's voice lowered to a dangerous degree. "Right. Your Grace."

But my wrist bore no magical band. I carefully adjusted my sleeve, keeping my eyes locked forward as my reality twisted around me. They stared at each other in silence for what seemed like ages, a pissing match if ever I'd seen one. And though I had no idea who the stranger was, I still would have chosen him over the prince, and that was enough to hold me as a silent witness to their unspoken war.

Eventually, the prince spoke to another man beside him. "Bring the Silk's ledger from Nightshade Row."

Somehow, the stranger beside me grew taller. "I'm surprised you have time for this production. What with the Lord of the Salt still on the run?"

I choked on my gasp at the mention of the man I was to find, bringing the attention back to myself. The stranger pulled me closer as the prince scowled. "Those of us with many important jobs find a way to manage it all, Thorne."

A heavy book was dropped onto the table. The prince dragged his finger down the ledger, searching for the name. I found it a millisecond before he covered it with his hand. "I can't help but notice you're not wearing a wedding band, beauty. You wouldn't be trying to trick me, now would you?"

The air between them crackled with barely concealed animosity. Thorne chuckled. The sound was warm but edged with something dangerous. "You saw me three days ago wearing that cloak, did you not? Certainly, you know I have better things to do with my time than claim strangers."

"Perhaps you should keep better track of your wife then," Farris bit out. "But that doesn't explain the ring."

"I left it on my bedside table," I lied, speaking for the first time, yet still feeling insignificant in the conversation.

With a slight tug on my shoulder, Thorne guided me to turn to him, sliding his thumb under my chin, forcing me to stare into hazel eyes, framed with simple glasses. My entire body relaxed at his touch. He was handsome. Stunning even, with dark brown hair peeking out from his oversized hood.

Flashing a small golden band, he lifted my frozen fingers to his lips and held eye contact with me as he kissed each one. "May I?"

This was it. The moment I solidified my choice. As if I'd had one at all. I swallowed the lump in my throat, though it did nothing to conceal the tremble in my voice. "Yes, of course." I hadn't blinked, but something within me stirred to life.

He slid the ring onto my finger, holding my attention for another moment before we turned back to the prince and he said, "Satisfied?"

"Just one last thing, Miss." He dipped his quill into a frosted inkpot. "Name? For the record, of course."

Thanking the gods that I'd been quick enough to spot his surname, I answered. "Paesha Noctus." Thorne's grip faltered on my shoulder, and I knew without looking that he'd hated this moment as much as I did. He'd stepped in and helped a stranger, but now, in his mind, he'd be bound to me forever. Anger rippled from him. But watching the ink bloom across the paper made me feel the same. All consuming regret immediately followed, caging me in as I felt my heart beat like the ticking of a clock. Another roadblock. Another problem. Another prison.

9

"Will there be anything else?" Thorne Noctus asked.

The prince lifted the heavy pouch from the table and dumped it onto the tax ledger. "I assume everything is here?"

"Assume away," Thorne answered with a curt nod.

The prince gritted his teeth. "Then you're dismissed."

"Good day, Your Grace."

My small bow was nearly imperceptible as my pretend husband tightened his grip and led me off the street, his gait so long and quick I had to run to keep up with him. I tried to fight free of his grasp, but I couldn't even manage that.

"Let go of me."

Sandwiched between two buildings, out of earshot of the crowd and the lurking Cimmerians, we continued to run until Thorne slammed to a halt and I nearly crashed into him.

"Seriously, let go." I yanked until he finally did.

"I think you mean, 'thank you.'" His chest heaved, as did a

thick, protruding vein on his neck. "What the hell were you thinking, going in there without a plan?"

I blinked slowly, my brain running, my mouth hardly keeping up. "You... If you... What choice..." I began to pace, though the alley was only about five steps wide. "I didn't..."

The brute reached out and grabbed my arm. "If walking and talking at the same time are difficult for you, try standing still."

"What the fuck did you just say to me?"

"If walking and—"

"I swear to every god in Etherium, if you finish that sentence, I will—"

He slammed a hand over my mouth, shoving me backward until I was pinned to the wall, then leaned over, practically trembling as he whispered in my ear. "Never, ever swear to every god. Have you lost your fucking mind?"

"You just told the prince we're married, and you don't even know me. If I've lost my mind, then you've completely lost touch with reality," I mumbled against his hand.

Thorne's eyes narrowed, his breath hot on my skin. "I saved your ass, didn't I? You were seconds away from going back to The Maw."

I wrenched my head to the side. "Saved me? You're delusional."

He pressed harder against me, his voice a low growl. "What was your plan, huh? Did you swing by home, change into this dress, and grab some coin? I've lived here my whole life and I've never seen you. Which means you're a Salt, and even then, I'm not certain you're from the city." He leaned in until his nose brushed mine. "I would remember these eyes. It's foolish to pretend to be a Silk. Everyone knows that."

I hated that I couldn't answer. My heart pounded in my chest, my own anger boiling over. I shoved him, but he didn't budge an inch. "Why?"

His cold eyes, a swirling mass of green and brown, grew. "Why what?"

"I didn't ask for your help. Why did you..." I couldn't speak the words, so instead, I gestured back toward the street.

"Claim you?"

"I'm not a fucking broodmare."

His dark brown hair fell across his face as he glared down at me through the round frame of his glasses, shoulders heaving as if he could hardly contain his own anger. "Because apparently we're both fools. Now let's go."

"I'm not going anywhere with you."

"Yes, you are. In the eyes of our kingdom, you're married to me. Which means you do as I say."

I bared my teeth, standing on the tips of my toes to get closer to his frustratingly handsome face. "There's not a man in this universe that I will ever answer to."

"Oh, I think there is, wife."

Fiery, hot anger surged through me. I could have handled it. I would have found a way to trick the prince and be on my way. It's what I always did. I was a survivor. I'd been a survivor my whole godsdamned life. "Call me that one more time."

He smirked, leaning until our foreheads touched, even though I was still on my tiptoes. "As you wish, *wife*."

I brought a swift knee up, smashing him between the legs. As he doubled over, I used the palm of my hand and jammed it into his nose. "Consider this our formal separation."

As I completed my sentence, a hefty body filled the space at the other end of the alley. A damn Cimmerian stood tall and broad and every bit as ominous as they'd always been.

Thorne grabbed my wrist and yanked me back to the wall, shoving himself against me as he leaned down, murmuring in my ear, "Don't do anything foolish." He slid his fingers under my hood, gripping my face as he leaned so close anyone passing might've thought we were kissing.

I narrowed my eyes. "I'm not an idiot."

"Jury's still out on that."

"I'm going to make your life a living hell," I promised.

"Shh," he hissed as the Cimmerian approached, his black robes billowing, so dark they nearly engulfed the silver emblem on his chest.

Nothing could hide the metal mask though, no matter how far forward his hood sat. The menacing face of anonymity was burned into my memory. This was the guard that held me by the throat in an alley. This was the guard that beat me with a whip until I couldn't endure the pain. This was the guard that ended Atticus's life. They were all the same. Even if I'd seen Thorne's wrath upon their fallen bodies. The masks made them one. One authority. One evil.

I couldn't help the way my body responded to the proximity of the guard. Couldn't fight the tremble, nor the short, stunted breaths.

Thorne's massive fingers slid behind my neck as he gripped my hair and forced my head back until I looked into his eyes. "I'll fight with you later. I need you to focus. Don't lose your grit. You're safe as long as I'm here. I promise."

"And what's going on here?" The Cimmerian asked, his voice echoing off the stone walls of the alleyway.

"What business is it of yours?" The hint of defiance in Thorne's tone, the challenge to authority, was unmistakable.

"By order of the prince, answer the question."

Thorne turned, his hold on me never wavering as he faced off with the Cimmerian. "The prince or the king? Who's ruling Stirling these days? Don't you have a certain crime lord to find? The one that's stealing from the entire city?"

"It's Tithe. You're to report for payment immediately."

"Go ask your prince, or better yet, the king you're supposed to serve for my information. Mine and my wife's taxes are paid."

I blanched at the ease of that word slipping from his mouth, and those fingers only tightened on me. Prick.

"You're playing a dangerous game."

"As are you," Thorne growled, staring down at the Cimmerian. "You stand here and pretend you don't know exactly who I am. Run along to your master and tell him I hurt your feelings. I can promise you, as long as he's getting a cut of my business, he doesn't give a fuck about them."

"I know exactly who you are, Thorne Noctus, but the prince would like to know who your wife is. Stand aside so I can get a better look at her."

He moved then, finally dropping his hand as he placed himself directly between the guard and me.

"How's the view now?" he asked, crossing his arms over his chest.

I panicked. So close to the crowd of people, so close to the prince and a horde of other guards. If a fight broke out, if the Cimmerian called for help, neither of us would leave this damp alley. I really needed him to shut the hell up and do what he was told, but there was a baser part of me that needed the safety he promised. Needed someone to protect me so I could compose myself.

The guard's masked gaze flickered past Thorne towards me before he let out a low growl of frustration. "Thorne Noctus, you're obstructing justice. Step aside."

"Justice?" Thorne laughed, a dry and humorless sound that echoed through the alleyway as I stared at the back of his broad shoulders, wondering if either of them would notice if I fled. "Whatever your master's goal is, it's certainly not justice. Let's call it greed."

"Problem here?"

My mouth went dry as two more guards approached, both with hands clenched into fists. Another three came from the other end of the alley, boxing us in.

"Step aside," the first crooned, knowing he was about to win this battle.

It seemed to take ages for Thorne to see reason. His giant ego must've stunted the function of his brain. What could he have possibly done in this situation other than acquiesce? As if it were some sort of pissing match between him and the guards, he didn't step off to the side, but rather he stepped back, gripping my hand in his fiercely.

Two of them inched closer as the original one reached forward, his gloved fingers grabbing my chin. Thorne's hold tightened, but he said no more.

"A woman has escaped the Maw. They say she used to be beautiful, before my brothers got ahold of her." He turned my face, studying it. "Red hair and green eyes. You wouldn't happen to know anything about that, would you?"

Though terrified, I forced myself to remember who I was. What I was. Not the woman beaten into submission, but the Huntress. A descendant of a powerful god and a woman that'd already known the lowest of low. I'd killed a man only days ago. I would not be afraid.

I pushed his hand away, my own steady and unyielding. My words followed suit in a whip of steel. "I don't know who you're looking for, but it certainly isn't me. And I'll thank you to keep your damn hands off me." As his eyes widened in surprise, I reached up and removed my hood, revealing my hair. "It might hold a faint red hue under certain lights, but it's unmistakably brown. And I think the eyes speak for themselves."

The guards looked among themselves, their masked faces concealing any trace of emotions, while their predatory aura began to wane. I held their gaze, daring them to contradict me, though I had no clue what we would do if they did.

"Now," I continued, my voice ringing clear and assertive in the stifling silence, "I've had quite enough of this. It's far too cold to be arguing over nothing in an alley." I pulled on Thorne's fingers, locked with mine. "Shall we, darling? I don't want to be late for lunch again. You know how much she hates that."

I didn't miss the way his thumb brushed over mine, an act as I slipped into the role he'd commanded of me so effortlessly. It took every bit of effort not to pull away from him. He lifted a brow toward the closest Cimmerian, who hesitated for only a second longer before stepping to the side.

We were down the alley, around the corner, and out of sight of the guards within a minute. I promptly jerked my hand out of the giant brute's grip. "What the hell were you thinking? Picking a fight? We needed no attention, and you might as well have put us in a spotlight."

"If I recall," he said with a growl. "You're the one that assaulted me and sparked their interest in the first place."

"Did you just fucking growl at me?"

He snatched the clasp of my— his cloak and dragged me forward until I was on my tiptoes, glaring up at him. "We need to let the dust settle around here on Tithe. Stop arguing with me and let's go."

I scoffed. "I'm not going anywhere with you. Get your hands off me."

He let go. But didn't pull away. "Don't you see what's happening? The prince is already hunting you. You want to face that alone?"

"I'm not alone!"

"Then go home," he said with a smirk. "I hope you don't mind if I follow. To make sure you get there safely."

"I'm perfectly cap—"

"I'll tolerate a lot, Paesha darling, but don't you dare lie to me. You're not from here and it's obvious. You probably came south to Stirling from Roundstone or Holland, but I'm telling you, with Farris's attention on you, there's nowhere you can go on your own that's going to be safe."

I lifted my hood back up to stave off the icy breeze circling my neck. "Why do you care, anyway?"

He held a hand out to me. "Because we're married now. And you either come with, or you end up back in the Maw. Your choice, darling."

10

The home before us nearly touched the sky, a show of both wealth and power. The front step sat almost directly on the cobblestone road before it, and the giant door with a golden lion knocker welcomed us into Thorne's home.

My icy fingers thawed in response to the sudden change of temperature when we stepped inside. It was a different world in here. A grand staircase wound up from the foyer, its carved wood railings polished to a rich sheen. Crystal chandeliers hung overhead, casting rainbows on the marble floors beneath. I'd only ever seen one place this exquisite. And the crime lord that owned it was long gone. I shuddered at the thought, hoping I hadn't just attached myself to a man worse than that.

"Go up the stairs, turn right, follow the hall all the way down. You can stay in the very last room until we figure out a plan for you."

"Let's get a few things straight, shall we? First, I don't take commands. You can take that one and shove it right back up your ass because that's clearly where you pulled it from.

Number two, I don't know who 'we' is, but if you're scheming something that has to do with me, I will sure as hell be a part of that conversation. And number three, likely the most important, so pay attention, don't forget that you need me to be here. You need the little lie you told to your prince to stand, and while I'm sure that wasn't the first mistake you've ever made, it doesn't make it any less foolish. I'm not your wife. I'm not your comrade, and I'm certainly not your friend. You will watch how you speak to me, or I'll march my happy ass right back out that door and leave you to answer for your own lies."

He reached for me and I flinched. His mouth curved into a dangerous smile as he unclasped the cloak at my neck. "All bark and no bite is so disappointing, Paesha darling. Had my friends and I not found you broken and dying in the Maw, I'd almost believe you. Now go wash up. You stink."

As he dismissed me, his gaze already wandering to the next matter of importance, I stood my ground for a moment longer, locked in quiet defiance. He might have had a point, but that didn't mean I was about to roll over and become his obedient puppet. With a huffing breath of frustration, I turned on my heel and began my trek up the grand staircase.

At the top, I turned right as instructed, finding myself in a long hallway adorned with artwork and lined with rugs of intricate design. The hall seemed to stretch out infinitely before me. The very last room nestled at the end of the hall was far from boring. It was palatial, layered with silks and velvets in jewel tones, an enormous four-poster bed dominated one side of the room with heavy curtains drawn back revealing plush pillows and ornate blankets. Was he expecting the king for lunch? Gods.

But what surprised me most was not the opulence or taste for extravagance displayed here. It was the massive bathroom. I walked inside, studying the intricate stained glass window before my hands reached out to touch the cold metal sides of the bath. The finish was so smooth. Maybe I should have given it a few minutes, let this reality sink in around me, made a plan for escape… something. But eh, I wanted a bath. I deserved a bath. And one could think in hot water just as well as they could curled up on that giant bed.

I shrugged off the heavy cloak and began peeling my worn clothes away from my sore, weary body. The clothes fell in a heap on the floor, revealing smooth skin not marred with bruises or cuts from the whippings. If I ever saw Archer again, I'd have to thank him.

I turned on the lavish bronze faucet and watched as the bath filled with steamy water that carried the scent of lavender and jasmine, as if even the simplest thing here was wrapped in luxury. How was that even possible?

I eased myself into the water, relishing the heat that pricked my frozen skin, my stiff muscles unfurling slowly under its coaxing. For a moment, I closed my eyes and let the luxuriant serenity wash over me like a balm. The silence of this place sank into my bones.

Alone and hopefully safe, my composure shattered like glass. I dragged my knees to my chest, laying my head down, and sobbed. I could only be strong for so long. I was human. Mostly. And the very faint trace of a god's power running through me was insignificant here. Just as I was. I hadn't been insignificant in a long time. Most knew I was the Huntress, but if they didn't know that, they knew I was a dancer. The Maestro's diamond. Beautiful, graceful, and guarded. I could stand before anyone and coax their desire forward in minutes. I could reach into their souls and drag their envy, their lust to the forefront of their minds. I'd been trained my whole life to do so.

None of that mattered now. Not as the clock ticked down and I was no closer to Quill than I had been when I'd made a foolish bargain with a god I had no business dealing with. What a fool I was. If his intention was to break me, he mastered it.

I sat in the bath until the water turned cold, the suds from washing and rewashing had long gone, and my body shook. I had no more tears to cry. Still, I couldn't be bothered to get out. This was the safest I'd been, even if it pained me to admit that I'd needed it. I rested my neck against the cold rim of the metal bath, ignoring the sharp chill that raced down my back. Cold was fine. Cold meant that I wasn't numb. That I was still breathing. I'd survived.

There was only one thing that could have pulled me from my frozen stupor. And as the smell of something rich and savory filled my room, I closed my eyes and sighed. The temptation of food was too strong to resist. With a sigh, I heaved myself out of the bath, my skin still glistening from the cold water.

Frozen to the bone, I padded out of the bathroom and toward the door, standing with my hand on the knob for several moments. Something was wrong, but my mind was sluggish. Only when I looked down at the puddle on the cold, stone floor did I register that I was naked. Any other time, I wouldn't have cared. Dressing in a warehouse filled with hundreds of people night after night gave one a skewed sense of modesty. A different kind of numbness. I'd danced on stage with little to no clothing, conveniently blocking my bottom half with props, but only for the audience. And even then, the Maestro would encourage a prop slip from time to time, depending on his goals. Which rats he was trying to catch in his trap.

Eyeing the dress and cloak, I couldn't bring myself to put them back on. I didn't care if I never wore either of them again. So I gathered the plush blanket from the bed, wrapped it around myself, and swung the door open.

I was prepared to walk all the way down the hall and find a kitchen if I needed to. The way my hunger gnawed at me now was painful. I'd had little more than rain water for days and days. It was a wonder I had any energy left at all. But then, I supposed I didn't. I'd been running on adrenaline.

A tray sat in the hall next to a pile of folded men's clothing. I listened intently, waiting to see if he would return, or at the very least discover where he spent his time in this place. When only silence filled the space, I let a tendril of magic loose, seeking the man that'd been my savior.

Nothing happened.

I shook my head and squeezed my eyes shut, trying again. No visions came, no string of power connected us. There was absolute silence on the other end of my power. Strange. But I was so tired, and all magic came with a cost. The first being a drain to my energy. I'd try again later.

With the blanket tucked around me, I gathered the tray and kicked the clothing into the bedroom before shutting the door with my hip. Each step was a burden as I slunk across the room to the bed and lifted the lid, forgetting about the clothes.

Thorne had delivered a feast fit for a queen, laid out neatly on a platter of polished silver. Tender roasted meats, fresh bread, buttery vegetables, and rich sauces to pour over them all. I began with the meat, tearing through it with an animalistic ferocity, my primitive hunger overpowering any semblance of manners. The warm juices trickled down my chin and I didn't care to wipe them off. I devoured the bread, dunking it into the rich sauce and stopping only to moan.

The flavors were incredible, vibrant and layered. Every bite was a symphony of taste that danced upon my tongue and filled me with a sense of warmth that began in the pit of my stomach and spread like wildfire throughout my body. I'd known what it meant to be starving at a young age. I knew if I ate like this, I'd be sick. Slow and steady was always the rule of thumb after days of no eating. But the flavor was so rich, I didn't care.

I'm not sure when I fell asleep, but I'm sure it was with a buttered roll in one hand and a chunk of tender meat in the other, still halfway through a bite I could no longer force down.

My sleep was fitful. No matter how I tossed and turned, I couldn't escape the feeling of a Cimmerian's hands on me. Couldn't forget the sound of my skin ripping beneath the lash of a whip. I couldn't escape Quill's cry and Atticus's old song, growing louder and louder until it drowned out everything and shattered the worlds.

When I woke, drenched in sweat, muted starlight filtered through the stained glass panes into my room. The moon was fat and luminous outside, its gentle glow coaxing me from my nightmares. The tray of food was gone. And, buried as I was in several blankets, it was clear the master of the house had sent someone in.

The dress and cloak I'd left in a pile on the floor were gone and the clothes I'd kicked into the room had been folded neatly and placed on a carved wooden armchair. Slowly, almost painfully, I rolled out of bed and made my way toward the pile. The coarse material was stiff in my hands and smelled faintly of leather and soap. My first instinct was to reject it, to return to the comfort of the bed. But I couldn't hide here forever.

The clothes were far too big. I didn't even bother with the pants. The shirt fit like an oversized nightgown and even then, I had to roll the sleeves a ridiculous number of times to use my hands.

Standing at the door, I tried again to use my magic to find Thorne. Darkness wrapped around my mind, blotting him out of the mental map I'd begun to build. There were other things, though. The book I'd touched from the man on the sidewalk was somewhere far north. The string of magic attached to Archer vibrated slightly. He was moving somewhere to the west.

But Thorne was somehow immune. I'd never met a person

immune to magic, but maybe that was his power. I opened the door as quietly as possible, listening for voices or footfalls, or anything to indicate he was awake, but was only met with silence. Padding down the hall, I peeked into room after room, scanning the spaces for anything of use. Because unfortunately for my new husband, I had no intention of sticking around.

The upstairs, full of bedrooms, was useless to me. Stepping quietly, drawing back only when the steps creaked, I began to hunt. The ground level held a simple layout. A long narrow corridor from the front door, with rooms on either side, much like the hall upstairs.

One door stood out among the others, half-opened, as if inviting me into its secrets. I stepped inside. This must have been Thorne's study, full of books and a large desk in the center of the room. A single shaft of moonlight streamed down, lighting an extensive map spread across one wall. The name Wisteria was inscribed in gold, as if crowning this world's existence. Stirling, the city I'd found myself in, was emblazoned at the southern tip of the map with surrounding towns dotted like loyal subjects at its borders.

I traced the threads marking boundaries and paths in my mind. I couldn't use my power to get there, since I hadn't been, but hopefully I'd remember as much as possible. The map was full of tiny push pins with numbered flags. Trying to find a key to them, I turned to the desk and began moving through the stack of papers. Most of it was financial transactions, records of sales and purchases, having no immediate relevance. Buried in the heap was a sheet of parchment. Ink faded at the edges but still legible. *The Hollow* was written in faded ink across the top. But what was even more curious was the list of transactions. He wouldn't have this if he wasn't directly associated with whatever the Hollow was. On the second page was a list of names, starting with his, followed by Archer and Harlow and a line of others. At the very bottom, nearly imperceptible and crossed through with a thick line, was the Lord of the Salt. No name, just the title.

But why was he removed? Had he died?

I put the papers back the way I'd found them, trying to remember what Thorne had said about the Lord of the Salt to the prince. Was he hunting him also? Maybe everyone was hunting for him.

Clearly, Thorne knew about the Hollow. And the Lord of the Salt was on the list, which meant he was involved with it somehow. If I stuck around a little longer, maybe Thorne would let slip what he knew of the place. But where did the Lord of the Salt come into it?

As the questions circled my mind, forcing me to debate my escape plan, I continued picking through the room. A golden quill sitting on Thorne's desk was tempting me. If I could find a buyer, I could probably guarantee myself room and board for a week on that alone. But it felt too obvious. He'd know it was missing and likely turn me over to the prince's guards as soon as he could. If he went that far, he'd probably also tell them I'd killed the guards just to spite me.

Leaving the quill behind, feeling like I'd passed some sort of arbitrary test, I began to really dig, shuffling through discarded papers with no idea what I was actually looking for. It's not like he was going to have a thousand answers to all my questions written out in a nice little explanation letter addressed to his future fake wife, but considering I knew nothing, everything was added knowledge.

Something strange was going on with Thorne Noctus. First of all, who randomly claims some stranger in the streets as their wife with absolutely nothing to gain from it? Second, and the most concerning was why... of every person I'd ever come across, was he immune to my power?

His book collection was boring, but probably useful. I preferred stories of fiction rather than tomes of a kingdom's entire history. But again, knowledge. I picked a random book and held onto it. I had to start somewhere and likely it wouldn't be missed. It was of no real use to me anyway once I'd read it, so honestly, I was just borrowing it and that was not the same as stealing.

Further along the inky darkness of the room, an old wooden filing cabinet beckoned me. Scars and dents from its years of service were proudly displayed on its surface. I opened the top drawer, revealing a sea of documents, letters, and maps, documents dated older than me, letters that bore crests, maps that depicted lands I didn't know. Which wasn't saying much. Based on the collected dust, I bet he never looked in here. This was likely one of those inheritance situations where the wealthy man's annoying son just swept in and took over.

The second drawer was less populated than the first, but a curious oblong object nestled in the corner caught my attention. It was wrapped in cloth so fragile and old that it seemed to partially disintegrate at my touch. I picked it up carefully and unwrapped it.

Though bound in gold, the treasure was nothing more than a blank notebook. No bigger than the size of my palm, with a matching pencil tucked into the binding, it took everything I had not to shove the book under my arm and run for it.

"Find something to your liking?"

II

Thorne's deep voice sent my heart plunging into my stomach, and I whirled around to face him, my hand clutching the golden notebook like a lifeline. He was standing in the doorway, half concealed by shadows, his bleary eyes catching the glimmer of fading moonlight. He looked like he hadn't slept for days. I tried to ignore the way his white shirt, rolled at the sleeves, clung to his broad shoulders, the fabric pulled taut as he leaned against the doorframe. These thoughts were fucking dangerous, but I had no control over them. Not as his loose suspenders drew my gaze down his muscled frame, and I caught myself wondering how his skin would feel beneath my fingertips.

His brown hair was a tousled mess, strands of it falling over his forehead in a way that made my fingers itch to brush them back, to let my hand trail down his stubbled jaw. Heat flooded through me at the unbidden thoughts, and I quickly forced my attention away from him.

My mind stuttered for a moment as I struggled to find an appropriate response, desperately pushing away the odd pull of his presence and the dangerous path my thoughts had taken.

"I've been down here causing a racket for ages. Took you long enough."

Heat raced across my cheeks. I'd been caught red-handed because the big bastard was quiet as a wraith. How? I had no idea. Swallowing my pride, I threw the book back into the cabinet and slammed the door, accidentally dropping the one I'd intended to keep.

He lifted an eyebrow, and it barely peaked over the dark rim of his glasses. I didn't miss the way his gaze fell all the way down my borrowed shirt, landing on my bare legs. I had no undergarments and there was no way he didn't know that. Not that I cared.

"Find something to your liking?" I mocked.

He blinked and the stern face from before returned. "If I did, trust me, you'd know."

His words hung in the air between us, thick with tension. I spied a smirk tugging at the corner of his mouth, satisfied with his retort. That smugness needed to go.

"Is that a threat or an invitation?" I asked with a teasing lilt to my voice, hoping to unsettle him. Yet, his eyes narrowed in amusement. He was enjoying this.

"Use context clues to figure it out." Thorne's voice was nonchalant, as if he were discussing the weather. He circled the desk, carefully placing each thing I'd moved back to the exact spot it'd been. "What were you hoping to find in my study?"

I moved to stand before the map again, deliberately plucking one of the pins from its home and moving it three inches to the left. "I'm nosey. If you leave your shit unlocked, it's like a treasure hunt for me. You've been warned."

I plucked two more pins in the time it took him to stride across the room. His gaze never left mine, even as he reached for them. The heat of his hand seared through me. I jerked my hand away, confused by my response to him.

With a calmness that covered his irritation, he took each pin away to replace them exactly where they'd been. He then snatched the book from my underarm, opened it to scan a few pages, and then handed it back.

"Interesting choice."

"It's not my fault you have bad taste."

A casual smile revealed a faint dimple hidden behind the scruff of a fresh beard. A beard?

"How long was I—how do you have a beard?"

"You were asleep for a couple days. You probably needed it, but I'm glad you're awake. The sun will be up soon, and we've got Lithe tonight. There's no possibility of missing it, of course."

A couple days? Days? I couldn't sleep for days. I didn't have time for that. What did that put the tally at now? Sixty-six, and that was purely a guess. I hid the panic at the sound of a clock ticking through my mind. I needed a plan. And quickly. But Thorne had a connection to the Hollow. Minimally, he knew of the Lord of the Salt or whatever his name was. Though I needed to tread lightly, this was at least a start. No need to push back on Thorne's plans just yet, in case he could lead me home.

"What's Lithe?"

"Let's call it a ball. In the Goddess of Lust's temple. Where clothing is optional after sunset." His gaze dropped as he watched me slide the papers on his desk back to where I'd put them. Something about the way his eyes trailed me burned. We were dancing. Even if he didn't know it. Each move, practiced and patient. But only just. "How have you never heard of it? What town did you say you came from, again?"

I held a blank stare. "I didn't."

He jutted a chin toward the map. "Pick one."

"Is this one of those 'show me where they hurt you'

94

moments? Because no thank you." I lifted a picture frame, studied the faces staring back at me for a moment and then put it back, face down, biting the inside of my cheek to keep from smiling.

He scratched his beard and his dimple reappeared seconds before he re-straightened the papers on the desk. "Humor me."

"Fine." I crossed the room to stand before the map, staring at the tiny pins before eventually pointing. "This one."

"No." He'd moved so quietly, I hadn't heard him approach. "That's Vercant. It was burned to ash in the Bloodleaf Conflict ages ago. The only people that live there now are outlaws."

"You did find me imprisoned, did you not?"

"I told you not to lie to me. Pick another."

"I'm really bad with directions and maps."

He clicked his tongue and gently grabbed my wrist, moving my hand until it hovered over a distant pin. His body was so, so close to mine. Too close. His voice was a deep rumble, sliding down my back. "This one."

I nodded, ignoring the burn where his hand touched mine. Focusing. "Exactly. I'm from…"

"Misby," he finished.

"Misby. You didn't let me answer."

"Tell me about the climate of Misby. Your main resource. Your father's surname. Tell me one small fact, anyone in the world, and I'll move on."

"There's a meadow in front of my old house that I used to dance in, even in the rain."

"Good. That's not incredibly specific. If you're going to lie, you have to avoid details that others might know on chance alone. But if that were your answer, then you couldn't be from Misby because anything that far north is a frozen wasteland year-round. There are no meadows, and it doesn't rain. It snows. The primary resource there is fur, and the most common surname is Daemon. Repeat that back to me."

I glared. "No."

"Listen," he crossed the room and opened the second drawer of the filing cabinet, pulling out the little golden book. "I don't care where you lived. I don't care what past you're running from. I don't care if you tell a thousand lies to everyone else. I only care about what affects me and my business. If you're going to lie, do it better. If you're going to steal, be sneakier. If you're going to murder a guard in an alley with a letter opener, don't fucking stick around for his brothers to find you."

He knew. I wasn't sure how, but he knew. And he'd wielded his arrogance like a weapon against me. Only the worst kind of people did that.

"Fine, you want the truth? You've got the majority of it down. I'm not going to tell you where I'm from or why I came to Stirling. I didn't know the guard was going to die, but he assaulted *me* first. He got what was coming to him. I'm not proud of what happened. I was in shock. But you got one thing wrong in your cocky assessment." I pulled my hand from where I'd held it tucked in the long sleeve of my borrowed shirt, revealing the coin bag I'd stolen from him while he'd placed my hand on Misby's pin. "I excel in the art of acquisition."

A hint of surprise lit his face as he reached for his pocket. "Clever, little thief."

"That's what I just said."

He pressed his lips together to hide the smile as he shook his head. "I have so many regrets right now. Tell me where you're from, Paesha Noctus."

"I'm not—"

"Tell me where you're from." His eyes flashed to the map and back to me.

"Misby."

"Good girl. And your surname?"

"Daemon. My father was a tanner before he died. My mother followed suit a few short years later. Of a broken heart."

"What a tragedy," he answered, with no inflection to his tone. "The orphan card will work."

"I'm twenty-eight years old. That's hardly an orphan."

"True, but that's one more thing about yourself you've unwittingly told me."

I drew back. "I'm not an orphan."

"Maybe not, but you *are* twenty-eight, are you not?"

"Judging by your infinite amount of wisdom, and the fact that you think I need to be taught how to survive, I'm guessing you're about a hundred and forty."

"No. But good guess."

He tossed the little golden book to me and I caught it with ease. "Was there a reason you were looking for this?"

"I wasn't looking for it. I just found it."

"While digging through my things."

"Yes."

He pulled off his glasses, and I was struck again by his handsome features. The dark lashes that hid behind the reflection of the glass, the dimple you had to work to see, the sheer size of the brooding man that seemed to care, at least a little, even if it made no sense at all.

"Look, on some level, you and I are going to have to come to an understanding. It's either that or you vanish without a trace, and I have to pretend like you died."

"Death or teamwork, what a horrible choice."

"Precisely. Which is why you must come to Lithe tonight, and you must play the role of the doting wife."

I wasn't a fool. I knew how bargains worked. I sauntered forward, placing my hand on his massive chest. "It sounds like you need me a lot more than I need you. But I'm not in the business of making bargains anymore. Sorry, husband."

He was as quick as a viper, grabbing my hand and pinning it to his chest. "Don't make me blackmail you, Paesha. It won't be pretty."

There it was.

The threat in his eyes, the card he held back, but we both knew he could play. He would have held onto it longer had I not forced his hand.

"Fine," I said, feigning annoyance, though I'd had no intentions of leaving just yet. "I'll play in your little show. But you better make sure I'm the best dressed person there. And clothing will *not* be optional. Then we're even. No more blackmail."

"This isn't blackmail. I'm just making a valid point. I lied for you. It was a selfless gesture. The least you could do is make sure I don't get burned."

"Next time, don't play with fire and that shouldn't be a problem, husband."

He nodded before holding out the golden pocketbook. "Keep it."

"What? No. I don't want that. It's probably your great, great grandfather's or something."

"Does it matter?" A sardonic smile graced his lips, a smaller version of the one he'd given earlier, not for show, but for himself, showcasing his single dimple. A confirmation that he'd won. "It'll just collect dust in the back of that old cabinet. Maybe you can use it to keep track of your lies, Paesha darling."

I'D TAKEN the damn book, of course. Determined to sell it the first chance I got. It was small enough to hide in a pocket and one never knew when the opportunity would arise. Thorne had something to hide and something to gain in all of this. I could wear fancy dresses and pretend for a crowd. I'd been doing that my whole life. But eventually he'd be the one to lead me to the Hollow. And I needed that portal more than I needed a clingy new husband.

I sat in the armchair of my assigned room, draped in a stunning gown. Like the night sky in fabric form, the darkness of the silk was broken up by thousands of tiny, twinkling gems that formed constellations across my body, from the crest of my shoulders to the gentle sweep where the fabric pooled at my feet. The whirl of stars embroidered on the sleeves were delicately stitched with platinum threads that gleamed under the lamplight, drawing eyes to the elegant path they traced down to the fine lace at my wrists, iridescent beads woven into the threading to mimic distant galaxies. It was quite possibly the most stunning thing I'd ever worn, and that was saying something, considering I'd once danced a show in nothing but rubies and diamonds strung together.

Thorne had brought it in himself around lunchtime with another tray of food. I'd lounged all day, biding my time with him as patiently as I could. There was a path back to Requiem here. I was certain. But if I rushed it, I'd risk losing it and I wasn't willing to do that when so many days had already passed.

I tossed the history book to the side, giving up on the boring accounts of lineage, opting instead to study the little gold book. Hesitant fingers traced the etched designs on its cover, the gold cool to the touch. I liked pretty things, but I loved valuable things. Anything coated in gold would likely save me from starving. That was the only security I chased in my life.

I unhinged the tiny clasp and opened it, surprised to see writing on the page I knew to be blank this morning.

Where are you from, Paesha darling?

I'd never seen him write in the book. In fact, I was confident he'd never opened it. There was something almost over-whelming about the urge to answer him and defile the old, delicate pages of his little book. But I couldn't bring myself to do it.

Not until a second line of words appeared below the first.

Cat got your tongue?

With a gasp, I jerked back and dropped the book on the floor. What the hell kind of magic was *that?*

12

The sun had begun to fade, my hair was done, my dress was perfect and a younger version of me would have waited until he called. I would have cascaded down the steps, commanding every second before walking past with heavy lids and a sweet smile, knowing how much he wouldn't care about the dress or the hair. He'd be furious I'd taken my time, and I'd relish in it. But when he barked my name for the second time, I completely ignored it, staring instead at the little book in my hand.

I opened the clasp again and slid a finger down the tiny pencil bound inside, reading the new line of letters.

We're going to be late.

"Can you see me?" I whispered, looking around the room for a sign of him.

Nothing.

I pushed the pencil free and held it just above the old page. Before I could think of something to write, a new line appeared.

I'm sure you look passable. We need to leave.

I scribbled furiously.

How do you know I'm looking at this?

His response was quick.

It's become quite clear that you revel in infuriating me. I assume you're dressed?

Assume away.

The door swung open in a fury, and the brooding man stalked across the room, snatched the book from me and clasped it shut. "You can play with this later. We need to leave."

"What if I was naked?"

"I paid a lot of money for that dress. I'm sure you put it on the second it was delivered. Women tend to like expensive things too much to resist them."

"You assume too much," I retorted, standing tall in spite of my pounding heart.

His gaze traced down my body, lingering for a moment before landing back on my face. "Yes, I do."

"Here." Thorne pulled a long box from his pocket and held it out for me. "You have to wear a mask. Do you need me to tie it on for you?"

"I'm fairly sure I can handle it." I moved to stand before the mirror and slid the black diamond mask over my face. It did nothing to conceal, only framed my eyes. With the knot tied, I glanced up to see him remove his glasses and place his own mask on. It matched mine perfectly, made of the same black diamonds, though his covered half his face.

With a curt nod, he turned to leave, polished boots echoing down the hall. I snagged the book and fell in line behind him. With fewer than three conversations in total, somehow he already knew exactly how to infuriate me.

As we descended the marble staircase, his heavy stare found its way back to me once more, eyes stormy and intense. He paused halfway down, waiting for me without a word. It was an unspoken command that I knew better than to ignore. This would be a game of wits and power between us, and while he carefully laid all of his pieces on the board with each show of irritation, I hadn't even begun.

I joined him on the landing, our bodies standing close together as he offered his arm. I hesitated before accepting. That brief pause was enough to make him sigh. His gloved hand slipped over mine and even through the thick fabric of his five-piece suit and my dress, a jolt of electricity passed between us. I wondered if he'd felt it too, but I was far too strong-willed to give him the satisfaction of acknowledging the way he'd rattled me.

We stopped at the door without a word. He slid a heavy, fur-lined cloak over my shoulders. It matched my gown in length and if he'd paid a lot for the dress, I knew he paid even more for the coat.

"The fur is from a bear."

"Thank you for that random piece of information." Of course, I knew what he was doing. If my family were truly tanners, I would have known that. But I'd let him continue to assume my ignorance for a while. I swung the door open before he could answer and nearly stumbled into the carriage waiting just outside the door. He caught my arm and helped me into it without a word.

"No stops tonight, Tuck," he said to the driver, and crawled in behind me.

Only then did it occur to me his house had been silent. There was no staff at all. He'd been the one cooking. He'd been the one to fold the clothes and lay them on the chair when I slept. He'd been the one to smother me in blankets while I slept for days. Odd.

As I settled into the plush velvet interior, Thorne took the seat opposite me. His broad frame filled more space than anyone I'd ever seen. The light from outside filtered in through the tiny windows, casting a warm glow on the angles of his face, highlighting them in gold and shadow. It occurred to me again how undeniably handsome he was, albeit his winning personality won him no favors.

His clothing was immaculate, a charcoal gray suit tailored with precision to accentuate his broad shoulders and trim waist. His hair was slicked back neatly, save for a few rebellious locks that brushed against his forehead, pairing nicely with his stern demeanor.

I watched as he pulled out a small silver watch from his pocket, eyes flicking to it before they moved on to the passing scenery outside. For what seemed like an endless moment, there was silence, broken only by the steady creaking of the carriage wheels against cobblestone and the occasional thud of hooves.

"You're staring," he said finally.

I slid open the little curtain beside me. "You take up the entire space. It's impossible not to. Was the bear from this cloak a relative?"

He reached over and shut the curtain after I'd finished gawking out the window, and I could have sworn I saw a hint of a smile.

"You'll need to be prepared for the night. Talk as little as possible and try to blend in. Don't spiral with your lies. You're not that good at it. A simple hello and a demure demeanor will be enough. We met in Misby. You were a lonely spinster, living off your dwindling inheritance. I was there for work. We met when your carriage was blocking a snow packed road. Your horse was lame, and I offered you a ride home. There will be no need for additional information, no matter how much the women press, state only those facts."

"How romantic," I answered with an eye roll, sliding the curtain back open. "I'd have rather been the town whore, but I can see why you went with the route you did. Quick question though, how many times a day do we... you know?"

He went about as rigid as he could. "Pardon?"

"You see, when a man and a woman love each other very much—"

"Stop it."

My grin was beaming. "You're shy? That's adorable. But let's circle back to the nature of the event. You did say clothing was optional at a certain point, did you not? You also mentioned it was an event for the Goddess of Lust? Not to mention, poor little old me has been trapped away, alone in a frozen tundra, for years and years. A woman has needs, just like a man, you know? And since we're dealing with a goddess, I'm assuming there will be power involved somewhere. Lusty power? So, for science, of course, how... satisfied am I? Dripping with need? Raw from friction? Scale of one to ten."

The flex of his jaw was the most gratifying thing I'd ever seen in my life. "Let's avoid diving into our personal business."

"Oh, come on. You know how women can be. I mean, you certainly *claim* to know everything. Don't let me down, husband. How often?"

His face was a mixture of disbelief and bemusement, a low chuckle escaping his lips as he shook his head. "You're a mischief maker."

I leaned forward, inching closer towards him. "How often?"

"Fine." He threw up his hands in surrender. "For the sake of your insatiable curiosity—and science, let's say... often."

My grin widened. "Often? That's so vague. A more quantifiable response would be appreciated."

He ran a hand through his hair, clearly frustrated by my line of questioning. But beneath it all was an underlying amusement that told me he wasn't entirely put off by it.

"Every day," he said finally, crossing his arms over his chest protectively.

"Once or twice a day? All day? Be more specific."

He rolled his eyes and turned away from me to hide his burgeoning smile. The handsome devil probably didn't want to admit it, but at the very least, I was entertaining him.

"Twice," he answered, stressing the word as if daring me to push him further, his gaze flicking back at me defiantly.

I drew the small golden book from where I'd tucked it in my cloak, unclasped the lock, and penciled a tiny two at the top of the first page.

He watched me carefully.

"Just keeping track of all the lies." I snapped the book shut and tucked it away. "Now, was that so hard?"

He scoffed and uncrossed his arms, gazing out into the distance as though seeking refuge from my relentless questioning.

I leaned closer to him, my voice dropping to a low whisper. "And just so we're clear, I'd rate it an eleven."

He nearly choked on his own breath as he turned to face me, surprise and mirth reflecting in hazel eyes. "Eleven? Out of ten?"

"You're quite the overachiever."

"That," he said, pushing the door open as the carriage came to a stop. "Is a fact I can support. Shall we?"

The biting cold of the evening air wrapped around the back of my neck. I moved to lift my hood, but he stopped me.

"You're not cold, are you? You, of all people? A woman of Misby?"

Dammit.

"I might hate you right now." I let the hood fall, noting how the rest of the women shuffling by were bundled and hustling. "And I'm pretty sure you planned for that."

"Oh, I hoped for it," he said, spinning on his heel and pulling me toward the giant temple in front of us.

I squinted through the cascading snowflakes, trying to make out our destination. The temple was a towering colossus of stone and metal, grand in a way that made me uncomfortable. There were people freezing on the streets here.

The entrance was a gaping maw swallowed by shadows. Two gargoyles guarded its steps, their eyes glowing with some otherworldly energy. Lanterns flickered around them, casting dancing shadows that made them seem alive; their snarling expressions stone-cold warnings to those who dared enter.

"No need to look so scared," he said with a teasing edge in his voice. His fingers squeezed mine reassuringly. "Just remember what I told you."

"Only two times a day," I muttered back. We started up the snow-dusted steps, the crunching sound of our boots against the icy stone echoing eerily around us.

"No. Head down. Avoid the prince. And most importantly..." He glanced at me sideways from behind his mask.

"Go unnoticed," I finished for him.

I'd never been in a temple that wasn't in ruins, and even then, it'd only happened twice. Temples were bad luck and everyone at home knew it. But here? It felt like standing in line to enter a castle. The music grew louder as we inched closer to the door, but more curiously were the eyes of the city, gathered around, huddled together for warmth, just to watch people enter. The Salt. Those with long faces, some steeped in ire, others in awe. I couldn't help but see myself in them. Knowing, had I been born to this world, I'd likely be standing there scheming for my rise in society. I was never one to settle. Only then did it occur to me that this was the event the little boy on the street was trying to sell tickets to.

Thorne led us forward, and while I fully expected to see a horde of Cimmerians outside, harassing the onlookers, instead two tall guards dressed in soft blue with gold embellishments squaring their shoulders stood rigid, watching the crowd. I cast my eyes down as Thorne pulled an invitation from a pocket on the interior of his suit and showed it to the guards.

With a silent shared look, they gripped the handles of the towering doors and pulled them open. "Welcome to Lithe."

13

Winter melted away as we stepped into the golden, dimly lit hall. Not only was it warm within the temple, but nearly sweltering. The crowded entry, full of masked people barely shuffling forward, might've been stifling if we had to wait there long.

Keeping my head down, I tried my best to mimic a woman I once knew that could hide within the shadows. *Make no eye contact, be no one.* Except, I'd always performed better when eyes were on me. When others couldn't tear their gaze from mine, they paid no mind to what my hands were doing. But today, right now at least, I was not here to collect a thing. Only pretend.

"Eyes up, wife. Pay attention, now. Getting distracted in a temple is the most dangerous thing you could do."

"And here I thought it was lying to the crown," I grumbled.

Thorne spun, all but closing me in with his massive shoulders. "Be careful what you say with that pretty little mouth. Especially here."

"You can't compliment me and command me at the same time, prick."

He moved a finger over my jaw, a sweet gesture for onlookers, though his tone was anything but. "If you think I enjoy the fact that I have to guide you like a fucking child, you're wrong. But here we are, nonetheless."

I reached up to straighten his tie, shifting it completely sideways instead of straight down as I smiled. "Maybe you should keep your mouth shut and just see where we end up. You know, practice some self-restraint."

"Every second with you is a practice in self-restraint."

I tilted my head to the side, narrowing my eyes. "Because you want to do naughty things with me? I knew it. We could say three times a day if it would make you feel better."

He rolled his eyes. Mr. High and Mighty actually rolled his fucking eyes. "There's something wrong with you."

"Childhood trauma. In case anyone asks."

He leaned closer, practically growling. "I'm not going to say that."

"You should. The shock on people's faces when you're blunt is entertaining. Oh, tell them you rescued me from a bear that'd taken me in as its cub as a child up in good 'ole Misby. That's fun. That's what I'm going to tell people. Why is your eye twitching?"

"A different kind of trauma," he answered, trying to hide his glare.

I gasped, reaching up to run my fingers through his hair as I continued to fuck with him. "Is that sarcasm? I didn't know you had it in you."

"Of all the people in the whole entire world I had to bind myself to..."

"What a lucky man you are, Thorne Noctus."

"Indeed," he answered, forcing a grin as he spun, snagging a glass from a passing tray and drinking the whole thing, hair now a complete mess. The night might suck but at least I could entertain myself.

Drinks flowed freely in the temple. Trickling laughter and a cacophony of voices settled around us as the richest in the city, with their beautiful gowns and finest suits, waited with palpable excitement. I wanted so badly to push to my toes and glance over the gathered crowd, just to see what all the fuss was about, but I couldn't. I had to remind myself what role I played. Uninterested, unamused. As if I'd done this a thousand times and nothing could shock me.

A tall, uniformed man approached and took our coats. Thorne pulled us forward, glancing back with a steady, reassuring look on his face as we squeezed by chattering people. Each person we passed fell silent. Some gawked, others whispered behind their hands.

I didn't know what I was expecting from a temple. Piety. Solemn moments. A great sacrifice or maybe a robed figure waiting to be praised, the Silk beseeching the gods to show favor? It certainly wasn't a room filled with scattered pillars, elevating naked men and women. Nor people hanging from the ceiling on ropes, moving as one like a giant ocean wave to the slow and steady beat of a drum.

Covered with gold paint, the performers danced, touching themselves while the sultry melody played, their elaborate masks hiding their true identities. I didn't mind, really. A naked body was hardly something of note when you spent enough time on stage, but here, it felt like a scandal. Like a secret law had been broken and only those privileged enough to walk beyond the doors were good enough to know about it.

The truth of the evening became abundantly clear. The Silks

used this celebration to revel in anonymity, allowing them to forgo any sense of propriety with a free pass to follow their baser instincts. They danced, touching themselves, touching each other. Kissing and stroking, sweat poured off their bodies.

I felt them before I saw them. Standing inhumanly still around the perimeter of the room. The Cimmerians. Panic raced through me the moment I realized the gravity of the evening. I'd poked fun at Thorne and pushed his comfort level, but maybe I should have been as serious as he'd been. I'd forgotten. I let myself forget them because it was easier than remembering, and now I had to stand before the guards and pretend like they hadn't taken a part of my soul.

I didn't realize I'd stopped moving until Thorne's massive body filled my vision. He placed two hands on my cheeks and forced my gaze away from the guards and onto him. "Tell me where you're from, Paesha darling."

"M-Misby."

"Good girl. And where did we meet?"

I spoke so quietly, my racing heart was all I could hear. "On a snowy road."

"It was the greatest moment of my existence," he said, stepping backward, pulling me with him. "You had snowflakes on your eyelashes and that beautiful scowl on your face." Another step. "You used such colorful language with your horse. I wondered if you were auditioning for a play. Tell me you remember."

The fear melted from me as we stepped onto the dance floor. "It was cold."

"Try harder," he commanded, his annoyed tone long gone.

"I'd been stuck out there for hours, and I couldn't feel my fingers or toes. The sun was setting. I thought I'd die that night. And then you came stomping around like you always do. Commanding the horse to be smarter and do better."

"And he was as stubborn as you are."

I managed a blink. "Did you just compare me to a horse?"

"There are worse things."

The sultry strains of music wrapped around me like a lover. Forgetting the Cimmerians, I wanted to dance. Really dance. To find something of myself that'd been lost while trying to survive this realm. Each note caressed my skin as much as Thorne did. His fingers were gentle, sending shivers down my spine and I couldn't help but lean into that touch and secretly, desperately hope for more. The room pulsated with an ancient rhythm, beckoning everyone to surrender to its seductive call. As if I'd heard those notes a million lifetimes ago, they forced me to focus on my body and the way each sweaty inch came alive before the man in front of me, instead of the danger lurking nearby.

I was an easy victim when it came to music and dance. They were my weakness. But Thorne was right there with me, moving as swiftly, his eyes locked on mine. He wanted a show? He wanted to convince them we were in love? It wasn't going to happen with imagined stories and planted gossip. It would come from actions. From forcing them to watch us.

I grabbed his tie and spun, pulling it over my shoulder as I pressed my back to his chest, sliding down as I moved. He held on, matching my tempo and every sway of my body as if he were trained, as if he were just as desperate for that connection as I was. But some of his steps were clumsy, and he watched his feet as carefully as he watched me. His hands were perfect though. Touching where I'd hoped he would, trailing where they shouldn't. No one else existed in our imagined spotlight. And if they did, I wouldn't have known because the man never once looked away from me. Nor I, him. Not when he brushed a thumb over my lips as he pulled me flush against him. Not when he smiled as I spun away and yanked me back as if he'd missed me right there beside him. Not even when the music melted into a different song and the tempo changed.

We danced for three songs, our forced display garnering enough attention to satisfy him. The music changed and all sense of the man that'd pulled me onto the dance floor turned to ice with the small line between his brows returning as he cleared his throat. "That should do for now. They won't expect us to stay together the whole night. The women will gather and gaggle over there."

"Your view of women is really awe-inspiring," I said, leveling my tone as we left the center of the room.

A stunning, curvy woman in a long red dress approached us. Her cropped blonde hair was perfectly curled to graze her chin, and she wore a hairpin in the shape of a moth. Her mask was similar to mine, covering only her eyes and doused in rubies to match her dress.

"Paesha, this is Harlow. Harlow, I don't think you've formally met my wife."

"Harlow," I echoed, meeting her icy blue gaze.

Her smile faltered for a moment, but she quickly resumed her poised demeanor. "Paesha," she greeted with a voice like soft silk enveloping the room. "A pleasure." She leaned toward me and whispered. "In case you're wondering, we have seen each other once before, under less... formal circumstances." She held out a manicured hand.

"I remember," I said coolly, taking it. A simple touch, the tiniest bit of power, and now she was marked. Harlow was the one with the men when they came to the prison to free Atticus, though seeing her now, formally dressed without a hair out of place, was entirely different. She was beautiful. But her eyes were discerning.

"I've been told the women gather and gaggle over there," I said, jutting my chin toward a group of others.

Harlow's head snapped to Thorne. "What is wrong with you?"

I bit back my smile, and he shot me a warning glance. If a show was what he wanted, then a show he would get.

"Oh my darling, don't be so curt." I moved to stand before him, sliding my hands up his broad chest. Only I could hear the small gasp as he looked at me through his black mask. Locking my hands behind his neck, I tugged him down to whisper in his ear. "I'm going to move every single thing in your house when you fall asleep tonight."

He grinned, showing far too many teeth as he whispered back. "I fucking dare you."

"Such language," I said aloud, swatting him away. "Save that for later. A woman can only take so much." I turned to Harlow. "We're on a two-times a day schedule."

He choked on his gasp this time, and I pulled away entirely. "What? Are we not discussing your tonic?"

The color rushed back to his face, and he didn't miss a beat. "If you're referring to the amount of liquor I've had to drink lately, then discuss away, but don't forget the reason."

"Oh no, dear. I meant the other one. For the rash?"

Harlow let loose a silvery laugh.

He grabbed me and pulled me close again, growling, "Stop it," in my ear.

"Do you two need a room? A coat closet?" Archer's warm voice came from behind us. He pulled a coin from his pocket and flipped it in the air before catching it and nudging me with a shoulder. "Nice to see you again." He dipped a chin to Harlow. "Harlot."

She glared. "Don't call me that, brother."

"We ready?" Archer asked, looking at Thorne.

His eyes flashed at me, giving nothing away before looking

115

at Harlow. "It's about to start. Make sure she stays away from the front of the crowd."

"You know I will." She linked arms with me and tugged. "I promise I won't leave you to the vultures."

I had no idea how much Thorne had told the woman about our situation, but she pulled me dutifully through the throng of people. Did she think we'd actually gotten married? Did she think he knew me before the prison escape? With no information, the only thing I could really do was keep my head down and my mouth shut. That was the best idea, anyway. People that listened more than they talked typically knew far more than those with a thousand things to say. And maybe someone here would know something about the Lord of the Salt or the Hollow.

The women stared down their noses at their friends. They gossiped behind their hands and pointed as they spoke. Each conversation, each word exchanged, was laced with a venomous sweetness. I couldn't help but feel like a moth drawn to a deadly flame, taking it all in. A terrible realization occurred. It wasn't beauty I beheld in this magnificent temple. It was decadence, excessiveness, it was sickness.

Lost in the murmurs of the chattering crowd, I barely heard the music fade. Still, I continued to study the people. I knew fine things. The way a real jewel glistened in candlelight versus an imitation. The subtle difference between silk that caressed the skin like a lover's touch and its cheaper counterpart that only hinted at luxury. The taste of true aged wine, rich and complex, compared to the diluted imitation that left a bitter aftertaste. The sound of genuine laughter, full of warmth and sincerity, as opposed to the hollow echoes of forced mirth. Those tiny bits of knowledge were paid for with every moment I spent living on the end of the Maestro's rope, chasing luxury and life, unlike the one I was born into.

But the people here? Dripping in jewels and fine silks? I'd bet my last coin none of them knew about suffering. None of them knew anything about the people standing just outside the temple, gathered around, just to watch them enter. There weren't such clear lines drawn in Requiem. The rich weren't above crawling into bed with the poor. Here, I can't imagine what kind of scandal that would be. And that's exactly what Thorne was worried about.

"Thorne told me this is your first Lithe. I think I should warn you before it really begins," Harlow said, stealing me from my thoughts. "It's going to be overwhelming at first, but the most important thing is to avoid the selection. Keep your head down. Your eyes are unique, and they will draw attention. As I'm sure you know."

"So I've been told."

She swiped a glass from a passing tray and handed it to me.

"Thank you."

"For the nerves," she said quietly, eyes pinned on a Cimmerian standing on the perimeter of the room. "We'll avoid them. And the women for now. Don't want to seem too eager."

We stopped walking, standing closer to the door than the dance floor, and about as far away from the head of the cavernous room as possible. I did everything I could to refrain from looking around. A woman in high society would not concern herself with beautiful carvings, golden ceilings or naked people dancing on a pillar.

Harlow grabbed another glass and finished it in three gulps. "Get ready. Eyes down."

I stared at the beautiful white floor laced with golden flecks as three low bells chimed, and the room silenced. As if I were hit by a tidal wave, the heat in the room became nearly unbearable.

I wouldn't claim to know a thing about the gods that ruled the realms. They'd all but abandoned mine long ago. But clearly not this one. And this temple didn't belong to a God of Shadows or a God of Moons or whatever else those assholes deigned themselves rulers of. This temple belonged to a goddess. One whose name I'd seen on an ancient tapestry hung in my old boss's office. And as the crowd fell to their knees, fine gowns be damned, there she sat beyond the dance floor, upon her throne, staring down at the people that clearly worshiped her: Serene, Goddess of Loss and Lust.

Slowly, almost reluctantly, as my heart hammered in my throat, I lifted my gaze to meet the piercing stare of the Goddess of Lust. Draped in sheer gold fabric, not an ounce of her perfect form hidden, she sat upon her elevated throne, a regal figure bathed in an otherworldly glow. Beside her, an old king sat, seemingly insignificant, a mere mortal in the presence of true divinity. But it was the goddess's smile that sent a chill racing through my veins, a smile that held the promise of untold power and unfathomable darkness. And she'd stared at me as if she knew all my secrets the moment I'd stepped through her doors.

"Shit," Harlow spat, keeping her head down.

She knew, of course. They all did, following the piercing gaze of the goddess. Serene rose from her seat slowly, eyes holding me frozen in place. The rest of the world could have fallen into a pit of fire, and I'd have never known it. I couldn't look away, couldn't bear the thought of it. I wanted only one thing in the entire world. Her. I wanted to touch her perfect skin and taste her. I wanted to brush my lips upon hers and...

Only when she looked away from me did the thoughts subside. Though an ache had grown between my legs. A desire to touch myself, right here in front of everyone, nearly smothered me. With a reluctant swallow, I cursed the goddess and her godsdamned magic. Anyone worth their death knew this temple was a dangerous place to be. What a fool I was to agree to this farce. I'd been a victim of the war between logic and desire in the span of minutes.

How weak I was.

"Stand, dear ones," the goddess said, her voice as pure as a child's song, echoing off of painted walls and stilling the flicker of the candles surrounding the room. "It's time to select the Paramour of Lithe. And as you all know, your king has been gifted with this honor." She turned, holding a hand toward the old king. "Come, Your Grace, select your Paramour and let us celebrate." He pushed himself up from his seat, standing only at the goddess's shoulder, his round belly and white hair aging him far more than the wrinkles around his eyes.

Everyone rose, but there was nowhere to run. Nothing to do but keep my head down and hope the Goddess hadn't truly been watching me.

"This is fine," Harlow whispered, slipping her hand around my bicep. "As soon as he chooses, we just have one little thing to do, and then we can get out of here. The Goddess will forget. It's fine. Completely fine."

"Which one of us are you trying to convince?" I asked as the crowd began to murmur with anticipation.

We sank backward, slipping behind shoulder after shoulder. Away from the attention, away from the crowd until I collided with a broad chest. I couldn't help but feel a sense of relief as I turned my head to find the stern face of my pretend husband. The last time I'd seen him, he'd been across the room. Yet he'd come for me, and try as I might to hate him, he was my only confidant in the world right now.

We locked eyes, and he dipped his chin in reassurance. "Steady."

The crowd bowed to the king, then clapped, though the sound seemed muted compared to the chuckle the old king released as the goddess whispered into his ear. Pink raced across round cheeks. He nodded to the goddess and together, they stepped from their dais and into the crowd.

It wasn't until the surrounding crowd parted and Thorne grew rigid behind me that I accepted I was well and truly fucked.

14

Standing before the round old king, I forced steel into my veins and lifted my chin, remembering who I was. Who I'd taught myself to be. Not just the role I'd assumed for Thorne, but the woman I'd become. Long before I'd stepped into this world.

"Might I select you to be tonight's Paramour, beauty?" The old king's voice was kind and soft. He waited patiently for an answer, though I was confident he'd never been denied in his life. Thorne might as well have been a mile away, for as useful as he could be in this moment. What was a Paramour? What did I have to agree to? I couldn't swallow the panic, nor could I force my hand into his. I simply stood before him, frozen like a damn fool.

"You can say no," the king whispered, leaning in. "Though I don't believe Serene will be pleased if you do."

So it wasn't the king I needed to worry about offending. But my grave had already been dug, and I was one foot in. Who would ever forget someone that'd denied the king and a goddess in one night? I didn't want to be remembered. As the gravity of the situation melted over me, I realized there was no chance of being forgotten now.

I curtsied, dipping as low to the floor as possible until the old man chuckled and whispered, "Rise, my dear."

Upon sliding my fingers over the king's gloves, I glanced back at Thorne. He wasn't watching me though. He was in a staring match with a grinning goddess perched across the room. Apparently we were both fools.

The king led me beyond the jealous glares of the onlookers and straight up the dais steps to the throne the Goddess of Lust sat upon. My thighs throbbed, and my skin prickled at her nearness. My body softened for her, eager for her touch. I refused to look at the stunning woman, keeping my eyes glued to her long, bare legs that shimmered like gold. I wondered what they might taste like. I wondered what kind of sound she would make, should I throw caution to the wind and fall to my knees before this hateful crowd. My heart pounded in my throat. My body swelled with desire. Only the firm grip of the old king kept me grounded. He patted my hand, never letting go, and for that small mercy, I was grateful.

"Your eyes, child," Serene said, placing a searing finger below my chin and lifting my gaze until I met hers.

I couldn't help the whimper that escaped, nor the pulse between my legs at her touch.

"They are so unique, Your Grace, are they not?"

"Quite... quite so." The king reached into his chest pocket and pulled out a handkerchief, wiping the sweat from his brow. "I believe we've selected the perfect Paramour."

"Indeed," the goddess said, flashing another look at Thorne. The draw of her sultry voice turned me to a puddle as I stood silent, remembering only to breathe, though I was now burning with need.

"Do you speak, girl?" Serene asked. "Or do you need extra motivation?"

"I speak." Though I wasn't sure if I would ever blink again.

"Lovely, little thing. I saw you with Thorne Noctus. You're a dancer?"

"In another life, perhaps." I pulled my chin from her touch and the way her eyes narrowed, the way she drew back, told me all I needed to know about the woman. She coveted absolute control, and should I do anything else against her will, that action would come at a price.

"What an interesting concept," she purred, pushing her raven hair over her shoulder. "Maybe someday you'll visit again and tell me all about your past lives. Perhaps you'll dance."

"If you wish it," I breathed, though I absolutely hated the fact that I'd inadvertently accepted her invitation. Looking into that stunning face, I wondered if falling beneath the thumb of such a being was exactly what I should have done. Where I might've found happiness. Only my baser instincts warned me this was simply her power and likely a direct path to misery.

"Take my hand, Paramour. Let us open the ceremony." The goddess lifted her palm. The hesitation was infinitesimal, but I knew she felt it as much as I did. Still, I wanted nothing more than to touch the serpent. To let her poison me. Because even though I hated the way my body responded to her, I was trembling and filled with a primal need to give her every ounce of ecstasy I could. But the moment my fingers connected with hers, indescribable, body-convulsing pain seared every nerve, devoured every inch of skin, shredded every piece of my soul until I nearly fell.

But I could not and would not be weak before the vicious crowd, nor a goddess that played her hand so easily. I would not let them see my fall. Though gasps ricocheted around the cavernous room, though some cried out in shock at my willingness to touch their goddess, I did not falter as I held the connection and slid my palm into hers.

"Very impressive," the siren crooned, leaning in to press her lips to my cheek. "Do come see me again, pet. I know you want to taste me. I can see it in those stunning eyes, and I promise you, it will be a glorious endeavor."

I would absolutely fucking not be returning, but in that moment, all I could do was nod and brace myself as she escorted me back down the steps and around the room, putting me on parade as the Silk she approached became noticeably weaker. She reached for several faces clearly familiar to her, kissing some, grabbing others between their legs or brushing her thumb across taut nipples and whispering into eager ears.

She delivered on whims of desire with a display of power, coaxing her amiable audience to lean into their desires, with no concern for the consequences. She was chaos in feminine form, and she was perfection. Years ago, I'd longed for that sort of devotion. I'd learned to command a room, a theater even, but here, she commanded the world. With as much effort as it took me to inhale. To blink.

The audience truly believed their masks gave them some sort of immunity to propriety, and perhaps it did. Perhaps that was the magic of Lithe. Perhaps that was the goddess's true power. Because how could one person feel guilty for something everyone in the room was feeling?

The trill of her laugh was intoxicating as she walked further and further to the back of the room, her grip getting tighter as she stopped before Thorne. "Your bride, Thorne Noctus, is she not?"

His glare was lethal. "She is."

Something in the way he'd claimed me felt different from the day we'd stood before the prince. He'd been a beast that day, unbothered by the prince, but now, as she stuck her hand out and waited for him to kiss it, he acquiesced so easily. Bent so amiably. I tried not to stew as those lips touched her. He was not my husband. I had no claim over the man. I wanted nothing to do with him. I'd be gone from this realm soon enough, anyway.

Serene whispered something in Thorne's ear, but I looked away, as any wife might've done. I couldn't forget the role. The reason we were here. Archer had joined his sister's side, and though Serene was so near, both watched the king rather than the goddess. Likely to keep her attention away from them. Couldn't say I blamed them for it either.

She continued on, avoiding the cloaked guards as we moved. Her first, then me, then the king following dutifully behind. Some didn't tremble when she drew nearer, completely unaffected, proving that she controlled the effects and direction of her sultry power and gave them a pass the rest of us were not afforded.

"Your Paramour," the goddess said, placing my hand in the king's once we stepped onto the dance floor. "Enjoy your evening, Your Grace."

With my arm tucked firmly into the king's grip, neither of us could resist the urge to watch Serene glide all the way back up to her golden throne, hips swaying beneath the sheer fabric, holding every pair of eyes in the room until she sat and gestured for the music to begin again.

My gaze met the king's. Warmth and kindness radiated from him. "Just a bit longer, dear."

There was a familiarity there, a gentle comfort that reminded me of my dear friend Hollis, an old man I'd loved and mourned until my soul ached. With a soft smile, I allowed the king to guide me across the dance floor, our steps falling into a graceful rhythm.

I didn't know gentle kings existed, but I had enough experience with men to see beyond vicious facades and masks. And though his actual mask covered his face from the top of his cheeks to his temple, the smile lines were there. The wrinkles that proved he'd spent many years in happiness. This was not a tyrant. Nor a man that ruled with an iron fist.

The onlookers watched in awe, likely captivated by the sight of a stranger dancing with the monarch. Their curious eyes burned into me, but I wouldn't shrink beneath their scrutiny. Instead, I held my head high, radiating an inner confidence that had been slowly kindling within me. As if I was no longer the lost and bewildered outsider, but a woman who had found her footing in this strange, unfamiliar world.

"Forgive me, Paramour," the king said, snatching my attention as he circled me in the center of the dance floor. "I know it must feel quite uncomfortable to have the attention of so many. If you'd like to keep our dance short, please say."

"I've never minded an audience, Your Grace."

"I don't believe we've met before," he whispered. "I'm quite sure I'd remember a set of eyes such as yours. Did your parents bring you to the castle as a child?"

"Actually, Your Grace, I've recently come from Misby."

Though it didn't seem possible, the king's rosy cheeks deepened as he smiled again, full of delight. "Truly? How wonderful! I used to hunt there when I was a boy. Tell me, what was your surname?"

I could just picture the smug look on Thorne's face if he knew how this conversation was going. Prick.

"Daemon."

"You can't mean Riccard? Riccard Daemon?"

"Oh no, no relation. But there are so many of us Daemons there these days, it's hard to keep track."

"Well, you're the prettiest Daemon I've ever seen."

"You flatter me, Your Grace. I'd heard you were a charmer,

but to stand before you is to know the truth. You have a kind soul."

It should have been a farce, a part I played to conceal the truth of who I was. But as we stepped back and forth, moving across the dance floor while the old man chuckled, his full belly laugh endearing, I knew it to be sincerely true. And something in that felt dangerous. Because how could a kind old man rule a kingdom and not be swallowed whole by power-hungry leeches?

"Can I tell you a secret?" he asked as we turned once more, the world fading away.

"I'm very good at keeping secrets." I winked and let him spin me until my black dress billowed along the floor in waves.

As soon as he'd pulled me close again, he admitted, "I dislike these types of events."

"Can I tell *you* a secret?"

"I wish you would."

"I think most people hate these kinds of events. While there's comfort on a stage, there's nothing like home."

"Well then. Isn't it lovely to find a kindred spirit amongst the monsters?"

His choice of words shocked me. I nearly missed the next step, but the king held on tightly.

"What kind of monsters might a king know?"

His all but hidden eyes glossed over as he looked past my shoulder, seemingly lost in a memory. "There are monsters in sheep's clothing, my darling, but there are also monsters that wear no masks. They are the most dangerous, for they have no need to hide their true nature. They revel in their chaos, and their honesty is their weapon. It's the ones who show you exactly who they are, without a shred of pretense, that you must fear the most."

I smiled, bowing as the music stopped. "I will take that lesson with me, Your Grace. Thank you for this honor."

He pressed a gloved hand over his heart and bowed back. "Truly, it's been my pleasure. Do try to visit the castle. I have so few visitors these days."

I gripped his hands. "I would love to."

He looked beyond me again, as if remembering the crowd, and his fingers tightened on mine. He straightened and pulled me toward him as if he'd meant to protect me. All sense of comfort was swept away in an instant. The Cimmerians had closed in, surrounding us.

15

Though the king stood at my side, his grasp gentle and his eyes discerning, fear settled in as the faceless Cimmerians formed a circle around us on the dance floor. There were no thoughts of Thorne, just survival as my vision darkened and the only thing I could see were prison bars and the blood on the floor. Hear the crack of the whip and the squeal of the wheel when I'd been stretched on the rack. Smell the rot of bodies left for the rats. I'd been to Death's court. That was not the fear here. It was the journey.

"Father," Prince Farris crooned, holding a glass in one hand as he stepped through the perimeter of robed guards. "You've not introduced me to our new friend. But no matter. I think we've met, haven't we, beauty?"

Phantom hands of fear held any words I might say from coming. I fought the urge to run.

"Tonight's Paramour, son," the king said with a flourish of his hand, though he didn't look either of us in the eye. "Her duty is done."

The prince sloshed his drink to the side, letting it spill as he continued. "And does our Paramour have a name, Father?"

The old man cleared his throat, straightening as if he meant to look down on his son, though the feat was impossible with such a height difference. "As is her right this evening, her name remains a mystery. Or have you forgotten the traditions of Lithe?"

I prided myself on knowing people. Reading them. The king meant to protect me with his sharp words, and I wasn't sure why, but I was certainly not upset about it. This was a game. Farris knew my first name, and the king knew my pretend surname. They both knew Thorne.

The prince reached for my chin, and I fought every one of my instincts screaming to pull away as he studied my eyes behind the black diamond mask. The leather texture of his glove rubbed my face, and the familiar smell reminded me of my old boss. I wondered which would have been worse: the wrath of a crime lord, of which I was intimately familiar, or the wrath of a prince, held beneath the fist of his father's rule.

"Farris!" The old king's bark of his son's name didn't dissuade him from squeezing harder.

The Cimmerians stepped closer as one. As if they shared a single mind with no spoken words. Maybe it was the proximity to the king, knowing he held ultimate authority here, but I could feel the fear melting into anger the longer the bastard gripped my chin in defiance of his father.

Narrowing my eyes, muscles tensed and fists at my side, I held my breath as he leaned closer, his words hot on my ear. "Come see me later, Paramour. I have just the thing to treat that defiant nature I can see in those stunning eyes." Without waiting for me to reply, he pushed me away and spun to his father. "Time for bed, Your Grace. I can take it from here."

"I'm quite capable—"

The prince tossed his head back and laughed, his shoulders relaxing, his stance melting into a different man than he'd been seconds ago. "You have an entire kingdom to run, Father, and we all know how much you hate these types of events. I'll have one of my men see you home."

The prince jutted his chin toward the closest guards, and they closed in around the old man, effectively cutting me off from him before I could say goodbye. As if on cue, the music transitioned into something far more pulsating, and the dance floor swarmed with all the people that'd been waiting around the edge.

Lithe had officially begun, and while I was relieved my part was over, I was equally concerned for that old king.

But I'd already taken on a world of problems and that wasn't one of them. I prepared myself to be bombarded by onlookers trying to figure out who I was, how they knew me, and as was common with high society, why they prematurely decided they were better than I was. Instead, they turned their backs, immediately shutting me out. Which was ideal.

With each slow beat of music, the gold painted dancers, naked on their pillars changed their pose. The goddess's power seeped down the walls, thickening the air until it was hard to breathe without feeling every inch of my skin come alive, over and over again.

I scanned the room for Thorne, easily picking him out. He stood a head taller than most of the crowd. A doting wife might've joined him, an adoring husband might've been waiting in the wings for me. Instead, he stood amongst a group of women, his posture casual, his laugh loud as they conversed. Though I hardly knew him, that relaxed state and joyful nature wasn't one I'd seen from him. Which begged the question, how miserable had our pretend marriage made the man?

I sank backward through the room, keeping my ears open

for mention of the Lord of Salt or the Hollow, shutting out the idea of Thorne entirely. They'd said we were leaving as soon as the selection was over, but clearly, the promise of a seductive evening had taken over. The music shifted to a lively tune, eliciting a pang of longing to join in the dance but I denied myself the pleasure.

With each passing minute, the temperature in the room rose, the heat pressing in until I could feel the sweltering in my bones. Sweat gathered at my temples and trickled down my spine. Each breath drew in warm, stifling air, leaving my mouth dry and parched. My dress clung to my skin, trapping the heat, making every movement uncomfortable. Men began stripping layers of their suits, tossing them at servants passing through the crowd.

I swiped a glass from a sweaty man carrying a golden tray through the room. With the glass inches from my lips, Harlow flashed in front of me, and before I knew it, the drink splashed down my dress and the glass shattered on the floor. I barely stifled a curse.

"Oh goodness, I'm so sorry," she said, louder than necessary. Sweeping her slender, red gown to the side so she could kneel to gather broken pieces. She shook her head and glared as if I were a petulant child, and she was my caretaker.

I knelt, plucking shards as she fumed. "What are you thinking?" She held a piece of the glass between us, "This is the goddess's crystal. Drink from it and you'll be poisoned with lust for the rest of your life. Everyone knows that. I swear, it's like you're trying to get yourself caught."

"Caught?"

"Of course I know you two..." her voice trailed off as she looked in Thorne's direction.

"I never asked for his help. And I'm not asking for yours now."

And it would be easier for me if I had less people to juggle my lies between. But one day soon, I would simply vanish and remain a mystery to them for the rest of their days. These conversations, even the run-ins with the prince's guard were trivial in the grand scheme of things. As long as I could avoid the Maw, I'd be home soon.

Large blue eyes widened. "I wasn't judging. I'm willing to help, of course. But I would think a respectable woman from Misby would know not to touch the goddess's glass. Doesn't she have a temple there?"

I stood, holding several pieces of the cursed crystal as carefully as I could. "I don't like the gods or the temples. I prefer to stay home and read a book. So probably, but that's not something I would know a lot about."

Her red dress glimmered in the warm chandelier light as she rose from the ground. "That's fair. I'm sorry, I just assumed..."

"Well, now you know."

She dropped the broken crystal on another passing tray. Her long, slender finger pointed to the floor so the half-dressed man could see the mess. "You might get someone to clean this."

"Yes, my lady."

"And take hers as well."

The man kept his eyes to the floor as he held his tray out, waiting for me to discard the glass. With a sigh, I handed over the broken glass, making eye contact with the man for a brief second before he slipped into the crowd.

Harlow smoothed her hands down her gown before adjusting her mask, looking pointedly over my shoulder. "I've just seen someone I need to speak with. A word of advice, don't touch anything... and try not to speak to anyone."

"Disappear. Got it."

With a shrug, she took my hand and squeezed. "We can talk later. I'll teach you what's important to know."

I forced a smile as she spun and walked away.

Confident I'd melt into the floor if I didn't cool off soon, I moved toward the door, taking in deep gulps of cool air each time it opened. I thought maybe I should leave. Use a little magic to hunt down Thorne's carriage and wait for him there, but just as I'd decided to, I caught a billowing flash of Harlow's dress. I watched as she laughed with a group of people. But it wasn't her laughter that held my attention, nor the company she kept, but rather the tiny steps backward. The subtle way she drew her company toward her as she moved.

I thought it was a strange habit until I caught her glance over a shoulder, making eye contact with Thorne. He had eyes only for her, watching... directing her through the space with subtle movements until she collided with a woman doused in jewels. Harlow grabbed the woman's wrist, apologizing, tipping sideways as if she were far more drunk than she'd been minutes ago. The woman sneered and said something I couldn't make out before turning away. But I didn't miss the gleam of that diamond bracelet as it fell into the small bag hanging from Harlow's wrist. Nor the eye contact she made with Thorne before spinning away. Thorne. Lord High and Mighty himself... paired with a beautiful blonde, were nothing but sneaky, little thieves. What were the odds? Considering he'd given me that title earlier with quick disdain.

I'd guessed as much with Archer, after watching the events of Tithe, but he'd helped that woman with the children. Had been part of a bigger plot to get her the red bag I'd watched someone steal. This was different. This was careless. In a crowd of rich people showing off their status... If I had seen them, anyone could have.

I kept my eyes locked on Harlow. She'd been quick. Sly. Nearly perfect. Except she didn't plan for the prince to be standing beside her. On collision, his guards moved in surrounding them as her bag flew to the floor. Watching over a short man's shoulder, I caught the brief look of panic race across her beautiful face, and I knew, without a doubt, the bracelet she'd just stolen had fallen out. Before I realized it, I was moving. Through the throng of people, twisting sideways and back, yanking my dress free from being stepped on as I closed in. With the prince's back to me, I scanned the floor, but I couldn't see anything until the tiniest glint of light reflected off the diamond bracelet, half hidden beneath the hem of a nearby gown.

Without pausing to think, I dropped to my knees, pretending to fix something on my shoe. My fingers brushed the cool metal, and I quickly slipped the bracelet into my bust, the weight of the jewels pressing into my skin. Harlow's jaw slackened as she watched me rise, understanding what I had done. The prince had a tight grip on her bare arm, and though I couldn't hear the words, the sharp tone was anything but kind and regal.

I needed a distraction, something that would draw the prince's attention away from Harlow and give her a chance to escape. She'd saved my ass with the tray, now it was my turn to save hers, or at the very least, try. My mind raced, but there was only one true answer, one talent honed not by magic, but through my own blood, sweat, and tears.

I took a deep breath and approached the prince, squeezing past the guards and between him and Harlow, though I knew it was a dangerous game. I let my body fall loose, pushing my breasts forward as I leaned in and slid a finger over his chest, pretending I'd had just enough drinks to not care about the repercussions with my new husband. "Your Highness," I said, bowing slightly, letting my eyes fall slowly down his slender body. "This is my favorite song. I was hoping we could dance?"

Dropping Harlow's arm, the prince turned to me, surprise

flickering in his eyes. He hesitated, then extended his hand. His grip, cold and firm. "Of course."

As we moved onto the dance floor, Harlow used the moment to shuffle away from the guards, toward the door. I just needed to buy her a little more time.

The prince was an excellent dancer, but he led with a firm hold and fingers that wandered far too low for comfort. I plastered a sweet smile on my face and let the music take over, sweeping me into a melodious place of comfort. I'd never heard the song before, but the pulse of the drums carried me without pause, each spin and step a balm to my rattled, realm-traveling soul.

"You're quite bold, Paramour. Will your new husband not be furious?"

Ignoring my pounding heart and every warning bell pealing through my mind, I let him pull me closer, let him wrap the ends of my hair around his fist, let him fall prey to the lust permeating the room.

"He certainly will be," Thorne said from our side, every bit the stoic statue as other people on the dance floor halted to keep from plowing into him when the music stopped mid-song.

Thorne's forced jealousy was exactly what would have been expected of him, and he'd played the part perfectly.

I smiled sweetly, patting his chest. "Don't be rude, darling. Our prince has asked for a dance."

"Yes, darling," Farris drawled, releasing my hair. "Don't be rude."

I watched the prince's gaze fall onto the fist balled at Thorne's side as he stepped just to the edge of the dance floor without blinking. Farris's laugh grated all the way down my spine as the music began again and I spun away, no longer swept into the sway of the song, but rather the role I was forced to play to keep all the pieces from falling apart. At this point, I was certain Thorne would be my quickest path to the Hollow. But how long would this charade have to continue? And would I be better off simply asking him?

My gaze flashed to his, catching the very subtle dip of his chin. He knew what I'd done to save Harlow. Maybe that would be a bargaining chip for answers. Farris brushed a strand of sweaty hair from my face. I clenched my teeth to keep from pulling away. I knew the hunger within his eyes. Hunger I'd catered to by throwing myself in his path. Perhaps the target on my back had grown, but when I was gone, none of it would matter.

The song ended with a long dramatic note and the prince clapped his hands, dark eyes locked on mine. "There are plenty of dances left in this night. Find me for your last." His words were not a plea but a demand. A threat even.

I forced a giggle and bowed before rushing to Thorne's side. The brooding man didn't waste a single second. Not one note, as he led me back to the dance floor and declared, "This dance is mine. And not just this one. Every last dance of every event for the rest of our lives."

The woman closest to us sighed as she looked at Thorne. He yanked me closer and whispered, "Good girl. Now finish strong and we can get out of here."

The music began with a deep, deep tone that carried dramatically through the room. But it wasn't the music that concerned me. It was the flash of power that locked onto me. The bone-deep rattle of pure need that jolted through me, causing me to go rigid.

Serene had struck.

Thorne, sensing my distraction, tightened his grip on me. His palm seared through the thin fabric of my dress, a hot touch working to ground me back to reality.

"Focus," he hissed, but it wasn't his voice that filled my ears.

It was hers. The haunting, seductive whisper from the golden-eyed goddess lurking somewhere nearby.

I pressed my body closer to Thorne, hating the whimper that escaped as I became aware of every place our bodies touched. The fabric of his suit brushed against my skin, soft and warm. It was addictive, this feeling of being held so tightly. His fingers tangled in my hair, pulling it free from the hair pins, letting it tumble down my back in a waterfall of curls that tickled.

My body wound tighter and tighter. The friction of my thighs touching, of his hands moving gently across the small of my back, the heat, the people crowding around us, kissing, removing clothing, it was all too much. A wave of need crested between my legs.

Thorne moved his hands up, gripping my neck as he leaned down, his warm breath dancing across my collarbone as he spoke. "It's the goddess's power. Try to fight it. Eyes on me."

"I think I need..."

"Not much longer."

Suddenly it was only him and I in an empty room as a faint song played in the background. With hands wrapped firmly around my waist, he lifted me, spinning us both, consuming me with his touch. His hands never left me, as we stepped in and out on time with the beat, he expertly overwhelmed my senses, keeping my mind on the steps and not how it felt to be touched by him. The way he looked at me as if I were truly his last everything didn't matter. The way he'd protected me and watched me was only a show. The way his fingers held me tight enough to appease a fraction of the ache was merely a performance by a poised man.

Before I knew it, the song was over, and he was leading us through the room in a rush. Archer was already at the door with our cloaks. I threw mine around me as we stepped out of the temple. The air, though freezing, was purifying; each breath washed away a layer of Serene's power.

The carriage ride back to Thorne's home was silent. I didn't want to go to his house. I wanted to go to mine. I wanted to stand at the entrance of the Syndicate house and watch a little girl with wild, curly hair come running for me with her dog at her heels. I wanted to eat Elowen's soup and argue with Thea over things that weren't really important. I was tired. So damn tired, and this night had been for Thorne, but tomorrow would be for me. He was either going to tell me everything he knew about the Hollow and the Lord of the Salt, or I would have to leave and find it on my own. I'd had enough of Wisteria.

16

I woke drenched in sweat, my stomach churning. Rushing to the bathroom, I barely had time to sink onto the cold floor before I was violently sick. I knew it wasn't real, but the body remembers what the mind tries to forget; every touch, every word, every tear shed because of the Cimmerians. My skin was stained by their touch, and every inch of me wanted to crawl out of my own body, my own reality, and escape.

Gritting my teeth, I pushed myself up from the bathroom floor, ignoring how my legs felt weak beneath me. I rinsed my mouth and splashed water on my face and neck. The icy chill helped soothe the fire, dousing the remnants of Serene's intoxicating power.

Dressed in Thorne's shirt once again, I padded back to the bed. Each shadow cast by the moonlight filtering through the window heightened my alertness. My mind was teetering, caught between the aftermath of Lithe and the lingering nightmares of my imprisonment.

My plan wasn't fully formed yet, but waiting around was

becoming more and more difficult. Another night passed. If I stayed with Thorne, he'd only draw the prince closer. Whatever crime ring they were running was none of my business, but the last thing I needed was the trouble bound to come with it. I'd sooner go back to Death's court and spend eternity knowing I failed the realms, than return to the Maw.

Last night, before I'd fallen asleep, I decided I couldn't just ask him where the Hollow was. He was far too smart, and he'd ask questions I couldn't answer. I didn't need him to question me more than he already was. As long as I was stuck in this world, I needed an ally. And though I wouldn't be sharing the whys of it, I'd be using him for as long as I could. I had time. I could wait a few days if I had to. Let him settle into a routine with me around before I started following him and figuring it out on my own.

After years of learning hard lessons on the rotting streets of Requiem, I would not, could not, easily trust a single living soul. One could only be burned so many times before the flames no longer hurt, and all that remained were the cold, hollow ashes of what had been. I would not lose myself to the fire again.

I considered using my power to get back to where I'd met the eerie boy that first day. Following the instructions to the Hollow just as he'd given them, but the first time I'd followed them, they'd led me to murder, prison and torture that haunted me. The second time had led me to Tithe. Forcing a different kind of torture onto me.

I pulled the blanket up, staring at the bedside table. My fingers brushed against the worn edge of the small golden book sitting there. Unclasping the latch, I flipped the cover open to find the number two still etched on the top of the page. Below it, a new message from Thorne had appeared.

Paesha,
I set a glass of water outside your door.
The nightmares will fade,
Thorne

I slipped the pencil free and considered writing something witty back. But I was exhausted, and playing this game with him was only a distraction from my escape.

Thank you.

Beyond the door, on a simple little tray, was a glass of water and three small books. I spent the rest of the night curled up on the chair, reading about a woman that rode dragons and fought in battles and died beside the man she never said 'I love you' to.

The warm rays of the morning sun cut through the cold draft in the room, gently stirring me from my state of half awake, half asleep. I stretched languidly, feeling the aftereffects of last night's reading adventure in the stiffness of my neck and shoulders.

The scent of fresh bread filled the air, drawing me like an invisible tether. Navigating through the hall and down the stairs, I passed ornate paintings with intricate patterns and faded portraits of men and women whose eyes followed me with cold indifference. I casually slid the lower left corner of one of the frames to the side as I walked by, leaving it tilted.

The dining room was near the front door, down a small hall beyond the staircase. I found it easily, following that tether as if it were my power luring me to food. Thorne was seated at a large mahogany table with a simple breakfast laid out. He hadn't seen me come in yet, too consumed by the paper he gripped like a lifeline in his hands.

I cleared my throat to announce my presence, and he slowly lowered the paper, staring at me through his round glasses, eyes falling to the hem of his shirt on my bare legs. I stepped into the room, snagging a piece of toast and sitting at the opposite end of the table.

"Paesha darling. Did you happen to switch the two paintings at the top of the stairs around last night?"

Sliding a pad of butter across my toast, I grinned. "I might've."

He said nothing more, raising his newspaper again, though I could see the white of his knuckles and it brought me an odd sense of joy. After several pieces of toast and a small bowl of fruit, three crisp knocks rattled the front door.

Thorne didn't move. So we sat there in silence, listening to the next three knocks followed by one more and then Archer's voice. "It's colder than Farris's balls out here, Thorne. Open up."

I bit back the smile as the brooding man at the head of the table lowered his paper again with a sigh, as if his world were filled with petulant children. Maybe it was. He slid his glasses to the tip of his nose to pin me with a look. "Will you be changing soon, so we can let our guests in, or shall we see how long it takes them to leave?"

I slid my chair back and stood, walking down the side of the table, before reaching all the way across to snag his steaming coffee and bring it to my lips, letting the shirt rise as far as possible on my bare thighs. "Open the door, *darling*. It's rude to keep our guests waiting."

The challenge in his eyes was unwavering as he also stood, plucking the coffee from my hands and placing it back in the exact spot I'd taken it from. He even twisted the handle.

With a subtle but deliberate turn, he moved toward the door. The winter breeze slipped into the hall, carrying with it a rush of crisp, invigorating air that licked my legs. I waited patiently, knowing the worst thing I could do to Thorne was remain standing until the company came in. They'd make their own assumptions, but as far as most were concerned, we were newlyweds. Besides, everyone had legs. It's not like I had my chest on full display. I looked down to confirm the buttons were secure as Harlow, Archer, and a rather rakish man stepped in. Harlow led the trio, her golden hair dancing around her shoulders like a blazing halo.

Without much preamble, they claimed their positions around the table. Harlow seated herself elegantly beside Thorne, her dress pooling around her in a wash of midnight blues and starlight silvers. Archer lounged on the chair next to mine, his boots stretched out and crossed at the ankles.

The third man was a tall, thinly built figure with an air of intensity. His brown eyes were deep set, shrouded in shadows. He had an uncanny resemblance to a hawk. Maybe this was the Lord of the Salt.

They'd come in dressed in finery and layers of clothing to keep them warm. It wasn't until Thorne looked at me and then my chair that I remembered I was still standing there, in nothing but a shirt.

As I took my seat, Archer nudged me. "Nice shirt."

I sat back casually, lifting a strawberry just to give my hands something to do. "I had so many choices this morning, I couldn't decide."

Thorne casually rolled up the sleeves of his white shirt until I was sure the width of his massive forearms would tear the stitching. "What my wife means to say is that she needs to go shopping. Harlow."

Harlow straightened in her chair. Only then did I realize she'd been staring at the third man. "You can drop the act, no need for pretend names. Everyone here knows the truth."

Archer tossed a grape into his mouth. "Harlot here told Wee Willy on the way over."

"Archie!" she squealed. "Don't call him that."

"It's fine, Har," the third man said. He turned to face me, holding out a hand. "I'm Willard."

It was the softest handshake I'd ever had from a man. "Nice to meet you. I'm Paesha."

"Lovely."

Out of the corner of my eye, I could see red bloom across Harlow's pale cheeks. I promptly pulled my hand from Willard's. I knew that color, that lingering gaze of hers.

"Indeed," Thorne responded, his eyes leveling on mine. "My wife has a unique charm."

There was no mistaking the soft emphasis on my fictitious title, the quiet assertion meant only for me. The small hum of amusement from Archer told me he hadn't missed it either. "Speaking of unique charms," Harlow began, looking back to Thorne. "I'm happy to take Paesha to get a new dress, but I have something to drop off at the Hollow before we can do that. And then she'll have to find her way back. We have that thing later."

The room fell into a tense silence at the mention of the Hollow. I kept my face calm and collected, when really I wanted to leap from my chair. I knew Thorne had been connected to the Hollow somehow, but this was all I needed. And I didn't have to wait to get it.

Thorne gave Harlow a look, dark brows knitted in confusion. "What thing?"

"It's the seventh," Archer said, pulling a coin from his pocket, letting it dance over the top of his knuckles as he expertly juggled it.

The room was silent for a moment, acknowledging without words that whatever they meant to do, I was not privy to know.

Thorne managed to cover his surprise with a nod, his lips pressing into a thin line. "Ah, right, the seventh."

Whatever 'the seventh' meant, it was important, and I'd bet my death it was related to the Hollow. Thorne rose from the table, carefully folded the newspaper exactly where the creases had been, and tucked it under his arm. "I've got to do the books for the Parlor today. I can try to find Tuck."

"No need. I'll go with the twins and be the third, Thorne. No problem," Willard said, rising from the table.

"Great," Thorne turned to me. "Will you be wearing my shirt to the Hollow, wife?"

I ran my finger around the rim of my glass, wondering if it was a good time to push his buttons or leave him alone. I couldn't jeopardize my invitation, but if I seemed too eager, he'd get curious. "Would that be frowned upon?"

Deep hazel eyes narrowed on me. Thorne ignored Archer's snort as he turned and left. I followed suit, heading to my room to throw on the dress I'd stolen after my prison escape.

I quickly braided my hair and slipped into the boots that were a little too big. And though I debated it, I snagged Thorne's golden pocketbook on the way out the door. This was it. The single thing I'd been waiting for since being dropped into this godforsaken realm. Should I truly find the path home today, maybe I could send him a message just to let him know he didn't need to pretend anymore.

Somehow, the biting cold didn't hurt my face so much today. I crept into the carriage beside Archer, watching him flip his coin through the air while he whistled. Harlow sat a little closer to Willard than necessary. No one spoke though. As we rode together, each block carrying us closer to my freedom, I couldn't help counting the minutes. Picturing Quill's eyes light up when she saw me. Sitting in Thea's bedroom and telling her everything that happened.

Through the winding streets of the crowded city, nestled within its heart, sat a building of no great consequence. Crumbling brick plagued the southern side, and though worn, it boasted the same walls as all the others. If I didn't look close enough, the spires along the buildings and history worn into the walls might've tricked my mind into believing I was surrounded by ancient castles and not a dangerous city. Anyone strolling by paid the building no mind at all, but I supposed that was the point if it housed a secret portal out of this world.

Archer and Willard hopped out of the carriage and walked around the building, but Harlow remained at my side. She looked nothing like the prim, proper woman I'd met at Lithe, nor the leather clad thief orchestrating prison breaks. Now she was hardened, shrewd. Like a mother protecting her babe. The many faces she wore were interesting. I knew women like her. I was one. If you wear a thousand masks, no one will know the real version of you.

"Beyond this point, anything you see or hear is not to be repeated. We need to know we can trust you." Harlow moved to stand in front of me, her hands on her hips, her mud-soaked clothes dry and stiff.

"Trust is for lovers and fools," I said. My eyes flicked over to the seemingly innocuous building. "And I'm neither. Take it or leave it."

She stared for several moments contemplating, though it was clear she'd already made up her mind about me. And if she hadn't, it didn't matter, because Thorne had. At least on some level, or he would have tried to keep me from coming. Harlow wasn't in charge, and that's all I needed to know. But then maybe Thorne wasn't in charge either and they all worked for the Lord of the Salt.

"Okay, well, this is the Hollow. The door on the south wall is always unlocked unless there's something major happening. I know it's not much, but the Salt can come here for food or shelter." She beat three times on the door, waited a second, and knocked once more.

"What? No secret handshake to learn? Disappointing really."

Her answer was a soft snort as the heavy door swung open, revealing a tall, round man with a curly brown mustache. His smile lit his whole face as he melted for Harlow. "Miss Harlow," he said with a chuckle, scanning her from head to toe. "Did you find it?"

"I left it in the carriage for you. It's pretty heavy."

He wiped his hands on the apron hanging loosely around his neck and not tied in the back as if he'd been about to take it off, and answered the door instead. "The best pots always are." His eyes flicked to mine. "Who's your friend?"

"Paesha, Jasper. Jasper, Thorne's new wife."

She flourished her hand between us and the man's smile widened. "Quite the looker, aren't you?"

"Well, aren't you charming?" I crooned, slipping into the role of a dainty woman.

He stepped to the side, cheeks blooming red. "Come in out of this cold while I get things settled. There's breakfast."

"Welcome to the Hollow," Harlow said, pushing the door to welcome me inside.

The smell of old wood and slowly simmering stew drew me in beyond the warmth. The Hollow lived up to its name as a cavernous expanse that swallowed the meager light streaming from the few scattered lamps. The large room was sparsely but practically furnished with cots of various sizes arranged in rows. They likely weren't comfortable, but they were better than sleeping in an alley and each had a nicely folded blanket on top.

Several people surrounded a wooden table dominating the

center of the room. Laden with a large spread of food, the ambiance reminded me of the Syndicate from Requiem; a patchwork group of people just doing their best to help others and make life a little easier in a harsh world.

My boots echoed softly against the worn floorboards as I shuffled forward, noting first an upstairs balcony that overlooked the enormous room, hinting at a private second level. I turned to find Harlow ruffling a child's hair as he held a bowl up to her with a toothless grin. She knelt, taking the bowl and sharing a secret with the boy before he trampled off.

I thought back to Tithe, to watching Archer steal to save the woman with the children. Then to Lithe, watching Harlow steal again. They were dressed in finery, as was Thorne, so they hadn't given away their livelihoods. They'd maintained it as a mask, allowing them to steal from the Silk and give to the Salt. They were heroes, in their own way. The Hollow was not a portal. It was a shelter.

But why here? Why had the God of godly things and a thousand names sent me here? From what I'd gathered, the Lord of the Salt was being hunted by the prince. Even Thorne wanted him caught. He'd goaded the prince about it. How was he to be the missing piece to this entire journey?

I sat at the long table, feeling my stomach sink into my toes. Everything I thought I knew, everything I'd hoped for was wrapped up in an assumption. And clearly I'd been wrong. There was no magic here. No portal unseen. No gossip about separate worlds or traveling between them. There was nothing here. And now, I had no plan at all, other than hunting for the Lord of the Salt and praying it was more successful than finding the Hollow. However, the Hollow had to be part of the equation.

I could leave. But where would I go? Someone here had to know something. Talk was cheap when people lacked entertainment and this was a honeypot of Salts. I needed to only consider my words and actions while watching them all. Listening to the Salt, but more so, watching the Silk. I had one motive. One goal. It wasn't being a charity case or a wife, but if that was the path promised in the bargain, then I'd trample down it with a hell hound's fury and a dancer's grace.

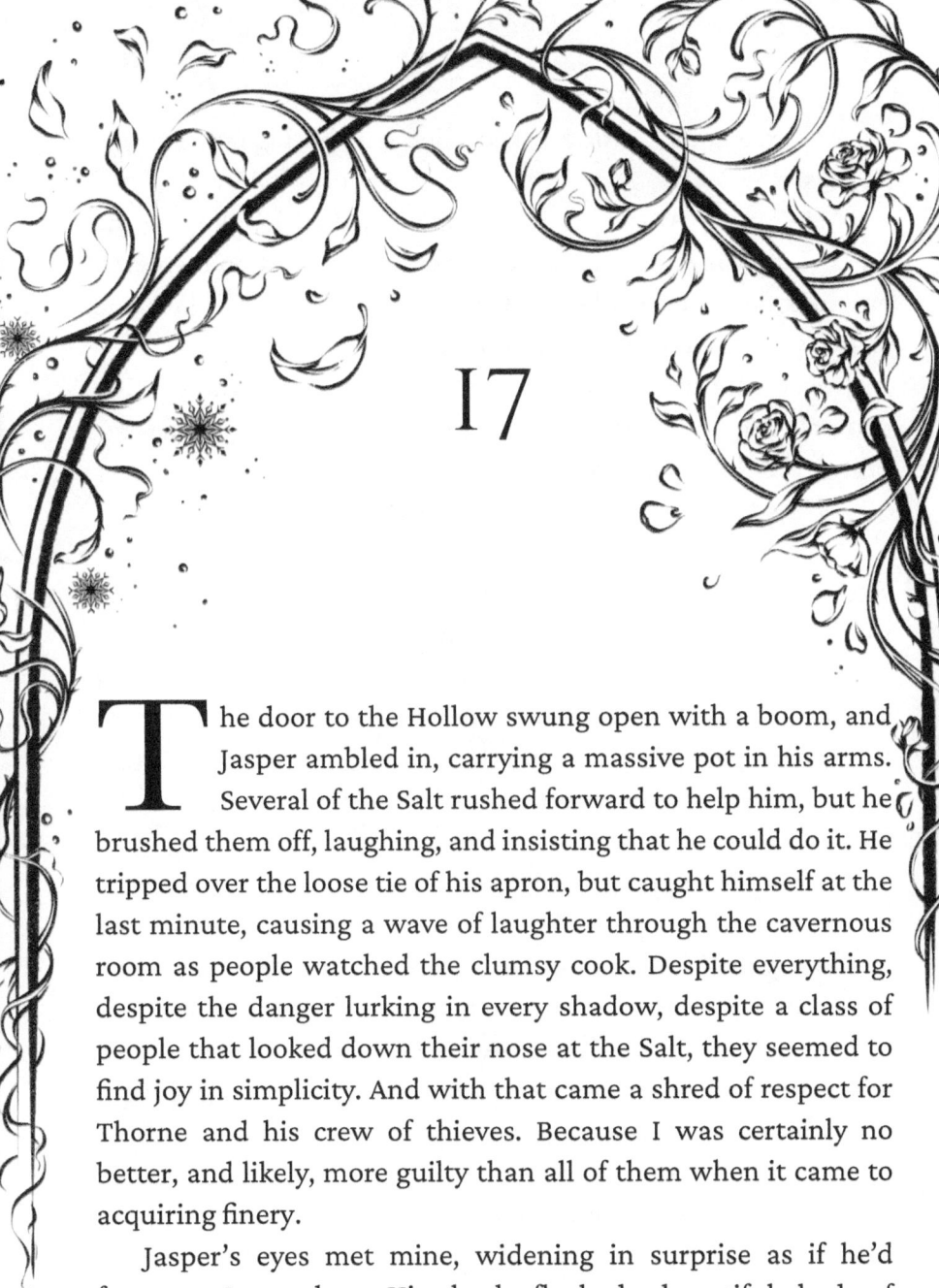

17

The door to the Hollow swung open with a boom, and Jasper ambled in, carrying a massive pot in his arms. Several of the Salt rushed forward to help him, but he brushed them off, laughing, and insisting that he could do it. He tripped over the loose tie of his apron, but caught himself at the last minute, causing a wave of laughter through the cavernous room as people watched the clumsy cook. Despite everything, despite the danger lurking in every shadow, despite a class of people that looked down their nose at the Salt, they seemed to find joy in simplicity. And with that came a shred of respect for Thorne and his crew of thieves. Because I was certainly no better, and likely, more guilty than all of them when it came to acquiring finery.

Jasper's eyes met mine, widening in surprise as if he'd forgotten I was there. His cheeks flushed a beautiful shade of crimson as he quickly straightened and hustled back to his kitchen, calling over his shoulder, "You lot can thank Miss Harlow for your stew tonight."

I didn't want to know where she'd stolen the pot from.

"You see now?" Harlow asked, sliding up beside me.

"I see."

"The prince would see us all hanged before he allowed the Silk to help the Salt. But I'd rather be dead than sit on my perch and look down at people that were born to this world the same as I was. Their blood is the same color as yours and mine."

I was sure it was foolish to show how little I knew, but I couldn't help my curiosity, and maybe showing a little vulnerability to Harlow would pay off.

"Why do they call them the Salt? And you the Silk?"

"A long time ago, this kingdom and some of its surrounding settlements used Salt as currency. The poor would mine it, the rich would confiscate it, and on and on it went until the rich converted their currency to coin, thus taking away the endless supply for the lower class, and creating a large divide. Those that worked the mines became the Salt, and those that profited, buying things of luxury to drape over their bodies became the Silk."

A little boy came barreling out of the kitchen full of laughter as Jasper chased him with a wooden spoon. Soon, two more children joined in, running circles around the old cook as he spun back and forth, pretending to sword fight them all with his spoon. My heart ached. Because maybe I'd have grown to be a Silk in this world, but I would have been born a Salt. I had more in common with both sides of this divide than any of them knew. But I never had a group of well-intentioned people putting themselves between me and starvation. I only had the Maestro. And he used me and my power to build his empire. He collected people, and I was the hunter. Willing to do whatever it took to ensure my next meal.

"How many Silk are there? To help?"

"They call us the Fray. It's a small number. Definitely not enough," she said with a sigh.

"How does it work? I don't know anything about Willard, but I know *you*... take things. Yet, we're going shopping for dresses?"

"Archer and I inherited our wealth when our grandmother died. Our parents passed away when we were young, and Grandmother Bramwell raised us. She'd likely be rolling over in her grave if she knew where we were spending her fortune. We have to walk a fine line though, making sure we keep up with the Silks, while doing everything we can to care for the Salt. Most Silk, they sleep on their fortunes. They don't notice when things go missing because they live and breathe in abundance. But sometimes a necklace is the difference between those kids eating for a month or the group of us, standing in black around an unmarked grave."

I teetered on the edge of my next words, wondering if I should ask. Wondering if she would tell me about the Lord of the Salt. How was a warehouse full of poor people the beginning of my path home? And with a rebellion group out here, where did the Lord of the Salt come in?

If the prince hated him, he'd certainly be one of the Salt. But if Thorne also hated him... I'd seen the fury in his eyes when he spat the name to the prince. What kind of common enemy would the prince and my fictional husband have? I decided not to ask. I couldn't risk it. If they knew I was looking for him, as it seemed everyone else was, they'd try to intervene at the very least. And I didn't need that.

So, I asked a different question. Something far less important, but enough to make me seem interested. "What do you do with the pieces you steal? How do you turn them into coin when they are so easily recognized?"

She smiled, her first genuine smile of the day. "That information is on a need to know basis, and right now, you don't need to know that."

"You talking about Alastor?" Archer asked, plopping down beside us.

"Gods, Archer, can you not keep anything to yourself?"

He shook his head. "I left my rebellion rulebook at home today."

"You're terrible," she said, standing from her seat. "We have to go if we're going to make it on time. Where's Will?"

Archer pulled his favorite coin from his pocket and flipped it into the air, catching it without looking. "Heads he makes it on time, tails he bails."

Harlow drew back. "He left?"

"I guess Wee Willy had something else to do this afternoon. He said he'd meet us."

She nodded slowly, smoothing her hands down her dress as if it were habit. "Okay, well that's fine. We can go then."

The smile on Archer's face faded as he took in his sister's disappointment. "Har—"

"No. It's fine. He's a busy man. I can't imagine what his daily schedule must look like."

Archer stood, hanging his arm over his sister's shoulder. "We were born eleven minutes apart. You think I can't tell when you're upset?"

Her eyes flashed to me. She turned, slipping out of his hold. "I'm not upset. We should go."

We followed her slowly out of the door and just before we got to the carriage, Archer showed me the tail emblem on his silver coin.

We rode through the streets at a casual pace, until the buildings grew wider apart and the streets smoother. Until the glass on the windows of the shops was clear and the people had shifted from somber and freezing Salts, into a world of Silks. Women with long gowns peeking beneath their wool coats carried bags from shopping and leaned in to whisper to one another. There was static in the air. Something buzzing from the people as they hurried around, speaking as if they all had secret news to share. But that was the way of people with no cares in the world. Holding secrets was a form of currency. Everyone could buy the finery, but whispers had no price.

The carriage stopped, and we crawled out, Archer taking each of our hands to assist, as a gentleman would be expected to do. Because even in the small company I kept, there'd been a transition on the journey. Long gone were the leather clad twins, breaking into the Maw. Harlow and Archer were Bramwell's now. And judging by the stares, that was a very important name to carry. The curiosity on the faces that stared at me was easier to decipher. They knew me only as Thorne's mysterious bride and the Paramour from last night's event. The cutting glances and hurried whispers told me all I needed to know as we followed Archer toward the large glass doors of a nearby shop.

I raised my spine until, no matter their height, I looked down at everyone. My pace quickened and even my breathing changed when I slipped into the role of the woman they meant me to play. No one was authentic here.

"This is Tulles. You're to find some things to start replacing the clothing that was stolen by the Lord of the Salt on your journey here. I suggest you consider the season. The winter will soon be over and spring will be in bloom. Darker colors for the rest of winter, something lighter, maybe floral for spring," Harlow said, giving me the reasonable excuse I'd need for shopping if I were to procure several things.

The world seemed to pulse with her words though, as if the mention of each season was a reminder of the giant clock

hanging above my head. I couldn't consider the seasons changing. Not when I'd been here for possibly weeks and that felt
suffocating. I had sixty-five days, if I was lucky. I didn't want to
fall into a routine. I didn't want to accept how things were here.
I only wanted to learn enough to find my path out. I could smile
at the right people and scowl at the others, if that's what was
required.

The single step leading up to the store was covered with a
thick layer of ice. Harlow tsked, shaking her head as she pushed
inside and let out a huff.

"You're trying to kill your patrons with that step, aren't you,
Thalena?"

"Save it. She's not in yet." A tall, skinny man walked around
a beautifully dressed mannequin, black hair falling into his eyes.
"But I'll see to the step before she gets here."

"Thank the gods." Harlow said, shoulders falling. "I've got
to prepare myself before I deal with her. Marik, this is Paesha
Noctus, Thorne's new bride. She was robbed on her way to Stirling. She'll need a full wardrobe, but we won't have time to fill it
today. Get her some new boots and a dress and a few sleeping
garments to get her through until we can do something more
substantial." She turned to me, eyes narrowing. "Such a tragic
thing that happened to all your pretty gowns. But Marik is a
member of the Fray and he'll get you squared away. Come, you
must see this piece by the window. I've been eyeing it for
weeks."

"I won't be needing the sleeping garments," I told the lanky
man with a wink. "I do like some give in the soles of my boots,
though, if you can manage it."

The second we were far enough away, she leaned in to whisper. "Consider every word and every movement when Thalena
gets here. She's got an eagle eye and she will gossip. It's her
favorite pastime. Your job is to make sure she's fully convinced.

Marik is one of ours. Willard got him this job months ago. He'll do as he's told and help buffer, but he can't know the whole truth. No one can. You've got the inner circle. That's me, Archer, Will and Thorne. Only the four of us know about your fake marriage. Then you have the Fray. That's every Silk helping the Salt. They only know what they need to know. Understand?"

"Don't tell the thieves I'm a murderer that escaped the Maw. Got it."

The corner of her mouth lifted, and a gleam lit her pretty blue eyes. "Precisely." Lifting the sleeve of a gown resting on a dress form, pretending to be interested in the fabric, she continued. "And not that I need to defend myself, but proper thievery takes an immense amount of practice. We won't ask you to do it. Just do your best to fit in here."

Pulling my hand from my pocket, I tossed her the coin bag she'd been wearing only moments ago with a sultry smile. "That little murdery thing with the Cimmerian was an accident, but I have my own skill sets."

She swiped the bag back, eyes wide in surprise. "How did you... When—"

She was interrupted by a gust of freezing wind as the door pushed open and a busty woman with too much rouge and a drawn on mole strolled in.

"That's Thalena," Harlow mouthed. "Try not to mess this up."

"Oh, my darling. No need to worry about me. I was born to perform."

18

rcher was the first one to the door of the woman's shop, greeting Thalena as she brushed the snowflakes from her black hair. He swept his arm behind his back and slightly bowed. "Thalena, so nice to see you again. Is that a new dress? It is, isn't it? You have the most incredible taste. Where can I get a jacket in that color?"

Thalena laughed, swatting him away. "Archie Bramwell, you big flirt. Stop that."

He looped his hand with hers and pulled her to a cluster of chairs in the middle of the store. "One day, that old husband of yours is going to kick the bucket and you and I are going to have a night on the town you'll never forget. I'll even let you buy me a drink."

Her gasp was less believable than her laugh. "You're a scandalous heartbreaker! You mustn't say such things." Her face turned a merry shade of pink as she sat, snapping her finger until Marik vanished into the back and reappeared with a tea tray.

I spent the next hour or so standing on a platform, staring at myself in a set of three mirrors as Marik tended to the measurements and hemming of the single gown I was to take home, making a note of others to be sent later.

"The seamstress will need to make adjustments, of course," I said, picking at the fabric. "That won't be a problem, I assume? And for the next, this shade is too light for my complexion in the winter. The fabric will have to be dyed." I snapped my fingers at Marik, feeling slightly awful for the act. "Are you taking notes?"

"Y-yes, my lady," Marik said over the pins in his mouth as he marked the gown for length. "Got it all in my head."

I hadn't asked about the price and honestly, I didn't want to know. Each coin the members of the Fray had to spend to maintain their status must have been a burden. To have watched that homeless boy in the Hollow and imagine him freezing in an alley while you slept warm in your bed had to do something awful to their souls. But at least it proved they had one. Whatever the details of the transaction, I forced myself to ignore it. *Lady* Paesha would never consider the cost of a single gown. And that was my role. So, I didn't.

Harlow and Archer sat with Thalena. The women had tea and gossiped in low whispers, while Archer sat with his ankle on his knee pretending to read a book. He might've fooled everyone else, but I'd watched his eyes. He hung on every word the women spoke. But then so did I because the topic had, of course, drifted to one of the biggest mysteries in Stirling.

"They say he has fiery red hair, but I think that's nonsense," Thalena said. "If the Lord of the Salt had red hair, he'd be too easy to spot."

"I bet you're right," Harlow answered, sipping her tea. "I hear he has some kind of magic that makes him invisible. They say he could be right here at this very moment and we'd never know."

"That's unlikely." Archer said, finally putting his book down.

"Several gods are on the hunt. If he was using power, I think they would know."

The gods?

As in plural?

What kind of man could run from multiple gods? Had I... Oh, shit!

Had I made a deal with a god to find the Lord of the Salt for his own gain and *not* to get home? Was I stuck here, hunting a man that even the gods couldn't find? It took everything in my power to school my face into something remotely calm as Harlow looked down at the man stitching my hem.

"Sorry, Marik. It must be awful to hear his name."

He solemnly dipped his chin before going back to his work. "Nothing to be done now, my lady."

Thalena finally addressed me. "Our poor Marik here... he used to be one of us. But his fortune was stolen from under his nose and now we've taken him in as a sort of charity case. I have a very big heart when you get to know me. Isn't that right, Archer?"

"The biggest heart in Stirling. That's what I always say."

It was a miracle she couldn't see through his lie, but she just smiled and nodded. Still, I didn't miss his wink in the reflection of the mirror when she turned away. I was beginning to panic that I hadn't done my job well enough. Hadn't quite laid it on thick enough. Since the Lord of the Salt was apparently every-one's enemy, even the *members* of the Salt, it was looking like I was going to be here longer than I wanted to be.

I stewed over his name and wondered why he'd earned the title as the fitting went on. Harlow watched the door closely. Likely either pining for Willard or planning her escape if this all went downhill. The unsightly business owner, with an abnor-mally long nose and permanent scowl, hadn't spoken another word to me, but the mirror betrayed her curious glances. I just needed to take it a bit further.

I traced my fingers along the waistband of the gown. "We should discuss this seam. Honestly, who is your head seamstress? Or do you have a tailor? Maybe I should speak to them directly."

"I'm quite capable of relaying notes," Marik answered with a glare.

I hadn't been given boundaries and fully intended on traipsing right over the top of them if it meant pushing my way toward more people that might know something about the Lord of the Salt. If the true currency here was secrets, then Thalena had to be a prime target for me.

"I've not seen you write down a single thing." I stepped from the platform, "and quite honestly, after being robbed seconds from entering this godforsaken city, I'd say it's not wise to trust anyone here… aside from my dear husband, of course." I spun, staring Thalena in the eye. "I'm sure you'll understand."

"I only hire the best," she answered, rising to the bait. "I've had each of my employees fully tested and their skills challenged to the highest limits to dress me alone. I would not lower my standards for my patrons."

"I'm not entirely convinced," I said, letting my eyes slowly wander through her exquisite shop. "I've seen no fewer than three snags and loose threads on your display gowns. Not to mention the rather underwhelming choice of fabrics. I require something far more refined, more… exclusive."

Thalena's eyes narrowed, and her posture stiffened. "Perhaps you are mistaken. My materials are sourced from the finest mills, and the craftsmanship is unparalleled."

I raised an eyebrow, feigning boredom as I trailed a finger along the hem of a nearby gown. "In your opinion. But for me, such imperfections are simply unacceptable. If this is the best you can offer, I'm afraid I must take my business elsewhere."

Truly, each piece was stunning. Most were made of silk or satin and in these frigid temperatures, I couldn't imagine choosing to put it against my skin. But what would someone who didn't have to spend time outside care?

Harlow cleared her throat. "I can speak for the quality Thalena's workers produce. We should get something to eat. Take a break. Archer?"

"Oh, I'm not hungry," I said, walking over to a wall of ribbons. "Shall we try another shop? Was the other one something starting with a 'D'? I'm so terrible with details."

Harlow's eyes widened to the size of saucers as she grabbed Archer's arm for backup. "She's kidding, of course." The laugh that followed was forced, but the glare at me wasn't. "Aren't you?"

I spun dramatically, lowering my chin as I lifted a brow to Thalena. "You're hiding something, aren't you?"

"I don't know wh—"

"I bet you're just like my favorite girl back home. She keeps her *best* inventory in the back."

Thalena paused. We both did.

She opened her mouth to retort, then snapped it shut. Then started again. "Marik, be a dear and bring Mrs. Noctus the Gideon dress. Slim the sleeve, drop the waist a fraction and pair it with the Tobens. Those will be the ones with the narrow strap." She turned to Harlow, whose jaw was on the floor. "I must be off now. I've got tea with Roswen."

"You can't stay for just five more minutes?" Archer said, pulling his coin from his pocket to flip it in the air. "That's too bad."

"You know how these things are," Thalena said.

"Thank you for coming by this morning. We appreciate the

promptness and attention to detail. I'm sorry for the... you know," Harlow said, eyes flashing at me.

"Don't be silly. It's a woman's prerogative to know what she likes. I welcome you to peruse any of the other dress shops in Stirling. You won't find another that's more suited for the ladies of society. Of that, I'm sure." She walked casually to the door before turning back to me, all pleasantries gone from her face as she pointed. "You should try on that hat, dear. It matches your strange eyes perfectly. Consider it a gift." She waited, tapping her fingers on her purse until Marik darted forward and opened the door for her. With a huff, she strolled away, leaving a trail of pungent floral perfume in her wake.

Harlow sank into her seat the moment the woman was out of eyesight. "Thank the gods. Paesha, what in the world were you thinking?"

"Don't be so dramatic. That went perfectly." I said sweetly, eyes flashing to Marik before placing the hat on my head.

Harlow looked back at the door again.

Archer dropped his coin in his pocket and stole a hat from a mannequin, flipping it expertly. It landed with a plop on his head. He sank into the chair Thalena had been sitting in, swinging his legs over the arm as he swept the hat away in another parlor trick, occupying his hands as he asked, "Do we think she bought it?"

Marik stood, gathering his supplies. "She did. Don't be too hard on Paesha, Har. If anything, I think Thalena finds her intriguing."

"She was supposed to win her over, befriend her even. Not start a godsdamn war with the biggest gossip in Stirling."

I lifted the edges of my dress, walking toward her to stare down my nose. "I did exactly what needed to be done. Weren't you paying attention? She was so distracted trying to prove herself to me, she didn't question any of it. If she believed for one second I was a Salt she wouldn't have bothered at all."

Archer's chuckle began quietly but quickly grew to a full obnoxious laugh as he watched his sister stand with her mouth hung open.

"This is not funny," Harlow said, swatting his arm. "Stop laughing."

"You don't have to be a mother hen in every situation. Look at her," he said, gesturing toward me. "She's got it under control."

"But how did you know about the dress in the back?"

When I used my magic, there were times when it would pull me like I was hooked on the end of a fishing line, blindly following a tendril of power until whatever I hunted was near. But there were other times, few and far between, when I could see slivers of space around my targets. Visions of spaces in shadow. Thalena's back room was the first I'd seen in Stirling, because something here with the magic was different, but I couldn't tell her that. When people learned of my power, they had a tendency to use me. I was done being used. Meddling gods, dead bosses, fictional husbands and otherwise.

I walked behind the folded partition and started unbuttoning the dress. "I used to know an amazing tailor. He always kept his best work a secret. But Thalena seems the type to collect her worker's finest for herself. I acted on a hunch. And I was right."

I dressed quickly in the first gown we'd decided on, hissing as Thorne's little golden book turned hot, nearly burning my skin.

His little love note inside was so endearing.

Paesha darling,
Since it's been a few hours, I'm going to go out on a limb and assume you're being difficult. Stop it.

Usually Right,
Thorne Noctus

I slid the pencil free and promptly drew a middle finger before signing,

Always right,
Paesha

Charming.
Would you happen to know where the vase that was in the entry hall went?

My house is vanishing,
Thorne Noctus

Sir Thorne Noctus the Third,
My room is boring.

Your new interior decorator,
Paesha V.

Paesha Noctus,
See how there's no V in your name? It's the same
as how there's no 'The third' in my name. And you
stole flowers?

I wasn't aware I was hiring,
Thorne N.

Thorne Noctus, the seventeenth,
You realize that I'm the only one seeing your messages,
right? There's exactly zero need to address them so
formally, other than to flex your pretentious muscles.
And about the flowers, I borrowed them. You can have
them back when they die. Promise.

Not to toot my own horn, but you can't buy skills like
mine,
Paesha

How's the dress shopping going? Thalena can be
difficult.

Biting my lip, I contemplated how much to tell him. But
Archer cleared his throat, and I knew they were waiting. I
quickly scrawled,

We're best friends now. See you at home, grumpy.

See you for dinner. Oh, and Paesha darling? You

really should consider art lessons. I have no idea what you've drawn up there.

Use your vibrant imagination, husband.

With the snap of the book, I walked out from behind the partition to see the twins standing at the door.

"Har, if Will isn't coming... maybe we should go up to the castle instead."

"That is not up for debate, and you know it," she said, warily. "Willard will be here. He promised."

"But—"

"Let's leave family matters off the table, okay? For one day. Please."

Archer glanced at me, clearly weighing how far he wanted to push her. "You know we have to do this."

"Stop it," she ground out.

She stared at the street for several moments, watching people pace up and down. Time stood still as she waited. We all did. I sat in the chair, listening to the quiet sounds of Archer's pacing.

He stepped behind his sister, softening as he placed a hand on her back. "He's not coming. If we don't go now, we'll miss it."

"I know," she whispered.

"We've always been the best team anyway, yeah?"

She nodded, taking a large breath in before she faced me. "We have an errand to run. You'll take the carriage and go straight back to Thorne's house. The driver knows how to get there."

"Listen, if you need help with something, I could—"

"No!" they both said at the same time.

Harlow pushed the door open. "Just head back to Thorne's."

I saw myself in her at that moment. The familiarity with the disappointment I harbored in my soul was vast. I'd lived a good portion of my life in that state. It was why I didn't trust a soul. A trait my parents had given me upon their abandonment.

"I'll see you later then."

We stepped out of the shop, splitting ways. They turned right, and I was to go left, and I did, until I was sure they could no longer see me. Then I hiked up my new dress and dashed into an alley, following them all the way through the city without either of them having a clue.

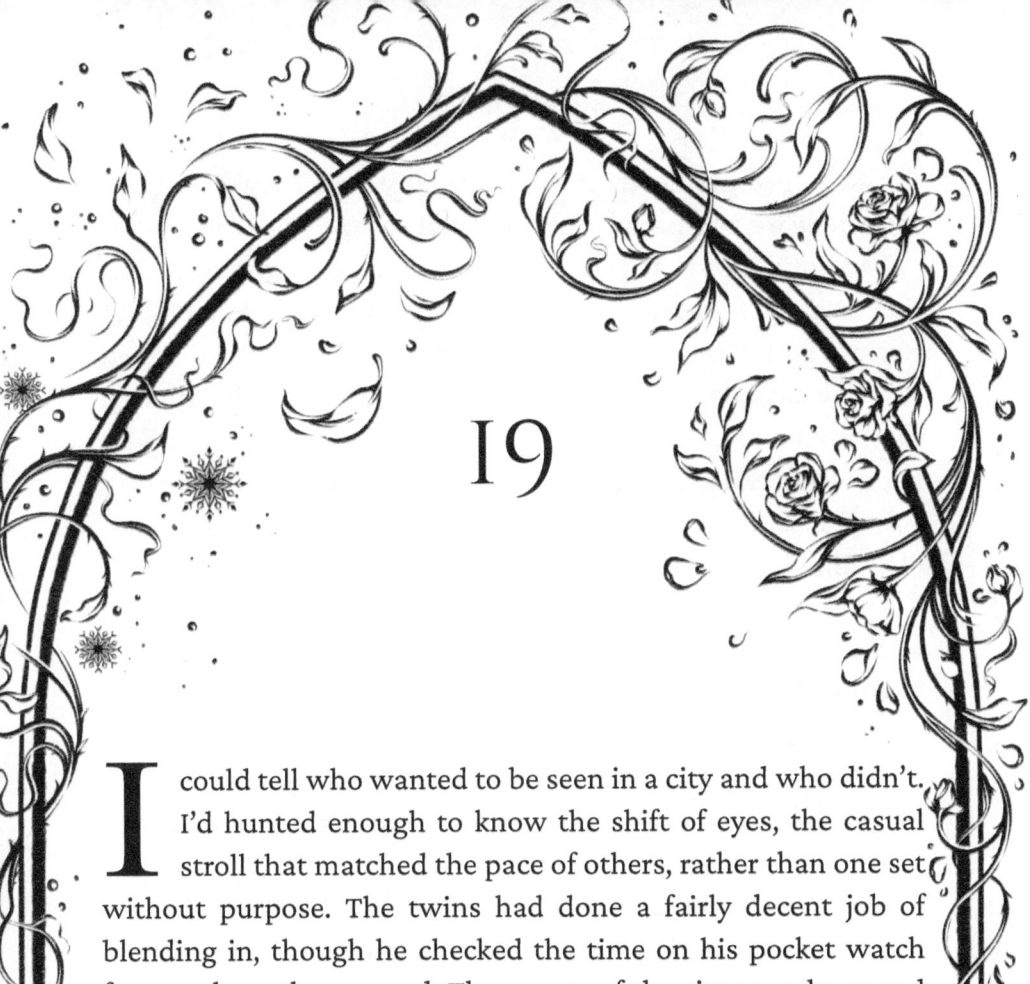

19

I could tell who wanted to be seen in a city and who didn't. I'd hunted enough to know the shift of eyes, the casual stroll that matched the pace of others, rather than one set without purpose. The twins had done a fairly decent job of blending in, though he checked the time on his pocket watch frequently as they moved. The streets of the city were busy and bustling, but I passed through with ease.

The Silk streets were different. There was never a break in the towering stone buildings. They lined the cobble streets like walls, with shop doors every twenty paces, luring in the rich. There were passes through the rows of buildings like very narrow alleyways, where a broad man could reach both of the buildings on either side with little effort. The alleys were a labyrinth on their own. I couldn't tell what would be on the other side until I walked down the steep steps they enclosed or around the winding corners.

Because the buildings were so close, once we passed a metal ladder, I pulled myself onto the roof. Crouching low, I crept to the edge, peering down at the bustling street. They'd stopped, seemingly for no reason, in the midst of the crowd.

A young boy darted out from a side street, weaving through the throng of people with practiced ease. He collided with Harlow, stumbling back. In that brief moment of contact, a flash of fabric passed from his hands to hers. Harlow quickly unfurled the bundle, revealing a dark, hooded cloak. She swung it over her shoulders, fastening the silver clasp at her throat. The cloak shimmered, the color shifting to match the hues of her dress, blending seamlessly.

No sooner had Harlow donned the cloak than another child, a scrawny girl with a shock of red hair, barreled into Archer. The girl mumbled an apology, pressing something into his palm before melting back into the crowd. Archer's fingers curled around the crowbar before he tucked it into his jacket, his eyes darting around to ensure no one had noticed the exchange. With a subtle nod to Harlow, they split up, each taking a different route forward.

I followed Harlow from above, leaping over the narrow alleys with a dancer's grace. She moved with purpose, her cloak rippling like liquid shadow as she navigated the crowded thoroughfare. The further into the heart of the city they got, the more Cimmerians I saw. All broad, cloaked and masked, all standing sentinel, watching over Stirling like it was prey.

Harlow stepped off the narrow sidewalk and into the street. She'd kept an eye on the clock tower looming above, because whatever they were planning, the timing must've been specific. She slowed her pace, walking carefully on the uneven street, gripping the edges of her cloak as she walked.

Behind her, a carriage adorned with intricate gold filigree zipped down the street, far too fast. Two large, burly men rode on the back of the carriage, guarding the chests that'd lined the tables at Tithe.

Good Gods. Were they going to try to steal the tax money from the prince? What an asinine, ridiculous... Harlow was way too close. I crouched lower, my breath catching in my throat as I nearly screamed for her to move. But with practiced steps, she seemed to be timing the approach.

The carriage slowed and a man on the seat in front shouted at her to get out of the way. She spun wide, flicking her cloak so it billowed around her. The second it passed, the tip of her cloak snagged on the wagon wheel and Harlow began screaming, clutching her throat where the clasp was far too tight. I leaped to my feet, no longer worried about being caught, as I dashed to the edge of the roof, ready to jump. Seconds before considering if I could fall so far and not break every bone in my body, I caught a glimpse of Archer sneaking out from the alley.

He darted behind the carriage, his movements quick and precise. He pulled the crowbar from his jacket and wedged it beneath a gleaming gold ornament adorning the carriage's rear. With a grunt, he tried to pry the piece loose, but it wouldn't budge.

I scanned the surrounding streets, my heart pounding. Two imposing figures in dark cloaks rounded the corner, their strides purposeful and menacing. Cimmerians. They were heading straight for the commotion caused by Harlow's nearly flawless distraction.

Realization struck me like a bolt of lightning. The third person, Willard... he was meant to be the lookout. Without him, Harlow and Archer were flying blind, unaware of the guards.

Glancing around, I spotted a stack of crates piled in the alley below. I leaped from the rooftop, landing on the crates with a muffled thud. The wood creaked beneath my feet but held firm. Just as I was about to dart into the street and warn them, a hand reached out and grabbed me, yanking me off the wooden crates and sending me crashing into the alley.

"Don't," Thorne snarled. "It's too late. You'll just end up caught with them."

"Some friend you are, sitting back while they get caught." I hissed, jumping to my feet, and dashing away. Consequences be damned. I heard him curse behind me as he followed.

"I just got here," he said as I ran through the narrow space. "Come back."

"I've never been good with orders," I called over my shoulder.

Bursting out of the alley, my heart pounding, I raced towards Harlow and Archer. The Cimmerians had to be closing in, but I couldn't see them from the street. Only the chaos as Harlow struggled with her trapped cloak, and Archer hadn't moved, still undetected on the side of the carriage. Thorne was hot on my heels, his footsteps echoing behind me. He dashed past, his movements a blur as he snatched the crowbar from Archer's grasp and wedged it beneath the ornament with a forceful shove. The gold piece popped loose with a satisfying crack.

I winced, confident the men with Harlow on the other side of the carriage would have heard it, but her commotion was loud enough to drown it out as Thorne and Archer hustled back into the alley. I ran to Harlow, shoving past the men, and yanked on the end of her cloak, now wrapped in the wheel. "How many times have I told you it's dangerous to walk in the streets?" I stared at her, letting my eyes flick the corner. The Cimmerians would be coming any second now.

She glared, but choked out an answer. "Too many."

I reached forward, releasing the clasp at her throat. "I'm so sorry about my friend," I told the men. Harlow stumbled back, rubbing her throat as she caught her breath. I grabbed her arm, pulling her away from the carriage and the gathering crowd.

"We're not worried about the cloak. If you want to use your dagger there to cut it free, that would be so helpful."

"You sure? Miss Bramwell?" one of the men asked, looking up at the clock tower and back to Harlow. "We can try backing up the carriage."

"No, no. It's not sentimental," she said. "I can tell you're in a hurry."

The man nodded, taking out his dagger and slicing through the cloak with a quick, clean cut.

"We need to go," I whispered urgently, my eyes darting to the corner where the Cimmerians would appear any moment. "Now."

Harlow gasped as understanding dawned on her face and she gave a quick nod. Together, we hurried down the street, away from the commotion. We ducked into the nearest alley, pressing our backs against the rough stone wall as we listened for any signs of pursuit.

"What were you thinking?" she hissed, her voice low and angry. "You were supposed to go back. If Thorne finds out..."

"I was trying to help. The Cimmerians were coming. You needed a third as a lookout."

"We were... It doesn't matter. We need to get out of here."

We darted through the alleyways, taking twists and turns to throw off any potential pursuers. My heart pounded in my chest as adrenaline coursed through my veins. Finally, we reached a shadowed alcove and ducked inside, pressing ourselves against the damp stone walls.

"My brother," Harlow huffed. "Did he make it out?"

Before I could respond, two figures emerged from the shadows. Thorne and Archer strode towards us, their faces grim. Archer held up the gold ornament, its surface glinting in the faint light.

"Got it," he said, his voice low. "But we cut it too close."

"It's the right one?" she asked, swiping the piece of gold he'd pried off the carriage and shoving it into the folds of her dress without examining it.

Thorne stepped forward, his coat accentuating the width of his shoulders in the narrow alley as he scowled. "Where was Willard?"

Harlow met his gaze defiantly, her chin tilted up. "He must have lost track of time. You know he wouldn't abandon us intentionally."

Thorne scoffed, running a hand through his dark, tousled hair. The action drew my attention to his hands. A glint of metal caught my eye, and I noticed a new ring adorning his left hand, sitting boldly on his wedding finger.

"Lost track of time?" Thorne repeated, his tone dripping with sarcasm. "If it weren't for Paesha, you two would have been caught." He turned, glaring at me. "And she was not supposed to be here. In fact, I explicitly forbade it."

Somehow I managed to speak, though my jaw hung open. "Excuse me?"

"Don't start," he answered.

I moved to Harlow's side. "There are exactly three people in the world that can forbid me from doing something. And I hate to break it to you, prick, but you are not one of them."

"Please share their names so I can hunt them down and beg them to talk some godsdamn sense into you."

"Me, myself and I. And as it turns out, we're booked for the next century." I spun, walking all the way down the alley before I pulled my hand from my pocket, lifting the golden ornament I'd just stolen from Harlow. "The next time you experts want to steal something, keep a better grip on it."

I thought I'd won that spat. Outsmarted a group of people that had clearly been raised to believe they were better than everyone else. But that was a fleeting thought as someone from far behind me answered. "What exactly have we stolen today?"

I should have felt him before I heard him, but I'd never be able to hunt the Cimmerians unless I saw them unmasked. Some had touched me, but that wasn't enough. Sight and touch were both required. My power had failed me, and I'd just given us all away.

My soul rattled with fear. Suddenly, I was just a woman, hanging from a ceiling by her arms while a plethora of robed figures surrounded me, taunting me, whipping me. Archer's sharp whistle that ricocheted off the looming buildings broke the spell of fear over me. I could not and would not let them break me now. I needed to focus if I didn't want to end up back in the Maw, alongside these people that had a community of unfortunate people depending on them.

I spun without answering the Cimmerian and hustled back toward the others. Thorne seemed to grow in size, as if every muscle in his body went taut, every corded vein aware of the danger aimed directly for us.

"That mouth of yours is going to be the end of us," he snarled.

"Thorne." Archer's whisper was hardly audible but warranted. Another Cimmerian had come around the other opening, puffs of his breath clouding his black mask as if they'd been designed to intimidate.

The two guards closed in on us, and Harlow's panting breaths grew in response. With nowhere to run, we reluctantly stood still, knowing we were being sandwiched between two of the prince's men in a narrow alley with no chance of escape.

"Falling on hard times, Thorne Noctus?" The Cimmerian's tone was anything but inquisitive as he spat Thorne's name.

"Surely it's not a crime to steal a punchline to a joke," he answered, melting into a relaxed stance as he faced off with the guard who'd closed the distance. "Perhaps a little context before you start making assumptions."

The Cimmerian clasped his hands behind his back. "If that's true, then certainly you wouldn't mind me searching your wife? One can never be too careful these days."

Hands buried into my pocket, I wrapped my fingers around the golden bauble stolen from the carriage, wondering what the hell I was going to do with it. "Shouldn't you ask for *my* consent?"

The other one laughed, the sound muffled by the metal clinging to his face. "We don't need permission."

I hated how scared I was of them. How hard it was to look at them and not feel every heartbeat rattling through me. But if they could sense my fear, they would only grow more persistent. More aggressive. So, I let my fear wrap around me like a shield, a mask. I stepped forward, glaring at the guard closest to Archer. "You put your fucking hands on me, and it'll be the last thing you do."

Everything after that was a blur. The guard rose to the challenge, coming for me. I swept around Harlow, dropping the stolen item back into her pocket undetected, pretending to cower from the man. But Thorne didn't know the plan, so when the second the Cimmerian put his hands on me, my fictitious, irrational husband grabbed the Cimmerian around the throat and slammed him against the wall.

As he slid to the frozen ground, Archer flicked his arm and the crowbar he'd been hiding up his sleeve slid free. I snagged Harlow's hand, forcing her to move just in time for her brother to take a solid swing. But he missed, and the remaining Cimmerian lashed out, snatching the end of the weapon and yanking Archer toward him.

Heart racing and without a thought, I let go of Harlow and spun around the guard before Thorne could catch me, kicking him right in the back of the knee. He stumbled forward. Archer yanked the crowbar free and tossed it toward Thorne. With a single slice through the air, he cracked the man on the back of the head, and the guard fell onto his brother-in-arms.

Thorne gripped my hand and yanked me toward him, away from the men that lay in the alley. "We need to leave. Now."

"You can't be serious." I stepped away to face him. "They've seen your faces. There'll be a hundred of these fuckers at your door as soon as they wake up and you know it."

His brows knit together. His fingers tightened on the crowbar. Just when I thought he'd fight me, he sighed and turned to Archer. "Take watch on that end. Harlow take the other."

Their fading footfalls were nothing compared to the choke-hold of fear pulsing within me as I prayed to every God I didn't know to grant us a few minutes to escape this. Thorne whipped his coat back and drew a dagger from his belt.

"Wait!" I put my hand on his wrist. "I know we don't have much time, but we should take their robes and masks. Maybe we can use them later."

The look he gave me, the way those eyes scrutinized me, was not something I was proud of. "Are you planning for more chaos, Paesha darling?"

"Preparing is not the same as planning. Now, hurry up. We can't waste time."

The Cimmerian guards were no more than men. Though a strange mark branded their forearms, beyond that, they were just someone's son. Someone's husband. Someone's friend. Or maybe they used to be. But as Thorne's blade sliced their necks, as they lay in a puddle of blood, they were no more menacing than any other.

We raced down the alley toward Harlow. Archer vanished into the streets on the opposite end and rejoined us moments later as we casually strolled along the Silk roads as if nothing had happened. As if Harlow and I weren't both hiding the infamous robes and masks of two dead men in the alley.

"Archer," Thorne said below his breath when the passersby thinned.

"I know," Archer answered, flipping his favorite coin in the air. "I agree."

"The Lord of the Salt?" Harlow asked, her pretty blue eyes flashing to my side as she adjusted the gold moth pin in her hair.

I tried not to react at all. I didn't hold my breath or look at their faces. I simply walked on, clenching my teeth as I held my composure, hoping like hell one of them would say something of value. But I did not expect Thorne's next words.

"It's time for my new wife to pay him a little visit."

20

The heavy door to Thorne's house clicked shut, and we were left standing there in silence. The questions thrumming through my mind hadn't wavered as we walked back. If anything, I had more now than I did an hour ago. And Thorne knew it. He was far too observant for his own good.

"Can I ask you something?"

"No."

"But—"

He sighed. "What was the point of asking for permission if you were going to do it anyway?"

"You know where the Lord of the Salt is? Who he is?"

"I've taken a recent interest in him. I have my theories."

"So you don't know where he is."

He peeled his coat off and hung it on a stand in the foyer. He'd already taken the robes and masks before Archer and Harlow left and hid them. "Is there a reason you're suddenly so interested?"

"Why do you want me to meet him? I'm not going to steal

179

from him, if that's what you're thinking. Just because I swiped that bauble thing from Harlow without you realizing it, doesn't mean my services are yours. I'm not your wife and I'm not your personal thief."

He closed the distance, leaning over me. "What if the Lord of the Salt took something that belongs to me? What if I need it back? Would you consider it then?"

I lowered my chin. "Absolutely not."

"What if it were life and death?"

I was so confused but also aware of the slight upper hand here. He needed something. "I might consider it if you answered my questions."

He dropped a heavy hand on my shoulder and forced me to turn, lifting the coat from my shoulders before hanging it beside his on the post. "The prince is hunting the Lord of the Salt. I find him interesting. The rest will have to wait until tomorrow." He tapped me on my nose just to be annoying. "Patience, Paesha darling."

"I hate it when you call me that."

"I'll keep that in mind," he said, before walking down a hall I hadn't been in.

Passing through the arched doors, we stepped into his kitchen. No cook... just as I thought. Yet, even without staff, its design and the items it held were a testament to Thorne's perceived wealth. The kitchen was expansive, almost twice the size of his study, and flooded with sunlight from the high windows, making the array of polished copper pots hanging from the ceiling glow like fire. The counter held a spectrum of spices in glass jars that sat half empty. He'd used them. He was his own cook. Coveting his privacy above ease. I hated how much I liked that about him.

Thorne washed his hands and picked up a knife, testing its weight before moving towards the baskets of fresh produce. He selected a large, ripe tomato, the skin dark red against the sunlight slicing through the windows. He diced with careful precision, each piece identical to the last.

"Why is there no staff? You could easily afford one. And you'd be lining the pockets of the Salt in a safe way."

His eyes didn't move from his work as he replied, "When I need work done, I employ them. But I prefer solitude and don't like strangers in my house."

"Then why not have me stay at the Hollow? Surely you can trust them to keep your secret. If you're really just protecting them."

I hadn't honestly considered this until it came out of my mouth, but maybe staying at the Hollow was a better option for me. Whatever path I was to find there would certainly be easier if I could *be* there.

He paused, sliding his glasses down as he pinned me with a hard look. "First of all, there are very few people that know you and I aren't married. I'd prefer to keep it that way. Second of all, and most importantly, Farris has a new obsession with you. His guards are intrigued. We don't need to lure them to the Hollow. This is the safest place for you."

"And you're so concerned with my safety, I'm sure," I said, rolling my eyes.

He set the knife down and began rolling his sleeves. "I did save you. So apparently I am. If you want to get yourself killed, do it on your own time, but make sure it has nothing to do with me, the Fray or the Hollow. I'll play the grieving widower for a few weeks and then go on about my business. But," he said, reclaiming the knife. "The fates are real, Paesha. And there's a reason our paths crossed."

I circled behind him as he continued slicing his vegetables, silently swapping two pots so they were no longer in order by size, and then a few spoons. Maybe if I annoyed him enough, he'd send me to the Hollow anyway.

"I'll have you know, your pathetic tampering hardly affects me," he said without turning around, now chopping a crisp onion.

Ignoring his comment, I went on to the spice jars and intentionally mixed them up. "Which one of us are you trying to convince?"

He followed right behind me, putting the jars back in place. "If you move these around and I grab the wrong one, it could ruin an entire dish, and then I would have to start from scratch," he said. "These aren't playthings. These are tools."

I smiled and sat on the counter with a swift hop. "That doesn't sound like someone that's unaffected. If you're going to lie, do it better."

He slid the final jar back into place. "I said it hardly affects me. Leaving a margin of error for annoyances is just practical."

"I will make a note of your practicality for future reference. Shall I write it in the book? I think I should, so I don't forget."

"Note keeping is very practical."

I narrowed my eyes. "Shall I add patronizing to the list as well?"

He smirked. "If you like to be thorough, but I think you really just prefer to be a pain in my ass."

"Look at us being so obvious with each other. We should celebrate."

"With alcohol?"

"Being driven to drinking so new in our relationship doesn't bode well for the future. I think you should consider giving it up. For me, of course."

"I'd rather stick this blade into my gut, Paesha darling."

"Let me get a towel first. Oh hey, your eye is twitching again. That must be new."

"Entirely." He crossed his arms over his chest. "Dinner's going to take me about an hour. Why don't you go and get cleaned up? Once it's done, I'll bring you a dinner tray."

"But I could help—"

"Given your affinity for touching every single thing you can," he said, throwing a glance at the copper pots, "I think you'd be more useful anywhere but here. Besides, I can't trust you."

I jumped down. "Oh, don't flatter yourself. I wouldn't poison you."

"Poisoning wasn't my concern. Though now that you've mentioned it..."

I walked to the door. "I haven't taken the idea completely off the table, so don't tempt me."

I THOUGHT he'd be there when I opened the door after he knocked, but instead, the tray sat on the floor with a single flower. He'd made tomato soup with basil and though it was comfort food, something that soothed my soul, the jarring loneliness trumped the minuscule comfort of a warm meal. We'd killed two men today and though not by my hand, I'd spoken the words. I'd chosen that. And we never looked back. We never mentioned it after walking away. Simply bantered with each other in the kitchen and that was that. Life went on.

Lying in bed, the tips of my hair dampening Thorne's shirt, I stared at a chip in the teacup I'd stolen from the kitchen. I didn't want to think about the Cimmerians, but as I closed my eyes, their faces were all I could see until I fell asleep.

REQUIEM APPEARED around me like an inkblot on paper, rippling outward until I stood in a place I'd been a thousand times in my life, tucked into the corner of the Maestro's office, silent as a wraith as the memory unfolded before me. I tried to rush forward, to forbid this memory from unfolding, but I was stuck in the same place I'd been that day.

"Five minutes ago you had no use for the child at all, Visha," the Maestro said, leaning back in his leather chair, his halo of red hair gleaming in the lantern light. "What's changed?"

The brothel owner stood on the other side of the desk, leaning all the way forward as she blew a puff of smoke into my boss's face. "Five minutes ago, she was just some kid one of my girls found abandoned in an alley. Five minutes ago, she was a debt. Another mouth to feed." She tapped the edge of her long cigarette on the Maestro's desk, eyes flashing to me with a scowl before she continued. "We all know you collect pretty things. Even... powerful things. Perhaps she has more value than I realized."

"Of course she does," the Maestro answered, coolly.

"Then I'll take double and no less. No terms. No conditions. She's yours fair and square. Until her parents come looking for her. Then that's your problem."

My heart beat so loud, I knew it betrayed me. I knew the stagger of my breath and the worry in my eyes would make things worse, so I didn't let myself look down for a second. I couldn't look into the eyes of a babe and be anything but weak. Broken. My throat grew thick as I watched Lady Visha take her coins and walk out of the Maestro's office.

I wanted to scream at her to come back. To tell her of the life she'd condemned this innocent little girl to. But I locked those toxic thoughts into my mind and kept my eyes on the vintage map pinned to the wall.

No blinking.

No breathing.

The tension in the air grew heavy as the Maestro slowly spun in his chair. "She's quite beautiful, don't you think, Huntress?"

I nodded, though I hadn't looked, fighting the way my arms wanted to wrap around the child and shield her from his vision. He knew what he was doing. He knew why he called me here. He knew my plight.

"Can I see it?" he asked, slumping back in his chair. "The scar?"

Internally, I was screaming. Burning. Running. Fighting. But my face was stoic. My hands, steady. If I spoke, the emotions pulsing through me would betray everything. The scar was mine. The emotional payment, mine.

I glanced at the other corner of the room. Something was wrong. Someone was missing. There had been... the pain of a thousand blades shot through my broken memory. But I could not fall, I could not scream. I felt my body move, that day still playing out, though it was twisted. Wrong. But I couldn't figure out how.

My trembling fingers gripped the edge of my shirt. I owed the Maestro nothing. I'd gone my entire life free of his magical bonds. I was here to dance. He'd taken the only other stage I could have, so we'd made our own kind of arrangement. I could dance in his dark burlesque show, and he would give me... errands to run. People to hunt. Things to collect.

I closed my eyes, remembering the feel of the spotlight on my skin. The magic of music and the obliteration of existence when I was consumed on a stage by steps and turns and beats and rhythm. Dancing was forgetting. Dancing was escaping. And the audience's rise and applause were proof that I'd found a way to carry them all with me into that space where nothing else mattered.

The memory still burned. Searing my skin as I was wholly aware of every second since, yet trapped in a body that knew so very little. I couldn't change my memories though, and that was probably the most frustrating part of it all.

I stared down at the Maestro, my fingers gripping the edge of my shirt so tightly my knuckles turned white. His eyes bore into me, hungry and expectant, like a predator sizing up its prey. He didn't need to see the scar. He had no interest in seeing my bare skin. This was a power move. A reminder of who was truly in control. The room seemed to shrink around us, the walls closing in, suffocating me.

Slowly, agonizingly, I lifted the hem of my shirt, exposing a sliver of skin above the waistband of my pants. A single tear slid down my cheek. I turned my head, unable to bear the weight of his gaze as he leaned forward. I could feel his stare intensify, fixating on that small patch of flesh as if it held the key to my stubborn will. Because maybe it did.

With shaking hands, I lowered the band of my pants, just enough to reveal the jagged scar that marred my skin. Red, raised and puckered, it was a permanent reminder of the choice that had been stolen from me. The choice to one day bear a child, to feel life growing inside me, to become a mother. That dream had been ripped away, leaving behind only this ugly mark.

The Maestro reached forward, his fingers outstretched, greedy to touch the scar that branded me. To claim ownership over the most intimate part of my being. I recoiled instinctively, jerking back and letting my shirt fall, concealing the mark once more.

His eyes flashed with annoyance at my defiance, but a cruel smile played at the corners of his lips. "Most think you're just a beautiful face and lucky to be the deluded descendant of a god. But we both know the truth, don't we? How smart you are. How cunning you had to be as a child to survive on those wretched streets. How I saved you. Made something out of nothing." His voice purred as he spoke to me. As if he were introducing the next act on his stage and not setting the scene of a bargain he'd waited my whole life for. "Imagine what you'd be if I hadn't found you. You cannot deny I rescued you, can you?"

I turned away from him, but I could picture the curl of his mustache as he spoke, the light in his dark eyes as a well-laid plan finally came to fruition. A very small part of me began to wonder if he'd been the one behind my stabbing. Had he twisted and tightened the coil on that dancer's jealousy so far, she couldn't stand it any longer? Or had he bargained with her behind my back? My childhood savior had always been cunning and dangerous, but was he also a monster?

"No," I whispered.

"Good," he said, drawing out the word as he stood from his chair, circling the desk until he no doubt stood beside the tiny child. "Then you be grateful that, once again, I've become your savior. There will be a cost for this, of course. But you can be her mother. They say she is only two. She'll never know, my beauty. You can have her."

The word was trapped in my throat, my freedom, the walls that held it back. I could take her in. Love her. Keep her safe and warm. Protected. A fiery tear trekked down my cheek, betraying the emotions I tried to keep caged.

But I couldn't do it. I'd seen too many sell their souls to the Maestro for bargains they thought they wanted, only to come crawling back when they realized what they'd asked for was never what was really best for them.

"She will be stunning. You could teach her to dance. Make a little family."

"No," I managed, digging my fingers into my palms to remind myself that pain was only temporary discomfort.

The room shrank even further, the air growing thick and heavy, pressing down on me like a physical weight.

"Why? Why would you refuse such a generous offer? I'm giving you the chance to have everything you've ever wanted. A child of your own. A family. A purpose beyond the stage."

I fought every instinct pushing against my skin, telling me to tread lightly as I stood solid. "I'll watch the kid for you, sure. Keep her out of trouble, no problem. But I'll never bind myself to you and you know that. We've been doing this for twelve years. I dance because it's my choice. You pay me a fair wage and it works for both of us with no contracts." I circled him, showing him my wrist and reiterating, "I'll never bind myself to you. Not for all the children in the world."

For the first time in my life, the calm, cool nature of the Maestro was shaken as he drew a hand back and struck me across the face. The mark burned, but the scream of the child I still hadn't looked at sliced through my mind, white hot and terrified.

Gods. She had power, mighty power.

"This is a mistake," the Maestro ground out through clenched teeth. "After all these years, will you prove to be as useless as your father? After all I've done for you. Since the day we met, have you ever gone hungry?"

I said nothing. And though my fingers twitched, aching to soothe the pain on my face, I didn't move. I'd never give him the satisfaction.

"Answer me!" he roared.

"No," I said, tears of fury betraying me as they raced down my cheeks. Still, I didn't look at him, didn't move my eyes from that fucking tapestry on the wall.

"Did you have everything you needed? Shelter? Clothes. Even your godsdamned ballet lessons. And what was it all for? If you will not bend your will to mine." He stormed forward and gripped the edge of my shirt, pulling me to him. "Shall we summon Death and let him take her? Save her the misery of this existence."

"Do what you will." My words betrayed my heart, but really there was no choice here at all. I could not become indebted to him. I would not. Not for all the innocent souls in the world.

His fist twisted in my shirt before he melted back into the calm facade he'd always carried. The snarl faded into a forced smile, the rigidity of his shoulders fell away, but the fire in his eyes would always be his tell.

I forced myself to meet his gaze, to stand tall and unwavering in the face of his rage. My heart pounded in my chest, the ache of longing and despair threatening to tear me apart from the inside out. But I couldn't let him see that. I couldn't let him know how much his words affected me.

"I imagine if I ever had a daughter, she would be just like you, Huntress. She would have that fire and that stubborn will. She would never break or bend. And she would be just as beautiful." His eyes flicked to the corner before he looked back at me. "Perhaps I should be proud of your unbending nature. After all, it is the one thing I've taught you." He rested a hand on the knob, turning back to look at the child, whose tiny sobs were so hard to bear, I could hardly hold myself upright. "Her name is Quill. Do something with her. She's valuable, and now mine. You are never to be her mother. That's the choice you've made. You will protect her and teach her, but she belongs to me. Should you do anything to spoil the way she looks at me, I will make sure those closest to you pay the price."

My breath came in ragged gasps as I fought back the sobs that threatened to tear me apart. The weight of my choice, of my refusal to bind myself to the Maestro, even for the sake of this innocent child, crashed over me like a tidal wave until I fell to the ground and crawled around the desk, my heart pounding in my ears.

There, huddled in the corner, was the most beautiful child I had ever seen. Her wild, curly hair framed a chubby face. But it was her eyes that drew me in, two endless pools of the deepest blue, like the sky after a storm.

I reached out a trembling hand, my fingers hovering just inches from the child's face. She flinched back, her expression wide with fear and uncertainty. Slowly, gently, I lowered my hand, offering it palm up in a gesture of peace.

"Shh, it's okay," I whispered, my voice barely more than a breath. "I won't hurt you. I promise."

Quill's eyes darted from my outstretched hand to my face, searching for any sign of deception or malice. Smart kid. Tentatively, she took a tiny step forward, then another, until her small fingers brushed against my palm. In that moment, a spark of connection flared between us, a bond forged in the flames of shared pain and loneliness.

I held my breath as she inched closer, her movements hesitant and unsure. Then, with a sudden burst of courage, she stumbled forward, her chubby legs carrying her straight into my waiting arms. I caught her against my chest, cradling her tiny body as if she were the most precious thing in the world.

And at that moment, she was.

I rocked her gently, murmuring soothing words into her ear as I stroked her wild curls. The scent of her, like sunshine and wildflowers, did something to my soul and I felt a wave of love so fierce it stole my breath away. But when I pulled away she'd aged, no longer the toddler with the sweet, baby face she had when we met, but the child I'd loved through all of her milestones.

"Remember when you saved me?" she whispered, both

hands on the sides of my face, squeezing gently to get my attention.

The world around us had changed, jarring my mind as I tried to keep up, though something rang through me, a warning to pull away. But I had no control. The walls of the Maestro's office melted away like wax, replaced by the familiar confines of the warehouse behind the theater. The trappings of the dark burlesque show, racks of glittering costumes, props and set pieces, and the heavy velvet curtains that shrouded the stage filled the cavernous space around us.

Quill's hands were soft and warm against my cheeks as she held my face, her eyes wide and imploring. "Paesha, please," she begged, her voice trembling with emotion. "Please, let me save him. He's all alone, and he needs me. I know he's covered in dirt, but he's cute. I promise."

My heart swelled with love for this child, for the compassion and empathy that shone so brightly in her eyes. Even in the midst of this dark and twisted world, Quill's pure soul remained untouched. The Syndicate had built a wall around her, protecting her from the vile outside world as best we could. She'd become ours, though she remained within the ownership of the Maestro.

I covered her hands with my own, marveling at the way they had grown over the years, from chubby baby fingers to the slender digits of a young girl. "A puppy is a lot of work, Quilly."

Those big, blue eyes stared up at me, filling with tears. "I can share my dinner and he can have half my bath days. And I'll walk him, even in the rain. I can love him. And you can love him. And we can play with him. And probably he can dance when I teach him. He's my family now. Our family. Orin said I can keep him if you say I can. Please? Pretty please?"

Of course he did.

"You don't feed that dog an ounce of your food, do you hear

me? Your belly is always full before his. You never go without for the sake of a dog."

A brilliant smile broke across Quill's face. "That means a yes! Because you say nos when you mean no. But that wasn't a no, so it's a yes."

I forced a playful glare. "You sure?"

"As sure as sure can be, because we're best friends, right?"

I felt myself turn to the mirror, leaning forward to check my lipstick. "Of course we are, kid."

"Don't you want to see him? I already named him Boo. Because he was scared when I found him in the alleyway, but now he's not so scared. Just a little smelly."

"Show starts in an hour," I said.

But she was already gone, darting out the door of the warehouse. I'm not sure where she'd stashed the pup, but she came back only seconds later. Walking backward, careful not to bump into anything as she hid the little pup from me. "Are you ready?"

"Ready." I crossed my arms over my chest.

She turned and my breath caught in my throat, a wave of icy fear washing over me. There, cradled in Quill's arms, was not a helpless little dog, but a sleek black snake, its scales glistening like polished onyx in the dim light of the warehouse.

No. This was wrong. This was not what happened that day. I fought against the walls of my mind, pushing and pulling, begging to leave this nightmare.

The snake coiled lazily around Quill's slender arm, its forked tongue flicking out to taste the air. But it was the eyes that stole my breath, twin pools of molten gold with intricate hourglasses etched into the irises, the black sand within trickling endlessly from one bulb to the other.

"Quill, listen to me," I pleaded, my voice trembling with barely contained panic. "That's not a puppy. It's a snake, a dangerous one. You can't keep it as a pet. Please, put it down and come away from it."

But she didn't hear me. Because this was a memory, twisted and gnarled, but a memory.

"You could pet him," the child said, staring up at me. "He's not a biter, right Boo? No bites."

My stomach tightened as I watched the serpent wrap itself around her neck. My heart seized in my chest as it coiled tighter around Quill's neck, its scales glinting like black diamonds. The snake's hourglass eyes bore into mine, mesmerizing and terrifying all at once. Its forked tongue darted out, tasting the air, tasting my fear.

"Quilly, please," I begged, my voice cracking with desperation. "Put it down."

But when she looked back up to me, she'd changed too. Her eyes morphed into the same horror as the serpent. "Aren't you coming to save me?" she whispered. "Time's running out."

I lunged for her, breaking free of the hold the memory had on me. But the second my will became my own, I was falling. Falling. Falling. Fast and hard, with no sense of direction.

Fragments of the twisted memory flashed before my eyes, taunting me with their distorted images. Quill's face, once so innocent and pure, was now marred by the serpent's sinister gaze. The Maestro's cruel smile, his fingers digging into my flesh as he demanded my obedience. The scar, a jagged reminder of the choice that had been ripped away from me.

I screamed, certain I'd die from such a dangerous height as I plummeted into an endless pit. And then the faces of the fallen Cimmerians came to me again, holding hourglasses as they begged me to show mercy, blood dripping from their masks like tears. I looked down to find the crowbar in my hand, and try as I might, I could not refrain from striking them. Another scream.

Another strike. Until my voice was raw, and they began to chant my name.

Paesha.

Paesha.

Further and further I fell until my body jerked and suddenly I was awake, covered in sweat, panting, and staring into the wild eyes of Thorne Noctus hovering above me. It'd been his voice ricocheting through my dream.

I couldn't put words together. I only moved fast enough to hang over the edge of the bed and vomit all over the floor.

21

"How do you sleep at night?" I asked Thorne, hovering over the toilet as he held my hair back. "How do you close your eyes without feeling the weight of the lives you've taken?"

"Don't fool yourself. There's no sleep for the wicked."

I lifted the glass he handed me to my mouth and swished the water around before spitting. "Are you wicked? Truly?"

"To some," he answered honestly, before lifting me off the floor.

He'd cleaned my mess while I hugged the toilet, consumed with guilt and fear and memories that would never leave me. But he hadn't left either. He'd stayed. With little effort, he put me back into the bed, pulling the blankets up to my chin. "Sleep now. Don't dwell on the darkness."

"There's horror in the daylight, too."

He walked back toward the door and for a moment I thought he'd leave, and I'd be left to my own misery, my own poisoned thoughts, but instead he grabbed the chair and hauled it back to the bed, sitting beside me.

"I think I can manage without a sitter," I said, evoking the most annoyed tone I could muster, though I didn't mean an ounce of it.

He pulled the gold frame glasses from his nose, carefully folded them and set them directly beside my stolen teacup. "Yes. You probably could. But I didn't open that for discussion. For both our sakes, go back to sleep, or by next week we'll be deliriously tired. There's only so much nighttime screaming a man can take."

"Well, that's not true at all," I answered with a faint smile.

He didn't indulge my humor, choosing instead to cross his massive arms over his chest and close his eyes. "Go back to sleep, Paesha darling."

WHEN I WOKE, he was gone. The chair was placed back in the exact same spot and angle it'd been, and the little teacup was replaced with a matching one, sans the chip.

"I liked the chip in my teacup," I said, strolling into the kitchen after dressing, noting he'd set the table in here rather than the dining room this morning.

He was already at the stove, back turned to me as he cooked in a five-piece suit as if it were just casual wear. "Last time I checked, that teacup was mine."

Everything was in its place, just the way he liked it. I sat at the table and poured myself a cup of tea, careful not to touch anything else. He was expecting me to, though. I could tell by the way his shoulders stiffened, how he paused just before flipping the eggs. He was waiting for something.

I smiled to myself, letting the steam from my tea warm my face. He brought the plates over, setting mine in front of me. I didn't move a thing. Instead, I took another sip to hide the smile, though I could feel his eyes on me. I lifted my fork and began eating.

He stared longer than necessary. His gaze flicked to the salt, then back to me before saying, "You didn't touch the salt."

I drew back, palm to chest, feigning confusion. "Why would I? Afraid your food is too bland?"

He frowned. Clearly he was waiting for me to move something, hide something, anything. I paid him no attention, taking another drink before setting the teacup back onto the small plate, spinning the handle to mirror his setting exactly. Right where he'd placed it this morning.

He sat in his chair, tapping his fingers on the edge of the table. "No comments on the table setting? No urge to move the sugar bowl today?"

I meet his gaze, smiling innocently. "Everything looks perfect. You're in a weird mood today, aren't you?"

He stared at me hard. The confusion on his face, the narrowing of his eyes was comical, like he was sure I was up to something, but he couldn't figure out what. I took a bite of my toast, savoring the way his jaw tightened just slightly. Adorable, really. In an aggressive, know-it-all, annoying man kind of way.

He leaned forward, clasping his hands together. "No temptation to... rearrange anything at all?"

I shook my head, letting my smile widen. "Why would I ruin such a perfectly organized breakfast?"

"I'm glad we can agree on that question," he said, though his scrutinizing gaze lingered. Without breaking his stare, he lifted his newspaper, peering at me over the top of the fold. "We have a meeting late this afternoon. I'll be leaving in an hour. Can you manage here on your own for a while?"

I smiled, letting him think the worst. "I think I can manage just fine."

His knuckles turned white. I thought for sure he'd rip the

pages as we danced around his reluctancy. But instead, he slowly lifted the paper, covering his face. And though we sat together for half an hour, he never turned a single page.

THE FRONT DOOR clicked shut quietly, but the turn of the lock was far louder. As soon as the echo of his departure faded, I ran down the stairs, threw my coat on and stood at the window, watching him disappear down the winding road that stretched in front of his house.

The world outside was a palette of grays and whites, monochromatic proof of winter's grip. I fucking hated it here. But it'd be no different back home. Maybe a bit more wet, but still freezing. Bare trees stood tall and stark against the gray sky like skeletal sentinels, their branches swaying slightly in the biting wind, casting faint shadows on the empty flower boxes sitting beneath the windows on the expensive homes on the street.

I waited until I couldn't see him anymore before unlocking the door and letting myself out. I prodded the sleepy power within me, but still I couldn't lock onto Thorne. I even tried his coat to no avail. So I followed the direction I thought he'd gone until I saw his bulky outline in the distance. A sharp left turn, then two rights and another left. He was zigzagging through the city with a purpose only he knew.

On high alert for the Cimmerians, I carefully followed Thorne for ages, turning in nonsensical directions, wondering if he was hunting the Lord of the Salt and if so, why had he so casually mentioned a meeting with him the day before. Nothing made sense, not the sharp corners, the winding stairs, not the way I watched him duck into alleys for seemingly no reason. He was easy enough to track though. He'd stopped to chat with a man standing outside of a tobacco shop for a few minutes and even lingered outside a bakery, watching as the baker set out trays of fresh buns.

He was quick to move when he remembered whatever his task was, and I was happy to follow, learning the streets, marking the buildings as we went. He made a sharp turn around a distant corner, and I waited just a moment before following. Except when I did, he was gone. I walked further, sure there was only one way to go, but he seemed to have vanished. I checked for doors along the street, but there were none in the alley.

Thorne's golden pocketbook warmed against my thigh. I'd forgotten I'd even brought it, but as I slipped the book from my dress pocket and opened the page, I went rigid.

Lost, Paesha darling?

I spun slowly, staring up into Thorne's handsome face. "I've never been lost a day in my life, thank you very much."

He crossed his arms over his chest, leaning against the building. "That's a bold claim. Anything in particular bring you all the way over here?"

He knew I'd been following him. Of course he did. All the turns and confusion were simply to bait me. His version of my game. But I couldn't and wouldn't give in to his upper hand. I'd figured out the lay of the city well enough to know exactly where I was, save a few of the outlining streets. "I should think it was obvious."

He smirked. "How so?"

I snapped the book shut and slipped it back into my pocket. "The Hollow is right up there. I was going to see if Jasper, I think that was his name, wanted a hand, since there's nothing for me to do at the house."

His lips twitched. "But why are you in the alley? The next street would lead you straight there."

I lifted my hood. "Because the closer buildings block the wind and it's cold."

He moved in closer, pulling my hood further forward. "I hate to break it to you, but the wind is northbound today. It's pushing through this alley faster because there's nothing here to block it. You'd have been warmer on the main street."

"What are you doing here, anyway?"

"Just waiting for my wife to catch up."

"I'm not your... I wasn't..."

He held an arm out for me. "Shall we then?"

"I hate you," I said, taking his arm. "I'm probably going to have a public affair with Jasper and rock your perfect world, Mr. Noctus."

He strode forward, pulling me along. "Please consider anyone but Jasper. I'd hate to have to fight the cook."

I bit the inside of my cheek to keep from smiling.

WHILE THORNE WENT UPSTAIRS to do whatever he needed to do, I sat near the giant hearth in the old building, letting the small bit of warmth seep into my bones. The Hollow was quiet, with a few people sleeping on cots along the far wall, all sharing the same cough. A woman, a doctor of some sort, based on her care of the Salt, went from bed to bed, checking temperatures, making small talk and changing bed linens. A burly man followed her. He carried the blankets and handed her things as she asked for them, and though he remained silent, he held a smile as they moved.

"I really could be helpful," I whispered for the third time as they passed. She swiped her curly red hair from her face and shook her head. "The last thing we need is more people coming down with the illness, right Tuck?"

The large man nodded, and thanks to the light of the fire, I could just make out the faint trace of a scar cutting through his brow and ending at the height of his cheek. "If you really want to be helpful, we could use a new pot of tea," the man said, his low voice calm.

I was in the kitchen with less than a thought, rummaging through the various containers to seem helpful, when really I was searching through their things for signs of a portal. I knew it wasn't here. Something told me it wasn't, but still, I hoped. I sank into the pantry, only to find baskets of dried food and fruit. The cabinets were full of boring, standard kitchen utensils, pots and pans and the like. There was absolutely nothing indicative of a secret society, even. Just a damn kitchen. With food. Annoying.

I found what I needed for tea, aside from a missing kettle. Instead, I warmed a pot of water on the coals in the stove and did my best to steep the loose leaves. Upon delivery of the cups, Thorne had returned, along with Willard, Harlow and Archer. Willard had an arm wrapped around Harlow's shoulder and she looked as if she were settled there. As if that's where she believed she was meant to be. Archer, on the other hand, seemed less than thrilled, maintaining his distance while Thorne barked out orders.

"It's important he be there no later than four. We can't have another incident like yesterday, Will."

"Understood," the shrinking man said.

The door to the Hollow slammed open and Jasper strolled in, carrying a towering stack of wooden bowls. He swayed to one side, and the stack followed, threatening to fall. With a chuckle, he over-corrected, going in the opposite direction, tripped over his feet and landed in a heap on the floor with all the bowls crashing down around him.

Harlow rushed forward, grabbing his hand and heaving until the clumsy cook was on his feet again. "Are you okay?"

He lifted his apron and swiped it across his forehead. "I had a feeling that was a bad idea. Did you, uh... hear the news?"

I didn't miss the way his eyes flashed to me before Thorne.

"I did."

"What happened?" Harlow asked, returning to Willard's side.

"The Lord of the Salt was almost captured last night. They say he was trying to break into the castle and the prince caught him. He's being held in the Maw."

"How long until we think he escapes this time?" Archer laughed as he and I collected the bowls from the floor and set them on the long table.

My ears were burning, trying to collect every morsel of information without seeming too eager. If the Lord of the Salt was trapped in the Maw, could I get to him? I knew where the secret entrance was. But did I have it in me? Unless... was this a set up? Nearly all of my present company had been there the day I escaped. Were they waiting for his capture? Would they help free him? At what cost?

"He's already free," Thorne said. "There's word he was out before the gates were locked."

Jasper's eyes twinkled. "Slippery little thief, isn't he?"

"Are we sure today's a good day?" Harlow asked, tucking closer to Willard's side.

"Yes. Paesha meets him now." Thorne's eyes swept over me. "She's curious and curious creatures cause all kinds of chaos when left to their own devices. Don't they, wife?"

"Did you just... is there a reason you're using alliteration? Are you having a stroke?"

Archer barked a laugh, slipping a hand over my shoulder. "I'm with Thorne. Let's just get this done."

I'd never been so grateful for a man in my life. I couldn't seem eager, but beyond my mission, my curiosity was piqued. They clearly knew how to find the Lord of the Salt, but they'd also made it blatantly obvious they weren't fans. He'd stolen the man from the dress shop's entire life from under him. Whatever this crew wanted with him, it couldn't be good. I thought back to the dead bodies in the Maw, to the ones in the alley yesterday. There were no lines, no boundaries for Thorne. He was ruthless when he needed to be. The problem with that was my bargain. I needed the Lord of the Salt. And if that meant I had to stand between him and the Fray, then that's where my loyalty would lie.

Thorne casually strode forward, lifting Archer's hand from my shoulder. "Let's think about the way we're presenting ourselves to outsiders, Bramwell."

Archer took a step back. "All yours, boss."

"Actually, no. I belong to no one," I said, walking away from all of them. "Are we doing this or what?"

I didn't miss the way Thorne's jaw tightened as he nodded, gesturing toward the door. "After you."

We melted into the hustle and bustle of the city just as we'd done the days before. Keeping our eyes down as we passed the Cimmerians lurking in the alleys and along the streets. We wound our way back toward the Silk side of the city. Beyond the shops and small street vendors, we turned only when the wall of buildings stopped. The entrance to our destination appeared as if out of nowhere, set back from the street, where the other buildings had practically sat on top of it. Passing the four pillars that seemed to reach toward the sky, we walked over the brick drive, worn from years of carriages and horses passing through. It seemed as if this place didn't belong. Even among the elite of Stirling, even with a castle looming in the distance, it was grander somehow. Different.

"There's no way the Lord of the Salt is here," I said, mouth open as we shuffled toward the door. "He'd be too easy to find."

The others said nothing, as if speaking outside would damn them. As if the Lord of the Salt would hear their thoughts and target them. We stepped through the doors, and had I not seen it with my own eyes, I might've believed we'd crossed into a different world. But then, I hadn't been inside many of the Silk buildings yet. Maybe this was the standard. The space was full of chattering people. Their secrets traveled through the curls of cigar smoke. Dark wood paneling, rich and polished, circled the room, illuminated by the warm glow of golden sconces.

Luxurious, tufted leather couches in deep burgundy were scattered about the floor, inviting guests to sink in. To let go. To get lost in a place that promised luxury and scandal in a single card game. The floor, smothered in richly patterned carpet, muffled the soft murmurs of scattered conversations. It reminded me of home. Of a place where deals were made with a handshake and fortunes decided with the turn of a card.

Above, a grand balcony overlooked the main room, its railing intricately wrought in dark iron. This was clearly a sanctuary for the city's elite, a space of indulgence and intrigue where every glance and every gesture carried weight, where power played in silence and whispers.

Archer pulled a stack of chips from his pocket and sat at a table with ease, the dealer acknowledging him with a nod before sliding a card across the table.

Harlow grabbed my hand and squeezed. "Keep an open mind," she said before slipping away, tugging on Willard who followed her toward a group of Silk sipping on tiny glasses and scrutinizing every move in the room as they whispered among each other.

Keep an open mind? I would absolutely *not* be doing that. But the warning settled into me all the same, probably having the opposite effect of her intention. What the hell were these people up to?

Thorne continued on, pulling me through the room, his grip on my hand tightening as we passed a few card tables poised for play and a bar lined with dark mahogany holding bottles of liquor reflecting like jewels in the low light.

Although some looked his way, most kept their eyes on me as we climbed the stairs, walked all the way down the rich wooden balcony, and disappeared down a hall smothered in tapestries. All the textures and carpet could only serve one purpose, a fact the Maestro learned long ago. Whispers never carried through well-insulated spaces.

Thorne rested his hand on the knob of the only door at the end of the hall, his posture growing stiff. "Beyond this door, there's a line. Wherever your loyalty lies, consider the line. Consider the lies you're willing to tell and who you are. If you thought the streets were dangerous before, this will darken everything. The edges of danger will sharpen. I know it seems like I made this decision for you, but it's your choice now."

There could be no choice for me. Not really. I needed this introduction. And though I could feel the reluctance like fingers around my throat, though I knew the man beyond the door was friend to no one, I needed him. And starting now, I'd have to figure out why. But there was still a role to play with Thorne. A place at his side until I didn't need him anymore.

"Tell me why it matters to you if I meet him."

"Dead Cimmerians lead to questions and there are four now. In this city, no matter who you are, everyone has to answer to someone. Unfortunately for us, that someone is sitting on the other side of this door."

I nodded. "Okay then. I'm ready."

He twisted the knob and swung the door open, gesturing for me to enter the dark room. I stepped in, unable to see much beyond the faint outline of a huge wooden desk and a leather chair facing the wall behind it.

I waited, letting my boots sink into the plush carpet as Thorne closed the door behind me, walked around the desk and sat in the godsdamn chair. "It's a pleasure to meet you, Paesha darling."

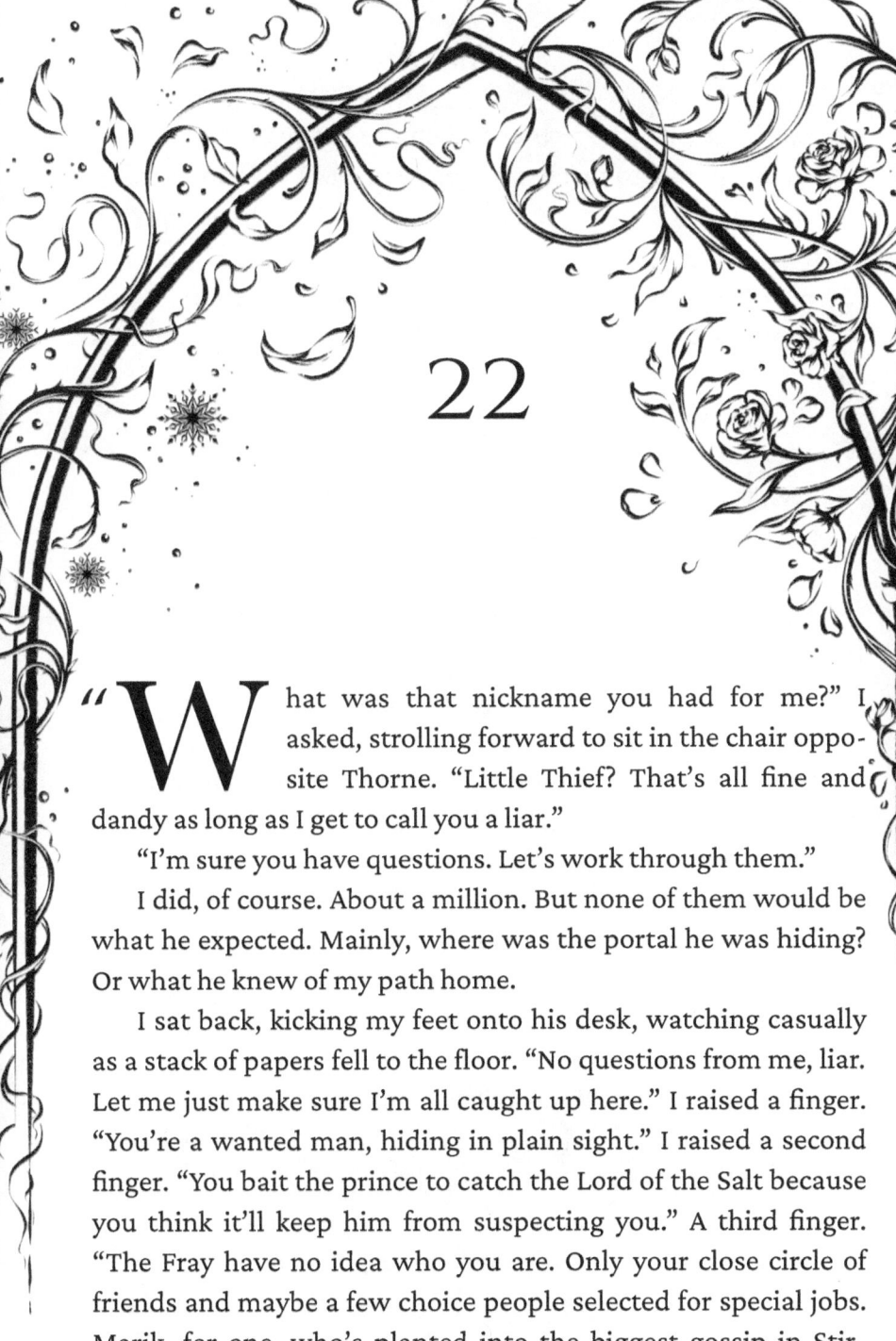

22

"What was that nickname you had for me?" I asked, strolling forward to sit in the chair opposite Thorne. "Little Thief? That's all fine and dandy as long as I get to call you a liar."

"I'm sure you have questions. Let's work through them."

I did, of course. About a million. But none of them would be what he expected. Mainly, where was the portal he was hiding? Or what he knew of my path home.

I sat back, kicking my feet onto his desk, watching casually as a stack of papers fell to the floor. "No questions from me, liar. Let me just make sure I'm all caught up here." I raised a finger. "You're a wanted man, hiding in plain sight." I raised a second finger. "You bait the prince to catch the Lord of the Salt because you think it'll keep him from suspecting you." A third finger. "The Fray have no idea who you are. Only your close circle of friends and maybe a few choice people selected for special jobs. Marik, for one, who's planted into the biggest gossip in Stirling's shop and given a tragic backstory to make him a charity case." Another finger. "Aside from the murder, you're really out

207

here stealing from the rich and giving to the poor, while being rich yourself, just to throw everyone off. Does that about cover it? Oh, sorry, let me rephrase that. Does that about cover it, *liar*?"

He scowled, his eyes flashing to the mess. "Just about."

"Hate to break it to you, but it really wasn't that big of a mystery. You're all terrible liars."

"You knew?" he asked, eyebrows knitting together.

"Of course I knew."

"What gave us away? And do be specific."

I shook my head, forcing a dark smile. "I'll never tell."

His hazel eyes, more brown than green in the dark room, scrutinized me for a moment before he stood and strode across the space, pausing at an old sideboard. There was something there in that look. Something that heated me more than I wanted it to.

He bent down, opening the doors to reveal an array of bottled spirits, and selected two, one a deep amber and the other a clear liquid, holding them up for my inspection. "Pick your poison," he said, a glint of challenge dancing in his gaze.

I tilted my head to one side, considering. The darker was doubtlessly aged and of fine quality, the type of drink that warmed you from the inside more than his piercing gaze and brought an untamed burn with each sip. Yet the clear, it promised something different. Something unknown.

Blinking, I finally pointed to the amber. A smile twitched at the corner of his lips as he uncorked the bottle with his mouth and poured the two glasses. When he was finished, he brought the drink over to me. "You're here because you have a choice to make. You've seen too much, and we need more than blind hope that you'll keep your mouth shut."

Three knocks sounded on the door, followed by a pause and one more.

"Come in," he said, his voice full of authority, though his eyes never left mine.

"She knows?" Harlow asked.

"She does. Though you could have given her more than a single hand of cards before you interrupted us."

"Sorry boss," Archer said, shuffling into the room and shutting the door behind him as he faced me. "You in?"

Thorne lifted a brow.

"I'm... listening," I said, taking the glass Thorne held out, ignoring the way my skin burned where our fingers brushed. "Cheers, husband."

"You don't get to be a member of the Fray without an initiation." His eyes swept over me. "I'm in charge. You don't get a say. You don't get an opinion. You do as you're told. Understand?"

"I said I was listening, that's as much as you're getting from me."

"Hardly anyone knows the Fray exists. Those that do seldom bite the hand that feeds them. We don't deal with leaked secrets well. If you get caught and even think about snitching, I'll kill you myself before you ever get a chance to follow through. You want out, I'll find the Story Snatcher and have him take your memories from the last few days. Decide now."

I sipped the liquid, letting it burn a glorious path down my throat as he walked back across the room and poured drinks for everyone else. Sitting with what he'd said, I knew how careful I needed to be. How little I could actually trust any of them.

"I don't do bargains."

"This isn't a bargain. It's a choice. You're in or out and that's all there is to it. But if you stay, you earn your keep. Do you have magic you've been hiding, Paesha darling?"

The subtle gasp from Harlow could've been a roar in the quiet room. "Thorne."

He threw his hand up without looking away from me, those glorious eyes burning. I couldn't look away. Could hardly breathe before the man that commanded more than just the room. "We have to know the risk she poses."

Having magic was a risk? Interesting.

"I don't have magic," I said.

His eyes lingered, searching for anything beyond the surface of my lie before he nodded. "Good girl. Hopefully that means Farris will get bored with you quickly." He poured himself another glass and moved until he was directly in front of me, sitting on the edge of his desk as he looked down. "This is the Parlor. Owned by me, Thorne Noctus. It has nothing to do with the Lord of the Salt. In fact, he's a bit of a nuisance around here." He reached forward and took the empty glass from my hands, setting it on his desk before he crossed his massive arms over his broad chest. "Now, the decision is yours. In or out."

If Thorne was being hunted by gods and I'd been sent to find him, maybe that meant other gods were helping hide him. And if that were the case, if the fates were as real as he seemed to believe, and my path lay with him, maybe I could actually pull this off. Maybe I really could get home, reunite with Quill, and save the realms while I was at it. Minimally, this gave me guaranteed shelter while I worked out where I was supposed to be.

I took a deep, calming breath before standing, swiping Thorne's drink from his hand and tossing it back. "I'm in."

Archer held his glass out to me from the door. "Welcome to the chaos."

"I knew you'd join," Harlow said, pulling a small dagger from her pocket, expertly flipping it in her hand and holding it out toward me. "I got you a present. If you get into a jam, stick them with the pointy end."

I hesitated, scrutinizing Harlow more than I had before. "Are you secretly a badass, blondie?"

"Don't let it get to her head." Archer smiled. "She hates people and dresses and always has a weapon handy."

"Pants are so much more practical," she said, taking her own drink.

"If we could get back to the point here." Thorne reclaimed the seat behind the desk. "We don't have a lot of time. Paesha, you take your cues from Archer tonight. This job cannot fail. There are months of work riding on it. Your role is the same as it has been. You're my new wife." He smiled, showing the rare dimple as his eyes narrowed. "You're madly in love with me. Your goal is to distract Archer's target with your... charm. I'm sure you can find some of that somewhere if you dig deep enough."

I walked forward, careful to tread over the pile of papers on his floor as I sank back into the seat across from him. "Do you keep it dark in here for the act? Does it make you feel more important? Because I can hardly see you and I don't like making plans in the dark. Feels wrong."

"Don't be difficult," he said. "This is serious. We can't have mistakes."

"What'd you say? I can't see you."

I loved pushing that man's buttons, and he made it so, so easy.

Harlow's laugh surprised me. She walked forward and spun a small knob on the wall. Several lamps bloomed to life, their flames warming the space. "It really is creepy when you keep it so dark."

Thorne's lips formed a thin line.

"Back to business. When you say 'madly in love', where do I rank on a scale of noticeable adoration to dangerously obsessive? Just so I'm clear."

Something flashed across his face. A look I hadn't seen from him before, not confusion, nor calculating. Not an emotion at all. Just a light that answered before his words did. "Dangerously obsessive would be a hard level to prove."

I smirked, running my finger over the knife Harlow had given me. "Would it?"

"Thaaaat's actually creepy," Archer said, reaching to take the blade. "Let's maybe have a lesson with weapons before we start playing with them."

"What are we stealing?" I asked, sliding the dagger into its sheath and pocketing it before he could take it. I knew my way around a blade well enough.

"Nothing that concerns you," Thorne answered. "You've got a pretty face. Use it. Don't press boundaries. Don't stray from the plan. Prove you can do the job without messing it up, then we'll decide what use you'll have to the team."

"I'm more than just a pretty face, Thorne."

He leaned closer, folding his hands. "I'm sure you'd like to think so."

"Better watch that mouth of yours. It'd be such a shame if your obsessive wife stabbed you in your sleep."

"I'd love to see her try."

"You certainly do strike me as the kind of man that would prefer to watch."

He grinned, his gaze flicking to my lips. "Only if you put on a good show."

I arched a brow, leaning in just close enough to make him hold his breath. "Careful, there. I never do anything half-heartedly."

"Good. I'd hate to be underwhelmed."

"You two need a minute? It seems like maybe you need a minute," Archer said, backing toward the door.

"Don't be silly. We're just flirting," I answered, eyes glued to Thorne. "Isn't that right, husband?"

His dimple was showing again. "Indeed... Shall we?"

I stood, straightening the sleeve of my gown as he circled the desk and offered me an arm. Batting my eyelashes, I managed a small curtsy before taking it. "Lead the way, handsome."

Thorne led us down the stairs, into an alcove hiding a door to a room clearly only meant for his staff. He left shortly after, giving a warning about the importance of our mission, but no additional information.

The room itself was much larger than I expected and just as grand as the Parlor. Mirrors lined one wall from floor to ceiling, amplifying the glorious array of textiles and disguises before me. Sconces lined the space, all but one identical in finish. Beyond those, garments hung from hangers like leaves from a tree in autumn.

Archer's instructions were thorough and clear as we stood side by side, peeking out into the giant room full of impeccably dressed Silk. "All you have to do is come join the conversation and be friendly. See that platform in front of the table?"

I nodded, eyes tracing over the gold box at the head of a round table surrounded by high-back, leather chairs.

"Old Victor loves a beautiful woman and with a dancer in front of him on the platform *and* the attention of the Paramour, who happens to be Thorne's new and mysterious bride, he won't be able to keep his wits about him. When I've got the bag, I'll stretch. When you see the signal, you can go. If he gets handsy, Thorne won't like it. So keep a respectable distance. We use the Parlor as a distraction for the big jobs. Thorne only lets certain members of the Silk in. You have to be an elitist to make it through those doors. Because of that, people pine to get in and some pay for it too. Thorne takes a back seat to most of the Parlor's dealings. His role is more of a distant observer. Someone they all want to get close to, and no one can. See that woman over there with the long cigarette?"

I nodded, locking onto the way she watched Thorne, who stood on the balcony, leaning against one of the pillars, reading a damn book, of all things. But I'd learned enough about him to know he was watching the crowd more than the ink on the pages.

"She pays the man at the door a diamond once a month just to get in. He turns it over to Thorne. Thorne sells it to her husband, who owns a jewelry store. He gives it back to her and round and round they go, just pouring money into the Parlor, which in turn, feeds the Hollow for a good couple of days. And every once in a while, she'll show up wearing something extra shiny and leave without it."

"Don't these people notice you're stealing and selling their stuff?"

"Nah," Archer said, letting the door snick shut. "Most of the rich don't pay much attention to what they have in surplus. Also, that's where the Vale, well… the black market comes into play. One of ours deals with Alastor. He pays a low price and then whatever he does with it from there is his own business. He doesn't make it easy on us, but hopefully tonight changes that. We've been working on this for months."

"You nervous.?" I asked.

He pushed his shoulder into mine. "Just try not to mess it up."

I rolled my eyes. "Don't worry. I won't."

The back door to the room opened and a woman with tight black curls came bustling in, clutching her cloak around her as the freezing wind raced through.

"Well?" Archer asked. "Where is she?"

The woman shook her head. "Caught by the Cimmerians. She's not coming."

"We really need her."

"I don't know what to tell you, Archie. I can't very well go plead her case. You know that. She's being tested."

"Paesha, this is Rosy. Rosy, Paesha. Thorne's wife. She's helping keep Victor distracted tonight."

Rosy sucked a sharp breath between her teeth. "Good luck with that. Emaline's not coming, Arch. I don't know what to tell you."

The deep rumble of a man's laugh came from the Parlor seconds before there was a light tapping at the door. "On our way," Archer said with a gulp, eyes wide.

"You're going to have to really keep his attention. It's just you and I."

I nodded, feeling his nerves as if they were my own. "Tell me something about him. Anything. What's his job?"

"He's a Silk. He doesn't have a job."

"Okay. Does he own businesses? Give to charity? Visit a temple? I need something to go on here."

Rosy snorted. "He loves the temple all right... Serene's lusty one, to be specific."

I put my hand on Archer's shoulder. "I've got this handled. Don't worry."

"Give me some time to get him settled. Then it's all you." His nervous laugh as he left the back room was less than reassuring.

"I'm not going to be able to keep that man's attention with a riveting conversation, am I?" I asked the woman as she slipped out of her boots.

"Not a chance," she said with a wink before pulling her dress over her head. "And I can't help you, honey. I've got to help Harlow and Will entertain his partner. Just in case."

The way she undressed without a thought reminded me of being backstage before a show. No one cared about what could be seen because we'd shown almost all of it on stage, anyway.

I'd grown numb to human anatomy. But it did give me a brilliant idea.

"Do you have time to help me get this dress off?"

She snorted. "Yes. But no."

"I'm serious. I need to get out of this immediately."

"The boss will burn this place down before he lets his wife walk out there in anything but a floor-length gown and sleeves long enough to cover your fingertips. He's nice until he isn't. Don't be foolish."

"No one knows me," I said.

"You've got the most unique eyes anyone has ever seen. We all know you, even if we've never met you. But most of this crowd was at Lithe, Paramour. They know exactly who you are."

"I've got an idea, but we're going to have to be quick."

"Famous last words," Rosy answered, ripping at the string on the back of my dress. "If I lose my job over this, I'll find a way to make you suffer."

ROSY WAS ACTUALLY A GEM. She'd left the room, and just as I'd asked her to, ordered the band to play something smoother than the peppy song they'd been repeating. She'd handed out jeweled veils to all the workers and bid them to put them on, so I would not be the only one disguised.

I stepped out of the back room, hardly able to see, but there were enough details seeping through the jewels to guide me toward the table Archer had pointed out. Still, as I walked, with little more than lace and diamonds covering me, my heart hammered. The attention of the entire parlor on me added to the tension. The pressure to get this right for Thorne. Each step I took felt like a proclamation, each sway of my hips, a command. A duty, but one I'd asked for.

The music swelled around me, and though I knew Archer looked away, focusing only on Victor, it felt as if the rest of the room were mine. And I'd commanded many rooms. Many crowds. Many stages. But as a giant shadow filled my peripheral vision, I knew Thorne had descended from his perch, likely in full protest of my decision to walk out of that back room almost naked.

A seductive melody seeped into my bones, urging me to move. And so I did, letting the music guide me as I stepped up on the platform. Victor stopped talking to Archer mid-sentence, his attention all mine as if it were wrapped around my fist as I danced, slow at first, then gaining momentum, spinning, sway-ing, twirling and the music trailed through the Parlor, sinking into my soul. Speaking the only language I ever wanted to know.

My focus should have been on Victor. That was the test, wasn't it? The initiation. The big target. Keep his attention long enough for Archer to make his move. But the fire resting beneath my skin came from another. The man that had shifted closer.

Thorne's scorching gaze traveled along the curve of my waist, grazing the arch of my back and tracing the line of my bare legs. I reveled in it, allowed myself to succumb to the intox-icating rhythm as my body moved gracefully to the surrounding beat. A smirk played on my lips as I thought of him. Of the look of disapproval on his handsome face. Maybe, for once, he'd break through the walls of self-discipline he'd built around himself. But he couldn't do that here. Not now, when this moment was so important. He was trapped beneath my control and I loved it.

Old Victor shifted forward, leaning over the small round table between us. Whatever conversation he'd been having had been long abandoned as I danced for him, but not really. I couldn't take my mind from Thorne just feet away.

I extended an arm, the gauzy fabric of the veil trailing behind me like wisps of smoky desire. Victor's eyes followed the movement, his own longing blatantly obvious in the hungry look he cast my way. Subtly, I beckoned him closer, knowing Thorne would be watching his every move, but also fully aware that keeping him in my grasp would make Archer's job the easiest.

Twirling once more, I lost myself in the rhythm of the song. Raw power surged through me as I noticed Thorne stepping forward; his tall and commanding figure cutting an intimidating path through the crowd that had gathered.

Gliding toward Victor like a phantom in the night, the layers of my disguise billowing around my shoulders, I reached a single hand toward him. He sat at rapt attention, eyes wide and mouth slightly agape, as if he'd seen an angel descend from the heavens.

Panic set in as Thorne drew closer. He'd give us both away if he couldn't control himself. He made no effort to hide the anger on his face as he watched me edge toward Victor. His hand flexed at his side. But this was his game. His months of planning. He's the one that knew what was at stake tonight.

Beyond the speckled jewels and gossamer masking my face, our eyes locked for a fleeting moment, sparking a connection that rocked me, nearly sending me off the side of the platform. His smirk at my misstep was infuriating. I needed only to keep the charade a few moments more. Victor, with his eyes glued to me, shifted in his seat again. I pushed my hips forward and then back, spinning to give him a glimpse of my entire body. My grip around his attention tightened as Archer made his move.

Seconds later, Archer slowly raised both hands in the air with a dramatic yawn. The sign. We'd pulled it off. And Thorne had managed to maintain his distance. I waited for three beats of music before stepping off the pedestal and circling through the room, walking past each of the other dancers, stroking my fingers over their skin, though none of them were naked or even partially aware of what was happening.

The song's final note came just as I closed the door to the back room, ripped the veil from my face, and quickly stepped back into my dress. I thought he'd come. I thought for sure the door would slam open and Thorne would come barreling in with all of his anger and all of his self-righteous attitude, swinging it like a hammer at me. But I stood in silence, beyond the low murmur of the next song, the laughter of the Silk, and the soft shuffle of gambling chips.

After carefully tying the corset on my dress so it didn't look rushed, I slipped Thorne's ring back onto my finger, fluffed my hair in one of the mirrors, and double checked the door. I was alone. I drew in one steady breath before approaching the sconce with more wear on its finish than the others. I knew a secret door when I saw one. I also knew most wouldn't have questioned it, hidden halfway behind the mirrors. But it just so happened I was on the hunt for a hidden door.

My nerves rattled, sending wave after wave of anticipation until my hands were a sweaty mess. I'd found the Hollow. I'd found the Lord of the Salt. And now this. And while I wasn't sure I could be so lucky to find a portal home hidden within the backroom of Thorne's little shop of thievery, a girl could hope. Pray. Even beg.

"Please," I whispered, closing my eyes as I turned the metal handle, and the wall gave way.

23

My face fell and my shoulders slumped as I took in the darkness of a stairwell before me. Nothing glowing, nothing magical. Nothing that felt out of place in this world. Dammit.

The air smelled a bit like him. Like worn parchment and an empty inkpot, like the final tendril of smoke from a snuffed-out candle. I could nearly feel him shuffling up these narrow steps, broad shoulders brushing the sides of the walls as he avoided as many people as possible in his own establishment.

Feeling my way forward, step after step in the dark, my fingers traced over the smooth texture of polished wood until they stumbled upon something smooth and metallic. A brass handle. Holding my breath as if the silence were a fragile glass about to shatter, I pressed down and let the door swing open, the passageway depositing me into Thorne's dark study.

He stood with his back to me, spinning only when the creak of the door gave me away. His eyes were dark with anger, disappointment etched on every line of his face. "What were you thinking?"

"You know, I was just sitting in the back room thinking, 'I'd sure like to get my titties out today.' Those were the exact thoughts in my pretty little mind."

He stalked forward. I backed away. He took another step, and I moved away again, colliding with the bookshelves. Thorne pressed a hand to my throat, stroking my jawline, though I could feel the anger within the tremble of his fingers. I couldn't lie, even to myself. I'd needed this fight from him. This anger. Finally, he'd broken. Finally, he'd shown a bit of the rage I'd seen in that alley the day he'd claimed me as his wife. That vulnerability wrapped itself around me like a vice.

"Do not mock me."

"Mock you? *Mock you?* I saved your ass with mine."

"No one asked you to do that."

I shoved him away. "That's exactly what you asked me to do. Shall I repeat the pretty face comment you made? The woman that was supposed to come in and dance was caught by Farris for something. Do you seriously think my conversational skills are so good Victor wasn't going to notice Archer elbow deep in his fucking pockets? Men are so easy. So, so easy. Show them a nipple and suddenly they forget how to string together words."

He said nothing, but his eyes narrowed with fury.

"Don't think I didn't see you watching me," I said, baiting him. Pushing him. "Don't think for a second I missed the way you drooled over me dancing. And you know what that means to me? Absolutely *nothing.*"

I had to bite my tongue to keep from revealing more about myself. He didn't need to hear it. I'd be gone soon enough and none of them would matter anyway. But maybe now, he and I could find some genuine common ground. Because the clock was ticking, and I needed to get the fuck out of here.

He stalked forward again, closing the space between us until

I was dwarfed by his massive size. He brought a hand up to the bookshelf, shifting his weight until he loomed over me. "Must you lie to me?"

I snorted. "Careful, husband. The conceited man buried in your veins is showing."

He smiled. Not the handsome dimpled smile, but something far more menacing. "Shall I let him out to play with you, wife? Is that why you're trying to push me?"

The way the low tone of his voice rumbled sent a wave of something warm and welcome straight through my body.

"Are you angry-flirting with me?"

He leaned closer. Until his glasses no longer reflected the light from the room and all I could feel was the warmth of his breath on my ear as he whispered, "Absolutely. And let's get one thing straight right now. Everyone knows I do not share. And this body," he said, skimming a finger down my arm, "belongs to me in public. Should you ever bare it again, I will let my baser instincts win and you will see exactly how a monster devours his prey. Piece by bloody piece."

His words sent a shiver down my spine, both thrilling and terrifying me. I couldn't let him see how much he affected me though. I had to stay in control.

"Is that a threat or a promise?" I asked, tilting my chin up in defiance.

"Which would you prefer it to be?"

I swallowed hard, pulse racing. The air between us crackled with tension, the kind that could ignite at any moment into an inferno. Part of me wanted to push him further, to see how far I could take this dangerous game. But the rational side of my brain screamed at me to stop playing with fire.

"Neither," I finally said, ducking to the side to put some distance between us. "But it's nice to see you rattled in your cage."

He moved a hand through his dark hair. "And who has the key to put you back in yours?"

I think I hated him. But also, I was pretty sure I didn't. Still, he had no idea how relevant that question was. Nor that he was the key holder.

Thorne ignored the knocking on his office door as he rolled his white shirt sleeve halfway up his forearm. I was beginning to think that habit of his was to distract his mind. But gods, it distracted me too.

"Take the scowl off your face. You have a part to play."

"Right," I glared, baring all of my teeth. "Dangerously obsessive."

His hands were on me again, gentle, yet pressing as he pushed me back into the bookcase, leaning down to whisper, "Continue to push and you'll find out just how obsessive *I* can be." His breath was hot against my ear, sending another shiver down my spine that I tried, and failed, to suppress.

I smirked, meeting his gaze, even as my heart pounded wildly. "Promises, promises."

He chuckled darkly, his fingers trailing down my arm, the touch as light as a whisper but leaving a blaze in its wake. "Careful. I always keep them."

I shook my head. "Liars don't keep their promises."

Again, a knock came at the door. He crossed the room in four giant strides and yanked the door open. "What?"

"Willard caught Allun cheating again, and he's holding him at table thirteen."

With a deep rise and fall of Thorne's shoulders, he spun to me, holding a hand out. "Come, my darling. There's no need to spend your whole evening up here. I'd love to show you around."

And there it was. Just like that, the masks were back on, and we were cascading down the steps, hand in hand, sharing a smile that only he and I knew had fangs. His grip was too tight, my stride too slow. Everything about our official debut into his dark world was a battle. His hand wrapped around mine never faltered though. He never raced forward to embarrass my slow stride. And he never once looked at another woman in the room.

Willard sat at a table in a far corner of the room with another man, similar in age and handsome features. Harlow stood behind Will and though he wasn't part of the confrontation, Archer leaned against the bar across the way, watching as he casually sipped his liquor.

"Caught this one cheating again," Willard grunted, jerking his thumb towards Allun. "Thought you might want to handle it personally."

Thorne's grip on my hand tightened almost imperceptibly as he leaned in close to Allun. "Is that so? And here I thought we had an understanding, Newcomb. You know how I feel about cheaters and thieves. Especially on my wife's first visit. This isn't a way to welcome her, is it?"

Allun's mouth worked soundlessly, his face growing paler by the second. He shrank under Thorne's withering gaze. Licking his lips, he glanced around as if hoping for a miraculous savior. He pulled the tall hat from his head and loosened his tie. "I've had too much to drink, is all."

"Don't embarrass yourself. See yourself out and don't come back or I'll make a personal request to our beloved prince and see that your entire household is brought to justice."

Every shade of color melted from the man's face as he swallowed. He slowly rose from his seat, leaving the pile of chips in front of him as well as his hat behind. "S-Sorry, Thorne."

We stood side by side as the man ran from the building. Thorne motioned for the little band set up near the bar to begin playing again, and then led me across the room toward a section that had been roped off. He unclipped the rope and pulled me toward him, lifting my hand to kiss the ring that sat on my finger. I held my breath, waiting for him to end his little show, but he knew it. And it gave him fuel to keep going. "Smile, Paesha darling. The whole world is watching."

I sauntered forward, sliding my hands up his chest, moving to my tip toes. "Fetch me a drink, husband. It's going to be a long night if I'm to be stuck back here with you."

He laughed. Far too loud and far too long, but eventually, once I'd slid down onto the leather couch like an obedient wife, he walked away. I hadn't realized how much he'd been blocking my view of the room until his shadow was gone and I could feel every single pair of curious eyes studying me. I leaned back, studying nails that were in desperate need of a manicure until he returned. Drinks in hand.

"When was the last time *you* served someone in your little fun house?"

He smiled genuinely this time, his dimple showing. "This would be a first."

I took the glass of clear liquid and lifted it toward him. "To your good health then, my darling. May your meals always be warm and your wife, never lethal."

"WHAT?" he asked for the third time in the carriage on the way home.

"I've already told you, it's nothing."

"No one's ever told you how horrible of a liar you are, and it shows."

"That's not true at all. I'm an excellent liar. I just don't want to talk to you."

He sat back, the simple adjustment of his body causing the carriage to rock. "Fine."

"Fine."

He pulled a small book from his coat pocket and opened it. Though it was far too dark in the carriage for light reading, somehow he managed, turning pages by moonlight all the way to his house. I rubbed my hands together, staring out the window, feeling pulled down a path I knew I needed to walk but really only wanted to get to the end of.

I closed my eyes and thought of Thea. Wondered what she might be doing now. Was it nighttime at home? Had Elowen cooked dinner for the Syndicate? Had they rallied around Quill to make her feel better? My poor girl. She had so many that loved her, and though she was almost nine, it was still such a tender age to feel so abandoned on a repeated cycle. Left behind by her parents, passed on by a brothel owner, used by a crime lord. I'd done my best with her. Gave her the love and attention I'd known from my own father before he'd left me. But the realms would fall to Quill's fury, so I supposed nothing I had done mattered. Only what I would do.

So I sucked it up, pulled my head back into Wisteria and forced myself into a plan. I needed Thorne to need me as much as I needed him. And there was a very clear path. He just needed to be the one to see it. He liked his own mind too much to rely on the requests of others.

"A key?"

Thorne put his book down, looking at me over the top of his glasses. "Oh, we're talking now?"

"Yes."

"About a key." I paused. "And a broach, a pearl necklace, emerald studded cufflinks, a bag of betting chips, and oddly enough, a gold tipped walking cane."

He looked away, taking note of the items as I listed them. "How'd you know?"

"Because your little thieves? They aren't that clever. Most of them have tells right before they take something. Harlow always sweeps her eyes around the room. It's subtle, but foolish. If she catches the eye of one person a second too late, she's caught. Archer? He's good. But he keeps his hands in his pockets so much, people are going to start wondering if he's really just playing with himself down there. But when he's pulling a job, he doesn't do it. He makes sure his hands are out, but not flipping his coin. It's out of character for him. And Willard. Don't get me started on that guy. He's a crasher. Every time. Which is fine on the streets. Someone bumps into you, goes on about their business. No big deal. They don't figure out what's missing until later. But if your patrons start talking, swapping stories, it's not going to take long before they realize they all had a run in with Wee Willy."

"Clever little fox, aren't you?"

I shook my head before staring out the window. "No. I'm not trying to show off, Thorne. You're going to get caught. As my friend Thea would say, you have too many irons in the fire and you're missing the small details."

"I'll keep that in mind," he said, just as the carriage came to a stop. He crawled out and held a hand up to help me.

After we were out, he walked to the front and tossed the driver a small bag. "Thanks Tuck. Any news from Tilly?"

"Nothing new. Farris is circling. We're watching."

"One of ours was pulled for testing tonight. Emaline. The Cimmerians must have caught her doing something."

"I'll look into it."

"That's all for me tonight."

"See you tomorrow," Tuck said, clicking his tongue just before the horses sped away.

As if he'd only just realized, Thorne turned back to me and said, "That's the first time you've mentioned someone from your past."

"Don't get used to it. That life is gone now."

Protected. Locked away in my heart to keep them all safe.

The second carriage, the one that'd been following us, approached. Harlow, Archer and Willard crawled out and followed us inside. Shedding our coats at the door, we nestled into the sitting room, sinking into the couches. Harlow plopped down beside Willard, leaning on him as he wrapped an arm around her shoulder. Archer paid them little more than a glance. He took the leather chair opposite of Thorne's, propping his leg up on his knee as he checked his watch. I sat alone, waiting to be dismissed. Aching to take my boots off and get into the bath.

Thorne settled back in his chair, steepling his fingers beneath his chin as he surveyed the room. I expected him to launch into a lecture about the flaws I'd pointed out, to dissect each mistake with surgical precision. But instead, he simply gave Archer a pointed look.

The blond man reached into the inside pocket of his jacket and withdrew a brown paper package tied with a bit of twine. With deft fingers, he unraveled the knot, and the paper fell away, revealing an exquisite snuff box nestled in his palm.

The box was a work of art, gleaming silver embellished with intricate filigree that caught the firelight. A large emerald was set into the center of the lid, glinting with a mesmerizing depth of color. "Well done, Archie."

Archer preened slightly under the praise. "Snagged it right out of the old codger's pocket, thanks to Paesha here." I didn't miss the blush that crossed his face as he looked anywhere but at me.

Thorne cleared his throat, his eyes locking on to mine. "No need to revisit that foolish choice."

"Oh!" Harlow sat forward, suddenly far more engaged. "I heard Emaline was caught by a Cimmerian on her way in tonight. They say she cursed the prince and hit a guard."

Archer's face turned grim. "Talbot reported just as we were leaving. She failed her test and she'll be marked in the morning."

Thorne pushed a hand through his dark hair. "Best let Tuck know. I hadn't heard the update."

I couldn't ask what they were talking about without raising more questions about me. Whatever was happening was common knowledge, so I just had to sit back and take in enough context clues to figure it out. But I couldn't draw attention by silence. This game was a fine line.

I sat forward, matching Harlow's posture. "It seems strange that Farris is given so much power when his father is still around."

Willard snorted. "You'd be hard pressed to find someone that disagreed with that. It's unfortunate really. How well King Wendale has been cut off from the kingdom."

Whatever playfulness I'd learned to expect in Archer's voice had vanished, replaced by little more than a growl as he set the box on the coffee table between us and stood. "What I don't understand is why the people, *his people*, aren't forcing their way in. If he knew, he wouldn't stand for what's happening on the streets."

"You think too highly of him, brother," Harlow said, her tone careful. "There's no way he doesn't know what's happening. He's given up. You're going to have to accept that."

The boyish features in Archer's face faded away with his glare toward his sister. "I will not, and neither should you."

"King and prince aside, we need to talk about Alastor," Thorne said, breaking the tension. "We need better deals with the Vale."

"Oh yes, because gods are so much easier than the monarchy," Harlow said with a sigh.

Gods? Alastor was a god?

229

But I knew that name. I held my breath, sinking into the couch, hoping my face hadn't given me away.

"Alastor runs the black market, Paesha. He's ruthless but the only avenue we have to sell our stolen goods without eyes looking back at us. The problem is, he won't deal with me directly. No member of the Fray may do trade with Alastor. He's forbidden it." Thorne said. "We've constantly got to work with a middleman, who takes a cut of the money."

"And the annoying part is," Willard continued, putting his elbows on his knees as he sat forward. "Alastor *knows* he's still dealing with us. He's forcing us to give these middlemen cuts, just to take away from our profits. Which is only hurting the Salt."

"He's going to be tough to bargain with. Even with that," Thorne said, pointing at the stolen box with his chin. "We'll need you for negotiations, Archie."

"I know you want me to do this, boss, but I think the best I'm going to be able to pull from him is a meeting."

"Use the artifact from Farris's Tithe carriage to lure him in. The man that built that carriage wants the artifact back because Farris stole it, and Alastor knows it. He'll get a good price for it. When you meet with Alastor to give him the artifact, tell him I need a meeting. If he agrees, give him the box you stole tonight."

"And if he doesn't? If I try to walk out of there with that thing, you're going to find my head on a pike in Prospector's Pointe."

Thorne stood, walking over to a large hutch sitting against the far wall. He opened the door, reached all the way to the back, engaged a mechanism, and a hidden drawer popped out of the side. He crossed the room and handed Archer a matching box from the drawer. "If he denies you, give him this one instead. And then get the hell out of there as fast as you can."

The power that typically sat dormant within me until I called it forward rumbled to life. The urge to touch both of those items, to mark them before they vanished, was pressing, suffocating. Desperate.

I didn't hesitate, jumping from my seat to sweep the original box from where it lay on the table. I smoothed a finger over the carving first, and then the emerald, bigger than any stone I'd ever seen.

Thorne's fingers closed over the snuff box seconds later. I hadn't even registered his movement. "Careful wife. Not every treasure is meant for mortals." He looked at me as if he'd really seen me in that moment. As if he'd known the way my power ached for rare trinkets. But also as if he knew he couldn't trust me. Which was absolutely true.

"If you already had the replica, why not bait him with that one?" Harlow asked.

"Alastor isn't a fool. There's a reason he runs the Vale. If he touches this, even looks at it close enough, he'll know it's not real." Thorne held the other box out for me, as if he knew how badly I wanted to see it. "Can you see the difference, Paesha darling?"

Harlow took my side, studying the replicated box just as I did. Similar in weight and finish, they were nearly identical. But Thorne wasn't wrong. There was a difference, something so subtle, I almost missed it.

"They look and feel exactly the same," Harlow said, touching both boxes.

"Do you agree?" Thorne asked, his eyes swallowing me whole as he waited. As if this had been an unspoken test and I couldn't fail.

"No." I answered, moving back to my seat. "He'll know the difference."

With a nod of approval, Thorne handed both to Archer.

"Keep the real one wrapped in paper, so you don't mix them up. And for the love of all the gods, do not open them."

"Why?" he asked, eyes wide as he shoved each of them into different pockets.

"That's not what's important here. Just do as I ask and mind your words carefully. We need this meeting. Our food stores are too low."

"I could go with?" Willard offered. "If you're nervous about it."

"He'll manage," Thorne answered, moving toward the door. "It's time to call it a night."

"Agreed." Harlow followed close behind, turning back to Willard. "Walk me home tonight. I'm too tired to keep to the shadows and I don't want to deal with the Cimmies."

Archer rubbed his hands together. "No need to bother Wee Willy, Harlot. I can drop you off first. I'll head to the Vale from there."

"Don't call him that," she said from behind a clenched smile.

"Aw." Archer punched Willard on the arm. "Willy knows nicknames are my love language, don't you, bud?"

Willard shared a friendly smile. "Yeah, yeah. I know."

Thorne's friends didn't dawdle, and I was grateful for that. It'd been a long day. As Thorne walked past me and up the stairs, I spun and wandered down the hall to his office, studying the spines of his collection of books. I chose three and slunk heavily to my room.

I unlaced the corset on the back of my dress and let it pool at my feet near the door, leaving me in just my thin silk chemise. Padding into the adjoining bathroom, I turned on the faucet, sending steaming water gushing into the large clawfoot tub.

I perched on its porcelain edge, trailing my fingers through the silky water. When the bath was nearly full, I shut off the water and shed my remaining clothes. Sinking into the deliciously hot water, I let out a sigh of pure bliss. The heat seeped into my bones, unwinding the tension from my muscles. I lay there for what seemed like an hour, ignoring the knocking on my door, and Thorne's gruff voice informing me he'd left dinner on the bed.

As the bath water grew tepid, I reluctantly emerged, my pruney fingers trailing droplets across the plush bath rug. Wrapping myself in an oversized, fluffy towel, I walked back into the bedroom, and to my surprise, all of my clothing was gone. The wardrobe doors hung open, revealing only bare hangers where the few things I'd collected had been. I searched the room, checking in drawers and under furniture, the towel clutched tightly to my chest. But my clothes were simply gone, vanished.

A flicker of suspicion ignited.

Thorne... two could play at that game.

Clad in nothing but the damp towel, I stormed out of the room, dripping water down the hall. Without hesitation, I raised a fist and pounded on his door.

"Yes?" he crooned softly, swinging the door open as if he'd been waiting for me. His eyes made a slow pass down my body, and honestly, I couldn't tell if he hated his inability to control that hungry look in his eyes or if he hoped for it.

"Where are my clothes?" I demanded, trying to ignore the way his intense gaze made my pulse race.

A lazy smirk curved his lips. "Clothing seems rather optional now, wouldn't you say?"

I glared at him. "You're such a fucking prick."

"You might've mentioned that before."

I narrowed my eyes at him, tightening my grip on the towel. "Don't play games with me. I know you took them. Give them back."

He pushed off the doorframe and stepped closer, invading

my personal space. The heat radiating from his body mingled with the lingering warmth from my bath, making my skin tingle. "And why would I do that? I think I enjoy seeing you like this."

I dropped my grip on the towel and let it fall to the floor in a heap. Thorne's eyes widened, his pupils dilating with unmistakable desire as his gaze raked over my naked body, lingering on the curves of my breasts. He swallowed hard.

I took a step closer, reaching up to shut his gaping mouth with a finger. "Take a good, long look because you're never going to see this again." With a defiant tilt of my chin, I turned on my heel and sauntered back down the hallway, slamming my door so hard one of his precious paintings crashed to the floor.

24

He was there when I woke up screaming, eyes wide, heart racing. I buried my face under the pillow and wished like hell I could have been sent anywhere else. The Cimmerians had broken me. They'd planted a fear of pain so deep in my soul, I'd never break free. It wasn't death I feared. It was the moments before, when I wasn't in control of my own body, of the pain they'd wreak. Of the tears and the fear and everything they'd likely spent years learning how to coax free.

Thorne knelt beside my bed, brushing sweaty tendrils of hair from my face. "They won't come here. You should know that."

"My mind knows it's irrational. When I'm awake, I'm free of it. But I can't help what happens when I sleep. The nightmares are worse than those days hanging from the ceiling."

His eyes narrowed as he sat on the edge of my bed. "Tell me about the nightmares."

I rolled over, closing my eyes. "Go back to bed, Thorne Noctus. I don't have it in me to do this with you right now."

"I want to help you," he whispered, placing a hand on my bare shoulder.

I lifted the sheets higher, making sure he couldn't see any more of my naked body. "I don't want your help."

"Then tell me what you want. Tell me why you're here. I know nothing of your past, your motives, your dreams. Tell me something. What makes you happy?"

I watched the flame in the lamp flicker as his questions filled the space between us. I didn't want to answer, or even be kind to him. I wanted to stay mad and guarded. But I needed him to trust me. I needed him to believe that I could be useful to him, even if I was starting to question the fact. So I decided to tread lightly. Give a little, but stay on guard, safe behind the walls I'd forged for years and years. "I came to help a friend of mine and somehow we got separated. She's in Death's court now, and I'm here. With nothing and no one. I don't have dreams, only nightmares. And my decision to walk out into your Parlor naked wasn't made without thought. I need you to know that. I was trying to help."

"I know," he said, his voice only a whisper. "I'm sorry about the clothes. They'll be back before you wake."

"I don't care about the clothes. Not really."

The bed rocked as he stood. I let him get a few paces away. "Will you stay? Just until I fall asleep again?"

Rolling over to face him, I waited, watching him weigh the pros and cons, knowing he didn't have it in him to make a single decision without thorough consideration.

After a long moment, he let out a soft sigh. "All right. I'll stay until I know your nightmares are gone."

Relief washed over me as he crossed the room. He grabbed the same chair as the previous night and carried it back, its legs scraping lightly against the floor as he positioned it beside me.

I watched him through heavy-lidded eyes, his tall frame

looking slightly too large for the delicate furniture. He reached over to the nightstand where the stack of books I had borrowed from his study rested beside the little chipped teacup I'd stolen back. Long, deft fingers skimmed over the leather-bound spines before selecting one with a well-worn cover, its gilded title faded. I'd been weak, but he'd bent. A win.

THE DAYS PASSED like molasses sliding down a roof in the dead of winter. I worried and worried about Quill and my ticking time. I followed Thorne around the city, invited but bored out of my mind, and mostly, I kept my eyes and ears open for mention of a door, passage, portal, or even the Keeper, Reverius, god of all the things and names and pain in my ass. We hadn't seen Harlow or Willard, we'd made few trips to the Hollow, and Archer was busy trying to secure a meeting with Alastor, who was apparently giving him the run-around. Thorne had replaced my wardrobe ten-fold, and by the end of the week, I was running out of reading material. Half the study bookshelves were empty, but the piles grew in my room. As did my careful collection of other bits and bobs around the house.

My prized possession was still that chipped teacup, its beauty lived in its flaws, a reminder that perfection was never what made something worth keeping. And though he'd replaced it twice, and questioned how I managed to keep finding it, I continued to steal it back, setting it on the bedside table for him to see each time he came crashing into my room late at night.

I'd grown tired of sitting around by hour two of day one, and with the weight of my days pressing down on me, by day three I couldn't take it anymore and feigned a headache when Thorne announced he was off to run whatever errand he needed to with his driver.

I'd slipped out of the house fifteen minutes later and headed straight to the one place I thought I'd never go back to. Serene's temple. There was no plan if the prince was there. I'd simply have to play the part of a worshiping mortal and take my chances. She'd invited me, I'd returned. It was that simple. I couldn't tell her a thing about my bargain. But maybe gods gossiped and fuck if I wasn't tired of sitting around waiting on fate to figure it out.

The temple, slightly southwest from Thorne's home sat on Banshee's Run. And if that wasn't a sign, I didn't know what was. Still, it was just as I remembered it, save the king's guards standing watch outside. I supposed a goddess needed no such protection. In fact, I was sure she invited all walks of people into her little steamy dominion. As I crossed the threshold, the air thickened with a dizzying blend of jasmine and sandalwood that coiled around me like a lover's embrace.

Just like last time, every surface was adorned with gold and silk, but despite the opulence, an eerie silence filled the space, broken only by the sound of dripping water, a rhythmic pattern that echoed through the cavernous halls feeding off the main room where Lithe had been held.

I followed the sound like a siren's call. I knew it was fucking stupid, but so was waiting for answers to just magically show up. The temple seemed to breathe around me, the walls pulsing as if they were embodying the motion of countless lovers who had come before.

As I walked deeper into the temple's heart, the sound of falling water grew louder until I stepped into a golden bath-house and saw her reclining against the tiled edge of a sunken bath. Naked and resplendent, Serene's skin glistened. Raven tresses spilled over her shoulders and breasts like rivulets of ink. Noticing my presence, her lips curved into a sensuous smile.

"You've returned, Paramour," she purred, her voice a melody that seemed to vibrate my bones and make my skin tremble. "Come closer. The water is divine."

As if in a trance, I walked. The steam from the bath curled around my ankles, beckoning me closer. With each step, the room grew more intoxicating, clouding my thoughts with a haze of desire. As I reached the edge of the sunken bath, I couldn't help but let my gaze travel the length of Serene's body. Her legs were spread invitingly, the water lapping at her inner thighs. Rivulets trickled down her skin, tracing paths I longed to follow with my fingertips, my lips. A flush crept up my neck as I dragged my eyes back to her face, trying desperately to focus on my purpose here. I didn't want to fuck a goddess. I didn't even want to speak to her. In fact, I hated the lack of control. Hated that I couldn't even breathe. And the narrowing of her eyes told me just how much she loved it. She knew what she was doing of course.

"Join me. The water will soothe your troubles, ease the burdens you carry."

I swallowed hard, my throat suddenly parched. The temptation to shed my clothes and slip into the steaming water beside her was nearly overwhelming. To let her touch chase away the paths that haunted me felt like the right answer. I bit the inside of my cheek, letting the metallic tang of blood coat my tongue, if only to remind myself of the true pain she'd caused me when I touched her.

Still, I needed to show her a semblance of respect if I wished to achieve anything other than an orgasm today, though I wouldn't be mad about that either. Preferably from anyone but her. With a deep breath, I closed my eyes. "Forgive me, Goddess, but I must respectfully decline your generous offer." The words felt like gravel in my throat, each syllable a struggle against the overwhelming desire that threatened to consume me. "I come seeking answers, not pleasure, though I am humbled by your invitation."

Serene's laughter echoed through the chamber. "Answers? What makes you think I would answer to you? Do you think just anyone could open the door to my temple, let alone wander through it to find me in such a state? I've done you a favor by letting you look upon me." She drew a hand from the steaming water and the droplets fell down her breasts as she looked down and said, "I will further that favor by letting you taste the water I bathe in. What more could a mortal want than that? Don't you wish to please me?"

Fuck no.

"Yes. But you asked me to dance for you before, and I've thought of nothing else since that moment. If you would allow me, Goddess."

Her eyes closed to slits. "I would believe you, had you not asked for answers first."

"Forgive me, Goddess," I said, bowing my head. "I do seek answers. But I would never presume to demand anything of you." That didn't feel like I was laying it on thick enough, so I kept going, trying not to fumble the words I would have rather vomited over. "I am but a humble beggar, hoping for a glimmer of your divine wisdom."

Serene regarded me silently for a long moment, her fingers idly tracing patterns on the water's surface. "And what answers do you seek, Paramour?" she finally asked, her tone deceptively light.

I'd thought about how I might ask this, the whole way here, and I wasn't sure if it would work or not but I had to try. I couldn't tell anyone about the deal with the big, bad god, but I could maybe skirt around that if she had any context. "I have a... task."

She yawned. "I grow bored already." She waved an arm and a man appeared in the water beside her. Not just any man, but Thorne. Thorne. Naked and glistening and fucking glorious. His hands roamed her body, caressing her skin with a reverence that made my heart ache, though I knew it shouldn't have. Maybe I wanted to do naked things with him, but I also wanted to kind of kill him on a daily basis at some point, so it really didn't mean much.

Serene tilted her head back, a soft moan escaping her lips as Thorne's fingers dipped below the water's surface. Her black hair fanned out around her, undulating gently with each ripple their movements created.

"Well, Paramour?" Serene purred, her voice thick with pleasure. "Care to join us now? I promise, the water feels divine, almost as much as the man."

Thorne turned his head to look at me, hazel eyes smoldering with desire. He extended a hand, droplets cascading down his forearm. "Come, wife," he murmured, his deep baritone sending shivers down my spine. "Let us worship you."

I stood frozen, torn between the overwhelming temptation and the nagging sense that this was wrong, a manipulation. "N... no, thank you."

The goddess stood from the water. Thorne, well, not Thorne, vanished and the entire room changed around us. No longer a bathhouse, but instead the hall where Lithe had been. She sat upon her throne, looking down at me, completely unamused. "I could lie and say I'm completely shocked that you were able to resist my power, but as there's been such an imbalance lately, I'll save us both the lie. Come closer."

All pretenses were gone. No longer the sensuous being she'd

been in the bath, with bedroom eyes and a silky smile, she simply stared at me hard, her gaze unforgiving as I did as I was commanded. She rose as I approached and gripped the sides of my face, though this time it didn't burn so strongly. If anything, the touch was merely a sting. As if the power she'd had during Lithe had completely dissipated. "Speak your question. But only one."

She played no more games and neither would I. "Assuming you know the task I've been given, how am I to complete it?"

"One should never make assumptions."

"True, but here we are."

The corner of her mouth turned up into a hint of a smile. "There's a god on your path soon. Eyes and ears open, Paramour."

"Which—"

She pressed a finger to my lips. "One question answered at no cost. I've been more than generous. Now leave before I change my mind about you."

I thought about Alastor all the way out of the damn temple and all the way back to Thorne's house. The god on the path. At least I was headed in the right direction. As long as he agreed to meet with us, though no one seemed convinced it would happen.

"I was pretty certain I bought clothing for you to sleep in," Thorne said, for zero reason whatsoever as we sat together in silence, both reading in the office.

I looked down at my dress, confused. "I'm fully dressed this morning."

"And I'm running out of shirts."

I snorted. "No one to wash your laundry, husband? You spend one night in that itchy thing and report back. Then we can discuss it." I flipped the page of the book I was reading, slipping back into the romance written across the pages.

"Good book?" he asked, pulling me right back into his study.

"I'll let you know when you're quiet enough for me to decide."

He set his folded paper on his desk. "You've been on that one for days. I'm sure you have an opinion by now."

"I think we both know you don't really want to know what's happening in here."

"Try me."

I straightened in my chair, seeing the opportunity for what it was. "In this one, our male main character has just laid the woman down by the fire and right now, he's got two fingers—"

"Changed my mind," he said, throwing up a hand.

"Checking her pulse because she's just fainted."

"That is *not* what you were about to say."

"Does Thorne Noctus have a dirty mind? What did you think I was about to say?" I asked, knowing full well this man was two fingers deep in a dripping vagina.

He leaned back in his chair, trying to maintain some semblance of composure. "No, I definitely do not."

"My gods, I think you do. I should have said tongue instead."

He leaned closer. "Two tongues instead of fingers? What the hell?"

"That feels like judgment. I don't care for your judgment, sir."

"It's not... I wasn't... You didn't even say tongues. What the fuck is happening right now?"

"You're wishing you had two tongues, I think. Honestly, you're creeping me out."

"I never said that."

I nodded, eyes wide. "I think you did. Maybe more of your subconscious than anything but wow, consider me enlightened.

I probably better hide these books from you. Imagine if I'd have mentioned the dragon tail in the one from last week."

Three knocks sounded at the door, followed by a pause and one more. Thorne let out a long sigh. "Thank fuck. Expecting someone?"

"That's Archer. He and Harlow always knocks the same way, but his is more aggressive."

"Huh. I never realized."

"Well, are you going to let him in or just sit there contemplating knock theory?"

He rose from his chair, closing the book he'd been reading and sliding back onto its very empty shelf. "Tomorrow morning when you're staring at that last piece of fruit and contemplating finishing it, do us both a favor and do it. You're so much more pleasant on a full stomach."

He smirked at my middle finger before leaving to answer the door. I waited a beat, and then leaped up, hustling to the door to eavesdrop down the hall. But there was no need because the two of them came walking in, and I had to quickly pivot and pretend like I was admiring an old painting of a woman with exotic eyes and gold shimmering on her skin.

It surprised me, mostly. Thorne's trust. For whatever reason, something he'd likely spent days considering, he hadn't tried to hide his life and his lies from me. Once I learned he was the Lord of the Salt, it was like he'd opened the door to that world and let me in, unrestricted. He hadn't spoken a word when he caught me reading his letters, hadn't taken many meetings in privacy. If I didn't know any better, I'd swear he was trying to lead me down the promised path without telling me he was doing it. As if it were an unspoken understanding between us. Maybe he knew I was trying to leave this world and whatever I discovered wouldn't matter in a few days, anyway. Maybe the real portal lay somewhere with Alastor. He was a god, after all. And clearly arrogant.

"Hey, Lady Salt, good to see you." Archer paused, stroking a thumb over his smooth chin. "Nope. Doesn't have the right ring to it."

"You'll get there eventually," I said, flopping back down in my chair. "Any luck with Alastor?"

He waited for Thorne to sit. "Actually, yes. He's finally agreed to meet with us. But only at the Hollow and he wouldn't say when. We're supposed to go there and wait for him to show up, I guess."

"An indirect agreement. How god-like," Thorne said, sitting back in his chair. "Did he give any sort of timeline? Are we to sit around for days? Weeks? Until the flowers in Prospector's Pointe bloom for spring?"

While Thorne and Archer discussed the exact phrasing and each detail of the agreement, I lifted my book to hide my face. If I could get back to the Hollow, really spend some time there, maybe I could figure out why it was so important. Or if it was at all. It might've just been a name Reverius had known. A direction and nothing more.

"How many gods do you know?" I asked, sliding the book down when their conversation slowed. "In person, how many?"

"Personally?" Archer asked, playing with a coin. "I've only ever met Alastor twice. And Harlow met Vesalia out and about one day. They don't really mingle amongst the mortals. We've gone to Lithe enough to recognize Serene as well."

Unwilling to ask any burning questions, I let my gaze fall on Thorne. "How about you?"

He stood, walking around the desk to pluck the book from my hand. "I don't think any mortal ever truly knows a god."

What a very political response.

He held a hand out to me and I took it. "Don't pack lightly, Paesha darling. The Hollow is cold at night."

The narrowing of his eyes said more than his words. Sleeping in only his shirt was the last thing he wanted.

"Then maybe you should bring more wood for the fire. There'd be plenty of room if you left your arrogance at home."

"You'd be bored by tomorrow."

"But I'd be warm."

He laughed, really laughed, and it took everything in me to ignore the way it soothed my soul. I balked at the thought. Maybe going to the Hollow was the best option. Putting space between us and the casual routine we'd been building was likely for the best.

"Just bring everything down you want to take, and I'll pack it away for you. There's a proper way to pack a trunk to optimize space and, based on your hoarding tendencies, it's fair to say you have no such talent."

"Do you just wake up and think of all the shitty things you might be able to squeeze into a conversation for the day before rolling out of bed, or do those little treats come to you sporadically?"

"It's a gift really," he said, face blank. "You open so many doors of opportunity."

"And here I thought the two of you were starting to get along," Archer said, rising from his seat.

I rolled my eyes before snatching my book back. "Trust me, this is tame."

"There's no time for reading. We need to leave."

"I'm going to save us both the headache and let you pack for me. Consider it a door of opportunity. You're welcome."

Archer laughed, shook his head, and walked out.

Thorne pulled the book out of my hand again. "Better make sure I don't forget to pack this one."

I reached into the deep pocket of my dress and pulled out another without looking at him. "Good boy. Solid plan."

THE CHAOS within the Hollow was greater than I'd ever seen it. Though I'd only been to the warehouse a few times, it was typically quiet, maybe even somber. But today, people were running back and forth, it was packed with children and the occasional adult, looking around as if lost. Of course Jasper was there, his apron tied on backward and a wooden spoon in his hand, face grim.

"What's happened?" Thorne barked, snatching Harlow by the arm as soon as she tried to shuffle by, a baby in her arms and another young boy clinging to her leg.

She passed the baby to another, and knelt down, whispering to the child and hugging him. He darted away, straight to Jasper. Harlow's eyes filled with tears. "Tilly," was all she could manage.

Thorne softened, pulling her into his massive arms. "Captured?"

She shook her head, burying her face. "Killed trying to keep Reuben away from the Cimmerians."

Tilly... Tilly... I'd heard that name. I'd seen it on some of Thorne's papers.

"Tilly ran the orphanage," Archer whispered into my ear. "You met her husband in the Maw."

The woman they'd saved at Tithe. The one that'd tried to give me courage. Atticus's wife. I held my breath, swallowing the gasp and the twinge of heartache for a woman I never knew.

"What are we going to do with all these children?" Harlow asked moments later, stepping back.

"The same thing you've been doing," I answered, though I

knew it wasn't my place. "Feed them, keep them warm, let them sleep with both eyes shut. That's the best thing you can do."

"We can't take them back to Tilly's," Harlow said, looking up at Thorne. "Farris heard Reuben has magic, and he completely destroyed the place trying to find him. He told everyone Reuben stole a chest from Tithe."

"He's twelve!" Archer scoffed. "Who's going to believe that?"

Thorne lifted a shoulder. "They don't need to believe it. He just needs an excuse to capture him. Reuben will be tested and bound by nightfall."

Harlow swiped away the tears and hardened her beautiful face. "Then I guess I better get going."

"Don't be ridiculous, Har. You know it's too late. There's no way you'll be able to get to him."

"I'll go too," Willard said, pushing around the children to join the conversation. "That's what we're discussing, right? Reuben?"

"It's a death wish," Archer said. "If you get caught..."

"I'll go too," I added.

"No!" Everyone but Thorne said in unison.

When they all realized the deep timbre of his voice was missing, they spun to him.

"I can help. Let me."

"I won't take the choice away from you. But if you're caught, there'll be no question about your death if one of the Cimmerians recognizes you."

He wasn't wrong. And the lingering gaze said everything I knew his words hadn't. If I was locked back into the Maw and somehow managed a second escape, I'd never sleep again. He wouldn't put his foot down. He wouldn't lord his command over me. But that only meant it was my job to be responsible enough to see the danger and shy away from it. And though he didn't know it, this wasn't my future. None of this was about me. I wasn't even supposed to be in this world. I didn't care. Not for them. Not for him. Not even for that little boy. And I was not a fucking hero.

"No, you're right," I said, taking a step backward. "I'll stay here. Maybe see if Jasper can use my help in the kitchen."

I wiped every thought from showing on my face as I returned his stare.

He waited. One moment and then two before turning his back to me and addressing the others. "Be quick, be smart, and don't risk yourselves for him. If you can't get him out, we'll reconvene in the morning."

"You're not coming?" Harlow asked, hand resting on what I assumed was a blade hidden under her skirts.

"I'm going to bait Farris into a chase with the *real* Lord of the Salt to keep as many of his men as busy as I can. Don't lead them back here. If you get the boy, take him to your place and wait for me."

It took every ounce of self-control I had to stick to my selfish plan as I watched them all walk out that door, knowing I'd touched that boy. I knew exactly where he was.

25

The walls creaked their lullabies to the night while distant snores spoke of dreams. Though a few adults were scattered through the room, most had gone, giving the children the time to acclimate and grieve. I imagined that choice meant they were sleeping in the alleys. The children, nestled on cots and snuggling on piles of blankets near the fire, deserved more attention than I could manage. No matter how much I'd tried to be present, no matter how many chins I wiped and bedtime stories I read, I'd watched the door like a hawk. Each moment that passed in silence was a burden. I should have gone. I should have told them about my power.

I'd used it, of course. Occasionally, the magic was strong enough to show me clouded visions of spaces and I kept trying and trying to see glimpses as I sat in the Hollow, forced smile on my face so I didn't rattle the children that had been orphaned twice in their short lives. No visuals of Reuben came to me, but I knew he wasn't in the Maw, which was my biggest concern. Instead, I felt the pull of magic leading me toward Serene, the

Goddess of Lust's temple. Not specifically there, but somewhere very close. And he hadn't moved at all.

I hardly had time to talk to Jasper. He managed the kitchen chores, while I had kept the kids entertained with stories about dragons and sword fights and death maidens tricked into marrying the wrong men. I spoke to them of giant beasts with great big wings, and witches stirring their pots. I remembered bits and pieces of my favorite stories and wove them together as much as I could. Until the yawns followed the sleepy eyes and, one by one, they went to bed. One girl, Lianna, had stayed up well past midnight, staring at the fire, knees clutched to her chest, little blonde ringlets brushing slender shoulders. She'd wiped her tears in silence, and I didn't shove myself in. She was mourning a woman that must've been a saint to wrangle all of these children, day in and day out. She'd earned those tears. Deserved the love these children had for her.

Eventually, after Jasper was long gone, Lianna sank to the floor, wrapping herself in blankets before the sniffles faded away and her dreams took her somewhere else. Anywhere else. When I was a child and the days were the bleakest, sleep was always a welcomed reprieve. I hoped she'd find the same.

Though I'd been told of a bedroom upstairs, I kept a cot near the door instead, waiting and watching for any of the crew to come back.

Any luck?

I'd written those two words into the little golden book a while ago, but no answer came. Which was probably for the best. Distracted bait would be dangerous. The moon and the song of the crackling fireplace were my only companion for hours. The fire was little more than charred logs before there was a sound at the door, a scraping at first and then a creak as it opened.

I lay stiff as a board, holding my breath, wrapping my fingers around the dagger Harlow had given me. Squinting through the dark as a shape took form, the first light of day haloed him and my heart sank. It was Jasper. He kicked a loose board and went tumbling forward, hissing and scolding himself. "Shh. Quiet, you old fool. You'll wake the lot of 'em."

He straightened himself and froze, turning to watch over the sleeping people until he was convinced he'd been quiet as a mouse. Then off he went, tiptoeing into the kitchen. I didn't immediately follow. I needed to see someone else walk through that door, but no one did and the twins were nowhere near.

Invisible, but there, the aroma of freshly baked bread drew me in less than an hour later, a symphony of flour, yeast, and sweet buttery notes pirouetting in an inviting waltz. I padded softly to the kitchen, lulled by curiosity and an inability to sleep. Because if I had a nightmare, the screaming would wake the children.

"Well, Miss Paesha, you're up early."

"I could say the same about you."

"An old habit from my previous work as a cook's assistant at a noblewoman's estate. Any word from our team yet?"

"I was hoping you'd heard something. Guess not?"

"Not a word."

"Damn."

"Care to jump in? Might take your mind off worrying about your husband." He gestured toward the counter littered with flour sacks, butter pots and eggs still nestled in their straw baskets. "A helping hand is always welcome at the Hollow."

Rolling up my sleeves, I admitted, "I'm not much of a cook beyond bread and basic soup, but I'm a quick study and I know my way around a blade."

"In the kitchen, we call them knives, Miss Paesha. Now, I've started the bread already. Perhaps you could help with the eggs. One egg cracked is one mouth fed." He gently kneaded the last bit of dough he'd made. "Our lot may not have much, but we are rich in company."

I gathered the eggs from the straw basket, careful not to break a single one. I could likely hide in the kitchen and be useful somehow while I snooped around, if I was patient and observant enough. And fortunately, I was proficient in both. Mostly.

"To crack an egg, you must be firm yet gentle. Tap it against the edge of the bowl and give it a soft squeeze." His large, callused hands moved through the air, mimicking the action.

I did as he said, holding the egg tightly in my hand. The shell shattered under my grip, dropping the yolk into a bowl on the long counter.

My technique drew a hearty laugh from the old cook. "You'll have to learn finesse, young lady."

"Hey, now. I was born with finesse."

He chuckled. "All the best women are."

From then on, I was at his side whisking eggs into frothy clouds, stirring pots of simmering oats sweetened with brown sugar and cinnamon. Jasper was magical. He took what little there was and made miracles out of it, simple ingredients transformed into hearty dishes that would warm souls as much as bellies.

He'd told stories because he believed I was so distraught waiting for my new husband to return. I had no idea if he knew Thorne was the infamous Lord of the Salt, but he certainly had no idea our marriage was a lie.

The little golden book never warmed against my skin, and I tried not to think about it too much. I mostly smiled and nodded, keeping an ear out for newcomers and occasionally using my magic to lock onto the three of the four I could. Harlow and Willard were together, somewhere near the vicinity of the boy, but Archer was moving through the city. That was all I knew.

We worked through the morning preparing the meager feast for those that would soon wake and some that had already popped into the kitchen to offer to help. Jugs of water boiled for tea while a small bit of bacon sizzled and popped in a cast iron skillet.

"Here's a funny one," Jasper said, collecting the spoons he'd dropped all over the floor. "Once, when I was working for the noblewoman, I was tasked with preparing a seven-course feast for her Silk guests. Everything had to be perfect, from the spiced wine to the roast pheasant. To make matters worse, the noblewoman had a temper as volatile as dragon's fire. It was enough to turn any man into a bundle of nerves.

"I remember it was the morning of the feast, and I had rolled out a massive pie crust on one of her expansive mahogany tables. I had to. There was no other working surface large enough. The flour dusted everything. It turned my arms and apron white, and even settled in my hair, turning my brown locks gray.

"But as I was about to lift the crust and wrap it around the pie dish, a hulking, ornate ceramic deal that looked more like it belonged in a museum than a kitchen, I felt a tickle in my nose. I tried to hold back the sneeze and forgot to pay attention to these clumsy feet, and I tripped on the rug.

"The pie crust blew up into the air like a sail caught in a gale, flour exploding off it in clouds of white. It landed on the chandelier hanging above the table. The kitchen staff watched in stunned silence as my lovely crust hung from those crystal pendants like some strange doughy curtain."

He paused as he dramatically mimicked his past shock with an exaggerated gasp and wide eyes.

"Naturally, I was horrified. Not at my lost pastry, which had taken hours to perfect but at the prospect of facing the noblewoman's wrath. I decided to climb up a ladder and try to remove the dough from the chandelier, but just as I reached for it, the noblewoman entered the kitchen."

While delivering his animated story, Jasper gathered three sacks of flour at once from where they'd been sitting on the floor. I had to snap my jaw shut to hide my surprise as he casually moved them onto the counter. Then I remembered the giant pot he'd carried the first time I met him. He was clumsy, sure, but he hadn't struggled. No ordinary man was lifting three sacks that were the size of me. Jasper had magic. And he'd used it so casually.

He ripped into one of the bags, spilling flour everywhere as he continued his story. "Her eyes found mine and then followed the path upwards to where my pie crust was hanging. The silence in that room could have curdled milk. She opened her mouth to say something, her face contorted in horror. But, just at that moment, the crust fell straight down and onto her head."

He paused again, his chest shaking with laughter at his own story. I couldn't help but share a small smile, the image of a haughty noblewoman wearing a crust hat now imprinted vividly in my mind. Jasper was a storyteller. And gods I loved stories.

"Needless to say, I was fired on the spot. I had to grab my things right there and then, didn't even get to see how my pastry tasted."

His infectious energy made our work feel lighter, the anticipation less daunting.

"And now," he added after wiping tears from his eyes, "I serve this hodgepodge of misfits here at the Hollow. And I wouldn't trade them for all the fancy cakes and pies in the world. Cooking is a lot like life. Sometimes you have to make do with what you have, and sometimes things don't turn out the way you planned. But in the end, it's all about the people you share it with."

These moments were odd. I didn't want to care. I didn't want to understand the people here and feel anything for them. I didn't want to lay my head on my pillow when I got home and wonder what had happened to them all in the years to come. I wanted my walls. I wanted the distance. I wanted to be selfish. But today, at the height of my worry, I just wasn't strong enough to keep it.

People were just people, after all. No matter what street they lived on. No matter what fabric they threw over their shoulders, what they valued. No matter the power we hid or the lies we told. And I couldn't pretend this place didn't matter or that these people and all their dreams were less important than my own.

I was about to respond when a commotion erupted outside the Hollow. Shouts and the clatter of hooves against cobblestones shattered the quiet space. Jasper's jovial expression instantly transformed into one of alarm. In a flurry of movement belying his age, he rushed out of the kitchen.

"Children, come quickly! Get the little ones. That's right." His arms flailed in the air as he stood near the table, gesturing wildly for everyone's attention. "Someone's spotted the prince's guard. We must hide."

The children, rubbing sleep from their eyes, stumbled out of their cots. Lianna herded them together like a protective mother hen, her blonde curls bouncing as she moved. Jasper ushered them down a narrow hallway, his large frame nearly blocking out the dim light.

With one of the youngest wrapped in my arms, I followed

close behind, my heart hammering against my ribs at the thought of the Cimmerians busting in. Jasper stopped before a nondescript door, yanking it open to reveal a small, dark space. Coats and cloaks hung from pegs, and a musty smell wafted out. A closet.

"In you go, little ones. Quickly now," Jasper urged in a hushed but firm tone. The children filed in one by one. Lianna, the few adults that stayed behind, and I all helped the smallest ones. Jasper handed out the thickest cloaks to wrap around them. "Not a peep, you hear? No matter what."

Wide, frightened eyes peered up at us from the depths of the closet, pale faces illuminated by the meager light filtering through the cracks. My heart clenched at the sight. These children, so young and innocent, huddled together seeking warmth and comfort after whatever trauma they'd experienced the day before.

Jasper pulled the adults to the side and whispered, "Stay with them. Keep them calm and quiet. Don't open this door for anyone but me or the others from our team. Understand?"

"What about you?" I asked.

"I'll see what all the ruckus is and report back."

Jasper slipped out of the closet, shutting the door with a soft click that resonated in the sudden, oppressive silence. Most of the adults shifted to the back. I settled down on the floor, cradling the babe close to my chest. The little one's warmth and gentle breathing were a small comfort amidst the tension.

I couldn't imagine how scared the children were. After the trauma from yesterday, there would probably always be a part of the older ones that felt a kernel of fear when it came to authority. Lianna held two of the younger ones, whispering soothing words I couldn't quite make out. A boy, no more than six, had silent tears streaming down his cheeks. I reached out and gently wiped them away with my thumb, offering a reassuring smile.

"No tears today," I whispered, so faint I wasn't sure he'd heard me at all.

I strained my ears for any hint of what was happening outside. Muffled shouts and the clanging of metal on metal filtered through, each sound making them flinch and huddle closer together. There wasn't much I could do, aside from passing the baby to another as I shifted to the front of the pack, placing myself between whatever may come barreling in and a room full of terrified children.

Footsteps grew closer and I pulled the blade Harlow had given me from my thigh, gripping it tightly as I forced steel into my veins. With a sudden whoosh, the door flew open, hinges creaking in protest. Light spilled into the closet, temporarily blinding us after the prolonged darkness.

As the silhouette in the doorway came into focus, I nearly dropped the blade. Harlow stood there, her blonde hair disheveled and streaked with mud and a mask covering the lower half of her face, but her eyes burning with relief. Beside her, clutching her hand tightly, was the young boy that'd crashed into me at Tithe. With a shock of fiery red hair and freckles that dotted his nose and cheeks, I doubted he'd be easy to hide from the prince for long.

"Reuben!" Lianna cried out, her voice cracking with emotion. The boy tore away from Harlow and dashed into the closet, flinging himself into Lianna's open arms. She hugged him fiercely, tears falling as she murmured incoherent words.

Harlow's gaze fell on the blade still gripped tightly in my hand. She gave an approving nod, a flicker of respect dancing in her eyes. "It's safe now. You can all come out."

The children began to stir, untangling themselves from the

huddle of cloaks and limbs. Filing into the hallway, I caught Harlow's arm. "What happened? Is everyone all right?"

She nodded. "Cimmerians gave chase. They tracked us almost all the way to the Hollow. Thorne and Archer led them off while Willard and I snuck Reuben in through the back. It was a near thing, but we made it, thanks to Willard's quick thinking. He yanked us into a nearby alcove to hide as the Cimmerians ran by and we were able to follow behind them. Everything is fine."

"Almost," I said, watching the door as we walked back into the main room. "But not quite yet."

"They should be back soon." She glanced down at the dagger still clutched in my hand and smirked. "Looks like you were ready for a fight."

"Old habits."

Harlow pulled her skirt to the side, revealing a lot of leg and a black leather strap holding a dagger. "Same."

Jasper and a few of the adults helped feed the children. Harlow and I busied ourselves just to pass the time. We took turns staring at the door, her waiting on her brother, me on a man that was supposed to lead me home. Thorne was likely a step on the path, just as the Hollow was, and I knew in my soul this meeting with Alastor was important for me. His part in this couldn't have been a coincidence. He was a god, afterall.

Time was such a bitch. It dragged like a slow, mournful tune when I begged it to hurry, then quickened to a wild tempo the moment I needed it to linger. And somehow, in this single moment, it did both, until finally the door slammed open and Archer and Thorne limped in.

I stared at both men in shock. Based on Harlow's tiny gasp, she hadn't missed the blood either.

26

Thorne stumbled through the doorway, his face pale and his jaw clenched tight with pain. Blood dripped from his left arm, staining the floor with crimson splatters. The fabric of his shirt was torn, revealing a deep gash across his bicep that oozed steadily.

"What happened?" I rushed forward to help support his weight. He leaned heavily against me, his breath coming in short, pained gasps.

"Later," he managed through gritted teeth. "Not here."

Understanding dawned as I glanced over at the wide-eyed children huddled together, their gazes fixed on Thorne's injury with a mix of fear and morbid curiosity. Nodding, I guided him towards the kitchen, away from their prying eyes, as he put very little weight on his left leg.

I helped him into a chair and quickly gathered supplies, clean cloths, a basin of warm water, and a needle and thread. Thorne watched me through half-lidded eyes, his face drawn with pain.

"Take off your shirt," I said, my voice surprisingly steady despite the adrenaline coursing through my veins.

He quirked an eyebrow, a ghost of his usual smirk playing at the corners of his mouth. "If you wanted me undressed, all you had to do was ask."

"I'm not playing with you. Do as you're told."

"It's just a scratch."

"Prove it."

Thorne huffed out a pained laugh as he struggled to remove his shirt with his one good arm. "Only because you asked so nicely."

I stepped forward to help, carefully peeling the blood-soaked fabric away from his wound. He hissed. The gash was deep and jagged, starting at his shoulder and trailing down to his bicep. It would definitely need stitches. And fortunately, I'd seen Elowen do this enough times, I felt confident. After dipping the cloth in the warm water, I cleaned the wound, my brow furrowed in concentration.

Thorne watched me work, his dark eyes following my every move. "You're surprisingly good at this. Patching up wounded men a common occurrence for you? Back in Misby?"

"My old boss liked violence."

He nodded, hissing again as I dabbed the gash. "Is that why you ran? Why you won't say where you're really from?"

"No. He died." Twice actually, but that was a story for another time. Or perhaps never at all. "Now, hush. I'm trying to concentrate."

I threaded the needle, my hands steady despite the weight of Thorne's gaze. As I stitched the wound closed, he remained silent, his jaw clenched against the pain. The only sound in the kitchen was his measured breathing and the soft slide of the thread through his flesh.

I tied off the final stitch and Thorne let out a long, shuddering breath. "Thank you."

I met his gaze. "You're welcome,"

He reached out with his uninjured arm, his fingertips grazing my cheek in a feather-light caress. I froze, my heart stuttering at the unexpected touch. Thorne's fingers lingered on my cheek. For a moment, the world narrowed to just the two of us, the kitchen fading away as I lost myself in the depths of his dark eyes. They held a vulnerability I hadn't seen before, a rawness that made my breath catch. He never lost control. Never rose to take the bait. Whatever had happened, rattled him. Which bothered me more than anything. This man had been unbreakable. Stoic. Studious. A rock. And he'd been shaken.

"Thorne, I..." My voice trailed off, the words stuck on my tongue.

He leaned in closer, his breath ghosting across my lips. The air between us crackled with tension that set my nerves on fire. I could feel the heat of his body, the steady thrum of his heartbeat beneath my fingertips as they rested on his chest.

Time seemed to slow, stretching out into an infinite moment as we hovered on the precipice of something dangerous. But then the kitchen door swung open with a bang, shattering the spell. I jerked back, my cheeks flushing hot as Willard strode into the room. If he noticed the charged atmosphere, he didn't show it. His brow was furrowed with concern as he took in Thorne's bandaged arm. "How bad is it?"

Thorne straightened, his mask of cool indifference slipping back into place. "Just a scratch. Paesha handled it."

"The arm is taken care of, but what happened to your leg? You were limping."

"It's just a bruise. I took a hard kick to the thigh."

The faint lines around Willard's brown eyes deepened. "I'll

never be able to repay you for this." He pointed to his stitched arm. "If you hadn't gotten there, I don't know what would have happened."

Thorne clapped a hand over Willard's shoulder. "I saw what you did, Will. When those Cimmerians cornered Harlow in that alley, you didn't hesitate. You threw yourself between her and them, shielding her with your own body."

Willard ducked his head, a flush creeping up his neck. "I did what anyone would have done. What you did for us."

But Thorne shook his head, his grip tightening on Willard's shoulder. "No. You fought like a lion. And thanks to your masks, they never saw your faces. Never discredit quick wit."

"I'm just glad we all made it back in one piece," Harlow said from the door. "But we need to take this upstairs with less prying eyes. The rest of the Salt are starting to trickle in. Anna's asking for you, Thorne."

"I had Jasper bring our stuff inside. Will, would you mind getting me a fresh shirt? I need to discuss something with my wife."

"Sure, boss."

He waited until the kitchen door shut completely before limping over to me, brushing a stray lock of hair from my face, and lifting my chin until I was staring into eyes that were becoming far too comfortable. "Farris is getting more dangerous by the minute. Desperate even. He's not happy that he can't have full control and he's collecting magic users."

"I gathered that," I whispered, too aware of his thumb on my chin.

"I pulled you into this because I thought I was saving you from something. But now, I'm wondering if I didn't damn you instead. He'll never stop, Paesha. He's going to push and push until his father is dead and he's sitting on the throne. And then he'll turn into a conqueror, spreading his wings and burning down cities all over this world. Men like him... they will never have enough. They'll never be happy."

My gaze shifted between his. Confused. "Why are you telling me all this?"

"Because you need to leave."

My heart dropped. For a second I thought he was telling me he knew. That he was to be my guide out. But I was wrong. He only meant him. He wanted me to leave him.

"I'm not—"

He raised his voice, anger flaring as if that would get his point across. "This isn't a life you signed up for. I damned you that day, don't you see it?"

Pressing my hands to his chest, I shoved. "I don't care that you're hurt. I don't even care that you're trying to be fucking chivalrous. If I wanted out, I would just walk out the door. You don't get to say my decisions are my own and then turn around and tell me to leave. I can help you. Let me."

He used the counter to balance himself, putting no weight on his bruised leg. The fire burning in my soul was, again, confusing. Was I fighting to be here because I had to get home, or was it because I actually had something to offer this realm before I went back to mine?

I wanted to ask him. The words were sitting right on the tip of my tongue.

What do you know, Thorne? What are you hiding?

But I couldn't do it. Not yet. Not while he sat on the very brink of forcing me out the door. He needed to need me. Only then would he trust me enough to help. And only then would I feel confident enough to ask for it.

"Come on, Fingers, It's just a game."

I lifted a brow to Archer. "Fingers?"

Sitting across from me at the giant dinner table planted in the center of the Hollow, he held up two hands and wiggled every finger. "Because yours are sticky."

I didn't blink as I slowly shook my head. "Absolutely not."

"Aw. Come on. It's the perfect name."

"Fingers is *not* a nickname. How'd you like it if I called you a random body part?"

Willard circled the table, filling my cup with a sweet red wine. "Anything's better than Wee Willy."

"Wee Willy is also an excellent nickname," Archer said, shuffling his deck of cards. "Now who's in?"

I glanced at Thorne leaning against the door to the kitchen reading a book, lost in his own world. As if he'd felt my eyes on him, he looked up, eyes locking with mine, stealing my breath. Gods I hated him for that power of his. A slow, lazy smile curved his lips as he closed his book with a soft snap and pushed off the doorframe, his movements fluid and graceful despite the slight limp in his step.

As he sauntered towards the table, I couldn't tear my eyes away from the way his shirt stretched across his broad shoulders, the fabric clinging to the hard planes of his chest. Heat bloomed in my cheeks and I quickly took a swig of wine, averting my gaze.

"I think I'll sit this one out," Thorne said, his deep voice sending a shiver down my spine. He slid into the chair beside me, close enough that I could feel the warmth radiating from his body.

Archer grinned, his eyes twinkling with mischief. "Suit yourself, boss. More winnings for me then."

Thorne leaned in closer, his breath hot against my ear. "My money's on you, Paesha darling."

I looked over at the children sitting before the fire, listening to Lianna read them a story. "You can't use money here. It's not right."

"Don't worry, we never play with real coin in the Hollow. It's all in good fun."

I turned to face him, our noses almost brushing. Up close, I could see the flecks of gold in his hazel eyes. "Archie boy here seems to play a lot of cards. You think I can beat him?"

I knew I could. The question was, how much of myself did I want to give away? But I couldn't help the desire to wipe the cocky grin off his face.

Thorne's lips quirked up at the corners as he whispered. "I know you can. Archer's overconfident. He thinks he's unbeatable. But you..." He trailed off, his eyes roaming over my face. "I've studied you. You're clever. Quick. You notice things others miss. Use that to your advantage. Don't get lost in his reactions. He'll try to bluff his way to a win."

I turned to Archer. "All right. I'll play. But I've never done it before, so you'll have to teach me."

Archer slammed the cards down on the table, eyes lighting with excitement as he fanned them out. "Excellent. We'll play Maid Marian. It's really simple. See this card here?"

I nodded as he tapped on the card with a woman on it.

"There are four in the deck but for the sake of this game, we pull the others out. She's the goal. We're trying to rescue her. Each player is dealt fifteen cards. The rest stay in the draw pile, including the Maid Marian. High card wins. We both put a card in the middle and flip them at the same time. Whoever has the highest card wins that round. You take both the cards you won and put them to the side and since you won, you get to draw a card from the draw pile. Your goal is to draw Maid Marian. She's worth fifty points. The cards you've won are worth their face value. Once Maid Marian is drawn, the game is over and whoever has the highest number of points wins. Simple enough?"

"I'm a learn-as-you-go kind of player. I think I've got the gist of it. Just go easy on me."

He winked, gathering the cards. "Beginner's luck will carry you through the first game. Don't worry. Anyone else want to join us?"

Willard spun his chair around, resting his arms on the high back. "I think I'll watch this time."

Harlow pushed away from the table, collecting the leftover plates. "I'm going to help Jasper in the kitchen. Join me, Will? An extra hand with all these mouths is so helpful."

His eyes flicked back and forth between her and the end of the table where we'd perched. "You sure you need another person in there fumbling around?"

"If you don't want to—"

"No, no. It's fine. I'll come help." He hopped up from his seat, spun it back around, and nudged me. "Good luck."

"She won't need it," Thorne said, wrapping an arm over the back of my chair. "I have a feeling she's going to be excellent at cards."

I turned to Archer with a smile. "All right, Toes, deal me in. But first, may I?" I held out my hand for the deck of cards.

Archer's brows lifted in surprise, but he passed them over readily enough. "Be my guest, Fingers."

I ignored the nickname and shuffled, the cards moving deftly between my hands, the worn edges soft beneath my fingertips, the faded images blurring as I mixed the deck with quick, practiced movements.

"Whoa, whoa, whoa. I thought you said you'd never played before. Did I just get tricked before the first card is dealt?"

"Ruthless," Thorne echoed with a chuckle, his finger blazing a trail of fire along my neck.

I smiled sweetly at Archer as I finished shuffling and dealt out the cards with a flick of my wrist. "I said I'd never played this particular game before. But I know my way around a deck."

Archer narrowed his eyes, studying me intently as he picked up his cards. One of the little boys came to sit beside him and he flashed the boy his hand. "This'll be interesting."

The boy nodded, sharing a missing-toothed grin. A few of the others gathered around the table, some taking seats, some just standing back to watch.

"This is when you'd normally place a bet," Thorne said. "You'd evaluate your hand and put as much in the pot as you wanted based on your confidence or lack thereof. Then, you'd play out the game and whoever wins would get the pot at the end.

I tapped my fingers along the stack of cards I hadn't peeked at yet with a smile. "I'll bet you dishes for the rest of the time we're here that I'll win."

"You can look at your cards before you make a bet," Archer said, moving around the cards in his hand.

"No need," I grinned. "Beginner's luck. Right?"

He hesitated, eyes lingering on his cards before swiping a hand through his hair. A tell, maybe. Was he nervous? Or setting a bluff?

"All right. I'll take that bet. I sure hope your hands aren't sensitive to soap and water."

"Nah, I'll be fine."

He huffed a laugh. "You hope."

I gathered the cards from the table, fanning them out for show. Watching. Waiting. I couldn't see his cards and he couldn't see mine, but I knew the Maid Marian card was eight down from the top of the deck and this was about to be a very short game.

He plucked a card from his hand a second before I made my choice and for the first flip, he counted down. "Three, two, one."

The smile vanished from his face as he laid eyes on my five. Archer's plan was immediately obvious. He'd played a four, testing whether I'd play a high card or a low card out of the gate. He certainly hadn't expected me to play in the middle just like him.

"So, that's nine points for me? I add the four and the five and I also get to draw. Is that right?" I asked, knowing the answer.

"You've got it," Thorne said.

I drew my card, knowing it was a nine before I slid it into my hand. "Ready again?"

Archer made his choice and I made mine. Again, we flipped them.

"Oh hey, good job," I said. sliding the ten and the one toward him.

Ten was the highest point card, and he'd only won a single point with it. Still he smiled, though I could see the tension in his shoulders as he drew his card from the deck and showed the boy. "Maid Marian is hiding."

The little boy pushed his dark hair from his eyes and leaned on Archie's arm. "Plenty of time to whoop her."

"There'll be no whooping," I chided, waiting for Archer to select his next card.

Archer's brow furrowed in concentration. The boy looked at him, made the exact same face and pointed to his pick. I could practically see the gears turning as Archer tried to predict my next move.

We flipped our cards in unison, the sound of the worn paper snapping against the wood. Archer had played a seven, a respectable card. But I had played my nine.

A collective gasp rose from the onlookers as I scooped up the cards, adding them to my growing pile. Archer's mouth pressed into a thin line, his eyes narrowing as he studied me intently.

I met his gaze with a serene smile, the picture of innocence. "Beginner's luck, right?"

He didn't respond, instead drawing his next card with a sharp flick of his wrist. The little boy patted his arm in consolation.

We continued to play, the tension mounting with each flip of the cards. Archer's pile remained small as I won round after round, my stack of cards growing ever higher. I'd given him a couple of small wins. On the seventh rotation, with Maid Marian next in the draw pile, I took my time, sliding my hand over my cards, pretending like I just couldn't decide what to do.

"What happens if you run out of cards before the Maid Marian is found?" I asked, knowing that wasn't going to happen.

He forced a smile. "Then the game is over, and you win by default."

"Well, that's not as fun, now is it?"

Archer huffed but said nothing back.

Thorne hadn't offered an ounce of advice. Hadn't weighed in or made a single sound as we played. For a man that lived to tell other people how to function, his silence was almost unnerving. His gaze was heavy on my profile, watching my every move like a hawk. Was he trying to read my tells? Gain some insight into my strategy? If so, he would be sorely disappointed. I had perfected every mask I wore long ago, showing calm indifference no matter what cards I held. And that was probably the biggest thing he and I had in common.

I finally selected a card, holding it between my fingers as I waited for Archer to make his choice. He hesitated, his hand hovering over his dwindling options. He licked his lips nervously. The little boy leaned in close, whispering something in his ear.

With a sharp exhale, he plucked a card from his hand and held it ready. We locked eyes across the table, a silent challenge passing between us. Then, as one, we flipped our cards. Archer had played a nine. A strong card, one that would have bested most others. But I had played my ten.

A shocked silence fell over the room as I moved the cards to my side and selected the top card from the draw pile. I gasped, putting on a show as I laid the beautiful woman face up on the table. "Maid Marian! I win!"

Archer stared at the Maid Marian card laying face up on the table, his expression a mix of disbelief and grudging admiration. Slowly, a rueful grin spread across his face. He shook his head. "Well played, Fingers."

The little boy clapped his hands in delight, his eyes shining with excitement as he echoed Archer's gracious loss.

Archer stood from the table, gathering up the cards. The dim candlelight caught the silver of his rings, and with a flourish, he presented the deck to me, bowing low in a gesture of respect. "I concede defeat to a worthy opponent. The dishes are yours to command, my lady."

I accepted the cards with a gracious nod, the corners of my mouth twitching with a suppressed smile. "You put up a valiant fight, Toes. Have fun with the suds."

Just as Archer was walking into the kitchen, Jasper walked out, nearly running into him. The old cook wiped his hand across his brow and laughed, stepping to the side to let Archer through before walking to the table to collect a couple bowls. I immediately jumped up to help, gathering the rest of the empty dishes.

"You'll have to excuse my state," the old cook said, gesturing to the dusting of flour down his shirt. "I've lost my apron."

"Again?" Thorne asked, taking the dishes from me, though I hadn't asked for help.

"Did you see it this morning, Miss Paesha?"

I handed Thorne the last two cups and spoke without thinking. "It's under the sink next to a bunch of glass jars."

The second the words were out of my mouth, I knew I'd made a mistake. There was no way I could have possibly known that. The old cook didn't question it for a second as he raised a finger into the air. "That's right. I meant to put it in the washing pile and tucked it down there with the soap." He swept back into the kitchen.

It wasn't the cook I was worried about though. It was the man at my side that never missed a single red flag. "Paesha darling," Thorne asked, hovering over my shoulder, his curious tone walking down my spine. "How could you have known that?"

I spun to look at him, panicking, but holding my practiced neutral face. "You heard him. He meant to put it in the washing pile this morning. I was helping him."

He shook his head, leaning closer. "I don't think that's what he said at all."

"Next time, I'll be sure to reiterate every word verbatim. Just for you."

Thorne's brow furrowed, clearly undeterred by my brush off. He opened his mouth to press further, but I quickly cut him off.

"Why are you making a big deal out of this? So I saw him stash his apron earlier. Who cares?"

"He had that apron on before he started cooking dinner and you haven't been in the kitchen since."

I held my stance. "You sure you didn't get hit in the head earlier? Might want to find that healer and have them check it out."

I tried to step around him, but Thorne's hand shot out, gently grasping my elbow. I froze, my skin tingling where he touched me. He leaned in close. "I know there's more to you than meets the eye, Paesha darling. And I intend to uncover all your secrets. One by one."

"So ominous. Have you been practicing?" I patted his chest. "Good luck with that." I said, and then promptly walked to the kitchen, Thorne's scrutinizing eyes burning into my spine as I left.

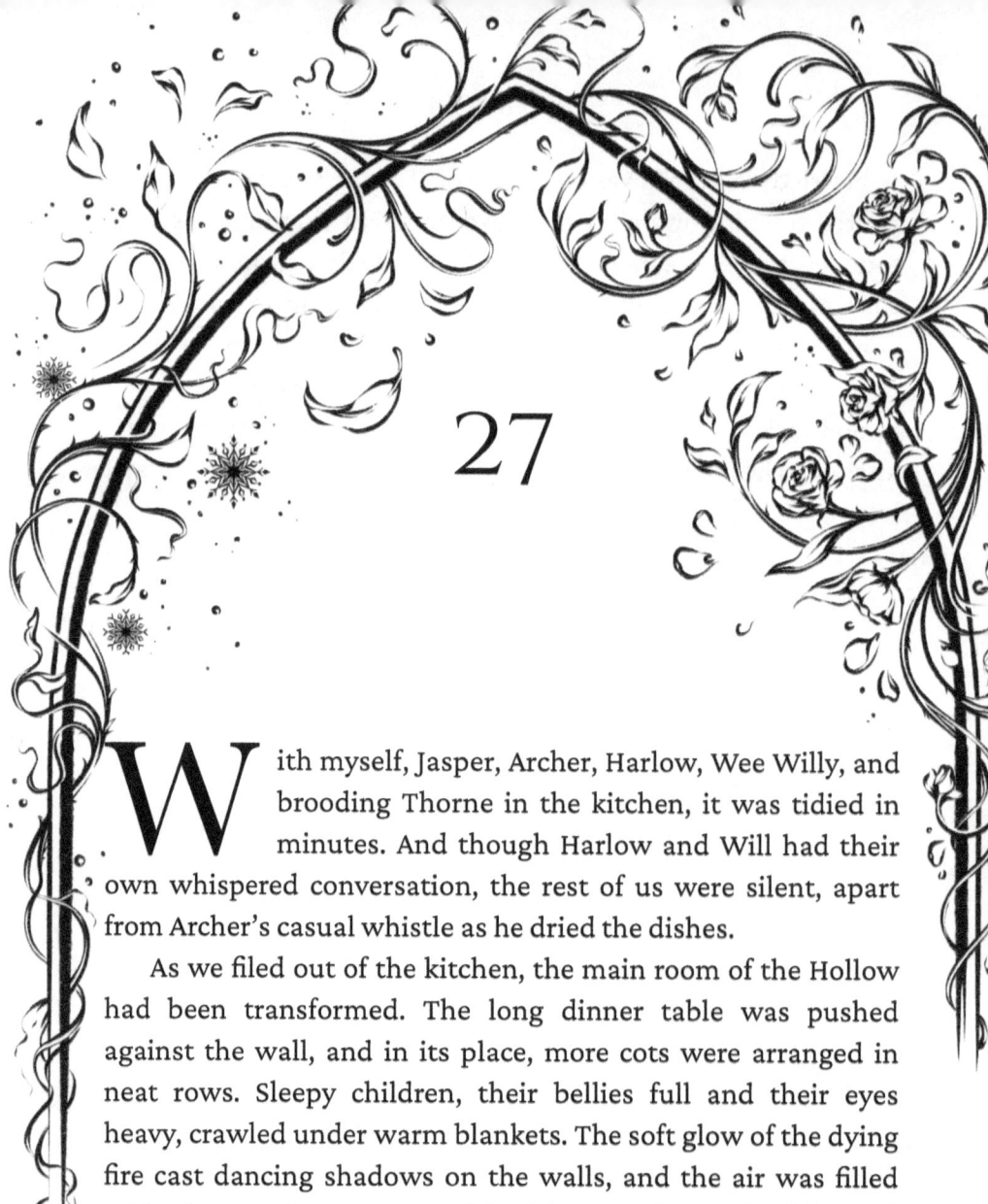

27

With myself, Jasper, Archer, Harlow, Wee Willy, and brooding Thorne in the kitchen, it was tidied in minutes. And though Harlow and Will had their own whispered conversation, the rest of us were silent, apart from Archer's casual whistle as he dried the dishes.

As we filed out of the kitchen, the main room of the Hollow had been transformed. The long dinner table was pushed against the wall, and in its place, more cots were arranged in neat rows. Sleepy children, their bellies full and their eyes heavy, crawled under warm blankets. The soft glow of the dying fire cast dancing shadows on the walls, and the air was filled with the gentle murmur of bedtime stories and whispered goodnights.

In the corner, a man sat cross-legged on a worn cushion, a battered fiddle cradled in his hands. He drew the bow across the strings, coaxing out a haunting, beautiful melody that seemed to weave itself into the thick air of the exhausted room. The notes rose and fell like the sighing of the wind, a lullaby for the weary souls seeking shelter within these walls.

I stood transfixed, letting the music wash over me. It stirred something deep within my chest, a bittersweet ache. The way each note carried left a pull on my body. A longing to move. To dance. To remember my own lullaby. One of pain and heartache, that always found solace in the long music notes.

"Is that your wife, Mr. Thorne, sir?" a small girl asked.

The child's question caught me off guard, bringing me back to the present with a jolt.

"It is," he answered, eyes falling onto me.

The girl gestured for him to come closer with tiny fingers. Thorne leaned down, his dark brown hair falling forward to obscure his face as the little girl cupped her hands around his ear, whispering something that made the corners of his eyes crinkle with amusement.

He straightened, his gaze finding mine. There was a softness in his expression that I hadn't seen before, a warmth. He made his way towards me, weaving between the cots with a grace that hid his injury.

"I'm told it's impolite not to ask my wife for a dance."

It wasn't a question, but there was a gentleness in his tone that made it feel like an invitation. Slowly, I placed my hand in his. Thorne's palm was warm and callused as it enveloped mine. He drew me close, his other hand coming to rest on the small of my back. The heat of his touch igniting a spark that danced along my spine.

We began to move, swaying in time to the mournful melody. The rest of the room faded away until there was nothing but the music and the man holding me in his arms. I was acutely aware of every place our bodies touched, the brush of his thigh against mine, the firmness of his chest beneath my palm, the whisper of his breath against my hair.

I let him lead me through the steps with confident ease, guiding me into a slow turn. As I spun back towards him, he caught me against his chest, his hand splaying across my back to press me closer still. My breath caught in my throat, my heart stuttering at the sudden intimacy.

This close, I could see the faint stubble shadowing his jaw, could count each individual lash framing his hazel eyes. Those eyes held me captive now, dark with an emotion I couldn't name. Or perhaps didn't dare to. But dancing was a language I spoke fluently. It was nostalgic and felt more like home than anything else. Dancing reminded me of where I needed to go, why I couldn't stay here.

I lost myself in the music and the feel of his body against mine, letting the rest of the world fade away until there was only this moment, this man. As the final notes of the song quivered in the air, Thorne slowly brought us to a stop. But he didn't release me immediately. Time stretched between us, the air heavy with unspoken words. I knew he had a thousand questions, but so did I. And somehow we'd found comfort in that space with each other. We were curious, but respecting the walls. What right did I have to push him for answers about his past, when I wasn't willing to share?

Slowly, reluctantly, he let his hands fall away. I immediately felt the loss of his warmth, a chill rushing in to replace it. Around us, the Hollow was settling into sleep, the crackle of the dying fire and the soft snores of children the only sounds.

But Archer sat at the table, head in hands, watching us with an obnoxious grin. Jasper was on his right, that satisfied look on his face not too different from Archer's. One of the two assumed we were newlyweds, but the other one knew better. And his grin was almost infuriating.

Leaving Thorne, I walked across the room to sit in front of Archer. "Stop it."

"Stop what?" he crooned.

"You know what."

"Aw. Don't give them a hard time, Archie. It's nice to see the boss in love."

"We're n—"

Archer leaped from his chair, the sharp scrape of wood cutting off my words. "My turn for a dance. Come on, Fingers. Show me what you've got."

I was grateful for his quick thinking, but annoyed I'd almost slipped up. I let him lead me into the space between the cots and the table, as we assumed a far more rigid stance than Thorne and I had taken. A few of the other adults danced, and some gently clapped to the music as we began. Archer was a clumsy fool when it came to dancing. I suppressed a wince as he stomped on my toes, his apologies mingling with the gentle laughter from the onlookers. But despite his lack of grace, there was a warmth in his smile, a genuine joy that was infectious.

As we spun and stumbled our way through the dance, I couldn't help but laugh along with him, the tension of the earlier moment with Thorne slowly easing from my shoulders.

"Can I ask you a question?"

His head bobbed as he mouthed the count of the steps, trying to lead me, though I was the one in control. "Sure."

"How do you and Jasper hide your magic from the prince? If having magic is illegal in Stirling."

"Having magic isn't illegal. It's just dangerous."

"But the Cimmerians can detect magic? They test people for it?"

He eyed me carefully. "Why do you ask?"

I flicked my chin toward Reuben snuggled in a blanket on the floor beside Lianna. "I want to make sure I understand how we're hiding the boy. And why."

Mostly that's what I wanted. Kind of.

"Ah. That makes sense. But it's a taboo subject. So I wouldn't go around asking random people."

"I didn't," I said, staring directly at him. "I asked you. We're friends, right?"

He grinned, showing all of his teeth. "We are now."

I drew back. "Don't look so excited. It's creepy. Just tell me about the Cimmerians."

"The Cimmie's have all been burned with immense power during Themis." He paused at the raise of my brow. "Don't get me started on that bullshit. But basically, we think there's something to the marking. Something giving them the ability to find traces of magic if they are close enough to a wielder using it. Because they were regular people, living their lives until Farris started collecting them. As I'm sure you know, the king is a descendant of Themis, God of Justice. Farris's power... It's unlike anything this realm has seen, and he's taken *justice* into his own hands, quite literally."

"So he makes laws, then forces people to break laws to survive, and then punishes them for it, building his own army."

"Not quite. As much as I'm sure it grates his nerves, Farris can't make laws. Not while the king is still living. No matter how much he walls his father off, no matter how much he wishes he was ruling already, there's nothing he can do about that. But may the gods help you if you are caught by Cimmerians with magic. They'll take your name and claim they are testing you. And then they'll hunt you until you commit a crime, lock you in the Maw until you confess, and then you're handed over to Farris, whose ultimate punishment is stealing your power and letting Themis bind you to him."

I gasped, nearly losing my footing. "Farris can steal people's power?"

Archer's eyes turned sad, flashing to Harlow, who sat perfectly still beside Willard. "He can take it. He just can't wield it. It's like he's trying to remove all the magic from the world, but we don't know why."

"All the more reason to stay the hell off the streets," I said, mostly to myself.

"You'll never be on the streets, Fingers," he said as the song faded to an end. "As long as you keep Thorne's last name, you're safe. They say he's a descendant of one of the first gods. Not even I know what his power is, though. But his family line is deep-rooted. Don't worry."

I didn't want to crush his feelings and let him know that Thorne's all powerful magic was nothing more than passing notes through a single notebook that occasionally warmed the skin.

"I'll take the next dance, miss, if'n you'll have me," one of the men said, sliding up next to us and pulling the old worn hat from his head to clutch it to his chest. "Promise I'm a better dancer than Archie boy."

I laughed, dipping my chin as I turned to him with a graceful curtsy. "It would be my pleasure, sir."

"Careful, Charlie," Archer said, punching him playfully in the arm. "Thorne'll have your neck if you get too close." He jutted his chin toward my brooding husband, staring at us over the top of his book.

"No need to worry about him," I said, letting Charlie take my hands. "He's all bark and no bite."

Charlie smiled sheepishly, sleek brown hair now a mess from where he'd removed his hat. "No offense, my dear, but I think we all know that's not true."

"Well, don't you worry then. I know his weakness."

He chanced a glance at Thorne and back to me as we swept across the floor, keeping true to his word about being a better dancer. "I think we all do now."

The sound of the fiddle swept us away, and I let it. Let the music fill my soul, command my body, let the sweat gather at the base of my neck and my breaths grow short as we spun and laughed and made a giant spectacle of ourselves, as quietly as possible. Careful not to wake the children but embracing the song.

"It's good for them," I told Charlie when he tried to muffle his laugh. "They need to know happiness exists in every corner of life. In sad places and in unknown moments, there's still joy to be found. They can't live their lives, never knowing what it means to let loose of the reins. When you're a kid, it's so much better to be woken from laughter than tears." I yawned, the weight of the long day and no sleep the night before bearing down on me.

"I suppose so," he answered, letting his smile show. "Guess I never thought of that."

"Thank you very much for the dance," I said as the song came to an end. "I'll see you tomorrow, I'm sure. Maybe you can teach Archer."

"Oh no, Miss Paesha. I'm on guard duty starting in the morning."

"Well then, maybe I'll bring you some breakfast."

"Don't burden yourself."

I shook my head. "It wouldn't be at all."

I'd forgotten the new plan. Thorne assigned four men to the roof on rotation to keep a look out for Farris and his men. They were to stay out of sight up there, but report anything suspicious. Every one of the men volunteered, but he'd promised them a wage, regardless.

I couldn't stifle my next yawn. The day's events gave way to a bone-deep exhaustion. My feet carried me back to the table where Thorne sat, his book now closed, his stare watchful. I sank down onto the chair beside him, my shoulder brushing his. The solid warmth of him was comforting, grounding.

Thorne stood, his movement commanding attention as he

looked over all the Salt seeking refuge, food and warmth from the Hollow. "It's time for lights out. We've all had a long day."

There was a chorus of murmured goodnights as people began to disperse, banking the fire and blowing out candles while shadows crept in, softening the edges of the room. Archer and Harlow lingered by the door, shrugging into their coats. Thorne joined them. He spoke in low tones and I couldn't quite catch what he was saying. Willard walked up, his expression serious as he nodded along to whatever Thorne was saying. After a few moments, they clasped hands and slipped out into the night.

Thorne held out a hand. "Come, wife. Let's get you to bed."

Too tired to protest the endearment, I let him pull me to my feet.

"I could stay down here. I don't mind."

There was no give in his voice. "Absolutely not. There's one room upstairs. Mine."

We made our way up the narrow stairs, the wood creaking beneath our weight. At the top, Thorne guided me down the hall with a limp to the room we'd be sharing. He closed the door and lit a small candle on the table, its warm light enveloping the room. It felt wrong to sleep here, knowing there were children on piles of blankets on the floor and sharing cots just below us.

But I knew the rules as well as the roles and there'd be no sense in arguing. Even to those that knew Thorne was a professional thief, we had to maintain our farce, parading as man and wife. Especially because I now understood things I hadn't before. If we were caught in the lie, if the prince decided that was treason, he would use his power to take both of ours and bind us to him forever. And I couldn't have imagined a more horrible existence.

Thorne moved to stand before me, lifting my chin until I looked into his eyes. "You mustn't think of them with pity. Most have too much pride to allow it and the children are safe and warm and together. Believe me, this room isn't a gift in the winter. The heat from the fire will hardly reach us."

"Are we flipping a coin to see who gets the bed?"

"No," he said, unbuttoning his shirt.

"You can't possibly mean... I'm not getting into that bed with you. And why are you taking your shirt off two seconds after you said it's going to be cold?"

"I don't sleep clothed. And if it offends you so much, take the floor. Makes no difference to me."

I drew back. "I'm not sleeping on the floor."

"If we'd have flipped a coin, and you lost, would you have taken it?"

I hesitated, caught off guard by his question. "You're supposed to be chivalrous and offer the bed to me."

"I'm rarely ever what I'm supposed to be, Paesha darling."

"Except for being an arrogant prick."

He walked forward and tapped me on the nose. "Except for that."

"You're a baby giant. How the hell are we both supposed to fit in that thing?"

Thorne watched me, his expression unreadable in the flickering candlelight. Slowly, he shrugged out of his shirt, letting it fall to the floor. My eyes were drawn to the expanse of his bare chest, the corded muscle and the scattering of scars. I swallowed hard, turning away, my mouth suddenly dry.

"I'll sleep on top of the covers," I said.

I could hear his annoying smile in his tone. "I had a feeling you'd come around."

He moved to the bed and slid beneath the quilt, the mattress dipping under his weight. I stood frozen for a moment, my heart pounding, before I forced my feet to carry me forward, refusing to look at how low he'd laid the quilt across his hips.

With a sigh, I fumbled with the laces of my dress. My fingers were clumsy, the knots refusing to budge. I cursed under my breath, tugging ineffectively at the stubborn ties. I'd undressed myself a million times, and of all days, of all times to be trapped within, it would be now. With those scrutinizing, know-it-all eyes watching me.

"Had I known you were incapable of removing your gowns, I might've offered to help these last weeks."

The teasing tone of his voice boiled my blood. "Can you please be less... *you* right now? I can undress myself just fine."

"Pull the longest string. The one to the left. And then the right. I will release the knot you've tied yourself into."

"Do you ever hear yourself speak and wonder where you get the audacity? When was the last time you put on a corset?"

He sat up on his elbows, staring at me with a grin. "Well, I don't make it a habit of putting them on myself, but I've removed more than my fair share."

"Oh hey, your lying tendencies are showing."

"I would never lie about that."

"Do I need to get you a book to keep track of your lies too?"

He grinned. "As long as it's made of gold."

"Do you talk just to hear your own voice sometimes? Because I think you do."

"Sometimes I talk just to hear your voice argue back. In that annoying tone you like to use when you're sure you're right and usually aren't. Would you please come here and let me loosen the fucking corset? At this point, it's just sad. And probably embarrassing for you."

"No, no. I'm fine."

"I won't offer again."

I spun and glared at him. "Good. Then maybe you'll stop talking."

"Maybe."

"I hate you so much, Thorne Noctus."

He chuckled, the sound infuriating me. "Who's the liar now, Paesha darling?"

"Still you."

After several more frustrating attempts, the laces of my gown finally loosened enough for me to shimmy out of the dress. I let it pool at my feet, standing in just my thin shift. The cool air pebbled my skin as I hurried to the bed.

I lay on my back, stiff as a board, acutely aware of his presence mere inches away. I stared up at the shadowed ceiling, willing my racing heart to calm.

Thorne shifted, and the mattress creaked softly. "Relax. I don't bite. Unless you ask me to, of course."

I scoffed, but some of the tension eased from my muscles at his teasing. "You're insufferable, you know that? Pure torture to even look at."

He smiled, showing that very annoying and not at all adorable dimple. "So you keep telling me. And yet, here you are. In my bed."

"Not by choice."

"I think there was a little choice involved," he countered.

I tried to turn, but there was no room. "Gods, were you actually a giant in another life? Scoot over."

Thorne laughed, a deep, rich sound that seemed to resonate through the small room. But he obliged, shifting his large frame to make more space for me on the narrow bed. Muscles taut and arms propping himself up as he faced me.

I dragged my gaze away, focusing intently on the flickering candle flame instead. But his presence was impossible to ignore, the steady rise and fall of his chest, the spicy scent of his skin, the heat radiating off him like a fireplace. It was maddening.

"A giant in another life, hmm?" His voice was low, almost a

purr. "Is that one of your special abilities? Seeing into past lives?"

I huffed out a laugh, still stubbornly refusing to look at him. "Hardly. It's the only explanation for your... excessive size."

"I can assure you, there's nothing excessive about me. Everything is perfectly proportional."

The suggestive note in his tone made my cheeks flush hot.

"Have you ever thought about your past lives? The concept has always intrigued me," he said, the philosophical bookworm showing his true colors. "Imagine walking around, a whole life of memories and things and attachments, only to leave it all behind and start over."

I couldn't tell him I'd seen it happen. A descendant of the Goddess of Life releasing souls to reincarnate and live again. Try for happiness again. It was real and maybe even something to look forward to, should one choose it.

"I've never given it much thought." I wiggled down, hating the cold seeping in. Hating how badly I wanted to crawl under the blanket. But fortunately, I was stubborn.

"Do you ever feel pulled to something random? Something that must be from a past life, because it makes no sense in this one?"

"Not that I've ever noticed."

"Take the chipped teacup," he pressed, his breath falling warm along my chilled skin. "Why does that mean so much to you, but the others don't?"

"I don't know. I picked it because it was flawed. It's not that serious."

"Hmm."

I turned to finally look at him. At the way his eyes held mine. "Why are you suddenly so interested?"

"Just killing time until you admit you're freezing and you need me to share my blanket."

"Gods, I hate you."

He traced a finger down my bare shoulder. "No, Paesha darling. I don't think you do."

His touch ignited a spark that raced through my veins, jolting me wide awake despite my exhaustion. I held perfectly still, hardly daring to breathe as his fingertip dragged a slow path down my arm, leaving a trail of raised flesh in its wake.

"Thorne..." My voice was barely a whisper, but in the charged silence of the room, it sounded far too loud.

He withdrew his hand, and I immediately missed the contact. Slowly, so slowly, he lifted the edge of the quilt in silent invitation. An unspoken truce.

Pride warred with practicality as I hesitated, caught between my stubborn determination to resist him and the bone-deep chill seeping into my skin. In the end, the cold won out. With a defeated sigh, I slipped beneath the covers, the heat of his body enveloping me like a cocoon.

I kept a careful distance between us, balanced precariously on the edge of the mattress. But even with that tiny space separating our bodies, I was intensely aware of him. The solid bulk of his frame, the steady rhythm of his breathing, his scent.

My heart thundered in my chest, pounding out a frantic rhythm that drowned out all rational thought. I squeezed my eyes shut, fighting the overwhelming urge to close the distance between us, to press myself against him and lose myself in his embrace.

"Paesha, look at me."

Against my better judgment, I turned my head to meet his gaze. His eyes, normally a swirling mix of green and brown, were darkened with an emotion I couldn't name. Or perhaps didn't want to. There was a question there, a challenge, a plea.

I swallowed hard, my mouth suddenly dry. "Thorne, I..."

He lifted a hand to cradle my cheek, his thumb gently tracing the line of my lower lip. "Don't overthink this."

I wanted to give in, to surrender to the magnetic pull between us. His touch was fire, his presence intoxicating. I was drowning in the man he was when no one was looking. The walls he let down for only me. The way he'd let himself be vulnerable in only select moments. It would be so easy to close the distance separating us, to claim his lips with my own and let the rest of the world fade away.

But something held me back, a whisper of doubt that cut through the haze of desire clouding my mind. This wasn't real. The connection between us, this undeniable chemistry, it was born of circumstance, of forced proximity and the adrenaline of shared danger. Outside the walls of this room, beyond the flickering candlelight and rumpled sheets, we were still strangers playing at being husband and wife.

I couldn't afford to let myself forget that, no matter how tempting it was to pretend otherwise. Thorne was a means to an end. My ticket to safety in a world that wanted to bind me. I couldn't get attached, couldn't risk my heart on a man I'd have to leave behind.

With a shaky breath, I pulled away from his touch. "I can't do this, Thorne. It's not real."

Hurt flashed in his eyes before he changed his expression, the walls slamming back into place. He withdrew his hand.

"I would never force you," he whispered. "But I am here."

I reached for his hand, pulling it closer to me. "I know. And I'm sorry."

Something strange passed over his face, as if he were searching for something deeper within me. Maybe only understanding, but that didn't feel like the whole story. He looked at me like he knew more. Saw more. And suddenly I was reminded that he was the key to my path home. And the only thing he'd truly proven himself to be was a thief who kept secrets well. I just wish I could figure out what he was hiding from me.

28

Dawn came far too early, pale light seeping through the curtains and pulling me from restless dreams filled with heated touches and whispered pleas. I blinked away the lingering cobwebs of sleep, disoriented for a moment. The warm weight of an arm draped across my waist brought the events of last night rushing back with startling clarity.

I lay perfectly still, hardly daring to breathe as I became acutely aware of every point of contact between Thorne's body and mine. We'd gravitated towards each other, our limbs tangling beneath the shared quilt. His chest was a solid wall of heat against my back, his steady heartbeat echoing through me.

Carefully, I tried to extract myself from his embrace without waking him. But as I shifted, his arm tightened, pulling me flush against him. I froze, my pulse thundering in my ears.

"Not so fast," he mumbled. "That's the first time you haven't woken me up in the middle of the night with hysterics. Let me enjoy it for a moment."

His breath tickled the sensitive skin of my neck, sending a

shiver down my spine. A traitorous part of me wanted to stay like this, cocooned in his embrace, the rest of the world fading away. But I couldn't let myself indulge in that fantasy. With a determined twist, I broke free and slid out of bed, the chill morning air prickling my skin. I didn't dare look back at him as I quickly gathered my clothes, needing to put some distance between us. Fifty-five days. If I'd only been in the Maw for a week, which was completely a guess, I'd already spent twenty here. And where seventy-five felt like plenty, fifty-five and only a trace of answers felt like a trap. It felt like the walls were pressing in. Time was running out. And I needed Alastor to get his shit together fast.

"Paesha." The gravelly timbre of his sleep-roughened voice froze me in place. Slowly, I turned to face him. His hair was endearingly mussed, his eyes still heavy-lidded. The sight of him, so disheveled and intimate, sent a flutter through my stomach.

"We should talk about last night."

"Let's not. There's nothing to talk about. Where's my trunk? Didn't we bring more clothes? I know there's a bathroom down-stairs. Is that the only one?"

Thorne sighed, running a hand through his tousled hair. "Your trunk is over there by the dresser. And yes, the bathroom downstairs is the only one in the Hollow." He paused, his gaze searching mine. "Look at me."

I kept my expression carefully neutral as I retrieved a clean dress from my trunk, refusing to meet his eyes. "Nothing happened, Thorne. We shared a bed, that's all. We were both exhausted and emotions were running high. Let's not make it into something it wasn't."

"Why are you fidgeting? Come here."

I busied myself, folding the dress over my arm, still avoiding his piercing stare. "I think we both know, whatever this is between us, it can't go anywhere. We have roles to play. Husband and wife in name only. Getting tangled up in feelings will only complicate things. You think you want more because that's an easy option, but it won't be easy at the end of this. Don't push."

He stood from the bed, letting the damn blanket fall to the floor, his pants riding low on his hips as he walked over, grabbed my face, and forced me to look at him. "Think about this. Where *is* the end? At what point can either of us walk away unscathed? We're married. And that's forever."

I gently grabbed his hands and pushed them away. "We aren't married."

His eyes flashed with a mix of anger and hurt. But before he could respond, I turned away, slipping into the clean dress, the cool silk whispering against my skin as I pulled it up. The bodice hugged my curves, the neckline dipping just low enough to hint at the swell of my breasts. Tiny pearl buttons marched down the back. It was a dress fit for a lady, not a thief's wife playing at being something she wasn't. And for once, there was no damn corset.

Before I could even try, Thorne's fingers were there, brushing against my skin as he buttoned up the back of the dress. His touch was gentle, almost reverent, as he worked his way up the row of delicate buttons. I held perfectly still, hardly daring to breathe as his knuckles grazed the nape of my neck, sending a shiver racing down my spine. There was something in the whisper of his closeness that wrapped around me, unsettling me. I danced dangerously close to the edge with him every day now. And I needed to fucking stop it.

"Talk to me."

"No. Stop pushing."

He snorted. "That's an awfully commanding response from someone that pushes buttons like it's a hobby."

"Pushing boundaries isn't the same as pushing buttons."

"Maybe I'm pushing your boundaries because I want to stand behind the walls you build around yourself. Maybe there's something to this thing between us."

I stiffened at his words. They were dangerous. Too much. His fingers paused at the top button, his hands still warm against my back, but his words wrapped around me tighter than the dress ever could.

"You're wrong, Thorne."

He sighed, his breath a soft exhale against my skin. "You know I'm not. Every damn day, every moment with you, it's different. You challenge me, you make me want to break every rule I've ever set for myself. You're stubborn and annoying and probably the worst possible option and yet here we are. Just tell me I'm not alone in this. Tell me you feel something. Tell me there's a reason you find comfort in me at night. Tell me something. Anything."

I shook my head, unable to say a thing. Worried I'd give myself away if I tried. The moment stretched between us, heavy with unspoken words and simmering tension. With a final tug, he finished fastening the last button. His hands lingered on my shoulders. His thumbs traced small circles that burned like brands through the thin silk. I wanted to lean back into his touch, to let myself melt into the solid strength of him. But I couldn't trust those feelings. I couldn't trust anyone.

Stepping out of his grasp, I turned to face him, my expression carefully composed. "Thank you," I said, my voice too loud in a space that was entirely consumed by him. "For buttoning my dress."

I moved towards the door, my skirts swishing softly with each step. I had to close my eyes. I had to draw in a steadying breath. I had to imagine a space without him in it. Because the temptation to turn back to him, to let myself fall into the warmth of his arms and forget the world outside these walls, was almost overwhelming. But I couldn't. I wouldn't let myself. Even though I knew he would.

Without looking back, I opened the door and slipped out into the narrow hallway. The air was cooler here, the shadows deeper. Muffled voices and the clatter of dishes drifted up from below, the Hollow coming to life with the new day, pulling me away from a conversation I wasn't ready to have. Thorne would put his mask back on, hide behind his walls again, and things would go back to a safe distance. Where he told me what to do and I told him fuck off and nothing was more serious than that.

Children darted between the tables, their laughter mingling with the clatter of dishes and the low murmur of conversation. The air was thick with the scent of freshly baked bread and simmering stew, making my stomach grumble in anticipation.

I wove my way through the controlled chaos, nodding greetings to the bleary-eyed adults nursing steaming mugs of tea. The clamor faded as I slipped into the bathroom and splashed cool water on my face, letting it soothe my flushed cheeks and clear the lingering cobwebs of sleep and confusion, and the panic of racing time from my mind.

Meeting my reflection's gaze in the spotted mirror, I studied the woman looking back at me. Her mismatched eyes were nearly vacant, her lips pressed into a determined line. She was nearly a stranger. Not the woman relishing the spotlight, but rather the one that was lost. Fighting a battle within herself. Maybe it was the lack of control that was suffocating me. Knowing there was nothing I could do right now. But I knew it was more than that. It was the friendships I could make so easily. The draw to become a confidant to Harlow, a friend to Archer. A lover to the man I'd shared a bed with. None of those things would make my escape easy though. If anything, they would make it harder. I needed the space. I needed to stay the course. But fuck if it wasn't getting harder to remember that.

With a final sigh, acceptance more than anything, I pushed off the sink and walked back into the massive space, ready to spend another day here, sitting around and waiting for Alastor, the leader of the black market—the Vale—to call a meeting. Waiting to see if this god was the next step on my path home.

I expected to find Jasper bustling about in his kitchen, his weathered hands kneading dough or stirring a pot, a dusting of flour on his cheek and a twinkle in his eye. But instead, I was greeted by the sight of Willard, leaning casually against the counter, his attention wholly focused on a woman I didn't recognize.

She was pretty, with a heart-shaped face and a riot of chestnut curls escaping from a messy bun. Her cheeks were flushed. Either from the heat of the kitchen or Willard's undivided attention, I couldn't be sure. They were speaking in low tones, their heads bent close together, intimate smiles playing at the corners of their mouths.

I hesitated in the doorway, feeling like an intruder in a private moment. But before I could slip away unnoticed, Willard glanced up, his eyes widening slightly as he registered my presence. He straightened, putting a bit of distance between himself and the mystery woman.

"So sorry to interrupt. I was just looking for Harlow." I walked forward, sliding a knife from the counter to twist it between my fingers as I casually said, " You might've seen her before. About this tall, blonde, drop dead gorgeous, lethal?"

"Is she here?" Willard asked, trying and failing to slide into a casual tone. "Mara was just asking about her, weren't you?"

"Oh, sure. Sure, I was." The woman gathered a few bowls in her hand and swept out of the kitchen.

Willard followed.

I stewed.

What was my role here? To be a friend to Harlow? Tell her what I'd seen? I didn't know if they were officially a couple. Would it be rude of me to assume? But I'd seen the way she'd looked at him. The way she shifted toward him in weak moments. Either way, Archer and I were in agreement for once on one thing. Wee Willy was absolutely going to be his nickname from now on. Asshole.

When Jasper came barreling into the kitchen, ever the lovable clumsy cook, my thoughts of Willy were quickly stolen as I jumped to work, going through the paces of the day before. He moved with a hurried, slightly clumsy step, narrowly avoiding colliding with the corner of the counter as he worked. With a huff, he dropped two sacks on the counter, sending up a small cloud of flour that dusted his wild gray eyebrows and the tip of his nose.

His weathered face creased into a warm smile. "Ah, Miss Paesha! You're up with the sun, I see. Early bird gets the worm, as they say. Or, in this case, the first taste of my famous cinnamon rolls! It's a rare treat for this lot today. I... *found* a heap of sugar."

He winked, then set about organizing his ingredients, humming under his breath. I watched him work, finding comfort in the familiar routine, exactly like a dance he'd practiced over and over.

"How'd you sleep? Not too cold up in that room, I hope. I've been telling the boss for years we could build a ground level room for him, but he refuses."

"I slept fine, but how often does he stay here?" I asked, a bit surprised.

"Well, now that he's gotten himself a bride, I don't think it will be too often at all. Soon enough, you'll have little ones to look after."

My heart wrenched at the thought of that. Even if I were to stay and the realms burned around me, even if I were to fail and forget everything as the God of Things and Stuff and all the names had said, I'd never have children. Not one. Not ever. I'd only ever have Quill. And she wasn't mine. Not truly.

Still, I smiled and nodded and turned my back to him, concentrating on anything but those feelings of loss that'd consumed me years ago. I cracked the eggs and dumped them into a bowl, one by one. But Jasper read my face. I must not have been great at hiding it, because he was by my side seconds later. His hand, weathered and warm, closed over mine as he gently took the egg from my fingers. "Miss Paesha," he said softly, "forgive an old cook's assumptions. I spoke without thinking."

I blinked rapidly, trying to hide the sudden sting of tears. I hadn't dwelled on this in so long. "It's all right, Jasper. You couldn't have known."

He studied me, his kind eyes seeming to see straight through to the heart of me. "No, I couldn't have. But I recognize that look, that pain. I've seen it before, worn by women who carry a grief they keep tucked close to their heart."

This wasn't a safe space. These weren't secrets to let loose with a person I hardly knew. I schooled my face and turned away. "Let's keep it to ourselves, for now."

He immediately changed the subject. No more words needed. "You're meeting with Alastor soon. Are you nervous about that?"

"Should I be?" I asked, plucking another egg from a basket.

"Yes. Alastor isn't a crime lord or black market transient, Miss Paesha. He's a god. An old god."

"I thought all gods were the same age. Ancient or something."

"No. Not at all. And they say they gain their power from the love of the people of the realms. Only the darkest of people worship a God of Lost Things. Lost hearts, lost souls, lost friendships. Some whisper that he's the patron of thieves, the master of all things hidden and illicit. Every criminal worth their silk in Wisteria has ties to Alastor, whether they know it or not."

I'd heard of the Gods of Lost Things before, but I wouldn't give myself away, especially when they were missing a vital piece of information about him. "Why would a god concern himself with the mortal world? With petty criminals and black markets?"

He leaned in closer, eyes shifting between mine. "Legend has it, Alastor was banished from Etherium lifetimes ago. Cast out by the other gods for some unspeakable transgression. They say he wanders the realms, collecting lost things, drawn to the shattered and discarded. Some even whisper that he gains power from the suffering of mortals, thriving on their pain and desperation."

The idea of a god who fed on misery, who reveled in the darkness of the human heart, was exactly what I thought the gods were, anyway. None of this shocked me. I knew living in a realm with no gods was a blessing. They meddle. They lord over the people. Fuck that. But I'd play the shocked, delicate flower here, if only to hide my past. "My mother used to call Serene the Goddess of Loss and Lust. Isn't that the same as a God of Lost Things?"

"No, Serene and Alastor are not the same at all. Serene may revel in the sensuous pleasures of lust and the bittersweet ache of loss, but Alastor... he is something else entirely. Where Serene finds power in the fleeting nature of desire and the poignant sorrow of a broken heart, Alastor feeds on the deepest, darkest despair. He is drawn to the lost and forsaken, to the shattered remnants of hope and the gaping wounds of the soul.

"Imagine a child, abandoned and alone, wandering the streets with nothing but the clothes on their back. Imagine the anguish of a parent searching for a lost child, never knowing if they are alive or dead. Imagine the gut-wrenching pain of losing everything you hold dear, your home, your family, your very sense of self. That is where Alastor thrives. He is the patron of the truly lost, the god of those who have been cast aside by the world and left to rot in the shadows."

Alastor was the god of my own trauma. Definitely not a coincidence. "And Thorne's ready to willingly meet with him? Seems like a terrible idea."

Jasper sighed, his gaze distant. "The boss has a complicated history with Alastor. Theirs is a relationship born of necessity, of secrets and favors traded. I don't know the details, and I've never asked. But I do know that Thorne would never put you in danger, not deliberately."

"That's true enough," Thorne said from the door, surprising both of us. Freshly bathed and wearing a finely pressed suit, he leaned in, snagged an apple and forced a glance my way before continuing. "I've got to run over to the Parlor to get the ledger. I'll likely be back before anyone realizes I'm gone, but if Alastor happens to show, stall him."

"You got it, boss," Jasper said as Thorne walked out, refusing to acknowledge me. Or the sting of my rejection.

We worked in silence after that, except for his cheerful hum and the few times I saved him from slipping on the flour dusting the floor. We washed up together and even sat together at the long table afterward, watching our meal be appreciated.

Willy hadn't avoided me like I expected him to. Instead, he'd sat with us, a little girl on his lap, teaching her how to pronounce her alphabet. Something in that confidence made me question the assumptions I'd drawn. Maybe he and Harlow weren't in a relationship at all and I'd only assumed they were.

When Harlow and Archer walked in, removing their coats and stopping to say hello to several of the people tucked into the

Hollow, I watched her eyes. Waited to see how long it would take before she sought him out. But she didn't. Instead, she held a tight smile and walked up the stairs with Archer not far behind.

I excused myself from the table. The second floor of the Hollow was quieter, the bustle and chatter from below muffled by the floorboards. I paused at the top of the stairs, straining to hear the low murmur of voices coming from down the hall where Harlow and Archer argued in hushed, urgent tones. I crept closer.

"— can't keep doing this, Archer. It's too dangerous." Harlow's voice was strained, pleading.

"I know what I'm doing, Har. It's not my first time."

"That's exactly my point! You're reckless, always throwing yourself into the thick of things without a thought for your own safety. One of these days, your luck's going to run out and you'll end up in the grave, just like her. You need to let this go."

"You can't make every decision for me for my entire life. Think about what that security would do for you." Archer's voice softened until I couldn't hear much beyond, "Let me finally pay you back, Har. Let me do this to make up for you losing your magic."

"You're not in debt to me, brother."

Just as I was about to turn away, I heard the creak of floorboards behind me. Heart leaping into my throat, I spun around to see Willy stomping up the stairs, his brow furrowed in concern. Panic jolted through me at the thought of being caught eavesdropping.

Without thinking, I reached for the door handle and pushed into the room, plastering a bright smile on my face. "We made breakfast."

"Not hungry," Archer said, a scowl on his face as he walked out, brushing my shoulder and clipping Willard's on his way.

"I'll be down in a minute," Harlow said, not bothering with false happiness. She stood by the window, her arms wrapped tightly around herself, as if trying to hold together the fractured pieces of her composure.

"We've got tea with the Whittaker's at three and I've promised my parents we'd stop by after dinner."

Harlow turned then, clearly annoyed that Wee Willy hadn't read the room at all. "You'll have to tell them I'm busy. We're waiting for a meeting with Alastor."

He scoffed, walking forward to grip her shoulders. "We both know he's going to drag this thing on for weeks. I've canceled with my parents three times. We must be there. It's not open to debate."

She leaned into his touch, and I stood frozen, unsure if I should walk out or tell her about Mara and let them figure it out. There was something so foreign, yet so familiar, about witnessing this moment. As if it were déjà vu, but I knew I'd never been here before. So, I stood like a fool and waited for her to answer. Hoping she'd stand her ground. But she didn't.

"All right. We can't keep pushing them off. They'll start to wonder, and we don't need anyone asking questions about our free time."

"Perfect," he said, brushing a kiss to her cheek. "I'll see you downstairs in a bit?"

He didn't even wait for a response, just walked out. All this time, I wasn't sure, but never because of her. His actions hadn't indicated a committed relationship and Harlow's resolve seemed so tough, even moments before when she was talking to Archer. But not with Willard. Which begged the question, what was he lording over her?

"You okay?" I asked, kicking the door to the room shut.

She let out a shaky laugh, the sound brittle and sharp-edged. "Just a typical morning in the Bramwell household.

Archer being a stubborn fool and me trying to keep him from getting himself killed."

I wasn't sure how to respond, so I said nothing, walking over to stand next to her. She didn't settle in the silence though. Instead, she nudged me with a shoulder. "Want to go up and give the new guards a break? Get a little fresh air?"

"Absolutely."

Her shoulders sank in relief. "Thank the Gods. I think there are only two up there. We couldn't spare four men. They're probably so tired."

We slipped out of the room, and the chatter from below faded as we climbed the other stairs, the air growing cooler with each step. At the top, a wooden door with a heavy iron latch barred our way.

Harlow lifted the latch and pushed the door open, letting in a gust of crisp morning air. We stepped out onto the rooftop, and immediately I regretted not grabbing our coats. Still, the view stole my breath. Stirling stretched out before us, a sprawling city of stone tiled roofs, winding cobblestone streets, and towering spires that pierced the pale blue sky. In many ways, it felt ancient, but if one looked close enough, that didn't seem right at all. Not compared to Requiem, a city riddled with rot and decay. The misery was the same in both worlds, though. At least there was that. Familiarity in suffering. The morning sun was drowned out by the low mist that settled over the highest buildings, even drowning the castle on the hillside in the distance.

Two guards, Charlie and one other I didn't know the name of, turned to us, their expressions a mix of surprise and relief. They'd been hunkered down behind the low stone parapet, keeping watch over the streets below. Harlow nodded to them, a silent dismissal, and they gratefully retreated back into the warmth of the Hollow.

We took their place, crouching low to stay out of sight. The rough stone was cold against my palms as I peered over the edge, taking in the city.

Harlow settled in beside me, her keen eyes scanning the winding alleys and shadowed doorways for any sign of trouble. Her body was tense, coiled like a spring, ready to snap into action at the first hint of danger. I could feel the restless energy emanating from her, the need to move, to do something other than be still.

She drew a slim blade from the folds of her skirt and twirled it deftly between her fingers, betraying countless hours spent honing the skill. Much like Archer and his love of coins. I watched, transfixed, as the knife danced across her knuckles, the deadly edge never once grazing her skin. It was a mesmerizing display, a testament to the lethal grace coiled within her deceptively delicate frame.

We sat in companionable silence, the only sound the soft whisper of her blade cutting through the air and the distant clatter of the city coming to life below. I knew there were a thousand questions I could ask, a hundred ways I could try to draw her out and forge a deeper connection. But I didn't want that. Nor did I need it. The fewer people I had to say goodbye to, the better.

And as if I'd timed it, a clocktower, lost in the mist of clouds, chimed the hour, reminding me that my days here were numbered and I really needed to get the hell out of here. I had faith that Alastor was the key. That maybe he'd brought things from different worlds into his little black market, and if he could get items across the realms, then maybe he could carry people as well. And while I considered asking Harlow, she wasn't safe either. I couldn't trust them. But I needed them to trust me.

"How long were you in the hall?" she finally asked, turning those bright blue eyes to me. "Did you hear everything?"

I weighed my options, but the hesitation was enough to answer her unspoken question.

"I'd barely come into my power when the prince took it." She turned, looking back over the city. "Archer and I were near the castle walls, just twelve years old. We were messing around, throwing rocks and waiting for our grandmother to get done with her meeting with the king. Archer threw a rock, it hit Farris's carriage as it was passing by. Farris got out, huffing and puffing as teenage boys will do, and picked a fight with Archer. He had no idea he was the prince when he took a swing at him."

I swallowed my gasp, trying to keep my reaction subtle as she continued.

"I'll never forget the look on Farris's face. The smile as he stood up from the ground and called the king's guards over. Harming or insulting royalty is an act of treason, punishable by death. Even at a young age, Farris sought law breakers. Not because he cared about justice. But because he loved the punishment. He forced his guards to grab Archer. Everyone was screaming. At least it seemed like it. Maybe it was only me. I flung myself to the ground at the prince's feet, begging him to show mercy. Begging him to take me instead of my brother. No one knew Archer had power at that point. But they'd heard of mine. So Farris grabbed my wrist and made me swear I'd meant it. I'd pay for Archer's mistake. And I did. Because we'd already lost our mother and father and... I couldn't lose him too. So, I agreed to give him my power. And he took it, right there on the street, never breaking contact with me as he wrenched something from my soul that I was never meant to be parted with."

I couldn't imagine the horror. Being separated from my power would be like splitting my soul. There couldn't be a worse fate, surely. "I'm so sorry that happened," I said moments later, if for no other reason than to break the agonizing silence.

"It's done now," she whispered. "I've moved on, but he

hasn't. I don't think he ever will. Not until Farris is rotting six feet under and he's the one to put him there."

"But if—" My power burst to life within me. Warning bells pealing in my mind. I'd locked onto Farris as she spoke, my magic taking on a mind of its own. "Farris is coming," I said, grabbing her hand.

She ducked, training her eyes back onto the city below us. "Where? I can't see him."

"He's on the other side of the street."

"But how could you..." She gasped. "You have magic."

"There's no time. Come on. We have to warn the others."

Regret followed every single footstep as we ran. I'd just given away a secret. And I wasn't sure I could trust Harlow to keep it.

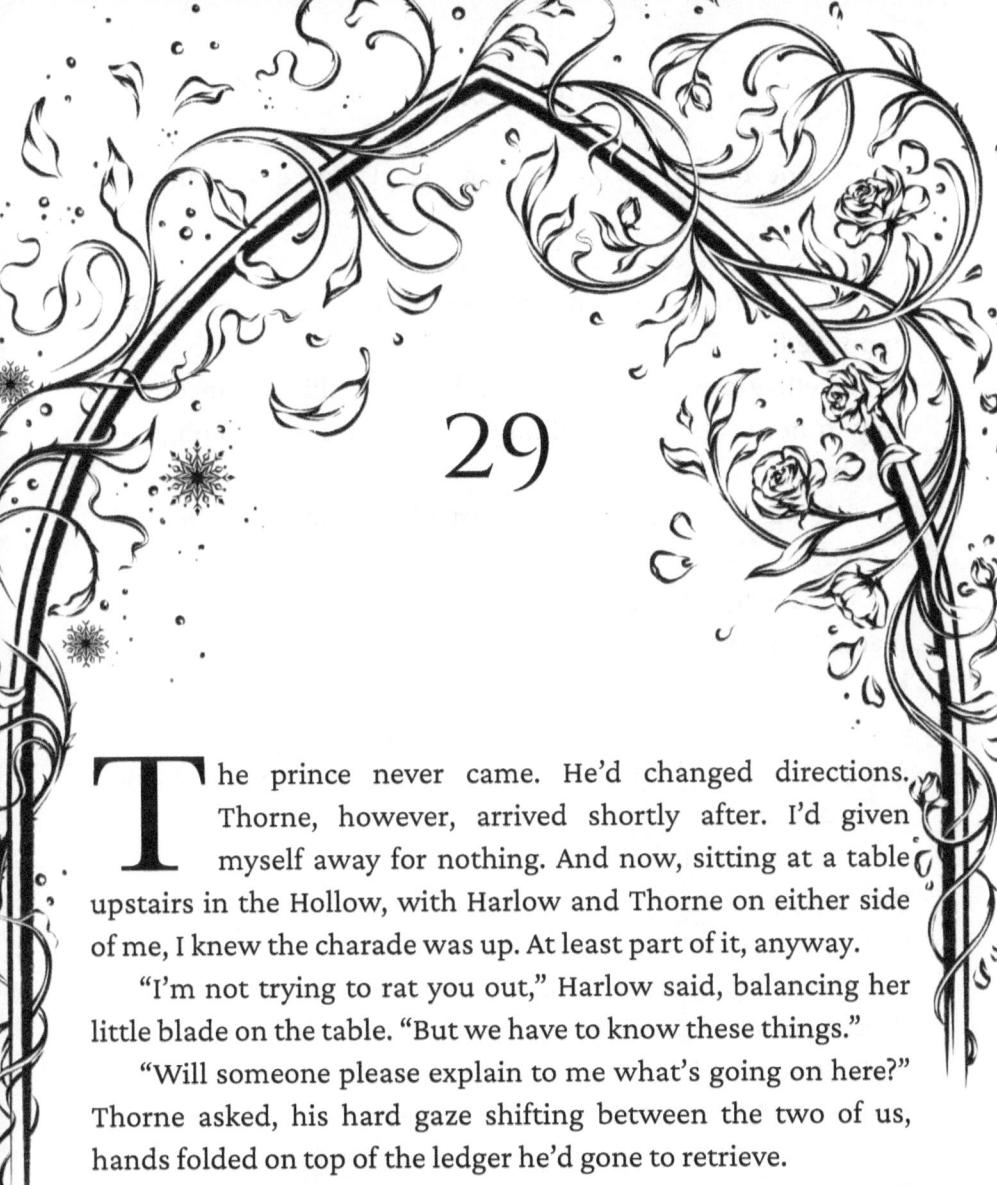

29

The prince never came. He'd changed directions. Thorne, however, arrived shortly after. I'd given myself away for nothing. And now, sitting at a table upstairs in the Hollow, with Harlow and Thorne on either side of me, I knew the charade was up. At least part of it, anyway.

"I'm not trying to rat you out," Harlow said, balancing her little blade on the table. "But we have to know these things."

"Will someone please explain to me what's going on here?" Thorne asked, his hard gaze shifting between the two of us, hands folded on top of the ledger he'd gone to retrieve.

Harlow looked at me, clearly giving me the option to tell him before she did it herself. I knew it didn't come from a dark place. Not from jealousy or distrust, but because having magic was so, so dangerous here. And I'd been so reckless with it, not knowing any better.

"I didn't know it at the time, but the reason the Cimmerians put me in the Maw... was because one was close enough to detect the magic I was using that day. I hadn't seen the one that came for me until it was too late."

Thorne looked at me, sliding his glasses down his nose. "And?"

I glanced at Harlow and back to him. "I have magic."

Still confused, he looked between us. "I know. What happened?"

"Well, nothing happened," Harlow said, shifting uncomfortably in her seat. "Paesha thought the prince was coming, and that was all."

"He was." I argued. "He was just a few blocks away before he turned."

Thorne leaned forward, his intense gaze pinning me in place. "I knew you had magic, but not its ability. How did you know exactly where he was?"

I swallowed hard, my mouth suddenly dry. There was no point in trying to hide it anymore, not with them both staring at me expectantly.

"I can kind of sense things. If I've touched and seen something, my power allows me to find it. If I focus on someone, I can track their location, sometimes see through their eyes for a moment." Though I hadn't been able to see a single target since I'd been to Wisteria, come to think of it. Even the way my magic had alerted to Farris's proximity earlier felt different. Off. I hadn't used enough power to really test what it was like here, but it wasn't the same as home. That much was certain.

Thorne sat back, his expression unreadable as he processed. I was surprised he didn't take his damn ledger out and start making notes.

Beside me, Harlow let out a low whistle. "That's a rare gift. No wonder the Cimmies were after you."

"It's not something I advertise," I replied, my voice tight. "For obvious reasons."

"But why did you lie when we asked?" Harlow sat forward, resting her elbows on the table.

"Because I didn't trust you."

"Fair enough," she answered. "But wh—"

"Thorne!" Archer's sharp, urgent voice echoed down the hall.

"We're in here," Harlow answered back.

The door slammed open to reveal Archer heaving as he leaned into the frame. "He's coming. Charlie spotted him. You ready?"

Thorne took a long, deep breath. "As ready as I can be. Make sure he sees the children on his way up. Don't hide them. He needs to know what we're doing here is not selfish."

We waited in silence, Thorne thrumming a finger along the table as the minutes passed by. The heavy tread of footsteps echoed in the hallway, growing louder with each passing second. I glanced at Thorne, noting the tension in his jaw, the way his fingers flexed against the worn leather of his book.

The door swung open with a creak, revealing a towering figure silhouetted against the dim light of the hall. Alastor stepped into the room, his presence filling every corner, pulling the shadows in close like a cloak.

He was a massive man, easily matching Thorne's considerable height. Though I knew him to be old, ancient even, he didn't look a day over forty. But he had that way about him. The undeniable attractiveness that marked him as a god. Broad shoulders strained against the fine black fabric of a buttoned shirt, the garment doing little to conceal the corded muscle beneath. But it was his face that drew the eye. Harsh, brutal beauty, all sharp angles and cruel lines. A latticework of intricate tattoos covered every inch of exposed olive skin below his jaw, the dark ink seeming to writhe and shift in the flickering candlelight.

Piercing green eyes swept the room, lingering on each of us in turn as Wee Willy and Archer took their seats at the table. The god, who looked more like a criminal than any criminal I'd ever seen, sat last, steepling his tattooed fingers, letting his presence swallow the room whole.

"Thorne Noctus," he said, finally.

"Alastor Erevar."

The two men stared hard at each other, an unspoken war happening before another word was said. After a long moment, Thorne leaned forward, his voice low and even. "I asked you here to discuss a proposal. One that could benefit us both, as I'm sure you know."

The god's lips curved into a humorless smile, revealing a flash of white teeth. "Always straight to... present business with you. No time for pleasantries? And here I thought we were old friends."

Thorne ignored the jab, pushing the ledger across the table. "The Fray is expanding. We need more goods than ever before, but our current trade routes are becoming problematic. The Cimmerians grow bolder by the day, and more and more are falling to the streets."

Alastor flipped open the ledger with a casual flick of his wrist, his eyes scanning the neat rows of numbers and coded entries. "And you think I can solve this little dilemma of yours? Oh, no. Not even that. You're hoping I care enough."

"The Vale is the most extensive black market network in the realm. Your routes are untouchable, your methods unparalleled. An alliance between our organizations could change everything. With your resources and our reach, we could keep the people here fed and clothed, even in the face of Farris's tyranny. The Salt need us now more than ever."

"If I didn't know any better, I'd say you cared. But I think we both know that's not true. You'd have to have a heart to care." Alastor studied Thorne for a long moment, his green eyes glittering with a predatory light. "That was a pretty speech, delivered with conviction. But this isn't about altruism. The Fray need my help to survive. Without access to the Vale's dark corners, you'll wither on the vine, choked out by Farris and his dogs. Don't circle the truth, Noctus."

Something in my heart twitched. This wasn't my battle. It made no difference to me if Alastor agreed to do business with Thorne or not. In fact, I wasn't sure if I needed Alastor more than I needed Thorne at this point. But I had to draw a line somewhere. I couldn't leave this room and look into the faces of those children downstairs and not see myself years ago, hungry, tired and all alone. The resources keeping everyone here warm and fed would eventually run out. And then what?

Thorne's jaw clenched, but remarkably, he held the god's gaze steadily. "We're the only thing standing between the people and starvation. Between hope and despair. Surely that means something. If there are no people, there's no one to worship the gods. No power to be grown."

Alastor slid the ledger back across the table with ease. "I think I'll pass."

I leaped from my seat so fast my chair fell over. "How could you walk by those children and deny them a meal? You're the God of Lost *and* Broken Things? Can't you see how broken this entire place is?"

"Some give me that title, but not all. I must say, you care more than I thought you would, Huntress." He shifted forward, all of his godly attention on me. "Those eyes are incredible. You're a perfect blend of the gods you descend from."

I couldn't process what he'd said. Stumbling past the fact that he'd called me Huntress, a name surely given to him by Reverius. He'd known exactly who I was, what my power was. But I focused on the other words until my knees felt weak.

"Gods?"

A knowing smirk played at the corners of Alastor's mouth. I could feel Thorne's eyes on me, searching, questioning, but I couldn't tear my gaze away from the god.

"You didn't know," Alastor stated, his voice a low purr. It wasn't a question.

"Everyone with power descends from gods. Of course I knew."

Of one, but not two.

He shook his head slowly. "No, no, Huntress. Born of two, loved by two, your reincarnated soul descended. Not the body. Not the blood."

"Are you saying..." I stepped closer, moving around Harlow until his presence was nearly choking me. "Two gods had a baby, and a new god was not born?"

The tattoos on his skin seemed to darken with his eyes. "You're asking the wrong questions." He stared directly at Thorne as he answered. "Gods are not born like mortals. Gods are born of emotion. Etherium is full of demi-gods, waiting around to kill their parents and take their place or give up and descend to a mortal realm."

"I think we're done here," Thorne said, standing at the other end of the table. "I do hope you reconsider working with the Fray, Alastor. So, so many people could suffer if you do not."

"Don't threaten me, *mortal*. You have no idea the things I'm capable of here. The things I've dreamed of doing. Let me make myself perfectly clear. If I ever see you again, you'll wish to be broken and beg to be lost."

Again, a battle happened in the silence that followed. In the way Alastor rose slowly from the table. In the way that his knowing eyes burned through Thorne before flicking to Archer as he said, "All paths, broken or whole, lead to the prince. But you already know that, don't you, Archie boy?"

His tattoos shifted as he made one final glance toward me and stormed out. Something in my soul rattled, longing to reach out to him. To force him to tell me more. Was that message really meant for me? Why had he used that word?

30

Panic set in, wrapping itself around my throat like a vice as I realized I was lying in a glass coffin. I tried to scream. To cry. To breathe. But no sound escaped my lips. My vocal cords had been paralyzed along with my legs, my entire body.

Surrounded by damp earth and decay, I'd been discarded under a sorrowful sky. Interred, but not covered, forced to see the world above me. Two Cimmerians stood as guards at the foot of my grave, but rather than watching the world, they watched me. Their breath, coiling before them in the frigid air, seeped from the carved masks like smoke from a demon.

Turn around. Gods. Turn away.

I couldn't think or feel beyond their eerie stares.

Cold seeped through the coffin. Snowflakes drifted lazily from the gray sky, landing softly on the glass inches above my nose. They melted slowly, the droplets sliding down the pane like the final notes of a requiem.

Each shallow breath became a struggle. My lungs burned with effort. A shadow shifted in my peripheral vision, beyond the headstone I could see but not read, marking my fresh grave. Hysteria bubbled up inside me but I couldn't give it a voice. I couldn't release the scream trapped in my throat as I tried and failed to twist and turn and break free of the invisible chains holding me frozen in place.

I needed to get out. To escape this prison before it became my tomb. I focused every fiber of my being on moving just one finger, just one toe. But my limbs remained still and lifeless. Betrayed by my own body. By my irrational fear of the Cimmerians stroking my terror like it brought them pleasure. The frantic beating of my heart echoed off the walls of my casket, stealing the tail end of every breath I managed. But I still couldn't move.

Desperation was an animal, wild and untamed, clawing at the edges of my reason as it crept in like a shadow at the corners of my mind. I told myself I could get out. I convinced myself the air would last, someone would come, this couldn't be the end. But as the minutes dragged on, that hope curdled into something ugly, something frantic.

As if shattering through a wall, my body relented, giving in to my desperate need to move. To cry. To scream and scream. For him. For Thorne. The only person in the world I thought would come. But he did not.

I thrashed against the confines, my hands slamming into the coffin lid until my knuckles bled, smearing the glass. I couldn't stop. I had to keep moving, fighting, as if sheer force of will could crack the walls around me. But nothing gave. The glass held firm. And their gazes never wavered.

The absolute horror of being so helpless hit me right in the chest. I pounded on the coffin harder, tears burning down my face. My chest tightened, my throat closed in, and I was left gasping, choking on sobs that only they could hear.

Through my tears, beyond the bloodied glass and the

sentinels, another shadow passed by. Panic surged, and I tried to scream again, to pound on the lid, but no sound came from my throat. My body refused to move again, frozen in place, helpless. I blinked hard, trying to focus. A small figure came into view... Quill, dressed in black, clutching a bouquet of dead peonies to her chest as she cried. She moved toward me and the Cimmerians vanished, clearing the way for me to manage a breath. Her pale face hovered over the glass, blue eyes wide and unblinking. She stared down at me from where the guards had stood and tilted her head to the side like a curious bird.

"Help me!" I mouthed, trying to scream, but my voice stayed trapped inside, buried along with me.

I watched her lips move, but I could not hear her. Still, hope flickered in my chest. Until she sat down, cross-legged, right on top of the snow-covered coffin. She began arranging the withered flowers carefully on the lid, like she was laying out a fragile bouquet on a table.

"They're all gone now. Thea and Elowen and even you. I gave the grave digger three extra coins to bury you at night. Don't you remember, Paesha? Don't you? Remember. Remember. You remember him, don't you? You love him."

I shook my head, forcing words that wouldn't come before. "I don't... I've never been in love. Listen to me, Quilly. I know you're hurt. I know you're sad, but you are not alone. This isn't real. I'm coming. I promise I'm coming."

She cocked her head to the side again, tilting it a little bit more and a little bit more until the unnatural angle twisted my stomach. I pressed my hands to the glass, finally able to move again. She put hers in the same spot, lying on top until our noses were nearly touching. And then she was there. Not the eerie child that'd haunted me, but Quill, my Quilly. I could see her beyond the deep circles under her little eyes.

"There you are," I whispered.

Her tears began to fall, transforming into grains of sand. "I miss you. Why did you leave?"

"I'm so sorry. I'm coming home. I'll never leave again. I promise. Never again. Find Thea. Let her help you until I get there."

She moved her tiny fingers along the glass. "You promise you're coming?"

I nodded, opening my mouth to swear it when a giant serpent emerged from the sides of my coffin.

"Quill, look out!"

Its obsidian scales glistened and it moved with a sinister grace, coiling its massive body around the glass coffin, tightening its grip like a noose. I tried to scream, but terror stole my voice, leaving me mute and helpless as the creature's forked tongue flicked out, tasting the air inches from Quill's face.

She let out a bloodcurdling shriek, scrambling backwards, her hands slipping on the icy glass. The snake's eyes, twin hourglasses filled with black sand, fixed on her. It slithered over the coffin lid, its heavy body making the glass creak and groan under its weight.

Quill's tears turned to rivulets of crimson, staining her pale cheeks as she trembled, frozen in place by the serpent's stare. It coiled around her. Tightening, constricting. It was one thing when I was the victim of my nightmares, but when it was her? I couldn't take it. My heart could not see beyond the pain on her face. I pounded against the glass. I screamed. I cried. I begged, thrashing around until something warm surrounded me. I fought against the restriction, pleading to be free.

Only when Thorne's deep voice commanded me to wake, did I leave the horror behind. Shaken, eyes wide, it took several minutes for my heart to settle, for me to realize those were his arms surrounding me and not the confines of a glass coffin.

"There you are," he whispered, brushing the mess of hair from my sweaty forehead.

I blinked, drawing away from him, letting my eyes settle on my bedroom in his home. A place that'd been a blessing, but as the days passed, also a curse. I pushed away from him, moving to stand next to the window, if only to see the first rays of sun in the distance.

"Still mad?" Thorne asked, coming to stand beside me, his arm brushing mine as we watched out the window.

We'd come back to his place and when I'd pushed for more information about Alastor, confident he knew more than what he was letting on, he refused to say anything at all. We'd hardly spoken for days after that. Every night, the dreams came though. Every night, Quill was begging for me to return home. Sometimes the Cimmerians were the ones to haunt the nightmares and sometimes it was Quill, but no matter what, Thorne was always there to wake me. Even when I'd tried to stay up all night and failed, he'd come barging in and shook me awake.

"Just tell me what you did to make him hate you so much. You're hiding something."

He let out a long sigh. "This doesn't need to be an argument."

"You're hiding something."

He grabbed my wrist and pulled until I was looking into the depths of his hazel eyes. "You're hiding something, too. Tell me what he meant when he said all paths led to the prince."

"I don't know what he meant. He looked at Archer."

"He looked at you, too. Are you in business with Farris, Paesha? Does he know who I am?"

"If I answer that," I said, pulling away, "then you have to answer something for me."

He waited a beat, searching for my question before I asked it.

"And then we're done with this silent treatment you've been giving me?"

I nodded. "I'm not in cahoots with the prince. I had never met him before Tithe. Your secrets and your identity are safe with me." I backed away. "I think you're one of the good ones. This world is full of greedy, cruel people, and I think you're self-less. To your own detriment sometimes, but that's your choice. I promise you, I have not, nor will I ever make a deal with Farris."

"Don't make promises you can't keep."

I grabbed his wrist. "I promise. Your turn. Why does Alastor hate you so much?"

His shoulders dropped. "Some years ago, I took something from him. He's holding onto a grudge that we may never see end. Gods are strange. Their grasp on time is not the same as ours. They speak in riddles and do small things that won't matter for centuries."

"Then give it back. Whatever you took, give it back."

"It's not that simple."

"Was it the snuff box Archer traded with him to get a meeting?"

"No. That was sentimental, but nothing more than that."

My eyes found the little golden book on the bedside table, a burning question so strong on my mind, I couldn't help but ask. "Where does your power descend from? Which god do you think gave you the ability to send private notes?"

He swiped his glasses from his face and began to pace the room, waiting for an eternity to begin, as if he were at battle, deciding whether he should share. "I've actually been trying to research the gods, mapping who we know has power to which god it might've come from. It was strange, because some make perfect sense, like Archer's ability to heal would come from a healing god for sure. I don't know all their names, but I'm

317

working on it. Some are less guarded with their secrets than others."

"Okay. Let me ask you something else." I tumbled through the meeting in my mind, trying to remember the words. "He said... I mean, I know I'm a reincarnation. We all are, right? Or we're on our first life, but odds are, we're reincarnations." I couldn't tell him how familiar I was with reincarnated souls. Couldn't tell him that I'd seen the Life Maiden give that choice back to a massive amount of people. But he'd been the one to bring it up before with the teacup, not me. So maybe he knew something.

"Was there supposed to be a question in that?"

I rolled my eyes. "I'm getting there. Born of two, loved by two, something about my reincarnated soul descending. Not the body. Not the blood."

He lifted an easy shoulder. "I told you they speak in riddles."

"I'll show you some leg if you try to break it down for me."

He ran a finger through his tousled hair. "Am I supposed to pretend you're not showing me *all* of your legs right now?" Walking forward, he gripped the collar of my oversized shirt and yanked me toward him. "This is mine, you know."

I swallowed. It was meant to be a joke, but damn was he distracting. "Can you please focus?" I whispered. "I've been stewing on this for days."

He moved closer. "Do you think I haven't? Do you think every word spoken in that meeting hasn't haunted me? I was young, I made a stupid decision and I'm still paying for it. Everyone is paying for it. Imagine living with that much regret every single day. Imagine knowing people are suffering more than they need to be because of a reckless decision made in haste. But you make it really fucking hard to concentrate when you parade around here like this all day, keeping your distance, stealing my shit, moving everything you can get your hands on.

I can't pretend like you don't exist, even when you're mad at me. Nor do I want to. But fuck if you aren't trouble in a t-shirt right now, wife."

"I'm sorry," I managed, not bothering to pull away from his grip, even as I stood on tiptoes.

"That's the curious thing." He leaned so close his breath whispered across my lips. "I don't think you're sorry at all. In fact, I think you enjoy tormenting me. You push my buttons just to see how far you can go, don't you?" His grip on my collar tightened, drawing me impossibly closer. "You're playing such a dangerous game, Paesha darling."

"Maybe you should push back. Take off your masks."

He dropped me to my feet. His hand slid up, fingers tracing the line of my jaw, thumb brushing over my cheek in the lightest, most maddening touch. "You're not nearly as fearless as you pretend to be. Because you know, if I did, there'd be no going back. And I don't think you're ready for that."

My heart hammered, every nerve on edge, but I managed a smirk. "Maybe you're the one who's scared."

His gaze dropped to my mouth, lingering there a beat too long before snapping back up to my eyes. "If that's a dare, you're about to regret it." He leaned in close, so close his breath mingled with mine, his lips barely a whisper away. My head swam, every inch of me screaming to close that tiny, torturous gap, to bridge the distance he was purposely drawing out.

"Then make me regret it," I murmured, refusing to back down.

"Have you learned nothing, Paesha darling. Regret is the root of our problems."

He stepped away, his words like ice as he tucked his hands into his pockets and turned his back to me. He meant our fictional marriage as much as his past mistakes with Alastor. Even if he hadn't directly said it. That truth stung, even if he was right. Because in all the days since that meeting, I'd hardly taken the time to think of him. Of the guilt he must have been feeling.

I'd been consumed by my search. By pouring through his little notes of discarded information, by listening anytime Tuck, the carriage driver, came to report on the prince. I'd avoided him, but not really. There wasn't a single thing he did that I wasn't a step behind him. Undetected mostly, but around. Still, I wanted nothing more than to reach out, to smooth my hand over his back and promise him we'd figure it out.

I couldn't. I had to remember my purpose, the reason I was here. Getting tangled up in Thorne's complicated past, in the undeniable pull between us, would only make leaving that much harder when the time came. And it would come. Soon. Because Alastor had to be the key. And maybe even the prince. And I had forty-nine days left to find my way back to Requiem.

He turned then, his eyes meeting mine. In that moment, I saw a flicker of the man beneath the persona of the Lord of the Salt and wealthy owner of the Parlor, a glimpse of the weight he carried, the scars he tried to hide.

Before I could act on the impulse, he walked to the door. "I'll likely be gone most of the day." His tone was brisk, businesslike. The walls firmly back in place. "Jasper has a list of supplies the Hollow needs. If Archer comes by today, can you make sure he gets it? It's on my desk."

I nodded and he walked out.

The day was long and boring, much like the others this week. I'd left shortly after he did, cloaked and avoiding the Cimmerians as I walked around, noting the way the chill in the air wasn't so biting, the way the sun began to show itself through the mist in the middle of the afternoons, the way the water stopped freezing in piles on the street. I couldn't help but mark the places I'd been as I wandered, though I did my best to steer far, far away from Farris and his men, who'd hardly been in the streets. But no matter where I went, what leads I'd followed, I couldn't gain a single clue as to the whereabouts of the Vale. I'd tried to find that damn snuff box, only to wind up seeing it in the window of the jeweler's shop. He'd sold the fucking thing. So much for sentimental. Failing another day, I went home.

I plucked the little golden book from the lace band I'd been wearing around my thigh to keep the book with me. I hated that he hadn't used it once all week. Flopping down on my bed, I slowly opened the page and let my fingers trace the only thing on the page that hadn't vanished. The number two.

Sliding the pencil from its tiny holder, I touched the lead to the paper, contemplating what I should say to him. I didn't need a single thing. He'd seen to that since the moment I arrived. Still, this wasn't about need. It was something else. Something I didn't want to think about.

> *Thorne Noctus, Lord of the Ledgers,*
> *Are we having soup for dinner again? Is there some-*
> *thing I can do to start it?*
>
> *Bored at home,*
> *Paesha V.*

I waited, moving the pencil between my lips as I willed him to answer me. Eventually, Thorne's beautiful handwriting graced the page.

Paesha N.

We've got an invitation for dinner at the palace tonight.

Still working on your alphabet, I see.
Thorne also N.

I nearly dropped the pencil.

You didn't think to mention that this morning?

I was distracted.

By the legs?

The legs, the arms, the eyes, the mind. Take your pick, Paesha darling.

This thing is complicated, you know?

I held my breath the entire time I waited for his next response. I didn't know where I was spiraling to. What I was saying to him. I didn't know what I wanted. How I could have it, even if I did know. I had to leave. And tonight, with the prince at my fingertips, I'd have to decide if I was ready to start asking questions. I couldn't keep doing what I was doing, that much was obvious.

Eventually his answer came through, dancing across the page in such mesmerizing swirls, I almost forgot to read the beautiful words. I traced my fingers over his elegant script.

It's only as complicated as we make it. Life is messy. Relationships are messy. But sometimes beautiful things grow from chaos. You're infuriating, and I'm tedious. You're stubborn, and I'm worse. You're mischievous, and I need control. There are about a million reasons why this can never work. And if you don't think I see that, you're wrong.

As long as we're on the same page.

I couldn't stomach writing those words, but I knew I needed to. I knew we both needed the space.

I'll be home in two hours. Wear something decent. Both the king and Farris will be there.

As if I'd go in rags.

As if I'd let you.

I bit my bottom lip.

We should really consider an intervention for your massive control issues.

I'm not sure I can allow that.

Reread that and tell me how it makes you feel. Deep inside.

Are you smiling right now, Paesha darling.

Maybe.

Excellent. I'll be home soon.

I PAUSED IN THE DOORWAY, my breath catching at the sight that greeted me. Thorne stood by his desk, silhouetted against the fading light, a crystal tumbler dangling from his long fingers. With a book in hand, lost to the present world, he sipped, his crisp white shirt tugging against his suspenders. He swallowed, the strong column of his throat bobbing.

His eyes swept over me as I walked in, taking in my figure-hugging dress that clung to every curve. The neckline dipped daringly low, more than hinting at the swell of my breasts, while the skirt flared out at my hips, swishing around my legs as I walked. I had pinned my hair up, a few tendrils escaping to frame my face.

Under Thorne's heated gaze, I felt a flush creep up my neck. The air between was charged with tension that had been building for weeks, simmering just beneath the surface of every interaction. He set down his glass and book, approaching me with a measured stride, eyes never leaving mine. When he reached me, his fingers ghosted along my bare shoulder, trailing fire in their wake. By some miracle, I held myself perfectly still beneath his blazing touch.

"Can you tie the back? I couldn't reach."

"Turn around," he commanded.

Something in the way his knuckles kissed my skin brought my entire body to life in a way I'd never known. Gods, I hated him. How easily he controlled me. How desperately I wanted him to.

"Are we flirting or fighting tonight, just so I'm ready?"

"I'm not sure yet," I whispered, reaching for his glass and taking a drink to cool myself off.

His voice was a low rumble I felt in my bones. "You're stunning. Every set of eyes will be on you."

"Let them look. Maybe you can use it as a distraction. Send me to seduce someone in a dark corner. I can be very persuasive. Plus I still have this pretty face and all."

He plucked the drink away and finished it before sitting it back on the desk. "That will never, ever be the plan. You're to play the obsessive wife tonight. No one else exists but me. Understand?"

"And will you be the obsessive husband?"

He reached forward, gripping my throat tenderly as he brushed his finger against my jaw and pulled me closer. "That's the only kind of husband I want to be."

31

Hand in hand, we walked up the castle drive together. I couldn't hold back the warmth in my soul at the thought of meeting with King Aldus again. He'd been so friendly when we met at Lithe, and though tonight would be a test of our fictional marriage, his kind eyes and belly laugh were something to look forward to. And of course, Farris would interfere, as was his standard, stepping right into my trap.

Marble columns soared overhead, supporting an intricately carved art piece depicting scenes from what I assumed was Stirling's history. Ghostly faces stretched out of the stone, as if held behind sheer fabric. I couldn't imagine the time and skill it must have taken to create such detailed artwork. But none of the Silk hustling into the palace looked up. None were in awe, or even aware of the tiny details. The veins on the leaves etched into the stone. The texture on the hooves of horses and points on the tips of the spears.

Liveried servants bowed low as we passed. I wondered if they lived up here on the hilltop, or if they walked every day to serve their king. Or, as I noticed the silver emblems on their chests, were they actually working for the prince.

I'd thought through everything I might say to Farris. How I might lead him to talk about other worlds without knowing why. How I might distract him from the truth by dangling just enough information about the Lord of the Salt to pique his interest. I hated to do it, but I needed to. Because if Thorne wasn't holding the keys to a door, then his secrets were the currency I needed.

Thorne's presence was magnetic. His hand drifted to rest possessively on the small of my back as we made our way through the palace. Every heartbeat, every step felt like a betrayal. And he had no idea what I intended to do. How I might unmask him if it came to that. My stomach felt uneasy about it, but I just had to believe this was the path. Still, I'd never be able to look at myself in the mirror again. I was setting myself up for the ultimate betrayal. But what choice did I have with only fifty something days left? Maybe even forty, depending on how many days the Maw had stolen from me.

The sound of a violin drifted from somewhere in the hall, low and mournful, wrapping around me like smoke. Each note pulled tighter, like strings wound around my ribs, squeezing until I could hardly breathe, setting me on edge. Preparing me to fall.

Thorne watched, gauging every flicker of my expression as if he wasn't sure I could keep the mask in place. But he was wrong. I had no intention of breaking our facade, even with my questions for the prince. I'd still be Thorne's wife, a cunning thief's wife. But I was confident I could lead Farris through the conversation without revealing everything. Only enough to barter a trade. I'd seen enough deals made with fine print. I just needed to walk him into the trap first.

Thorne's hand, warm and firm, was the only thing keeping

me grounded, and yet it felt like a weight around me, circling me with his trust. Trust he'd given without question. Which was undoubtedly the most foolish decision of his life.

He shifted, sliding his fingers across the small of my back. The heat of his touch seeped through the thin silk of my gown, branding my skin until I was hyper aware of him, of the danger coiled in his large frame, the subtle tension thrumming just beneath the surface as if *he* commanded the room and not the royals.

As we crossed into the grand vestibule, the music changed, a haunting melody echoed off the grand walls as a hush fell over the crowd. Guests turned, eyes tracking us, the whispers rising in our wake like the rustle of leaves in an autumn breeze. I lifted my chin, meeting their curious stares with a cool, unruffled gaze as if nothing could touch me, not even the truth gnawing at my chest. Let them look. Let them wonder. Let them see. Tonight, I would be untouchable. Fully Thorne's and nothing else, as far as they were concerned.

Thorne's hand was steady, grounding. He moved us through the crowd, nodding to familiar faces, exchanging brief words with acquaintances. I caught glimpses of faces I vaguely recognized from Lithe and the Parlor. Wealthy merchants, minor nobles. That was about it. There were far more strangers, men and women draped in sumptuous fabrics and glittering jewels, their eyes sharp and assessing behind painted smiles.

The whole world was watching. But his grip on me remained gentle yet unyielding. I glanced up, catching the look in his eyes, a calm confidence I didn't deserve. The music shifted, rising in an elegant crescendo, a perfect backdrop for deceit. It should've given me courage. Instead, it felt like a warning, sinking into me, telling me to stop, to pull back. But I couldn't. I needed that information. And after tonight, I'd have to leave.

Even if it shattered him.

The ballroom wasn't full. There weren't enough people to get lost in a crowd, which was unfortunate, because it meant everyone stood out. Everyone had a reason to keep the prince's attention. And maybe he'd meant for that. But I needed privacy with him.

"Those are the gods," Thorne whispered, lifting his chin to a group of stunning people, practically glowing as they shut out the room and spoke only to each other. "Try not to focus on them. We don't need the added attention tonight."

I nodded, unbothered by gods when the room was peppered with Cimmerians. But Thorne's firm grip on my hand was steadfast. The way he subtly placed himself between me and each of them as we moved was the smallest gesture that planted itself within the trenches of my heart. He knew my fear, my trauma. He knew it and would not see me falter because of it. And I was an awful person for what I was willing to do to him.

The prince, with his dark hair slicked back and a band of ceremonial medals across his chest, stood in a far corner, speaking to a small group gathered around him. He smiled and chattered as if he weren't ordering the torture of his people within the catacombs of his city. As if the warmth in his father's castle spread throughout their kingdom and there were no sick men dying in the alleys or children starving in the streets.

"How can he just stand there and smile?"

I hadn't realized I'd said it aloud until Thorne answered. "Careful, wife. This is a dangerous place to lose your composure."

I moved to stand before him, placing my hands on his broad chest, sliding them up until they gripped the lapels of his jacket. "I disagree, lover. I think this is the perfect place."

His jaw tightened. His breath shortened. He stared down at me with that dimpled smile and it might as well have swept me away with it. Smoothing a thumb over my bottom lip, he stared for a moment, long enough for my heart to begin racing. "Gods, you're a ravishing little menace." His voice was low, reverent, like he was saying a prayer meant only for me.

The air between us thickened as his thumb lingered, tracing my lip with a touch so gentle it was maddening.

I blinked, trying to break the spell with a whisper. "If you keep looking at me like that, I might forget we're pretending."

He leaned in closer until his lips grazed my earlobe. "Then forget."

The world outside faded. There was only Thorne, only his breath falling down my neck. His hand cupped my cheek, tilting my face upward, and the promise in his eyes set my skin on fire. He had no idea that behind each of his movements, he was begging me not to betray him and my resolve was waning. I was growing weak for him.

"I don't want to forget," I whispered, with no conviction at all.

But he only smiled and shifted away. "Liar."

"So, this is your new, mysterious wife?" A woman sauntered toward us, dripping in jewels and fine silks, ripping us away from a moment I needed. She took a long drag from her cigarette, exhaling the smoke in a lazy plume as her piercing gaze raked over me from head to toe. "How lovely to finally meet you, Paramour. I've heard so many rumors. None true, I'm sure."

"I'm sure," I repeated, face natural as I looked down my nose at her.

"Paesha darling, meet Lady Selia Berch," Thorne said smoothly, his hand wrapping around my waist as he pulled me to his side. "An old acquaintance."

Selia arched one perfectly manicured brow, her ruby red lips curving into a smirk. "Is that what we're calling it these days?"

Thorne stiffened. "That's what we called it those days too, Selia."

She threw her head back and laughed, swatting his chest. "Of course, I'm only teasing. Always so serious, Thorne Noctus."

She turned her eyes to me again, tapping her long cigarette on a passing tray with no regard for the drinks. "So, Paramour. You seem to have appeared from nowhere. What's your story? Spare me no details."

I leaned into Thorne, molding my body to his side as I fixed Selia with a cool smile. "There's not much to tell, really. Just a simple girl swept off her feet by a dashing stranger. You know how these love stories go. A few kisses later and he couldn't keep his hands off me. The rest is history."

I reached up to straighten Thorne's red tie, my fingers lingering on the silk as we locked eyes. His hand tightened on my hip, pulling me impossibly closer. His heart beat strong and steady beneath my palm. "Not history. Eternity, my darling."

Selia's eyes narrowed as they darted between us, taking in our intimate posture, the way we gravitated towards each other. Something ugly flashed across her face, there and gone in an instant, replaced by a brittle smile. "How charming. Young love is so precious, isn't it?" She sighed wistfully, flicking ash from her cigarette again. "Enjoy it while it lasts, my dear. The shine tends to wear off rather quickly around here." She looked at the clock. "That's odd. I thought we'd be seated for dinner already."

"His Royal Highness is not here yet, Lady Berch. Or hadn't you noticed?"

The small gasp that caught in my throat was muffled by Selia's screech. "Your Grace, I hadn't heard you approach."

Neither had I. And that was rare for me. Though again, something felt off about my power. A reminder that Wisteria was not like Requiem. It was muffled in a strange way. But also imbalanced. I'd felt him coming from so far away on that rooftop, and here, he'd snuck up on us.

"Remind me not to invite you to the Hunt," he chuckled, snagging a glass off a nearby tray as those dark eyes slid to where Thorne held me pressed against him. "Paramour. Lovely of you to join us. I believe there were bets as to whether your husband was going to finally let you out of the house."

I had to think beyond the fear thrumming through my veins. Suddenly, his nearness reminded me how callous he was. How he'd ripped a man's tongue from his mouth in front of his whole kingdom. And he was hunting magic. Could he sense my power? I couldn't help what little escaped when I touched new things. It was automatic for me. I tried to hold as still as possible, not even shifting my feet along the floor as I answered. "Good evening, Your Grace." I managed a small curtsy, considering my words. "I'm afraid it's me keeping my husband tied up at home, rather than the other way around."

"Chains or cuffs?" Farris asked, not missing a beat.

"Your Grace," Thorne said with a dip of his chin, pressing his fingers into my back as if he knew I'd answer that question with a reckless answer. It took so little effort to reach around and pinch his fingers. No one noticed, except him, of course. "I believe my wife was using a figure of speech."

"Pity for you," the prince replied, hardly looking at Thorne's face as he returned his attention to me. "How have you found our city? Similar to home? Vercant, was it?"

"Misby," I corrected, fully aware of his test and the eyes that fell on us, the silence of the room listening in.

He snapped his fingers. "That's right. You know these Silks. Sometimes they gossip so much the details are muddled."

"I can imagine it's hard to keep up with so many people and so many places, don't you think, my darling?" I swung my focus to Thorne, batting heavy lashes as I looked his way. I didn't expect to be so taken aback when he smiled down at me. Nor to be lost in a moment, right there in front of the crowd waiting for us to slip, confident we were lying. But he'd never looked at me like that. He truly was a master at disguising himself. No wonder they could never catch the Lord of the Salt. His masks were flawlessly applied.

"Indeed, my love. The endless sea of faces can be quite overwhelming. The key is to let one steal all your focus."

"Are you calling me a thief in front of our prince?" I asked, a single subtle hint.

"Only of hearts."

I turned back to the prince, a coy smile playing on my lips. "Misby is a beautiful city, Your Grace, but it pales in comparison to Stirling. The architecture, the fashion, it's all so captivating. I bet one could travel the realms and never see another place quite like this one."

"I'm certain there are many parts you've yet to see." His gaze dropped from my eyes to my chest and lingered too long, pinning me beneath his gaze. Two of the Cimmerians moved as one. As if it'd been planned. Stepping closer and closer. The sound of their breaths behind the masks yanking me into my nightmares. I tried to fight the panic by clearing my throat. The prince reached forward, gripping my hand.

Thorne stiffened beside me. His fingers tightened, digging into my hip.

"This is such a simple ring. Not at all what I expected from you, Noctus."

There was something odd about the way he held my palm. Something dark and dangerous about the way his eyes found mine again, searching yet strange. "Do you have magic, Paramour? I'm sorry, it's Paesha, isn't it?"

"Yes. I mean no. But yes."

He lifted a brow.

"I don't have magic. I used to wish for it when I was a child, of course. How incredible it must be for you. But sadly, that was not a blessing I was gifted. You were right about the name, though. I'm impressed. You must have a perfect memory."

Prince Farris's hand was uncomfortably hot against my skin, his grip just a little too tight to be polite. His dark eyes bored into mine with an intensity that sent a chill down my spine, despite the warmth of the crowded ballroom.

"No, not quite. Let's speak again soon. Find me after dinner. I find you... interesting."

He withdrew immediately. The Cimmerians that'd gotten far too close took a step back. I couldn't figure out why. What'd happened? But relief melted over me all the same.

I couldn't ignore the way my skin crawled. Couldn't fight the sound of those fucking chains echoing in my mind. I couldn't escape the trauma of the Maw. Suddenly, my palms were sweating, my heart racing. Sheer panic threatened to swallow me whole until Thorne's capable fingers began to swirl on my back. His presence calming me. Steadying me. As if he knew when my dreams weren't filled with Quill's face, they were haunted by the carved masks and my own blood. The lullaby of my death, playing on repeat.

"Thank you, Your Grace," I said with as much poise as I could, bowing again to the prince as he walked away.

A conversation with him was exactly what I'd come here hoping for, but the longer I stood before him, the more I realized there was absolutely no way I'd be opening myself up to Farris. If Thorne wasn't worth my secrets, the prince wasn't worth an ounce of my time.

But the man who was? The one that might know more about this kingdom than anyone else with ties to Farris, but also every other path throughout his kingdom... was the king. My last hope.

What had he called me? *A kindred spirit amongst the monsters.* There was something about him. Something that felt safe, even in the trenches of Serene's dark temple. Surely, we could talk tonight. Maybe I could even convince him to help me without having to give away the existence of the Fray, the identity of the Lord of the Salt, the Hollow, all of it. But maybe he should know there were people out there serving his kingdom, when he wasn't.

My heart began to race, rejuvenating me as I realized this was the obvious answer all along and I'd been so blinded by the people around me to see it. The Lord of the Salt had taken me to Lithe. Reverius's path began there. That's what Alastor was trying to hint at. It was where I'd met the prince, *and* where I met the king. He was the next step. I knew it as confidently as I knew my own name.

I just needed to find a way to get him alone. To create a distraction. Maybe the Lord of the Salt had come to King Aldus Wendale's dinner after all, he just needed a small introduction.

32

"Sit by me at dinner, won't you?" Lady Selia Berch asked, though I'd nearly forgotten she'd been lurking beside us while the prince had come.

"I'm afraid we've already made other arrangements," Thorne answered, pulling me away. "But do enjoy your meal, Selia."

After she was out of earshot, he scanned the room, looking for our next audience.

"Don't bother," I said, adjusting my earring until, as if I'd planned such a thing, it clattered to the floor, rolling until it landed directly in the center of a group of people who'd watched our exchange with the prince closely. I tugged on Thorne's hand, shoving our way into their group. "Pardon me, I'm so sorry to interrupt. I think I've dropped my—Oh, there it is."

I pointed near a man's polished shoe. He stepped back, bending to pluck the ruby earring from the ground. He considered the weight of the jewel before dropping it into my palm. "Exquisite."

"Thank you," I answered, pretending to be shy as I turned to my husband.

His fingers brushed my palm as he took the delicate earring, eyes careful as he played his part. "Allow me, my darling."

I tilted my head, baring the graceful column of my neck as he stepped closer. The spicy scent of his cologne enveloped me, mingling with the aroma of expensive perfume and aged whiskey that permeated the air. Carefully, almost sacredly, Thorne swept the loose strands of my hair back, his knuckles grazing the sensitive skin just below my ear.

My breath caught as he fixed the earring in place. To an onlooker, it would look like an intimate moment between newlyweds, lost in their own private world amidst the glittering crush of nobility. But I could feel the weight of the stares on us, the barely concealed whispers and speculative glances as the surrounding circle stepped away, just enough to give the others in the room the space to watch.

"I think everyone is staring, husband," I said, fully aware they could all hear me.

Thorne's hand lingered, his thumb tracing the delicate shell of my ear before trailing down to rest possessively at the nape of my neck. "Let them. I want them to see how utterly infatuated I am with my beautiful wife."

He pulled me closer until our bodies were flush, the hard planes of his chest pressed against the softness of my curves. The heat of him seeped through the layers of silk and lace separating our skin, igniting a fire low in my belly. I could feel the steady thrum of his heartbeat, the rise and fall of his breathing, and for a moment I let myself forget that this was all an act.

My hands slid up the fine linen of his jacket, coming to rest on his broad shoulders as I gazed at him from beneath lowered lashes. "Is that so? Then perhaps you should kiss me. Give them something to really gossip about."

A muscle ticked in his jaw, his hazel eyes darkening to molten gold as they dropped to my lips. Time seemed to still, the chatter and music fading to a distant hum as Thorne cupped my face in his large hands, his thumbs sweeping across my jawline.

I held my breath. The only thing that existed was Thorne, the solid heat of his body against mine, the rough calluses of his fingers as they traced the delicate lines of my face, the magnetic pull that drew me fatefully closer.

Slowly, achingly slowly, he lowered his head, his lips hovering a hairsbreadth from mine. I could almost taste him, the faint hint of whiskey and spice and something uniquely Thorne. My eyes fluttered closed of their own volition, my hands fisting the lapels of his jacket as I waited for the moment when he would close the final distance between us and claim my mouth with his own.

But the kiss never came.

Instead, Thorne's lips brushed against my skin, missing my mouth entirely. His breath fanned across my cheek as he lingered there. "Patience, wife. This ruse will never be the reason I claim those lips."

I glared, trying not to show the tinge of heat rushing through my body. Refusing to let him see how flawless his mask had been. But he'd seen it, of course. He'd planned for it.

Bastard.

His chuckle as he pulled away was equal parts endearing and infuriating. If the rest of this room hadn't fallen for our show, they were liars, because the gods knew I had.

A woman in the group nearby swatted her husband, stealing the focus of the room as she scolded him. "If you looked at me like that, maybe I wouldn't have to seek my thrills elsewhere."

The man sputtered, his face turning an unbecoming shade of puce. "I beg your pardon, madam?"

She stumbled over her words. "Only a joke, Varyn."

Their bickering escalated, drawing the attention of the other guests like moths to a flame. I let out a slow breath, grateful for the reprieve from prying eyes. Thorne's hand slid down my back as he guided me away from the squabbling couple and into a private corner. No Cimmerians, no people. Just us.

"Quick thinking with the earring."

"They'll question the missing kiss."

"But they won't question the way you looked at me."

"I'm excellent on stage."

"Undoubtedly." He bit his bottom lip to hide that fucking smile.

I locked eyes with him, my gaze full of venom. "I hate you."

His lips quirked, but movement across the room caught our attention. Archer and Harlow had walked in, their faces serious, shooting glares at one another as they collectively reached for drinks and went in opposite directions, though Harlow hadn't taken her eyes off Archer, as if she couldn't trust him to be left alone.

"Please tell me he's not thinking of stealing tonight," I said as she approached.

"No, no. Nothing like that. But I didn't want him to come at all. He thinks... the king... Well, it's not important what he thinks. If Prince Farris gets a wild idea about him... he knows he has magic."

"He'll be fine," Thorne said, eyes locked with Archer. "You can trust him."

"I don't think it's her brother she's worried about trusting," I said, adjusting the bottom of my gown.

She scoffed, but changed the subject. "We don't usually come to these. Who've you seen?"

"Farris and his usual crew. We've got a few gods tonight. Selia already made her presence known. Henry Dravenor, Varyn

Lethros, Elin Lindberg. A few others, but no one of note," Thorne said, as if speaking from a ledger he'd burned into his mind.

She looked around the room, studying faces. "Where's the king?"

"We're waiting for him to enter the dining hall, I think. He's late." I answered.

"A king is never late," Harlow said, taking a sip of her drink as her shoulders relaxed. "Maybe he just won't show, and we can all go home."

"A girl can dream." I slipped my arm around Thorne's.

"No Willard today?"

She let her shoulders fall. "I asked him to come with, but he thought it would be rude since he wasn't formally invited."

"Well, sorry to leave you, but we have to go mingle with the people and prove we've seen each other naked. See you later?"

She winked with a smirk. "Good luck."

As Thorne and I made our rounds through the glittering room, exchanging pleasantries with Stirling's Silk, a strange sensation prickled at the back of my neck. As if time had slowed, the chatter and laughter of the guests faded to a distant hum, their movements turning languid and dreamlike.

I blinked, trying to clear the sudden haze from my vision. When I opened my eyes again, the room had transformed. The chandeliers overhead now cast a soft glow, the light shimmering and dancing like stars plucked from the night sky. The marble floors beneath our feet rippled and flowed as if we stood upon the surface of a moonlit lake.

Thorne's hand tightened on mine, his brow furrowing as he sensed the shift. We exchanged a glance, a silent question passing between us. Before we could question a thing, a figure emerged from the shimmering mists that now swirled at the edges of the room.

She was tall and willowy, her warm skin luminous in the otherworldly light. Hair the color of spun silver cascaded down her back in loose waves, catching the light like strands of starlight. Her gown, a mix of pale gold and ivory, clung to her frame like a second skin before flaring out into a train that pooled at her feet.

As she drew closer, her pale blue eyes, flecked with shards of gold, reminded me of sand. Her full lips curved into a smile as she glided to a stop before us, the air around her shimmering with an odd glow.

"Huntress," she said, her voice a melodic lilt that seemed to resonate through my bones. "I have been waiting to meet you."

Beside me, Thorne tensed, his grip on my hand tightening almost painfully. But I barely registered the pressure, my attention wholly captivated by the goddess that'd just used a name I preferred to keep hidden.

"Don't worry, your secret is safe with me," she said, eyes sweeping around the room as if the people around us, frozen in time, would hear.

"Who are you?"

She laughed, spreading her arms wide as she said, "My sweet child. How very innocent. I'm Vesalia, your Goddess of Time. Of course, you've heard of me."

"And me," came another voice from behind. "Bellatora, the Goddess of War and Ruin."

I opened my mouth to speak, but the words died on my tongue as the room became a battleground of swirling chaos, the air crackling with electric tension. Bellatora stood tall and proud, her presence stealing the air from the room.

Her hair, a vibrant shade of crimson, fell in wild curls past her shoulders, each strand seeming to dance with a life of its own, like flames licking at the air. A smattering of freckles dusted her high cheekbones, circled her golden eyes, and covered the bridge of her nose.

Colors clashed violently, merging into a kaleidoscope of fierce hues as if painted by the strokes of a warrior's brush. Thorne's grip faltered under the weight of the new presence, his fingers slipping away. Panicked, I reached out for him, only to find empty space where he'd stood, swallowed whole by the vision delivered by the Goddess of War.

Abruptly, the chaos ceased, leaving behind a silence so profound it echoed like the aftermath of a fierce battle. Disoriented and breathless, I struggled to find my footing amidst the remnants of the chaotic storm. As I steadied myself, relieved to be back in the castle with people moving as they had before the women approached. Thorne snatched my hand and yanked me toward him, glaring daggers at the goddesses.

What kind of man would dare?

I inched back, staring at his face, looking beyond the familiarity of it to find something more. But he was nothing like them. His skin was scarred. His eyes were stunning, but normal. And with a single dimple, he was far from perfectly made. No. Thorne was not a god. But he was certainly foolish. Believing himself to be invincible as he stared down two goddesses at once.

I elbowed him, hoping he'd take a hint even though he knew far more about dealing with gods than I did. Maybe it was fine to take things from them and argue with them. Maybe it was even fine to hate them.

"You have questions," Vesalia said, her voice a purr that seemed to caress my skin. It wasn't a query, but a statement. "Don't worry, darling. We have all the time in the world. Time is a curious thing. It bends and stretches, twists and turns. What was, what is, what will be... they are all connected, all part of the same grand story." Her eyes were curious. Intoxicating. The flecks of gold seemed to move, drifting slowly between the two.

"Remember that thing I said about riddles?" Thorne asked.

I moved closer to him, and he slipped a hand onto the back of my neck, tracing tiny circles with his fingers as he scanned the room, likely to make sure someone was watching his show of affection. Though at this point, I didn't know if anything mattered. Not while standing before two powerful beings with the whole of the room more interested in the words spoken than the movements. Even the prince moved closer. Eyes on us once more.

"Don't be so hateful," the redhead chided. "My sister is merely curious about your new bride. And since the little mortal king is taking his time to make an entrance, bumbling old fool, we simply had to come meet her ourselves."

"Yes. Taking his time," Vesalia echoed, sliding her eyes to Thorne with a menacing smile. "Keeping time can be maddening."

"If only there—"

Bellatora's words were cut short by a sudden commotion at the front of the room. Raised voices mingled with gasps of shock, the sound rising like a swelling tide and crashing over the gathered guests. Heads turned, craning to see the source of the disturbance.

I stood on tiptoe, trying to peer over the sea of silk and jewels. At the grand entryway, a cluster of guards in royal livery huddled together, their faces pale and drawn. They spoke in urgent whispers, casting furtive glances between the cluster of gods and the prince.

Beside me, Thorne tensed, his hand tightening on the back of my neck. "Something's wrong."

Before I could respond, a tall, severe-looking man in a black uniform stepped forward, whispering into Farris's ear.

Farris stumbled backward, hand on his chest. "What do you mean my father is missing?"

33

"Are you sure you're okay with this?" Thorne asked for the thirtieth time.

We'd fled the castle in a flurry, all four of us cramming into a carriage to race home after the news of the missing king. The second we were far enough away from the Cimmerians, I began searching for the little old king who'd been so kind to me. I'd never gone for that visit and I regretted it now more than ever. I could have asked him. I could be home by now. And I wasn't willing to think about how much that thought hollowed me. I wouldn't be human if I didn't care for these people. It was that simple.

With him gone, Farris would rule in his stead. Make the laws, do whatever he wanted, and that was dangerous for everyone. Including me.

Harlow grabbed my hand. "Well?"

I fought against the muffled tones of my power, digging deep to lock onto anything that would connect me to the missing king, but nothing sat at the other end of my power. Only a void. And it took me far too long to realize why. "It's not going to work. He wore gloves. And a mask at Lithe. I've never touched him, and I haven't seen his face."

"Dammit. So we have no way to track him?" Thorne asked.

"Not like this."

Archer shifted, his shoulders pushing into Harlow in the cramped space. "The king never leaves the palace without a full retinue. Hell, he never leaves the palace at all anymore. For him to just vanish..." He trailed off, the unspoken implications hanging heavy in the air.

Harlow leaned against the carriage wall, hands nestled in her lap. "We know who's got him. We probably even know where he's being held. I mean, come on, it's so obvious."

I nodded. "The prince held the party to keep everyone distracted and give himself an alibi. He's got motive, means, and opportunity."

"It's a possibility we can't ignore," Thorne said grimly. "But speculating won't get us anywhere. And right now, the king isn't our first priority. We've got to lock down the Fray. The second Farris is in control, everything changes." He knocked three times on the carriage roof, giving Tuck, our coachman, the signal to head toward home.

Moments later, when Thorne rested his hand on the metal knob, his back straightened. I'm not sure if the others noticed such a small thing. And I'm not sure what it meant to be so acutely aware of his movements.

The ticking was subtle at first, a quiet backdrop to the creak of the door's hinges as Thorne swung it open. But as we stepped across the threshold, the sound swelled, growing louder with each passing second until it was a deafening cacophony.

Cuckoo clocks. Hundreds of them, covering every available surface of Thorne's once pristine home. They hung from the walls, perched on shelves, even dangling from the ceiling on thin chains. A sea of intricate wooden cases, gleaming brass pendulums, and delicate, painted faces.

And, as if on cue, they all burst to life, cuckoo birds springing from their hidden nests with mechanical precision. The inharmonious chorus of chirps, whistles and chimes crashed over us like a tidal wave, drowning out all other sound. It was maddening. Disorienting. As if we'd stumbled into some bizarre, nightmarish wonderland.

I pressed my hands over my ears, trying in vain to block out the relentless noise. Beside me, Harlow's eyes were wide with shock, her lips moving soundlessly as she stared at the chaos.

"This is what you get for mouthing off to the Goddess of Time," I yelled.

Thorne's face turned red as he strode forward, grabbing the nearest clock and wrenching it from the wall. The delicate wood splintered in his grip, gears and springs spilling from the shattered casing like mechanical entrails. He hurled it to the ground, the impact sending shards of painted wood skittering across the polished floor.

Harlow and I covered our ears, hardly muffling the sound as Archer joined him. The men moved through the room like a whirlwind of destruction, smashing and shattering every timepiece they could reach. But for each one they destroyed, two more appeared in its place, materializing out of thin air.

Chiming.

Calling.

Ticking.

Ticking.

Chiming.

On and on they went, reverberating through my bones and rattling my teeth. I sank to the floor, pressing my hands tighter against my ears to block out the maddening noise. Squeezing my eyes shut, I began to rock back and forth, humming tunelessly under my breath, fighting the urge to walk out.

Harlow was not so tolerant. "Fuck this. Stop pissing off the gods, Thorne." She shook her head and walked outside, cheeks flushed.

How could he have been so foolish, so arrogant, to think he could speak to the gods as equals? To believe that his words held any sway over beings as ancient and powerful as them? He'd been rash. Unfiltered. Perhaps I'd thought he was more. Different, simply because he seemed so mysterious. But this was a lesson well learned. Thorne was just a man. Arrogant and absolutely paying for it.

I stared at him until I was sure he could feel my eyes burning into him. His were wild. The ongoing barrage of chiming birds drove him to madness in minutes. The ticking grew louder still, more frenzied, until it was an off-key roar that shook the walls.

Thorne spun in a circle, his jaw clenched tight. He stalked forward, closing the distance between us until he sank to the floor in front of me. Archer said something and ran out of the house after his sister, but the noise was too much.

"She's reduced us to cowering wrecks, driven to the brink of madness by something as simple as sound. This is meant to be a lesson in piety."

"You think I don't know that? You think I'm not acutely aware of how much control they covet? I won't cower before them, Paesha. I won't let them dictate every damn move."

"You should have controlled your anger as well as you like to control everything else."

He ran a hand through his disheveled hair, the dark strands standing on end. A mirthless chuckle escaped his lips, his smile perfectly cruel. "Let's not pretend you're innocent in all this. You're the one they're really interested in. The 'Huntress'. Whatever game they're playing, you're a key piece on the board. Tell me why. Use your fucking words and tell me your secrets. You have to trust me by now."

How could I look him in the face and tell him the only thing I wanted to do was leave him? But maybe he needed that. Maybe he needed to hear a small piece of the truth. But no matter what I wanted, the words wouldn't come. Couldn't.

None can know of this bargain or where you come from. Only me.

The only thing I could do was fight back. Poke the beast Thorne kept hidden away. Maybe then he'd stop trying so damn hard. Or maybe he'd finally be the one to open up. I lowered my chin. "Don't sit there and pretend like you're not hiding something, too. You don't talk about your past. And don't think I haven't looked. Other than some old books and a few worn pages, there's not a single thing, no old letters, no keepsakes, nothing that tells me who you really are. You're a mystery in your own home. And do you know why I haven't asked?"

He didn't answer, only clenched his jaw, as he so loved to do.

"Because I don't want your secrets. I don't want to know the truth. Whatever you're hiding, you can keep hidden. I have my own shit to worry about."

His eyes narrowed as he pushed, ever the studious man, seeking answers. "And what might that be? You can tell me. Let me in."

"Oh, no. You don't get to ask questions you aren't willing to answer. In fact, you can sit right here and stew on it."

Anger flared hot and bright in my chest, temporarily drowning out the maddening chimes. I pushed myself to my feet, the fury simmering beneath my skin propelling me forward. I stomped up the stairs, down the hallway, and into my borrowed bedroom without looking back at Thorne. I didn't acknowledge the weight of his glare because what I'd said was true. I needed no more reasons to care about the man when I was gone. He could keep his fucking secrets and I could keep mine.

I shut the door firmly behind me. For a moment, I simply stood there, my back pressed against the solid wood, eyes closed as I drew in a breath. Searching beyond the chaos of sound for a semblance of peace. Slowly, I opened my eyes. With purposeful strides, I crossed to the dresser, my fingers closing around the delicate handle of the chipped teacup perched atop one of the infernal clocks.

"You first," I whispered, tucking it into the pocket of my coat.

I gathered my belongings with swift, angry movements. Even the little golden book that had been my lifeline to Thorne these past weeks. A few dresses, a spare cloak, a pair of sturdy boots. I bundled them haphazardly into my arms, not caring about wrinkles or creases. I wasn't too proud to take these things with me, knowing I'd need them to survive. I'd played the beggar in the past. I knew how this worked.

Yanking on the door, I marched down the hallway. The incessant ticking and chiming of the clocks pursued me, a mocking reminder that I'd never hear a clock the same way again. Stomping down the stairs, my eyes fixed straight ahead, I refused to look at the chaos of shattered wood and twisted metal that littered the floor. Thorne stood amidst the destruction, his broad shoulders heaving, hands clenched into fists at his sides. As I reached the bottom step, Thorne's head snapped up, eyes locking onto mine. For a moment, we simply stared at each other.

"Where do you think you're going?"

The audacity of that tone grated every one of my nerves. *Prick.*

"Anywhere but here."

"You can't just leave."

"I think you'll find I'm really fucking good at leaving." With that, I strode out the door, never looking back.

There was really only one place I could go. One place I felt safe enough. And though the night wasn't as cold as this terrible world had been when I arrived, with a heavy mist in the air, it still didn't take long before I was soaked through and shivering.

I wove through the shadowed streets, my senses on high alert as I clung to the edges of buildings and darted through narrow alleys. My teeth chattered, fingers numb where they clutched my meager bundle of belongings.

But I couldn't let the chill slow me down. Not with the threat of Cimmerians prowling the city and the news of King Aldus so fresh. I kept my head down, using the curtain of my damp hair to obscure my face from any prying eyes. When I was certain no one was nearby, I reached out with my power, letting it unfurl like gossamer threads seeking the familiar signature of the Hollow. My magic brushed against the worn stone of the Hollow's foundation, and I breathed a sigh of relief. Picking up my pace, I hurried along, guided by the gentle tug of power.

But as I turned a corner, my skin prickled with sudden awareness. The hairs on the back of my neck stood on end, and a shiver raced down my spine that had nothing to do with the bone-chilling rain. I wasn't alone. I quickened my pace, my heels splashing through puddles as I darted down a narrow side street. I strained my ears, trying to hear past the steady patter of raindrops and the frantic pounding of my own heart.

There. The faint scuff of a boot on cobblestones, the whisper of fabric brushing against a wall. Someone was following me, matching me step for step, keeping to the shadows. I scanned the alleyway for any means of escape or defense. But there was nothing. No convenient pile of crates to topple in my pursuer's path, no rusted pipe to wield as a makeshift weapon.

But those would not be needed, not as a large, familiar

frame finally stepped into the light. Thorne said nothing at all, striding up to me with a stoic face. He simply took the clothing and offered me an arm.

I hesitated for a moment, my pride warring with the undeniable pull I felt towards him. His eyes were unreadable in the dim light, but I could sense the tension thrumming just beneath the surface. With a sigh, I placed my hand on his arm. Because no matter what had happened, he would not see me suffer. It didn't matter what his past was. He was still the man that found me in the rain. The man that would do what he thought was right, no matter the consequences. Kill a man to save a stranger. Risk his name to save a city. Stand up to a god to hold onto his pride.

I kept my gaze fixed ahead, not daring to look at him, afraid of what I might see in his face. As we navigated the twisting streets, I couldn't help but notice the way he sidestepped puddles and ducked beneath low-hanging eaves with barely a thought. Something about his silence felt strange, but nothing more than the fact that he didn't follow me inside, choosing instead to brood and let me have my space. As I crossed the threshold into the Hollow, warmth enveloped me like a comforting embrace, chasing away the bone-deep chill from the rain.

I made my way through the quiet hall. Lianna raised her head from her spot on the floor, and I pressed a finger to my lips to keep her quiet. She shared a sleepy smile and laid right back down. As I climbed the stairs to the upper floor, my mind stayed on Thorne. Distance between us was better in the long run. Safer. It would make my leaving easier.

Reaching the room that had become my sanctuary within these walls, I pushed open the door, the hinges creaking softly. Inside, the space was just as we'd left it, the narrow bed neatly made, the small desk cluttered with papers and ink-stained quills from when he'd tried to work here.

I pulled the little teacup free and set it on the desk, turning the handle so it was perfectly placed. I opened the book, eyes falling over the two etched into the top of the first page before snapping it shut and tossing it.

Curling into the bed, I pulled the blankets up and hoped like hell, with Thorne gone, the nightmares wouldn't linger long enough to wake the children. Hours later, I lay in that familiar spot, cursing every god I could name and even the ones I couldn't. Being afraid to sleep without someone close by was ridiculous. I knew it. My brain didn't.

The door creaked open. I held my breath, eyes closed, pretending to be asleep as Thorne strode in. The bed dipped beneath his weight. Still, he said nothing, kicking off his boots and sliding in beside me. Moments later, with the heavy scent of his whiskey swirling through the air, his breaths slowed and he fell asleep. Something in that peace was enough for me to follow suit.

When I woke, he was gone. But he'd moved the teacup to the table on my side of the bed and propped his golden pocket book up beside it, clasp open, pages fanned. My heart was not ready for what I'd read within the pages.

Dearest Paesha,

As a man, a simple man really, that cherishes the written word, and history and knowledge, I cannot explain how deeply a mystery calls to me. At first, I thought that was the pull. I thought this charge between us was nothing more than unanswered questions. And I'll admit for a time, there was comfort in that space. Where neither of us answered to the other and we were fine. Guarded. Careful.

But as the days have passed and you've continued to stroke the curiosity swirling through my life, I can't pretend I haven't begun to wonder. I find it quite fitting that you've been curious about me. And while there are parts that will always remain mine, locked away in my heart, this truth is for you. A parting gift, if you wish it, but please know that I do not.

A lifetime ago, or so it seems, I fell in love with a woman who wrote my name across her heart and kept it. She was daring, like you. She pushed. Like you. She was everything. The sun. The stars. The space between realms. Whatever the ether was made of, it was her.

And I knew the day she died in my arms, the blade buried into her was also the evisceration of my heart. I knew I'd never recover. For years, I wandered through life as a ghost, a pale imitation of the man I once was. I sought solace in the pages of ancient tomes, losing myself in the tales of heroes and legends, becoming one to those that needed it most, anything to escape the gaping void that consumed me.

But then you arrived, a whirlwind of fire and steel, shattering the carefully constructed walls I had built around myself. And I did that to myself the day I asked the prince to write your name beside mine. That fact isn't lost on me. I know the role I forced you into blindly. And I'm sorry for it. You could have never known you were committing to pretend with a broken man. But now you do, and I hope you'll take this for what it is. A peace offering. I'm not asking you to like me. I'm only asking you to tolerate me.

But if you wake and your heart is heavy, if the walls are too high and you cannot go on with this charade, then so be it. I will handle the consequences and you can walk away freely. I offer my protection for as long as you need it.

Yours,
Thorne

34

Sliding my finger along the gold handle of the teacup, as I pictured Thorne setting it beside me, turning it just so, I settled into his words. Really heard what he'd said. He was just a man. And he'd have been awfully boring if he didn't have a past. In fact, the best people I'd ever known were shaped by trauma. And how could I fault him for telling me nothing, when I'd lived in his home and done exactly the same thing?

With a sigh, I pushed myself up from the bed, the floorboards creaking softly beneath my bare feet. Snatching one of my gowns from the pile I'd brought, I prepared myself to see him, and I walked down the stairs. Would everything be different now with one little argument, intensified by the maddening sound of clocks?

I was careful not to wake the sleeping people. He sat at the table, alone, a steaming cup of coffee in front of him, face blocked by the newspaper. I didn't linger, instead making my way to the bathroom, grateful to find it empty. I washed and dressed quickly, mindful of the others beginning to stir.

But try as I might, I couldn't stop my thoughts from drifting to Thorne. So, I put my hair in a simple braid, letting it fall down my back and walked out of the bathroom, choosing to slide into the seat next to him. Several of the adults had woken, but most kept to their spaces, and some had already left.

Thorne sat perfectly rigid, poised in a five-piece suit, still hidden behind his morning paper, though the coffee was no longer steaming. I reached for his cup, lifted it to my lips and let the warm, bitter taste slide down my throat. He slowly lowered the paper, just enough to look at me over the fold with a brow lifted.

"Morning, prick."

"Morning."

He was careful, the tone of his voice soft, and I didn't think it was for the sleeping warehouse.

I cleared my throat, meeting his gaze. "Thank you. For the letter." I fidgeted with the handle of the mug, tracing the delicate pattern with the tip of my finger. "You didn't have to share that with me. I felt pressure last night and I pushed back. I shouldn't have."

Thorne set the newspaper aside, giving me his full attention. He reached forward, his hand hovering near mine for a heartbeat before he pulled back, curling his fingers around his mug, stealing it back instead.

"You should always fight if you feel backed into a corner. Never apologize for that. We all have our secrets, our scars. I won't pry into yours. When or if you're ever ready to share them, I'll be here to listen. Until then, I'll follow your lead. As I promised."

I swallowed past the sudden lump in my throat, a pang of longing lancing through me. I wanted to tell him everything. But I couldn't. So, I thought I'd start small.

"You see all these children lying on the floor? What do you think when you look at them?"

He sat back, letting his eyes sweep over the room. "I'm overcome with pity."

I nodded, sliding the newspaper away from him so I could fold it in all the wrong places. Something familiar. "I don't feel pity for them at all. I feel hope. Hope because they found their way here, to safety and warmth and food in their bellies. Hope because they have each other, a community to belong to. Hope that this is just the beginning for them, not the end. Because when I was a child," I finally managed to look him right in the eye. "I had nothing. The streets were wet, cold and dangerous. The alleys even more so, and I wasn't welcome in the opium den my father fell victim to. We had a spot that was just ours behind an old bakery that would throw out moldy food once a month. I'd had to fight the rats for it, but it was something. My childhood is full of memories of huddling in a corner, watching my father waste away, his once bright eyes glazed and empty. He'd forget to feed me for days. Eventually, he forgot me altogether."

Thorne's fingers tightened around his mug, his knuckles turning white. He said nothing, though, letting me continue at my own pace. He was so good at being silent. But those that listened, learned.

"I learned quickly how to fend for myself. How to pick pockets and scavenge for scraps. The streets became my home, the other urchins my family. We looked out for each other, sharing what little we had. But always being one step away from starvation was hard. Don't look at these faces with pity, Thorne. Try pride." I handed the paper back, its edges crumpled with a touch of chaos that warmed something in me. "Pride isn't about having all the answers. Sometimes it's just letting yourself see the worth that's already there."

Thorne accepted the crumpled newspaper with a kind smile, his hazel eyes softening as they met mine. "Thank you for trusting me with a piece of your past. I'll work on the perspective."

He smoothed out the newspaper with careful hands, refolding it along the proper creases. The simple, methodical action seemed to calm him. "I'm not going to make any assumptions here. You're going to have to tell me what you want to do going forward." His eyes flashed to the ring on my finger.

"The king is missing. The prince is only going to get more dangerous. We have a warehouse full of orphaned children, one of which we know the prince wants. It's important to me that we find the king. If you'll help me do that, then I am yours for now. I'll play the doting wife. I'll sleep in your bed, which really is far too small, by the way, and I'll do whatever it takes to help you keep these people fed for as long as I can. But one day, things may change, and I need to know, if that day comes, it will come without questions and roadblocks."

"You have my word." The space between his lips parted, a question immediately lingering there. But he held it back, respecting the careful truce. Instead, he took my hand in his, rubbing his thumb over the ring on my finger. "I've only just realized I don't deserve you, Paesha darling."

"Mhmmm. I think everyone already knows that."

He leaned forward, tapping me on the nose. "If I'm to work on pride, you should work on humbleness."

"Honestly, that sounds awful."

Much to his chagrin, I took another drink of his coffee, the cool temperature souring the taste. I scrunched my nose, and he laughed, but quickly ducked down, scanning the room to make sure he didn't wake the children.

The door opened, and Jasper came hustling in with two great big bags of flour under his arms. Thorne flew from his seat, rushing forward to help. But Jasper insisted he was fine, crossing through to the kitchen.

I squatted next to Lianna, whose head had popped up when the door slammed shut. "Can you wake the rest of the kids, get your beds made up and hands washed for breakfast?"

She nodded, and I waited around long enough for her to wake the oldest first. She was young, maybe eleven or twelve, but they'd all clung to her as fiercely as Reuben had.

Stepping into the kitchen, I stopped at the door frame, taking a moment to simply observe. He'd taken his jacket off. With his sleeves rolled up and his vest already dusted with flour, he worked a ball of dough. The muscles of his forearms and shoulders flexed with each movement.

Jasper hovered nearby. "If it gets too sticky, just add a bit more flour. Once your consistency is the same throughout, don't overwork it. Just smooth the edges... that's it. Just like that. Then we put it here and cover, letting it rise."

Thorne glanced up, catching my eye as I lingered in the doorway. He flashed a wolfish grin and my heart stuttered at the open, unguarded expression, so different from his usual controlled facade.

"Care to join us?"

"And here I thought your talents lay solely in thievery and charm," I teased, sauntering over to stand beside him at the counter. "Oh, and being bossy."

He dusted his hands off on a towel before reaching out to tuck a stray lock of hair behind my ear, his fingers lingering against my skin. The look he gave me was one of gratitude. Of sliding right back into our familiar space, with maybe a little more compassion for each other. "I'm a man of many talents, Paesha darling."

Tuck walked in, shutting the door behind him as he moved to stand across from Thorne. "Now a good time, boss?" His honey brown eyes flicked to me and I realized I'd never really got a look at him in daylight. He'd driven the carriage, swung by at night to give reports, but he was a busy member of Thorne's inner circle.

Daylight revealed details I'd missed, shoulders broad enough to block the doorway, brown hair falling carelessly to his collar, a beard threaded with silver. He was a man of quiet menace, like a wolf lurking just at the edge of the firelight.

Thorne's shoulders tensed, his expression shifting from playful to serious in an instant. He wiped his hands on a towel and turned to face the burly man, his stance wide and commanding. "It's never good news when you're running this late. What's going on?"

"It's not good, boss. With the king missing, the prince has the Cimmerians out in full force. They're sweeping every street, every alley, turning over every stone. They started at the castle and now they're making their way down through the city, leaving no door unopened."

I stepped a little closer, drawing in every detail, the worry in my soul for the people of this world evident on my face, no doubt.

"Any word on where they think the king might be? Or who could have taken him?" Thorne asked.

Tuck shook his head. "Nothing concrete. Just rumors and speculation at this point. Some are saying with King Aldus locked in the castle these last years, it's a foreign power trying to sweep in. Others, and most, to be quite honest, think it's Prince Farris. An inside job makes more sense. But he's going out of his way to put on a show, if that's the case."

"Of course he is," Jasper said, wiping a hand across his brow. "Instill fear, then offer yourself up as a solution. People will be begging him to take the throne, just to end the invasive searches."

"He's not going to end it until he's had a proper search of every street, business and home," Tuck said.

The door swung open again and Brigid, the healer I'd brought tea to on my first visit to the Hollow walked in. She glanced at Thorne and smoothed her auburn hair from where it'd fallen out of her messy bun.

"Thorne, Jasper. Oh hi, Tuck. And Paesha, wasn't it?"

I nodded, moving to pour her a cup of tea, fading into the background as I listened to their conversation. Thorne had never kept me out of meetings but over this past week, I was listening from a door rather than being welcomed in. This was the first time I found myself in the middle of the conversation. I kept my hands steady and my face neutral as I selfishly devised a plan.

Brigid gratefully accepted the steaming mug of tea, cradling it between her slender hands. She took a small sip, her eyes fluttering closed for a brief moment before she spoke again. "I hate to be the bearer of bad news, but we're running dangerously low on medical supplies. Bandages, antiseptic, painkillers... we're scraping the bottom of the barrel here."

"How long can we stretch what we have?" Thorne asked.

She shook her head. "A week, maybe two if we're very careful. But with the increased Cimmerian presence, we'll see a rise in injuries. People are scared, desperate. They'll take more risks to avoid capture."

Jasper cleared his throat. "I'm afraid the kitchen's looking the same way. I've been skimming the top of the stock carts for the castle at night."

Thorne jerked around. "I told you not to do that. We don't do jobs alone, Jas."

"Well boss, we emptied Tilly's supply at the orphanage and there wasn't much. With the extra mouths to feed, I did what I had to do. But now they've moved the supply and I can't get to it."

Tuck stepped forward, his burly frame casting a shadow across the flour-dusted counter. "I think it's time we seriously consider how long we can keep going. I hate to say it, you know I do, but we can't pour from an empty cup."

Thorne raked his fingers through his dark hair, the strands standing on end as he shook his head. I took a slow step toward him, moving my hand to cover his. I had no idea things were so bad. I thought back to the words I'd flung at him, letting them burn into regret. He had no keepsakes. Nothing of his past. Hardly anything that said who he was. Not because he was hiding it. Because he was selling it, for less than its value, because Alastor was mad at him. And when he realized he couldn't keep that charade up, he started stealing. He was funneling everything he had to the Salt. And I'd thrown it in his face like he was just trying to hide himself.

Thorne pulled a small book from the inside pocket of his discarded jacket. "How many people? All in, what's our tally these days, Tuck?"

Tuck rubbed a rugged hand down his beard. "Last count was near seven hundred. That includes the orphans, the elderly, the Fray and the infirm we've taken in."

I moved the scattered flour on the counter top into a pile, keeping my hands busy as I casually asked, "Have you guys thought of leaving this place behind? Instead of just enduring?"

"How are we supposed to march seven hundred people out of their homes?" Harlow asked, shutting the door behind her and Wee Willy as they walked in. "We can't just go knock on another kingdom's door and ask for help. We'd be found easily. Hunted for sport."

"That's true." I drew the last word out, staring up at the ceiling. "It's almost like you'd need to leave Wisteria. Go to some other realm."

I needed to do this, to make moves here. Thorne had promised to help me find the king. And with that, hopefully a way home, but if we couldn't find him, if the prince had already killed him, I needed a plan B. Maybe even a plan C before I started beating down the temple doors and throwing myself at the feet of the gods. They couldn't all be happy to see the realms burn, could they? Not that I could come right out and ask.

"Wouldn't that make life so much easier?" Thorne asked, firmly planting a fist into the dough. "But we're not going to get anywhere sitting here wishing for impossible ideas."

"I guess it's just easier to wish for the impossible than deal with reality," I said, covering my tracks as Archer joined us.

Brigid nodded. "If we could do that, we might as well just wish Farris into Death's Court."

Archer nodded once to Thorne before adding, "I'd steal his fucking coin and hope he got lost in the Ether. What'd I miss?"

"Everything's falling apart, supplies are running low, and Farris sucks," I answered.

"And the king?" he asked, glancing at Tuck.

"Still missing."

They had no idea. Not a single one of them gave the slightest reaction to my question beyond its impossibilities. I'd never felt more stuck and confused in my life. Why was I here? Why this place? It'd be so much easier if I was searching for a door, but now more than ever, it was clear I wasn't. And even if we found the king, his involvement was only a guess. An excuse to keep myself away from the prince. The answer needed to be more clear. Especially when the problems just kept stacking. Unless... unless I was meant to help these people in order to go home.

Gods.

Was that it? I'd been so blind and distracted by all the

moving pieces, all the possibilities, I hadn't seen what was right in front of me. Of course. I'd spiraled in every other direction, nearly gave this crew away and I'd missed the obvious. Every sign. The Hollow? The Lord of the Salt? Alastor's mention of the prince and broken paths. We needed to find the king, but not because he was the answer, he was a missing piece of the greater puzzle. They needed a solution and I needed to get home and those were not two separate journeys. Only one. One path.

I let my eyes fall on Thorne. On the hard set of his jaw and the worry line between his brow. He wasn't a stepping stone. This place wasn't a small piece. Somehow, helping save all them, as was his ultimate goal, would carry me home. It was him. It'd always been him.

Thorne nodded, his jaw set in a hard line yanking me back into a room where the world felt more clear. He turned to the healer. "Brigid, take stock of everything we have left. Prioritize what's most critical. We'll scavenge what we can over the next few days, and I'll try to get you some help."

"Consider it done."

"Jasper, same for the kitchen. Ration portion sizes if you have to. Nothing goes to waste."

Jasper pulled two loaves of bread from the oven. "I'll stretch everything as far as I can but the more the prince destroys, the more Salt will come. There are thousands of Salt in the city. Our operation can't sustain that if word gets out. And it will when people get desperate."

Thorne's beautiful, sad eyes turned to me next. "You don't mind helping Jasper in the kitchen while we work on that job we discussed, do you?"

I gripped his fingers tighter, grateful he still meant to find the king. "Not at all."

"We keep this quiet for now. No need to cause undue panic. Let the rest of the Fray know to keep an eye on the Salt as best they can. Tend to your duties, but keep your eyes and ears open. If you hear anything about the king or the prince's plans, report back immediately. Understood?"

A chorus of 'Yes, boss' echoed through the kitchen. Thorne dismissed them with a curt nod, and Tuck and Brigid filed out, grim determination etched on their faces. Thorne braced his hands on the counter, his broad shoulders slumping as if the weight of the world rested upon them.

I laid a tentative hand on his back. "We'll figure this out."

WE'D GONE BACK to the house day after day, each one a tally mark in my mind. Forty-three days remained and the pressure from the countdown was gnawing at me. But we were doing everything we could. We took what we could, picking through everything in Thorne's house of value to sell in the Vale. But Alastor had kept his word, refusing any kind of deal with the Fray, forcing a middle man into the equation, so what was sold versus what came in was honestly sad and not enough. And after days in the kitchen with Jasper, creating a detailed inventory and menu, as more and more people began to shuffle in, cast out from their homes in the prince's show of strength, the truth was becoming glaringly obvious. We were going to run out of food.

"We're in this together, right?" Jasper asked, wrapping his scarf across his face.

I took his arm as we walked down the street, bathed in the midnight shadows of Stirling. "I'll never be able to sleep at night if those kids are hungry."

"Tossed and turned myself the last three days. Eventually the watered down soup is just going to be water," he said, patting my arm, but I could see the tears pooling in his eyes.

I'd never met someone that cared so hard for everyone

around him, no matter the cost to himself. Jasper was kind, yes, but he was so loving, and so bright, it broke something in me to see him cry. He was breaking. The Fray was breaking. And if we had to rob a garden to feed everyone for a few more days, then that's what we had to do.

"I've done this a few times," he admitted, shoving his hands into his pockets. "Just keep an eye out. Remember the signal, Miss Paesha?"

I adjusted my hood to be sure my face couldn't be seen as we stood on a narrow street, closed in by two buildings. "Yes, but a crow's caw is probably the worst signal ever. I haven't seen a single bird over here."

His huff was muffled by his scarf. "We're close enough to the city's edge. It'll be fine. Besides, it's not right. I planted this garden and I know there's warroot ready for harvest. You should have seen it. Rows upon rows of vegetables and herbs. The warroot, in particular, was my pride and joy. You can't see them from above the ground, you know? That's why they survive the winter. The roots swell beneath the dark, cold soil.

"That's also why they won't have harvested them. They don't know they're in there. It's food gone to waste if we don't get them. And the hearty warroot stores really well. The prince claimed taking my garden was 'necessary for the good of the kingdom.' Ha! More like necessary to line his own pockets and keep his thugs well-fed."

I patted his arm where it held mine. "I'll be right here the whole time. Promise."

"I'd never steer you into danger, you know that right? I don't want you to be afraid."

"Everyone in this city is in a prison, even if it doesn't have four walls and bars. What the prince is doing to the people is wrong. It's inhumane. But there's usually freedom on the other side of fear. And if freedom means taking back what's rightfully yours, what's meant to help people, then I'd face a whole lot worse than fear to see it through."

He nudged me with his shoulder. "Then let's dig up some freedom, shall we? Besides, it's not like they guard this place anymore. A picked over garden doesn't seem like a place the prince would be worried about these days. Especially with the Maw filling up."

I couldn't think about that. Couldn't consider the story of the woman who'd been dragged away from her husband and children because the prince had claimed she spat at him. The woman who conveniently had power, though her husband had confessed to Thorne it was little more than controlling the flicker of a candle's flame.

I stepped in front of Jasper, pulling his hood forward. "Be so careful and so quick. Don't risk your life for vegetables, you clumsy fool."

His eyes twinkled as he grabbed my wrists. "In and out. Promise. Got my lucky apron beneath my coat."

"Best get to it then."

I had a clear view of him, watching through the dim light as he hustled across the street and stood motionless for a moment, sizing up the tall garden gate. He wrapped his hands around two of the thick iron bars. A low groan from the metal accompanied a shriek as it began to bend.

I swept my eyes down the streets, hoping no one had heard. There was nothing, no movement at all. The bars gave way, slow at first, but then they twisted apart like they were no more than soft branches, the vines wrapped around them snapping in protest. In one smooth motion, Jasper had created a gap wide enough for his round frame to slip through.

Still no movement. No lights in the nearby houses. Good. As the seconds turned to minutes and I couldn't see him, I tightened my grip on the hilt of my knife, scanning the street again, my pulse quickening.

Still clear.

But they would know someone had come. And I doubted they'd blame the Lord of the Salt for garden robbery. The gate was bent, the wall destroyed, and the earth inside disturbed. It wouldn't be that much longer, though. And then we'd be gone before anyone noticed the destruction. But the evidence of his power would remain.

As I scanned the darkened street again, my heart hammering against my ribs, two shadows detached from the inky blackness. They moved with an eerie, fluid grace, their forms seeming to ripple and blur at the edges like wisps of smoke. Cimmerians.

I pressed myself farther into the alley, ignoring the way my skin came alive with panic, the way I couldn't breathe, the way the edges of my vision darkened, willing myself to become one with the stone at my back. The guards drew closer, their black cloaks swirling around them, the silver masks glinting dully in the faint moonlight. They were wraiths, nightmares given form.

But they weren't.

Only men, I told myself. *They're only men.*

I held my breath, not daring to make a sound when they passed the mouth of the alley. As they neared the garden gate, I tensed, my fingers tightening around the hilt of my knife until my knuckles ached.

What could I do? Certainly not run after them with the dagger. Two against one? And if I'd learned anything from my time here, where two marched, many more followed.

I parted my lips, letting loose the agreed upon signal, praying to whatever gods might be listening that Jasper would hear the caw and stay hidden. As I knew they would, the guards paused. Time stretched and warped, seconds bleeding into agonizing eternities as they surveyed the twisted metal bars, the gaping hole like a wound in the wrought iron.

One of the guards tilted his head. A gloved hand reached out, trailing along the bent bars. Beside him, the other stood perfectly still, a statue carved from obsidian and malice. They could feel the magic used there. That would be enough to draw them in. I only wished we'd had an army on the other side. That we'd laid a trap for them rather than the truth. Behind those bars was just an old cook, doing his best to secure vegetables to feed the hungry.

The Cimmerian, tracing the twisted gate, stepped back. He exchanged a wordless look with his companion. Then they turned away and continued down the darkened street, their black cloaks billowing behind them like the wings of crows.

I was frozen, hardly daring to believe our luck as they receded into the shadows. Only when they turned a corner and vanished from sight did my shoulders sag with relief. Jasper's head popped up over a garden wall a moment later, his eyes wide above his scarf. I gestured frantically for him to hurry. In seconds, he scrambled through the gap in the twisted bars, a large sack slung over his shoulder, bulging with his precious warroot. He moved with surprising speed for a man his size and age, his feet barely touching the ground as he darted across the street towards me.

"Never again. That was too close." I threw my arms around him. "Never again, you old fool."

"There, there. Nothing to worry about. Like I said." He pulled a handkerchief from his pocket and wiped it across his forehead. "Nothing at all."

Just as Jasper and I turned to flee back down the alley, a wall of black appeared. A dozen Cimmerians stood between us and escape. They moved as one, a silent, deadly unit, spreading out to cut off any escape route. My nerves rattled, panic clawing its way up from my gut. Jasper turned to me, eyes wide, fingers gripped tightly around his sack.

Then all hell broke loose. The guards surged forward in a tide of darkness. Jasper shoved me behind him, dropping the sack. "Run! Get out of here!"

"Not on your life," I snapped back.

"There's no escape. They will take one or two of us this night. You choosing to stand there won't save me. Now run!"

I'd fought a horde of charging soldiers in the belly of a castle before. I'd waded through bloodshed and fought with everything I had to save a little girl, and yet this... I knew he was right. Those were not trained soldiers and Death's Maiden had been at my side. This was different. Guaranteed torture lay at the far end of the alley, moving toward us. Adrenaline shot through me, forcing my mind back to a place where they'd strapped me to a table, back to a place where I'd bled and been starved for days. Back to a place where I'd licked rain water off the floor to keep from dying.

And so, like a coward, I spun and ran. I ran far and fast. I ran like Jasper's life depended on it... because it did. I ran with tears burning trails of fire down my cheeks. I ran. And ran. And ran. Until my lungs were fire, and my legs grew numb. Until the screams of pain from an old cook no longer echoed along the streets. Until I slammed open the door to the Parlor and dashed upstairs, ignoring everything as I crashed into Thorne's office.

He jerked to his feet and surged around the desk, eyes wide in terror. "What happened?"

I couldn't force myself to speak. Instead, I shook my head and flew into his arms, sobbing.

35

arlow and Archer stood side by side, dressed in full black leather gear, cloaked, masked and poised, just as they'd been the first time I saw them. These were the thieves. The Fray. Those that worked for the Lord of the Salt.

Though he'd hated it, Thorne had agreed to my plan. We all changed into similar garb and raced through the city, headed straight for the Maw. They'd saved me. We could save Jasper and if I had any luck in the entire world, we'd find a little old king down there as well. We hadn't studied the rotation of the guards, had no idea when we'd be able to get in. We just ran, knowing once we got there, we'd need time to watch, wait and learn.

But when I'd panicked at the door, when I'd needed only a moment to collect myself before we went in, Archer and Harlow had gone in first and come out way too soon with terrible news.

Harlow swung her hand toward the secret entrance to the dark labyrinth under the city. "You can check for yourself, Thorne. There's nothing down there but blood and bones."

"Do you think—"

Three trumpet blasts cut through the early morning air like a knife, their ominous notes echoing off the stone walls of the city.

"Oh, fuck!"

"Themis," Harlow said.

I didn't have time to ask before Thorne's hand tightened around mine and he darted down the street, his long strides eating up the ground. Harlow and Archer flanked us. We raced through the twisting streets where the city was just beginning to stir, shutters creaking open and sleepy faces peering out of windows. As the trumpet's call faded, a new sound took its place: the rising tide of panicked voices and hurried footsteps as the citizens of Stirling reacted to those three notes.

"We can't save him," Harlow snapped, yanking Archer back. "We can't. We need to stop."

"What's happening?" I asked as we paused.

"It's Jasper." Her sadness mixed with the hatred so much that hot tears welled in Harlow's eyes. "We're too damn late. Again."

I dared to ask the question burning on my tongue. "Farris is taking his magic, isn't he?"

Thorne nodded, face indiscernible behind his mask.

"I need to see it."

"You don't," he growled.

But I did. Because nothing in this world made sense, and I needed to know why. I needed more information. All of it. As much as the thought of witnessing the horror made me sick, I knew I had to see for myself. If helping the Fray, the Salt, this whole kingdom and all the fucking realms, really boiled down to helping the Fray defeat their villain, I needed to watch him in action.

Thorne's grip tightened on my hand as he met my gaze, his hazel eyes darkening with concern. For a long moment, he simply stared at me, searching my face as if trying to gauge my resolve. Finally, with a curt nod, he turned and led us down a steep side street, away from the growing commotion with Archer and Harlow right behind us.

We moved swiftly and silently. His steps never faltered and each of mine were filled with worry for that old clumsy cook that I should have never agreed to help. If I'd have said no, if I hadn't come, none of this would be happening. The guilt was enough to swallow me whole. There was a reason Thorne didn't want Jasper doing runs, he cared about him. I cared about him. And there'd be no turning back from this day.

As we neared the heart of the city, the streets began to widen, the buildings growing taller and more ornate, I'd definitely been here before. Thorne veered suddenly to the right, ducking into a nondescript doorway that opened into a dimly lit stairwell.

We scaled the narrow steps until my legs burned with the effort and my lungs strained for air in the close confines. Just when I thought I couldn't take another step, we emerged onto a flat rooftop. Moving to the edge of the building we laid, shoulder to shoulder to shoulder, belly down staring at the city square, catching our breaths.

"This is Prospector's Pointe," Archer said, scooting closer to me.

"She's been here," Thorne said, jutting his chin toward the far side of the square. "I put that ring on your finger right there."

Archer pointed. "See that gold circle down there on the ground? It's the center of the city and where every royal spectacle has happened since Stirling's birth. Kings have been crowned, weddings have commenced, and every person sentenced to death by a royal has stood in that very spot. You come here on a normal day, and no one steps on it. It's bad luck."

"Look!" Harlow gasped.

The prince walked forward, standing now in the center of Prospector's Pointe, the gold circle gleaming beneath his polished boots. The rising sun reflected off his inky hair, slicked back, not a strand out of place. The Cimmerians formed a half circle behind the prince, several rows deep, their black cloaks and silver masks a chilling contrast to the prince's regal attire. They stood as still as statues, an impenetrable wall of darkness.

But it was the ragged line of prisoners that drew my eye and turned my stomach. They huddled together, their faces gaunt and haunted, clothes hanging in filthy tatters from their emaciated frames. Some bore the marks of torture, bruises, half-healed cuts, fingers bent at unnatural angles. They blinked owlishly, flinching at every movement as if expecting a blow.

I knew intimately what their minds felt like, how their bodies ached. It stirred another wave of guilt within me, because I'd been saved by fate alone, and they hadn't. I didn't notice my trembling hands until Thorne wrapped a heavy arm over my shoulder.

There, at the end of the line, was Jasper, who only a day ago had been puttering around the Hollow's kitchen ladling out soup with a smile. Now he sagged between two Cimmerians, his face a mask of bruises, his left eye swollen shut. Blood crusted his torn shirt and his hands hung limp and useless at his sides. Even from this distance, I could see his chest heaving with labored breaths, each inhalation a painful battle.

The shocking transformation wrought in so short a time was disgusting. How could they have broken him so thoroughly, so quickly? What horrors had they inflicted upon him in the bowels of this terrible, terrible place?

Thorne's arm tightened around me, his body rigid with barely suppressed fury beside me. Rage rolled off him in waves. I could see it in the white-knuckled grip of his fingers on the roof ledge. Archer made a low, wounded sound, quickly muffled behind his clenched teeth. Harlow's face was a blank mask, but I saw the glimmer of unshed tears in her eyes. They'd had so much more time with that man than I had. Whatever I was feeling, they were likely drowning in.

Prince Farris raised his hands, commanding the attention of the growing crowd.

"We won't be able to hear him from all the way up here," Thorne said. "Not clearly anyway."

"Will he kill him?" I asked, hating the words the second they left my lips.

"No. Not likely. It'll be far worse than that."

We watched as Farris turned and marched directly in front of Jasper. Jasper desperately shook his head as the prince leaned in to speak to him.

"Farris's power won't let him exact justice unless there's truly a crime committed. And even then, he'll give Jasper a choice," Thorne said. "There'll be no question about his crime. They know as well as we do that Jasper shouldn't have been in the damn gardens."

"I still can't believe it," Harlow said. "We've warned him for months. He said he wouldn't go back."

"It's my fault," I confessed. "He said he knew where there was more food and I offered to help after we finished inventory again last night."

"He knew better," Archer said.

"Maybe, but we can't fault him for rash decisions. He feels responsible for keeping everyone fed. It's been weighing on him every day," Thorne answered.

"I don't understand how the king doesn't know this is happening if it's such a spectacle. Why has Farris been given so much space in a kingdom that isn't even his. Not yet anyway."

"Simple," Archer said, narrowed eyes pinned to the prince. "The king has a very filtered view of what's happening in his kingdom. His advisors are too afraid of Farris to say anything against him, and Farris has absolute control over his father's public appearances."

I said nothing more, remembering Lithe and the way that'd played out. Farris had sent his father away with the Cimmerians. The Goddess was the only other one that had access to him that night, aside from me. And Farris had hardly let us finish the first dance.

We watched in silence for several moments. Holding our breaths as the prince grabbed Jasper by his bound wrists and dragged him to the center of the point.

Harlow spoke, her voice hollow as she explained. "Farris is telling him that his choice is to either die or give away his... his power."

I knew why no one would choose death. It was the reason his face was already marked with bruises and blood, why he limped and his hair was matted. The Maw was a statement to the prisoners. Death would not come swiftly, but rather in the bowels of a place that would tear the skin from your body first, coaxing you to change your mind.

"You don't have to watch, Har." I whispered, taking her hand. "I don't need the words."

"Yes, you do," she argued. "You need to see it and feel the world weep. That power was never meant to be taken and now it'll be lost forever."

Sure enough, Jasper fell to his knees before the prince, arms up as he clearly begged for mercy. But Farris simply grabbed his hands, speaking sharp words to the silent crowd.

As Farris's hands closed around Jasper's, a blinding flash of light erupted from their joined palms. Jasper's back arched. His mouth opened in a silent scream as tendrils of energy, shimmering and incandescent, began to stream from his body into Farris. Mesmerizing and horrifying all at once.

Harlow made a choked sound, halfway between a sob and a snarl. Her fingers dug into my arm but I hardly felt it. Slowly, agonizingly, the light between them faded. Jasper sagged in Farris's grip, his skin ashen. He looked diminished, hollowed out. A vital spark had been ripped from his core. Witnessing such a violation made my skin crawl. The prince released him, and he crumpled to the ground like a marionette with its strings cut.

Harlow's body shook with silent sobs. She might've cried for Jasper's loss of power, but there was no doubt she was also mourning her own. Living in a moment she'd had all those years ago. Likely prodding at the missing piece of her soul. I pulled her close, wrapping my arms around her as she buried her face in my shoulder. She'd been tough. Sharp. Exactly what was expected of her in almost every moment but this one.

Beside us, Thorne and Archer lay still as stone. Thorne's eyes, those captivating eyes that could flash with mischief or darken with intensity, now glistened with unshed tears. He stared at Jasper's crumpled form, unblinking, as if by sheer force of will.

With a sharp gesture from Farris, two Cimmerians stepped forward. They grasped Jasper's limp arms and hauled him roughly to his feet. His head lolled forward, but still his feet moved. Still, he tried to right himself.

A figure glided forward and the air shimmered around them, an aura of power that set my teeth on edge.

"Here? He's going to do it here in front of everyone?" Archer asked.

"What's happening?" I asked as Harlow whipped around.

"Oh, gods. That's Themis, isn't it?"

God of Justice. Interesting.

Thorne lifted a shoulder. "I can't see his face. But yes, it is. This is his specific flavor of justice."

"Why do the gods just blindly work for Farris? It makes no sense. What does he possibly bring to the table?"

All three heads turned to me, all three confused, drawing back.

"You don't know?" Thorne asked.

"I never paid any attention to gods before," I admitted, giving a small bit of truth. In reality, the gods had abandoned Requiem.

"Gods draw power from notoriety. The more people that acknowledge them, even through fear, the more power a god has."

"I know that," I lied, "but that doesn't explain why they work for him."

"They don't work for him," Archer said with a huff. "Royalty is always favored by the gods. It's like they get a certain amount of tolerance for bullshit because they usually create a modicum of chaos and the gods love chaos. Farris might think they work for him, but they show him favor so he will put them on a pedestal. They're drawing power from every mortal that learns to fear or worship them. And Farris has power here. A different kind than they do, but they leech off him and the heads he turns. The gods need the mortals more than mortals need gods. They do nothing for us. Not a fucking thing, other than create problems."

"For all we know, there are gods on the outside silently making moves, trying to help us" Harlow said in contradiction to her brother.

He snorted. "It's not likely. What power would they have in Wisteria to make a difference? If no one speaks their name, no one goes to their temples, they aren't showing up."

"That's why I visit the temples of the silent gods," she

hissed. "Because I haven't forgotten, and I have hope. Maybe you should give it a try sometime."

"I left hope and reason on my mother's tombstone," he said tightly, all sense of the lighthearted gambler gone as he pushed her.

"Watch," Thorne whispered to me, drawing me back to Jasper.

The glowing, cloaked figure leaned in close, whispered something to Jasper, who tried with every effort to pull away again, and then grabbed his bare forearm, branding him with power, just as they'd said happened when a Cimmerian was marked. And just like that, a mark appeared on his forearm.

"There's nothing to be done now," Archer said, voice solemn. "He'll be cloaked and masked. He's one of them now."

"I think I've seen enough," I whispered as Jasper was handed a folded robe and began to undress in front of the crowd as if they didn't exist.

The hurried walk back to the Hollow was a somber one. Still dressed in leathers, we couldn't risk being seen and the weight of what we'd witnessed hung heavy over us. When we returned, Harlow clung to Willard, whispering what'd happened as he consoled her. Shortly after, she transformed back into the perfect Silk, and disappeared into the daylight. Archer had stayed, chatting with Brigid and a few of the other adults lingering about.

Thorne led me, heavy-footed, directly up the stairs, ushering me to bed in the middle of the day, trusting the rest of the Fray to handle the workings of the Hollow so we could finally sleep. Jasper was gone. Completely lost to us, and with that would come a complete change in the kitchens. But that was a problem for tomorrow, even while the midday sun poured in.

Thorne crawled in the bed, and before either of us was asleep, wrapped his heavy arm around me and pulled me close.

And I let him. Because I just didn't want to feel alone. Not this day.

"Sleep, Paesha darling. Tomorrow will be a better day."

"Don't tell lies," I yawned. "It just keeps getting worse."

Sleep had taken me quickly, the emotional and physical exhaustion was far too much to bear. But only minutes later, a commotion from downstairs forced us both awake. Thorne was out of bed and throwing his boots back on in seconds. I followed quickly behind. We raced down the stairs, chasing the shouts of a familiar voice. But neither of us were prepared to see Jasper standing there, in the flesh, screaming for someone to cut his damn arm off.

36

"Please," Jasper begged, falling to his knees at the door, still covered in blood and bruises. "You know me. I'll do anything. I can't belong to him."

Archer rushed forward and Thorne caught up as they grabbed the crying man by the arms, hauling him to his feet. He sagged between them, the anguish deepening the wrinkles on his face.

"You're safe here. We won't let anything happen to you," Thorne promised.

But Jasper shook his head wildly, tears racing down his face. "No, no, you don't understand! I can't be one of them. I won't! Please, just take my arm. Cut it off, burn it, I don't care. I can't bear this mark! If he gets to me, I'll betray you. Don't you see? You need me to protect you. Kill me or cut it off. You must."

He broke free of the men and thrust his forearm forward, the angry red brand seared into his flesh. The intricate symbol, a circle broken in half by swirling lines, seemed to pulse and writhe, as if alive. I swallowed back a wave of nausea at the sight, my heart clenching.

Thorne and Archer exchanged a grim look over Jasper's bowed head.

"I hate to say this, but how do we know it's not already too late?" Archer asked.

Jasper shook his head wildly just as the door slammed open and Harlow and Willard came rushing in. She ran across the room to Jasper and hugged him.

"Thank you, Miss Harlow. Thank you for saving me."

Thorne's head whipped around, glaring daggers at Willard.

Willy's eyes widened, a slight tinge of fear showing through. "She wouldn't take no for an answer. They threw him in a carriage while the others were being bound. We got him and two more free."

Harlow pulled away, spinning to throw Thorne's glare right back at him. "He risked everything for fucking vegetables. He paid his price. He's lost his magic and that's enough. Jasper's one of us. We don't let him fall. Now, get your shit together because this arm is going."

Thorne's jaw clenched, a muscle ticking beneath the stubble shadowing his cheek. He held Harlow's defiant gaze for a long, tense moment before letting out a slow breath. "You're right. We take care of our own."

"Thank you. Oh gods, thank you," Jasper said, clamoring forward, tripping on his boot and falling to Thorne's feet. He hugged his legs, crying. "Thank you."

Thorne glanced around the room, taking in the resolute faces of the Fray gathered close. Even the children sat silent and wide eyed. "Brigid, get your medical kit. Willard, find something to use as a tourniquet. Archer, I need you to hold him steady and do as much as you can... otherwise." His tone brooked no argument, each word sharp and precise as he hinted at Archer's magic without coming right out and saying it. "Paesha, get these kids out of here."

It wasn't going to work. There was no way. I knew the magic or at least something similar because I was bound to the Maestro for years and I'd seen people try this. But how could I tell them that? Hours ago they had to explain to me exactly what was happening. But this wasn't Requiem. Farris was not the Maestro. And the magic here wasn't the same. I buried my doubt and got moving.

"Come with me," I told Larcan, the man standing near the kitchen door. "Grab your fiddle."

He nodded gravely, eyes glued to Jasper. "I'm afraid it's not going to be loud enough."

I moved around the room, shuffling the children toward the closet we'd hid in numerous times over the past weeks. "Grab your blankets and go quickly. That's right. Hustle."

Lianna and Reuben stayed back, whispering back and forth in harsh tones.

"Come on, you two. We need to go."

Lianna turned to me, but kept her eyes on Reuben. "Tell her."

I glanced back and forth between the children. "Tell me what."

"We can trust her. It's okay," Lianna said, coaxing him forward.

He nodded, though the fear in his soft eyes held him frozen in place. I knelt down, taking his hand. "You can tell me. I promise I'm very good with secrets."

The boy, in desperate need of a haircut, nodded, leaning forward. His red hair fell into his eyes as he cupped a hand around his mouth and whispered. "I can help him."

"Help him how?"

He glanced at Lianna for reassurance before answering. "I can make him go to sleep. I'm not the best at it yet, but I can help."

I smiled at him, heart racing as I tried to remain steady. "Are you sure?"

He nodded. "I'm sure."

"Archer," I called, pulling the boy along. "Reuben here is going to be a hero today."

After explaining to Archer, he ran a hand over his chin, debating. "I can't let him watch this. He's just a kid."

"Here," Lianna said, pulling off her scarf. "Take this and wrap it around his eyes. That would be okay, wouldn't it, Benny?"

Reuben hesitated. Brigid yelled for Archer.

He kneeled beside the boy. "Benny, huh? I love a good nickname. And we're friends, aren't we Benny? Remember that card trick I showed you? When we get all done with this, I'll show you an even better one."

His eyes lit up. "Really?"

Archer nodded, "And I'll cover your ears, so you don't have to hear anything if you want me to."

"Promise?"

"Promise."

"Come on," I took Lianna's hand, and we rushed to the closet, listening to Brigid bark orders.

"Tighten the tourniquet. Cut off as much of the blood flow as you can."

I threw my hands over the girl's ears and rushed her forward, hustling into the closet. The haunting strains of Larcan's fiddle filled the air, rising above the commotion in the main room. The melody wove through the space, mournful and bittersweet, singing of sorrow and resilience in equal measure. Speaking to the part of my heart that loved music.

I settled on the floor, pulling the children close as the music swelled. One of the babes burrowed into my side, her small hands fisting in my shirt. I stroked her hair, murmuring soothing nonsense as the older ones huddled together, eyes wide and uncertain.

Larcan stood just inside the closet door, his eyes closed as he lost himself in the music. His bow danced across the strings. In my mind's eye, I could see Jasper laid out on the table, his face pale and drawn, slick with sweat. Brigid bent over him, her expression one of grim determination as she worked. Thorne and Archer standing on either side as Harlow and Willard helped hold him down. And Reuben with his blindfold, while he attempted to save Jasper from the trauma of remembering this foul moment.

But then the screams started, faint, at first, muffled beyond the fiddle.

The door flew open and Reuben dashed inside, eyes full of tears. "I wasn't strong enough to keep him asleep," he confessed, hugging Lianna.

I grabbed his little face and forced him to look at me. "Listen to me. You were brave and strong, and you did your best. That's all a hero does. Do you understand me? You did your very best and you're a hero now. We're all so, so proud of you."

He nodded past his tears. The screams grew louder, piercing through the soothing notes of the fiddle. Agonized wails of unimaginable pain, of a torment beyond comprehension. They rose and fell in jagged crescendos, each one more heart-wrenching than the last.

I held the children tighter, pressing their faces into my shoulders, trying to shield them from the horror. But there was no escaping it. The sound seeped through the cracks. Under the door. Through the walls. It filled the small space, suffocating and inescapable.

Finally, after what felt like an eternity, the screams began to fade. Larcan's melody slowed, the notes stretching out like molasses, each one a balm to frayed nerves. The children stirred against me, their small bodies uncurling from the tight knots they'd wound themselves into.

A soft knock. Three taps and the door flung open.

"It's all right," Thorne announced. "You can all come out now."

One by one, the children filed past me, their faces pale but resolute. Reuben clung to Lianna's hand, his eyes still red-rimmed, but his chin held high. I tried preparing myself for whatever we might see out in the main hall, thinking only of that until I brushed past Thorne, still standing at the door. His hand shot out and caught my wrist. With a swift tug, he pulled me to him, engulfing me in his strong arms. The unexpected hug knocked the breath from my lungs, my face pressed against the solid warmth of his chest.

For a moment, I stood frozen, my mind struggling to catch up with the sudden shift. I thought back to the way I'd needed him after Jasper was caught and realized, in his weakest moment, maybe he needed me too.

Slowly, tentatively, I raised my arms to wrap around his waist. My hands splayed across his broad back, feeling the muscles beneath his shirt. He tightened his hold, one hand coming up to cradle the back of my head, long fingers threading through my hair, holding me desperately close.

"You ready to run yet?"

His question shocked me. If only he knew. "Not quite yet."

THE WHOLE of the Fray had done their very best to keep the children shielded from the horror that'd crashed into the Hollow. After a long discussion, it was decided it was best for

Harlow and Willard to usher the children, a few at a time, to Harlow and Archer's house. It couldn't be a permanent placement, but since their grandmother had passed and just the two of them lived there, it made sense, just in case there was lingering danger with Jasper.

Exhausted beyond belief and dragging by nightfall, we did our best to put together a dinner for the Salt that'd sought refuge in the Hollow. I was beginning to see the thin line between the Fray and the Salt of the Hollow. Most of the Salt needed help and were all hands in when it came to spreading the work. The Fray were those mostly on the streets, moving goods, acquiring what they could, whispering into the Salt's ears about where to go for help. But everyone worked.

Everyone had a role to play, and the community that came with it was beautiful. One of laughter in small moments and shared stories. Of camaraderie and giving, even when you had nothing to truly give. There wasn't a single thing about this group that didn't remind me of the Syndicate back home. And maybe that's why I'd fit in so well. I knew this life. I'd been here for many, many years, even if the people at the table wore different faces. Their hearts were the same. Their struggles were the same. We were the same.

Jasper was somewhat dazed, but Archer's magic had sealed the wound, keeping him free of pain, though I wondered what trauma lingered. What hole couldn't be healed by the loss of his power.

"Do you think it worked?" Archer asked, handing me another clean bowl to dry and stack as we washed dishes together after dinner.

"He'll have to stay hidden now, regardless. He can't go home."

"He didn't have much of a home anyway. Just a room up by

the castle one of the Fray lent him. What do we think life as a one-armed cook will be like?"

"Doesn't matter," I said, shifting my weight because my legs were so, so tired. "The point is he'll have a life."

I sighed, setting down the bowl I'd been drying and leaned heavily against the counter. The Hollow was settling into an uneasy quiet, the usual chatter and bustle replaced by a somber hush. Even the creaks and groans of the old building seemed muted, as if the walls were holding their breath.

Archer nudged me. "I'm going to head home, unless there's something else we need to get done? I bet Harlot has her hands full with all the kids."

"Nah. I think we're good here. Thanks for... you know. All the help."

He scrunched his nose. "You're the newbie here, Fingers. I should be thanking you." He tossed his rag down and walked out of the kitchen.

I didn't hear Thorne approach, lost as I was in my own thoughts. It wasn't until his hands settled on my shoulders, warm and solid, that I startled back to awareness. A small gasp escaped my lips as his fingers dug into the tense muscles, working out the knots with a gentle but insistent pressure.

"You're wound tighter than a clock spring," he murmured, his breath stirring the fine hairs at the nape of my neck.

"Is that a Goddess of Time joke?"

Thorne chuckled, a low rumble that I felt more than heard. "Not an intentional one, but I'll take credit for accidental wit." His thumbs pressed into the base of my skull, rubbing small circles that sent shivers cascading down my spine.

I let my head fall forward, my chin nearly touching my chest as I melted into his touch. His hands were like magic, coaxing the tension from my body with each sweeping pass. Slowly, methodically, he worked his way down the column of my neck, kneading the corded muscles until they loosened beneath his fingers.

A soft sigh slipped past my lips, my eyes fluttering closed as I gave myself over to the sensation. The rest of the world fell away, the low murmur of voices from the main room, the weight of the day's trials. There was only Thorne. The heat of his body at my back. The mesmerizing glide of his hands on my skin. The spicy, masculine scent of him.

Lost in the hypnotic spell of Thorne's touch, I almost didn't register the slam of the front door, but there was no mistaking the voice as Archer ran across the Hollow, shouting for Thorne.

He burst into the kitchen, eyes wild, darting between Thorne and me as he fought to catch his breath. "They're coming," he gasped, one hand braced against the doorframe. "The prince... Cimmerians... headed this way."

Thorne cursed under his breath. In an instant, the tender, attentive man was gone, replaced by the hard-edged leader.

"How long do we have?"

Archer shook his head.

I ran for the door. "Minutes, at most. He's moving fast."

"A whole damn army of them," Archer managed.

"Get the hell out of here, Arch. Tell everyone. They aren't breaking any laws by sleeping in the streets. They'll be safe." He snatched my hand without another word and yanked me toward the stairs. "We have to go this way. The Salt are safe, but we aren't."

I yanked free of his grip the second we were up the stairs, darting into the room we'd shared, and though it pained me, I left the teacup behind, choosing instead to swipe only his golden book, and the stack of ledgers he'd left on the small desk. But he surged past me, swiping the teacup anyway, as the prince's voice could be heard shouting down the street.

We moved like wraiths, dashing up to the rooftop as silently as we could. None of the Fray's guards were there and there was no time to ask ourselves why. We peered down over the edge of the building just in time to see the Cimmerians fan out along the street. Just in time to see Brigid caught by the throat.

"Fuck," Thorne's curse was nearly silent, but the anger rippling off him was unmistakable.

"Come out, come out wherever you are," the prince sang, striding with a happy bounce in his step.

I gripped Thorne's hand. "It was Jasper, wasn't it? He probably told Farris everything before Harlow and Willard even got there."

"You would think," Thorne said, pointing. "But look."

Jasper was scrambling into the back of a covered cart with several other Salt. "He can hear Farris. But he's not listening to him. He would have had to come out if he was bound to him."

And of that I was certain. I knew the tight noose of a magical bond. There was no bending, no wavering against your master's absolute rule.

"Show your faces, little rats," Farris said, heading toward the front door of the Hollow.

Cutting his arm off had actually worked. But there was no time to think about that now. Not as Brigid's scream ripped through the night. Not as it was abruptly cut off by the quick snap of her neck. Not as Thorne froze, and his breaths stopped coming.

"Look at me," I said, gripping his face. "Look at me, now."

But he didn't move, didn't take his eyes off her as she was tossed to the side, her unmoving body discarded like it meant nothing at all. My stomach turned at the way her twisted body landed.

"Thorne," I tried again. "We have to go. He's coming. He's coming right now. We need to run."

His face was all hard lines and stone as he spun to me. "Maybe I don't want to run anymore. Maybe it's time to stand and teach that little prick a fucking lesson."

"You can't," I pleaded desperately. "He's too powerful and there are way too many. We have to get out of here. Please... Please."

My begging broke the spell. "One day. One day, I will break him."

"Great," I said, tugging him toward the next building. "But not this one."

Thorne and I raced across the rooftop, our feet pounding against the weathered shingles. The cool night air whipped at our faces as we leapt from one building to the next, the gap between them a yawning chasm that threatened to swallow us whole. But Thorne moved with a feline grace, his muscles coiling and releasing with each powerful stride, and I found myself drawn along in his wake, my own body responding to his lead as if we were two parts of the same dance.

Once we were far enough away, once the chaos was behind us, though I knew it grated on him to have abandoned everyone, we redirected and headed straight for the Parlor. "We can stay there tonight. I don't have a bed, but I've got blankets and couches and we can make do until tomorrow."

"What's tomorrow?"

"I've got a few things I need to do, then we regroup and pay a little visit to Vesalia."

"The Goddess of Time? Why?" I asked, matching his long strides with two of my own.

"Because we can never go back to the Hollow and I need her to get her fucking clocks out of my house."

"I'm not sure you should be the one to ask," I said, looking past the reflection on his glasses. "You don't really make friends easily."

"I'm not concerned with being her friend."

"Oh, okay, great. Today was such a lovely, casual day. We should definitely stir the pot and pick a fight with a goddess tomorrow."

He stopped hard in his tracks. "Just so we're clear, she started it."

37

"They can't know we were part of the prince's raid," Thorne said, pulling me through the back door of the Parlor. "I promise you can sleep soon, but we need to make sure they know we've been here first. We're going to have to make a show of it."

We hustled upstairs, landing in his office. He crossed the room in three strides, stopping to pour a drink from a decanter. He slammed it back before refilling. I stood there, watching him, knowing he was hurting and angry and his mind was carrying him through every memory he'd had of Brigid. Of his responsibility for her life and ultimately her death.

He walked back to me, glass in hand, staring down. With perfect ease, Thorne raised his hand, hesitating for only a second before sliding his fingers up my collar bone, stopping to let his thumb rest on my racing pulse.

"Settle, wife. I need you to be able to focus. Let go of everything we're running from and be present."

It wasn't the night that had me so rattled. I'd become numb to chaos, it seemed, but his commanding tone, his beautiful eyes, his caring nature, his pain... those would easily be the things that unraveled me.

He held out the glass, the amber liquid sloshing gently against the crystal. "Here. This will help."

I accepted the drink with a steady hand, daring to stare him in the eye as I took the first sip, letting it burn down my throat, spreading warmth through my chest and belly. I followed it with another, never breaking eye contact.

"Good girl," he said, slowly wiping a drop from the corner of my mouth with the pad of his thumb before taking the glass back. "Now play nice with me for an hour and I'll let you sleep all day tomorrow."

"Let's be clear about something, husband. You don't *let* me do shit."

He leaned in close, narrowing his eyes. "I think I do."

I knew what he was doing. Baiting me, pushing me into a mindset ready for a crowd of curious Silk. But it was completely unnecessary. I didn't need direction. Nor coaxing. I knew exactly what was expected of me, and now that I'd realized my fate was tied to him, he was about to get more than he bargained for.

I let him have this moment. Let him watch as I settled in, taking a long deep breath before I grabbed a suspender and yanked him closer, a coy smile lifting my lips. Running my fingers through his thick, dark hair, I messed it up before I spun and jerked him toward the door. Drink in hand, he let me pull him down the steps, eyes burning into my back as we walked purposefully through the crowd of laughing, gambling, unruly Silk, losing themselves in their guilty pleasures, not caring an ounce for what was happening outside of their cushy comfort zones. All eyes turned our way as we cut a path through the revelry. Whispers followed in our wake, speculative murmurs hidden behind gloved hands and lace fans.

He plopped down on the couch, letting the last of his drink

splash onto the carpet, though I knew, without a doubt, that small mess grated every one of his nerves. Thorne loved order. And control. But he'd never crack because most of all he loved his masks.

I sat in his lap, throwing my legs up onto the couch. Thorne's hand immediately settled on my thigh, his long fingers splaying possessively over the silk fabric of my dress. The heat of his touch seared through the layers, igniting a slow burn beneath my skin.

Leaning into him, I rested my cheek against his shoulder, letting my own hand wander, trailing along his chest. His fingers dug into my thigh, a silent warning, a reminder of who he thought held the reins.

Tilting my head, my lips grazed the shell of his ear as I whispered, "Is that all you've got, husband? A little touch of my thigh and you think they're all going to run to the gossip mill? You've got a point to prove here. Do better."

His eyes met mine, dark and fathomless. "For them or for you?"

I held his gaze, unflinching, even as my heart raced. "For them, of course."

This was the dance we did, forever circling, forever pushing, forever testing the limits of our twisted bond. Thorne's hand slipped under the slit in my dress, moving up my thigh. Back and forth, he brushed his fingers. Slowly. Achingly so. They teased and tested my resolve.

I moved my fingers into his hair, winding the long strands through my fingers as I leaned into him, stretching to drag my tongue along the bottom of his earlobe. Testing how far I could push him until he broke.

His fingers found the lace trim of my undergarments. "Tell me when you want me to stop."

I wouldn't be the first to break.

He pressed lightly, sliding a bit further up and my chest rose and fell, my breath hot against his neck. He was playing with fire, and I loved it.

"You're asking for trouble," I whispered.

He smirked, that dimple on full display. "Don't lie, Paesha darling. You asked. I'm delivering."

His fingers, barely hidden beneath the drape of my gown, brushed the damp lace of my undergarments and I sucked in a sharp breath, my thighs clenching involuntarily. Thorne's lips quirked in a self-satisfied smirk as he leaned in close. "Tell me to stop."

"I could. But I'd rather be a scandal."

With a mischievous grin and eyes for only me, he pushed the flimsy fabric aside, his fingertips gliding through the slick heat he found there. He moved with deliberate slowness, circling, teasing, stoking the ache building low in my belly.

My breath caught in my throat as Thorne's skilled fingers danced over the sensitive flesh right here in front of everyone. Hidden but only just. I bit my lip to stifle a moan, my hips rocking subtly against his hand, seeking more of his electrifying touch. Around us, the murmur of the crowd faded to a distant hum, my entire world narrowing to the exquisite sensations Thorne coaxed from my body.

"Eyes on me. If you look away, I'll stop."

"Only you could command me, threaten me, and pleasure me in the same breath." I managed, my voice full of weakness for him as I stared into eyes that held me on the edge of control.

He moved with maddening slowness, tracing delicate patterns that had me quivering with need. Feather-light strokes alternated with firmer pressure. His thumb brushed over my clit, and I couldn't stop the breathy gasp that escaped my parted lips.

"That tiny hitch in your breath is going to be my undoing,

wife." Thorne's eyes were molten as they held mine, dark with desire and a primal sort of satisfaction. He relished having me at his mercy, pliant and desperate. His fingers delved deeper, sliding easily inside, trailing the flames that licked along my nerve endings.

I gripped his lapel tighter, my knuckles turning white as I fought to maintain a semblance of composure, even as my body threatened to unravel. Thorne's fingers curled inside me, finding that spot that made my toes curl. I couldn't hold back the whimper, my head falling to rest against his shoulder.

"That's it, darling. Let go for me."

His words, rough with desire, were my undoing. The coil that had been tightening low in my belly snapped, my release crashing over me in wave after exquisite wave. I shuddered in Thorne's arms, my face buried against his neck to muffle my cries of ecstasy. He held me through it, his fingers never ceasing their wicked dance, wringing every last drop of pleasure from my trembling form.

As the last aftershocks faded, I slumped bonelessly against Thorne's chest. He withdrew his hand from beneath the gown and lifted his fingers to his lips, holding my gaze as he slowly, deliberately licked them clean. My breath hitched at the sight, desire building within me once more. He leaned in close, his lips brushing my ear as he whispered, "You taste like honey and sin, darling. I could feast on you for hours and never be sated."

He shifted until our lips were a hairsbreadth apart, his breath mingling with mine.

Time slowed, the anticipation stretching taut between us. The rapid thrum of his heartbeat beneath my palm echoed the wild cadence of my own. His eyes, those captivating hazel eyes that could see straight through to my soul, dropped to my mouth and for one selfish moment, I wished I never had to leave him. I wished I could promise him forever and keep my word, because fuck if I wasn't falling. And there wasn't a doubt in my mind that he would be right there to catch me.

A flurry of movement in the center of the Parlor broke the spell over us. One of the Parlor workers came rushing forward, weaving through the throng of Silk. Her pale face was pinched with worry, tendrils of dark hair escaping her neat bun to frame her delicate features.

I reluctantly pulled back from Thorne, straightening my gown as I shifted to a more respectable position on his lap. He kept one arm wrapped securely around my waist, his fingers digging possessively into my hip even as he turned his attention to the approaching woman.

"Uhm, Mister Noctus, sir," she said breathlessly, dipping into a quick curtsy. "Forgive the intrusion, but there's a matter requiring your immediate attention."

Thorne's brow furrowed, a flicker of annoyance passing over his handsome face before he smoothed it away. "Can it wait, Hannah? As you can see, I'm rather... occupied at the moment." His fingers flexed on my hip, emphasizing his point.

Hannah's eyes darted to me, her cheeks blushing before she leaned forward and whispered. "It's Brigid, Sir. I'm afraid she's been..." She swallowed, tears filling her eyes. "Tuck brought her body."

As if ice had been splashed over both of us, everything changed. Thorne slipped his mask back on, taking a commanding tone as he forced her to focus on his words. "You will not speak of this to another person. Clear? You fix your face. You take a breath. You stand straight and smile down at me. Then you will turn, walk over to Mr. Vendrake and offer to fill his drink for him. Nothing dire has happened. There cannot be any indication that we are connected to what has occurred tonight. Do you understand?"

She nodded.

"Good, girl."

Thorne tossed his head back and laughed, waving a hand through the air as if shooing Hannah away. She plastered a smile on and spun, doing exactly as he'd directed, but she shook slightly on her heels as she walked.

Every moment he continued to sit there, stroking the back of my neck grated on him. I could feel it in the firmness of his touch, see it in the depths of his eyes. But he was smart and patient, and when he eventually held a hand up to guide me to my feet, I could feel the tremble there.

"Would you mind going upstairs without me?"

A question. Not a command.

"I can come. I can help."

He slid his hands to the sides of my face, staring down. "I need you well rested for tomorrow. Vesalia is interested in you, which means she'll make it impossible for me to find her without you. You have to be sharp."

I nodded. "Wherever you need me, that's where I'll be."

He paused, rubbing his thumb over my jaw line. "I hope you mean that."

THE SECOND I WAS ALONE, exhaustion hit me like a tidal wave. My limbs felt leaden, each step an effort as I trudged up the stairs to Thorne's office. I pushed open the cabinet door with more effort than it should have taken, pulled one of his shirts from a hanger and changed before snagging his little golden book from the desk and curling up on the couch. I'm not sure what I could have done if he ran into some kind of trouble, but at least it was something. His goals were mine for the foreseeable future and I needed to be whatever asset I could.

But when I clicked open the book just to check, five words appeared on the page.

Go to sleep, Paesha darling.

I wrote back.

Don't tell me how to live my life.

And then promptly fell asleep.

I woke to the tinkling of ice in a glass and peered through tired eyes to see Thorne behind his desk, leaning against the window frame, hair a disheveled mess, glasses at the tip of his nose, swirling his whiskey as he looked over a ledger.

I pushed myself up from the couch. The worn leather creaked beneath me as I shifted, the sound drawing Thorne's attention. He glanced up from the paper, eyes meeting mine over the rim of his glasses. A small, tired smile tugged at the corners of his lips.

"I didn't mean to wake you," he said, his voice low and rough with exhaustion.

I shook my head, my bare feet whispering against the plush rug as I padded over to him. The early morning light filtered through the window, highlighting the dark shadows beneath his eyes. He looked worn, the weight of last night's events etched into every line and hollow.

Without a word, I plucked the ledger from his hands, ignoring his half-hearted protest as I set it aside on his desk. He watched me but made no move to stop me. Gently sliding the glasses from his face, I folded them carefully before setting them down as well. His eyes, unobstructed now, bore into mine with an intensity that stole my breath. Flecks of gold and green danced in their depths, captivating me.

Slowly, deliberately, I perched on the edge of the desk, the worn wood smooth beneath my palms. Thorne's shirt rode up my thighs as I settled, exposing an enticing expanse of skin. His gaze flickered down, his Adam's apple bobbing as he swallowed hard. Grabbing him by the front of his shirt, I yanked him toward me. He stepped between my parted knees, his large hands coming to rest on the desk on either side of my hips, caging me in while the heat of his body seeped into mine, chasing away the lingering chill of the night. I tilted my head back to meet his gaze, my breath catching at the raw hunger I found there.

"You shouldn't tempt me like this. Not when I'm barely holding on by a thread."

I trailed my fingers along his jaw, relishing the scrape of stubble against my skin. "Maybe I want you to let go. You don't need to control every single moment. Give me this one."

His voice was reverent, almost sad. "You don't know what you're asking for."

I leaned in closer, my nose grazing along the side of his neck. "I know exactly what I'm asking for. Let me in. Trust me. Let yourself feel something real, even if it's just for a moment. Not for an audience. Not for the prince, or the gossip mill. Take something that you want for yourself. Be selfish, but gods help me, do it slowly."

"There was a time I took what I wanted without thought, and the cost became a cycle of loss. Now, here I am again, standing on the edge of all I know, drawn to you like a song calls to the heart. You're the note that could shatter the silence, the promise of something more than just survival. But if I give in, if I risk this... I'm afraid I'd lose the one thing holding me together. I lean on logic because wanting you feels like the beginning of something vast, something unstoppable, and gods, I don't know if I'm strong enough to survive it."

"Letting someone in doesn't make you weaker."

Thorne's hands flexed on the desk, the wood creaking beneath his white-knuckled grip. I nipped lightly at his earlobe, soothing the sting with a flick of my tongue, battling his logical brain, coaxing the irrational side of him to come out and play with me.

A low groan rumbled up from his chest and I smiled. "Shall I beg, Husband?"

He shifted closer, releasing the desk to wrap my hair around his fist, pulling me toward him. His hand tightened in my hair, his grip just shy of painful as he tilted my head back, searching my eyes as if he could see every one of my secrets within them. "What if I taste of heartache?"

"What if I taste of healing?"

His resolve crumbled, the last of his restraint shattering like spun glass. He captured my lips in a searing kiss. His mouth slanted over mine, hungry and demanding, his tongue delving past my parted lips to stroke along my own. I melted into him, my fingers tangling in the folds of his shirt, holding him to me as if he might disappear. He kissed me like a man starved, like I was the air he needed to breathe.

His hands skimmed up my bare thighs, igniting sparks in their wake. Higher and higher they crept, pushing the fabric of my borrowed shirt up until it bunched around my waist. I gasped into his mouth as his fingers dug into the soft flesh of my hips, anchoring me to him.

He kissed a fiery path along my jaw, down the column of my throat, his lips and teeth and tongue painting a masterpiece of sensation on my skin. I arched into him, my head falling back, a breathless moan escaping me as he found that sweet spot just below my ear that made my toes curl. He lingered there, no doubt leaving a mark for all the world to see. A brand. A claim.

And then he stepped away. Spinning so his back was to me, shoulders heaving.

It was too much. I was too much. He thought of her, and his heart wasn't ready to let go. And mine wasn't ready to stay.

"I'm sorry," he whispered.

I moved down from the desk, walking over to gather my dress I'd left on the floor. "Don't you dare apologize to me for knowing what it means to love someone with your whole heart, Thorne Noctus. Don't you dare."

38

"I'm honestly underwhelmed. Is that a word? I'm pretty sure it is. All this time I thought this was just a clock."

"Stop talking. You're embarrassing yourself," Harlow told Archer, though I'd caught the smile tugging on her lips. "How many temples have you been to? If you had to guess?"

"Just Serene's, so one," he said back, staring up at the giant clock ticking above us.

"Ever?" Harlow and I asked in unison.

"Fine. Maybe more. I don't remember."

"You don't have to go in if you don't want to, Archie," Thorne said, swinging an arm over his shoulder.

"Listen," he said, shoving Thorne's arm away until he escaped his hold. "I'm pretty sure she'd like to use our bones as clock handles. And you're reckless when it comes to pissing off the gods. Do I want to go in there? No. But am I going to? Yes. Because my house is full of orphans, and sure, they're okay, but I'd rather it be full of silence."

"They can stay as long as they want," Harlow glared.

Much to all of our disappointment, it'd taken three days for Vesalia to agree to meet with us. Three days of displaced Salt. Three days of alternating cat naps on couches at the Parlor with a rotation of Salt staying wherever we could hide them in the city. Three days of glances at Thorne and subtle touches and nothing more. But finally, we were here, standing at the base of the clock tower that I'd never have guessed was a temple.

"It makes more sense to put as many orphans as we can in Thorne's house. You're in the heart of the Silk district. There's no way we can keep hiding everyone over there," I said.

"This is why we're friends," Archer agreed, ducking away from Thorne to move to my side. "Always the logical one."

I rolled my eyes. "You're just saying that because I beat you at cards again this morning."

"I didn't let you shuffle. You couldn't have cheated. Tell me your secret, Fingers."

Harlow knocked on the door again, winking at me. She'd been the secret, of course, swapping his deck of cards when he wasn't paying attention. Passing time with a bunch of thieves was, at minimum, entertaining.

"Did she not say three o'clock?"

Thorne slipped his hand around mine. The first committed touch in days. "She did. And it will be three o'clock on the dot. Not a second earlier."

I spun to him as the bell began to toll. "And will you be playing nice today?"

He forced a smile. "I will if she will."

"Well, we're all going to die," Archer said as the bell stopped and the door swung open, welcoming us into the Goddess of Time's temple.

The space was nothing like I imagined, as if stepping through the door had taken us to a different place. A different time, though I knew that to be impossible. Magic, however? Power? That could trick the eye into almost anything.

The temple gleamed under the soft flicker of lanterns, their light catching on white stone walls. Standing close to the wall, I traced my fingers along the gold trim that circled the room, intricate patterns twisting beneath my touch like they were spun from threads of time.

Thorne tugged me toward him. "Touch with your eyes, Paesha darling."

Above us, massive clocks were embedded in the walls, their faces glowing faintly. The steady, quiet ticking echoed through the space like a dissipating war drum. Cold, white sand shifted beneath our boots as we walked, leaving shallow imprints in its fine grains. The place was so bright, so pure, it was hard to believe it existed in the heart of a city so broken. Ahead, an enormous golden door loomed, framed by massive hourglasses spilling dark grains in a measured cadence, as though counting out the final bars of a song.

I couldn't shake the feeling of being watched, of something old and powerful lurking just beyond sight. The clocks grew louder, the sound sinking into my bones until at once, they stopped. It wasn't silence, not really. It was a pause, a moment where time held its breath, waiting.

The door swung open and Vesalia all but floated out, her long silver hair glistening as much as those pale eyes of hers did. Her smile was almost venomous. She gestured toward the largest clock. "Right on time. How absolutely delicious! Come." She spun, her deep red dress flowing behind her in waves.

Archer looked around. "You guys heard delicious, right?"

"Grow a pair," Harlow said, the first of the group to follow the goddess beyond the golden door.

"I did," he said, following her. "Apparently they shrink in times of terror."

"Untrue," Thorne whispered into my ear.

"Shockingly, I didn't need confirmation." I said, letting him go in first.

We followed Vesalia into a grand chamber, the walls lined with more clocks of varying sizes and designs. Some were simple and elegant, others ornate and intricate, but all ticked in perfect unison, a symphony of measured time. In the center of the room stood a massive, golden sundial, its shadow slicing across the polished floor like a blade.

The goddess perched on the edge of a plush velvet chaise, crossing her legs with feline grace. She gestured for us to sit in the chairs arranged before her. We did so warily, after Thorne deliberately grabbed the chair meant for me and slid it all the way over until it butted up against his chair. And Archer, never one to miss a trend, did the same with Harlow's, making an absolute scene of it, letting the legs groan across the white marble floor.

"So," the goddess purred. "To what do I owe the pleasure of this visit?"

Thorne leaned forward, his expression serious. "The clocks you gifted me? I'm sure you'll remember them. They need to be removed from my home. Immediately."

She tossed her head back and laughed. "Oh, my darling, I gifted you a lesson. Not the clocks."

He glared. "Lesson learned."

"Time is my domain. I alone decide when a lesson begins and ends."

Harlow shifted uneasily, shooting me a worried glance. I could feel the tension radiating off Thorne, see the muscle ticking behind his stubble as he struggled to rein in his temper. Something about the gods changed him. Twisted him into a man with no control.

Vesalia's eyes slid from Thorne to me. Her lips curved into a slow smile. "Bold of you to bring the Huntress. I can only imagine that was a calculated move."

Thorne let his rigid body relax, slipping into the man he needed to be to bargain with a goddess. "She's here because she is my wife. Her power has nothing to do with it."

The goddess waved a dismissive hand. "Wife, Huntress, it matters not. Labels are such fleeting, mortal constructs. She is a woman out of time, plucked from the fabric of fate and woven into your story." Her gaze bore into me, ancient and knowing. "I see you're sleeping better than when we first met. The circles have vanished. How charming."

I did not cower. I'd had about enough of these damn gods. In that, Thorne and I were the same. "We've barely slept in days waiting to meet with you."

"Not the quantity. The quality. How fleeting your memory is." Vesalia laughed, the sound like tinkling crystal echoing through the chamber. She rose from her chaise in a whisper of silk, gliding over to stand before an ornate grandfather clock. One I'd seen before, hidden in the depths of a serpent's fucking eyes.

This bitch.

It was her. Her meddling. Her nightmares. Her torture. My despair. She'd ruined almost every single night I'd spent in Wisteria. But why?

Vesalia ran a delicate finger along the clock's polished wood, tracing the intricate carvings. "Time is a curious thing, is it not? It can be a great healer or a cruel mistress. It can bring love or sorrow, clarity or confusion. And for some..." Her eyes flicked to me again. "It can be a prison."

Thorne tensed beside me, his hand tightening on the armrest. "Enough with the riddles, Vesalia. We came here for a simple request. Remove the clocks from my home. You've had your fun."

But time *was* a prison. At least for me. And the walls were closing in with every night that passed. Each day. And she knew that. Holy shit. She knew. Which meant... if I could see her alone. If I could ask her...

The goddess turned to face Thorne with a mocking smile. "Nothing is ever simple with you, Thorne Noctus. You, who wear so many masks, play so many roles. The devoted husband, the cunning thief, the benevolent lord. Have I listed them all? Which is the real you, I wonder? How weak are you?"

"He is not weak, Vesalia. May I call you Vesalia? I think I will." I stood from my chair and crossed the room, staring at the hands of the clock beside her, poised to strike.

"I don't think that would be wise, Huntress."

"I think this clock is off." I traced a finger along the face, tilting my head as if studying it intently. "For a Goddess of Time, I would expect nothing short of perfection. And yet, this one seems to be running just a hair slow. A fraction of a second, perhaps, but still... one must wonder."

Vesalia's eyes narrowed, a flicker of irritation passing over her lovely features before she smoothed it away with a practiced smile. "My clocks are never wrong, mortal. They keep the rhythm of the universe."

I hummed a noncommittal sound as I moved to the next clock, a towering masterpiece of gears and golden filigree. "If you say so. But you know, I've always found time to be rather subjective. Fleeting and fickle, bending to the whims of perception." I glanced over my shoulder at her, a mischievous glint in my eye. I had no fucking clue what I was talking about, but I held her attention as surely as her breath.

I ran my fingers along the intricate engravings on the clock's face, tracing the swirling patterns. "Take this design, for instance. Beautiful, to be sure, but rather... busy, don't you think? So many flourishes and embellishments. One might argue it distracts from the clock's true purpose."

I moved on to the next, a sleek, modern creation of brushed steel and careful lines. "Now this, this is more my style. Clean, efficient, no unnecessary frills. It knows what it is and doesn't try to be anything else. Admirable, really."

Vesalia's lips pressed into a thin line, her eyes flashing with barely contained ire. "I didn't bring you here to critique my decor, mortal."

"You didn't bring us here at all. We walked." I reached into the clock, and despite her gasp, spun the hand backward.

Behind me, Archer made a strangled sound, halfway between a gasp and a cough. Harlow elbowed him sharply in the ribs. I knew I'd lost my ever-loving mind pushing a goddess. But Thorne had done it with minimal repercussions.

The Goddess stormed forward, snatching my hand and wrenching it backward.

The world blurred and stretched around us, the grand chamber and its ticking clocks fading into a hazy background. Suddenly, we were alone, standing in a small, circular room, the walls lined with mirrors that reflected our images into infinity, and hourglasses. So many hourglasses. But it was not the fact that each one held a different color sand that made them horrifying. It was the people trapped within. Some stared back, mirroring the shock I tried to hide, some slept, others scowled. This was Vesalia's prison.

"You dare to touch my clocks?" she hissed, her pale cheeks flushing with anger, as she commanded my attention. "You don't understand the intricacies of time. You fool."

I ignored her. Walking around the room, dragging a finger over the hourglasses, leaving the glass smudged just to irritate her.

"Don't touch!" she yelled.

"Yeah, yeah. Shame on me. Listen, I know you know something about me." For the first time since I'd entered Wisteria, I forced myself to say the words aloud. Pushed and pushed to speak of where I'd come from. Of Quill. Of Thea and Elowen. Of my chosen family. A path. A Fera. But no matter how hard I tried. No matter the words sitting on the edge of my tongue, I could not speak them aloud. The bargain didn't care that she already knew. I was not allowed to tell her.

"Cat got your tongue, Huntress?"

"Tell me what you know." There. Not a direct confession of anything. Just a question.

She sauntered forward, grabbing the sides of my face, burning my skin. "It is not for you to ask what I know."

Her grip tightened on my face, her nails digging in like talons. Her eyes, once a pale, ethereal blue, now glowed with an unholy light, swirling like molten gold. The air crackled with energy, the mirrors vibrating in their frames as if resonating with her fury.

"You are nothing more than a pawn in a game far beyond your comprehension," she snarled. "A mere mortal, stumbling through the threads of fate, tangling them with your clumsy fingers." She leaned in close, her breath hot against my cheek. "I have seen the tapestry of your lives, Huntress. I have watched you weave your way through time, leaving chaos and heartache in your wake. You think yourself clever, but you are a child playing with forces you cannot possibly understand."

I tried to pull away, but her grip was iron, unyielding.

"I should kill you here and now, but there is one that saves you. One hope. One child. Go home, Huntress. Your pa—" She screamed, yanking her hand away from me as she looked down at her gnarled fingers.

With no warning, Vesalia's eyes glazed over, her expression going slack as if in a trance.

"No," I screamed, lunging for her, grabbing her by the arms, no matter the consequences. "What were you going to say? Say it. My path. That's what you were going to say, isn't it? Tell me."

She blinked slowly, her gaze unfocused and distant. The anger and fury that had twisted her features moments before melted away, replaced by a dreamy, almost serene look. "Do you see it?" she whispered, her voice soft and reverent. "The sands of time?" She looked back at me, eyes pale once more, blinking rapidly. "What... why are you here?"

"What the fuck just happened?"

The goddess waved her hand, and we returned to the chamber with the others. Thorne and Archer launched themselves out of their chairs, surging for me. Thorne's large hands cupped my face, tilting it toward the light as he studied the angry red marks left by Vesalia's nails. The muscles in his jaw clenched and unclenched, a tic pulsing at his temple as he fought to control his temper.

"What did you do to her?" Archer growled.

Vesalia merely smiled, a serene curve of her lips as she settled back on the velvet chaise, smoothing the folds of her gown. "I don't remember."

"Nothing," I said, pulling away from them both. "She did nothing."

I glanced at Harlow, desperate for help. She stood, clearing her throat, her voice steady as she addressed the goddess. "Vesalia, if I may?" She waited for the goddess's nod before continuing. "We didn't come here to cause problems, though some in my party may have forgotten that. We simply came to humbly ask you to remove the clocks from Thorne's home, so that he may take in Stirling's orphans. However, if you feel that he has not learned his lesson, I offer a compromise. What if you left only one clock? One that the children would see every day and hear the soft ticking of, so they would know who helped them in their time of need. Imagine the devotion from minds so young. Imagine who they might grow to love."

Smart. Harlow's compromise was offering power, even if she hadn't directly said it.

"I will take the clocks from the home, but there still must be a price paid for the Huntress's actions. Who will pay with their time? Will it be the one that holds a secret?" Her eyes flashed to Harlow, then slid to Archer. "The one that knows the secret?" She looked at me. "The one that's chasing?" And then to Thorne. "Or the one that's scrambling?"

Harlow's secret? Could she have been referring to her sacrificed power? To her struggling relationship with Wee Willy? Everyone had secrets. And a goddess would make a mountain out of nothing if she thought it would cause chaos. None of these vague ideas mattered except what she'd said about me. I was chasing. Running down a promised path blind and guided by hope and desperation. But the others had no clue and I could only hope they wouldn't have questions when we left.

For some reason, Vesalia had an invested interest in me going home. Which meant she didn't want to die. Even if that prick of a god I'd bargained with did. The problem was, as soon as she'd tried to speak of it, she'd forgotten what she was going to say. Because Reverius, God of Whoevers and Whatevers and Realms and Keys and shit, had another name. One that Ro had only called him in my mind. *The Keeper of Memories.*

This fucker had sent me to a dangerous world and refused to let anyone help me get back. Sure, there was a path, but he'd blocked it repeatedly in his own suicide mission. Or so it seemed, but that couldn't be right either. Because why bother sending me here at all, if that were the case? The answer was so clear, and yet so difficult. Thorne stood on the path, sure, but there were no meddling gods allowed. Maybe that was Reverius's way of protecting me. Bastard.

The others bickering back and forth yanked me from my spiraling thoughts.

"Seriously, heads or tails," Archer said, a coin resting on the tip of his thumb. "I'm not going to let you offer yourself up as bait without trying, Thorne. Let me do this."

Thorne rolled his eyes and shoved past Archer, moving to my side. "I will pay your cost."

I slid my hand into his, remembering the way her grip on my face had burned. Reverius had protected me. I had to believe he would again. "I'm the one that made her mad. Let me do it," I whispered.

Thorne turned, gently moving a finger over my cheek. "Her price will only be time. You heard her. Go back to our home. Get everyone settled in. I'll come as soon as I'm free."

There would be no arguing as Vesalia clapped her hands together, stood once more, and walked over to the largest clock. She twisted a lever and the entire face swung open, revealing a door. The room beyond was nothing more than concrete walls and sandy floors.

"How long?" I asked, trying to keep the desperation from my voice.

"Don't take away all the fun, Huntress."

"I will fuck with every one of your clocks. Every single one in the entire city. I will make it my personal mission to hunt them down, and change them all, minute by minute so none read true." I clenched my hands at my side, feeling empowered by the fact that a god was protecting me. "How. Long? You must speak the terms of your bargain for it to be agreed upon."

Her eyes lit with fury. "Seven months."

"Absolutely not." I turned to Thorne. "We can find another

place. We don't need that one. Hell, we can stay in the Parlor. We'll figure it out."

He looked beyond me. "One week, Vesalia. You can have one week."

"It would have only been a day before your Huntress stepped in, but a week with Thorne Noctus sounds delightful. I agree to your terms. Right this way."

39

I'd taken the little, chipped teacup from the Parlor and set it on my bedside table. I'd stared into the reflection of the giant gold clock in the dining room, watching each second of each minute tick by. A week was nothing to most. Certainly not Vesalia, an immortal with all the time in the world. But it was a lot to me. I'd needed him to be here. We needed to move forward with his cause. Secure the children, find a king, maybe kill a prince. I wasn't sure. But the seventy-five days were flying by and each one reminded me that Quill was getting further and further away instead of closer.

The only thing I could do was take the time and use it to my advantage. Learn something, let the space between Thorne and I be exactly what it needed to be. Space. Because at the end of this, come hell or high water, I was going to leave. And there'd be nothing but space between us then. And so, so much time.

As if he could have heard my thoughts, that little golden book burned at my thigh. Warm at first and then growing increasingly hot as I was warred with myself to open it. I could have. But what good would deepening my relationship with Thorne do? That's all that would come from being available to him for a week. I'd be his distraction from whatever hells Vesalia wrought, and he'd dig himself a little further into my heart.

With very little resolve, I walked away from the sitting room and hustled upstairs, throwing the book into the bedside table and slamming the drawer. I wasn't proud of the fact that I stood there. Wasn't proud of the way I held the knob in my hand, let go and grabbed it again. But I was proud when I walked away. When I chose to protect my heart as fiercely as I'd protected Quill these past seven years. Maybe I wasn't her mother. But I was the closest thing she had, and she was the closest I would ever get to being one.

I paced in front of the door, the moonlight shining through the line of windows above it. Waiting. And waiting. Until three soft knocks sounded. I whipped the door open to find Archer there, a sleeping child in his arms, one clinging to his free hand and two more behind.

"Thank the gods," I said, stepping to the side to let him in. "Actually, fuck them, but I was beginning to worry."

I ushered the children in, kneeling. I swiped the threadbare hats from their heads, revealing a curly haired blond boy, Alex and his cousin Amara, not the youngest but nearly there at only five and seven.

"Okay?" I asked, looking over every inch of them. "Ready to get settled in?"

Amara rubbed her sleepy eyes. "Yes, Miss Paesha."

I smiled, taking Alex's hand. "Go on up the stairs and turn that way." I pointed. "There are several rooms and beds. Stay together but pick your favorite. I put blankets at the end of the bed. Be sure to take your boots off."

They were so tired, their strides long and leaden.

"What took so long?"

"Wee Willy decided we needed to wait an extra hour just to be on the safe side."

"And he's in charge now?" I asked, taking the little one from Archer's arms.

He pulled Sigrid from where she'd clung to his leg. She was older, ten maybe, but she'd always been the quietest of the crew. "Harlow always lets him decide." He looked over his shoulder to make sure no one else was coming. "And I don't get it, Fingers. She's always been so tough. She doesn't give in on *anything* with me. But he says 'jump' and she says, 'Would you like me to come back down too?'"

I smiled, looking up at him. "Maybe she loves him."

"Yeah, but why? And also, how does that make him in charge of everything?"

"Come on. Let's get these sleepy kids up to bed and then I'll tell you the story of what happens when a man and a woman fall deeply in love."

"Stop it. That's my sister."

"Yeah, well, I'm pretty sure Cressida is someone's sister too and last week you didn't have a problem—"

"Point taken," he said sharply. "Tiny ears, Paesha. Tiny ears."

By the time it was all said and done, all thirteen children were accounted for. Some of the beds were crowded, and we'd taken blankets from every place we could. But it wasn't until Jasper came in, his cheeks rosy with a genuine smile, despite his arm, that I felt somewhat at peace.

I needed to know he'd be taken care of, too. And if that meant the prince came knocking on this door and I had to hide everyone in Thorne's empty wine cellar, then I guess that's what that meant. But I wouldn't do it alone. Briony had come in with the last group of Salt around midnight. Apart from how much the kids attached themselves to Archer, she was next in line.

I'd taken a step back from the little ones, knowing if I spent too much time with them, I'd never be able to leave. But Briony was almost always there, the first to dry tears and the first to scold bad behavior.

That evening, with Thorne gone, but the house entirely full, the adults sat around the dining room table.

"What do you know about her?" I asked Archer when she left the room to get a cup of tea, keeping my voice low enough to avoid cutting into the table's many conversations.

"Momma Salt... er uh, Tilly, the woman that ran the orphanage, she raised Briony. Several of the Salt that came through the Hollow were hers. Tilly was always respected on both sides of the line and folks were willing to help her, no matter how deep or shallow their pockets were. I think the Salt feel beholden to these kids. Like helping them is paying tribute to Momma Salt."

"Good. That'll make it easier when—"

He raised a brow, pinning me with those baby blues. "When what?"

Dammit.

Archer was kind and gentle, playful and generous. But he wasn't safe. No one here was safe.

"Well, eventually Stirling is going to need another orphanage, don't you think? The prince is likely already wondering where these kids are. Especially Reuben."

He leaned back in his chair, locking his arms behind his head. "What's your end goal, Fingers? What does this look like for you in, say, three years?"

His posture was casual, but his eyes were not. Archer was smart, decisive, always three moves ahead. And fuck if he wasn't growing on me. But there were others in the room and the fact that it'd fallen silent wasn't lost on me. Tuck, sitting at the far end of the table, stared right into my soul as he waited for my answer.

"From where I'm sitting, it's hard to tell. We've heard nothing about where the king might be. Farris is still doing his raids, but it's hard to believe he's searching for his dad when the fruit of his labor is growing his Cimmerian army and removing magic from the world. If we find the king, and he's alive, which is doubtful, then I think he'll take an audience with me. I think that's the right move and I have to believe it's still possible. He's still alive somewhere.

"If I get an audience, I can expose everything Farris is doing. Then Farris falls from power. The kingdom goes back to some form of peace, and everyone lives happily ever after."

"Couple things," Archer said, sitting forward. "If this could be solved by an audience with the king, it would have been done. But as long as Farris is breathing, he's not going to let that happen. He controls every foot that steps into that castle and the bigger his army grows, the worse it gets."

"Then we start chopping off the arms of the Cimmerians," Jasper said, piping up from his seat beside Tuck. "We know it works."

"Or we kill the prince," Tuck said, staring at Archer now. "Just cut off the head of the snake and the body will fall."

Archer raised his glass in the air. "Here's to *just*."

The room silently raised their glasses and drank. I slid my hand around the rim of my cup, walking through what I knew, what I'd assumed, where I'd landed in my mind, wondering if this was a safe place to say it. But mine was only a theory.

I glanced at Tuck and he was still watching me. I tilted my

head toward the open seat on my right. He promptly rose, stretched and came to sit closer, with Archer and Jasper moving in to listen. Building a wall of shoulders.

"I have a theory," I whispered, prepared to lace a few lies in where I needed to cover my own tracks. "It might be just that. I haven't sorted it all out yet, but what if Farris is giving the magic he's stealing to the gods? And what if that's why none of them try to stop him? When we were with Vesalia, there was this moment. She pulled me into another space. You were there, Archie. You saw it."

He nodded.

"She told me the power feels different in this world. Like it's not as strong. What if Farris is trying to help the gods and in turn they are helping him? What if this isn't a war against the people? Not really. What if it's the gods vying for power and this realm is where they are pulling it from?"

"Then we're in far over our heads," Tuck whispered before sitting back once more. I studied their faces, letting the theory race around their thoughts. In that moment, I felt a pang of longing, wishing Thorne was here. His mind would have been running rampant with theories.

"Can we all agree that step one is finding the king?" Archer asked, pulling the conversation back in. "Even if this is a god's war and not our own, we're being used as minions. We'll turn into foot soldiers. If we can't get to Farris because he's protected by the Cimmerians *and* the gods, then we have to find King Aldus and make him see reason. If he can set up a meeting with Farris, we can ambush and take him down."

"Well, that's the second part of my theory. We can't find the king. We've had people searching all over the place. Tuck, you even managed to get in the Maw again yesterday, right?"

Tuck sighed. "It's ah..." He cleared his throat. "It's bad down there. We've swept the castle too. It's hardly guarded. They know the king isn't inside."

I took a steady breath, steeling myself for their shut down, though I knew I needed to push us into action. "We need to do something reckless. And we need to do it before Thorne gets back."

Jasper shook his head. "This sounds like a bad idea, Miss Paesha."

"It's definitely a bad idea. Because we have to figure out where all the Cimmerians from the castle are. We've seen them in the streets, sure. We know Farris has some around him. But there's a horde of them hiding somewhere and I think if we find them, we'll find the king."

Tuck scratched his neck, drawing away from the table as if he could remove himself from the idea. "It's too dangerous. And I'm standing by my original theory that the king is already dead."

"If the king were dead, Farris would already have had his funeral and taken the throne," Archer argued.

"Then what the fuck is he hiding him for?" Tuck asked.

I finished the rest of my tea, letting the question linger until I was ready to speak the answer. "Unless he's not the one hiding him."

You could have heard a pin drop. The entire world fell silent.

"What do you mean?" Archer asked.

"What if it's a god?"

Jasper blew out a long, slow breath. "I think you're onto something."

I finally, finally let my eyes fall to him. The most important man in the conversation. "Tell us what the God of Justice said as he bound you to Farris."

Jasper's face paled. "I'll never forget those words. Themis, he said... he said, 'I bind your will. Your heart shall beat as one with your Cimmerian brethren, your loyalty unwavering, your obedience absolute. With each pulse, feel the threads of fate entwine, drawing you ever closer to your prince's desires. With each pulse, you will become an extension of this being, a vessel for my ambition.'"

"Well that makes no sense," Archer said.

"Sure it does," Jasper argued. "Cutting off my arm worked because there hadn't been enough time passed for me to feel drawn to the prince. Not enough heartbeats, if you will."

I let the smile unfurl as I watched the other's faces, seeing the truth behind my wild theory.

"Yes, but that's not the most damning part of that revelation," Tuck said, echoing my thoughts. "The Cimmerians are bound to the prince, sure. But they're also bound to Themis's ambition."

"Son of a bitch," Archer said, leaning so far forward the back legs of his chair left the ground. "If this is a battle against the gods, we're fucked."

Tuck shook his head. "We've always been fucked, brother. The battlegrounds have just changed."

"Which one of us is going to tell Thorne when he gets back?" Jasper asked.

All heads turned to me.

"I don't know about you boys, but I'm not about to sit around and wait a week to find where the Cimmerians are hiding. This is still a theory. We're counting on Jasper to remember every single word, and we're still making assumptions based on it. I prefer proof. And I think it's time to do something instead of sitting around here, waiting for more terrible shit to happen."

"Got a plan?" Archer asked.

"Yeah, but it's dangerous."

"We need to wait for Thorne," Tuck said.

Jasper nodded. "I agree."

Archer kicked me from under the table before saying. "Yes. We'll wait a week and as soon as Thorne gets back, we make a plan."

I stared into his eyes, knowing he didn't mean a single thing he'd said. "All right. It's decided. We wait a week."

40

That night, I lay in bed, staring at the bedside table. I knew what lay within, tucked away in that innocuous drawer. The book. The lifeline between Thorne and me, a tether that connected us even when we were apart.

My fingers itched to reach out, to slide open the drawer and grab it, to feel its warmth against my skin. To trace the intricate engravings on the cover, to let my fingertips skim over the gilded edges of the pages. I longed to open it and see his familiar scrawl flowing across the parchment, to read the words.

Something snarky. Commanding. Just shy of nerdy. Gods, I hated that I missed him. But being around these kids made me miss Quilly too. The way I'd taught her to count while she brushed her teeth. The way she'd race up the stairs two at a time to beat her dog Boo to the top. The way she'd be so sleepy, her eyes hung heavy, and still insist on one more dance.

I rolled onto my back, staring up at the intricate molding that adorned the ceiling. In the dim light, the swirling patterns seemed to dance and shift, morphing into images from my memories. Quill's face, her bright blue eyes crinkling with

426

laughter as we twirled around the kitchen, our bare feet slapping against the worn wooden floors. The way her small hand fit so perfectly in mine, her trust unwavering as I guided her through the steps of a waltz. The memories of Quill battled the longing for Thorne and that didn't feel fair to either one of them. There was no choice here. Not really.

In truth, I felt more alone here and now than I had since Thorne's rescue. I hated the companionship he'd given me. The long looks and the lingering touches. They confused everything. But at least with those things, I wasn't alone.

I'm not sure if it was comfort, desperation or loneliness that drove me, but one second I was lying there, deep in my feelings and the next, I yanked the book free of the drawer and held it against my chest, the warm cover pressing into my skin through the thin fabric of his shirt. The golden engravings dug gently into my palms as I clutched it tightly.

The book radiated a soothing heat, just like Thorne's random hugs. But I knew what it meant. And I knew how dangerous giving over to that baser need would be at the end of this path. So, I tucked the book under my pillow and willed myself to sleep.

"WAKE UP, sunshine. We've got a full day of hunting. Heh. Hunting with the Huntress. That's fun. Hey, wait, why do you get a cool name and I don't?"

I rubbed my eyes, looking past the blurry outline of Archer toward the open window, where the cool morning breeze moved in, reminding me that another damn day had passed. And my days were more numbered now than ever. Thirty-seven. And six more would be spent without Thorne.

"You could have used the door, you know?"

"Nah. Thought we better make a plan before we expose ourselves."

I rolled my eyes, kicking the covers free and swinging my feet to the icy floor. "Give me five minutes with no talking."

"Not a morning person. Got it."

I glared at Archer's freshly shaven face. "That's talking."

He raised his hands in mock surrender before his eyes fell down past Thorne's shirt. "Damn Fingers, I should have been calling you Legs this whole time."

"I will actually kill you."

His eyes gleamed with mischief. "Right. Sorry. Five minutes. Got it."

He sat down in the chair by the door, put his ankle on his knee and began to whistle. I grabbed a pillow and launched it across the room at him before going to the bathroom to wash up.

"Nobody likes a grumpy goose," he shouted after I shut the door.

"What was the point of coming in the window if you're going to wake the whole house?"

"That's a really good question. I'll ponder it for the rest of the five minutes."

I dressed quickly, splashing water onto my face and brushing my teeth, staring at myself in the mirror to see past the way this realm had dragged me down. Not unlike Requiem, just in different ways.

I pulled the black leathers from the hook on the back of the door and swung it open to find Archer standing there, staring at his watch.

"Wi—"

"No." He held up a finger. "Three, two, one. And go."

"You know how your sister seems to be annoyed with you very easily?"

He grinned, showing all his teeth. "I'm not going to dignify that with a response. I'm simply charming. I can't be cut-throat all the time, Fingers."

"I'm not going to dignify *that* with a response," I said, sliding Harlow's gifted blade into the sheath on my thigh.

He crossed his arms over his chest. "Now that you're finally ready to go, what's the plan?"

"Hmm. I guess I thought it was obvious. We need the king, right? And the king is missing? What's another word for missing?"

His brow lowered. "Absent?"

"Try *lost*. And guess what Alastor is the god of?"

Archer crossed the room, slumping back into the chair, running his fists through his hair. "I'm not sure that's a good idea." All sense of the lovable oaf was gone as his face turned serious. Hard even. "If Thorne found out we were—"

"Do you want to find the king?"

"Yes, but—"

"Are you an adult?"

"Paesha, you don't understand."

"I'm tired of sitting around letting everyone else run these streets. I'm the Huntress. I'm the one that needs to do this. I know it. And you can either come with and help, or you can sit right there and wait for me to get back. I told you last night it was reckless. I stand by that, but I'm still going."

"You can't just walk into the Vale. You'll never even find it."

I smiled, lowering my chin. "I already know where it is, thanks to you lingering around it. And if I have to steal something fucking shiny for a meeting with Alastor, I'll do it. I'm done playing games with gods on their terms."

"IF THORNE KILLS me for this, I'm taking you to Death's Court with me."

"That's not the threat you think it is," I said, following Archer through the city.

The Vale was not above, but in fact below Stirling, similar to the Maw. Archer insisted there were no connecting paths between the two and I could do nothing but take his word for it. It made sense though, if Alastor was the master of the Vale, he wasn't going to put his black market right under the nose of the Cimmerians. And likely, the Silk weren't meandering down here to shop. The rich thrived on the minions they kept for every dark job. We passed through one of the narrowest alleys. The kind of place that made the hairs on the back of your neck stand up, that had you glancing over your shoulder with every echoing footstep. The walls loomed high on either side, the bricks crumbling and covered in a patchwork of grime. Bits of broken glass and debris crunched underfoot.

We moved quickly, Archer's hand a vice around my wrist as he tugged me along, taking sharp corners, moving up steep stairs only to turn and jog down another set. But I followed him effortlessly, letting our cloaks keep our identities as hidden as possible. When I thought there was no way we could possibly go farther down, he tugged us right, and we slipped past a half-broken door, hanging off rusted hinges.

I had to hand it to Alastor. If I were trying to hide in a city this big, I'd have picked this place too. But of course, as a God of Lost things, he'd know how to take a place and make it exactly that. Lost. Hidden. His alone.

"You'll have to show your face to the guard, but say nothing and keep those eyes down. If they figure out you're Thorne's wife, we might not make it out of here."

"Hey," I said, tugging on his hand to pull him back. The

worry on his face was almost unsettling. "We're walking out of here. There's no question about that. I promise."

"Don't make those promises." He stepped closer, pushing my hood away. "Eyes down, okay?"

I nodded, staring only at his feet as the light faded and we stood in almost complete darkness before another door. There were no words exchanged. Out of the corner of my eye, I could see Archer produce something from his pocket. Beyond that, we stood and I held my breath until the door creaked open and we were given access to the Vale.

The cavernous space sprawled before us, air thick with the scent of incense and the hum of whispered deals. I let my eyes sweep the room once. Let my magic anchor me to this place before I stared at the floor once more. Golden lanterns hung from the ceiling, so far away, it felt like we were truly buried in the heart of Wisteria. Merchants stood like statues behind their stalls, jewels and relics glittering in the dim light. No one spoke to us, yet I felt the weight of every gaze as we passed through, the kind of eyes that only dangerous people wore.

Archer walked beside me with slow, deliberate steps and I could sense the tension in the way his fingers flexed at his side. He didn't need to look around. He knew we were being watched just as well as I did. Prey in a den of wolves. Each glance over the wares, every subtle movement, was a promise that here, fortunes were made or lost with a single misstep. Because the Vale wasn't filled with honest, hardworking people. This was where the cruelest thrived. Where mercenaries and murderers meet on equal ground.

Still, Archer didn't falter. His stride remained steady, his eyes forward, as if daring anyone to act. His silence was sharper than any blade, a warning all on its own. I adjusted my cloak, more for comfort than warmth. We weren't here for the trinkets or the whispers of fortune—those things were distractions. Yet, the deeper we ventured into the heart of the Vale, the more I felt like we were walking into a trap that had already been set.

I had no idea what Archer's plan was to lure Alastor out. All I could do was keep my head down and have a little faith in him, as he'd asked me to do. At the far end of the galley, past the final stall, he stopped to talk to a man, leaning in to whisper. I chanced another look around the space, nothing big enough to draw attention, just enough to see the table to our right, lined with jewels and ornate golden ornaments.

"Alastor is a very busy man. He doesn't have time for unscheduled visitors."

I lifted my face enough to see his dark eyes flicked to me for a moment before settling back on Archer.

Archer leaned forward, bracing his hands on the edge of the table, his tone melting into something deep and dangerous. "We're not leaving until we speak with Alastor."

The man chuckled, the sound devoid of any real mirth. "You're in no position to make demands here, boy." He snapped his fingers and the shadows along the walls shifted, men detaching themselves from the darkness like wraiths.

I tensed and beside me, Archer remained still, but I could see the coiled readiness in the set of his shoulders.

"Maybe you didn't hear my friend," I said, lifting my face, holding my chin high as I stepped between the man and Archer. "We're not leaving until we meet with Alastor, so be a good boy, and go fetch."

"I'm not your godsdamn dog," the man said, raising his fist to strike me.

But as swift as the dancer I'd always been, I spun to the side, swiping the sword from the table, and I would have had it to his throat, had Archer not been far quicker. He had the man on the ground, boot to throat.

I turned again, pressing my back toward Archer as I held the blade in my hands, adjusting to its weight. A dagger was not my weapon of choice, but I'd battled a Hell Hound to near death with a sword.

This I knew.

The men crept closer, a pack of predators circling their cornered prey. Heart racing, wondering if I'd guessed wrong and completely fucked us, I adjusted my grip on the sword. Beside me, Archer's breaths came steady and even, his body a coiled spring ready to unleash at the slightest provocation. We were outnumbered and outmatched and about as foolish as they came.

But before the dogs could descend, a strong steady voice carried down the space. "Now, now, boys. What have I told you about bloodshed before noon? It's bad form." Alastor stepped from the shadows, his tattoos writhing like smoke on his skin as he stared only at me. "The Huntress comes at last. I must say, it took you long enough."

"Yeah, well, I've been pretty busy trying not to die, so there's that."

Alastor snapped his fingers and the men retreated back to their shadowy perches. "You two, follow me. I imagine if you were willing to fight my wraiths, you must have something very valuable to share." His eyes flicked down to the sword in my hand. "Interesting choice. Perhaps you should keep it."

"Is it expensive?" I asked, staring him right in the eyes that matched one of mine perfectly.

"Quite."

"Then I think I will."

We walked in silence, save the tip of the sword I purposefully let drag across the stone floor, staring straight ahead, scowling as we walked.

Archer bumped my shoulder once Alastor was far enough

ahead and whispered under his breath, "How'd you know he'd come?"

"Easy. I'm his descendant, and he has something he wants to share with me."

"That would have been nice to know before I thought we were about to die," he hissed.

"Has anyone told you you're a tad dramatic?"

"Has anyone told you you're a terrible friend?"

I paused. "Actually, yes. Pretty much everyone I know."

He flashed a side eyed glance at me. "Take comfort in the fact that you don't surround yourself with liars."

"I'd say you handled yourself well enough. Surprisingly."

He tilted his head. "Surprisingly?"

"Charming people aren't usually dangerous."

"Well, that's not true at all," Alastor said, butting into the conversation I hadn't realized he could hear. "The most dangerous beings I know are actually quite charming. When they want to be."

Archer beamed. "You think I'm charming."

I twisted my mouth to hide the smile as we entered Alastor's meeting room. The space was nothing more than an office with deep red rugs on the floor, a desk, and walls and walls of books that called for me to stay and read them all, though every single shelf had gaps where a book was clearly missing and each of the spaces had filled with dust and cobwebs.

"Sit," Alastor said, handing us each a drink. "Show me what you've brought."

"I hate to be the bearer of bad news, but we didn't bring anything for you. In fact," I sat, taking a long pull from the glass he'd handed me and set it on the desk before placing the sword across my lap. "I'm just going to level with you. I'm tired of the riddles and bullshit. We know the gods are hiding the king and we're here to ask you where he is."

Archer choked on his drink. Really choked, coughing and sputtering, taking several moments to regain his composure. "What my friend here is trying to say," he said, with a rasp, eyes watery, "Is we *think* certain gods *might* be responsible and we'd be so grateful, the most grateful, if you could provide any insight. Isn't that right, Paesha?"

I narrowed my stare at Alastor. "No. I meant what I said."

Alastor chuckled, soft at first and then it grew into something loud, and unnerving. Once settled, he sat forward, clasping his hands on his desk. "You're so much like Irri, Huntress. You come by that mouth honestly, I'll tell you that. But you've got it all wrong. The gods do not benefit in this realm. In fact, most hate it. With muted magic and constant turmoil, all eyes are on that insolent prince. Gods draw power from emotion and praise, piety. But no one is looking to the gods for guidance. People stopped casually praying in Wisteria a long time ago. Now it's just desperation, which is fine, but it just doesn't have the same ring to it, you know?"

"I'd think the god of lost things could find the most important man in this realm that's missing. I don't really give a shit who's worshiping who or whatever, so forgive me if I don't trust a word you're saying. "

He leaned back, kicking his feet up onto his desk, boots thudding against the wood. "You'd be foolish to."

"Where's the king? Let's not play games."

"What makes you think I know where the king is?"

"For starters, you answered my question with a question. And to follow up on that, as I said, but maybe I need to speak slower, you're the God of *Lost* and Broken things, are you not?"

"I hold those names, yes."

"What does that mean?" Archer asked. "Sir... God, sir."

He shook his head, looking up at the ceiling as he folded his arms over his broad chest. "You mortals have such a way of asking the wrong questions. Let me help you. Repeat after me. Alastor, most benevolent and patient,"

He gestured, waiting until we repeated the phrase, though it boiled my blood. "Alastor, most benevolent and patient."

He smiled. I glared.

"What is the most important thing you have to tell us?"

Archer dutifully repeated the words, no hesitation. I was not so compliant.

"Important to whom?"

"Ah, ah, Huntress, speak the words to get the answers you need, not the ones you seek."

Truly, the king's location was not the most important information I needed. But I wasn't sure if he knew that. The Goddess of Time knew about Quill, but did they all? Was he about to spill my secret to Archer? Did I care at this point? With the clock ticking down and the walls moving in, maybe I didn't. Still, I hated this game. Always the damn games.

I kicked my feet up on his desk, mirroring him as I stared, but when he refused to move a muscle, when he did not blink and flecks of gold began to show in his eyes, reminding me that I was facing down a god and I needed to tread lightly, I begrudgingly repeated his words. "What is the most important thing you have to tell us, oh great and mighty asshole?"

I braced myself. Ready for any answer. I needed so, so many.

His eyes darkened. "It might surprise you to know you're not the first to call me that."

"It doesn't."

"Careful, Huntress. There are plenty of gods killing off their descendants these days. I'd hate for you to become another tragedy."

"Dying is not a threat to me. I'd rather be in Death's Court than this hell hole."

"She doesn't mean that," he told Archer. "Our Huntress has

a flair for the dramatics as well. In answer to your question, the most important thing I have to tell you is that your soul has lived many, many lives and this will probably be its last. While I'm sure you would prefer to live eternity in Death's dark court, that will likely not happen. You are not only the Huntress but also the Hunted." He turned his gaze to Archer, pulling his feet from the desk to sit forward. Hands clasped once more, the tattoos were as still as simple ink and not the magic I believed them to be. "And since I'm feeling quite generous today, Archer Bramwell, let me be quite clear. Chop off the head to kill the snake but be wary of the venom."

"Very helpful," Archer answered, nodding.

"Now, if you'll excuse me, apparently there's another brawl on the floor. To their credit, none of *them* have snatched a seven-hundred-year-old sword for protection."

I jumped to my feet. "No. Wait. I have more questions. I'll give you back the sword."

He stopped before me, lifting the sword to examine it while he said. "You already know the answer to your most pressing question," he said. "And keep the sword. It was yours long before it was mine."

41

Archer and I decided our trip to the Vale was best kept between us for now. We'd gone to see Marik and gather bolts of fabric Thalena had decided was out of fashion. It mostly gave us an excuse to have been gone, but we could use as many blankets as we could find.

"Easy does it now," Jasper said, standing behind Lianna in the kitchen, directing her moves as she seasoned broth in the pot on Thorne's beautiful stove.

There wasn't a moment in this house that didn't come with a memory of him and each second that passed, I braced myself a little more and a little more for the excuses I would give for why I hadn't opened that damn book.

Harlow giggled from beside me, sleeves rolled up, working with Willard to make a few loaves of bread.

Jasper leaned over Lianna's shoulder, his eyes focused on the simmering broth. "Now, add a pinch of thyme. Not too much, just enough to bring out the other flavors."

Lianna nodded, her brow furrowed in concentration as she carefully measured out the herb and sprinkled it into the pot.

The savory aroma wafted up, mingling with the rich scent of the bread rising on the counter.

Jasper took a long, deep breath. "Good, good. Now give it a stir, nice and slow. Let all those flavors meld together."

With his remaining hand resting lightly on her arm, he guided Lianna's movements as she stirred the broth with a wooden spoon. Despite the challenges of his missing limb, Jasper seemed at peace in the kitchen, finding happiness in teaching his little apprentice.

Across the room, Harlow and Willard worked in tandem, their hands dusted with flour as they kneaded the dough. They moved in a synchronized dance, their bodies brushing as they reached for ingredients, sharing secret smiles over the mounds of flour. In these stolen moments, the weight of the world fell away.

Briony bustled around carrying a tray with a steaming pot of tea and an assortment of mismatched cups. She set it down on the worn wooden table with a clatter. "Nothing like a little break to keep the spirits bright."

But my spirits weren't bright. They were missing a man I had no right missing. She poured the tea, the fragrant steam curling in the air. We didn't have much, truly, but we'd been able to salvage the herbs and teas stored away from the Hollow. Tuck was on a mission to clear out anything that was left in the Hollow tonight with several other members of the Fray. I didn't know all the details, but I worried about Archer and the dangerous advice Alastor had given him about the snake head. The worst thing he could do was try to be a hero, but there were times when it seemed like he might break away from the restraints his sister put around him. And though he didn't know it, I had to believe it was because she knew him best and whatever he wanted, whatever secrets he hid, would lead to something far more reckless than talking back to a god.

Willard abandoned his kneading and came over, snagging two cups from the tray. He carried one over to me, the faded pattern smeared by the flour on his fingers. "Long day?"

I accepted the tea with a grateful smile, inhaling the comforting scent of bergamot and honey. "Short day."

The heat seeped into my palms, reminding me of a woman who'd been like a mother to me, and how we'd sit around a fire in the winter, drink warm tea and share stories, me mostly of dance and her of her son's mischief when he was a boy. The homesickness was nearly palpable as I sipped and sat quietly, letting the others live the life they would always have while I mourned the one I may never see again, may never even remember, realizing that Thorne's absence made me homesick too.

But the warm cup only reminded me that time was passing, and Wisteria was warming as well. Seventy-five had turned to thirty-seven so quickly and time was running out. Alastor had all but confirmed I was on the right path, but as time ticked by, I couldn't help but feel the pressure mounting. At least I'd done something today. And yesterday. Facing off with two gods back-to-back had to count for something. Even if it was only stirring a simmering pot.

Willard leaned against the counter beside me, cradling his own cup. For a moment, we simply watched the others, content in the companionable silence. Then he turned to me, his dark eyes serious beneath dark lashes.

"You going to Marielle's dinner party tonight?"

From what I'd gathered, Marielle was one of the wealthier members of the Silk, known for her lavish parties. Thorne had mentioned something about the invitation, but neither of us had taken it very seriously.

"No. Doesn't seem like it'd be a good idea without Thorne here. Those things are only for us to make a scene and prove a point. We've... done enough of that. Besides, I'd spend the night having to answer questions I don't want to. Harlow and I were talking earlier about a girls' night in. Maybe doing some brainstorming on a long-term plan for the kids."

His brow furrowed, lips pressing into a thin line. "You can't," he said, the words coming out harsher than I think he intended. "Harlow needs to be there tonight. We both do."

I straightened, my fingers tightening around the delicate teacup. "And why is that?"

"It's what's expected. Marielle is one of the most influential members of the Silk. If we don't show up, it'll be noticed. People will talk."

He shifted, turning to face me fully, his eyes imploring. "We've worked hard to build up our reputation and make the right connections. Skipping out on this dinner party could undo all of that. It could make us look weak, like we're not serious players in the game."

"What's wrong?" Harlow asked, wrapping a hand around his waist as she glanced between us.

"Paesha isn't going to Marielle's tonight. She said you were planning to stay here, but you know you can't, love."

I frowned, setting my empty cup down beside his, clearing my throat. "I understand the importance of keeping up appearances, but at what cost? We're in the middle of a crisis here. And you're worried about what some wealthy socialites will think if you miss their fancy dinner party?"

Willard's jaw clenched, a muscle ticking beneath the smooth skin of his cheek. "It's not that simple. You know that. Everything we do, every move we make, it's all part of a larger strategy. We have to play the long game here. We need their resources."

"We get them from the Parlor."

He leaned in closer. "The Silk may seem frivolous to you,

with our extravagant parties and idle gossip, but we wield more power than you realize."

Harlow's eyes widened. Her hand slipped from his waist as she took a small step back, creating a sliver of space between them. "You act like I don't know that. Of course I understand the importance. But surely, just this once, we could make an exception. Look around you. This is what matters right now."

His face hardened, his shoulders squaring as he drew himself up to his full height as if lording over her was the better approach. "We're going to the dinner. I've already said we'd go."

I saw the flicker of defiance in her eyes. The war behind her smile. The grit in her.

"You don't have to go, Har. If you don't want to," I said, clearing my throat, rubbing the weight that seemed to be growing in my chest. "There's plenty to do around here."

Wee Willy looked at me like I'd grown a second head before he turned back to her. "Of course she'll go."

She sank. "Of course, I will. If it means that much to you."

I deflated just as he took her hand, lifted a brow to me, and walked out of the damn kitchen. She looked over her shoulder and mouthed 'I'm sorry,' and I couldn't help but feel bad for her. She was worth so much more than the rises and falls he took her on. Giving in to her in small moments, only when it played to his advantage. And she just let him. I couldn't shake the feeling of understanding, even if I'd never experienced such a thing, I felt in my soul that I had. But maybe that was one of my supposed past lives peeking through, willing me to see him for what he was. Just another man pulling the strings and her, just another woman, capable of so much more, but following because that's what was expected. I almost felt bad for her. Almost.

Later that night, I lay in my bed, blankets folded to the end, wondering when it'd gotten so hot outside. When Tuck had come by to do a head count and light the fire, I had to ask him not to.

I'd gone to bed early and pushed the golden book away from me, wondering if Thorne's magic had anything to do with the way I was overheating. If so, I needed to give him a piece of my mind. I flipped open his book, *my book* prepared to let him have it, only to find a few simple words.

Paesha Darling,
Tell me you miss me, and this will all be worth it.
~Sincerely, Lost in Time

> *Always so needy.*
> *~Sincerely, Found in Bed*

I waited a beat, wondering if he'd know I finally replied. A bead of sweat dripped onto the page. Setting the book to the other side of the bed, I slid out, stumbling toward the bathroom to splash cool water on my face. Every limb was heavy. The room was spinning by the time I crept back into the bed.

It's been two days.
~Testing my patience

> *Oh, good. You're practicing your counting while you're*
> *there. I was so worried you'd be bored.*
> *~Eternally Amused, and slightly missing you*

Slightly?
~Tell me more

I fought to hold my head up, desperate to keep my attention on him without alarming him. Desperate to feel our connection from the fog moving in over me.

I don't think you know how signatures in a letter work.
        ~Casually doing whatever we want now

Tell me about your day.
~Let me live vicariously

                    Don't be so

Not finishing your sentences now?
~That's beneath you

...

Paesha

...

Paesha?

...

Tell me what's happening.

...

Where the fuck are you?

I could see the words. I just couldn't lift my hand to answer.

Couldn't put together enough thoughts. I was more tired than I thought. So, so very tired. I closed my eyes for just a minute.

And then it was daytime and Archer was hovering over me, shaking me, screaming, though I couldn't hear him.

I closed my eyes again. So very tired.

"No!" I heard him yell, more clearly this time, but still like I was underwater, and he was above.

"Water?" I knew I'd said it, but my lips didn't move, and my limbs didn't move and I didn't make sound and I couldn't feel a thing and suddenly the world was heavy. And hot.

Archer's ice-cold fingers gripped my face, startling me. So scared. Like a cat. A little bitty kitten. I liked cats. Quill had a dog, though. He was a very good boy.

"Who was in your room? Who poisoned you?"

"Poisoned? The cat."

"Who's the cat? What do you mean?"

"I'm not mean, you're mean."

Archer panicked, pulling away. Pulling his hair. Scaredy cat.

I closed my eyes for one baby second and then I was in the bathtub. With my clothes on.

"Don't die. Don't die." Archer yelled. "Help! We need help!"

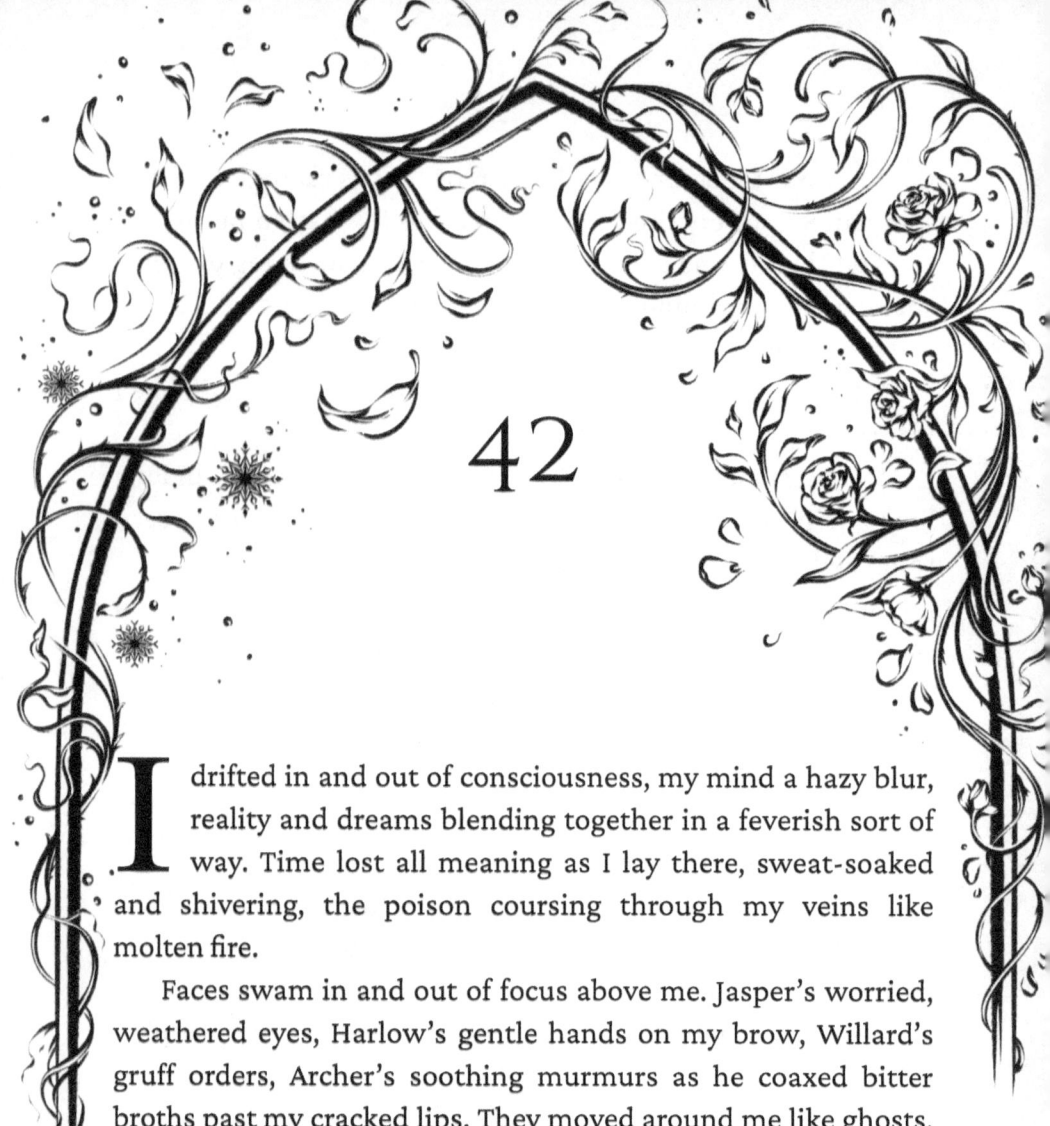

42

I drifted in and out of consciousness, my mind a hazy blur, reality and dreams blending together in a feverish sort of way. Time lost all meaning as I lay there, sweat-soaked and shivering, the poison coursing through my veins like molten fire.

Faces swam in and out of focus above me. Jasper's worried, weathered eyes, Harlow's gentle hands on my brow, Willard's gruff orders, Archer's soothing murmurs as he coaxed bitter broths past my cracked lips. They moved around me like ghosts, their voices muffled and distant, as if reaching me from across a great divide.

"... getting worse... we need to find the antidote..." Archer's words, tight with barely suppressed panic.

"... Thorne would know... time..." Harlow's reply, heavy with fear and indecision.

"... running out of time..." Jasper's somber assessment, his hand a comforting weight on my shoulder.

The world tilted and spun, colors bleeding together in a sickening kaleidoscope. I squeezed my eyes shut against the dizzying onslaught, a low moan tearing from my parched throat. Cool hands cupped my face, thumbs brushing over my feverish cheeks. I leaned into the touch, desperate for any shred of comfort, any anchor in the storm. But when I opened my eyes, the hazy outline of Thorne was fading away. My heart had hoped he'd come, but in reality, he couldn't.

I longed for his strong arms around me, his low voice murmuring reassurances in my ear. For the way he'd sat at my bed to make sure I could sleep beyond the nightmares. I ached for the safety I felt in his presence, the unshakable knowledge that he would protect me.

And Quill, my sweet girl. Memories of her danced through my fevered dreams, her bright laughter as we raced through the rain-soaked meadow, the scrunch of her nose as she battled bath time, the fierce love in her eyes as she declared me to be her chosen family.

I could hardly breathe, each attempt grew more and more difficult as Wisteria tried to end me. Hot tears leaked from beneath my lids, carving tracks down my face.

"You're going to die, aren't you, Fingers?" Archie asked, swiping a sweaty lock of hair from my face.

I blinked beyond my tears.

"I hope it doesn't hurt. Oh gods, what if it hurts?"

I couldn't tell him how numb I'd become. How the only pain I felt was the crack in my heart. I'd failed.

Had I been able, I might've jumped at the crash downstairs. Instead, my eyes rolled back. The breaths were too hard to take.

"Where the fuck is my wife?" I heard the roar, but couldn't make myself stir. Not as the next crash sounded. Not as someone fell to the floor. Not as strong arms lifted me, and my head lolled back.

"... cloak... godsdammit."

Words. Focus Paesha.

"... dare die on me."

I knew that voice. My anchor. My path.

Pain.

I felt pain. Jarring me. Breaking me. Waking me. Killing me.

It surged through me in waves, not just rattling my body, but splintering something deep inside me, cracking open places I didn't know could hurt. It wasn't just pain; it was despair, raw and relentless, scraping at my ribs, peeling me apart. Every breath was a battle, ragged, shattered, like trying to gulp down fire and smoke like breathing wasn't something I deserved to keep doing.

I tried to move, to claw my way back to him, to find his face, even just for a second, to burn it into my memory before everything slipped away. But nothing in me worked anymore. My limbs hung useless, dead weight, hollow. All I had left was the awareness of his heartbeat, pounding fiercely under my ear where he held me close. It was so strong, so alive, and I felt the bitter ache of it.

His arms tightened around me, a silent plea, as if his grip could stitch me back together, as if he could force me to stay with him through sheer desperation. I wanted to whisper his name, to reassure him, but my lips stayed numb. My thoughts turned sluggish, and again I couldn't tell if Thorne was real or some fevered hallucination born of the ache in my chest. I had called for him so many times in my heart, in the nights when the loneliness had felt too wide, too deep. Maybe this is just my mind's way of giving me a final kindness before everything went dark?

The air was thick, choking, the sharp tang of incense and perfume mingling with something darker, more sinister. Voices swam at the edges of my awareness. Disembodied sounds, fragments of life happening somewhere far away from me, life I would no longer be a part of. But Thorne kept walking, his breath sharp and broken, his words spilling out like something vital, like every syllable was the only thing keeping me tethered to him. To this world.

"Stay with me, darling. Please."

I wanted to tell him I was sorry. That I tried. That he had been enough. But no words would come, just the sound of my heartbeat slowing, fading into the heavy silence between us. I was slipping. And no matter how tightly he held me, I couldn't find my way back. The world flickered in and out like a dying flame. Moments of sharp clarity punctuated the void, but they were fleeting, slipping through my grasp before I could hold onto them. His voice, though? It cut through. Thorne's voice. The path. Always him.

"Please!" His words were a ragged sob, torn from him in desperation. "You have to help her. You know you do."

The weight of his plea pressed against my heart, an ache deeper than the pain, deeper than the darkness. A murmur responded to his frantic words, low and measured, but I couldn't make out the voice. It came from the shadows, indifferent, detached. It didn't care about me the way Thorne did. Nothing did.

"... deal... will die..." His voice broke on that last word, shattered like glass, raw and jagged, like saying it made it too real. His breath hitched, his chest heaving beneath me as if he was trying to breathe for the both of us.

The other voice cut through the haze, deeper, more commanding now, but still blurred at the edges. "There's a price. You know that." The tone wasn't unkind, but it wasn't compassionate either. It was just... final.

Thorne's hand clutched mine, trembling. "I don't care. I'll pay it."

The silence that followed felt too heavy, too long.

"Then she will pay it." Even as I drifted in the nothingness, I could sense it, the weight of the choice looming over us like a storm ready to break. I wanted to scream, to reach out and stop him. Not this way. But I couldn't move. Couldn't speak. Couldn't even feel the beat of my own heart anymore.

Something cold brushed against my skin, a faint pressure at my wrist, and then a sharp, icy pain shot through me, pulling me back, dragging me toward the surface. It was like being yanked out of water, gasping for air I couldn't quite catch. My body seized, and I felt Thorne's arms tighten around me, felt the tremor of his breath as he held on.

"Open your eyes, Huntress."

My eyelids fluttered open, but the world remained a blur of shadows and hazy shapes. Thorne's face swam above me, his features distorted by the shimmering air, but I could still see the raw anguish etched into every line. A figure moved at the edge of my vision, a man that seemed to absorb the light rather than reflect it.

Alastor.

He spoke. The words washed over me, indistinct and garbled. I strained to understand.

Cool fingers brushed my forehead, and with the touch came a searing bolt of agony, arcing through my nerves like lightning. I gasped, my back twisting as the pain consumed me.

"You ... agree... four broken souls... to me... cost... live."

I arched again as the pain hit me once more.

"Come on, Paesha," Thorne growled, closer. Clearer. "Agree."

Alastor was closer now. "Use your words."

With monumental effort, I forced my eyes open, blinking against the wavering shadows that danced at the edges of my vision. "Y—yes."

That single word was all I could manage before the darkness returned with a vengeance.

"Set her down," Alastor roared through the haze.

"No!" Thorne growled back.

Cold fire exploded around us, yanking me to full aware-ness. Blue flames erupting from nowhere, engulfing us in an instant. My body, already a battleground of pain, seized with the shock of it, and I could feel the flames curling around me, sharp and biting like shards of ice, but it wasn't the kind of heat that would burn skin. It was something far worse. Consuming. Burrowing into every crack and fissure inside me, wrenching the poison from my blood with excruciating precision.

Maybe it wasn't poison. Maybe it was the venom Alastor had warned Archer about. And this was his final moment. Exacting a cost from Thorne for whatever he'd taken. Maybe I was just his payment for thievery.

Thorne's grip didn't falter, even as the fire licked up his arms, wrapping around us both like a living thing. His muscles tightened. Hands trembled. His breath came in ragged bursts, and through the haze, I heard the low, guttural sound of his suffering. But he didn't stop. He didn't let go.

The flames danced higher, growing more violent, wrapping us in a vortex of flickering blue light. I tried to scream, but the sound was trapped in my throat, swallowed by the fire's roar. It twisted and surged, carving through me.

"Thorne," I tried to say, but my voice was nothing more than a strangled whisper. His name tasted bitter, filled with ash and pain, slipping between my lips as I lay limp in his arms.

"I'm here. Focus on me. Focus on the song."

The song? Something dark and haunting began to stir through the chaos. He hummed a melody, ancient, full of grief, the notes winding through the crackle of flames like a lullaby for the dying. But this was no lullaby. It was an anthem of loss, pulling me back from the edge.

"Listen," he commanded. "Focus on the melody. Imagine the dance."

My body spasmed, the fire surging again, and I whimpered, feeling myself slipping. His arms tightened around me, his voice rising over the roar of the flames.

"Focus" he rasped. "The steps. The dance. I need you to dance with me, Paesha. Do it now."

His words struck something deep within me, an instinct older than memory. My mind clung to the rhythm of his song, the slow, haunting pulse of it. I could see the movements in my mind, the turn of the body, the sweep of the arm, the weightless glide of feet across stone. The steps, not the pain. The dance, not the fire.

The fire twisted around us, fierce and consuming, but for a heartbeat, I wasn't burning. I was dancing. Dancing in an ocean of blue flames threatening to drown us.

"That's it. Keep moving with me."

His song darkened, the melody twisting into something deeper, a mournful cry that reached into my core. The fire surged again, and I whimpered, my back arching in his arms. His pain became mine. His voice, ragged and broken, became the only thing anchoring me to the world. The fire crawled up his arms, turning the skin raw, blistering, but still he sang, his breath hitching with every note. His body shook, but he kept carrying me, never faltering. And I danced.

Alastor loomed in the distance, watching. His shadowed form barely visible through the flames, as if our torment was nothing but an idle curiosity to him.

"Don't stop," he growled, his lips brushing my ear. "Imagine the next step. Another turn. Another breath."

I tried. Gods, I tried. But I was breaking. Shattering.

"Thorne..." I tried to speak, tried to tell him it was too much, that I couldn't do it anymore. The words dissolved on my tongue.

His arms tightened again, pulling me closer, and I could feel his pain in the tremor of his breath, the ragged edge to his voice. His song was faltering, breaking with the weight of his own suffering, but he didn't stop. He wouldn't stop.

"The dance, Paesha. Focus on the dance. One more step. One more... breath."

The fire surged one last time, and the world narrowed to the space between us, the heat of his breath against my skin, the raw agony in his voice. Everything fell silent.

The flames dulled to a distant hum, and for a moment, I felt weightless, suspended between life and death. Between the blue fire and the man who had refused to let me fall.

43

I woke with a gasp. My eyes flew open as I jolted upright in bed. For a moment, panic seized me, the memory of searing pain and sapphire flames still vivid in my mind. My hands flew to my chest, expecting to find charred flesh and blackened skin, but there was only the soft fabric of my nightgown, damp with sweat.

Slowly, the fog of terror lifted, and I took in my surroundings with growing confusion. I was in my room at Thorne's house, tucked beneath the familiar weight of the blankets.

I pushed myself up on shaky arms, my body aching. I groaned as I swung my legs over the side of the bed and willed my eyes to focus beyond the ache rattling through me.

I was alive. Somehow. Impossibly. I had survived.

But Thorne... The memory of his anguished face haunted me, the desperation in his voice as he begged Alastor to save me was something of nightmares. He'd carried me into the heart of the flames, holding me close even as the fire consumed him. Alastor had told him to leave me, but he'd refused, walking through for me. But... why? This thing between us, it wasn't

454

nearly as strong as that gesture implied. Or had I been blind? Refusing to see what was in front of me because I knew the inevitable? He'd burned for me. And what did fire that healed the broken do to someone that was whole?

Needing the comfort of my power, I tugged within, coaxing it forward as a small tether on the other end wrapped around the golden book. With trembling fingers, I reached beneath my pillow to grab it, wondering if I'd tucked it under there in my poisoned, delusional state. I let it fall open in my lap.

The pages were blank, the parchment pristine and unmarked. I traced my fingers over the empty pages, willing them to reveal something, anything. A sign that he was all right, that he had survived the ordeal just as I had. But the book remained stubbornly silent, offering no reassurance, no solace.

My mind grew increasingly heavy. The pull on my limbs too much. With all of my will, I shoved the book back under the pillow, lay back down and fell back asleep.

"Miss Paesha?" Jasper's soft voice dragged me from sleep in what felt like moments later. With a deep line between his brows, he held a steaming cup out to me with his only hand. "You must drink."

I eyed the cup warily, realizing that I couldn't trust a soul. Not even this one. Someone had poisoned me, and I wasn't sure how. Aside from a single visit to Alastor, I'd been here. Only here. Surrounded by nothing but familiar faces. Alastor had mentioned venom, but I'd been in the kitchen with everyone before I had gotten sick. Briony had made tea, Willard had handed it to me, Jasper had been there. Harlow and Archer had been there.

I turned away from Jasper without a word, giving him my back, letting my stomach whirl with the motion. How long had it been since I ate? How many days had passed? How long had I been in Wisteria? The days were impossible to count. Even at my best guess, I had no idea how long I had left. The hourglass controlling my fate was emptying quickly. And if I thought about that for too long, I'd probably be sick.

"You have to eat something," Archer barked at me later. "You can't wither away and die in this bed."

I rolled again, realizing it was darker outside now. I'd fallen asleep.

"I can if I want."

He knelt down in front of me. "It wasn't me. You have to know that, don't you? I got you these myself in the kitchen. Watch." With slow movements, or maybe that was just my weak mind, he lifted a small finger sandwich from the plate and took a bite, then followed it with a sip of the tea.

I watched him chew, swallow and stare me right in the face, more serious than I'd ever seen him. "Now eat."

I rolled back over.

"That's fine. Your bed has two sides."

He stomped around to the other side, crossing his arms over his chest. I wanted to trust him more than anything, but instead, I closed my eyes to hide the tears. "Where is he?"

"In his bed. We've moved the children that were in there to a different room. The space is tight but we're making it work."

"Is he hurt?"

"Eat and I'll tell you."

A tear slipped free. "Alastor said I was the Hunted. Some-one's trying to kill me. And it's probably someone here."

"Hey," he said, squatting down. "We don't know that. I'm betting it wasn't and I rarely take a bet I can't win. We were at the Vale. It could have been Alastor or that guard pricked you with something and we didn't realize it. Or someone at the Parlor even, with a slow acting poison. You were sick for days and days. Five in this bed alone. Something that takes that long doesn't happen all at once." He grabbed my hand, blue eyes a sea of solemnness as he looked at me. "I'll take a bite and a sip of everything you eat if you want me to. I'll go first, Fingers. You can't give up."

"For all we know, you're already poisoned. Slow-acting, remember?"

"Then we tighten the house. We move the kids somewhere else. The Salt back to the streets or the Hollow at their own risk. No one but your approved list of people gets in or out."

I shook my head, swiping away the pesky tears. "No. We don't displace dozens of people for the comfort of one."

"We do if that one is you."

With reluctance, I pushed myself up on one elbow and took the small sandwich from Archer's outstretched hand. The bread was soft and yielding beneath my fingers, the edges perfectly trimmed. I brought it to my lips, inhaling before taking a tentative bite.

The flavors burst across my tongue, cool and refreshing, a welcome respite from the bitter tang of paranoia that had taken up residence in my mouth. I chewed slowly, each movement of my jaw a monumental effort. Archer watched me intently, eyes tracking every bite, every swallow, as if he could will me back to health through sheer force of concern.

When the last morsel was gone, he pressed the delicate, chipped teacup into my hands. "I know this is your favorite cup. Not sure why, though. It's broken, in case you didn't notice."

I let myself smile, breathing in the fragrant steam wafting from the tea. As I drank, Archer settled himself more comfortably on the edge of the bed. He began to talk, his voice a low, steady murmur that washed over me like gentle waves lapping at the shore. He spoke of inconsequential things at first, the antics of the children as they adjusted to their new surroundings, Briony's valiant attempts to wrangle them into some semblance of order, the way Harlow had thrown herself into the role of caretaker with a ferocity that surprised no one. He spoke of Willard's increasing agitation, the long hours he spent sequestered in Thorne's study, poring over the few things Thorne had kept. Mostly his ledgers and a few history books.

Gradually, as the tea settled warm and heavy in my belly, Archer's words took on a more somber tone. "We tried to find the antidote, you know? But that's hard when you have no idea the source of the poison. Then Thorne showed up, early, in case you didn't catch that five days comment. He burst through the door like a man possessed. You should have seen it. Scary fucker. We sort of guessed the Goddess of Time told him what was happening after Harlow went banging on her door, begging to take his place so he could come back. Vesalia refused of course.

"Thorne carried you out of here like you weighed nothing. Wouldn't let any of us near you. Just wrapped you up in his cloak and disappeared into the night. We didn't know... we thought..." He swallowed hard, his Adam's apple bobbing in his throat.

I set the empty teacup aside, my fingers trembling slightly as I reached out to lay my hand over his. "Thank you for staying. For fighting."

He knelt closer, leaning on the bed. "You'll both get better, and then it's back to business. That's what we do."

"Can I see him?" I asked, not daring to look Archer in the eye.

He stood, putting his hands in his pocket to pull out a coin, rolling it between his fingers before he answered with a heavy sigh. "He doesn't want anyone in there. When Alastor's men dropped you two off at the front door, he demanded we leave him alone. He hasn't let anyone in since."

In the middle of the night, when the house was still and silent, the moon lit my bedroom floor and I couldn't stand it any longer. I rolled out of bed. Actually rolled, dropping to the floor, the pain of it stealing my breath.

I couldn't find the strength to rise, so I dragged my exhausted body towards him. Every inch was a battle. My arms trembled with fatigue as I moved closer in a desperate crawl. Down the hall, past the doors hiding sleeping children and others in need, beyond the single crooked painting he'd refused to sell.

I paused outside Thorne's door. Uncertainty coiled in my gut. He had made it clear he wanted to be left alone, that he didn't want anyone to see him. And I'd avoided him until I couldn't take it. But the need to be near him, to reassure myself that he was alive, that we had both somehow survived the fire, overrode any hesitation.

Reaching up, I turned the knob slowly, half expecting it to be locked, but it gave way easily beneath my palm. The door swung open on silent hinges, and I crawled into the room, my heart lodged in my throat.

The curtains were drawn, but slivers of moonlight slipped through the cracks, painting the space in shades of silver and shadow. The air was thick with the scent of medicinal herbs and the coppery tang of blood. And there, in the center of the large bed, lay Thorne.

Someone had been here. Someone had tried to help him. Thank the gods. Except not the gods because fuck them. He was a tangle of blankets and bandages, his normally golden skin pale and drawn. A sheen of sweat glistened on his brow.

I pulled myself up, using the bed frame for support, my muscles quivering with the effort. I crawled in beside him, the cool sheets a balm against my feverish skin. Thorne shifted, a low moan escaping his chapped lips as he turned towards me, his eyelids fluttering open.

For a long moment, we simply stared at each other, drinking in the sight of one another, alive and breathing. His eyes, normally a vibrant mass of brown and green, were dulled by pain and exhaustion, but they still held me captive, searching my face as if memorizing every detail.

The silence stretched between us, heavy with unspoken words and emotions too raw to voice. I traced the lines of his face with my gaze, the sharp angles softened by the moonlight, the dark stubble shadowing his jaw. He looked vulnerable like this, stripped of his usual masks and defenses, laid bare by the healing fire of meddling gods.

Slowly, hesitantly, I reached out, my fingertips grazing the edge of the bandage wrapped around his chest, a physical reminder of the price he had paid for my life. I swallowed hard, tears pricking at the corners of my eyes as I followed the path of the bandages, mapping out the extent of his injuries.

"Thank you," I said simply, no other words feeling significant enough.

He managed a ragged breath. "You don't get to die until I say so."

"Always so commanding," I whispered, letting my eyes fall shut, feeling whole in a way I'd missed with his absence.

As we lay there, side by side in the moonlit room, an odd sense of déjà vu washed over me. The scene felt familiar, like a half-remembered dream that lingered just beyond the reach of consciousness. In my mind's eye, I saw flashes of another time, another place, a cozy bedroom bathed in the warm glow of a crackling hearth.

A man lay beside me, his face obscured by shadows, but his presence was achingly familiar. I could feel the warmth of his body, the steady rise and fall of his chest as he slept, the rough calluses of his hand as it rested on my hip. We were tangled together, limbs intertwined, fitting like two pieces of a puzzle that had finally found their way home.

The details of the room sharpened, coming into focus like a painting slowly revealed. An apartment full of couches and there were... spoons? We'd bought spoons together that day. I could feel the love that permeated every inch of this space, the sense of belonging, of safety, of home.

The vision shifted, the edges blurring and reforming, and suddenly I was standing in a rain-soaked meadow, the scent of wildflowers heavy in the air. The man stood before me, his features still indistinct, but his presence a tangible force, drawing me in. He reached for me, his hands rough and warm as they cupped my face, his thumbs brushing away tears.

"I've been waiting for you. Waiting for you to remember."

I leaned into his touch, my eyes fluttering closed as I breathed him in. It was a scent I knew, a scent that meant comfort and desire and an aching, desperate mourning.

"Remember what?" I whispered.

He pulled me closer, his arms banding around me, strong and unyielding. I melted into him, my body molding to his as if it had been made to fit there, in the circle of his embrace. His heartbeat thundered beneath my cheek, a steady, reassuring rhythm that tethered me to him, to this moment.

"Us." he breathed, the word a reverent sigh against my hair. "Remember us, my love."

44

I gasped awake, heart racing, the dream slipping away like water through my fingers. For a moment, I was lost, caught between worlds, the rain-soaked meadow, and the dark bedroom. The scent of wildflowers lingered, a ghost in the air, fading as the room came into sharper focus.

Thorne lay beside me, his face tight with pain, even in sleep. His brow furrowed. His jaw clenched. Each shallow breath dragged from his chest like it cost him everything. Blue flames flickered in my mind, the memory of his arms tightening around me as they devoured him.

I stared, torn between guilt and gratitude. He'd walked through fire for me. Suffered. Burned. And for what? What was I to him that he would endure that kind of agony?

There'd been a price, though. A price that I had to pay. A mysterious bargain with Alastor. And so help me, if I was bound to another person again, if I lost my life and free will in that hazy agreement, I would never be able to look at Thorne the same way. I'd sooner see the world burn than lose myself to it.

He shifted, a soft moan slipping from his lips, barely a

sound, but enough to break me. Without thinking, I reached out. My hand brushed his brow, smoothing the lines of tension. His skin was too hot, feverish. Still, he leaned into my touch, as if, even in sleep, he sought me.

Another breath. Shallow. Ragged. But he didn't wake.

What had I done to him? What had I *cost* him? Why was I getting better, and he wasn't?

I forced myself to pull away from Thorne, every inch of me screaming against it. My body protested, leaden and sluggish as I dragged myself out of the warmth of his bed to the floor that bit into my feet, cold as ice. A shiver shot up my spine, my legs wobbling beneath me.

One last glance. I couldn't help it. His chest rose and fell, slow and shallow, sweat glistening on his skin. I turned away, each step toward the door a battle. Every muscle burned, exhaustion wrapping its arms around me, begging me to stop.

But I didn't.

When I finally made it to my room, my eyes landed on the bedside table. A steaming cup of tea. A bowl of porridge. They sat there, waiting, welcoming, and yet wholly unsettling.

A knot formed in my stomach.

I brought the tea to my lips, the fragrant steam wafting up to caress my face. But as the rim touched my mouth, I froze. Of course I was still paranoid. The tea rippled, a miniature ocean in the cradle of the cup, and for a moment, I swore I could see a sinister swirl of color, there and gone in a blink.

Poison.

The word whispered through my mind, insidious and relentless. Threatening me. But I had to let it go. I couldn't let the fear consume me. Not now. Not when there was so much at stake. If I started seeing enemies in every corner, suspicion in every kind gesture, I'd be lost. Paralyzed. And that was a luxury I couldn't afford.

I forced myself to breathe deep. With each exhale, I tried to release the tension coiled tight in my muscles. My gaze drifted around the room, taking in the small details I'd missed before. The vase of fresh flowers on the dresser. The stack of books on the nightstand. The quilt draped over the armchair in the corner. These weren't the signs of people trying to kill me. These were signs they cared. And they'd been here. They'd fought for me when I was dying.

So, I drank the damn tea. I drank the tea and ate the porridge, bland as it was, and decided to hell with it. If I was going to die in a realm of chaos and lies, then at least I wouldn't be hungry. And at that rate, maybe the realms deserved to fall. What good were they to me if I was dead?

A soft knock on my door was my only warning before Harlow stepped in, eyes wide to see me sitting on the edge of the bed, with an empty bowl, no doubt.

"You're up."

"I hadn't noticed."

She smiled. "And your winning personality is back."

"Baby steps."

She eyed the empty bowl. "Archer made us give him a bite of that before he'd let me bring it up. He's been sleeping in the office chair or that one in the corner."

"Well, maybe he likes me more than everyone else."

"Hey, I like you just fine."

"Calm down with your swooning. My migraine can't take it."

"I'll try to control myself." She walked across the room with as much grace as a woman that grew up in court might've, then flopped down on the bed, locking her fingers together at her stomach as she stared up at the ceiling. "On a scale of one to near-death, how are you feeling?"

"Five, why?"

"Because two of Alastor's thugs are at the door asking for you, and I'm debating how to kindly tell them to fuck off. Thought maybe you'd have some advice."

"Always better to get right to the point with men. If you smile, they think you want something from them, and if you scowl, they think they need to correct you. Stick with a solid 'fuck off' and go on about your day."

She giggled but didn't immediately get up.

I traced the hem of the blanket, cautious but desperate. "Can I ask you something?"

"Sure. But I can't promise I'll know the answer."

"How many days have passed since Tithe?"

She drew back, looking at me. Still, she counted in her mind, fingers slightly moving before she answered. "Forty-six. Why?"

I swallowed, trying to keep my expression neutral. I'd been out for nine between the poison and healing then. Dammit. That left me with only twenty-nine days, minus however long I'd been in the Maw. A week? So only about twenty two days to go, if I was lucky. I couldn't panic, though. I couldn't show an ounce of concern. "I was just wondering how long Thorne and I have been... pretending. That's all."

She rolled back over with a sigh. "Have you seen him yet?"

"I went in last night. He's in bad shape."

"He yelled at me yesterday, but he needed help. Your skin didn't burn, but his is charred. Any idea why?"

"We had to walk through some kind of fire. And he shielded most of me with his own body."

"I can't even get Willard to walk beside me some days."

"That's because he's a dick, but who am I to judge?"

She rolled her eyes. "All right. I'll go send the goons on the front step away. You good? Need anything?"

"I'm fine. I'll come down and see the kids after a really long bath."

She stood, smoothing her dress before walking out, chin high as if she were preparing for battle. Smart woman.

I'd no sooner stepped out of my clothes before the door to my bedroom slammed open. I snatched the towel and wrapped it around myself, hustling to the closed bathroom door.

"I told you she's resting," Harlow barked.

"Don't look like she's resting to me," a deep voice said. "Sounds like she's in the bath. Maybe I should go have a peek."

My heart skipped a beat as I stepped away from the door, swiping my dress from where I'd laid it across the counter.

Harlow's voice cut across the room like a blade. "If you so much as think of opening that door, I will fucking gut you. Got it?"

There was a scuffle. I threw the dress over my head and yanked the door open to find Harlow, standing with her foot on one man's throat and a blade in the leg of another. "Why do men always doubt me?" she asked, eyes flicking to me before turning back to the stabbed man. "It's the dress, isn't it?"

"Alastor—"

"Can wait," she bit back, glaring at the goon on the floor.

The man with the blade in his thigh stumbled.

"Oh, for god's sake, you're making such a mess." She looked down at the one on the floor. "You. Stay."

In one fell swoop, she yanked her blade free, wiped it on the man on the floor's shirt and flung her skirts back, exposing the slit and easy access to her thigh. She slid the blade home and grabbed the bleeding man by the collar. "Go sit on that chair while I get something to clean this up. If either of you move a single finger while I'm gone, I'll hunt you down."

She spun to me next, throwing her hands on her hips. "Take as long as you like, friend. I've got this handled."

My mouth twisted, but I didn't say a word, just let the door shut and twisted the lock before stepping into the bath, grinning from ear to ear. I knew she was fierce. I had no idea she was actually lethal. Not really.

There was not another sound from the other side of the door. Not one as I bathed, soaking my hair, letting the water wash away every dreadful thing that'd happened. I knew what would happen when I stepped out. Alastor had come to collect on whatever debt I owed him. And I needed five more minutes to accept the chaos already surrounding me before I added any more.

Eventually I dressed, feeling half human at least, plaited my hair and stepped back into the room, only to find Harlow, Archer, Tuck and Willard standing shoulder-to-shoulder with their backs to me, arms all crossed, staring down at Alastor's two thugs sitting on the floor.

"Playing nice?"

"I'm always nice," Archer answered without taking his eyes from the men. "She's ready now. Tell her what you need to."

The one with a bandage wrapped around his leg scowled. "We're not delivering a message. If your friend here had any brain cells, she would have listened."

Harlow spun, facing me. "You were right. I scowled, and he tried to correct me. Hurts less when I remember stabbing him, though."

I shared a cruel smile with her. "It usually does." Stepping through the wall of Fray, I knelt before one of the men. "What can I do for you, boys?"

"The boss wants you. You're to report to the Vale... well, an hour ago."

"Like hell she's—"

I cut Willard off with a hand. "I can speak for myself, thank you." Looking back at the leather clad men, both scared and heavy set, with arms wider than my thighs, I wondered if Harlow had felt an ounce of fear before she'd attacked them.

"Like hell I'm going with you. Crawl back to your boss and tell him I said no, thank you."

They shared a wary glance.

Tuck stepped forward, grabbing one from under his arm and hauling him to his feet. "You heard the lady. Best be off."

They didn't argue at all as they left the house, though I did wonder why Alastor sent these two. They wore scars and rough skin but had no resolve at all. That night, when the house had finally fallen to silence, I changed into my leathers, strapped the sword to my back, threw my cloak over it, and crept into the city, getting lost in the shadows gifted by the full moon, as I used only the power necessary to find my way back to the Vale. But the fear I'd had with the Cimmerians was waning. The trauma they'd caused barely scratched the surface if I took a step back and looked at everything I'd been through in my life. So, I moved without fear. Without hesitation, through a city, a world of hatred.

The man at the door hadn't said a word when I approached. Hadn't asked for a thing. I swept my hood down, pulling the sword from my back free. He took one look at my eyes and let me into the Vale. Once inside, I replaced the walls of the cloak, unbothered by how the crowd, the supposed worst in the city, watched me.

When I reached the door Archer and I had taken the meeting with Alastor in, I didn't bother knocking. I simply let myself in, sauntered through the room and plopped down in the open chair, throwing my feet up on his desk as he sat, watching me.

"Right on time."

"Why'd you send the world's worst lackeys to collect me?"

Alastor leaned back in his chair, steepling his long fingers. His emerald gaze raked over me, assessing, calculating. A slow smile curved his lips, but it held no warmth. "They served their purpose. Got your attention, didn't they?"

"You could have just sent a note."

He chuckled. "Where's the fun in that, Huntress? Besides, I find people are more likely to heed a summons when it's delivered with a bit of... force."

"If that's your idea of force, you should pick up a book sometime. Reunite yourself with the common language."

Alastor's smile sharpened. "They were told not to use violence and they aren't too good with words. Learning curve and all that." He rose from his seat, moving with a fluid grace. Rounding the desk, he perched on the edge, looming over me. "Now, you're here because we have unfinished business, you and me. A debt to settle. You've already agreed to the terms, so that's easy enough, but I thought I'd remind you what you owe me for that precious little life of yours. Now, give me your hand."

I narrowed my eyes at Alastor, warning bells screaming through my mind. His casual demeanor did nothing to put me at ease. If anything, it set my nerves on edge. Gods were never to be trusted, especially when they acted as if they were doing you a favor.

Slowly, I withdrew my feet from his desk and sat up straighter, squaring my shoulders, though I was terrified of the binds that would come from this conversation. "Remind me of the terms, then. Exactly what is it that I owe you?"

Alastor tsked, shaking his head as if disappointed by my question. "Four broken souls, Huntress. That was the price. Four lost, shattered names delivered unto me. Did the poison addle your mind so thoroughly that you've forgotten already?"

"I remember," I said evenly. "But I also remember that you never specified a timeline. Or what qualifies as a broken soul. Seems to me there's quite a bit of room for interpretation there."

Alastor's eyes flashed, a brief flicker of annoyance breaking through his mask of amusement. "There is no room for interpretation just because your mind doesn't remember what your mouth agreed to. You will find four broken souls and deliver their names to me, or your eternity will belong to me. Don't worry, Huntress. I did not steal your freedom. Nor your free will. I am not as cruel as some. Now. Hold out your hand."

I did as I was told, though I could hardly swallow. I'd have to do this before I went home or I'd never be able to complete the bargain. And as it was a deal with a god, there would be no loopholes. But I had twenty-two days to complete the Keeper's bargain. Time was ticking, and I wasn't sure I was any closer now than I had been.

Alastor's grip tightened around my palm, his skin impossibly warm against my own. A shiver ran down my spine as his power washed over me, ancient and vast, a yawning chasm that threatened to swallow me whole, though a tendril of it was familiar. Mine. Ours.

Slowly, almost imperceptibly at first, a soft golden light began to emanate from his skin. It started at our joined hands, a gentle warmth that spread up his arm, gradually engulfing his entire being. The light pulsed in time with an unseen heartbeat, growing brighter and more intense with each passing second.

I watched, transfixed, as the glow intensified. Alastor's features blurred, his edges softening until he was little more than a silhouette wreathed in shimmering gold. The light danced across his skin like a living flame, casting eerie shadows on the walls of the room. It filled the air until I could taste it on my tongue, feel it humming in my bones.

"Look," he commanded, his voice a distant echo, as if speaking from the bottom of a well. "Do you see the mark within me?"

"It's kind of hard to miss the giant, shiny man holding my hand."

"See beyond the gold. Look harder."

There was nothing at first, only the shimmering blinding light, but as I stared, wishing for this moment to end, a trace of black danced along the edges of the gold. Tainting it.

"There," he said, pulling his hand from mine, breathing away the golden light. "Find the broken, deliver their names to me."

"Why couldn't I see that before?"

"A mortal will show their broken soul at a moment of weakness, but a god may always choose what form to share. And mine are none of your concern. To see the broken is a gift, power that only my descendant carries."

Descendant. As in one...

I let my eyes fall to the floor, considering that final thought until another struck me and whipped back to him. "I deliver to you your own name. Alastor, God of Lost and Broken things."

The shadows hidden within the tattoos on his arms writhed as a hard smile formed. "No, Huntress. You don't know enough about my name to try to deliver it to me, but nice try. However, I would like to help you. Offer you a bit of advice." He stroked a thick finger across the bottom of his jaw. "You should be careful of the company you keep."

I rolled my eyes, well aware of who he meant. "Oh yes, a man who literally carried me through fire to make sure I live is the worst of the worst. Little hint, I don't trust gods. Especially not ones that make bargains with desperate people. I'll find your broken souls because I have no choice, but I'll never give you say over what happens in my life. I don't care what kind of ancestral claim you think you have over me. I belong to no one."

"Or so you think."

"Let me make it simple, Alastor. You're just the keeper of scraps no one else wants. The god of leftovers and left behinds. So don't waste your breath trying to give me advice, because I know exactly what you are. You're just like them. Every other god that's foaming at the mouth for scraps of more power. You're a puppeteer. But when this is over, I'll cut the strings and walk away."

He moved so fast, god-like precision snapping through the air to clinch my throat and drag me toward him. "There's a line between sass and disrespect, mortal, and you're going to find yourself dead before you learn the difference if you aren't careful. I've broken a lock on you, and I've saved you once, healed what was broken out of loyalty to Irri. But I won't do it again. Tread lightly."

He squeezed. And squeezed. Until I couldn't breathe. Until there was no doubt he'd left bruises on my neck with his warning. I couldn't swallow over his fingers, couldn't blink beyond the pressure in my eyes. "Break free of your chains and stop learning your lessons the hard way," he demanded, throwing me to the floor and storming out of his office.

He was a fool to trust me there, truly. But I knew a test when I saw one, so I kept my hands to myself, threw my hood back up and left. Sulking all the way home while contemplating what lock had been broken. And how Irri, a name I'd heard but couldn't place to save my life, had anything to do with anything.

Thorne was there when I walked into my room, sitting heavily on the bed, the golden book in his hands. I tried not to look at him with resentment. He'd tied me to Alastor, but I couldn't be mad at him for it because the only other choice was death.

Though slow, he stood wincing, glancing over me with deadly attentiveness, eyes locked on my throat. He jerked upright, all sense of weakness gone in a flurry of movement. "Who the fuck was dumb enough to put their hands on you?"

45

"Last night you were barely conscious and burned to a crisp, how are you standing in my room right now?"

"I gave in and let Archer heal me. Don't ask him about it though, he has a hard time using his magic when his sister can't. Now," Thorne said, wavering as he stood, "tell me about those fucking marks on your neck."

I closed the door behind me, stepping closer to him. "You bound me to a god, and I answer to him now."

He swiped a palm through his hair. "I didn't bind you to Alastor... If I'd had any other choice... You must know how much that killed me. I thought he'd say no. But he was the only one I could trust to fix what was broken. It was poison. Archer can't heal that. His power accelerates the healing process and if he'd have tried..."

I nodded. "I would have had less time. I understand."

I didn't want to. I wanted to be so incredibly furious. And deep down, I was. But not with Thorne. With myself, for ever taking the bargain with the God of Shiny Muscles and Probably Grass or something.

"Tell me what happened." His eyes locked onto my neck again and I couldn't help but wonder if Alastor had known what these bruises would do. If he'd left them to send a message meant for Thorne just as much as they were a lesson for me.

"It was just a simple misunderstanding. It probably looks worse than it is."

He closed the distance between us, moving slowly, his hands gently coming up to cup my face as he examined the bruises. "This is more than a misunderstanding. He hurt you."

The dangerous edge to Thorne's voice barely contained the rage simmering beneath the surface. I knew he'd go after Alastor if I let him, consequences be damned. But that would be the biggest mistake of his life. And he'd done enough.

"I'm fine, really." I tried to pull away, but Thorne held me fast, his eyes searching mine.

"You don't have to protect him, you know. Or me, for that matter. I can handle Alastor."

I searched his eyes. "Don't you see? This isn't a game. It's not even a fair fight. We cannot stand against the gods. Look at what happened. You were locked away without so much as a thought. And me? Now, I'm... I don't even want to get into it."

"Into what?"

My heart raced. I'd spoken without thinking. And I'd never be able to walk myself out of it if I wasn't careful with my words. But he stared at me. Into my soul, rubbing his thumb over my cheek, drawing the answer further and further to the tip of my tongue as if I could just speak the truth to him. But I couldn't, so I looked away.

Thorne sighed heavily, his thumb brushing over the bruise on my throat with a feather-light touch, tracing the pattern with a reverence that made my breath catch.

"You're not alone in this. I'm here, whether you like it or not."

I let my hands linger on Thorne's chest, feeling the steady thrum of his heartbeat, the warmth of his skin, a tangible reminder of his strength. He was here. Alive and whole and right here.

"Paesha..." he murmured, my name a plea and a prayer on his lips. "Talk to me. Let me help you."

The urge to confess, to unburden myself of the secrets I carried, was a physical ache in my chest. I wished I could.

"I can't," I whispered.

Thorne's gaze held mine. Slowly, giving me time to pull away, he leaned in until his forehead rested against mine. His breath fanned across my cheeks, warm and intoxicating. This close, I could trace the faint lines of exhaustion and pain etched into the corners of his eyes. Even battered and weary, he was beautiful in a way that was so unfair.

"I'm not going anywhere. Whatever you're facing, whatever Alastor has demanded of you, I'll be right here. Beside you. Trust me."

His words washed over me, a balm to my frayed nerves and battered heart. I couldn't tell him though. Not fully. Even though the truth hung between us like a blade waiting to fall, the Keeper's bargain was absolute.

Still, with Thorne's strong body so close to mine, his scent wrapping around me like a caress, I allowed myself to lean into him. Just for a heartbeat. Just long enough to draw strength from him. His thumbs brushed my bottom lip as if he were remembering... longing for another kiss.

"I do trust you," I whispered as he dragged me into a hug. "Maybe it's you who shouldn't trust me."

"And why is that?" he asked, pulling away.

"Because I'd rather die on my feet than live on my knees."

"And I'd rather spend eternity on my knees if it meant keeping you safe."

"You don't mean that, Thorne. We both know you don't. You're afraid to lose someone you care about, but you can't sacrifice yourself for me."

"Maybe that's your problem, thinking you have to face all of this alone. Tell me something real, Paesha. Just one damn truth."

"Why? What would that change?"

"It's called trust. Maybe you've heard of it. You don't open yourself up. Not to one damn person around you. At this point, I'm convinced you even lie to yourself."

My heart began to race, recognizing this battle for what it was. "You think trust is just spilling your past to someone?"

He scoffed. "It's certainly more than this endless push and pull. Why can't you just let me in?"

"Because you don't want to see what's inside, Thorne."

He moved toward me, refusing to accept the subtle space I'd put between us. "How would you know that?"

"What about you? You keep me in the dark just the same."

"You're deflecting."

"And you are too."

"Fine. What do you want to know?" he asked, crossing his arms over his chest, the only sign I needed to see. He wasn't really willing to open up. If he was, he wouldn't have built that little wall.

"Why you're willing to burn for someone you don't know shit about. Why you care so damn much about people you know you can't save at the end of this."

"Maybe because I want to believe someone's worth fighting for."

"Someone, or me?" The words were out of my mouth before I thought about them.

"I should think that was obvious. Look at me and tell me

you can see what's right in front of your face. I think you can, you just won't."

"Don't turn this on me."

He lifted a brow, moving closer. "Why not? I've tried to get close to you, but every time, it's like you're building walls before I can even knock on the door."

"Maybe there are things I can't just share. Maybe it's for your own good."

"Or maybe that's just what you tell yourself so you can keep hiding."

"It's not hiding, Thorne. It's survival. I've been surviving on my own since I was a *child*.

"Then survive with me. I'm right here, for gods' sake."

"I can't. You don't understand." I said at last, my voice barely above a whisper as I held the brittle walls of my resolve in place. My secrets were my own, whether I wanted them to be or not.

"Then make me understand. If it's the gods, if it's Alastor—"

"It's not about him. It's... it's just not that simple."

"It's never simple with you."

"And you don't want it to be. Admit it. If I laid it all out, every bit of my past, you'd turn away."

He moved closer again, daring me to step away. "Try me."

"You think you know me, but you don't."

"Funny, I thought I did. I think that's why I'm standing here, still fighting for you."

"Then stop. Because one day you're going to regret it."

"Maybe I already do."

My back was against the wall before I realized I'd actually taken the step. "Good."

"Is it good?" he asked slowly, prowling toward me as he reached forward, pressing his hand to the bruises on my throat again. "Do you want me to walk away?"

I knew I needed him. And not just for the Keeper's bargain, but for reasons far more dangerous to my heart. I couldn't look him in the face and lie about that. Not as I broke my own heart to push him away, so I let my eyes fall to the floor. "Yes."

He lifted my chin. "Tell me you don't mean that. You can be mad. You can be mean. But don't fucking lie to me."

My throat tightened, unshed tears burning behind my eyes. I squeezed them shut, fighting against the swell of emotion rising in my throat. Fighting against everything inside of me. Why did he have to make this so hard?

"Paesha, please." His voice was softer now, almost pleading. "I just want to understand. I want to be there for you, in whatever way you need me. But I can't do that if you keep shutting me out."

The bargain looming over me, caging me, sent a wave of anger through my veins. This man deserved an ounce of truth and I hated that I couldn't give him that. Still I tried. Still I ran for the ledge of honesty and jumped, shoving so hard against the walls of the bargain, the words poured from me. "You want to understand? Fine. Let me spell it out for you. I'm not just here by chance or coincidence. I didn't stumble into this mess. I'm here because I made a deal, a bargain with Reverius, the Keeper of too many things to fucking say. I'm trying to leave. I need to go home. I have to go and somehow you're the path."

I stumbled backward, wide eyed and confused. I'd said the words. How? Why now when I'd never been able to before? And then it hit me. Alastor. The realization rocked me. He'd tampered with the bargain somehow. That was the lock. And he'd broken it.

Thorne stared at me, his eyes wide with shock and something else. Hurt. He shook his head, stepping back as if he'd been hit in the gut. "You can change your mind. You can stay."

I didn't trust myself to speak. My heart raced, pounding

against my ribs like a wild thing desperate to escape. I braced myself for his reaction, for the anger, the betrayal, the accusations.

But they never came. Instead, Thorne closed the distance between us in a single stride, his hands coming up to cradle my face with a tenderness that shattered me. His thumbs brushed over my cheekbones. "Tell me about the bargain."

I knew what he was doing. Searching for the loophole to keep me here.

"If I don't find a way home, back to a little girl that really needs me, then the worst of the worst happens. Eventually, all the realms will fall. And it will be my fault. She will go through so much anguish and be so angry she'll burn the worlds. I have twenty two days, I think, and then I'll forget. He'll take my memories and only leave me knowing that I was responsible for all of it."

I tried to break away, but he held me so, so close. "Then let the worlds burn, Paesha darling. I'll carry you through the flames and we'll stand in the ashes together. You'll forget, but I will make you remember us."

"Don't you see? This... whatever this is between us, it can't happen."

His words were desperate. "How can you look at me and tell me you are walking away?"

"That was always the plan. Always."

His beautiful, aching eyes narrowed. "Then change the fucking plan."

The hurt on his face was breaking something I never knew I had within me. I reached for his face, stroking the stubble there. "I wish I could. I wish this were only about me."

"It is." He grabbed my hand, leaning down to place his forehead to mine. "Be selfish. Stay with me."

"I won't remember her, Thorne. I won't remember. And I can't accept that. I'm sorry."

Slowly, I extracted myself from his arms, each movement an agony, like tearing away pieces of my own flesh. His hands slid down my arms, catching my fingers in a desperate grip. His eyes blazed into mine, filled with a maelstrom of emotions, anguish, desperation, and a longing so deep it stole my breath.

But as he'd always so masterfully done, he slid his mask back on. Indifference taking the place of everything simmering below the surface. He would never beg, and I would never break, and between us, it could never be. He saw the truth just as I did and accepted it in turn. Now stoic, and every bit the Lord of the Salt, he dipped his chin to me. Raised my fingers to his lips, kissed the wedding band on my finger, and walked out.

46

Days passed in a melancholy haze, the world muted and distant. I moved through Thorne's house like a ghost, drifting from room to room, my footsteps echoing hollowly on the polished floors. The children's laughter, once a balm to my battered soul, now grated on my nerves, a painful reminder of the life I was fighting to return to and the one I was resigned to leave behind.

I caught glimpses of Thorne in the hallways, fleeting moments that left me aching. He was giving me the space I needed. Respecting me, even when it hurt. Nothing with Thorne was serious enough to truly contemplate staying here. We both knew that. It would have just been the easiest way for him to cope with his prior loss without having to fully move on.

Our eyes would meet, a brief flash of connection, before he looked away, his jaw clenched, his shoulders rigid. The air between us was heavy with unspoken words, with the weight of the truth he finally knew. The secret he had kept for me.

In the solitude of my room, I found myself reaching for his

book, my fingers tracing the gilded edges, hoping against hope to find a message from him. But the pages remained stubbornly blank. I stared at the empty parchment until my vision blurred, willing his familiar handwriting to appear, desperate for any scrap of connection. I knew it was wrong, but I was so weak in small moments.

He'd left the house. I'd eavesdropped on check-ins with Tuck as much as I could, but other than a few unverified sightings from drunk people claiming they'd seen the king, there was still nothing there. The Fray was just as strong as ever though, tightening together as the city fell further to ruin. If nothing else, that was movement. Progress for Thorne's cause, which was ultimately my cause.

The marks on my throat faded after the first day, but the memory of Alastor's cruel grip lingered. I'd tried using magic to hunt for the broken souls, latching on to what I'd known his to look and feel like, but there was nothing there. He'd said it would only show in weak moments, but when I'd tried to see beyond each of the people carrying on around the house, they were nothing more than I'd always known them to be.

"Wanna give me a hand, Miss Paesha?" Jasper asked as I walked into the kitchen.

I managed a smile. "Did you just make a joke, Jasper Boon?"

"Archer gave me the idea yesterday."

"Of course he did."

I joined Jasper at the worn wooden table, taking in the sight of the mismatched assortment of ingredients that'd been laid out in front of us. Bags of rice, cans of beans, a few onions, and a handful of spices, the humble beginnings of something hearty and filling.

"What are we making?"

"Bean stew and lots of it. We've got over thirty mouths to feed now, and not a lot to feed them with."

I rolled up my sleeves, the simple task a welcome distraction from the turmoil of my thoughts. "Then let's get to work."

Together, we measured and poured, Jasper instructing me on the proper ratios as I rinsed the rice and mixed the ingredients. He hummed a cheery tune as we worked, his deep baritone filling the kitchen with a sense of warmth. He'd walked into the counter more times than not, and he'd slipped on the water he'd dripped on the floor and sent a pan flying across the kitchen. But he never wavered. His spirit was unbreakable. And maybe I needed that when I felt so broken.

"Now, the key to a good bean stew is to let it simmer low and slow. Gives the flavors time to meld together, makes the beans nice and tender."

I nodded, stirring the pot as instructed.

"Smells good, doesn't it? Nothing quite like a hearty stew to lift the spirits."

He reached for the salt, but in his enthusiasm, managed to knock over the container, sending a cascade of white crystals across the table. "Oops! Can't let that go to waste."

Jasper scrambled to scoop up the spilled salt, his movements clumsy and uncoordinated with his single hand, so I stepped in.

As we cleaned, Archer strolled into the kitchen. He paused in the doorway, casting me a wary glance. His blue eyes, usually sparkling with mischief, clouded with concern. I'd been distant, lost in the depths of my own thoughts and fears. Archer, with his uncanny ability to read people, had undoubtedly sensed the shift in me, the melancholy that clung to my skin like a shroud.

He opened his mouth as if to speak, but seemed to think better of it. Instead, he crossed the kitchen and reached for a knife, joining Jasper and I in our task. The rhythmic thunk of the knife against the cutting board blended with the gentle bubble of the stew, a symphony that filled the sunlit kitchen. Jasper continued humming. The song was so soothing, even if it was slightly off tune. I'd missed music. Missed dancing. I even missed the stage. But there were things here I would miss too. Once Thorne accepted the truth for what it was, I knew he'd do the right thing and help me figure out the path. His curious mind was likely already stirring about what it could mean. Which was likely why he was included in the journey.

I glanced up, my heart stuttering in my chest as Thorne stepped into the kitchen. He looked tired, shadows lingering under his eyes, his usually impeccable suit slightly rumpled. But even disheveled, he was breathtaking, his presence filled the room, commanding attention without uttering a word.

Our eyes met. He cleared his throat, adjusting his glasses as he looked up from his book as if he weren't expecting us to be here. But then, of course, he wasn't, because for a very long time, he'd been alone in this house. He'd preferred solitude.

He greeted each of us with a nod. "I see you've been busy."

Jasper grinned, oblivious to the world. "Bean stew. Nothing better to feed a hungry crowd. Care to join us? Many hands make light work, as they say."

"Two hand jokes in one day? Have you been practicing?" I asked, trying desperately to break the tension.

"You know, when you sit down to think about it, there really are so many. I'd rather laugh than wallow. Self-pity serves no one."

Thorne's gaze flickered to the bubbling pot, then back to me. For a heartbeat, I thought I saw a glimmer of the old warmth in his eyes. But it was gone as quickly as it appeared, replaced by a polite mask of indifference.

"Thanks, but I'm afraid I've got other things to do." He turned to me, his expression unreadable. "Paesha, a word please? In private."

My heart leapt into my throat. I nodded, setting down my knife with hands that suddenly felt clumsy and unsure. Following him out into the hall, I forced my hands into my pockets to keep them, well, *not* on him.

"Have you been well?"

My brows dropped. "I guess?"

"Good. Good."

"Was that all?"

He adjusted his glasses again. Maybe it was a nervous habit. "No. Uh, Archer thought maybe you should come to the Parlor with us tonight."

"Did Archer think that?" I asked, loud enough he would hear me in the kitchen. "We're letting Archer think now?"

"Hey!" he yelled.

Briony slid past us in the narrow hall, one child on her hip and another gulping away his tears. "Excuse me," she said with her eyes down. "Sorry to interrupt."

Thorne took a calm, deep breath.

I managed a smile as she stepped into the kitchen, shutting the door behind her. "Feeling a little cramped?"

"I'm working on a safe place for this lot, but I'm also considering staying at the Parlor for a while."

Oh.

"Oh. Yeah, okay, that sounds like a good idea. Get some space."

"Yeah."

I nodded, my throat suddenly tight. Of course, he needed space. Who wouldn't, with the house overflowing with people, the constant noise and chaos? The woman pretending to be his wife, desperate to leave him? But still, a small, selfish part of me ached at the thought of him leaving, of putting even more distance between us.

I turned away, not wanting him to see the disappointment in my eyes. "Right. Well, I should get back to the kitchen. Jasper's probably wondering where I am."

Thorne's hand caught my elbow, gentle but insistent. "Paesha, wait."

I paused, my heart hammering against my ribs. Slowly, I turned back to face him, steeling myself for whatever he might say.

His brow was furrowed, eyes searching mine. "I think you misunderstood me. When I said I was considering staying at the Parlor, I meant... I thought we both could. Together."

My breath caught. "Together?"

He nodded, his thumb rubbing small circles on the inside of my elbow, sending shivers racing down my spine. "It would give everyone more room here, let them spread out a bit. And it would allow us to keep up appearances. We are supposed to be married, after all. And your time is running out, is it not? We can't hide behind these walls until you leave."

I wanted to address the last bit he'd said. Explain myself. Find a way to make him understand. But he was stubborn, and foolishly so, when he thought he had a lesson somewhere to teach, so I bit my tongue and nodded. "Okay. Today?"

"Can you be ready in an hour? I wanted to make sure Briony is okay to stay with the children permanently. She can have my room if she wants it."

"Or mine," I offered, feeling something selfish about another woman sleeping in his bed, though I knew I didn't have the right.

But he knew, of course. The narrowing of his eyes, the small flattening of his lips. It wasn't just me holding back, but at least this was a place of common ground.

"I'll see if Tuck will come by more. Security checks and stuff."

"Yeah. That's a good plan. And we could always stop by if you were feeling homesick or anything."

"There will be nothing here that feels like home. I've already packed up most of the study. I saved a few books for you, but that's pretty much it."

An hour later, I stood in the foyer, a small bag clutched in my hands. It felt wrong, leaving like this, abandoning the Fray to fend for themselves in a house that wasn't truly theirs. But Thorne was right. We needed to keep up appearances. We couldn't very well hide away forever, no matter how much I might wish to.

Thorne descended the stairs, his own bag slung over his shoulder. He'd changed into a fresh suit, the navy fabric impeccably tailored to his broad frame. He looked every inch the powerful lord, confident and in control. But I didn't miss the weariness in the set of his shoulders, the tightness around his eyes.

The carriage ride was silent. Full of unasked questions and more wary glances. By the time we made it through the Parlor and up the stairs, I was sure he was going to drop me off and run the other direction, but instead, he pressed a steady hand to the small of my back and pushed the door open.

I gasped. "You got us a bed?"

"Well, given our current circumstances," Thorne said, his voice carefully neutral as he closed the door behind us. "I had it brought from the Hollow. We can't take turns on the couch forever. Or not forever. The foreseeable future, I guess. What do we have? A week? Two?"

"Don't do that."

He lowered his glasses. "Do what?"

I sighed. "Nothing."

I set my bag down, letting my gaze wander over the room, taking in the little touches that made it undeniably Thorne's space, the stack of leather-bound books on the desk, the half-empty decanter of liquor on the sideboard, the faint scent of whiskey and spice that clung to the air.

Taking one step toward the desk, I got a sudden wave of déjà vu. Of standing in an office as rich as this one. Of watching Visha, the brothel owner, give Quill away, of the Maestro forcing me to show him my scar. But there was something else. Someone else. Lingering in the corner. Tainting the memory as if he'd been there. But no one else had been in that room that day. I was sure of it. Something in my memory protested, though. Willed me to see beyond a veil over my mind.

"What's wrong? What's happening?" Thorne asked, coming to stand before me. He gripped my shoulder, lifting my hand with a finger. "Poison?"

I could see the fear as clear as the floor beneath us. I grabbed his wrist. "No. I just had this odd sense of... Well, it's not important. It's just Ezra was—" I choked on my gasp.

As soon as the syllables left my tongue, they dissolved like mist in the morning sun. I blinked, the odd sense of familiarity fading as quickly as it had come, leaving me disoriented and unsure.

Thorne's grip on my shoulders tightened, his eyes searching mine with an intensity that unsettled me. "Who's Ezra?"

I shook my head, the remnants of the memory already slipping away, like sand through my fingers. "I... I don't know. It was just a strange feeling, like I'd been in a room like this before, with someone else. But it's gone now. I can't quite grasp it. Must've been something from a dream. Strange."

Thorne's brow furrowed, concern etched into the lines of his face. His thumbs rubbed soothing circles on my shoulders. "You sure you're all right? You looked like you'd seen a ghost for a moment there."

I managed a shaky smile, trying to dispel the lingering unease that coiled in my gut. "For a moment, I thought I had. It's gone now. Just a weird sensation. I don't even know an Ezra."

As the words left my lips, I couldn't shake the feeling that I did.

"Here." Thorne snagged a book from his desk. "We have a few hours before we need to make an appearance downstairs. Maybe settling in with a book will help."

It hadn't. No matter how many times I scanned the page, I had no idea of the main character's name. I couldn't tell you what he looked like, or even the type of story I had. My mind just circled and circled the war happening within my thoughts. Had he been someone in passing? One of the Maestro's many collections?

When Archer came a while later, I hadn't even moved through the first five pages.

"Bad news, boss," he said, taking the seat beside me, his cloak folded over his arm. "Tuck says Farris is making an appearance at the Parlor tonight."

Thorne dropped his paper onto the desk. His eyes flashed to me. "Can you tell if he's close?"

I nodded and had his answer within a minute. "He's only a block away."

"Shit," he said, jumping up from the desk. "Rosy's targeting the Cummings tonight."

"Best she doesn't," Archer said, standing.

I got to my feet as well, ready to zip downstairs behind Thorne. Archer grabbed my wrist, flashing me a look. I narrowed my eyes but didn't catch his meaning.

"Come on, wife. We've got a show to put on."

"Actually, that's the other thing I came to tell you. We were sort of talking at the house and... it's obvious something bad happened between you two. Now I'm not one to pry and I'm sure you'll be right as rain soon, but... if the prince picks up on it? Or if the Cimmerians catch a whiff of her power, you know what's going to happen."

Though Thorne hesitated, looking at me before letting loose a long sigh, he nodded. "I'll tell them you're under the weather. You better stay up here just to be safe."

"But I could help," I protested. "We've always put on a good show."

Archer cleared his throat. "You know I'm right. We can't take chances. Sorry, Fingers. But I can stay with you, if you want. I brought my cards." He turned his back to Thorne, winking at me at least three times.

I managed a look over his shoulder at my fictional husband. His face was completely unreadable.

"It's fine. I can stay. We don't need to make anything worse," I said.

Though his shoulders dropped, though he sighed in relief, he still asked, "Are you sure?"

I dipped my chin and watched as he walked out of the room.

"I know you've been sulking about for days, and I can't stand it anymore. Let's go have an adventure." Archer whipped the cloak off his arm, showing off the two Cimmerian robes and masks.

"Have you lost your mind?"

"This is the perfect opportunity. Farris is going to have so many guards here with him tonight, and Thorne will keep him occupied. This is a really solid plan."

"If you're so sure, then why don't we tell Thorne, just to make sure everyone's on board with a suicide mission?"

He grinned, pulling something from his pocket. "I'm one step ahead of you. I wrote him a note. He loves to read."

"If the prince doesn't kill you, he will. You realize that, right?"

"Well, he'll have to get in line behind Harlow. Now, are you coming or not? We have a lair to find."

I rolled my eyes, taking the robe and mask. "I already know where it is, but something tells me you knew that."

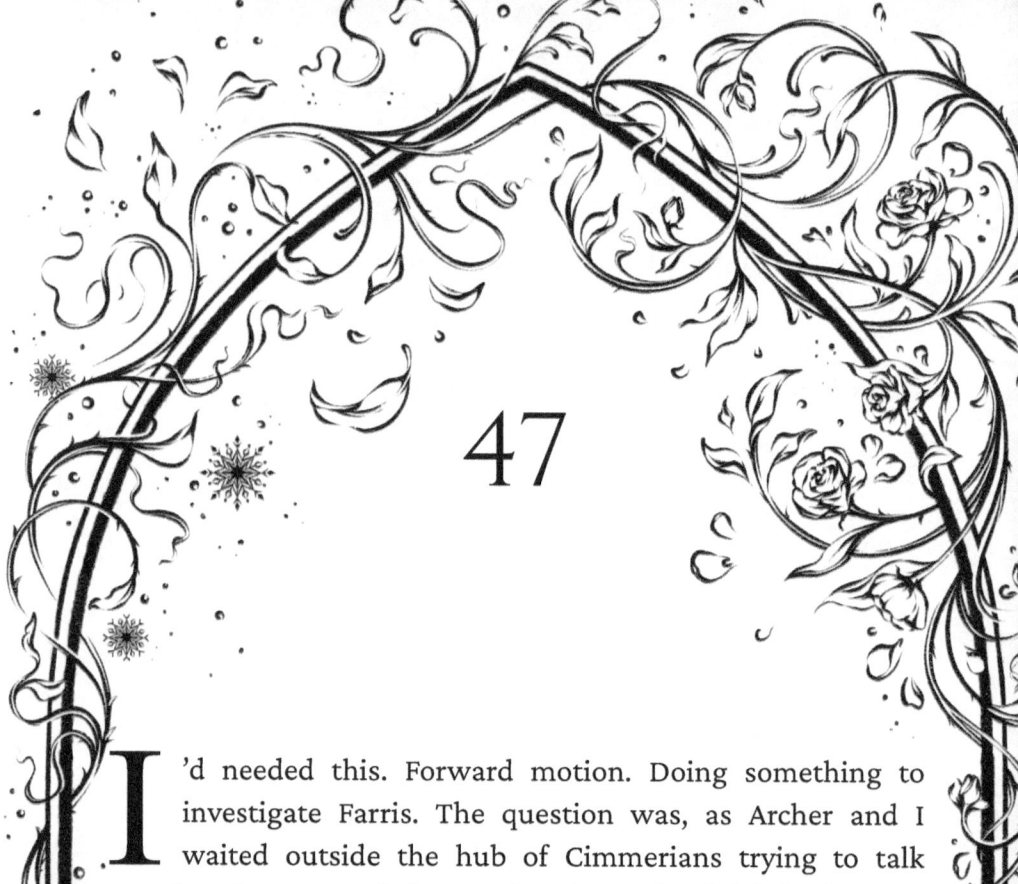

47

I'd needed this. Forward motion. Doing something to investigate Farris. The question was, as Archer and I waited outside the hub of Cimmerians trying to talk ourselves into committing to the plan, why did he? This was reckless on a good day. Especially because if I touched anything new, I'd use magic. And if that happened, they would all know. That's why I'd put gloves on. But it was dangerous all the same.

"You're sure it's down here?" he asked for the fourth time.

"If I didn't know any better, I'd say you were having second thoughts. We can go back if you want to?"

I hoped like hell he didn't. I hoped beyond hope that somewhere down in these catacombs was the answer I needed. Be it a few broken souls, or a door I could use after I found them.

"I'm not going back, Fingers." He shook his hands beside him. "Just preparing mentally."

"The only thing you have to do to prepare to become a Cimmerian is have no brain activity at all. No thoughts. Just don't speak. Keep your chin down and fade into the background. The robe fits well enough."

He nodded, sticking his head out from around the wall to peek down the underground tunnel again. "Remember the signal. If you get overwhelmed, we leave. No questions asked. And don't touch anything. There are women Cimmerians, but not many. Farris finds them weak. Maybe hunch when you walk, hide your... form."

"Archer?"

"Yeah?"

"I've got it. The only thing to do is commit."

"Right. Okay. It's just, I'm not worried about me. I'm worried about you."

"Hey," I grabbed his arm. "Stick 'em with the pointy end, right? I'll be fine. I don't think we should talk beyond this point though, so listen. If we were up on the streets, we would need to go about half a block down this way in distance. Then there should be a turn to go right and then another two blocks or so, and there's something there. A room, a door. Something. Every night I've checked on him, he inevitably lands somewhere around here. And the only reason I know is because we're directly under Prospector's Pointe, now."

Archer took a deep breath, sliding his mask into place. "Don't fall behind. Let's go."

The sight of him so close, in full Cimmerian garb rattled me for a second. My mind knew it was him, but something irrational still hated the way he'd stood so close. We pressed on through the dank, winding catacombs, the stench of mold and decay clinging to the air, thick and suffocating. The weight of the coarse robes tugged heavily at my shoulders.

Archer and I moved in silence. Our steps were swallowed by the damp earth beneath us and the soft drip of water echoing through the vast, empty spaces. He followed the directions perfectly, never straying. His shoulder brushed against mine and I was grateful for the small, steadying presence in the dark. As we rounded a bend, a group of Cimmerians loomed before us, their black robes billowing in the draft. My breath hitched. A single heartbeat stretched into eternity. But they merely nodded, greeting us as if we belonged because you'd have to be half mad to come down here by choice.

I swallowed, grateful to be so completely covered, as flashbacks of my welcome to Wisteria threatened to choke me. Archer nudged me. Subtle, but enough to ease the pressing panic. We did our best to blend, trying to mimic the purposeful stride of the other Cimmerians.

I kept my head down. Archer walked with the air of someone born to this world of shadows, his shoulders high, gait firm. Everything he needed to be to make me question whether he was the man that brought me down here. He was a perfect performer.

The bowels of the city swallowed us whole as we moved deeper, but ahead torches flickered from wrought iron sconces and clusters of Cimmerians drifted through the tunnels like wraiths, their murmured conversations barely breaking the silence. I strained to catch anything. Some clue, some whispered fragment of knowledge that might betray the king's whereabouts or the prince's plans, but the Cimmerians were well-versed in keeping their secrets close.

The tunnels shifted. Rough-hewn stone gave way to smooth, polished walls, no longer the grim underbelly of the city but something far grander. Artwork now lined the walls; grotesque scenes of battle and horror in every one. Our footsteps were muted by plush carpets, the luxury a jarring contrast to the grime we'd left behind.

And yet, it was a sign. The prince's taste for finery was unmistakable and honestly welcome. Now we just needed to ditch the group around us. I kept my eyes down, ignoring the creepy marble statues of terrifying beasts that stared from alcoves. Their blank, unblinking eyes tracked our every step.

There was no time to break away from the group because beyond the next set of doors, we entered an anti-chamber full of robed men. Some huddled together in the middle, some scattered throughout the cavernous room. All terrifying.

Archer and I exchanged a glance from behind our masks. We were in the belly of the beast now. Every instinct screamed at me to turn back, to flee before we were discovered. But we pressed through the room, shoulder to shoulder, driven by desperation and a reckless need for answers.

Slowly backing away from the others so as not to be suspicious, I tilted my head toward the door in the back of the room. We needed to find a way to get in there. But before we could even try, the screaming began.

The sound. Pure, unadulterated agony sent chills racing down my spine. It was a sound I knew all too well, a sound that had haunted my dreams for longer than I cared to remember. Beside me, Archer's back straightened, his posture going rigid with sudden, terrible understanding.

He knew that voice. I think we both did.

Archer stepped forward, his movements measured and deliberate, a predator stalking its prey. I followed close behind. We approached the huddle of Cimmerians in the center of the room. They stood in a tight cluster.

Gods, if Archer did something reckless right now, there was no way we were getting out of this alive. Another guard entered the room. He strode towards the huddle of Cimmerians, his presence commanding, authoritative. At his approach, the robed figures stepped back, parting like a dark sea to reveal the battered, broken form of our Tuck.

He lay curled on his side, his face a mess of blood and bruises, one eye swollen shut. His chest heaved with each labored breath, his hands clutching at his ribs as if trying to hold himself together.

"Tell me what you were doing in the Maw or I'll start by ripping fingernails and end by ripping skin."

That voice. I'd heard it before as well. He'd been the one to torture me. To break me.

"Fuck off," Tuck managed, spitting toward the Cimmerian.

The Cimmerian's boot connected with Tuck's already battered ribs with a sickening crunch. Tuck cried out. He curled in on himself, his breath coming in short, pained gasps. I found myself matching them. Reliving that pain, yet completely frozen in shock at the scene. The guard crouched down. He grabbed a fistful of Tuck's hair and wrenched his head back at a cruel angle. Still, I could not breathe.

"You've got spirit, I'll give you that," the Cimmerian hissed, his voice like gravel. "But spirit won't save you here. Nothing will. Not unless you start talking."

He leaned in closer. "Let's start with the woman. The one that escaped. The one that killed at least three of my brothers. She used the same tunnel we found you hiding in. Where is she?"

My heart did not beat. Every inch of my body fell numb. They were still searching for me. And Tuck knew almost everything.

His good eye fluttered open, defiance burning bright despite the pain etched into every line of his face. "I don't know what you're talking about," he rasped, his words slurred by his split and swollen lips.

The Cimmerian snarled, slamming Tuck's head against the floor. A wave of dizziness threatened to pull me under. But I couldn't look away, couldn't tear my gaze from the horrific scene unfolding before me.

Archer pressed himself into my side. An anchor. A reminder

of who we were meant to be in this moment. The masks we wore. The stage we stood on. But still, I could hardly think beyond the man.

The Cimmerians took turns torturing Tuck, their movements precise and methodical, a sickening dance of cruelty and pain. One used his blade, the edges jagged and rusted, tracing thin lines of crimson across his exposed abdomen. Another brought a set of pliers, clamping them around Tuck's fingernails and twisting, wrenching, until the nails tore free with a nauseating, wet pop.

Tuck writhed on the cold stone floor, his body convulsing in agony. His screams echoed off the walls, raw and primal, a sound that would haunt my nightmares for years to come. I stood frozen, my breath trapped in my lungs, my heart a leaden weight in my chest. Every fiber of my being screamed at me to move, to act, to do something to stop this. But I was paralyzed, rooted to the spot by a terror so profound it taxed my soul.

"Where is she?" the guard yelled.

Still, despite the brutality inflicted upon him, Tuck remained defiant, unwavering in his silence. He clenched his jaw against the screams that threatened to tear from his throat, his one good eye blazed with a fierce, unyielding loyalty. Even as his blood pooled on the cold stone beneath him, even as his body shuddered with each fresh wave of agony, he held fast to the secret, guarding it with the last shreds of his strength and will. Guarding me. And I could not go to him. I couldn't crumble to my knees and thank the man I barely knew. I couldn't tell him he wasn't alone. Or that he was brave. Or kind. Or the purest of men. I could do nothing. Absolutely nothing.

Archer's fingers dug into my arm. Slowly, inch by painstaking inch, he pulled me backwards, towards the unwatched door. The one that might lead to answers, to some clue that could justify the horrific price Tuck was paying.

We moved like ghosts, sliding through the shadows, hardly daring to breathe, afraid to draw attention to ourselves. The Cimmerians' focus remained locked on Tuck. Their cruel laughter and taunts mingled with his ragged, panting breaths, a macabre symphony that filled the chamber.

At last, we reached the door, our backs pressed against the aged wood. With a final, furtive glance at the grisly scene, Archer's hand closed around the handle. He turned it, slowly, carefully, the soft click of the latch almost lost beneath the din of torture.

He cracked the door open far enough for us to slip inside unnoticed. The moment I could tell the room was empty, I fell to my knees. The mask slipped from my face, clattering beside me. I barely noticed. I was consumed by the horror, by the gut-wrenching guilt that threatened to tear me apart. They ripped and tore and broke him, piece by agonizing piece, and we'd just fucking walked away.

Archer's hands were on me then, gripping my shoulders, trying to pull me back from the brink. "Don't you do this," he ordered. "Don't you break. Not now. Not here." His words, full of their own emotion, cut through the haze of my anguish like a blade. "Tuck's sacrifice will be for nothing if we get caught now. We have to focus. We have to find whatever we can and get out of here. For his sake, as much as ours."

I nodded, swallowing hard against the lump in my throat. Archer was right. Falling apart now would only put us in more danger. He helped me to my feet, his grip strong and steady. Together, we turned to face the room, our eyes scanning the shadowed space for any clue, any scrap of information.

The room was dimly lit, the air thick with the musty scent of old parchment and leather. I took a staggering breath, forcing myself to shut out the sounds seeping in from the antechamber. This was undoubtedly Farris's office. The walls were covered in deep, velvet drapes, to muffle the sound or camouflage the stone walls beneath, I wasn't sure, but it made one thing very obvious. It'd be so easy to light this place on fire. And if need be, I wouldn't give it a second thought. The stone would stop the flames, but not before everything within burned to ash.

A massive desk dominated the center of the office. The chair behind it was equally grand, its high back and armrests upholstered in the color of midnight. Despite the grandeur, there was a noticeable lack of things I'd expected to find. No towering bookshelves lined the walls. No maps or charts were spread out across the desk. For the most part, the space was... empty.

"I'll check the desk," Archer said. "You see if you can get into that cabinet."

I nodded, moving towards the large wooden cabinet that stood against the far wall. The doors were firmly shut, likely locked, but I had to try. I gave a firm tug on the handles. As expected, the doors didn't budge. But I could have sworn the damn thing moved. Archer was already rifling through the desk drawers, his movements quick and efficient, born of years of practice. We didn't have time for me to fiddle with a lock or make any wrong guesses here, but I was confident.

Bracing myself, I shoved against the side of the cabinet with all my strength. At first, there was no give, the heavy wood unyielding beneath my hands. But I whipped the gloves off and leaned into it, putting my whole weight behind the effort, I felt it shift again. Just slightly. Just enough to send a thrill of hope sparking through my veins.

I pushed harder, my muscles straining. The cabinet groaned in protest, its bulk scraping against the floor. And then, with a soft, whispering rustle, the heavy velvet curtain beside it rippled. Moved. As if disturbed by a breath of wind where none should be.

Heart pounding, I abandoned the cabinet and turned my

attention to the curtain. It moved easily, sliding back to reveal a hidden alcove, cleverly concealed behind the heavy fabric. I gasped, my eyes widening as I took in the sight before me. The small space was filled with a chaotic array of papers and maps tacked haphazardly to the rough stone walls. Faded parchment covered in scrawled notes and hasty sketches formed a dizzying patchwork, layer upon layer of secrets.

But it was the map at the center of the wall that drew my attention, its surface a riot of colors and symbols. It was a detailed rendering of the city. Every street and alley were meticulously charted, every building and landmark carefully marked. And scattered across its surface, like a constellation of mysteries, were dozens of small, brightly colored pins.

"Archer," I breathed, my voice barely above a whisper. "Come look at this."

He was at my side in an instant, his own search momentarily forgotten.

"Do you think this is where he's searched for the king?" Archer asked, his finger hovering over a cluster of red pins near the city's eastern edge. "All these markers... we knew he'd been systematically combing the city, but this is so intricate. Specific. Does this mean he really doesn't know where the king is?"

I lifted the frayed edge of one of the papers tacked to the wall with the letters L-O-T-S scrawled across the top. "I don't think this map has anything to do with his father. I think it's where he's been hunting for..." I didn't dare say Thorne's real name aloud, "the Lord of the Salt."

"No, look," Archer said, pointing. "The blue pins have dates. The red don't. I think it's both. This one marks Tilly's orphanage and the date it was raided. All the blue are recent."

"What do you think the gold are?" I asked, tracing my fingers over the map.

Archer stepped back, studying for a while, cocking his head

to the side. "I'm pretty sure he's marking where he's captured magic users. And look at this." He produced a book from the pocket of his Cimmerian robes. "This was in his desk. The title's so worn, you can't see it. But open the first page."

I took it from him, fanning the pages as he continued to study the map. I pulled the book closer, squinting. "Scientific Exploration of Power Transference?"

"What do you think it means?"

"It means Farris isn't helping the gods. Just like Alastor said." I held the book open to a specific page with several notes in the margin. "He's harboring the power and has no idea how to transfer it or use it."

"Then what the fuck is the point of taking it, other than erasure?"

"Looks to me like he wants to use it, but doesn't know how." I gasped, stepping backward until I collided with the other wall. "That's why the gods aren't smiting him or whatever. They want what he's harboring and I don't think any of them know how to get it."

Archer and I stared at each other in stunned silence. Farris wasn't just hunting magic users to eradicate them, to stamp out the power. His motives were far more insidious, far more dangerous. He was stockpiling power, amassing it like a dragon hoarding gold. He wanted to harness that power for himself, to bend it to his own twisted will. And as of now, the gods were letting him think he had control.

I wanted to celebrate figuring out one piece of the puzzle, but I couldn't. Not when the cost had been paid for with Tuck's blood.

Archer's voice cut through my thoughts. "Paesha, move."

The panic in his tone sent me rushing forward, but only far enough for him to reach out and spin me, forcing me to take in the other map. The one opposite of us, and completely foreign.

"What is this place?"

Archer guided me forward so we could lean in. I traced the faint silvery lines of threads marking the mountains and forest wondering why he'd hidden this away. Why was it important? Secret?

"This looks a little familiar but I've never seen these before. This silver pattern is so strange. And look at this red dot," he said.

But before I could run my fingers over it, the commotion from outside of the main room grew. Leaving everything behind, we rushed out of the alcove. Archer shoved the cabinet back while I grabbed my gloves and the masks we'd left on the floor. He plowed into me, slamming my back against the wall a fraction of a second before the door swung open, concealing both of us.

I carefully slid Archer's mask into his hand, holding my breath as Farris Wendale walked in with a horde of guards behind him and the only thing saving us was a door that would be shut at any moment.

48

A rcher and I slipped our masks back on with trembling fingers. The metal scraped against my skin, the eye holes constricting my vision to narrow slits. My heart pounded a furious rhythm against my ribs as we edged along the wall, trying to blend seamlessly into the crowd of Cimmerians now filing into the room, hoping like hell Farris didn't have some strange magical link to actually *feel* the real ones.

Prince Farris strode to his desk, his black robes swirling around him like a dark storm. He moved with a predatory grace, all coiled power and barely restrained violence. The Cimmerians parted before him, a sea of shadows bowing to their cruel master.

Farris sank into his chair. He steepled his fingers, his cold gaze sweeping over the assembled guards. The silence stretched. Taut and oppressive, broken only by the ragged, wet gasps of Tuck's labored breathing from the outer chamber, yanking on every fiber of my heart. He lived. At least he lived. Though I had no idea how we were going to get him out of here.

"The Parlor was completely useless. Just as I knew it would

be. Noctus is far too fragile to be dealing in anything but gambling. And he's completely distracted by his new... bride. We mark it off the list. Take him off the Hunt as well. Now," his voice lowered to something far more lethal. "Someone tell me how the fuck that oaf Jasper Boon was freed from my mark. What have we learned?"

The Cimmerians shifted uneasily, a ripple of fear passing through the ranks. No one dared speak. To draw Farris's attention was to court death, surely. I pressed further against the wall, trying to make myself as small and inconspicuous as possible. Beside me, Archer was unmoving, tall, strong, every bit the Cimmerian.

One cloaked figure stepped forward, his voice wavering slightly as he spoke. "There's word he severed his own arm, Your Highness. Perhaps if the mark is severed, the bond is broken."

Farris's head snapped up, his eyes narrowing to icy slits. "Shall I cut your arm off to confirm the possibility of that?"

"N... no, Your Grace. It was just a rumor. It's impossible."

In a flash, Farris was on his feet, stalking towards the guard. The man shrank back, but there was nowhere to run, nowhere to hide from the prince's wrath. But it wouldn't work. Jasper was saved because of the time between the marking and the severance of his forearm. Enough time hadn't passed to bind him. The words of the binding made that perfectly clear, though I had to wonder if Farris had ever bothered listening to Themis's words.

Farris's hand shot out, fingers curling around the man's throat in a brutal grip. He lifted him off his feet with terrifying ease, the Cimmerian's legs kicking feebly as he gasped for air. "Did you just say no to me?" He turned his head slightly, addressing another Cimmerian standing nearby, frozen in fear.

"Did you hear the utter nonsense that just spilled from this fool's mouth?"

"Y-yes, Your Grace," the second Cimmerian stammered.

Farris's lip curled in disgust. His grip tightened, and with a sharp, violent twist, the sickening crack of bone echoed through the chamber. The Cimmerian went limp, his masked head lolling at an unnatural angle as Farris released him, letting the body crumple to the floor like a discarded puppet. "Get rid of that," he said, snapping his fingers and pointing toward two of the guards.

"You two," he said, and my heart dropped into my stomach when his hand swung around, pointing straight at Archer and me. "Go get my father's advisor."

Archer and I said nothing, moving as deliberately as possible out of the room, shutting the door with no intentions of returning. The antechamber was completely empty, save a single massive man curled up in the middle. We rushed forward.

"Tuck! It's us, Tuck. Archer and Paesha."

He jerked, barely managing a moan.

"We have to go. We have to get out of here right now."

"Archer, look at him. He can't move at all. He's completely broken. You're going to have to heal him if you want any chance of getting out of here."

Archer's head snapped to me. "The Cimmerians are too close for that much power. And we don't have time. We need to run."

"Go." Tuck managed.

"Get him well enough to move and speak." I ran to the other end of the giant room, guarding the door. "If the door to the office opens, pretend to punch him and we'll walk out. But hurry up."

There was no time. He knew it. Still, I was patient, feeling the panic bubbling beneath my skin. Any second now, someone was going to come back in here and we'd all three be in the Maw. Especially if they got a single taste of Archer's magic. It was dangerous, but we knew that going in. Archer hissed when he laid his hands on Tuck, calling his power forward, wincing as if it pained him. As if he could feel the guilt that came with his magic weighing on him. Because Archer hated his power, no matter the good it did.

"Listen," I said, falling to my knees beside them. A bit of color had returned to Tuck's blood-stained face. "That's enough power. Any more and they'll come for sure. The best thing we can do is buy Tuck time. We've got maybe a minute more before the prince sends someone out here to find us, less probably. Tuck, you're going to have to get yourself hidden. Can you do that? Leave this chamber and find somewhere to hide. I'll find you. I promise."

"I can manage it," he said, gripping my fingers. "I'll manage it." He turned to Archer. "You did good, Archie boy."

"We could run. Right now. We could run," Archer said.

"Or we get the advisor back in that room and the prince carries on without raising any alarms. Tuck has time to hide. We can leave as soon as the others do. It's the only way to buy time."

Tuck tried to stand and fell. He needed every bit of help from Archer and I just to get to the door, but once he was up, he propped himself against the wall to stay that way.

Archer nodded. "You're right. We have to go back. Use the wall, Tuck. Follow it to a dark alcove and keep your eyes open."

We didn't have time to watch him go. Instead, we turned in the opposite direction. I had to fight the instinct to run, to make up for the lost time with Tuck, but the Cimmerians never ran, their gait was an ominous pace.

"Any idea where we're supposed to find the advisor?" Archer asked.

"No, but the next Cimmerians we see, you disguise your voice and ask."

We strode down the dimly lit corridor, our footsteps echoing off the stone walls. Rounding a corner, we came upon two guards stationed outside a heavy wooden door. They stood at attention, their eyes glinting from behind their masks. Archer straightened his shoulders, drawing himself up to his full, imposing height. He stepped forward, his voice a low, menacing growl as he addressed the guards.

"Where's the advisor?" he demanded, the words clipped and harsh. "The prince wants him. Now."

The guards exchanged a glance. For a heart-stopping moment, I thought they might question us, see through our flimsy disguise. But then one of them jerked his head towards the door behind them. "He's in the holding room. Been there for hours."

Archer nodded curtly, not bothering with thanks. We turned, moving towards the indicated door with fabricated confidence. We found a small, simple room inside, harboring a short man, likely the age of the missing old king, with a balding hairline and bushy, white eyebrows.

"Finally," the king's advisor said. "I was beginning to think I'd been forgotten."

In true Cimmerian form, we said nothing, owning the intimidating presence as we simply turned and walked back out of the room, down the corridor, and past the blood stains in the antechamber. Archer hesitated, likely unsure if he should knock but in the end decided to just open the door and walk in.

The Cimmerians parted, and we remained in the back, letting the advisor through to stand before Farris's desk. The prince leaned back in his chair, a slow, predatory smile curved his lips as the room went deathly silent, the assembled Cimmerians hardly daring to breathe lest they draw their master's ire.

"Advisor Ricken," Farris drawled, his voice a low, sinister purr. "So good of you to join us. I trust your accommodations were to your liking?"

The old man shifted uneasily, his aged hands clasped tightly before him. "Your Highness, I must protest this treatment. As the king's most trusted advisor, I—"

Farris cut him off with a sharp, humorless laugh. "I know your position without the name tag. Why else do you think I've invited you?"

The prince rose from his seat. He moved around the desk with a sickening grace, circling the trembling advisor like a shark scenting blood in the water.

"I... I trust that you are still searching, Your Highness. For your father?"

Farris's smile widened. A cold, cruel thing really. He stopped his pacing, coming to stand directly in front of the trembling advisor and one gloved hand reached out, gripping the old man's chin, forcing his head up to meet that icy gaze. Archer nudged me, as if reminding me to focus on the words.

Was he searching? It could have been a show. Still, the map circled my mind. If he'd marked where he was looking for the king, then he must've been right? But the other map, the red dot... was he hiding the king there, instead? Wherever that place was.

"Of course I'm still searching. My men scour the city day and night, leaving no stone unturned. It pains me deeply, the thought of my dear father out there, lost and alone, perhaps in grave danger."

The prince released his grip on the advisor's chin, letting his hand trail down to rest on the man's hunched shoulder. He squeezed, the gesture a mockery of comfort. "But we must be realistic. The king has been missing for so long now. With each passing day, hope dwindles. We may have to face a harsh truth soon. He may never be found."

Advisor Ricken's eyes widened, his weathered face draining of color. "Your Highness, surely it's too soon to make such dire proclamations. The search must continue. The council will not accept—"

Farris silenced him with a wave of his hand, the black leather of his glove catching the flickering torchlight. "The council will accept what I tell them to accept. In my father's absence, it falls to me to lead. To make the difficult decisions for the good of the kingdom." His voice dropped to a silken whisper, each word dripping with venom. "The council will come to see the wisdom in supporting their new king. Their only king. And when that day comes, dear Advisor Ricken, I do hope I can count on your... loyalty."

Farris was making it really hard for me to believe he had nothing to do with the king's absence. But the question remained. If he really did have something to do with it, why hadn't the king's body been found? Surely that would push his agenda forward. Maybe this was the show. Maybe he was trying to make it look like he had King Aldus when really he didn't. Maybe he thought planting those thoughts in the council would force them to do whatever Farris said, in order to save the king's life. Never to return to his castle, but to live.

"O-of course, Your Highness. I live to serve the crown."

A slow smile spread across Farris's cruel features. His gloved hand moved to cup Ricken's cheek. "Such a good man," he crooned. "So devoted. So eager to please. I'm certain your faithful service will be remembered and rewarded when the time comes. In fact, I'd love for you to join me on my Hunt. I'll send the information later."

Farris patted Ricken's cheek once more, a final, mocking gesture of affection, before stepping back. He surveyed the room, his cold gaze sweeping over us. "You're all dismissed. Return to your duties. I want reports on the search efforts by sunrise."

After bowing, we moved with the tide of bodies, letting it carry us through twisting passageways and up narrow, winding stairs. As soon as we could, we broke off from the group, sinking into an alcove until they were long gone.

"We need to find Tuck."

Though nervous, I coaxed my power forward, wrapping around the giant man as quickly and as faintly as I could. "This way."

We found him hiding behind one of the terrifying carvings in the main corridor of the catacombs. I stood watch as Archer used a bit more of his magic to help heal Tuck in another small burst. Enough to let him run. Because the Cimmerians might not have noticed Tuck wasn't there when they left the room, but someone was going to figure it out. And then it'd be a man hunt.

So we hustled. Me in the lead, carrying us out, with Tuck sandwiched between, though surprisingly, he'd been able to keep himself erect. Even run. Though I didn't let myself think too much on that. On the risk Archer had made, using so much of his unique power in the catacombs. The dank air grew fresher as we ascended, the oppressive weight of the depths falling away. We shed the masks and robes and ran like hell for the backside of the Parlor.

But our arrival was not one of celebration and shared secrets, not as Thorne paced just outside, head snapping up as soon as we came into view. Eyes of malice glued to us with no question of his murderous intentions.

49

Thorne's dark gaze burned into me. Actually burned. I could feel the heat coating my skin. The evenings had grown warmer, but not this warm.

"Put your teeth away, husband. You're snarling at the wrong people."

Thorne's eyes slid from me to Archer, narrowing to slits of barely contained fury. "What the hell were you thinking? Risking your lives on some irresponsible, unapproved mission?"

Archer met Thorne's glare unflinchingly, his own jaw set in a stubborn line. "We can't sit around here and wait for everyone else to do dangerous things. I didn't join the Fray to let others fall. Look at Tuck. If we hadn't been there tonight, he would have died. And he puts himself at risk every day while we do what? Attend dinners and lift jewels when we can? This was necessary."

Thorne scoffed, taking a step forward. "Necessary? Necessary to put her in danger? No. It served *your* purpose, and that's all."

"Boss," Tuck tried to cut in.

511

"And what is my purpose, if not the same as yours?" Archer bit back, absolutely fuming.

I moved between them, placing a hand on Thorne's chest. His heart pounded beneath my fingertips in a furious rhythm. "Enough. I am not a child to be coddled and sheltered. I made the choice to go with Archer tonight and I would do it again in a heartbeat."

His gaze searched mine, but I met his stare unflinchingly, refusing to back down. "In case you've forgotten, I am my own person. I don't need your permission. This is my life, Thorne. These are my damn choices. And if you can't respect that, then I guess you need to step aside and let me go."

He closed all the space between us. Every inch. Grabbing the hand on his heart, smoothing his finger over the ring on mine. "I will *not* let go. You want someone to be reckless with, Paesha darling? It will be me and no one else." He turned to Archer. "Go back to the house. Try not to get yourselves killed. I'll see you in my office in two days and not a second before."

Archer locked eyes with me, the sentiment clear. If I didn't want to be left with this brooding, furious man, he wouldn't have left me. Consequences be damned. And gods I loved him for that.

"I'll be fine. I'll see you in two days. I'll tell him everything."

"You should have told me before you went," Thorne seethed as they walked away.

"And what would you have done? Forbidden it?"

"I would have come with. I would have made sure you were okay."

"*I* made sure I was okay. I am my own protector. What would you have done differently with Farris knocking down the Parlor door? Left him to it? Welcomed him to do as he pleased with everyone in there? We both know this is where you were supposed to be."

"If something had happened..." his words faded into the warm breeze. "This is what I get for giving you space."

My eyebrows shot up. "Space? Is that what you've been doing? Small glances and half sentences because you're giving me space? What if I don't fucking want space? What if I want you to help me? Or at least stand beside me. Or gods, hold me. I know I'm leaving, but I'm not gone yet."

I didn't know what I was saying. Of course I wanted space. Every second with him was dangerous. Every minute, a jerk on my heart, begging me to forget everything. Allowing me to. I'd never been the hero. I didn't need to be. And it killed me every day. But a few more days with this man in peace was worth an eternity without him. And I had to let that be enough.

"You're right," he said softly. "I haven't been fair to you. I thought... I thought if I kept my distance, it would make it easier. For both of us. When you..." He trailed off, unable or unwilling to finish the thought.

I knew what he meant. When I left. When I abandoned him and this world and everything blooming between us.

I reached up, catching his hand in mine. "I don't think I want easy, Thorne."

He melted, the ferocious man changing back into the studious one as he placed his forehead on mine, haloed in pale moonlight. "Then I am yours. However you will have me, I am yours. And I'll help you however I can. Because I'd rather have memories full of your touches than regret."

As we stood there, foreheads pressed together, hands intertwined, the first drops of rain began to fall. Soft at first, a gentle patter against the cobblestones, but quickly they built to a steady rhythm, the cool droplets kissing my skin.

Thorne's free hand came up to cup my cheek, his thumb brushing away the wetness. Whether it was tears because I was so frustrated and so torn, or rain, I couldn't be sure. His touch was gentle, reverent, as if he were handling something infinitely precious.

"Paesha, I—"

Whatever he'd been about to say was lost as a crack of lightning split the sky, the thunder reverberating through my bones. The heavens opened, rain coming down in earnest, drenching us both in seconds. But we didn't move, unwilling to break this moment, this fragile connection forged in the midst of chaos.

Thorne's hair was plastered to his forehead, rivulets of water running down his face, catching on his lips. Those lips, I couldn't tear my gaze away from them.

I tilted my face up to his and slid the water-spotted glasses from his face. Thorne's gaze held mine, his hazel eyes dark with hunger. Slowly, giving me time to pull away, he lowered his head, his breath ghosting across my lips.

I ached for him with every fiber of my being. The physical pain of it was a hollow feeling in my chest that only his touch could fill. I wanted to lose myself in him, to forget the cruel twists of fate that brought us together only to tear us apart. I wanted to memorize every angle of his face, the taste of his skin, the way his body fit against mine like we were two halves of a whole.

Thorne's hand moved from my cheek to tangle in my rain-soaked hair, his fingers curling possessively around the strands. The first brush of Thorne's lips against mine was achingly gentle, almost hesitant, as if he couldn't quite believe this was real. That I was here, in his arms, kissing him back. The rain poured down around us, but I barely felt it, lost in the heat of his mouth, the slide of his tongue against mine as the kiss deepened.

I pressed closer, molding my body to his, needing to feel every inch of him with a desperation born of too many denied moments. Thorne groaned into my mouth, the sound vibrating through me, igniting a fire in my veins.

The rest of the world fell away. The Parlor, the city, the cruel games of gods and monsters. In that moment, there was only Thorne and the storm. Because he was the storm. His touch seared me, branding me as his, and I knew, no matter what the future held, a part of me would always belong to him.

He walked me backward, never breaking the kiss, until my shoulders hit the rough stone wall. Thorne's body was a delicious weight pinning me to the wall. His mouth broke from mine to trail searing kisses down the column of my throat, his teeth grazing the sensitive skin. I gasped, my fingers digging into his shoulders, anchoring myself to him as the world spun dizzily around us.

"Thorne," I breathed, my voice hardly recognizable to my own ears, thick with need and longing. "Please..."

He pulled back just enough to meet my gaze, his eyes nearly black with desire, gold flecks glinting like embers in the darkness. Rain dripped from his lashes, from the sharp angles of his face. He was wild and beautiful and dangerous. A force of nature barely leashed.

His hands skimmed down my sides, fingers hooking into the waistband of my soaked pants. "Tell me to stop," he rasped, his voice a low rumble that I felt in my bones. "Tell me now, Paesha."

I moved to my toes, sliding my tongue across the base of his earlobe. "And if I don't, will you fuck me against this wall, husband?"

His grip on my waist tightened, fingers digging into my flesh through the drenched fabric. "Is that what you want, wife? For me to take you here, where anyone could see?"

"Yes," I breathed, the word a desperate plea. "Shall I beg?"

"Oh, no, darling. You shall scream."

I cried out as he hoisted me up, my legs instinctively wrapping around his waist, the hard length of him pressing against my aching center through his clothes. Thorne's mouth crashed down on mine in a bruising kiss, his tongue delving deep, claiming me, consuming me. I was lost to him, to the storm raging inside me, my whole body reduced to the places we were joined.

Thorne broke the kiss to nip sharply at my bottom lip. "Look at me."

I obeyed, my heavy-lidded gaze meeting his, seeing the tempest of lust and possession and something infinitely more terrifying reflected back at me. Something that looked perilously like love.

"You're mine," he growled fiercely, one hand fisting in my rain-soaked hair again. "I will leave this world behind. You will go and I will follow. Today. Tomorrow. Forever. Every lifetime."

Something in his words, in the lines he spoke, yanked at my consciousness, pulling me from the moment, from Thorne's arms, from the streets of Wisteria. I gasped, my body going rigid against him as a flood of memories crashed over me, vivid and visceral, stealing the breath from my lungs.

I was on my knees in the mud, icy rain pelting my skin, plastering my hair to my face. Sobs wracked my body, tearing from my throat in raw, agonized howls that barely sounded human. Grief consumed me, a yawning chasm in my chest where my heart used to be.

Had I loved before? Maybe. I couldn't remember his face. Nor his voice, nor the way his arms had felt around me, but I thought he was there. He was real. But just as fast as those thoughts had come, they vanished, leaving me ice cold and confused.

"What's wrong?" Thorne asked, searching my face for an explanation.

This man. This strong, caring, beast of a man had loved and lost and still looked at me like that. Did it matter? If I had once had a lover I couldn't remember? Everyone had a past and whatever mine was, it was laced with heartache and mourning. Just like his.

"It's... it's nothing. I just had this weird memory and now I'm suddenly so, so tired. I'm sorry. Can we go inside? Maybe it's the rain."

Thorne's brow furrowed with concern, his grip on my waist loosening as he gently lowered me back to my feet. The loss of his warmth was immediate, the cold rain seeping into my bones, but it was nothing compared to the ache in my chest. The memories, fragmented and fleeting as they were, had shaken me to my core.

"Of course." He brushed a sodden lock of hair from my face with a tenderness that made my heart clench.

We made our soggy way into the Parlor. The warmth of the interior was a welcome respite from the storm. We took the private stairs, and his hand never left the small of my back.

"Get changed," he whispered, so hesitant it was clear he was trying to understand what'd just happened. "I'll go downstairs and give orders to lock up."

"Okay," I whispered, hating what I'd made him question as I searched his eyes for understanding.

He swooped in, pulling me into his arms, wrapping them so firmly around me I knew he meant to protect me from whatever haunted me. We stayed like that for several minutes. Letting everything that had overheated calm back down to a simmer. But eventually, reluctantly, he pulled back, pressing a soft, lingering kiss to my forehead. Then, with a final squeeze of my hand, he left.

Alone, I let out a shuddering breath. Acknowledging and hating the absolute push and pull of our connection. In small tasks. In big ones. In the way we spoke. The way we looked at each other. The way we fought. The way we cared.

The room suddenly felt too big, too empty without him. Shivering, I peeled off my rain-soaked clothes, letting them fall to the floor with a wet plop. I pulled one of his shirts out of the cupboard and slipped it over my head. I raked my hands through my hair enough to braid it before crawling into the bed and pulled out the gold book, writing

I'm sorry. I think it's just been a long day.

I was asleep before I heard him creep back into the room, kicking off his boots and sitting on the edge of the bed with a sigh. But at least he'd joined me. At least we'd come back to a place of peace compared to this morning. He laid down slowly, wrapping a strong arm around me and quickly fell asleep.

By morning, the tension had long dissipated.

"Tell me where you stand. Do you think he has the king or not?"

I drew back, nearly falling out of my chair at his desk. "The mighty Thorne Noctus is asking for my opinion? Are you feeling well, sir?"

He tried but failed to hide his smirk. "I said I'd help you. So, I'm helping. What do you think?"

"I'm so torn. I thought for sure I'd get an answer if we went and then there were signs for both. I can't believe he's a really amazing liar. He was really angry about needing his father to be found, but equally nonchalant about taking his place. Honestly, I'm more confused now than before we went."

He opened his mouth but I threw a hand up. "Don't bother with that comment. I don't regret going."

Three familiar knocks sounded at the door, followed by one more. All hint of playfulness melted from his face.

"Be nice," I said.

"I'll be nice if you be smart."

"Did you just call me... not smart?"

"Not at all." He grinned showing far too many teeth. "Come in, Archer."

Archer stormed into the room, holding some kind of white hanging flower by the root. "I know it hasn't been two days and if you want to fist fight me in the hall, fine. But the first snow-drop bloomed last night." He held out the plant. "You know what this means."

"Gods, Archer, you couldn't have waited for us?" Harlow snapped, gulping down breaths as she leaned against the door frame.

"No. You're slow." He walked into the room and dropped the plant on the table. "We need a plan."

Thorne leaned back, crossing his arms over his chest, the smile gone. "You can't begin to imagine how much I despise your planning skills these days, Bramwell."

"You wanted to be included. I'm including you." He plopped down beside me, jutting a chin in my direction. "Nice to see you didn't kill each other last night."

"I'm not sure he's out of his murderous phase yet. Be careful," I whispered loud enough for Harlow and Wee Willy to hear as they approached from behind. I leaned forward and grabbed Thorne's coffee from where it sat in front of him, ignoring mine entirely, which garnered a blast of his attention. "What's with the flower, anyway?"

"Well, Paesha darling," he answered, sliding my cup to sit in front of him. "That's the first bloom of spring, which means, Farris will officially announce the Hunt. Assuming it was seen by someone other than our flower thief here."

"This wasn't the only one," Archer said.

"I keep hearing about the Hunt, but is it just what it sounds like? A bunch of men ride out on horses and kill an animal? Drink too much and start telling stories of their near death at the conquering? What's the big deal?"

Willard clicked his tongue and shook his head. "Every year, after the first snowdrop bloom, Farris announces his Hunt. If they bloom in the city, it means the snow's melted in the mountains. Him and some of his favorites... gods, mortals, courtesans, whoever, they join a caravan of carriages and go up to the countryside. They camp for days and usually the Hunt is for an animal, but also, because it's Farris, some poor unfortunate soul usually faces a tragedy. Though none would ever admit that. There hasn't been a single year where everyone came back alive."

"So, I have a plan." Archer sat back in his chair, refusing to make eye contact with Thorne as he turned to me. "It's a good plan, but it might be dangerous."

I lifted a shoulder, taking a drink. "I like a good plan."

"Your eyes light up when someone mentions danger. Did you know that?" Archer said, a smirk on his face. "That's why we're friends."

"Yes. It's quite endearing," Thorne rumbled.

Harlow cut in. "Can we get to the point?"

"Don't you see it? This is how we'll know once and for all if Farris is hiding the king."

"Here we go," Harlow said, throwing her hands up. "It always comes back to the king."

He spun to face her. "You want Farris to rule, Sister? Really? As far as I'm concerned, we're the only ones standing in the way of that happening."

"So what's your plan?" Thorne asked, shocking us all as he shifted the attention in the room.

"You're willing to hear it?" Archer asked, mouth agape. "I thought for sure I was going to get shut down."

"He's agreed to be more helpful. Haven't you, husband?" I asked with a grin as I took another sip of coffee.

He didn't bother answering, just lifted a brow toward Archie.

"We let them get a half a day head start. Paesha uses her magic to follow, we camp in woods outside the hunt, then at night, or when they all leave to hunt, we slip into the tents and find the king. We never have to do anything when they are around. It's completely safe."

Wee Willy walked around the desk to sit on the edge, facing Archer. "Nothing is completely safe where gods and royals are concerned. And why would Farris take his father to the Hunt if he's trying to hide him? It makes absolutely no sense. It's far too dangerous."

"That one's obvious," I answered. "Farris is too paranoid. He's not going to leave the king to be handled by anyone else. If he has him, King Aldus will be there. Likely knocked out and bound, but he'll be there." I looked at Thorne. "You wanted to be invited. Consider this your invite. We're going hunting."

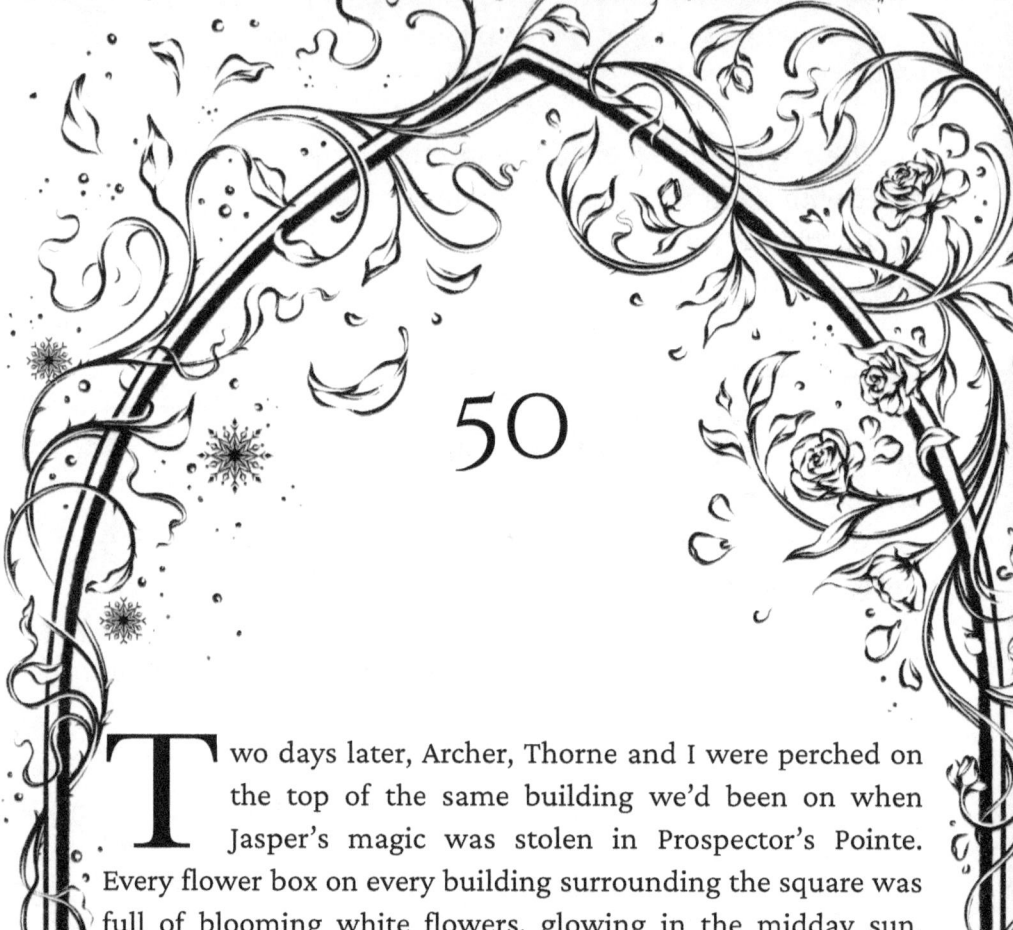

50

Two days later, Archer, Thorne and I were perched on the top of the same building we'd been on when Jasper's magic was stolen in Prospector's Pointe. Every flower box on every building surrounding the square was full of blooming white flowers, glowing in the midday sun. Farris and his horde of Cimmerians stood front and center as a line of ornate carriages were stopped just behind the golden circle.

"Do you guys see what I see?" Archer asked, an edge to his voice.

"We see it," I said, feeling a cool sense of dread melt over me.

All the gathered Cimmerians wore deep green robes, rendering the black ones we'd planned to take completely useless.

"We'll think of something else. See what it looks like when we get there," Archer said, not willing to doubt this trip for a second.

We watched from our vantage point as the gods and mortals

that had been selected for this year's Hunt arrived in the square. They were a dazzling sight, dressed in textures, furs and glittering jewels. The few gathered gods seemed to glow with an inner light, their beauty and power almost painful to look at. They loved a good show though, love their growing power from the worshiping of others, even if that worshiping was really envy, hatred, or even malice. The emotions are what fed them, just like fear had fed Death in his court. This was an important event for each of them. The chosen Silk looked small and insignificant next to them, but there was a hungry gleam in their eyes, a desperation to prove themselves worthy of this disgusting honor, yes. But they wanted to be close for Farris. They wanted the power he was hoarding.

One by one, the selected favorites climbed into the waiting carriages. Each one bearing the royal crest, a stark reminder of who controlled this grand spectacle. On the sidelines, the Silk that hadn't been chosen watched with envious eyes. They preened and postured, their bright spring wardrobes a riot of color against the muted backdrop of the city.

Once the caravan was gone, Thorne adjusted his glasses, checking his watch for the third time. "They're late."

"They aren't," I said, curling around my power. "They're down by the carriages with Tuck."

Archer rolled his eyes. "I bet they're arguing. This has Wee Willy's name written all over it."

Thorne's lips thinned into a grim line. "Perfect."

I nodded, already moving towards the rusted access ladder. "Why haven't one of you punched that guy in the nose yet?"

"Willy is a good guy," Archer answered. "He's just a terrible boyfriend. But the second I start talking shit to Harlow, she shuts down. Her life, her choice. We just support her. But as soon as she gives up on him, I get first dibs."

The muted sounds of the city engulfed us as we hiked back

down. The distant clatter of carriage wheels on cobblestones, the low murmur of conversations drifting from open windows, the cry of a street vendor hawking his wares. Stepping onto the bustling street, a far more familiar noise took precedent though.

Raised voices, sharp with anger and frustration, cut through the din of the crowd. Thorne's head snapped up, his eyes narrowing behind his spectacles as he sought Harlow and Willy, arguing behind the carriage with Tuck sitting dutifully at the helm, eyes locked on Thorne. Before they knew we were close, their voices carried.

"I'm not a child, Willard!" Harlow's hands were clenched into fists at her sides, her posture rigid with barely contained fury. "I can make my own decisions. I don't need your permission."

Wee Willy loomed over her. "It's too dangerous. Can't you see that? Farris is unpredictable. This whole Hunt is a farce, a twisted game. I won't let you risk your life for another of your brother's foolish plans."

"Let me?" Harlow scoffed, tossing her head. "Since when do you get to 'let me' do anything? I'm not some delicate flower that needs protecting. I'm a member of the Fray, same as you. And I think we both know I'm far more skilled."

"This is different. We have no idea what we're walking into. Have you ever been to the Hunt? Because I haven't. All I know are the horror stories that follow everyone home. You cannot go and that's final."

Archer and Thorne rushed forward.

"Don't," Harlow said, throwing a hand up to stop them both. She took an easy step toward Willard. "I have done every single thing you've ever asked of me. I've gone willingly to places I didn't want to go. I've had dinners with people I don't care about. I've watched your mother push other women into your path with no regard for me. And I've done it all silently.

Obediently. I've loved you since I was a girl. You were my first crush. Every time you gave me five seconds of attention it filled something broken in me. So, I've let you have the upper hand, even when those feelings have dissipated. Even as you've changed. I want to love you more than I actually do right now, and that says more about you than me. I'm going to the Hunt and you are not and that's the end of this conversation. Archie, please take my bag from Willard."

She said no more, and climbed into the carriage.

"Har, wait," Willard said, lunging for her.

Archer stepped in the way, blocking the door as he placed a hand on Willy's chest to hold him back. "She's spoken her peace. She can make her own decisions. Just give her some space."

"When her decisions involve you, it's bound to end in trouble, or have you forgotten why she has no magic? Harlow, come back out here."

The hurt look on Archer's face was all I needed to insert myself. I knew we had to tread lightly. If a member of the Fray went rogue, everyone would go down. But I'd had enough.

"Who do you think you are, talking to him like that? Or her, for that matter? Let me make this clear, you need to drag yourself home, stand in front of a mirror, and figure out why you're acting like a complete jerk. I saw you in the Hollow, Willard. You know I did. I've kept quiet out of respect, but don't push your luck. Go home. Cool off. Give her the space she deserves. And maybe by the time we're back, you'll have realized being a man doesn't make you better. It just means sometimes you have to shift your balls to sit down."

Willy turned every shade of red, fists clamped at his side. He opened his mouth to speak, but Thorne's heavy hand landed on his shoulder. "I wouldn't," he said simply.

"But she—"

Thorne lowered his chin. "No."

Pretty sure I'd never been more attracted to that man than I was just then.

Archer stepped around me, his voice laced with sadness. "No one here is trying to fight you. We're only asking you to give her the space she's requested. You can talk when we get back."

I hated the woman I had to be in this moment. And then I realized Harlow likely felt the same way. So, I left them behind to crawl into the carriage, sliding in beside her. I took her hand. Silent tears slipped down her face as she stared out of the small window.

"It would be so easy," she whispered. "If I stayed with Willard, if I let him dictate my life, my choices, I could have a kind of peace, you know? The peace of complacency, of never having to fight for what I want or who I am. Or wonder what things would be like outside of it. I would never have to think of what's missing because things would just become routine. Monotonous. No matter what it did to me on the inside. Eventually, I would stop feeling pain. And in the end, at least he'd keep our secrets. Maybe that's worth the flames."

"Stop setting yourself on fire for someone who'd rather tell you to find water instead of putting you out themselves. You don't have to conform to him. Or anyone else, for that matter."

Though Harlow cried silently, turning back to the window, I could almost feel her heartache radiating off her in waves. The air in the carriage grew heavy, thick with the weight of her pain. She turned to me, her blue eyes shimmering with tears, a sad smile playing at the corners of her lips.

"You know, I've never been whole since I lost my mother and then my power. It's like these two huge parts of me were ripped away, leaving this gaping, jagged hole that nothing can fill. And sometimes... sometimes it's just easier to take the silent road. To let someone else make the choices, to not have to think or feel or fight for myself so I'm not the one that needs saving."

Her words struck a chord deep within me, rattling my nerves enough to make me sit a little straighter. As I looked at Harlow, really looked at her, I saw it. There, just at the edges of her form, was a faint ripple. A distortion, like heat rising off sun-baked stones. And around that shimmer, a thin line of deep black absorbed the light, an inky void that made my eyes ache to look at it directly. The darkness pulsed in time with the ripples. A macabre heartbeat.

The mark of a broken soul, a spirit shattered by grief and loss. A wound that went far deeper than flesh and bone, a scar that could never fully heal. She'd been here this whole time, and I had no idea. But if I gave Alastor the name... if he knew it was her, he could help her. I had to sit on my hands to keep from reaching out to touch the void. It called to me, purred across the space like a lover coaxing me forward and the only thing I could think of beyond the need to caress the darkness, was if Harlow was a broken soul because she'd lost her magic, then Wisteria was full of broken souls. And that included Jasper.

But that couldn't be right, could it? I'd seen him at his lowest low. I'd seen him beg the prince to spare him. And worse, had watched him beg for deliverance, opting to lose his forearm rather than be bound to Farris. There was no black in that moment. Nothing that made him any more than a sad man. So was it both? The loss of a parent paired with the loss of her magic? Or was it just her capacity to feel things deeper, something different about Harlow that marked her?

The carriage door swung open, startling me from my trance. Archer and Thorne climbed in, the small space suddenly cramped with their long legs. Archer's sharp gaze darted between Harlow and me, his brow furrowing with concern as he took in the tense atmosphere.

"Har," he began, his voice characteristically gentle, "Why are you still with that asshole? You know you deserve better, right?"

Harlow sighed, tearing her gaze away from the window to meet her brother's eyes. The shimmer around her dissipated as she blinked away her sadness. "It's best for everyone if I stay put."

"Absolutely not," Thorne said, crossing his arms over his chest as Tuck whistled once and the carriage took off. "If you choose Willard, fine. But you are *not* going to stay with him for other people's benefits. Not even his own. He's not committed to you. If anything, he's stringing you along for his own appearances. If you don't want to be with him, it's done."

"You know what he'll do," she whispered.

"If you're worried about him giving away our secrets, then he shouldn't be a member of the Fray, anyway. Say the word and I'll pay a visit to the Story Snatcher and he'll never remember a thing."

The world melted over me, stealing all sense of reason. My ears rang. I forced a breath. Two. Keeping my eyes trained to the ground. That was the second time I'd heard of the Story Snatcher. And I'd bet my life I'd already met him. In the form of a little homeless boy. A little homeless boy who'd asked for a story of love and then snatched it away.

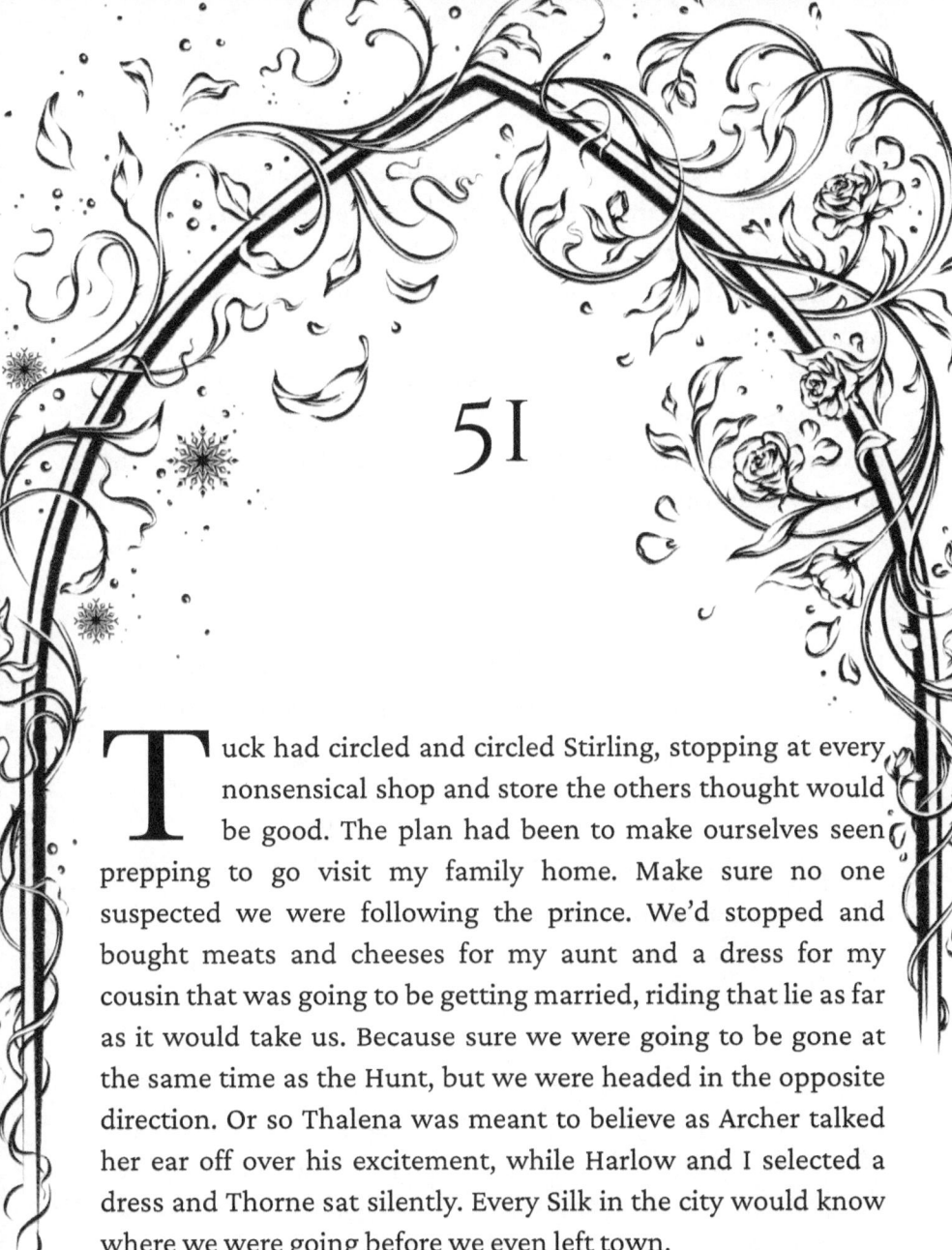

51

Tuck had circled and circled Stirling, stopping at every nonsensical shop and store the others thought would be good. The plan had been to make ourselves seen prepping to go visit my family home. Make sure no one suspected we were following the prince. We'd stopped and bought meats and cheeses for my aunt and a dress for my cousin that was going to be getting married, riding that lie as far as it would take us. Because sure we were going to be gone at the same time as the Hunt, but we were headed in the opposite direction. Or so Thalena was meant to believe as Archer talked her ear off over his excitement, while Harlow and I selected a dress and Thorne sat silently. Every Silk in the city would know where we were going before we even left town.

Harlow had been the perfect friend, gossiping with the ladies about Thorne and I, convincing them it was such a delight to be invited to come and how she and my cousin had become pen pals. We talked about shit that didn't matter. Ribbons and fashion and even the weather and the spring blossoms. Anything to make our story convincing, including drop-

529

ping a few nuggets of gossip just because. And then we were off, not toward my family home, unfortunately, but half a day behind the prince's caravan. And by the time we were done, no one in the city would question a thing. It'd been a flawless performance.

We'd stopped just outside the prying eyes of the city, and I finally got my first glimpse of the world beyond Stirling as we ditched the carriage, leaving Tuck behind as we mounted the horses several members of the Fray had brought. I'd known there were mountains in the distance, of course, because I could see them from the rooftops, but the grass was turning a vibrant green out here in the open, and the warmth of the sun was hidden beneath the chill of a breeze. More proof that the season was changing. As if I needed that damn pressure from the universe.

As I swung my leg over the saddle and settled onto the horse's broad back, Thorne mounted up behind me, his chest pressing against my back as he reached around to take the reins. The warmth of his body seeped through the layers of my riding clothes and only then did it occur to me just how long this day was going to be.

Harlow was seated onto her mount with little effort, and Archer followed suit on his. We'd agreed to take as few horses as possible, but we'd need a third for the king. As he settled into his saddle, Archer flashed me a roguish grin, leaning down onto the horn. "Ready to chase down a prince, Fingers?"

I returned his smile. "You're far too excited, Toes."

His smile fell. "We talked about that. 'Toes' is weird."

"And Fingers isn't?" Harlow asked, the sorrow from the morning growing more dull the farther away from Willard we got.

"Actually, no it's not, Harlot. Fingers the Bandit is too long, obviously."

"If you want to keep fair, we could start calling you Toes the Menace," Thorne said.

"Fuck all the way off," Archer answered.

With a click of his tongue and a gentle squeeze of his heels, Thorne urged our horse forward. When I glanced back and saw the dimpled smile, my favorite of his, I couldn't help but follow suit. Archer and Harlow fell in beside us as we set off at a brisk trot. The rhythmic pounding of hooves filled my ears as we rode, the wind whipping through my hair and tugging at my clothes. The farther we got from Stirling, the more the tension in my shoulders eased. Out here in the open, with nothing but rolling hills and endless sky stretching before us, I felt a sense of freedom I'd only ever known at the Syndicate house back home.

Thorne's strong arms bracketed my waist, holding me steady as we navigated the uneven terrain. Every now and then, his breath would tickle the back of my neck, sending shivers down my spine that had nothing to do with the cool spring air.

Beside us, Archer and Harlow rode in comfortable silence, their horses close, heads bent together as they conversed in low tones. I caught snatches of their conversation on the wind. They spoke of their mother, even their grandmother, who'd raised them. But there was something else. Something they spoke of so quickly, they'd argued and stopped talking altogether.

As the sun began to dip toward the horizon, painting the sky in shades of orange and pink, Thorne called for us to make camp for the night. I typically never needed enough power to feel drained. Occasionally I was exhausted, but not like this. Because no matter what I did in Wisteria, there was something wrong with my magic. Where I might have felt a jerk, a pull in a direction, chasing down Farris, pinpricks were all I had to guide us. No matter how I burrowed down, no matter how I pushed, still it felt muted. We found a sheltered spot near a bubbling stream and set about unpacking only what we needed. With heavy lids and half a day of yawning, I didn't protest when the men offered to take turns on watch. I simply snuggled down in the rolled blanket and fell asleep without dinner.

After what seemed like only minutes, Thorne was shaking me awake. The horses were already ready to go, Archer and Harlow were mounted and somehow I'd slept through it all.

"You could have woken me sooner," I whispered once we were on the road.

"Or I could have let you sleep. A simple thank you will suffice."

I rolled my eyes but still thanked him as I settled in, resting against his chest. As we rode on, the rising sun warmed the air around us, but it was the heat of Thorne's body pressed against my back that sent tingles across my skin. His strong thighs cradled mine, the hard muscles flexing with each sway of the horse. I found myself acutely aware of every place we touched, his broad chest against my shoulders, his hips nestled snugly against my backside, one arm around me to grip the reins, the other splayed comfortably on my abdomen.

With each mile, each hour spent sandwiched together, the air between us seemed to thicken. My body ached, and not because of the long ride. As if sensing the direction of my thoughts, Thorne shifted behind me, his hips rocking subtly against me in a way that made heat pool low in my belly. I bit my lip to stifle a gasp, my fingers clenching around the saddle horn.

I cleared my throat, trying to focus on anything but the delicious friction of Thorne's body against mine. We had a mission, a purpose. I couldn't let myself get distracted, no matter how tempting the distraction might be.

Thorne leaned in close, his lips brushing my neck as he murmured, "Something bothering you, Paesha darling?"

His low, rumbling voice sent a shiver down my spine, goosebumps erupting across my skin despite the growing warmth of the day. I twisted in the saddle to shoot him a mock glare over my shoulder. "Tease."

Thorne's answering chuckle was pure sin. "I have no idea what you're talking about."

Beside us, Archer made an exaggerated gagging noise. "Ugh, get a room, you two! Some of us are trying to keep our breakfasts down over here."

I rolled my hips forward, letting myself rise and fall just enough with the horse to warrant Thorne's grip tightening on my thighs.

"Stop it."

I kept my tone innocent. "Stop what?"

"You know what you're doing," he growled.

I pushed further back, feeling just how much he really wanted me to stop as his rock-hard length pressed against me. "You started it."

"If you think I'm too proud to share a horse with Archer, you're wrong," he growled.

I tossed my head back and laughed. Truly. Purely laughed. "You would never."

"You underestimate me, Paesha darling. I'd give up all my pride if it meant hearing that laugh again. I'd share a thousand horses with Archer, if it meant your happiness."

"Hard pass," Archer said.

I sat up straighter, suddenly acutely aware of the prince. "They stopped."

All sense of playfulness fell away from Thorne. "How far ahead do you think they are? Can you tell that?"

"A couple hours at this pace. Maybe one if we hustle."

Thorne dug his heels into the horse's flanks, urging it into a swift canter. Archer and Harlow matched our pace. I reached out with my magic, letting it guide me like a compass needle, pulling me closer to the prince and his entourage.

As we crested a hill, a vast forest sprawled out before us, the trees towering like ancient sentinels. I pointed towards the tree line, following the insistent tug of my power.

"They're this way. Not too far at all."

We urged our horses forward, plunging into the cool shade of the forest. The trees closed in around us. As we wound our way deeper into the woods, the trees grew older, taller, their trunks so wide it would take five men with arms outstretched to circle them. But just beyond them, past the forest, sat Farris's caravan nestled down below in a valley at the base of a mountain.

"We'll stay up here," Thorne said quietly, guiding me off the horse. "We have the perfect view to keep an eye on them and hopefully we're far enough away, the gods won't sense us."

"We know the Cimmerians need to be closer, right? To detect magic?"

"All good on that front," Archer said.

Thorne nodded. "We'll take watch in rotations. Look for our best opportunity. With the gods down there, I highly doubt any of them are doing anything productive tonight."

We made camp, opting for no fire as we set all of our blankets out and sat in a close semicircle. With the horses tied up, Archer handed out a bit of the meat and cheese we'd acquired from Stirling and we ate while staring down and watching the revelry.

"The tents are massive," Harlow said.

I pointed to a round little man that swayed with a drink in his hand before ducking into another of the tents. "Is that the king's advisor, Archie?"

"Yes, but what the hell is happening over there?"

A train of people poured out of the central tent, the glowing

Goddess of Lust leading the way as those that followed her danced and sang, completely naked. Their laughs carried over the music and trailed all the way up to the forest.

"Actually, you know what, nevermind. I absolutely don't want anyone to speculate on that one," he said, drawing back in disgust.

As the night wore on, the revelry in the valley below only grew wilder. The flickering light of bonfires cast dancing shadows across the canvas walls of the tents. Laughter and music floated up to us on the cool night breeze, punctuated by the occasional shriek of ecstasy or roar of drunken merriment. It was a scene of debauchery and excess, the prince, the gods and their chosen mortals indulging in every pleasure.

I couldn't tear my gaze away from the spectacle, equal parts repulsed and fascinated. Beside me, Thorne sat still as a statue, his sharp eyes scanning the camp below, cataloging every detail. The prince lounged on a plush divan outside his tent, a goblet of wine in one hand, the other idly stroking the hair of the beautiful courtier draped across his lap. If I didn't know he was so disgusting, I wouldn't judge, but as it was, I wanted to pluck my eyes out.

"Wait a minute," Archer said, sitting up taller. "Wait a godsdamn minute. We know they didn't carry those tents and couches on their little caravan, right? I didn't see anything big enough to haul that stuff, did you? A full-size couch, for gods sake."

"Well, no, Archie," Harlow answered. "He'd have had someone set this up days ago. Probably the day of the first bloom."

"Exactly," he said, rubbing his hands together. "He had a plan."

"I'm not following why that's such a surprise," I said.

"Doesn't it look familiar, Fingers? We've seen this. The

mountains are there, see, and we're in the forest. And the water is off that way. This was the map from his hidden room."

I gasped, orienting myself until the landscape matched. "You're right. And the tents must be the silver strings."

"And that means the red dot is there," he said, pointing to the far right.

I shook my head. "No, the dot was on the left side, remember, closer to the water?"

"There are thirty-two tents down there, Archie. None more guarded than another. But several haven't been used at all and it's likely, if the king is down there, he's in one of those. We won't have time to scour all of them," Thorne said, hardly blinking.

"We know the prince has mainly been in or around the center tent. It's not likely he's staying there," I said, then pointed farther left. "Bellatora, the Goddess of War and Ruin is camped down in that one. In fact, I think most of the gods are on the north side."

"How many gods are here?" Harlow asked.

"Three," Archer and I said in unison.

"Four," Thorne corrected.

"Serene, Bellatora, Vesalia and who else?" I asked.

"Orathis," he answered, pointing to a man that sat outside with several women in a circle, his shoulders covered in layers of pelts.

"I've never heard of him," Harlow said, narrowing her eyes on the man. "What's his divinity?"

Thorne tilted his head up, staring at the canopy of trees above us as if trying to pull information from a book he'd once read. "He's easy to spot because of his furs and golden curls. Orathis Varyn, God of Nature and Wild Beasts."

Archer snorted. "Is there a book in Stirling you haven't read? Know-it-all."

"Are the gods crawling out of the woodwork to get close to Farris now or what?" Harlow asked, hugging her knees to her chest.

"I think they are," I answered. "They want the power Farris is hoarding. And I think *he* wants it for himself. He just doesn't know how to use it, so he's leading them on."

"Has anyone counted guards and other people?" Archer asked.

"There are forty-five Cimmerians down there. More than I've ever seen in one place," Harlow said quietly. "I think we would have had free roam of the city, had we stayed home for the week."

"I left Tuck with a few instructions. He and the boys have their own missions this week. He's to stay the hell away from the Maw for the foreseeable future. Everyone is, including you two," Thorne said, giving the twins a pointed glare.

"You couldn't pay me to go back down there." Harlow turned her attention back to the chaos down below.

"Tell me again about the map," Thorne said, the authoritative tone to his voice still lingering.

I lifted a shoulder. "It was just a map. The mountains were there. There was water on this side, which I don't see now and then the valley."

"There's a river that runs through there. You can't see it from here because it's below that ridge. But I need more information. If you picture the map in your mind, how big was the dot? Were there others? Did you see the whole map?"

I closed my eyes, but Archer answered. "I'm telling you, it was right over there."

I shook my head again. "No, I really think it was the other side, but even still, what are we going to do? Search every tent on that side—" I jerked upright. "Oh!" Answering the tiny tug on my magic, I followed, letting it lead me down below. "He brought the map. It's down there in that tent across from him. Why would he have brought it?"

Archer scoffed. "Probably because he doesn't want to leave a road map to his father lying around for anyone to find. Come on. We can all agree the king is down there, right? All these Cimmies, the detailed plan ahead of time, multiple gods, including new ones? It's so suspicious."

"Archer, if you had to narrow it down to a tent you think the king's in, could you?"

He shook his head. "I know he's on the right, but I couldn't tell you specifically which one because the tents were just silver strings."

"I hate to break it to you, but I don't mess up directions. Let's call it a gift. From a god. When I was born. Because," I waved my fingers in the air, "magic. I'm telling you that dot was on the left, I think toward the top, but scouring even half the tents on both sides isn't going to be a stealthy, quick thing. What if we just went down and got the map?"

"Right now?" Archer asked.

"No!" Thorne, Harlow and I answered together.

"We sleep in shifts. Wait for them to leave to hunt, hope the gods go with for the sport of it, and then we're in and out. Get the map, confirm the red dot, grab the king, and get the hell out of here as fast as we can."

"What are we going to do with him once we've got him?" Archer asked. "It's not like we can just throw him back in his castle and wish him well."

"That's tomorrow's problem. Let's secure him first."

The only thing I could think of as the conversation faded away was the little old king I'd met at Lithe. How his rescue, and my part in leading this team here, was why this was my path. And once he was secure, he would hopefully have the answers for how I was to get home. He was so, so close. And I felt so torn.

I'd bonded with these people, and though Thorne had said he would return with me. What if he couldn't? What if something changed and he didn't want to? Could he just leave everything he'd built here behind? And could I really ask him to do that?

Harlow shifted restlessly. She'd been unusually quiet since we'd made camp, her gaze distant and troubled. She turned to face Archer. "Are we sure about this? Rescuing the king, I mean."

"What do you mean, Har? Of course we're sure. He needs us. It's why we're here."

Harlow shook her head, her soft golden curls catching the fading light filtering through the trees. She bit her bottom lip. "I know, but... what if we're wrong? What if the king isn't even here? We're risking so much on a hunch, on scraps of information we've pieced together. Look at all those Cimmerians. Plus the gods. It genuinely feels like a trap."

She was right, of course. Logical. We didn't know for certain the king was here. We were running on faith, on the desperate hope that we could put an end to Farris's unofficial reign of terror. For me, it was so much more. However, faith was a fragile thing, easily fractured by doubt and fear.

Archer straightened. "You know we can't sustain this way. We can't afford to feed a fraction of the city forever. The operation is failing. The Fray are struggling now more than ever. We need the king to step in and set it right. But you'd rather walk away empty-handed? What are you even saying right now?"

"I'm saying this is a bad idea. Look down there and see the trap. We all know they hunt more than animals on these things and we're sitting up here discussing walking right into it. If you're all too foolish to see this for what it is, then fine. But I'm not going to sit back and watch you die. I thought this was a good idea. It's not. It's not worth our lives. Minimally, it's not worth your power. Trust me on that one."

Archer's eyes flashed with anger. "So that's it then? You're just going to give up, let Farris win because you're afraid? Since when do you back down from a fight, Harlow?"

Harlow's voice became a low growl. "Don't you dare accuse me of cowardice. I have sacrificed everything for this cause, for this family. I lost my power, my future, because of a choice you made. And I have never once held that against you. But I will not let you lead us to our deaths on some fool's errand, all because you think things will change when you get the king alone and you can tell him the truth. It's not going to work, Archer, and I just can't understand why you care so damn much. I want to, but I can't."

"You know why I care. Why *she* cared."

Harlow spoke through her teeth. "She never wanted him to know. Honor our mother and let it go."

"He's our father. I'm never going to let it go."

52

Archer jumped to his feet, pacing like a wild animal. Thorne and I remained quiet, but the surprised glance we'd shared was more than enough to make sure we were on the same page. Eventually, Archer went back to the horses and Harlow watched him with sad, tired eyes, that dark glowing rim around her returning as she drew her knees to her chest, hugging them close.

Her words were barely audible at first. As if she'd held them so tightly to her heart for so long, letting them go was like losing a treasured piece of herself. Like she was betraying her mother. "Our mother... she loved the king with all her heart. It consumed her, that love. Like a fire burning too bright, too fast. She was one of the queen's ladies-in-waiting before the king and queen were married. Always by her side, privy to the most intimate moments of the royal couple's lives as they courted. And somewhere along the way, amidst the glittering court functions and quiet palace halls, she and the king fell into a forbidden affair."

She paused, her eyes distant, as if seeing the past play out before her. "When she discovered she was pregnant, they say she was overjoyed and terrified in equal measure. She knew the scandal it would cause, the danger it would put us all in if his betrothed were to find out. So she did the only thing she could think of. She wrote the king a letter, pouring her heart onto the page, telling him of the precious life growing inside her... and then she ran."

A single tear tracked down Harlow's cheek causing the black aura around her to ripple wildly, latching on to her sadness like it fed her broken soul. She continued. "She fled to our grand-mother's estate in the countryside, a place they'd been together before, hoping against hope that the king would come for her, that he would choose her and their unborn child over his promised queen. But she never sent the letter, too afraid of what might happen if she did.

"Our mother died when we were just babes, never having told a soul the truth of our parentage. I think it was a broken heart. It was our grandmother who finally revealed the secret to us on her own deathbed, pressing that unsent letter into my hands with her final breath."

I reached out, laying a comforting hand on Harlow's shoulder. She leaned into the touch, as if drawing strength from me. Thorne remained silent, but I could see the gears turning behind his sharp gaze, piecing together the implications of this story.

"Don't you see?" Harlow whispered. "Archer has been chasing this dream for years, this desperate need to confront the king, to make him acknowledge us as his true heirs. I still have the letter and he wants me to give it to him. We're two years older than Farris. But I know what will happen if he finds out. The king isn't going to protect us. Farris is going to hunt us. That's how this ends."

"You've been working to save this kingdom because it's yours," I whispered, finally understanding the whole story.

"No. We've been doing it because it's the right thing to do. Archer thinks we're the rightful heirs. I know we're just the bastard children of a lost king."

Hours later, after Harlow decided to go talk to her brother, Thorne and I were left to keep watch. I nudged him with my shoulder once I couldn't take the quiet anymore. "Bet you never saw that coming."

He looked at me over the rim of his glasses with a half smirk. "Actually, I had a hunch. I just never thought they'd confess it."

"You did not."

"They fight about it all the time, if you pay close enough attention. It was bound to come to a head. But Harlow isn't misguided in her fear. It's the same fear her mother had for a reason. The queen was a vicious woman, and her son is obviously worse."

"Why would the king have married her then? If he was so in love with their mom? That's the real question here."

He ran a hand through his dark hair. "Of course the king would have had to be married to hold his crown. That's how it works here. I'm sure Farris is already searching for his wife. And, I can't say for sure, but Harlow and Archer do everything with their whole heart. They've always jumped two feet in. If their mother was anything like them, then I'd say the king's heart was also broken. And men tend to do irrational things when they're hurt."

"Speaking from experience?"

"Quite honestly, yes."

Everything in me wanted to ask a thousand questions but we'd been down this road and it never ended in a happy place. One day, when all of this was over, maybe the walls would fall as well as the masks and we could stop dancing around each other. I didn't need to know who his parents were, nor what kind of trauma he kept locked away. But maybe I wanted to know his favorite meal as a child. Or where he went to escape the world when it was too dark to handle. Maybe I wanted to know about his studies and travels and the people that affected his life beyond the Fray.

Maybe he wanted that from me too. Just the little things. Except there was a part of my past I couldn't remember. A man. He'd come in small moments, but with that came so much heartache, I don't think I wanted to remember him. Maybe I'd actually wished his memory away to save my heart. Maybe I understood the king more than I knew.

"Did you bring my little book?" Thorne asked quietly, some time later. The fires had burned down to red hot coals, and the music was long gone. Only scattered hushed conversations drifted up the hill to us now.

"Of course I did. It's in my pack. Why?"

"If you stay up here and watch tomorrow, the three of us can go down. If something is coming, you can warn me by writing in it, and you can give direction as needed."

I shook my head. "I need to be down there. I need to touch the king and see his face as soon as possible. That way, if something happens, things go bad, I can always find him again. He's too important to everyone. We can't risk it."

"To everyone, or to your great escape?" he asked, the irritation in his voice obvious. "Maybe Harlow's right and we need to reevaluate."

"I need to get home and I won't hide that desire from you now that you know the truth, Thorne. I made a deal, and the days are ticking away. I think I have around fifteen left. I'm doing my best to stick together and do this as a team but keep that tone and see how fast I change my mind. You don't have to come with me just because you lost yourself in the moment. I won't hold you to that. But you do have to let me go at the end of this."

He nodded, lifting a rock from the ground and tossing it into the trees. "I'm going to wake the others. We should get some sleep."

I spread out our blankets while he did just that. I'm sure he wanted distance. Time to think about what I'd said. Time to figure out how to change my mind. But I was selfish, and I didn't want distance. Not when our time together was fading away. So, I laid his blankets next to mine, and when he laid down beside me. I curled up to him anyway, laying my head on his chest. And just before I fell asleep, his chest rumbled as he whispered, "Souls don't meet by accident and every time I'm with you, I know I'm exactly where I'm supposed to be, even if there's no logic to it. And I meant every damn word I said."

"Are you sure?" Archer asked, leaning against a tree as he squinted down to the dwindling party.

"I'm sure," Harlow nodded. "It would have been so much easier if we could have used the black Cimmerian robes, but it's like you said, it's your life too and we can't keep up the charade forever. We're running out of options. So we're doing this."

Archer walked forward, putting his arms around his sister. "I won't tell him about us. I promise." He turned to Thorne. "And you're just going to stay up here? And send letters in the little book? That's the plan?"

"Unless you have a better idea," Thorne answered.

I knew he hated the idea, but to the others, he hadn't opposed it. He'd chosen to support me and let me be the one to go down. It was the most logical thing to do and when it came to Thorne, he was nothing, if not logical. To an annoying degree if he so wished it.

Thorne drew a circle in the dirt with a stick and we gathered around, giving him the control he needed. "Pretend the camp is a clock. We'll communicate location with times. If I say six o'clock, it's the lowest, central point, make sense?"

"Yes, for the perimeter, but what about the inside? Say a guard is coming in here," I said, pointing to a spot within. "How will I know?"

Thorne considered for a moment, studying the rough map he'd sketched. "All right, for the interior, we'll use a grid system. Imagine the camp divided into nine quadrants you'll read left to right, top to bottom. Top left *perimeter* would be ten o'clock, but the interior is quadrant one. Center is quadrant five. Got it?"

I nodded.

"Archer, what's the quadrant?" he asked, pointing to one of the nine squares he'd drawn.

"Six interior, three o'clock on the perimeter."

"And this one, Harlow?"

She flipped her dagger in her hand. "If they're on the outside perimeter, it's six o'clock. If it's interior, you'll say quadrant eight."

"Paesha?" He pointed to another square.

"Center of the clock, quadrant 5. That's where the big tent is and we're headed to quadrant eight for the map."

"Good. Now commit this to memory. It's simple but effective. A quick way to convey critical information without getting bogged down in details. I won't send irrelevant warnings. Stay together and stay sharp."

Archer and Harlow looked equally focused. Last night's disagreement was set aside or forgiven entirely, I wasn't sure.

"Remember," he continued. "Speed and stealth are key. Get in, find the map, then the king, and get out. No unnecessary risks. If something feels off, trust your instincts, and pull back. We regroup here and reassess."

I kept the book tucked into the waistband of my pants,

pressed against my stomach. The three of us made it as far down as we could without being seen as the God of Wild Animals or whatever led the prince and most of the party north through the mountain pass.

With Thorne keeping watch from above, we crept down the hillside, moving silently through the underbrush. I wanted to be calm, wholly aware of everything around me, but I couldn't help the way my heart raced, the thrill of anticipation mingling with the icy tendrils of fear.

Most of the tents stood empty, holding the camp in an eerie quiet, and only about ten Cimmerians remained patrolling the perimeter. There was no way to know who was hiding in which tents, though. We paused at the edge of the trees. The book warmed against my skin. I slipped it out and read Thorne's message, scrawled in neat, precise handwriting:

Two guards approaching quad eight from the perimeter at 4 o'clock. Wait for them to pass.

I showed the note to Archer and Harlow, and we crouched down, huddling close together as we watched the guards stroll by, their green cloaks fluttering in the breeze. They seemed at ease, unaware of our presence mere feet away. After several tense minutes, they rounded the corner of a tent and disappeared from view.

"Let's go," Archer breathed. "Quadrant eight. Stay low and move fast."

We darted from the tree line, weaving between the tents. The small tent loomed before us, tantalizingly close. Harlow reached it first, pausing at the entrance and cocking her head, listening intently. After a moment, she nodded and slipped inside, Archer and I close on her heels.

The only light was the cloud covered sun filtering in through the thin fabric of the tent walls. Crates and trunks were stacked haphazardly around the edges, leaving a small, open space in the center. No one was inside, thankfully.

Harlow and Archer stood at the door, weapons out. I dashed across the space, moving the crates as quietly as possible, knowing the map was buried beneath them. The book heated against my skin again. I pulled it out, squinting to read Thorne's message in the gloom.

Approaching from six o'clock. Hide. Now.

My heart leapt into my throat. "We need to hide!"

Archer and Harlow's heads snapped to me, eyes wide. We scanned the small space desperately, looking for somewhere, anywhere to conceal ourselves. Harlow pointed to a large trunk in the corner, its lid propped open.

We ran for it, squeezing behind because there was no way we would all three fit inside. It certainly wasn't fool proof, but it was the only option. Huddled behind the trunk, barely daring to breathe, we waited as the sound of heavy footsteps approached. A shadow fell across the entrance of the tent, and I kicked myself for choosing not to bring the sword from Alastor. I had my blade, though, and Archie and Harlow were both armed.

Hunkered down, we never saw the guard duck inside, but when he took a step forward, his boot crunched on the dry grass. Archer's hand tightened on the hilt of his dagger as he brought a finger to his lips. I nodded slowly.

The Cimmerian moved. Checking behind each stack of crates. He was thorough, too thorough, and it was only a matter of time before he found us. I closed my eyes, silently praying to any god that might be listening.

A loud commotion erupted outside, shouts and the clash of

metal on metal. The guard's head snapped up. He hesitated for a moment, torn between completing his search and investigating the disturbance. With a muttered curse, he turned on his heel and ran out of the tent.

Seconds later, the flap ripped open, and Thorne was there, my bloodied sword in hand, heaving, eyes locked with mine and frantic. "New plan. Anyone that approaches dies. Let's go."

I could have thrown myself into his arms right then and there and sworn to never leave him. But there was no time as I rushed back to the crates. "Help me move these. The map's under here somewhere."

Thorne was at my side in an instant, his strong arms making quick work of the heavy crates. Together, we tossed them aside, desperation fueling our movements. Archer and Harlow kept watch. Thorne worked beside me, his eyes darting between the growing pile of discarded items and the tent flap.

"Here!" My fingers closed around a rolled parchment buried at the bottom of the last crate. I yanked it free, nearly toppling backward. Thorne's hand shot out to steady me and I unfurled the map with shaking hands, my eyes scanning the familiar lines and symbols, as more commotion grew outside the tent.

"He moved it," I said, across the space. "We would have both been wrong, Archer. He rotated the configuration and the dots at the top now."

"Twelve o'clock," Thorne said "Right between the god's tents."

Harlow glanced back from the door, her face pale. "We need to move. Now. Before they realize what's happening, and cut off our escape."

"Just run like hell. Get to the king. Paesha has to touch him. If he's incapacitated at all, do what you can to get him out of the tent. Take this," Thorne said, snagging a blanket from the top of one of the discarded crates. "Drag him on a blanket if you have to and get the fuck out as quick as you can."

"You're not coming?" I asked.

"I'll be right behind you. Now go!"

He left no room for argument.

With a last, lingering look, I turned and followed Archer and Harlow out. We ran, keeping low and darting between tents. Focused solely on our destination at the top of the camp. As we neared, a group of guards spotted us. They charged with a shout, weapons raised. Archer and Harlow met them head on, knives out. I ducked around the fight, my heart in my throat, as I kept running, dashed into the tent with the king and slammed to a halt, pure shock ripping the air from my lungs.

53

There was no king sitting in the heart of the tent. But, instead, a bloodied and bruised Jasper, sobbing, and a horde of Cimmerians standing along the far wall.

Harlow was right. It'd been a godsdamn trap and never once had I thought to use magic to find *him*.

Thorne burst into the tent mere seconds behind me, his eyes wild, chest heaving. He took in the scene. For a heartbeat, the world held its breath. Then he exploded into motion. He lunged forward, the sword a blur of silver as he sliced through Jasper's bonds. With a grunt, he hauled the terrified man to his feet and shoved him towards me as the Cimmerians sprung into action. Jasper stumbled, nearly falling.

"Run, Paesha!" Thorne roared, his voice raw with desperation and something else, something fierce and primal. "Get him out of here!"

No.

No!

My world shattered. The air between us heavy with

unspoken words and unfulfilled promises that would never be kept. Every inch of space felt like a chasm widening with each racing heartbeat. Thorne turned, our eyes locking for what felt like the last time, the weight of his sacrifice sinking into my chest like a blade.

"No."

But he was already moving. His body slammed into the oncoming wave of Cimmerians, the sword arcing in the dim light, a storm of fury and strength that wouldn't last. Harlow and Archer had hands on me before I knew what was happening, dragging me away as I screamed. And screamed. Begging to go back. For them to let me go. To try to save him.

I would have given it all away. All of me, to rip myself free and run to him, to die at his side, if that's what it took. But Harlow's grip tightened, and Archer's arms dragged me away.

"No!" My voice broke. Tears burned my eyes. My chest ached as if it might collapse in on itself. "Thorne! We need more time," I screamed. "We need more time."

But he didn't turn again as the flap to the tent dropped between us.

I jerked, twisting, and turning.

Archer's fingers dug in. "Paesha, stop! He's buying us time. We have to use it."

"He'll die! You know he will." The words tore from my throat, a sob catching on the jagged edges.

"He knew the risks. This was always a possibility."

Jasper stumbled along beside us, his eyes wide with shock, his breath coming in short, panicked gasps. Still he ran.

Still I fought.

Still we moved.

The clang of metal on metal and the shouts of fighting men faded behind us as I was dragged away from the camp, crashing through the underbrush. Branches whipped at my face, thorns tearing at my clothes as Archer and Harlow pulled me through the forest, away from the camp, away from Thorne. My heart shattered with every step, the pieces scattering behind me like breadcrumbs, marking a trail back to the man I think I could have let myself love. The man I was leaving behind.

Finally, when my lungs burned and my legs threatened to give out, Archer barked out orders. "Pack up the horses. There's one for you too, Jasper."

"I'm not leaving. You pack your horses and run like cowards. Go ahead. That man walked through fire for me, and I'll be damned if I won't return the favor, even if it means I have to burn the whole camp to the ground. Piss off every god from there to Etherium. Call down Death from his dark court and beg for revenge. I will do it."

Beside me, the old cook was a blubbering mess, his body shaking so badly he could barely grip the saddle horn with his one good arm. Archer and Harlow worked with grim efficiency, their movements quick and purposeful as they packed up our meager supplies.

"Why are you here?" I ground out, frozen in place, as I stared at Jasper. "Why the fuck are you here at camp?"

"I... I know the boss told me not to, but I was down by Nightshade Row. There's an old Silk that gets an order from the grocer every three days and she throws out what she doesn't use. I was—"

"A damn fool. How are we supposed to trust you? How the fuck are we supposed to accept that we just traded you for *him*? Why should we believe you're not still bound to the prince? You offered yourself up as bait, didn't you?"

Jasper's old eyes fell to the ground.

Archer slid a careful arm over my shoulder. "Hey," he whispered, voice low and slow, as if talking to a wild animal. "We know he's free, remember? We watched Farris kill a Cimmerian over it. We saw him disobey a direct order. He was never bait. We'd have had to know he was here for that to be true. The prince always *hunts* someone and you saw how pissed he was at Jasper. He was probably going to die up here. I know you're upset, but don't take it out on him."

I swiped away a tear and dropped to my knees, staring back at the camp, willing Thorne to come racing up the hill. "I'm sorry. I didn't mean it." Mostly.

Archer dropped beside me. "You stay, I stay."

"Well, if you're both staying, I am too," Harlow said, turning to Jasper. "You can take the spare horse back, if you want."

I could feel his eyes on me. "I... I think I'll stay. If that's okay, Miss Paesha?"

My emotions were a torrent of anger and sadness. There was nothing logical in this moment. Lashing out at Jasper. Begging to go to my own death. Threatening to anger every god out loud. Thorne had pinned me against a wall, shoving his hand over my mouth the last time I'd done that. And I think I fell for him in that moment. I think I'd been falling every day since.

"I'm sorry," I whispered, not bothering to look at him as I stared straight ahead. He'd been beaten, bruised, lost his fucking arm... he'd been captured, tied up, beaten again, by the looks of him, and I'd been terrible. Terrible to an old man that'd been nothing but kind to me. But a whispered apology was all I could manage.

I stared down at the camp below, the midday sun casting long shadows over the wreckage of our escape until the tents looked like tombstones. The few guards that moved were too far away to make out clearly. They were searching, no doubt, for signs of us. For him.

For Thorne.

I pressed my palms into the damp earth, the coolness grounding me in the moment, but it did nothing to stop the ache.

"He's not coming back," I whispered, my voice a raw rasp of finality that tasted like ash on my tongue. "We left him."

Harlow dropped beside us, her lips drawn into a tight line, her hands resting on the hilt of her knife. "Do you think they saw us run up here?"

I didn't move. Didn't answer. Couldn't. My eyes locked on the tattered tents, every part of me begging for one last glimpse of him. One last sign that he'd— A flash of movement. There, near the largest tent, a figure staggered through the wreckage.

No. It couldn't be.

"Paesha..." Archer's voice was low, cautionary, but I barely registered it.

I rose on unsteady legs, my heart slamming against my ribs. The figure moved with purpose. Steady. Determined. Gods, I knew those broad shoulders. I knew them like I knew my own heartbeat.

"Thorne?" I breathed, the word barely a whisper, as if speaking it too loudly might break the moment. He was alive.

I didn't think. Didn't care about the distance or the eyes that might spot me. Consequences be damned, I launched myself down the hill, my feet slipping and sliding on the loose earth, the world narrowing to a single point. My pulse roared in my ears, breath coming in sharp gasps as I tore through the branches snapping beneath my boots.

"Thorne!"

And then I was there. I crashed into him with all the force of my fear and relief, throwing my arms around his neck, pulling him to me as if I could never let go. His arms closed around me, solid and strong, and I clung to him, burying my face against his chest.

Thorne's arms tightened around me, holding me close as if he, too, feared I might vanish if he let go. I breathed him in. His heart pounded against my cheek, a furious rhythm that matched my own.

"You're alive," I whispered. "I thought..."

Thorne's hand came up to cradle the back of my head, his fingers tangling in my hair. "You said we need more time. I couldn't deny you that."

But the moment was fleeting, shattered by Archer's urgent shout from the hilltop. "Move your asses, they're coming!"

Reality crashed back in with the distant shouts of the guards. We ran, Thorne's hand gripping mine, our feet pounding against the earth as we raced up the hill. My lungs burned, my legs ached, but I pushed on, fueled by a desperate need to put as much distance as possible between us and the horrors of the camp.

Archer and Harlow had the horses ready, dancing nervously, ears flicking back and forth at the commotion rising from below. Thorne practically tossed me into the saddle before swinging up behind me, his strong arms encircling my waist as he grabbed the reins.

We tore out of there like Hell Hounds were snapping at our heels. The horses' hooves thundered against the ground. The wind whipped at our faces. Low-hanging branches snatched at our clothes, leaves blinding us in a whirl of green and brown. But we didn't slow. Didn't dare.

I clung to the saddle horn. It was only when the horses began to falter, their sides heaving and lathered with sweat, that Thorne finally reined us to a stop in a small, sheltered clearing. I slid from the saddle on shaky legs, my heart still racing.

Thorne dismounted beside me. His hand immediately found mine and our fingers laced together as if afraid to let go. Archer and Harlow and Jasper gathered close, their faces drawn and haunted in the dappled forest light.

"We'll stop only long enough to let the horses rest. We're going to have to push them hard. We'll tell everyone we were ambushed by the Lord of the Salt on the road and lost everything. Jasper, you can't be seen returning with us. You're going to have to hide outside of the city until I send someone to come get you. And then you bunker down. You can't go back to the house. You might have to room with Tuck at his place for a while."

I couldn't help but circle the burning questions in my mind as Thorne processed our next moves. Questions I was too afraid to ask. To speak aloud as if it would shatter this common devotion between us. But how had he done it? How had he faced over twenty Cimmerian guards and walked out of there? So far, he'd said nothing of his identity. Wasn't concerned at all about the fact that he'd been seen. Which meant he'd either killed them all or... no, there was no alternative. The few guards left standing were only those few that'd been left outside and could have never seen our faces, only our backs.

We rode through the night, the darkness broken only by slivers of moonlight filtering through the clouds. Thorne's solid presence at my back was a comfort, his arms a protective cage around me as we swayed with the horse's gait. The adrenaline of our narrow escape had long since faded, replaced by a bone-deep weariness, but still, we pressed on.

As the first pale fingers of dawn began to paint the eastern sky in delicate shades of pink and gold, the air grew lighter, and I settled into a state of cautious relief. We'd made it through the night.

Ahead, rising from the morning mist, the outline of the city walls took shape. Stirling. And I never thought I'd be so happy to see a city I hated more than anything. We left Jasper and all the horses behind as planned and crept into the city with nothing but each other. The Parlor was a welcomed sight. Our bed, heaven, as we both crawled in, bodies leaden.

I drifted into a fitful sleep, my mind still reeling from the events of the past day. At first, there was only darkness. A blessed emptiness that promised respite from the chaos and terror. But then, slowly, insidiously, the nightmare began to take shape.

It started with a sound. A steady, rhythmic ticking, like the beating of a monstrous heart. Filling my ears, growing louder and louder until it drowned out everything else. I stood in a vast, shadowy hall, the walls lined with countless clocks of every shape and size. Grandfather clocks loomed like ancient sentinels, their pendulums swinging in eerie unison. And everywhere, that incessant ticking pounded against my skull.

As I moved deeper into the hall, the clocks began to change. Their pristine faces cracked and splintered, oozing thick, crimson blood that dripped onto the floor in glistening puddles. The ticking grew erratic. Grating. A cacophony of broken gears sank into my mind and squeezed until I couldn't breathe or think beyond the pain.

I stumbled through the nightmarish hall, hands pressed over my ears in a vain attempt to block out the maddening ticking. But as I moved, the clocks began to change, twisting into grotesque imitations of the people I'd met here.

Harlow's face appeared on a small, delicate mantel clock, her usually vibrant blue eyes now dull and lifeless, staring accusingly at me from behind a cracked glass face while crimson tears leaked, leaving glistening trails down her beautiful cheeks.

Beside her, Archer's likeness sat within a towering grandfather clock, his features contorted in a silent scream, mouth stretched abnormally wide in agony. His hands, once so steady and sure with a blade, were now gnarled and broken, reaching out from the splintered wood as if pleading for help that would never come.

With each step, another familiar face appeared. Tuck, Jasper, Rosy, Briony... even Thorne, face twisted in pain on a cuckoo clock with a little bird that burst from his chest, a blackened, twisted thing with razor sharp talons.

The ticking grew to a sickening crescendo, the jagged, inharmonious sounds clashing and crashing against each other in a maddening symphony. I clapped my hands over my ears, trying desperately to block out the noise, but it seeped through my fingers.

And then, with a final, resounding clang, the clocks stopped.

Silence fell over the hall. Suffocating. Thick and heavy, it pressed down on me until I could scarcely draw breath. My heart raced, the only sound in the sudden quiet. One by one the figures fell, like marionettes with their strings cut, until the hall was littered with the bodies of everyone I'd grown to care about in Wisteria. Glassy eyes stared sightlessly at the vaulted ceiling, mouths frozen in silent screams.

As I stood there, a small figure emerged from the shadows at the far end of the hall. Quill stumbled forward, tiny hands outstretched, grasping at the air as if trying to reach me, her wild curly hair matted with blood.

"You left me! You promised you'd protect me, but you left me! And then you fell in love. You forgot *him* and fell in love with another. Will you forget me too? Mother?"

Guilt and anguish ripped through my chest, stealing the breath from my lungs as I tried to move, to run to her, to gather her small, broken body in my arms and beg for forgiveness. But my feet were rooted to the ground.

I fought and fought until a deep voice, an urgent voice of steel and reason cut through the nightmare, yanking me back to reality.

Thorne looked down at me wide-eyed. "Okay?"

I nodded, ignoring the tear that slipped free as I gulped down air.

"That's the first nightmare you've had in a while."

"Because I'm running out of time," I whispered, ignoring the fact that Vesalia was the real culprit behind that special fucking brand of torment.

54

With the rising of the sun and the reality that another day had passed, I snuck out of bed, gathered my leathers and my sword, and crept downstairs to the bathroom. I washed my hair, scrubbed the dirt and grime from every crevice, brushed my teeth, braided my hair, and dressed. I thought I'd get away without his protest, but as I swung the door open, he was there, leaning against the opposite wall, arms folded over his chest.

"Going somewhere, Paesha darling?"

"I have to go to the Vale and meet Alastor. And before you say anything, I need you to know that it kills me, too. If I could find a way to put these worlds together, I would. I don't want you to have to leave them, Thorne. And I don't want to have to leave you. But those are the choices right now. Maybe. If we're lucky. But there's a little girl that needs me. She needs me far more than you do. And even if I hadn't made a foolish deal with the Keeper, I would still have to go."

He stared at me for a long time, eyes shifting between mine, likely studying every shade of green and blue he could find within their depths as he heard the words repeated in his mind.

"Tell me about her," he said, taking my hand. "Come. Sit with me and tell me about your girl."

I let Thorne lead me to a small sitting area. He kept my hand clasped in his, his thumb tracing soothing circles on my skin as he waited patiently for me to gather my thoughts and open up about something I'd kept guarded, as if I were protecting her somehow.

"Her name is Quill. She's not my daughter by blood, but... but I love her as if she were my own flesh and bone." I closed my eyes for a moment, picturing Quill's cherubic face, her wild riot of dark curls, the way her eyes sparkled with mischief and intelligence far beyond her tender years. "I worked in a place called Misery's End for a wretched man called the Maestro. He owned a dark burlesque show and was Requiem's greatest crime lord. He had the power to bind me to him if he could ever catch me in a bargain. But I was smart. Even when I'd been stabbed and lost my ability to ever have children, he tried. He purchased Quill from a brothel owner to dangle her in front of me like bait. But I didn't take the deal. I refused him. The Syndicate and I, those are my friends, we rallied around her and raised her, protected her as best we could from him. I ended up bound to him for another reason." I closed my eyes, trying to remember why. Drawing a steadying breath as if it would come to me, letting the words flow, grasping at each one until they made sense. "I loved another man. And I bargained my freedom to the Maestro to save his life. He died, and I was bound anyway. I'd missed the loophole in the bargain."

As I spoke the words aloud, Thorne's grip tightened on my fingers. As if he could anchor me, save me from the sad memories. I opened my eyes to find his tracing every inch of my face.

"I have to go back. I have to complete the bargain with Alastor and I'm running out of time, Thorne. I'm sorry."

He closed his arms around me, pulling me to his chest. "I know I should have a thousand questions for you, but none feel like they matter right now. If she's important to you, then she's important to me, too. The rest can wait until later. We'll find a way. I promised. But going to Alastor before you have a name is pointless. He won't let you out of the bargain."

"I have a name," I confessed.

He drew back. "You never told me."

"Believe me, there hasn't been time."

"Are you going to tell me who it is?"

"I'm afraid to give it to another person, just in case it breaks the magic or the bargain somehow."

"Okay. That's smart. Let me get washed up and changed and we'll go together."

"Thorne, he hates you. I really think I need to go by myself."

"We don't play with the gods by ourselves, Paesha darling. Give me fifteen minutes and I'll be ready to go."

"HE WAITS OUTSIDE," Alastor said, brows lowered, his handsome, godly face stern as he glared at Thorne but refused to speak to him.

Thorne adjusted the sleeve of his suit jacket casually. "I won't touch a thing, Al. Pinky promise."

Alastor's tattoos whirled and writhed along his arms and neck. "You want to know what I think you can do with your promises? Or shall I start making some of my own with our lovely Paesha?"

Thorne's calm stature wavered, that tiny tic in his jaw betraying his ease. For a long, tense moment, he held Alastor's gaze, a silent battle of wills playing out between them. The air crackled with barely restrained power causing the hair on my neck to stand on end, the ancient god and the puzzling man locked in a stalemate. Finally, with a curt nod, Thorne stepped back.

I turned to Alastor. "Lead the way."

With a final, pointed look at Thorne, Alastor spun and strode down the main hall of the Vale, his long strides carrying him past the masked merchants and silent lords mulling about. I hurried to keep pace as he turned just past his office door and led me deeper into his dark world.

The narrow corridor twisted and turned, the air growing colder with each step. Sconces flickered to life as we passed, acutely reminding me of the magical fire that'd saved my life, freed me from a piece of the Keeper's bargain and maybe singed a part of my soul. I wanted to ask. To know what that power was. How a God of Lost and Broken things could heal poison, but those questions were not burning. Not yet. Perhaps when I had the fourth and final name and I could be done with this god, I would find the courage to ask.

We descended a winding staircase, our footsteps echoing in the heavy silence. The air grew musty and damp. Ancient and forgotten. What secrets lay buried in the bowels of the Vale, hidden away from prying eyes?

At the bottom of the stairs, we came to a door, scarred and pitted with age. Alastor placed his palm against the weathered wood and murmured something under his breath until the tattoos hidden beneath his sleeve crept over his hand and whispered across the door like smoke. It swung inward on protesting hinges.

Alastor stepped aside, motioning for me to enter. "After you."

I walked into the cavernous room, eyes widening as I took in the wonders laid out like scattered traps luring me forward. The space seemed to stretch on forever, the far walls lost in shadow. Towering shelves lined the room, crammed with a quirky assortment of objects. Ancient tomes bound in cracked leather, jars filled with shimmering liquids, ornate boxes carved with intricate symbols, weapons of every description from crude stone blades to gleaming swords. Shattered mirrors and clocks with no arms.

I moved deeper into the room, each step light and careful, as though I was performing on a sacred stage, though no audience watched, save for the towering god at my back. I couldn't explain the draw to dance, to move. As if something in this hidden treasure recognized a piece of me that'd been missing since I stepped into Wisteria.

Nearby, a shattered mirror caught my attention, reflecting fragmented glimpses of mismatched eyes, of myself, some younger, some older, some not me at all. They whispered of lives I hadn't lived, or maybe ones I already had.

The quiet song of a violin filled the air, the melody haunting and sweet. And there, draped over a forgotten throne, was a wedding dress, its lace frayed and stained red. So still yet filled with the ghosts of an unfinished waltz. Everything around me hummed with a quiet energy, aching to be remembered, to be held. And I could feel it all, the push, the pull. I held back, afraid of the danger that would come from touching a god's treasure.

"Don't touch anything," Alastor warned as if he knew my mind. Though I supposed, as a touch of his power coursed through my veins, maybe he knew the unexplainable pull to random items.

"You feel it, Huntress, don't you? The power of curiosity. The draw to the lost. The mark of my power?"

I nodded. "The first time we met, you said 'born of two, loved by two, your reincarnated soul descended. Not the body.

Not the blood.' What did you mean? Because a goddess told me your blood runs through my veins. But that's not true, is it?"

"It is not," he said, walking forward to collect a shattered hourglass, letting the fragments of bones slip through his fingers and onto the floor. "Your soul carries your power, not your blood." He glared at me with those dark, dangerous eyes. "Do not learn this lesson the hard way, as your past lives have done. Never trust a god. Not one."

"But why would she lie?"

"One can never be too sure of a god's motive. But you're... unique. A rare soul descendant, not a blood descendant. There is a difference. You're likely the blood descendant of some bastard who stumbled into a whore house hundreds of years ago in the realm you were born to, but your soul is older. More. The Huntress and the Hunted. Fated and damned."

"My soul carries my power. Not my blood?"

"As is the case for most of the prophesied, but that's not why you're here, is it? You've brought me a name. The first of four."

I nodded.

Alastor stepped closer, his dark eyes glittering with an unnerving intensity. He seemed to loom larger, the shadows in the room deepening, gathering around him like a living cloak. They struck hard and fast, winding around my wrists and ankles, swirling over my neck, lifting me off the ground.

Alastor circled me, his footsteps a slow, deliberate cadence. He leaned in close and whispered in a language I couldn't understand. The words were liquid and dark, flowing over me like black silk, leaving a prick of bliss in their wake, a sense of comfort mingling with fear. There was power in those syllables, ancient and primal.

"Give the name to my Remnants," Alastor commanded, his voice a low rumble that resonated through my chest. "Speak it aloud and let them taste it on your tongue."

I swallowed hard, my mouth suddenly dry. The Remnants pulsed eagerly, their inky tendrils curling around my jaw, tracing the seam of my lips as if in anticipation. For only a second, I tasted the tang of betrayal.

"Harlow Bramwell."

The Remnants pulsed. Then sank into the sensitive flesh on my neck just behind my ear, jolting through my veins. Then they were gone as fast as they'd come. I dropped to the hard floor in a heap, blinking, willing the room to come into focus.

"Will you..." I swallowed. "Will you fix her?"

Alastor tsked, walking close enough his boots filled my vision. "No."

A sudden burst of golden light filled the room, blinding me, searing my retinas and forcing my eyes shut. It grew brighter and brighter until I felt it seeping into my skin, my bones, my very soul.

With a gasp, I was yanked out of the dark chamber and into a vision so vivid, so visceral, it stole the breath from my lungs. Gone were the towering shelves of lost treasures, the watchful god, and the weight of ancient power. In their place was a world of blinding white snow, crimson blood and bitter cold.

Snowflakes nestled on half-open lids as I lay in the arms of a man I loved, staring into his bewitching, distraught face as he rocked me back and forth. Thorne. Beautiful, broken Thorne. The frigid air seared my lungs and heat leached from my body, replaced by a bone-deep chill that left me shivering violently. My arms were too heavy, as if the world was pulling me down and every breath was a battle against it, each one weaker than the last. Thorne's warmth was the only thing left in a world turned cold. My vision blurred with pain and tears.

"Please. Please, Winter, don't go."

My heart twisted. I didn't want this. His memory. But I couldn't pull myself out of the vision no matter how hard I fought against the violation. What kind of sick and twisted game was Alastor playing at? Because I was her. His beloved. And he was fighting a losing battle.

The world was already slipping away.

He pressed his hand harder against my side, trying to stanch the flow of blood, but it poured through his fingers. His face twisted with grief, with terror, and his voice... so low, so broken, was barely more than a whisper. "Please," he begged, his lips brushing against my forehead as his tears fell, warm and wet against my skin. "Please don't leave me. Not like this."

His words were thick with despair, and my heart twisted painfully in my chest. I wanted to stay. I wanted to promise him I wouldn't leave, to reach up and wipe the tears from his beautiful face, to tell him everything would be okay, but I couldn't move. My body, her body, was a weight I could no longer control. The cold had claimed me. All I could do was look up at him as my vision blurred and his face grew dim.

"Please, please..." Thorne's voice broke, shattering like fragile glass. His fingers trembled as he held me, as if the sheer force of his will could keep my soul tethered here, keep me alive a little longer. "Don't you fucking die. That's not how this was supposed to go. We need more time."

His forehead pressed against mine. And the way he shook? Like the world was crumbling around him. He kissed my hair, my cheeks, my forehead. Each touch was frantic. His tears fell faster now, splashing hot onto my skin. I was so cold, I barely felt them anymore.

"I'll fix this," he sobbed. "I'll fix you. Just... stay with me. Please, just stay."

I wanted to stay. Gods, I wanted to stay with him, but I couldn't. My breaths were slowing, the rise and fall of my chest growing fainter, and I could feel the moment he realized it. His body tensed, his grip tightening like he could pull me back from the edge, but we both knew.

"Thorne," I tried to whisper, but it was nothing more than a breath, lost in the wind.

"No, no, no," he chanted.

I felt his heart breaking, heard it in every tremor of his voice, every gasping breath he took as he rocked me gently in his arms. The warmth faded from his touch, the sound of his voice grew dimmer, and the light slipped from the world.

I wanted to tell him she loved him, that even though I wasn't truly her, I felt every piece of his agony and her unyielding devotion. I felt it in every tear that had soaked into my skin, in every word he whispered like a prayer.

But it was too late. I was already gone, and the last thing I saw was the look on his face, twisted with pain, shattered by grief. The last thing I heard was his roaring scream, promising revenge.

55

With a sudden, jarring wrench, the vision of Winter's death dissolved, the icy landscape shattering into a million glittering shards that rained down around me before fading into nothingness. I found myself sprawled on the cold stone floor of Alastor's hidden chamber.

With a groan, I pushed myself up on shaking arms. He'd loved her so thoroughly, so perfectly. And somehow I had to walk out of this room, look him in the face as if I knew nothing, as if I hadn't violated a sacred, precious memory of his, and carry on about my day.

Alastor watched me with an unreadable expression. He'd loosened his tie and rolled his sleeves, sitting back against a table with his arms crossed over his chest.

"Why? Why force me to witness his pain, his loss?"

He tilted his head. "I didn't choose what you were shown, Huntress. The Remnants can be quite ruthless when it comes to memories."

"But they weren't *my* memories, and that's fucked up. But

let me guess, such is the way of gods. I seriously hate you all so much."

He smirked. "She does learn."

I glared. "I have the name of another broken soul to give you. Do you want it, or are we going to continue these ceaseless lessons?"

The plan was dangerous. But if Harlow was broken because of her lost power, then maybe Jasper was a lost soul as well. Maybe the realm was crawling with them and I could end this bargain today.

Alastor pushed off the table and strode over to me, narrowing his eyes. "Give me the name."

"Don't you want to send your Remnants to violate my personal space first, or was that just for fun?"

"The name, Huntress," he demanded.

"Jasper Boon."

He dropped his chin to his chest and scowled. "Jasper Boon is not a broken soul. He's nothing more than a clumsy fool and mediocre cook. Consider this your first and last warning. Lie to me again, and I'll make you wish you'd died from that poison."

I HADN'T LOOKED Thorne in the eye the whole way back. And based on his lingering stares, the throat he cleared a thousand times, and the tension building between us, I could tell that it was making him crazy. But there were no words. There was nothing I could say that wouldn't just be hurtful. I would guard that memory of his with my whole heart.

"So, who was it?"

Winter's frozen fingers flashed into my mind. I shook the image away. "Who was what?"

"The broken soul," he said, unlocking the Parlor's door and pushing it open so I could enter first.

"Harlow," I said with a heavy sigh. "And before you ask, he never meant to mend her. I'd hoped he would, but he only took down her name."

He walked straight to the bar and poured two drinks. "But if she was one, then—"

"I tried. I gave him Jasper's name and pissed him off."

"He is a moody fucker. All right, so that's one down, three to go. How'd you figure out Harlow?" He held the glass out to me.

"Can we maybe eat something before we get morning drunk? I mean, I'm not judging, but I'll be asleep in an hour if I drink that right now."

"Oh, we're making smart decisions today. Perfect. Let's head over to the house, grab something to eat, and see if we can catch Tuck. You can tell me about Harlow on the way."

"There's not much to tell. Apparently, when broken people are in a low state of mind, their aura sort of glows black if their soul is broken. I saw it on our trip."

He shook his head, leading me back out the door. "Doesn't really give us anything solid to search for unless we want to start hanging around the graveyard."

I drew back. "Are you ever shocked by your logical thinking or are you so used to yourself you don't recognize the genius in that mind of yours?"

"I don't... I'm not—"

"It was a rhetorical question, Thorne. Don't ruin it with an answer."

He nodded, swiping his fingers through his hair and grinned until his dimple showed. I couldn't hide my smile as I slid my fingers through his and we walked back to the house. That damn smile of his called to my soul, and he had no idea. But to be fair, I'd only just now realized.

WE'D BEEN at the house for hours. The Salt had rallied around the children, taking turns with the little ones as Briony established a schedule. They used the dining room for learning, the study for nap time, and they'd split the chores. It felt like the Syndicate house in Requiem. Where everyone knew their role, everyone had a job, and things got done with ease. They'd even planned for a garden and several members of the Fray had committed to collecting seeds from the unsuspecting Silk they worked for. All with Briony at the helm, sliding into a role she was born for, it seemed.

"We were at the Vale today," Thorne was telling Tuck, who sat in the kitchen with his hands wrapped around a steaming cup of tea, the only sign of his torture, the one jagged scar running from his ashy brown hairline to his brow. "Barrows was down there, dealing with a masked jeweler. Know anything about it?"

"We're testing him out. Either Alastor hasn't caught on that Barrows is working for us, or he's taken a liking to our Paesha and he's giving us the in to trade directly. If I had to guess, I'd say it's the latter. When's the last time Alastor didn't know what was happening in the Vale?"

Thorne nodded, leaning against the counter with his arms crossed, a hand towel tossed over his shoulder from when he was drying dishes. "That was my guess, too. We need to make sure Briony has everything she needs for the kids. Have Barrows start coming by to check on her."

"You shifting the chain of command, boss?"

They exchanged a glance. Something so subtle I don't think anyone but me picked up on it. "There's something else that needs my attention right now. I'm hoping I can count on you and Archer to head the Fray, get yourselves organized, keep the wheels rolling."

Tuck's eyes flashed to where I stood at the sink, and guilt flooded me. But I had to be selfish, no matter what he thought.

"It's a smart move," Tuck said, surprising me. "If you pull back from the Parlor and make it obvious your marriage is your priority, the heat will likely fade. We can move easier if that happens."

"Jasper should be coming into the city with Walters later today. Archer was supposed to let him know last night on his way home. I want everyone to lay low for a while. Do nothing unless we're desperate. No missions, no heists, no jobs at the Parlor. Everything is by the books until I say otherwise. Do what we must to survive, and nothing more. Farris is up to something dangerous."

Tuck sighed. "Who's going to let Archer know?"

As if on cue, the kitchen door swung open. "Let Archer know what?" he said, strolling in, snatching a coin he'd tossed from the air, only to flip it again. "Oh, sorry, everyone. I didn't realize we were having a meeting today. Har!" he called over his shoulder. "Meeting in the kitchen."

"Well, it's an impromptu meeting, but pull up a seat."

Harlow strode into the kitchen, eyes tired, but her dress was as perfect as her posture. "Do we have news?"

"I have some where you're concerned." Thorne tossed the towel from his shoulder, and walked to the center island, leaning against it as he stood across from her. "The Story Snatcher was in the Vale this morning."

I was certain everyone could hear my tiny gasp at his admittance, though no one turned. Thorne hadn't mentioned that little tidbit to me. But there'd been no child in the Vale that I'd noticed. Unless I had it wrong and it wasn't that creepy boy I'd met my first hours in Wisteria. Or maybe the Story Snatcher changed forms.

Thorne continued. "While Paesha was in her meeting with Alastor, he and I had a talk. You don't have to answer this now, certainly not with an audience. But the choice is yours. As of this morning, Willard no longer remembers the Fray. His view of us aligns with the rest of the Silk. He has no memory of it. Not a single mission."

She stumbled back in shock. "I didn't mean—"

"You know him better than we do, and you don't trust him. Which means, we can't either, even if he's made some great choices for us in the past. We have to do what's best for these children, Har. I know he's a decent man with good intentions, but that's not enough. It's never going to be enough."

She nodded slowly. "Okay."

"He still remembers you. None of that was touched, unless it was tied up with the Fray, and if it was, those memories were replaced with half truths. Just enough for him to believe himself disconnected from the Lord of the Salt. However, if you wish to break away from him, you're free to do that now. There's no threat to us."

Harlow's entire posture changed. She grew inches. Color blanched her cheeks. Tired eyes opened. She was free. Thorne had freed her from a man that'd weighed her down so thoroughly, she'd grown to know nothing else. She didn't hide the tears as she flew across the kitchen and threw herself into his arms. "Thank you. Oh, gods. Thank you. I was so tired of burning."

"I'm still going to call him Wee Willy," Archer mumbled.

"Well, it's not a lie," Harlow said matter-of-factly, and walked out of the kitchen beaming when her brother groaned and covered his ears.

Hours later, Larcan, the fiddle player, tapped his foot in the corner of the study as Lianna and two of the other children danced around me. It wasn't quite ballet, but they were trying, and dance was my second language. One I'd almost stopped speaking. Harlow and Briony were taking turns reading books to some of the little ones, and Archer hunched in the corner with Reuben and two other men as they explained to the boy Maid Marian. But Archer had secretly already taught Reuben how to play, and they'd won three consecutive hands.

Watching the children dance and laugh, seeing the Fray bond with the children, my heart swelled with a bittersweet happiness. This crew had become so special to me in such a short time. The thought of leaving them behind tore at my soul a bit, but it also felt like a sliver of a conclusion. As if all of this was pushing me toward the end of the path. Each of these things we'd done had been for Thorne's cause and were, in turn, a step on the path.

As if sensing my mood, Thorne glanced at me over the paper he was reading. "Five more minutes with our favorite dancer, ladies," he told the children. "Then, I'm afraid we need to get going."

I smiled at him and turned back to the eager faces of Lianna and the other girls. "All right, my little ballerinas, let's make these last few minutes count, shall we?"

As I clapped my hands, Larcan struck up a lively tune on his fiddle. "First position, arms rounded, chins up!" I called out. The girls scrambled into place, spines straight as arrows, toes pointed.

I walked among them, gently adjusting an elbow here, tilting a chin there. "Remember, grace comes from the core. Imagine a string pulling up from the top of your head, elongating your neck." I demonstrated, and they followed, looks of intense concentration on their small faces.

"Now plié... and relevé!" They bent their knees in unison, then rose up on their toes, arms floating at their sides. "Beautiful! You're all naturals," I praised.

Their faces glowed with pride and joy as they moved to the music, leaping and twirling with abandon. For a moment, the darkness of the world fell away, and there was only the pure innocence of orphaned children.

We left in a flurry of 'goodbyes' and 'see you soons'. The warm evening air carried us all the way back to the Parlor. We passed Tuck at the door. He dipped his chin and shared a wink with Thorne and kept walking as if we hadn't seen him at all.

An eerie silence greeted us within the Parlor, broken only by the haunting melody of a lone violinist perched on the stage. The usual din of chatter, clinking glasses and raucous laughter was conspicuously absent.

I glanced around, unease prickling along my spine. Something was wrong. And we'd wasted hours of this day at the house. The gaming tables stood abandoned, their felted tops bare of cards and coin. The bar, usually a hub of activity, was deserted.

Thorne's hand found the small of my back, a reassuring touch that did little to quell the growing sense of wrongness.

"Where is everyone? It's never this empty in the evening."

"Tomorrow, we do everything we can to get you home. We'll perch at the graveyard and can even go to a temple if we need to. But we don't need to live every moment at the edge of our seats." He turned to me, cupping my face in his hands as he looked down. "What if there's only passage for one on whatever your path is? What if I can't go? What if the gods decide they need me here more than there? I know you want to go. You think you have to. But give me one single night to convince you to stay."

I gazed up into his eyes, every emotion surging through me. He didn't understand. I'd told him everything and still he hadn't understood.

"Thorne, I..." My voice trailed off, the words sticking in my throat.

He leaned down, his forehead pressing against mine. "Just one night, Paesha darling. That's all I ask. Let me give you a reason to stay."

I closed my eyes, taking a deep breath as I completely lied to him. "Okay. You have one night to convince me."

56

A faint strain of music drifted through the Parlor. Thorne led me to the center of the empty gaming hall, his hand warm and steady in mine. He pulled me close, one arm encircling my waist as the other held my hand against his chest.

We swayed to the gentle tune. Our bodies moved in perfect sync while the world around us faded away until there was nothing but the music, the dance, and the heat of Thorne's body pressed against mine. I rested my cheek against his chest, breathing him in.

For a moment, I allowed myself to let go and imagine a life here with Thorne. A life free from the burdens and expectations of the knowledge and memories I carried. And those that eluded me. A life where I could wake up every morning in his arms, where we could build a future together. It was a beautiful dream, but that's all it could ever be.

He tightened his hold on me as he whispered, "Stay with me. Right here in this room. Don't let that beautiful mind of yours wander quite yet. Let me paint the picture.

"Imagine waking up every morning in our bed, tangled in sheets with the sun streaming through the windows. I'd pull you close and kiss you softly, savoring the feeling of your warm skin against mine. We'd linger there. We'd worship each other. I would love you, Paesha. I would love you flawlessly.

"Eventually, we'd make our way downstairs to steaming cups of coffee. The orphans would come running in, their faces bright with smiles and laughter as they told us about their dreams and plans for the day. We'd sit together, one big happy family, sharing stories and reveling in simple joys.

"After, you'd go to check on the older children's studies and training while I met with Tuck and Archer to discuss business. But it would be different from now, less danger, more focus on helping the Salt and building a brighter future for Stirling."

He paused, twirling me away with the crescendo of the song, letting his beautiful story wash over me until he pulled me close again, lifting my chin until I stared into his eyes. "And at the end of the night, we would crawl back into our bed, lost in each other once more. I would worship every inch of your body, trailing kisses along your soft skin until you trembled beneath my touch.

"I'd take my time, savoring the taste of you, the sounds you made. My hands would map these beautiful curves of your body, committing every sigh, every gasp, every shiver to memory. I'd tease you, stoking the embers of your desire until they burst into flames.

"When you were aching for more, when you begged me with these enchanting eyes, I'd finally give in. I'd settle between your thighs, and with excruciating slowness, I'd make you mine." He trailed his hands down my arms. "We'd move together until the world shattered around us. I cannot give you the worlds, Paesha darling. But I can give you ecstasy." He paused, though the song hadn't ended. "Let me worship you. Let me show you that I can be enough."

I met his intense gaze. "Actions speak louder than words. Show me."

"Leave us," he ordered the violinist, his voice a low rumble against my mouth. The music cut off abruptly and hurried footsteps retreated, the door closing with a soft click.

Something flared in Thorne's eyes, hot and hungry. With a low growl, he claimed my mouth in a searing kiss. His tongue delved deep, tangling with mine in a dance as old as time. I clung to him, my fingers tangling in his hair, holding him to me as if letting go would mean letting it all go, and I wasn't ready for that moment just yet.

Without breaking the kiss, Thorne lifted me from the ground. I wrapped my legs around his waist as he carried me across the Parlor, setting me down on the edge of the bar. He broke the kiss, his breathing heavy as he rested his forehead against mine. "Stand on the bar," he commanded.

I did as ordered, moving to my feet to stare down at him. He pulled a chair over, flipped it around and rested his arms on the back as he sat, eyes never leaving mine. "Undress for me."

I met his unwavering gaze with steel in my veins as I tucked my thumbs into my pants. Slowly, teasingly, I pulled, letting the fabric slip down my legs to pool at my feet. My shirt followed seconds later. Thorne's stare was molten as it raked over my body, taking in every newly exposed inch of skin. Thorne's hands clenched the arm of his chair, but he made no move to touch me, content for now, to simply watch. My skin flushed and tingled under the heat of his gaze.

"You're exquisite. A goddess made flesh."

"It's too bad you sent the musician away. I would have danced for you."

He lowered his chin. "Do it anyway."

And so I did. Swaying my hips in a slow, sensual rhythm, my bare feet gliding across the smooth wood of the bar top. The air was electric against my naked skin as Thorne watched me with rapt attention, his eyes dark with desire.

I lifted my arms above my head, letting my fingertips trail down my own body, feeling the intensity of his gaze like a flame against my skin. "Like this?"

His jaw tightened, but his eyes remained fixed on mine, unwavering. "Perfect. Don't stop."

So I didn't. I spun slowly, giving him a long, deliberate view as I ran my hands down my waist, my hips rolling to a rhythm that was made just for us. I felt myself losing any sense of the room, lost in the thrill of his attention. Holding a steady rhythm as I moved, I slid my fingers down and down, imagining they were his as I held eye contact with him and lowered myself toward the bar, twisting, bending, sitting so I could spread my legs and watch him jerk with surprise.

"You're torturing me, you know that?" he said, his voice low, dangerous.

"I thought you could handle a little torture."

"Careful, darling. You're playing with fire."

I smiled, letting my eyes fall to his lips. "It's fine. I prefer the heat."

A slow smile spread across his face as he leaned in, his eyes filled with promise.

He crooked a finger. "Come here."

I stepped down, walking toward him, my hips swinging with each step. He spun the chair around, sitting down again, and when I was close enough to touch he reached out and grasped my hips, pulling me to stand naked between his spread thighs. His hands skimmed up my sides, fingers dragging deliciously against my sensitive skin, until he cupped my breasts.

Pressing a gentle kiss to my navel, he rolled my nipples

between his fingers, tugging gently, and I arched into his touch with a soft moan as sparks of pleasure shot straight to my core.

"So responsive," Thorne praised. One hand slid down my stomach to delve between my thighs and he groaned when he found me already wet and wanting. "Good girl." He grabbed my leg and lifted, propping my foot on his knee as he kissed my inner thigh, that stubble of his brushing against my resolve. "Now tell me this is only mine."

"So demanding."

I gasped as he circled my clit with a finger.

He surged to his feet, claiming my mouth in another searing kiss as he walked, him forward and me backwards. The edge of a gaming table hit the backs of my thighs and Thorne lifted me effortlessly to perch on the felt covered surface.

Cool air kissed my heated skin. He urged me to lay back on the red felted top that was soft beneath me, a decadent contrast to Thorne's rough hands as they mapped my body, leaving trails of tingling awareness in their wake.

He kissed a path down my neck, pausing to suck at a point of my shoulder that had me clutching at his hair and arching off the table, seeking more of his touch. His lips continued their journey south. His mouth trailed kisses of fire in its wake as he lavished attention on my breasts, drawing each aching peak into his hot mouth in turn. He kept moving down until he paused at the scar on my abdomen. I thought for a second it would be over. That he'd remember what that wound meant for me and my future, but instead, he brushed the most tender of kisses over the slightly raised flesh, smoothing it with a finger, and then continued moving down. When he finally reached the center, I trembled with need, my core throbbing and slick with desire.

"Look at you, spread out for me like a feast," Thorne murmured against me. "Tell me, do you still taste like sin?"

And then his mouth was on me. His tongue tasting me as I bucked against him. He held me down on the card table, gripping my hips. He worshiped me with his mouth. Sucking and licking and thrusting until stars burst behind my eyelids and I cried out my release.

"That's it, darling," he praised, working me through the aftershocks. "Let go for me. Only me."

When I finally floated back down, body limp and sated, Thorne was there, gathering me into his arms and kissing me deeply, letting me taste myself on his tongue. The hard length of him pressed insistently against my thigh and I reached between us, intent on returning the favor, but he caught my wrist.

"Not yet," he growled. "I'm not done with you."

In one smooth motion, he flipped me over onto my stomach. Thorne's hands skimmed down my back to grab my hips.

"You have the most spectacular ass, and I've been forced to stare at it in my shirt for far too long without touching." He gave it an appreciative squeeze before landing a sharp smack that made me yelp and arch into his touch.

"Such a good girl, taking what I give you." Thorne soothed the reddened flesh with his palm before trailing his fingers through my legs. "You're so wet for me, aren't you, darling?"

There was a brief rustle of fabric as he freed himself from his trousers, and then he was there, the thick head of his cock nudging my entrance.

Thorne's voice was a low rumble. "Tell me you want this, wife. Tell me you need me like I need you."

I moaned, pressing my ass against him, desperate for more. "I'll tell you whatever you want, just... please."

With a low growl, he surged forward, burying himself to the hilt. I cried out at the stretch, clenching around him as he filled me so completely.

Thorne groaned, his fingers digging into the flesh of my hips as he held himself still. I whimpered. Bent over the card table, I leaned, rocking back on my heels, silently begging him to move. And then he did, pulling nearly all the way out before slamming back in, setting a punishing pace. The table creaked beneath us. The plush red felt rubbed deliciously against my sensitive nipples with each powerful thrust, the dual sensations sending sparks of pleasure zinging through my veins.

He slid a hand in my hair and tugged, pulling my head back as he snapped his hips forward again and again, driving into me with a primal urgency. Each powerful thrust sent shockwaves of pleasure radiating through my body, building and building until I was teetering on the edge of oblivion.

"That's it, darling." His voice strained with the effort of holding back his own release.

I shattered. Fluttering and spasming as ecstasy crashed over me in wave after blissful wave. Thorne's rhythm faltered, his hips stuttering as my climax triggered his own. With a guttural groan, he buried himself to the hilt, spilling deep inside me as he chanted my name like a reverent prayer.

We stayed like that for a long moment, both of us struggling to catch our breath. Eventually, Thorne pulled out, leaving me feeling empty and aching in the best possible way. I turned to face him and he pulled me to my feet, hugging me, claiming my mouth in a languid kiss, pouring every ounce of tenderness and affection into the slow slide of his lips over mine.

"Stay with me."

I said nothing, lost in the bliss of the moment as he lifted and carried me up the stairs, his steady heartbeat lulling me into a state of drowsy contentment. He shouldered open the door to his office and crossed to the bed, laying me down with a gentleness that contradicted the raw passion of our moment downstairs.

Thorne crawled in behind me. He pulled the blanket up and

his arm snaked around my waist, pulling me back against his chest until there wasn't an inch of space between us, skin to skin from head to toe.

I sighed, melting into his embrace.

He nuzzled into the crook of my neck, his lips grazing the sensitive skin there. I shivered, arching into his touch as his hand slid up my side, fingers tracing patterns on my skin. Slowly, he brushed my hair aside, exposing my neck to his wandering mouth. He pressed a soft kiss just below my ear and then froze. I felt his breath hitch, his body going rigid behind me.

"What is this?"

Confused, I tilted my head, trying to see what had caught his attention. "What's what?"

His finger traced a spot behind my ear, sending a jolt of strange energy through me. "This tattoo. A snowflake. When did you get it?"

I frowned, reaching up to feel the skin he'd touched. It tingled beneath my fingertips. "Very funny. I think I'd remember getting a tattoo behind my ear."

Thorne sat up, gently turning my head so he could examine the mark more closely. His brow furrowed. "Paesha, I'm not joking. There's a snowflake tattoo behind your ear. It's small, but it's definitely there."

I scrambled out of bed and hurried to the mirror hanging on the wall. Pulling my hair aside, I angled my head, straining to see. And there it was. A perfect, intricate snowflake, no larger than a coin, etched into the skin on my neck behind my ear. The lines were so fine, so detailed, it looked almost like frost clinging to a windowpane.

And then it hit me like a bolt of lightning. Alastor. The memory he'd shown me, of Thorne cradling Winter's dying body in the snow. The cold. The ice. The snowflakes drifting down to settle on her still face.

The Remnants must have marked me. A reminder of the forbidden glimpse into Thorne's past. His deepest pain. Though I couldn't tell him the whole truth, afraid to twist this night into a painful reminder for him, I gave him just enough to understand. "Alastor left this when I gave him Harlow's name."

"A snowflake?"

I shrugged, lying to him a second time tonight. "Maybe it means she'll be whole by next winter. Maybe it's a promise."

"He's a god. Unless he spoke those words aloud. I can promise you it isn't."

"Well, there's nothing to be done about it now."

I should have been far more cautious when dealing with Alastor, though I'm not sure the outcome would have changed. I crawled back into the bed and let him wrap me in his arms once more, purposefully slowing my breathing until he thought I was asleep. I just couldn't tell him any more lies today. He hadn't deserved any of them. Eventually though, we really did fall asleep and when he woke up before the sun and snuck out, I waited until I couldn't hear him anymore before I got up and dressed into my leathers.

I let my eyes linger on the golden book on his desk for several moments before I snatched it, with every intention of telling him I was going to head to the graveyard. But he'd beat me to the punch, his words appearing on the page as if he were standing there writing them.

Good morning, Paesha darling.
You looked so peaceful lying there asleep. I didn't want to wake you. Just going to pay a visit to our friend Alastor.
~Hoping you're still naked when I return,
Thorne Noctus

Ice shot through me. He was going to do something reckless, and he was completely alone.

Gods, Thorne. Wait. There's something I need to tell you.

But he wouldn't listen. Stubborn fucking man as he was, had already made up his mind. I ran for the door and swung it open, bolting down the stairs, shoving the book into my pocket as I raced outside. But Thorne, broad shoulders, and brooding, wasn't there. Instead, it was Jasper, doubled over, panting, arm pressed against the side of the building as if he'd run a mile.

"Thorne?" He asked between gulping breaths. "Archer?"

I spun toward the street, torn between helping Jasper or going after Thorne.

"He's not here. Neither of them is. I'm sorry, Jasper, but I really have to—"

The one-armed cook stood up straight, no longer struggling as he let out a sharp whistle and all hell broke loose. Strange men, all very bulky, emerged from around corners, from alleys, from behind bins. They moved with a lethal grace, circling me like a pack of wolves closing in on their prey. I whipped around, heart pounding, searching for an escape, but there was none.

The pounding of my heart was the only sound I could hear,

drowning out all other noises in my head. I turned back to Jasper, betrayal and confusion warring in my chest. His face was etched with sorrow, his eyes haunted and apologetic.

"You lied. You were bound to the prince this whole time."

"No!" he said, lunging, trying to reach through the men. "I was never bound to the prince." But before I could demand an explanation, before I could even draw breath to scream, a heavy blow landed on the back of my head.

Pain exploded behind my eyes. The world tilted and spun as my knees buckled. I reached out blindly, fingers scrabbling against the rough brick of the Parlor wall as I fought to stay conscious. But it was a losing battle. Darkness crept in at the edges of my vision, narrowing my world to a pinpoint of fading light. The last thing I saw as I crumpled to the filthy cobblestones was Jasper's anguished face.

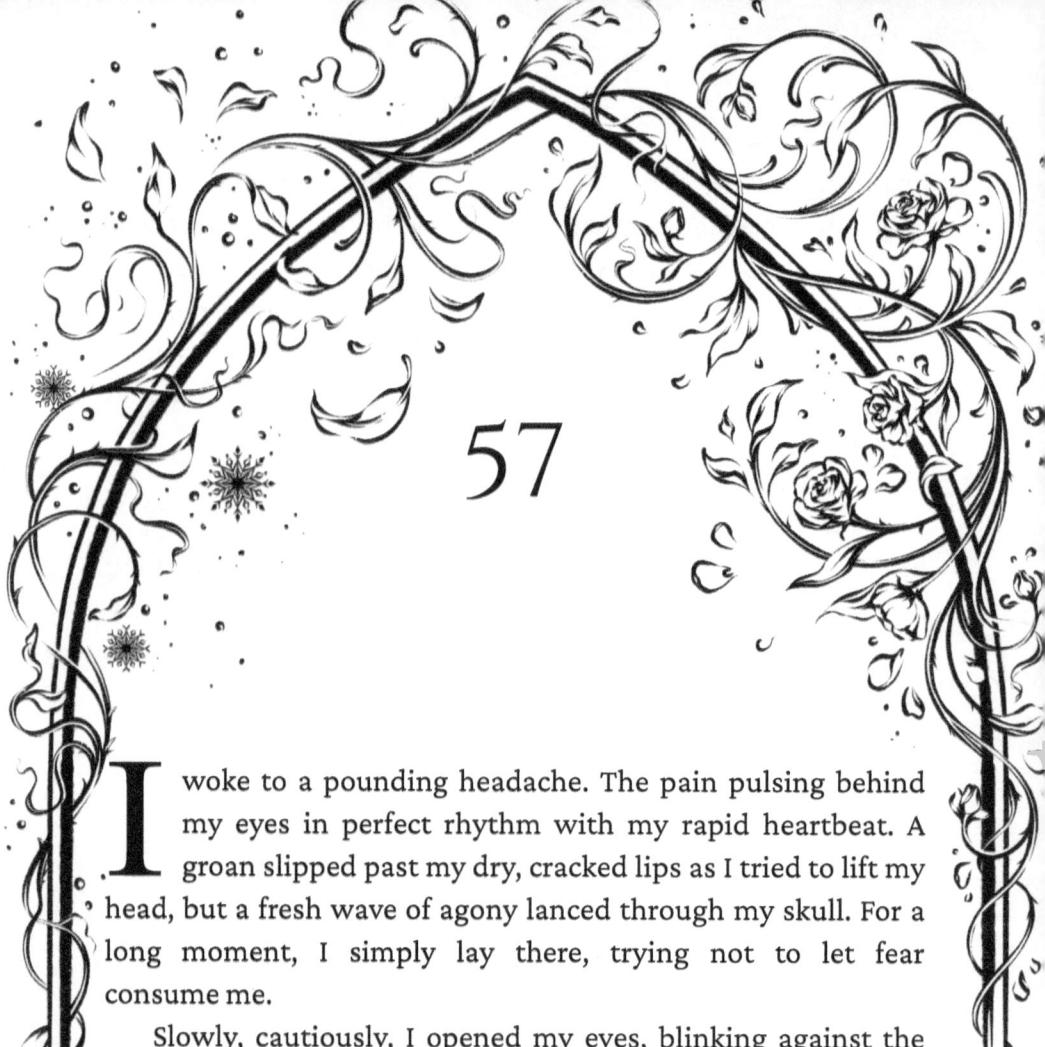

57

I woke to a pounding headache. The pain pulsing behind my eyes in perfect rhythm with my rapid heartbeat. A groan slipped past my dry, cracked lips as I tried to lift my head, but a fresh wave of agony lanced through my skull. For a long moment, I simply lay there, trying not to let fear consume me.

Slowly, cautiously, I opened my eyes, blinking against the dim light that stabbed into my brain. The room was small, the walls a dingy gray, the air stale and musty. A single, narrow window set high in the wall allowed a thin shaft of sunlight to filter through, casting long shadows across the bare floorboards. Was it still morning?

Whoever Jasper worked for hadn't thrown me into a prison cell, thank the gods. Actually, no. Fuck the gods. Every single one of them. The space was just a room, mostly bare, with a single, worn chair and a lumpy mattress shoved against the far wall. But there, curled up on that mattress, was a figure I hadn't expected to see at all.

I rushed forward, gently placing my hand on his shoulder as

I shook him awake. King Aldus Wendale, clutching his crown to his chest, peeled his eyes open and gasped.

"Have you—" He cleared his throat. "Have you come to rescue me?"

I shook my head, trying to keep the sadness from my face. "I wish I had. We've been trying to find you since the moment they announced you were taken."

He heaved himself up onto one arm, swinging his short legs to rest on the floor as he rubbed his eyes.

"Are you hurt?"

The old king shook his head. "Only my pride, dear. Only my pride."

The ripple of black surrounding his frame was so faint at first, I almost missed it. But the longer he sat, hanging his head, the more I noted the wear of his life on him. The heartache was there, as if it were tangible. And then I thought of Harlow's story. Of her mother. And I wondered if he'd carried that with him all this time.

"We have to try to get out of here."

"They won't allow me to leave the room, I'm afraid."

"Do you know where we are?"

He took a deep breath, looking up at the window. "I can smell the flowers sometimes. That's all I know."

"I hate to ask this, but I need to know," I said, taking a deep breath to prepare myself for the answer. "Was it Farris?"

The old king's eyes grew distant. A heavy sigh escaped his lips before he spoke, his voice soft and tinged with a profound sadness. "No, my dear. It was not Farris, though I fear he may be involved in some capacity. Despite what the people believe, I have never officially named him as my heir."

He paused, as a small, sad smile tugged at the corners of his mouth.

"The line of succession is a delicate matter, one that requires

careful consideration and wisdom. I had hoped, perhaps foolishly, that Farris would grow into a man worthy of the crown.
That he would learn compassion, humility, and leadership. But
as the years passed, I began to see the darkness within him and
on his thirteenth birthday, when he was to be titled, his mother
died. No one questioned why there wasn't a celebration because
they were all so focused on the funeral and the heart of a little
boy who grieved in a way that I've never seen. He grew angry.

"I can't say I was any better. My heart was gone long before
Farris was born and most of my time had been spent going
through the motions of life without the fire I used to have. If I
die before Farris can be named, the succession will fall to my
council."

There was nothing frantic about his movements, no sense of
fear within him, which worried me the most. It felt like he'd
given up, though a part of me was beginning to understand he'd
given up a long time ago. That's why Farris was able to keep him
shut off from his kingdom. This man... as kind and gentle as he
was, was never built with the ruthless resolve kings must have.
And that was the real tragedy of a monarchy. To keep it, you
could never truly be anything but subservient to your crown, no
matter the cost.

I tried to match his energy. Be calm. Still. Though my heart
was racing, and my head was throbbing and the only thing I
wanted to be doing was breaking down the walls. The deep
breath I took to contain my anxious nerves did nothing to settle
me. So, I pressed on. "I'm not here to blame your son, Your
Majesty, but we need an escape. How often do they come?"

I needed to stay sharp and focused for as long as I could. I
swallowed the nausea threatening to rise and gripped his
elderly fingers with trembling hands.

He leaned in close. "There is one main person, but he never
shows his face. Just comes to watch sometimes when they bring

food and water. No one speaks to me. It's as if they're waiting for something."

Waiting. Waiting for what? But the second I asked myself that question, it became glaringly obvious. It was me. It'd been me the whole time. The king's capture was a trap to lure me to him. I was the Hunted. And Alastor had been trying to tell me. Whoever it was, knew I'd touched the king. They knew I'd seen him. And they knew of my power. They just didn't realize the man had been masked, and he had gloves on. They didn't give a shit about the old man, only me. But why?

I pushed myself to my feet, ignoring the wave of dizziness that threatened to send me crashing back down. Slowly, I made my way to the door, testing the handle. Locked, of course. The window was too high and narrow to offer any means of escape. But desperate for clues, for an escape, I pressed my ear to the door and listened. Heavy footsteps were coming, though they seemed faint, somewhere down a narrow hall.

With my blood pumping and adrenaline rushing through, the tracers that filled my vision when I moved began to fade. The drag on my mind cleared. I scanned the barren room for anything of use, but there was nothing. Except...

I looked back at the door, then to the chair. The footsteps grew louder. I dashed for the chair, dragged it across the room and shoved it beneath the handle of the door on an angle, hoping it would buy me an extra minute. That was all I needed as I whipped Thorne's little golden notebook out and snatched the pencil.

Help. Jasper bad. Am captured. King here. Can smell flowers. Sun shining directly into the window near the ceiling. Facing West if past twelve.

The doorknob rattled. The king gasped. Thorne's response was instantaneous, though his beautiful writing was little more than scratches.

More!

But there was nothing else to give him. No other signs but... I could do something with my power. Something I'd never tried before. Seeking distance from familiar things. I burrowed down and whipped my power free as hard and fast as possible.

A slam on the door shook the whole floor.

Who was close by? I reached out for Archer first, praying he was close enough, but he wasn't. The magic trailed off for a while. Then Harlow. Then Prospector's Pointe. Then I reached for Serene's temple, and everything seemed so far. Magic surged through my veins, searching, seeking, straining to find anything familiar, any landmark that would anchor me and help Thorne find us.

The door shuddered under another heavy blow. I pushed harder, power flowing outward like an invisible net, skimming over the city, through winding streets and towering buildings until... there! The clock tower. It was close, so close, I could almost feel the vibrations of the bells on the other end of my lifeline.

Clutching the pencil, I began to write the word, but the door exploded inward with a deafening crack, splinters of wood from the chair spraying across the room as it toppled uselessly to the side.

Two men surged into the room, their faces twisted with malice. One of them was somehow familiar, though I couldn't place him.

"What've you got there, kitten?" he asked.

"It's just a notebook. It's nothing."

He held a hand out. "Then give it over."

The king was in good shape. He had no markings, so physically he was fine. What was the true danger here? What would they do?

"No. I don't think I will." I'd learned to be disciplined as a child. And now I needed to be unbreakable.

The first man lunged. I spun away with a dancer's grace, tucking the book into my waistband. I ducked, feeling the whoosh of air as another blow missed my head by inches. Instinct took over, years of dance and Thea's sword fight training guiding me as I moved with a woman's fury pushing me to fight back. I managed a vicious kick, catching one in the knee. He stumbled, cursing. I raced for the open door, confident I'd make it, but his partner was already on me.

I couldn't fight them both. Hell, they were so large, I didn't think I could manage one without a weapon. Still, I had to try. They came at me together, a whirlwind of fists and snarls. I gave ground, dodging and weaving, trying to keep them at bay more than actually fight back. The notebook dug into my back. If only I'd had a few more seconds...

The thought cost me. A meaty fist crashed into my cheek, snapping my head back and filling my vision with stars. Whatever I'd slightly recovered from since waking, came racing back with a vengeance. I wavered on my feet and knew immediately that I stood no chance. Tasting the blood trickling from my lip, I barely managed to avoid the follow-up blow.

"Stop this at once." The king's pointless demand cut through the chaos. He grabbed the broken chair and swung it wildly at my attackers. If not for the seriousness of the situation, it might've been comical, but at least he was sweet enough to try.

The men turned, sneering. One lashed out, almost lazily, and sent the elderly monarch tumbling to the floor. His cry of pain was terrible. I threw myself at the nearest thug, slamming my knee into his groin. He doubled over, retching. But his companion seized the opening. An iron grip closed around my arm, wrenching it up behind my back until my shoulder screamed. I stomped backward, aiming for his foot, but he'd been ready. Twisting savagely, he hurled me across the room.

I hit the far wall and crumpled; the breath whisked from my lungs in a rush. Gritting my teeth, I pushed myself up on my hands and knees. But a boot crashed into my ribs, flipping me onto my back. The man I'd kneed in the groin loomed over me, his face a mask of rage. He dropped down, pinning me with his weight, and drew back his fist.

I squeezed my eyes shut, holding my breath as I anticipated the blow that would surely shatter the bones in my face. The blow never came.

The weight pinning me down vanished as the man rose, his breathing harsh in the stillness of the room. I opened my eyes to see Thorne's notebook clutched in one of their fists and my heart stopped beating.

The men exchanged a look, silent communication passing between them, before turning and striding out of the room, their job done. As if they'd come just for that damn book. The door swung shut behind them with a final, damning click, the sound of the lock engaging like a death toll in the sudden quiet.

I fought the sting of tears threatening to give away my resolve. I'd failed. Failed the king, failed Thorne, failed me. And now, with the notebook gone, any hope of rescue had vanished with it. So, I'd failed Quill too.

But beneath the pain an ember of defiance still glowed. Stubborn. Unyielding. It was the same fire that had kept me alive in the Maw, that had driven me to survive against all odds. And it refused to be extinguished, even now. I dragged myself into a sitting position, my back against the cold stone wall. The room spun. Darkness threatened my vision from the second blow to my head in so many hours, so I closed my eyes, focusing on the ragged rhythm of my breathing.

In. Out. In. Out.

The king lowered himself painfully to the floor beside me, his weathered face creased with concern. "My dear girl, are you okay?"

I managed a weak smile, though it felt more like a grimace. "Never been better."

The king let out a surprised chuckle, then winced, pressing a hand to his side. "Ah, it seems laughter isn't the best medicine after all. Perhaps we shouldn't pick fights with our captors, eh?"

I turned to him, letting the fury buried within me peek through. "You can never destroy a monster without becoming one."

Minutes bled into hours, marked only by the changing light and the occasional sound of footsteps passing by beyond the locked door. No one came, not to bring food or water, not to check on us. As I thought over every memory with Thorne's band of men, I remembered my truth. One that kept me from slipping into misery. Every step I'd taken since coming to Wisteria had led me to this exact place. I'd never strayed from the path, even when I'd wanted to. I'd given days I didn't have to the Fray, to Thorne, trusting a god to keep his word and get me back to Quill.

"I need to ask you a question," I whispered, lying on the floor while the king took the mattress. "Have you ever heard of people traveling between the gods' realms? Not gods, but mortals actually crossing over into another world entirely?"

The old king was silent for a long moment. When he spoke, his words were slow and measured. "There are legends, ancient tales passed down through generations. Stories of men who stepped through shimmering portals or walked along hidden paths to journey to realms beyond our own."

He shifted on the thin mattress. "As a child, I remember my nursemaid spinning tales about a great hero named Octavian the Wayfarer. She said he discovered a secret door hidden deep within a mystical forest, a door that led him to a land of eternal summer where the air shimmered with magic and the waters were full of death. They're just stories, though. Derived from imaginative minds seeking an escape. Reality is far less exciting, I'm afraid."

The sound of hurried footsteps and urgent voices erupted outside. The king sat up, wincing, his face drawn with apprehension. I pushed myself to my feet, ready for answers. Ready for round two. Ready to run.

The door burst open and a group of guards rushed into the room. "Move. Now."

They were on us in seconds, dragging me and the king out. The guards' frantic urgency did nothing but inspire hope. Whatever had them so frazzled was a blessing for us and I just knew it had to do with a brooding man and his only family. The ones that did reckless things for hopeless people. And if I knew them as well as I thought I did, there was a blond man with a coin in his pocket at the helm, and his cautious, but dangerous sister at his side. Thorne was the planner, the man in control. But Archer was the hammer and Harlow, the blade.

After running down a narrow corridor, we were shoved unceremoniously into a carriage outside, the door slamming shut behind us with a resounding thud. The king and I huddled together as the carriage lurched into motion and when I took his hand in mine, I could feel the tremor of fear. "Have faith in your people because even when you forgot to fight for them, they never stopped fighting for you. Remember this night."

Screams erupted outside of the carriage as the king whispered, "I was so alone, but I never forgot to fight. I just forgot about the weapons."

"The people coming for us? *They* are your weapons."

"And you?"

"I'm not a hero."

"Then you better become the monster, dear. Just in case."

The carriage jerked to a halt, throwing us forward. Shouts erupted followed by the unmistakable clang of steel on steel. My insides vibrated with anticipation as I shifted toward the door. I knew I needed to wait. Give it a minute before I rushed into a horde of the strange guards, but I could hardly contain the adrenaline seeping into my bones.

The coach rocked as bodies slammed against its sides. The door was wrenched open and I tensed, ready to fight with every last ounce of strength I possessed if it wasn't one of the Fray. But a familiar man appeared, haloed by the dying light. Archer, his face grim, his sword, *my* sword, dripping red.

He flipped the hilt toward me with an ornery grin, hanging off the step of the carriage. "Stick 'em with the pointy side." And though I knew it killed him, he hadn't even acknowledged his father, choosing instead to wait for his sister as he hopped down and ran back into the chaos.

I wanted to search for Thorne, to take his side, ease his mind, if only for a second. But Harlow screamed, and I spun just in time to raise my sword and block a deadly blow. I gritted my teeth, drawing on every ounce of strength and skill Thea had drilled into me. But no amount of will power could overcome pure brute strength. Harlow though? She'd tossed a single dagger, and it landed in the man's back. He faltered. He staggered. And then he fell to the ground in a heap. A brief second of eye contact was all the thanks I could give before she was off again, like some nightmare vigilante set free from her cage.

Thorne burst through the fray, a whirlwind of lethal grace

and controlled fury. His sword crashed down, leaving a trail of crimson as he cut down every man standing between him and me. His eyes, the ones that could stop my heart with a single glance, were fixed on me, burning with an intensity that stole the breath from my lungs.

He moved like a man possessed. And then he was there, standing before me, his chest heaving, his hair disheveled, his face splattered with blood that wasn't his own. For a heartbeat, the world fell away. The chaos faded to a distant hum as he reached for me, a hand cupping my cheek with a tenderness that contradicted the violence swirling around us.

"You're late," I managed.

"We've got to work on your communication skills," he said, yanking me toward him, his lips crashing into mine in a desperate, searing kiss that left me breathless.

But the moment was shattered by a shout of warning from Archer. I spun, my sword arm blurring as I parried a vicious blow that would have taken my head. With a shout of frustration, I surged forward, slicing the man's arm clean off his body. He stumbled back, but Tuck was there. Waiting. The man was on the ground in seconds.

Thorne shoved me behind him. "Stay close. We're getting the fuck out of here."

He let out a sharp, piercing whistle that cut through the fight like a blade. The Fray responded instantly, moving toward us. They formed a tight circle around the carriage, a living, breathing barrier of unwavering loyalty for a king that might not have deserved them.

We'd lost a few, of that I was certain. But they had too. Only two men remained in the center of the street, the hilts of their swords raised. I glanced at Archer but he wasn't watching them. His eyes had gone wide, fixed on something just beyond us. A dagger flew, a gleam of death in the failing light, hurtling straight for him.

Harlow screamed.

And then she was moving, too fast, too reckless—her body a blur as she threw herself between him and the blade. Her breath caught, and for one horrifying second, the world stood still as the dagger buried itself deep in her chest. The sound of it, the only thing that existed.

My blood turned cold as she staggered, hands fluttering to the hilt. She tried to stay upright, as if sheer will could keep her standing. But the strength left her legs, and she collapsed into Archer's arms.

"Harlow!" His voice, the voice of a devoted brother, of a desperate friend, of a loyal man, was strangled, his arms wrapping around her, lowering her to the ground like she might shatter if he moved too fast. "Harlow, no."

He clutched her tight, and though I couldn't see it, I knew he was shoving magic through her, frantic to stop the inevitable. But the blood was already spilling from the wound, soaking his hands, her clothes. It spread, pooling around them as Archer's panic-stricken breaths filled the silence. With one hand pressing desperately against the wound, the other cradled her face.

Thorne moved through the night like a wraith, obliterating those left standing, but I couldn't bring myself to look away from Archer.

"Har," he choked out, his voice breaking on the single syllable. "Don't you fucking do it. Don't you dare."

Her eyelids fluttered, a weak moan escaping her lips as Archer cradled her against his chest, utterly defeated. His magic could not heal the dying, only rush the process and then he'd only lose her faster.

I stood frozen, my sword hanging forgotten at my side as I

watched the scene unfold, helpless to do anything but bear witness to Archer's devastation. But I couldn't stand there and watch him suffer alone. I couldn't look at her and not see every-thing this world was losing. So I ran, knowing there was nothing I could do but comfort them.

Harlow's hand drifted up, trembling fingers brushing against Archer's cheek, leaving streaks of crimson on his pale skin. "It's okay," she whispered, the words barely audible over the ragged sound of Archer's breathing. "It's going to be okay, Archie."

A broken sob tore from Archer's throat. "No. Not like this. Not now. You have to grow old and get wrinkly and I have to get bald and we have to tease each other. We were born together, we die together. That was our promise. That was our fucking promise. You don't get to leave me here alone."

A ghost of a smile touched Harlow's bloodless lips. "Always trying to tell me what to do."

Archer clutched her tighter, as if he could anchor her to this world through sheer force of will. "That's right," he whispered. "And right now, I'm telling you to stay with me. You hear me, Harlow? You stay with me."

But even as he spoke the words, I could see the light fading from her eyes, her breaths coming slower, shallower. Tears slipped down Archer's face as he rocked his sister gently, desperately.

"Remember when we were kids," Harlow breathed, her voice so faint now, I had to strain to hear it. "And I'd crawl into your bed during storms? You always kept me safe. My brother, my protector."

Archer's shoulders shook with silent sobs as he pressed his forehead against Harlow's, tears mingling with the blood on her face. "I'll always keep you safe, Har. Always."

Around us, the world had fallen still. The Fray stood in a

silent, mournful circle, their heads bowed, bearing witness to the heart-wrenching scene. Though it seemed impossible, even the night held its breath, saying goodbye to a silent warrior. A woman that'd spent her life fitting the mold of what everyone expected her to be rather than what she'd dreamed for herself.

I knelt beside them, fighting my selfish tears, fighting the jagged lump in my throat as I reached out to take Harlow's other hand. Her skin was cold, her delicate fingers so fragile in my grasp. I squeezed gently, trying to pour every ounce of love and comfort I could into that simple touch.

Harlow's gaze drifted to me, a flicker of warmth in those fading blue eyes. "Take care of him for me. Don't let him do anything stupid."

A choked laugh escaped my lips, more a sob than anything else. "I won't. I promise."

She smiled then, a serene, peaceful thing that shattered my heart into a million jagged pieces. Her eyes fluttered closed, her final breath leaving her in a soft sigh. And then she was still, her hand limp in mine, the rise and fall of her chest ceasing as her soul slipped away into the endless night.

Archer's anguished cry pierced the air, a sound of such raw, unfiltered pain that it physically hurt to hear. He clutched Harlow's lifeless body to his chest, rocking back and forth as great, heaving sobs shook him. It was pure agony.

With shaking hands, Archer reached into his pocket and pulled out his lucky coin, the one he always kept with him. A reminder of better times, of a life woven through with hope and purpose. He pressed the coin into Harlow's palm, curling her fingers around it in a final, tender gesture. "For the ferryman," he whispered, his voice broken and raw. "I'll never let you wander alone, Har. Not even in death."

58

Archer hadn't moved. Hadn't spoken. He stood as still as the grave before us, shoulders stiff beneath the weight of his pain, head bowed as the rain streamed down his face. He hadn't shed another tear in front of us, but I knew. I knew by the way his fists trembled at his sides. I knew by the way his breath hitched every time he exhaled. His silence was louder than any scream, more agonizing than any sob could have been.

The sound of the final shovel of dirt hitting the casket echoed like a thunderclap in the suffocating silence. Everyone had come. Willard, the Fray, the Salt and Silk alike, circling the grave of a woman who'd reached across the social barriers of this cruel world and left it a better place than she'd found it, even though it'd meant her life in the end. There was no going back. Harlow died last night, and the world felt emptier for it.

Even the king had come, hidden in a sodden cloak at Tuck's side, this broken soul the only one among us rippling across the graveyard. Archer had told him, of course. With an angry scream, he'd told the king that he'd been the reason for his own daughter's death. And though that hadn't been true at all, though I was always the target and the reason for the rescue, I hadn't corrected him. Hadn't had the heart to do so.

Serene had come, lurking around the outskirts of the grave-yard, her long cloak billowing in wind that didn't exist as she leeched off the broken hearts of the masses. Because in truth, she was the Goddess of Loss and Lust and though I'd always known that, it wasn't until now that I understood how the two might be connected. She fed off the aching emptiness grief carved into a heart, the way it left people vulnerable, raw, yearning to fill that hollow space with anything that might bring comfort. Lust, then, was not merely desire, but a desperate reaching for something, someone, to stave off the darkness.

In Archer's hand, crushed between his fingers, was a white lily. The flower he had carried all this way, soaked through by the rain, wilting just like she had, the last piece of her left in his grip. He stood there, staring down at the grave, as if he didn't know how to let go, how to move forward now that the last part of his sister was buried in the earth.

And then, slowly, his hand trembled as he released it. The flower fell, spinning gently, until it landed on the earth covering his sister's coffin. He didn't move. Didn't speak. Just stared down at the grave, like there were no words left to be said. None that could fix what had been broken. I watched the way his shoulders sagged, the way his chest hitched with breaths he was barely holding onto, and my heart shattered all over again. He had been holding it together, a threadbare facade, but he was slipping now. Breaking. And it was the kind of break no one could fix.

I stepped forward, hesitating for only a moment before I wrapped my arms around him. He didn't resist. Didn't pull away. He just... collapsed into me. His head dropped to my shoulder, and a sharp sob tore through him. The floodgate opened, and he fell apart in my arms, the weight of his grief too much to bear any longer.

There were no words of comfort I could offer, no platitudes that could ease the raw anguish radiating from him in waves. He clung to me like a drowning man, and I held him fiercely. He wept for her. And I wept for him. For the twin who had lost his other half, the one person who had always been there for him. And in that moment, as the rain poured down and the world seemed to shrink to just the two of us, I realized this pain, the pain of losing someone so deeply it wove into the fabric of your life, didn't go away. It lingered. It haunted. Because I'd spent years dancing with the ghost of a man that'd left me too.

Slowly, the mourners drifted away, their black-clad forms melting into the misty gray of the graveyard. Some lingered, murmuring quiet words of condolence to Archer before they faded into the gloom, leaving only the soft patter of rain and the distant caw of a lone raven.

I pulled back from Archer, my hands still resting on his shoulders as I searched his face. Grief had etched deep lines into his skin, aging him beyond his years. His eyes, once bright with mischief and laughter, were now haunted, shadowed by pain. But as I looked closer, dreading the telltale flicker of black that would mark his soul as broken, I still found nothing. Just the raw, human anguish of a man who had lost everything.

Thorne approached us, his own face drawn and somber. He placed a gentle hand on Archer's back. "Come on. Let's get out of this rain."

Archer nodded, seeming to rouse himself from the depths of his sadness. He straightened, squaring his shoulders as if physically bracing himself against the weight of a lonelier world. Together, we turned and began the long, slow walk back to the Parlor, leaving Harlow's final resting place behind us.

The city streets were nearly deserted, the usually bustling thoroughfares emptied by the relentless rain. It drummed against the cobblestones, running in rivulets along the gutters and pooling in the potholes. The few people we passed hurried by with their heads down, their faces obscured by dripping hoods and upturned collars.

As we walked, Thorne kept a steadying arm around Archer's shoulders, guiding him. I trailed a step behind. The silence stretched between us, thick and oppressive, broken only by the mournful whisper of the wind and the distant rumble of thunder.

Archer paused just over the threshold of the Parlor, his gaze sweeping the room as if seeing it for the first time. Every surface, every piece of furniture seemed to hold a memory of Harlow. The bar where she'd perched, laughing as she sipped her whiskey, the gaming tables where she'd leaned over Archer's shoulder, distracting his targets, the couch she loved the most, where she'd perfected becoming a thief.

"I can't do this right now," he said, backing away. "I can't be here."

"Where do you want to go? I'll come with you," I offered.

He shook his head. "I need space." And then he spun and walked back down the sodden street. Alone.

I turned to Thorne, worried for Archer, but he pulled me into his arms and kicked the door shut. "Just give him some time."

I didn't have time. None at all, in fact. I'd counted each one over and over in bed last night, unable to sleep. There was the unknown of my time in the Maw. I could have been there for 3 days, it could have been a week or more, but beyond that, sixty-three had passed. The winter had melted to spring, and at the very most, I had a week left to find my way back to Requiem.

"Did Tuck go with the king back to the castle?" I asked, begrudgingly letting my mind move beyond the heavy morning.

Thorne kissed my head, squeezing tighter. "King Aldus agreed to bring as many of the Salt under his protection as he can. He's offering them positions in his guard and throughout the castle. He knows he needs loyal people around him now more than ever."

I nodded, a flicker of hope sparking in my chest despite the sorrow that still clung to me like a second skin. Maybe peace would be the end of the path. "That's good. It's a start, at least."

"He's gearing up for the prince's return tomorrow. Fortifying the palace, doubling the guard, preparing for any potential threats. There's a sense of unease, like the entire city is holding its breath, waiting for the storm to break."

"It's not like the king doesn't see his son for the monster he is. He just accepted it was his fault and withdrew." I took a deep, settling breath, drawing the courage to tell Thorne everything. "The king was never the real target. It wasn't Farris that kidnapped him. It's someone else. Someone that's hunting me."

He stilled. "What do you mean?"

"Alastor has told me time and time again that I'm the Hunted. They never touched the king because he was only the bait for whoever is searching for me."

He shook his head. "No one is hunting you. Alastor is just meddling, as gods do. He likely just wants you to stay afraid of the gods. Because at least if you're afraid, then you'll be cautious."

"Either way, I have to go see him. I have another name and only days left here."

Looking down at me, his worried gaze shifted between my eyes. "But you don't know how to get back. Not really. Alastor's riddles and cryptic warnings aren't a map. They're breadcrumbs meant to keep you chasing after something that might not even be possible. He has his own motives. I can promise you that."

"I know you don't want me to go. But I can't just give up to appease you. You're forgetting the part where all the realms fall. Even this one."

"At least we'd be together when we burned."

He brushed a thumb over my cheek and I leaned into his touch, my eyes fluttering closed as I savored the warmth of his palm. When I opened them again, I met his gaze unapologetically. "I can't accept that."

I tried to step back, but he held me close. Close enough, as I stared up at him I noticed a dark mark beneath the collar of his shirt. One that was never there before. The top of a strange symbol, dark against his skin.

Without thinking, I reached out, my fingers brushing over the tattoo. "What is this?"

Thorne sighed, his eyes flickering away from mine for a moment before he answered. "I had to bargain with Alastor. To find you. When we realized you were gone, that Jasper had betrayed us... I was out of my mind with worry. I couldn't think straight. All I knew was that I had to find you, no matter the cost. And in my panic, I realized if they'd taken you right off the streets, someone had to see something. And no one has eyes on Stirling more than Alastor. If anyone was whispering, he was listening."

"So, I begged him to help me find you. And he agreed for a price. Because the fucker already knew where you were, so naturally he agreed."

I swallowed hard, almost afraid to ask. "What price?"

"It's not important now, is it? What's done is done."

There was the face. The one he made when the conversation was over. I hated it and understood it at the same time. Because my bargain had been my own for a long time too.

"What if Alastor is the one hunting me and this is a game to him?"

Thorne shook his head. "No one is hunting you. Alastor is playing games. We need to be careful with him."

"As long as we're both in his debt, I'm not sure how careful we can be."

"Then I guess we go together. Keep our guards up, eyes and ears open. Give him the name and nothing more."

ALASTOR HADN'T LET Thorne in, of course. He'd scowled at him as he always did and led me to the room of broken things again. After we entered and he shut the door behind him, he crossed his tattooed arms over his chest, lifting a brow as he waited expectantly.

"I've brought you the second name," I said, skin crawling at the thought of his Remnants creeping over me again.

Alastor's disappointment seeped from him as he shook his head and looked away. "All the pieces are before you and still you refuse to break through to the truth. Give the name."

The Remnants rippled, but they didn't surge forward, instead pooling at Alastor's feet like inky black fog lingering on a stage, waiting as patiently as their godly master.

"His Majesty, King Aldus Wendale."

The Remnants surged. They wrapped around me, tendrils of shadow sliding over my skin, leaving trails of icy fire in their wake. I gasped, my body going rigid as they crept up my neck, curling around my throat before white hot pain took me straight to the floor.

Again, I was whisked away from my own body and shoved into another memory. A remnant of the past. The vision shimmered into existence, enveloping me in a soft glow. I stood in a lavish bedchamber. The walls were adorned with delicate, hand-painted flowers and sunlight streamed through tall, arched windows, casting a warm, golden hue over everything it touched. There was joy in this memory. A sense of peace and love that melted over me like butter.

I looked down, marveling at the exquisite white lace gown I wore. The fabric was lighter than air, draping over my curves like a whisper, the intricate detailing so fine it seemed almost unreal. I clutched a bouquet of the most perfect roses I had ever seen, their petals a deep, velvety red.

The last vision had been a memory of Thorne's, but I wasn't immediately sure of this one. A woman, possibly on her wedding day but what was the connection? In the books I'd read since being here, the women wore white. At home, we wore black. Still, I was sure it was a wedding gown. I knew it like I knew how to breathe as if our minds had melded together. And she was happy. So uniquely happy. Every cell in my body was filled with the purest, most transcendent form of euphoria.

My reflection came into view as I walked to the mirror, and for a moment, I simply stared, transfixed by the vision. The woman in the mirror was radiant, like she held the key to all of life's joys. Her hair was a cascade of rich, lustrous red curls.

But as I leaned closer, my heart stopped. Those eyes... one a vibrant, emerald green, the other a striking, cerulean blue. Eyes that had haunted my dreams, that I knew as intimately as my own heartbeat. They were my eyes. The realization crashed over me like a tidal wave. This wasn't just a memory. It wasn't a glimpse into someone else's life, someone else's cherished moment. It was mine. A fragment of a past life. I couldn't stumble away, couldn't sit down. Couldn't break myself out of her mind. Her soul. My soul.

As I stood there, shocked, the heavy oak door behind me swung open with a gentle creak. The rustle of fabric and the soft tread of footsteps announced the arrival of another. My heart leapt, as I recognized the presence without needing to turn. It was him. My love. My soulmate. The man I was destined to marry on this perfect, sun-drenched day.

"My darling," I breathed, closing my eyes as my voice trembled with excitement. "You shouldn't be here. It's bad luck to see each other before the ceremony."

But even as I spoke the words, a smile played at the corners of my lips. I couldn't bring myself to truly admonish him, not when every fiber of my being ached to be near him, to bask in the warmth of his love.

He spoke no words. His footsteps grew closer until I worried something was wrong and lifted my gaze. But there was no stranger standing there at all, and the world seemed to tilt off its axis as Thorne Noctus pulled a long dagger from his jacket and plunged it into my back.

59

I'd loved a man once. I'd loved a man, and now lying on the floor of Alastor's chamber of broken things once more, everything came crashing back to me in a sickening wave of reality. I couldn't breathe beyond it.

Because I'd loved a man once.

He'd rescued me from the Maestro. He'd been my peace and my salvation. He'd carried me when I needed to be carried. He'd stood behind me like a beast when I needed strength. And he was so loving. So tender. He'd been patient when I didn't know how to love him back. But he'd grown forceful. Demanding. Controlling. And his name was Ezra Prophet.

Ezra Prophet.

Ezra Prophet.

And I remembered everything.

Including his face. With steady hazel eyes and rich dark hair, Ezra was unmistakable. Even as he masqueraded as a man named Thorne Noctus.

613

60

I dragged myself up from the floor of Alastor's chamber, skimming my fingers across the second marking on my neck. Using a broken shard of mirror, I took in the rose tattoo with petals falling like drops of blood with ease. What difference did it make when in a matter of minutes, my entire world had turned upside down?

Alastor was nowhere to be seen. Shoving steel into my veins, I walked to the door and rested my hand on the knob. I didn't want to see Ezra. I didn't want to look into those eyes and feel every ounce of truth he'd kept from me. I didn't want to know why he'd come here. Or how, when I'd left him behind in Death's Court. I only wanted space. Or to escape.

With a deep sigh, I swung the door open, surprised to see gray skies and cobblestone streets. I stood there for a long moment, letting the reality of my situation sink in. Alastor, in his twisted way, had granted me a bittersweet mercy. By giving me a different path to take, away from the man I'd thought I was falling for, he'd spared me the agony of facing Thorne. No, Ezra.

Questions swirled through my mind. The weight of betrayal pressed down on my shoulders as I began to walk, my feet carrying me aimlessly through the winding streets. He'd killed me. A past life version of me, anyway. He'd walked into that room, looked at a woman that'd loved him so purely, so fully, and stabbed her in the back. Because I was the Hunted and the Huntress, but he was the Hunter.

I'd also seen him cry, though. I'd felt him holding Winter's body and sobbing as hard as Archer had this morning at Harlow's graveside. And these people had known him for a lifetime. Not months. Nothing made sense. Not a fucking thing. In fact, it made less sense than it had this morning when I had no clue at all what the hell was happening.

And I think the only way I was going to be able to work it all out was to go back to the beginning. Back to a little boy with an eerie grin and a penchant for snatching stories. Luckily for me, maybe unfortunately for him, I knew exactly where to find the little fucker.

The streets weren't packed with Cimmerians, but they lingered as they always had. I'd learned the rooftops were a far less likely place to run into them. I crossed the city almost effortlessly, though it did take time. I tried not to think of how long Thorne had waited in the Vale for me. Didn't think about the little golden book that'd been stolen, nor how it would have heated my thigh the moment he figured out I wasn't coming back out to meet him. Minimally, he'd lied. Though something told me that barely scratched the surface of truths he had to tell.

The little boy stood under an umbrella, hopping from puddle to puddle as he counted out loud, singing a children's song about numbers. I strode forward. The boy remained oblivious, lost in his innocent play. I grabbed him by the collar of his coat, dragging him closer until we were face to face.

I couldn't help the snarl. "Hey! Remember me?"

The boy's eyes went wide with shock and fear, his small body stiffening in my grasp. His umbrella tumbled to the ground, forgotten, as he stared up at me with a mixture of confusion and terror. "I—I don't—" he stammered, his lower lip trembling. "I'm sorry."

I lifted a brow. "It's not nice to tell lies."

"Please, miss. I don't know you. I swear it!"

The boy's eyes shimmered with unshed tears. A flicker of doubt crept into my mind, but I pushed it aside, too consumed by the anger raging within me.

"You know exactly who I am. You stole my story, remember? In the marketplace, when I first arrived in this godforsaken city. You took my memories of being in love."

The child shook his head vehemently, tears now spilling down his freckled cheeks. "N—no, miss. I swear on the gods, I've never seen you before. Please, you're hurting me!"

"Paesha. Stop."

Ice raced through my veins. My chest tightened as I released the little boy and spun toward Thorne... Ezra... whatever. Whoever. "Don't you fucking talk to me. You're a liar. And I think you made a bargain with the Keeper of Memories to trap me here. You're a monster."

He stepped forward, eyes heavy and full of sorrow. "I can explain."

"No." Another familiar voice crooned, taking my side. "You've told enough lies." Alastor. The tattoos on his neck and arms writhed as he stood at his full height, glaring at Ezra.

The liar lowered his chin, glaring daggers at Alastor. The tattoo from their bargain rippled on his neck as if reminding him who was in debt to whom. Still, he growled, "This has nothing to do with you. Leave us."

I couldn't help but feel the power behind his command. The

connection to him even now when I didn't trust him at all. I cursed my weak heart and stood my ground as Alastor fought back.

"This has *everything* to do with me. Or have you forgotten she wouldn't be alive if not for my help? Nor would she have been rescued if not for my spies. She owes me two more names and it's time to collect on the third."

But I didn't have a third name. I hadn't had time to find another soul. And I was done standing in the middle of half-spoken conversations and implied meanings. I stepped away from both of them.

Thorne moved to stop me, grabbing my elbow, but I jerked away from him. "No. I'm not going to be a pawn in whatever game the two of you are playing."

"No one is playing games. I've told you this," Ezra said, his tone firm.

"You will take your fucking masks off when you speak to me. No more lies."

But Alastor didn't move. Didn't flinch at all, nor tear his gaze from the man I thought I'd loved... twice. "Give her the name."

I whipped my attention back to Thorne. "You? Do you have a broken soul? Are you..." My legs turned weak. I had to fight to remain standing. "If you have a choice to show it... it means... You're a god? And you knew. You knew I needed your name, and you kept it from me. You really did try to trap me here."

He took a step toward me, but I matched it, moving back. "Paesha. Darling. All of this is for you. Every life. Every choice. It's all always been for you."

I couldn't hear another word over the ringing in my ears. I stared Thorne right in the face, almost numb and Alastor knew. He'd planned for it. His Remnants surged from him, smothering my body, rippling, seeking the name from my lips.

"Give me the name," Alastor commanded.

"Thorne Noctus," I whispered, though I knew it wouldn't work. Still I'd tried, desperate to be wrong. For the betrayal to hurt less.

Alastor shook his head. "I need his *real* name."

I swallowed, staring deep into those beautiful hazel eyes as I whispered, "Ezra Prophet."

For a heartbeat, the world stopped. The Remnants froze. My heart ceased to beat. And as if it were from somewhere far, far away, Alastor whispered. "Wrong again."

I couldn't breathe. Couldn't think. Alastor commanded Thorne. "If you want to save her, give her your name, Keeper."

I stared at the man across from me as if I were drowning and he was the only hand reaching for me. I didn't want to take it. I didn't want a thing from him. But I had no choice.

A sliver of black rippled around Thorne's figure, confirming his broken soul before it melted into bright, vibrant gold. "My name is Reverius Hawthorne Noctus, Supreme Sovereign, the Unerring Arbiter of Beginnings and Endings, the Keeper of All Realms, the Keeper of Memories and I'm so fucking sorry."

The god of a thousand names.

The one I'd made the bargain with.

I'd seen him stand before Ezra in Death's court, but not really. I'd only seen a glowing light. Never a man. Never a form in the shape of a man. Because he'd been one and the same. A trick. A manipulation. Ezra was Thorne *and* Reverius. Three names and all the lies.

Overcome with betrayal and shock, I could do nothing but repeat his name in a choked whisper, "Reverius Hawthorne Noctus." The words felt foreign on my tongue, a name belonging to a stranger wearing the face of a man I thought I loved.

The Remnants surged forward, their inky tendrils burning

into the back of my neck and down my spine like white-hot brands. Pain exploded behind my eyes as the world tilted and spun. I tried to scream but no sound escaped my lips. The ground beneath my feet dissolved, colors blurring together in a sickening swirl until there was nothing but blinding white light.

With a jolt, I was wrenched from my body and thrust into another time, another place, another life.

The immediate heat, oppressive and all-consuming, burned into my skin. Sunlight beat down from a cloudless sky the color of bleached bone and sand stretched out in every direction, an endless expanse of shimmering gold broken only by towering dunes and the occasional skeletal remains of dead trees.

I stood next to Thorne in this barren wasteland as he held my hand, the dry wind whipping at the thin white shift that clung to my sweaty skin. The air shimmered with heat, distorting the horizon into a wavering mirage. Thorne's eyes were filled with a love so deep, so pure, it stole the breath from my lungs when he faced me. I wanted to scream at myself to run. Not to trust him. But I was frozen, watching through her eyes with no other freedoms as the memory played out.

With reverent fingers, he reached into his pocket and withdrew a ring, the metal glinting in the harsh desert light. It was a simple band, unadorned save for the intricate engraving of a flame etched into its surface.

"Marry me," he whispered, his voice raw with emotion. "Marry me and I swear, I will spend the rest of my days filling your life with wonders beyond imagining."

Tears blurred my vision as he slid the ring onto my finger, a perfect fit, as if it had always been meant to rest there. The metal was cool, a balm against the oppressive heat, and in that moment, I felt a joy so profound, and a love so deep, it rocked me. Because it was all a godsdamn lie.

He surged forward, capturing my lips in a searing kiss that

solidified every ounce of love, every shred of devotion I'd held in my heart into the press of his mouth against mine. His arms came around me, crushing me to his chest.

When we finally broke apart, he rested his forehead against mine. "Say yes, darling."

"So commanding," I whispered with a smile before nodding. "I would say yes in a thousand lifetimes, my love."

"Then I vow to find you in every one, just to hear it. And I will love you in every one, just to feel your heart beat with mine."

As I stared into his eyes, lost in the depths of his love, the shimmering heat at the edge of my vision rippled, taking on a more solid form. Slowly, as if stepping out from behind a veil of mist, another figure emerged.

My heart stuttered in my chest as I realized it was also my beloved. Another of him, identical in every way to the man who held me in his arms. The same tousled dark hair, the same chiseled features, the same broad shoulders and wide muscular frame. But where my love's eyes were filled with adoration, the other man's gaze burned with fury.

I looked between the two men, my mind struggling to comprehend what I was seeing. This must have been a trick of the desert heat, a cruel mirage conjured by the unforgiving sun.

"Rev?" My former self whispered, my voice trembling as I clung to the man who had just pledged his eternal love. "What's happening?"

He's a liar, I wanted to scream. *That's what's happening.* But I couldn't. I was trapped. Forced to watch and feel another tragedy at the hands of angry gods.

Before he could answer, the other man took a step forward, his hand reaching behind his back. In one fluid motion, he drew a sleek, black bow, nocked an arrow and let loose.

"Brother, no!" Reverius screamed, his voice raw with desperation as he tried to shield me.

The word 'brother' echoed in my mind like the chime of a clock as I was ripped from the vision. But not to stand back on the street with two warring gods. No. That would have been too damn easy. And clearly the Goddess of Time had to have her hand in the chaos too. Because why the fuck not?

61

Vesalia's smile was sharp, a cutting curve of crimson lips that held no warmth. Ancient eyes, gold and glittering with malevolent amusement, tracked my every breath, my every shudder of impotent rage as we stood side by side in an alley that faced Prospector's Pointe.

"You see now, don't you? The truth of the twin brothers. Both liars. Both manipulating you for their own gain." She paused, tilting her head. "Tell me you see it, Huntress."

"Go back to whichever hell you crawled from."

She glared, her eyes practically molten gold as she seethed, leaning forward to grab the collar of my cloak. "And what will you do if all the gods abandon you? Foolish mortal. Open your eyes to what's happening. The Fera is real. The threat she poses is real. Or have you forgotten you have a standing bargain with Reverius and you're running out of time? Lie in your grave like a victim or crawl out of it."

In a twist, I broke her hold and moved away. "You're a liar. You're all liars. You play games you think we're too stupid to see."

"Move away from her, Paesha. She's not your ally."

I whipped around to see Reverius standing there, hands in his pockets, leaning against the brick. He stepped forward. Gone was the tender lover, the studious husband. In his place stood a god, ancient and unyielding, his power crackling like a gathering storm as he spoke. "You think you know the truth now? You think because you've seen a few scattered memories, you understand the game being played?"

I shook my head, fighting back the swell of emotions threatening to break free. The confusion. The betrayal, the evisceration of everything I thought I might feel for him. I'd meant to be strong. To stand and fight against him for every one of my past lives, but I could hardly manage more than a whisper. "I don't understand any of it."

Vesalia hissed, her eyes flashing with restrained fury. "Don't speak to her as if she is a child, Reverius. She deserves the truth, not more of your honeyed lies."

Reverius rounded on her, his lip curling in a sneer. "And you think you're the one to give it to her?"

"At least I don't pretend to love her, only to betray her at every turn," Vesalia spat.

Reverius looked at me then, letting the truth hang in the air.

"Say it," I whispered, opening my heart for the final blow. "Tell me it was all a lie."

His cruel smile turned my stomach. "I do so love my masks. But you already knew that."

To hear the truth spoken so casually was like plunging into an ice-cold lake. He'd only pretended. None of it was real. Not one second. Not one kiss. Not one promise. I wanted to scream, to rage, to let the agony inside me pour out in a flood of bitter tears. But I stood frozen. Numb, as if my soul had been hollowed out. "Then your realms can fucking burn, but I guess that's what you wanted all along."

I turned and walked away, and neither of them tried to stop me. Though I could feel Thorne's gaze on my back, and I hated that I knew it was there. I hated him. A flash of movement caught my eye. Likely the whole reason Vesalia had chosen this spot. She'd wanted me to see him. Across the square, a familiar figure emerged from the shadows cast by the looming buildings. Archer, his blond hair gleaming in the muted light, strode towards Prospector's Pointe with a purposeful gait that filled me with concern.

He clutched a dagger. His knuckles were white around the hilt, his jaw clenched with determination. The haunted look in his eyes mirrored what I thought mine might look like. A soul shattered beyond repair.

Before I could move, before I could even draw breath to shout his name, the square was consumed by the deep, steady pounding of drums. Cold dread settled in the pit of my stomach as I turned toward the sound.

Farris and his Cimmerian guard marched into the square. The prince rode at their head, astride a massive black horse, his cloak billowing behind him like a banner of shadows. And Thorne hadn't cared at all. Hadn't made a single move. Because if it didn't serve him, it wasn't his problem. Archer wasn't his problem. Wasn't even his friend. But he sure as fuck was mine.

And in that moment, I knew what Archer intended to do. Knew it with a certainty that ripped my heart from my chest. Farris had taken Harlow's life long before she'd died. He'd lived the life Archer believed his sister deserved. Farris had taken advantage of every privilege and every power, while those around him had suffered. While she suffered. And he would never let that go.

I ran for him, desperate to reach him before he could do something that would surely end in his own death. The world blurred into a haze of muted colors and muffled sounds, narrowing down to the single, unwavering focus of reaching Archer before it was too late.

"Archer, stop!" I screamed. But he didn't hear me over the pounding of the drums and the clamor of the crowd. Or perhaps he chose not to, too lost in his own grief and need for vengeance.

I pushed myself harder, my lungs burning, my muscles screaming in protest as I wove through the throng of people. I broke through the last line of spectators and stumbled into the open space before the prince's procession. Archer stood feet away, his body coiled with tension, the dagger glinting in his white-knuckled grip.

"Please," I gasped, reaching for him. "Don't do this. She wouldn't want this. You'll die. There's no escape here and you know it."

His eyes met mine, a storm of grief and rage warring within them. His voice was a broken rasp as he spoke, each word laced with a pain so raw, it stole my breath. "She and I were born of the same cloth. We were a pair. Two halves of a whole. And she spent her life in misery because of him. He took something so precious from her, she never recovered. Because of me. Because I was a foolish kid with a big mouth. He destroyed her. Shattered her spirit until she was just a ghost of herself. And she died with that sadness still haunting her. I know you saw it, Paesha."

I grabbed his arm, pulling him from the edge of the opening, though he didn't come lightly. "Let me tell you something. It's important and you're not going to believe me, but you must. I know your heart is hurting right now. I know you buried your sister this morning and you feel like there's no life beyond grief. But I promise there is. I know this because..." I stared into his watery blue eyes, willing myself to speak the truth. "I've been to

Death's Court. I know Death. And her heart is no longer suffering there. Death would never allow that. And if she chooses it, she will reincarnate and she will live another life. She will be happy again. I promise. Last night was not her end."

He shook his head. Unwilling or unable to believe me, I wasn't sure. "You'll never understand. No one will."

"Think about what Harlow would want. She loved you more than anything in this world. She wouldn't want you to throw your life away for revenge."

"You don't get to stand there and talk to me about what she would want. It doesn't matter anymore. She's gone. And maybe not by Farris's hand or order, that revenge will come as well. But this. This is more. He deserves to pay for all of her sadness. Every day she suffered without her power, every day she was sad was his fault. And I'm done walking around the truth. I'm putting both of my siblings in the ground today, Paesha. And you're not going to stop me."

He was going to die. I was going to stand here and watch him die, just as his sister had. And what would Thorne do? Would he stand in the shadows of the alley and watch it too? Would he watch me? Was there a thrill to my heartache he fed from? Fury, deep and raw, heated across my skin. Every place he'd touched me burned. Every promise he'd made turned to ash. Because he could have saved her, too. And he didn't.

I turned back to the prince's procession, the cheering crowd fading to a distant hum. Farris sat with a triumphant smile as he waved to the masses. He lifted the severed head of some great beast, its lifeless eyes staring out at the sea of adoring faces. The Silks roared with bloodthirsty glee. I hated all of them. Everything about this world. This city.

The world slowed. The drumbeats faded to a distant echo as the cheers of the crowd muted to a muffled hum. Colors bled together, blurring at the edges until everything was cast in a strange, otherworldly haze.

Farris's triumphant smile froze on his face, a grotesque mask of arrogance and cruelty. Even his billowing cloak hung motionless, as if caught in an invisible breeze. I turned to Archer feeling heavy and sluggish, as if I were wading through thick syrup. His anguished expression was etched into his features, a portrait of grief and rage frozen in time.

"What's happening?" I tried to ask, but my words came out as a distorted whisper, the sound swallowed by the eerie stillness that had descended upon the square.

"This is the end of your path, Huntress."

I whirled to face Vesalia, the movement painfully slow.

But then it flickered. The hold she had on time, wavering. I'd seen that before. In Death's Court when Reverius had spoken to me in my mind. There'd been a flicker then too. An obvious weakness through a show of great power. I looked back at Farris, remembering Reveruis's words that day. *The amount of power the goddess used to bring a mortal to this realm was vast. She will feel the loss of that for centuries.*

Realization struck me like a blow to the chest, the pieces of the puzzle falling into place with sickening clarity. The flickering, the weakening of magic, the muffled sensation that had permeated this realm since my arrival, it all traced back to the prince. Farris. He was the key, the lynchpin.

I whispered, the words heavy on my tongue. "He's taking too much. Draining the magic even when he can't figure out how to use it for himself."

Vesalia's smile widened, a predatory flash of teeth. "Yes. Now you see what you must do. You must find what is lost to others, Huntress."

"Does Farris hold his power in his blood or in his soul like I do?"

The goddess smiled and reached into her flowing robes to reveal a long, black dagger. "In his blood, of course. Bring me the power and I will show you how to return to Quill."

Time burst free of her hold, and I snatched Archer by the collar. "You want to kill the prince? Fine. But we do it together."

62

I'd cried. I didn't think I would, but Archer deserved the truth. So, I told him everything. I told him of Requiem. Of Quill. Of Ezra's death. Of the years I spent in misery. Of the growth I'd found beyond my first love. And then of Death's Court. And Reverius's bargain. He'd held his breath as I told him of Thorne's true identity. Slipping his fingers into his hair as he tried to work it out. And then he'd pulled me into his arms and let me sob until I was nothing more than angry again.

"You don't need him," he said, wiping the last of the tears from my face. "I've got you now, okay? I'll protect you. And we'll find a way back to your kid. If the Goddess of Time fucks you over, we find another way. There are days left. Anything can happen in a few days."

"I don't think it's days, though. The Goddess of Time said this was the end of the path. And I don't know how long I was in the Maw. A few days is my best guess."

"Then we get this done before midnight. Just in case."

He never smiled. I'd hardly known Archer without a smile on his face and a coin in his hand. But this world had broken him, just as it'd broken me, and I truly didn't know if he would learn to find joy again. But there was no part of me that didn't want to be there if he did.

"Will you come with me?" I whispered.

He pulled me back into his arms and kissed the top of my head. "Of course I'm coming with you. There's nothing left here for me anymore. The kids are fine with Briony. Tuck's probably staying with the king. Farris will be in the ground. Tho—"

He sucked in a sharp breath, stopping himself.

"Call him whatever you want, Archie. He fucking does."

I knew he hadn't put together Thorne's hand in his sister's death. Or lack thereof. But one day he would. And when he raged and turned on the gods, I'd stand beside him then too. Because he was my family now. My brother.

THERE WAS NOT enough planning in the world to prepare oneself to kill a prince. Not one surrounded by Cimmerian guards fishing for power like it was air to breathe. We followed the muffled tendrils of my magic through Stirling on swift, silent feet. With the return of his father, we'd expected him to stay at the castle, at least one night, but he hadn't. Instead, he was nestled in the back of a whorehouse.

We slipped inside, our cloaks pulled low over our faces, blending seamlessly with the regulars. Being here was like being wrenched back into Lady Visha's place at home. It smelled of sex and sin, of smoke and liquor and bad decisions. It was decadent in fabrics and sparse in cleanliness.

Archer and I wove through the crowd using drunken stumbles, our movements exaggerated and clumsy. We leaned heavily against each other, pretending to laugh and whispering nonsense, playing the part of lovers seeking a private room for our use. The Cimmerian guards, stationed at strategic points throughout the main hall, barely spared us a glance.

Moans and sighs of pleasure drifted from behind closed doors as we made our way down the corridor that a prick of magic had pointed us to. At the end of the hall, two Cimmerian guards flanked the opening to a separate hall. Archer and I stumbled closer, our laughter growing louder, more raucous. We clung to each other, our hands roaming in a blatant display of drunken lust as we approached the guards.

I swayed and Archer caught me, though he crashed into one of the men, careful to keep me from touching anything, while he remained the barrier.

"Oops! So sorry, handsome. Didn't see you there." I kept my head down, to hide my eyes in the dim light.

The guard grunted. He shoved Archer back with a look of distaste. "Move along, you two. This area's off-limits."

"We just need a little privacy," Archer said, grabbing a pouch of coins from his pocket. "I'm sure you understand."

The masked Cimmerian snatched the bag from Archer's hand. "Down the hall, second door on the left. And make it quick. We won't cover for you if the boss comes around."

Archer flashed him a sloppy grin. "You're a real pal, you know that? We won't be long."

As soon as we turned the corner, our drunken facades dropped away. We moved with swift, silent purpose. Faint tendrils of my power drew us to the last door. Incense and the soft sighs of pleasure drifted through the cracks. Archer and I exchanged a glance. He reached for the handle, his other hand slipping beneath his cloak to grasp the hilt of his dagger. I mirrored his movements, my fingers curling around the cool metal of the one I'd gotten from Harlow.

We slipped into the room like shadows and the door closed behind us with a soft click. For a heartbeat, they had no idea death had come because they were too distracted by each other, by the roaming hands and rapid breaths. The woman's back was to us, and dark hair cascaded down her bare shoulders as she moved above the prince.

But, as if sensing the shift in the room, the woman stiffened. She turned her head, her eyes widening as they met mine over her shoulder. Her lips parted. She meant to scream and blow our cover but Archer moved like a snake. He leapt forward, his hand clamping over the woman's mouth as he wrapped his other arm around her waist, yanking her off the prince in one smooth motion as he cracked her in the back of the head and she fell unceremoniously to the ground.

Farris scrambled back on the bed, clutching a silk sheet to his naked body. But even in his haste, a smug grin stretched across his face as he took in the sight of Archer standing before him. "You've got to be fucking kidding me. All this time and Archer Bramwell is the Lord of the Salt?"

"You're dumber than you look," Archer answered.

The prince reached for Archer, his hands outstretched like claws. But I was faster. I swept in front and plunged the obsidian blade deep into Farris's chest. The prince's eyes bulged, his mouth gaping in shock as he stared down at the hilt protruding from his flesh. I pressed forward, driving the blade deeper, feeling it grate against bone.

"This is for every ounce of power you've ever stolen. For every person that suffered at your hands. For a woman with more grace and poise, more fire and passion than you could ever imagine. I'll see you in Death's Court, asshole."

I threw my power outward, invisible ribbons snaking through Farris's dying veins. I'd known what power felt like. I'd seen it countless times. It was easy to find. Easy to hunt. It called to me, whispering promises of unimaginable might as the edges of mine merged with what had been lost to the people of

Wisteria. The power was ancient, scattered, merciless, and unbending as it filled me. Until it grew too strong. Too heavy. Too searing. Panic rose within me. I whipped my head to Archer, but he didn't move, only stared. Staying back, just as we'd planned. In case things went terribly wrong. We had no idea what the power would do if he interfered. So he didn't.

I took and took and took, drawing from Farris until I couldn't breathe. Couldn't see. Until every mistake I'd ever made in my life felt like drops of water in the ocean of this choice. This power wasn't meant to be. And it was angry. So angry. Filling my veins with its own fury. Raging through me. Searing away the last vestiges of my control. The betrayals, the lies, the endless manipulations. They all coalesced into a white-hot ball of wrath that settled in the pit of my stomach, growing with each passing second.

I could feel the foreign magic pulsing beneath my skin, angry and restless, desperate to be unleashed. It whispered dark promises in my mind, tempting me with visions of retribution and power. The urge to give in, to let the magic take over and lay waste to everything in my path, was almost overwhelming.

Archer's hand on my shoulder yanked me back from the brink. I met his gaze, seeing my own anguish reflected in his eyes. He understood. He knew the siren call of vengeance, the all-consuming need to make those who had wronged us pay.

"We need to go. Now."

I nodded, drawing in a shuddering breath as I fought to regain a semblance of control on magic I had no business harnessing. The power bucked and writhed, resisting my attempts to rein it in. It took every ounce of my willpower to keep it contained, to stop it from spilling out and laying waste to everything.

With trembling hands and the taste of copper on my tongue, I let Archer guide me from the room, leaving Farris's lifeless body sprawled across the bloodied, rumpled sheets. I staggered through the whorehouse, my senses overwhelmed by the power raging within me. Colors seemed too bright, sounds too loud. The smell of perfume and sweat clung to the back of my throat, making me gag.

Archer's grip on my arm was the only thing keeping me upright as we stepped out into the night. The cool air was a blessed relief, but it hardly soothed the inferno in my veins. The cobblestones seemed to shift and undulate, the buildings looming over us like giants poised to strike.

"Clock tower now," Archer said, his voice strained with urgency. "Give that bitch the power, and let's get the hell out of here."

I nodded, not trusting myself to speak. It took all my concentration to keep putting one foot in front of the other, to focus on Archer at my side. As we hurried through the twisting streets, the power within me surged and roiled, a tempest barely contained beneath my skin. It tugged at me, insistent and unyielding, trying to pull me off course. Away from the clock-tower. Away from Vesalia's promise of a way home.

I stumbled. Archer's grip tightened. "Gods, are you going to make it?"

"The power," I gasped, my free hand pressing against my stomach as if I could physically hold it back. "It's fighting me. I need to use a little bit. I have to relieve the pressure."

On instinct alone, I tried to call a tiny bit forward, urging the magic to find the only thing I truly needed. Quill. But it bucked and raged, refusing to let me move. I crashed to my knees, the cobblestone street cracking beneath me.

Archer pulled me to my feet, but I couldn't move beyond that point. Not until I turned and let it lead us in the opposite direction. Far, far away from a greedy goddess. South. Beyond the graveyard, past Prospector's Pointe. Even past the Hollow, though my heart ached when I glanced at it. When I remembered a flash of strong arms holding me. The magic seethed as if it recognized the man in those memories for the evil he was and coated my mind with anger to protect me from falling weak.

Once we stood at the edge of the city, the magic finally stilled, its insistent tugging fading to a whisper. Calm. Tame. Letting me breathe. Which meant Archer could breathe.

"What the fuck is that?" I asked, pointing to the shimmering wall, gossamer thin and almost translucent, stretching as far as the eye could see.

"There's nothing out there," Archer said, studying my face and turning back to the darkness. "This is the eastern point of Wisteria. We'd have to go out the other way, go north to see anything more."

"Why can't you see this?" I reached forward, scraping my nails down the wall.

"You feel okay?"

I turned to Archer taking in the tilt of his brow, the concern on his face. He was full of so much worry, I thought he might be sick.

A melodic laugh echoed through the night. I spun, my heart leaping into my throat as Vesalia materialized before us, her silver hair gleaming in the moonlight. "Don't you see, Huntress? It's a veil. The barrier that has kept you trapped, muting the magic, dampening our power. Requiem is not in a different realm, child. It's merely behind this wall." She held a hand out. "Give me your palm. I will take the power and then I will show you how to walk time. I will let you cross the barrier and go home."

I couldn't wrap my head around the words. The truth. The godsdamn lies.

"I've been right here this whole time?" I hated the heartbreak in my voice. The complete raw emotion that poured from me as more lies from Thorne's mouth came to the surface. I'd told him about Quill in a vulnerable moment and not only had he already known of her, he promised to help me get back without ever meaning it. Whatever hearts were made of, mine began to unravel.

As I stared at Vesalia's outstretched hand, the power within me stirred, a warning hum that vibrated through my bones. It coiled around my heart, whispering cautions in a language older than time.

"Come now, Huntress. I offer you the key to your freedom. The path home to your precious Quill. Surely, you wouldn't turn your back on such a gift?"

The magic surged, an angry swell that crashed against my ribcage. It recognized the lie in her words, the trap hidden beneath.

I squeezed Archer's hand, mouthing, *Do you trust me?*

He squeezed back. "With my life."

I turned back to Vesalia, spine growing. Appearing from absolutely nowhere, stepping through space, it seemed, Reverius appeared. But to me, his name was Thorne Noctus, and he'd lied and lied and lied. He hadn't sent me to a different world. All this time. All this heartache and Quill had been right fucking here. On the other side of a magical wall.

"Whatever you're thinking, stop right now," Thorne ordered, that tic in his jaw that used to be adorable sending a wave of anger coursing through the tempest of power.

I stepped forward, making eye contact with the man behind them both. Hidden in the shadows, he smiled, dipping his chin, his Remnants circling him as I remembered something he'd said to me in anger. And I had finally fucking learned. I looked between Thorne and Vesalia, sweeping my hands to the sides. "You're both forgetting one very important thing. I hail from two gods, Alastor and his lost things, yes. But also Irri the Goddess of Broken things."

The stolen power roared to life, a maelstrom of raw, untamed energy that pulsed in time with the frantic beating of my heart. It surged through my veins, terrifying and insatiable. The magic I'd stolen from Farris, the magic that had been ripped from the very fabric of this realm now danced beneath my skin, eager to be set free.

A blinding flash of light exploded outward, ripping through the air like a star being born. The force of it tore through the ground. The stolen magic swelled, swirling in violent currents, and I didn't resist it. I surrendered to it, and let it consume me. Let it burn. Let them see the monster they'd made me into. I didn't care. Not for Thorne. Not for the realms. Not even for myself.

I was vengeance.

I was the reckoning they never saw coming.

The veil between worlds trembled, the thin barrier quivering as the two realms scraped against one another. Archer held my hand so tight it shook within his grasp. But he never let go. Not even when the veil crumbled, and tiny pieces of it rained down upon both worlds like all the stars in the sky had fallen.

The world fell silent and still. At peace and at war all at once. I turned, slowing, willing myself to tear my eyes from the gods long enough to finally, finally lay my eyes on home. I walked forward. With one foot in Requiem and one foot in Wisteria, we turned to face the gods once more. Prepared for all their wrath. All their vengeance. But they were gone.

Archer sighed. His posture had said he'd been prepared for battle. With the gods gone, his world likely felt a little lighter. Still, he seemed hesitant as he asked, "When was the last time you saw Thorne?"

"You didn't see him standing there?" I asked, feeling the blood drain from my face.

"No. Thorne has that mark from Alastor on his neck. That wasn't him. They're up to something. Or Thorne's in a world of shit and he's just lost his only allies."

I paused for a second. The last time I'd seen Thorne, the man with the mark on his neck was when he'd given me his full name, revealing the first of many lies. Everything else... It'd been Ezra?

He'd left Death's Court? As quickly as the realization melted over me, it faded. Nothing could surprise me anymore. And I didn't want to think about Thorne. I didn't want to care. Maybe somewhere deep down there was a trace of worry, but he didn't deserve that devotion from me. And one day my broken heart would know that, too. In the meantime, I'd lie to myself. I'd lie to everyone. Until the pain faded away and whatever had bloomed between us was nothing more than ash and faded memories.

"Here's the thing, Reverius is Thorne. The god that bound me to this veiled realm was Thorne. Not Ezra. The man that lied to my face this entire time so he could trap me here with my consent and take my memories? Yeah, that was still Thorne. I think the brothers want me dead. And I don't want shit to do with either of them. Wherever he is, I hope he's burning in his own pit of lies."

"Has anyone told you you're really fucking scary some-times?" Archer whispered.

"It's been mentioned."

The clock towers in each of the cities surrounding us chimed at once, the tones unnatural and screeching through the collided worlds like an angry, broken promise. As they faded, something dark stirred beneath my skin. The stolen power writhed, no longer content to simply burn, it wanted to consume. Inky tendrils, like Alastor's Remnants but somehow wrong, began seeping from my pores.

I told myself they were his. That he was testing me again. But deep down, I knew better. These weren't borrowed or stolen. They were mine. Born of rage and betrayal and something far more terrible than mere magic. They twisted around my arms, my throat, leaving trails of ice in their wake as they whispered promises of vengeance in voices that sounded too much like my own.

Archer stared at the city that seemed to have appeared from nowhere. "Vesalia's never going to let you forget. She led you to the water for a sip and you drained the fucking lake."

"What the hell do I care? She can get in line. Let them come. Let them destroy me. At least it'll be on my fucking terms. Because I'm entirely done. My soul is tired, and I know it. Whatever happens, this is it for me. The end. When they finally kill me, I won't come back again."

Not for them. Not for myself. I was done. Done with being anything but the monster they'd made me. Nevermore their victim. Nevermore their fool.

...To be continued in Evermore

EPILOGUE
REVERIUS

I couldn't move. Couldn't breathe beyond the walls of this fucking prison. But I could think. And think. And think. Of her face when the truth shattered whatever had bloomed between us. Of the darkness that crept into those mismatched eyes. Of the way she'd looked at me like I was nothing more than another lie.

Rage built within me, coating my throat until I could taste copper on my tongue. The barriers of my cage might hold for now, but they couldn't last forever. Nothing did. And when I broke free, when I finally escaped this godsforsaken hell, I would hunt her down. I would wrap my hands around that delicate throat and squeeze until the light left her eyes. Until her last breath carried my name to the endless void.

I smiled, remembering the weight of Paesha in my arms, the trust I'd cultivated, the love I'd let bloom. The memories would sustain me. Keep me warm in this frozen tomb until I could paint the walls with blood and finally end this game we'd played for far too long. "I'm coming for you," I whispered, watching another grain of red sand fall. "And this time, I won't fail."

Acknowledgments
Thanks for Reading!

Dear Reader,

Thank you so much for being here. For reading all these pages and loving me through the production of this beast. I couldn't do this without all of your support and encouragement. This book was the most challenging of my career to date. I'd convinced myself I could get this entire story into a stand-alone, because that's what the Never Sky series was supposed to be. But somewhere along the way, with stubborn Paesha in my ear, I realized we could either scratch the surface of her story and make it work, or I could start over and make it better and let her story be two books. So two books it is. Which of course, delayed everything by months. But, we're going to land in a much sweeter place because of it. You know what they say, right? The characters are telling us the stories and we're just along for the ride. Paesha was adamant that she get more floor time than Deyanira. But she's always loved the stage, so I guess that makes sense. Here's to hoping I never have another MC as hard-headed as Paesha for the rest of my career. Or I may need therapy.

To my husband, my ride or die, my love: Thank you for being my anchor in reality while I lose myself in worlds of magic and mayhem. Your endless patience, love, and belief in me mean more than I can ever put into words. This story exists because of the quiet moments you gave me, and the way you never stopped cheering me on. You're my greatest adventure. Thank you for believing in me, even when I doubted myself.

To my girls {and every other woman out there that needs to hear this}, I hope you see the strength in my female characters and know you have that in you. This world is hard to live in. They want to tell us that we are the weaker sex. We are the ones to be controlled. They are fucking wrong.

No one controls you.

No one can tell you what's best for you.

Burrow down. Find yourself in the anger you need to survive in this world and be exactly that person. Don't let them walk on you. Don't let them destroy you. It's okay to be soft. To be emotional. To be whatever and whoever you want to be as long as *you* choose it. There are no other options. Being a woman *makes* you strong. And the world wouldn't try to suppress you if they weren't scared of that strength.

To Melissa Roehrich, my bestie, the greatest soul in the whole world, you deserve all the success and all the dreams-come-true soaring your way. Your heart is truly the most pure place and this world is better for it. The beginning of this book started at your side in the Murder House, just as the beginning of Evermore did. And I hope every book for the rest of forever starts the same way. You make this whole journey so much sweeter, friend. I won't mention our ages like someone did in the back of her book, but when we're twice this number, and still watching Disney movies in the Murder House, just remember it all started with a dagger. The best friendships always do. Or so I've heard.

To Ali, Brit and Sarah, I don't know where I'd be without each of you. You bring so much to my table, there are days when I just sit back in awe of you. You spiral hard, you guide gently, and you support me better than I could ever hope for. I never have to be afraid to fall because you would never let me and there's truly magic in that power you each have. Thank you for every moment. You can never leave me.

To my Alphamore Team, Sara, Kelly, Jess, there were days when your eagerness and encouragement were the only thing that carried me through three am writing sessions. I'm so proud of where this book landed after being sifted through each of your capable fingers. Thank you from the very bottom of my heart for being on my team.

About the Author

Miranda Lyn is the best selling author of the trending witchy duology, Unmarked; her debut series, Fae Rising; and beyond with The Never Sky series. Miranda has spent the past two decades reading romantic fantasy novels, and the last handful of years crafting similar worlds steeped in heartache, adventure, love, and loss. Her past work has taken her readers into the heart of a witch, alongside the journey of a high fae, through the oceans with a siren and prowling the rooftops with Death's Maiden. Now, she's found the determination of a dancer with Nevermore and Evermore.

Check out our website for extras, character art, and exclusive content. www.authormirandalyn.com

To sign up for the mailing list and get access to more exclusive content and giveaways, please visit

https://www.authormirandalyn.com/subscribe

ALSO BY MIRANDA LYN

FATE BELONGS
TO THE BROKEN

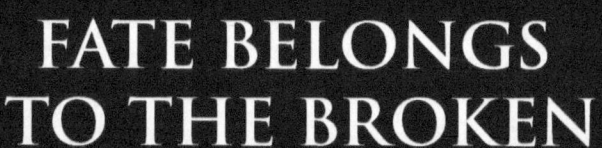

COMING NEXT
FROM

MIRANDA LYN